WYCLIFFE AND THE SCHOOL BULLIES

WYCLIFFE AND THE WINSOR BLUE

WYCLIFFE AND THE DUNES MYSTERY

W. J. Burley lived near Newquay in Cornwall, and was a school-master until he retired to concentrate on his writing. His many Wycliffe books include, most recently, *Wycliffe and the Guild of Nine*. He died in 2002.

By W. J. Burley

W.J.BURLEY

WYCLIFFE AND THE
SCHOOL BULLIES

WYCLIFFE AND THE
WINSOR BLUE

WYCLIFFE AND THE
DUNES MYSTERY

Wycliffe and the School Bullies
First published in Great Britain by Victor Gollancz Ltd under the
title *Wycliffe and the Schoolgirls* in 1976

Wycliffe and the Winsor Blue
First published in Great Britain by Victor Gollancz in 1987

Wycliffe and the Dunes Mystery
First published in Great Britain by Victor Gollancz in 1993

This omnibus edition published in 2011
by Orion Books Ltd
Orion House, 5 Upper St Martin's Lane
London WC2H 9EA

An Hachette UK Company

A CIP catalogue record for this book is available from the British
Library.

ISBN 9781407234168

Printed and bound in Great Britain by Clays Ltd, St Ives plc

www.orionbooks.co.uk

WYCLIFFE AND THE SCHOOL BULLIES

Prologue among the schoolgirls

ELAINE

'I can't eat all that, mum.'

'Of course you can, you need a decent breakfast inside you.'

'I shall be sick on the coach.'

Her mother, a little barrel of a woman in a spotless, white overall, stood over her.

'Be sensible, Elaine, you don't know when you'll get your next meal.'

'But I'm taking a picnic lunch to have on the trip.'

'I mean a proper meal.'

Elaine was fifteen, nearly sixteen, short like her mother but well proportioned. She was dark with large, soft eyes but a straight, determined mouth.

'I hope this Miss Russell isn't going to mind you coming dressed like that.'

'The letter said leisure clothes.'

'But jeans and a T-shirt . . . '

'Mother, I've told you, it's what the other girls are wearing.'

The Bennetts' dining room was little more than a wide passage between the bakery and the shop. At one end a glass door with a pattern of incised stars led into the shop; at the other a plank door, painted green,

7

opened into a little yard which led to the bakehouse. There, with two assistants, her father baked the crusty bread and yeast cakes which were the mainstay of the business. A business prosperous enough to pay Elaine's fees at Bishop Fuller's, a rather exclusive day-school for girls.

The plank door was pushed open and Elaine's father came in carrying a wire tray of bread rolls.

'That makes fourteen dozen, do you think that'll be enough, Dot?'

'There's nine dozen ordered . . . '

The shop, the bakery, their house were all one. Elaine was used to it, she had been brought up in the all-pervading, warm, yeasty atmosphere and rarely noticed it. Her mother looked after the shop with the help of a girl who was not much older than Elaine.

Mr Bennett went through with the bread rolls, came back and lingered. He was as tall and thin as his wife was short and fat and he was dusted all over with flour.

'Well, girl, you'll soon be off. Willie will take you to the school in the van. I've told him to pick you up at twenty to nine.' He stooped and kissed his daughter on the forehead. 'Have a good time and look after yourself.' He slipped two one-pound notes into the waistband of her jeans.

'Thanks, dad.'

'You spoil her, Sidney!'

'And why not?'

'Well, she's got enough pocket money already.' But Mrs Bennett's plump features were smiling.

At twenty minutes to nine a curly headed youth of nineteen or twenty pushed open the door from the shop and put his head round, 'Your carriage awaits, madam.'

Elaine kissed her mother and went out to the van. Willie followed carrying an enormous hold-all which was almost bursting at the zip.

ROSALINE

Rosaline Parkin stood with a cup of tea in one hand and a piece of bread-and-jam in the other. She was wearing jeans and a brassiere while her aunt ironed her T-shirt to dry it after a last-minute washing.

'Have you got everything else you want?' Her aunt could not have been more than fifty but her features had long since set in a mould of sadness and resignation. She was pale and she moved with slow deliberation as though any effort taxed her to the limit.

'I packed last night.'

'I suppose you've got enough money?'

'I'll manage.'

The little kitchen was a lean-to, its tiny window looked out on a brick-walled yard and the backs of the houses in the next street. Every minute or two a heavy lorry rumbled down the front street causing the doors and windows to rattle.

Rosaline had the thin, wiry body of a ballet dancer and her skin was white in startling contrast with her mop of jet-black hair. She had high, broad cheek-bones though her face narrowed to a pointed chin giving her a mischievous, elfin look. But her eyes were sullen and her mouth was hard. She had passed the eleven-plus selection test for Cholsey Grammar and she had become friendly with Elaine Bennett through inter-schools hockey. Now they were going on a community holiday with girls from several of the city's schools.

Her aunt finished ironing the shirt and handed it to her; she slipped it on.

'That's it, then. I'll be off.' She picked up a suitcase then dropped it again. 'Christ, I've forgotten my camera!'

'I wish you wouldn't speak like that, Rosaline.'

She dashed upstairs and came down with the camera slung over her shoulder. Her aunt looked at it and shook her head.

9

'I wish I knew where you got the money to buy that.'
'I worked in the Easter holidays, didn't I?'
'When will you be back?'
'Three weeks, I told you.'
'You'll write?'
'I wouldn't count on it, you know what I am.'
'Have you got your tablets?'
'I haven't had a fit for months.'
'I know that but being away from home . . .'
'Oh, forget it!'

Her aunt followed her to the front door. 'Look after yourself.' She stood watching while her niece walked up the dismal little street to the bus stop on the corner.

JANE

The kitchen at 37 Oakshott Avenue glowed in the morning sunshine; primrose-yellow walls, white and chromium fittings. The Rendells were at breakfast, seated round a plastic-topped table.

'You'll telephone if there's anything you want, Jane?'

'Yes, mother.'

'Are you sure you've had enough breakfast?'

'I couldn't eat any more.'

'Another cup of coffee?'

'No, thanks.'

'You usually have two cups.'

Jane's father intervened. 'She might not want to, love, going on a long coach trip.'

Jane was small for her age, thin and underdeveloped. She had straight, dark hair and a sad little face which might have been used in an appeal on behalf of deprived children. But with Jane it was heredity, she was like her mother.

'You're sure you've got enough spending money?' Her father was a grave, anxious man, almost morbidly meticulous.

10

'Yes, thank you, daddy.'

Jane went to the School of the Sacred Heart, a Catholic school though the Rendells were not Catholics.

'All the girls come from good homes and the fees are reasonable.'

Jane wore her school uniform, a black blazer with the school badge and a blue and white summer dress.

'The sisters said it would be best to wear school uniform on the trip but to take casual clothes to wear when we get there.'

'We shall miss you, Jane.' Mr Rendell's large hand closed over his daughter's and squeezed affectionately.

'I shall miss you, daddy.'

'Don't make her cry, Jim, she's going to enjoy herself. I've put a dozen postcards in your bag all stamped and addressed. If you haven't got time to write you can always pop one of those in the post.'

'Yes, mother.'

'You'll have Barbara Brooks for company.' Barbara was the only other girl from the School of the Sacred Heart who would be going on the holiday. 'You've always liked Barbara, haven't you?'

'I'll be all right, mother.'

'It's lucky it's a Saturday and that your father can take you to the school. If it had been a weekday we should have needed a taxi.'

It was a strange atmosphere. In the Rendell household nobody ever spoke a harsh word but all three of them seemed to be permanently tense. Harmony on taut strings.

Mr Rendell looked at his watch. 'Twenty-five to. We've got to pick up Barbara so it's time we were going.'

A pale-blue Cortina, six years old but looking like new, stood at the gate. Mr Rendell carried his daughter's case.

'Sure you've got everything?'

11

Mrs Rendeli was crying. She hugged her daughter, clutching at her thin little body.

SHEILA

The Jukeses lived on a council estate—14 Stoke's Road, in the Cholsey district of the city. Sheila was the youngest of three, her two brothers worked as machinists in a factory where her father was a welder. To everybody's surprise and tolerant amusement, Sheila had passed her eleven-plus test for Cholsey Grammar.

On Saturday mornings it was unusual for anybody to be up before ten or half-past so Sheila had the living room to herself. She was scraping butter on to slices of cut bread and slapping slivers of cooked ham between them. Sheila was plump with a large behind and a prominent bosom. Her jeans did not meet her blouse and a pink roll of flesh bridged the gap. She gathered her sandwiches into a polythene bag and put them in a haversack then she went to the bottom of the stairs.

'Mam!'

'What is it now?'

'I can't find my wedge heels.'

'They're in your wardrobe.'

'No. I've looked.'

Her mother muttered something inaudible.

Sheila went to the open dresser on which china was kept and took down a soup tureen from the top shelf. She lifted the lid and disclosed a number of crumpled one and five-pound notes. She slipped one of the fivers into the pocket of her jeans then, after a moment of hesitation, added three singles. Then she put the tureen back in its place.

There was a sound of footsteps on the stairs and her mother came in. She was Sheila thirty years on, her heavy breasts scarcely concealed by her nightgown, her features almost lost in fat. The first cigarette of the day hung from her lips. She dropped Sheila's wedge heels on the table.

'Where did you find 'em?'

'In the bloody wardrobe where I said. You don't look.' She glanced round the room and yawned. 'Any tea?'

'In the pot, it's not long made.'

Her mother poured herself a cup of tea. 'How you off for money?'

'I took eight quid out of the dish, is that all right?'

'Christ, your father gave you a fiver, you aren't going to the Costa del bloody Sol.'

'It's three weeks, mam.'

Mrs Jukes looked at the clock. 'You'll be late.'

'Tony said he'd take me on his bike.'

'Tony's still in bed.'

Sheila went to the bottom of the stairs and yelled. 'Tony!'

'What is it?'

'You got to take me to the school.'

Eventually Tom came downstairs, his eyes full of sleep, dressed in jeans and a shirt. 'O.K. Let's get it over with.'

Mrs Jukes stood in the doorway in her nightdress to see them off. The bike roared down the road with Sheila bouncing on the back, clinging to her brother with one hand and her haversack with the other.

The coach with twenty-four schoolgirls and a mistress on board sped along the A35. It was a hot, August afternoon but, because it was a Saturday, there was little traffic. Miss Dorothy Russell, thirty-nine years old, sat in front by the driver. She wore a light-blue dress patterned with huge white daisies which confused but did nothing to soften the aggressive angularity of her figure. She had light, brown hair, cut short and kinked at the ends to make it turn inwards; her features were small and sharp and she had a tiny mouth with thin lips.

13

'In a few minutes the old Roman road joins us, the one which led from Isca, that is Exeter, to Durnovaria which was their name for Dorchester.'

The girls looked out on the green landscape of subtle contours and unexpected shadows thinking their own thoughts. In the back seat Rosaline Parkin sat with Sheila Jukes and Elaine Bennett. Rosaline drew surreptitiously on a cigarette and let the smoke trickle slowly from her lips in a thin, grey spiral. Once she passed the cigarette to Elaine who almost gave the game away by a fit of violent coughing. Miss Russell turned round.

'Are you all right, Elaine?'

'Yes, thank you, Miss Russell.'

'She nearly swallowed the hole in her Polo mint,' Rosaline said.

There was a general laugh.

Miss Russell, who had not taught for seventeen years for nothing, remarked that she hoped it wouldn't prove carcinogenic.

'We are staying near Maiden Castle, a famous Iron Age fortress which fell to Vespasian in the first century A.D. Vespasian eventually became emperor.'

'Bully for him!' Rosaline muttered but only loud enough to be heard in the back seats.

Jane, with her friend, Barbara Brooks, sat primly in the seat behind Miss Russell, the only ones in more or less formal dress. Barbara was a complete contrast to Jane, she was pink skinned and she had kept a lot of her puppy fat though a figure was beginning to struggle through. Miss Russell turned to speak to them.

'Have you done the history of the Roman occupation at your school?'

Jane answered. 'No, Miss Russell, we did the eighteenth and nineteenth centuries for 'O' level.'

'But when you were younger, surely . . . '

'Oh, yes, I think we did about it in the third form but I've forgotten.' Jane blushed at the admission.

14

'You must read it up; Dorset is a most interesting county for that period.'

'Yes, Miss Russell.'

There was a derisive chuckle from further back.

The coach slowed down then turned off the main road into a narrow lane which had passing places at intervals. They jolted along for about half a mile then pulled into a gravelled drive which led to a gaunt, two-storeyed house with a pillared porch from which stucco was peeling.

'Well, girls, this is home for the next three weeks.'

The coach came to a standstill, the driver climbed down. Miss Russell stood while the girls trooped past her and out of the coach to gather in chattering groups on the gravel.

'Looks a crummy joint to me,' Rosaline said. 'God help us if we can't get into Dorchester in the evenings.'

'Get your baggage from the boot of the coach and assemble in the front hall.'

'How far is it?' Elaine asked.

Rosaline's thought had moved on. 'How far is what?'

'Dorchester.'

'Three miles.'

'We could walk, I suppose.'

Rosaline opened her dark eyes wide. 'Listen to the girl! Walk, she says. You should see me. There must be some farm lout or somebody with a car or even a motor bike.' She looked round the deserted countryside with obvious misgivings. 'We shall have to get organised.'

The hall was bare with a floor made of stone flags which extended down a passage on each side of a rather impressive staircase. There was no carpet on the stairs and the treads were badly worn. Miss Russell stood on the third stair to talk to them.

'Well, this is it! I hope that we shall all enjoy the next three weeks. I want us all to get to know each other better and to learn to live together as a community. There are five of the city's schools represented in our

15

party, all day-schools, and we shall probably find by the end of our stay that we have made new friends, had a few corners knocked off and learned something about ourselves.

'There are a few rules which I shall post on the notice board and I want you to keep strictly to them. They are not unreasonable and should not stop you enjoying yourselves.'

'Fat chance!' Sheila Jukes muttered. 'Stuck out here in the bloody wilds. She said it was near the town.'

'Are there any buses into town, Miss Russell?'

'Yes, quite a good service for a rural area. There is a bus stop about a hundred yards beyond the point where we turned off from the main road. But, and I must emphasise this as one of our most important rules, no one goes into town without getting my permission first.'

There was a general groan and Miss Russell moved up another step to command her audience more effectively.

'Quiet, please, girls. I want to give you some more details.

'There are two dormitories and twelve girls will sleep in each. Pamela O'Brien and Rosaline Parkin, will you come here, please?'

A slim girl with red-gold hair and freckles joined Rosaline to stand demurely a step or two below Miss Russell.

'I have a list of girls who will sleep in each dormitory and there will be no changes without my approval. The girls in each dormitory will be answerable to Pamela and Rosaline respectively, not only in the dormitories but in all matters concerning discipline while we are here.' Miss Russell cleared her throat. 'I will post the lists with a copy of the rules on the notice board.'

Miss Russell looked slowly round the group. 'Are there any questions?'

No one spoke.

Miss Russell came down the stairs and went over to the notice board of moth-eaten green baize to pin up the sheets. The girls crowded round to read them.

The dormitories were in the front of the house, each with two tall sash-windows looking out over the Dorsetshire countryside. The ceilings were ornamented with plaster mouldings and the skirtings were almost two feet high.

'Lady Chatterley summons Mellors to her boudoir,' Rosaline said, glancing round at the evidence of former elegance.

'You don't have beds in boudoirs.' Sheila Jukes flopped down on one of the twelve black-iron bedsteads.

'No? You do things your way and I'll do things mine.'

The two girls who had sat so primly on the coach were standing near Rosaline, waiting to be noticed.

'What do you want?'

Once more Jane was the spokesman. 'We want to know which beds we are to have.'

Rosaline looked them over appraisingly. 'Are you the Sacred Heart lot?'

'That's right.'

'Did they tell you to dress like that?'

'They said we should wear school uniform on the trip.'

'Christ!' She glanced along the rows of beds. 'You'd better have the two beds at the end—not that end—by the door. What are you called?'

'I'm Jane Rendell and this is Barbara Brooks.'

Rosaline shrugged. 'Too much for me, I shall call you Buttercup and Daisy.'

They had a meal at six-thirty and when the meal was over Miss Russell said, 'Now you have the rest of the evening to settle in. Bed at ten, lights out at ten-thirty.' She smiled. 'I should like to see Rosaline and Pamela in my room for a few minutes. My room is upstairs on the

17

main corridor and my name is on the door.' She paused for a moment, then added, 'There is a games room at the back of the ground floor next to the showers and toilets.'

'May we go into Dorchester this evening, Miss Russell?'

'Not tonight, Sheila, let's all use tonight to get really settled in.'

Rosaline Parkin, Elaine Bennett and Sheila Jukes had taken possession of beds at the far end of the dormitory. The two girls from the Sacred Heart were at the other end, by the door. They undressed demurely, careful not to expose their bodies while Sheila Jukes stormed about wearing only pyjama trousers and looking for the top.

'Which of you bastards nicked my top?'

At ten-thirty sharp, Rosaline called up the room, 'Put the lights out, Buttercup.'

Jane got out of bed and flicked the two switches leaving the room in darkness except for the pale lights coming in through the tall windows. Five minutes later Miss Russell opened the door.

'That's splendid, all of you; good-night, girls.'

'Good-night, Miss Russell.'

They could hear her footsteps until they stopped at the door of her room.

'All right, Buttercup.'

'What?'

'Put the lights on, you fool, she's gone, hasn't she?'

The trio put a table between the rows of beds and settled down to pontoon.

'Penny points.'

'I haven't got any change.'

'Neither have I.'

'All right, we'll play for matches and settle up in the morning.'

It was the first time Jane and her friend had slept away from home except when they were on holiday

18

with their parents. Jane lay in bed staring up at the elaborately moulded ceiling-rose from which a thin flex dangled absurdly.

Between hands Elaine Bennett said, 'What did she want you and O'Brien for?'

'Pep talk.'

Jukes said, 'And?'

'And nothing as far as I'm concerned. I left O'Brien there. I've had enough of that.' She studied her cards, 'Twist.' She took a card. 'And again.' She took another. 'And again—damn!' She threw her cards down. 'Bust!'

'Enough of what?' Elaine enquired.

'What do you think? Do you want me to draw a map? Our Rusty is one of those. Silly old cow, but I'll fix her.'

'Gosh, I don't think any of ours are like that.'

'Well, we've only got the one and that's enough.' She adopted a grotesque travesty of Miss Russell's speech. ''I want you to think of me as the mother you lost, dear . . .'' Hands like a randy billy goat.'

'Billy goats don't have hands.'

'No? Well, dear, you should know about such things.' Rosaline looked at her watch. 'Are we playing this silly game or going to bed?'

It was after midnight when the lights finally went out and some time later when Jane went to sleep, troubled in her mind.

Next morning, after breakfast, she tapped on Miss Russell's door.

'Come in.'

Miss Russell was standing in front of the dressing table mirror, doing her hair.

'What is it, Jane?'

'There's something I think you should know, Miss Russell. Some of the girls were playing cards last night until twelve o'clock—for money.'

Miss Russell continued back-combing her skimpy hair. 'Rosaline Parkin is in charge of your dormitory, Jane, you should talk to her about it.'

19

'But she was one of the girls playing, Miss Russell.'

Miss Russell put down her comb and came over. 'Now listen to me, Jane. You are here to learn something about living in a community and one of the things you should learn is self-reliance, another is loyalty. If some of the girls were doing what you say they were doing it was very wrong of them. But it is also wrong of you to come tale-bearing to me. Do you understand?'

'Yes, Miss Russell.'

'Then run along.'

As she reached the door Miss Russell called her back. As a good Anglican she had deeply-rooted suspicions of Roman Catholic institutions. 'I expect you are encouraged to do this sort of thing at your school?'

'I don't know, Miss Russell.'

'Well, you certainly will not be popular if you do it here.'

That night when Jane sat on her bed to take off her shoes the head and foot collapsed and she thudded on the floor while the whole dormitory laughed. She realised that Miss Russell had not kept her confidence but she did not suspect that there was worse to come. The next night her bed was soaking wet and she had to double up with her friend, Barbara.

On the fourth day Jane went to see Miss Russell again, this time her lips and her voice were trembling.

'I wanted to ask you if I may change with one of the girls in the other dormitory, Miss Russell.'

'No, Jane, you may not. You started off in a very foolish way and brought on yourself whatever it is that is happening to you now. You must take it in good part and make the best of it. If you start running away from the consequences of your own actions there is no knowing where it will end.'

Miss Russell looked at the thin, anaemic girl with a distaste which she could barely conceal. 'It is for your own good, Jane.'

'Yes, Miss Russell.'

The days were not so bad. They tramped all over Maiden Castle, they made two trips into Dorchester and saw the room where Judge Jeffreys is supposed to have conducted his 'bloody assize', the Shire Hall where the Tolpuddle Martyrs were tried and the County museum.

'We shall come again and devote a whole day to Hardy,' Miss Russell promised.

Pamela O'Brien seemed to take pity on the two girls from the Sacred Heart and made it her business to see that they were included in all that went on. Jane, emboldened by her kindness, confided her troubles but Pamela's response was disappointing.

'Oh, you don't want to worry too much about our Rosie, her bark is worse than her bite. If you put up with it for a bit she'll soon get tired.'

'It's not only her, it's the three of them,' Jane complained.

'Yes, well, they do stick together.'

The remainder of the three weeks stretched ahead interminably. She considered ringing her parents but she knew how upset they would be.

'We've been selfish, Jane, dear. We've kept you too much to ourselves instead of letting you mix with girls of your own age.'

Miss Russell's exercise in communal living had seemed like the answer to their particular need and they had paid the fifteen pounds, which they could ill afford, just as they paid Jane's school fees at the Sacred Heart, to give her the chance to grow up amongst 'nice' girls.

The climax came over the showers. Miss Russell's rules required that the girls should take a shower each morning, one dormitory between seven and seven-thirty and the other between seven-thirty and eight. They alternated on different days. Communal showers, after games, were common-place to the other girls but such thing were unknown at the Sacred Heart and Jane planned with Barbara to get up at six-thirty and so secure their privacy. In fact, Barbara liked her bed too much and so, each morning, in her dressing gown, carrying towel and soap, Jane stole downstairs alone. She was always back in the dormitory by the time the other girls began to stir and it seemed that nobody had noticed.

One morning, a week after their arrival, Jane went down to the showers as usual. Although sunshine was already streaming through the front windows the back of the house was still dimly lit and the whole place was as silent as the grave so that even a creaking stair made a startling noise. She hung up her dressing gown and pyjamas, threw her towel on top, kicked off her slippers and made for the nearest shower. She had just turned the mixing valve when Elaine Bennett dashed through from the direction of the lavatories, snatched up all Jane's things and rushed out leaving the door swinging. Jane was left wet and naked without even a towel. She did not panic but began a systematic search to see if there was anything she could wear or use to dry herself. She found a face-towel which somebody had left behind, dried herself roughly and then used it to cover herself as well as she could. She crept along the passage and up the stairs without meeting anyone until she reached the door of the dormitory.

'Here she is!' Sheila Jukes's voice.

The door was slammed and locked in her face. She could hear them giggling. She was about to try the other dormitory, to ask Pamela O'Brien for help, when Rosaline came sauntering down the corridor, hands in the pockets of her blue, quilted dressing gown, sponge-bag over her arm.

'Hullo, Butters, in trouble?'

She was too near to tears to answer and Rosaline stood, looking at her and smiling. 'Never mind, kid, it's only a joke. Your clothes are in Rusty's room, all you've got to do is to go in and get them.'

'But I can't go in Miss Russell's room like this!'

'Of course you can, she's not there, she's in the staff bathroom and you know how long she takes. Here, I'll come with you.'

A little way from Miss Russell's room Rosaline halted. 'In you go, I'll keep look-out.'

Jane had the door open and was about to go in when Rosaline called, 'Butters!'

She turned and in that instant the camera-flash went off. She gave a little cry and crumpled up where she was, sobbing hysterically.

Rosaline got her back to the dormitory, she was given her clothes and by breakfast time she had recovered sufficiently to go down with the others. In fact she was somewhat relieved, the trio had been nice to her and it seemed at last that she had been forgiven.

The following three days were the pleasantest she had spent since coming to the hostel. As far as she could tell Miss Russell had heard nothing of the incident and it was not referred to again in the dormitory or anywhere else in her hearing. They spent a day at Weymouth where they bathed and, though the weather broke, she enjoyed Miss Russell's conducted tour of the Hardy country. By the time she came down to breakfast on her third Sunday in the hostel she was beginning to feel relaxed and secure.

After breakfast she went, as usual, to look at the notice board and there, in the middle of the board, was an enlargement of the flash-light photograph Rosaline had taken. Standing, holding the knob of the door on which Miss Russell's name was clearly visible, she had half turned to the camera, clutching at the absurd towel with her free hand.

She rushed up to the dormitory only to find another pinned to her locker. They were everywhere, all over the building.

Miss Russell was almost inarticulate with anger. The trio were summoned to her room and interviewed

23

separately while the rest of the girls, including Jane, waited in the dormitories.

Rosaline came back from her interview unruffled.

'What happened?'

'Nothing happened. I said I'd fix her and I have, she's scared out of her tiny mind.'

Jane lay on her bed whimpering while the other girls maintained a deathly silence.

When Jane was called for interview she had a wild hope that she would now be vindicated, seen as the victim of a wicked persecution but the hope soon died. Miss Russell did not give her a chance to open her mouth.

'I do not want to hear anything from you, not one word! If I had the choice I would not have you near me but I have to tell you of the arrangements I have made. In an hour a taxi will arrive to take you to the station in Dorchester where you will be put on a train for home. I have telephoned your parents to expect you. Pamela O'Brien and Joan Simmonds will go with you to the station to see that you get on the train but apart from those two you are to have no contact with any of the girls. You will remain in this room until the taxi arrives and your things will be packed for you.'

CHAPTER ONE

Three o'clock on a wet January afternoon. Wycliffe sat at his desk reading an article in an old research bulletin: *Electrostatic Detection of Footprints*. The floor is dusted with minute expanded-polystyrene beads then, provided the omens are favourable, the beads which have not fallen on a recent footprint may easily be blown away while those which are in contact with a print remain to tell their tale.

The truth was that he was bored. For several days after Christmas and into the New Year professional crooks seem to call a truce or, perhaps, they are exhausted by their exertions during the great bonanza. Chief Inspector Gill, his deputy, was taking advantage of the situation to have some time off. Wycliffe felt lethargic and disinclined to settle to the routine of paper-work of which there was plenty. For his lethargy he blamed the heating and ventilating system against which he waged constant war.

He got up and went over to the large window which looked out over a dismal landscaped garden to one of the main highways in and out of the city. Double glazing. The damned thing wouldn't even open and the room was very nearly sound proof. Like being in a padded cell.

Outside rain fell vertically out of a leaden sky, cars

trooped nose to tail in ordered lanes, their screen-wipers beating time . . .

'Futile!'

He would have found it difficult to say exactly what it was that struck him as futile; the cars following each other like sheep, his job, or just life.

He was addicted to staring out of windows but from this one there was rarely anything to see but the endless streams of traffic. On a good day he might catch sight of the groundsman clearing litter, weeding or cutting the grass. It was a poor exchange for his old office which had overlooked a small public park where there were mothers and children, lovers and tramps and old gentlemen who each had a special seat on which to sleep in the sunshine. It could not always have been sunny but, in retrospect, it seemed so.

The telephone rang. He sighed and turned back to his desk.

'Wycliffe.'

Sergeant Bourne, his administrative assistant, reported the finding of a body in a flat in one of the new blocks near the city centre.

'Grenville House, sixth floor, a woman dead in suspicious circumstances, sir. The caretaker phoned the local station and they are passing it to us. Inspector Scales is on his way there with D.C. Dixon.'

'What do they mean by "suspicious circum-stances"? Why can't they say what they mean? Wycliffe was irritable.

'Perhaps they're not sure what they mean yet, sir.'

Bourne was good at putting the sting in a soft answer. Anyway it was an excuse to get out of the office.

Grenville House was one of the first fruits of a 'new community policy' for the city centre. Translated, it meant that the council wanted people to go back to live in an area from which the developers had turned them out. Grenville House consisted of fairly expensive flats over shops.

26

Wycliffe drove slowly in the afternoon traffic. The street lamps were on and, despite the rain, there were crowds of pedestrians milling around between the big stores where the January sales were persuading people to part with the money they had held on to over Christmas.

The entrance to Grenville House was between a furniture shop and a hi-fi establishment. A uniformed constable stepped out of the shelter of the canopied doorway and saluted as Wycliffe parked on the yellow lines.

'Flat 602, sir. Inspector Scales is up there with the doctor.'

The entrance was blue-carpeted, the lift smooth and silent. He got out on the sixth; a carpeted landing with four doors and a corridor with a notice: To Emergency Stairs. The door of 602 was open and in the hall a constable tried to make himself small. A card in a metal frame secured to the door read: Miss Debbie Joyce.

Scales was in the living room, a large room on split levels; up three steps to the dining area and the kitchen beyond. A large window, going almost to the floor, looked out over the grey city which, for the most part, had not yet sprouted above three or four floors. Scales was talking to the doctor who was in shirt sleeves and they broke off as Wycliffe came in. Scales was elegant. Not only was he the best-dressed man in the squad but his manner and general bearing suggested a top-ranking executive rather than a policeman. Wycliffe always felt foolishly diffident about giving him orders.

'She's in the kitchen, sir.'

'The kitchen?'

Few murders are committed in kitchens so if this proved to be murder the case had got off to an unusual start.

Wycliffe shook hands with the doctor, a wizened little man with a swingeing cold. The doctor took out a white handkerchief and blew violently.

'This damned weather!' He rubbed his nose and put the handkerchief away. 'She was strangled but I fancy she was knocked on the head first. She certainly received a blow to the base of her skull. I haven't moved her, of course.'

'Could she have struck her head in falling?'

'Possible, but I don't think so. You'll have to ask Franks when he's taken a look at her.' He sneezed. 'You'll get it all from him.'

'How long has she been dead?'

The doctor shrugged. 'A week? Several days, certainly. There again you'll have to rely on your experts.' He sneezed again. 'You won't want me any more? I've got work to do.'

'No, thank you for your help, doctor. We know where to find you.'

The doctor put on his jacket, picked up his bag and bustled out.

Wycliffe turned to Scales. 'She's been lying in there for a week?'

'It looks like it. The caretaker says she's a singer in the cabaret at the Golden Cockerel—the place in Judson Street.'

'A young woman, then?'

'Early to middle twenties. It's like this, sir: a week ago yesterday she told the caretaker of the flats that the club was closing for ten days for a face-lift and that she was going to London. She said that there was something wrong with her electric cooker and that she had asked the Electricity Board to send a man while she was away. She wanted the caretaker to let the chap in with his pass key. The electrician arrived this afternoon, the caretaker let him in and, together, they found her body.'

Wycliffe went up the three steps to the dining alcove and opened the kitchen door. The nauseating stench of putrefaction halted him for a moment.

28

'I opened the kitchen window. There seemed no point . . . '

'No, of course not.'

The kitchen was small but well equipped. White fittings with green patterned tiles on floor and walls. The body was lying partly on its right side and partly on the face with the head near the window which had a low sill paved with tiles. Rain spattered on to the sill through the open window. The dead girl wore a snugly fitting black jumper and slacks. She had a mass of black hair which almost hid her face but what he could see of it was livid and becoming bloated. The body was facing an open refrigerator. Fragments of a jug with a floral pattern were scattered for some distance around the body and the floor was stained, presumably where milk had dried on the tiles.

An electric kettle was plugged in but switched off and a teapot with two cups and saucers of the same pattern as the broken jug stood on a tray near the kettle. On the face of it she had been killed while she was making tea.

Wycliffe went back to the living room. 'Where's Dixon?'

'I've sent him to take a statement from the woman next door—604. D.C. Fowler is here too, he's doing the other flats in the building.'

Scales had tipped the contents of the girl's handbag on to the table. A cigarette pack, lighter, compact, lipstick, tissues, thirty-seven pounds in notes and some coin, a cheque book and banker's card. Scales pointed to a key ring with a yellow cockerel on the tab.

Wycliffe knew the club, a canopied entrance with a garish cockerel in neon lights over the door. It had a limited gaming licence and it was a favourite rendezvous for the city's wide boys. The place had been raided more than once but the proprietor, a Maltese called Bourg, was always a jump ahead. Ten to one the girl had got herself mixed up in some sordid intrigue and had tried to be too clever. He imagined a young face framed in that soft, fine, black hair.

'Futile!'

There was a commotion in the hall; Smith, the police photographer, had arrived with his equipment. Sergeant Smith was middle-aged, morose, and a martyr to indigestion. Lean and grey; his hair, his clothes, even his skin were grey. He acknowledged Wycliffe with the minimum of ceremony.

'Where is it?'

Soon he would be grumbling about the stench, the position of the body, the lighting, the space he had to work in and the inadequacy of his equipment but the grumbles were routine and only very new boys took any notice.

Debbie, he supposed, was short for Deborah though mothers are capable of anything. Well, Debbie had been murdered and the professionals, the specialists, were taking over, taking over her body, her flat and, as far as possible, they would take over her life as she had led it up to the moment of her dissolution. There were specialists for everything these days and it was getting worse.

A good witchdoctor could identify, convict and punish the guilty; in his spare time he could restore fertility to crops, cattle and women; treat the diseases of animals and men; drive out devils and make rain. What could he, Detective Chief Superintendent Wycliffe, do? Here at the scene of the crime he was redundant, waiting on his specialists. In fact, if he followed protocol, he would not be here at all, he would be sitting in his hermetically sealed office, sifting through reports, directing, co-ordinating and making more reports . . . To hell with that!

Perhaps he was in for a bout of 'flu, there was a lot of it about.

There was little furniture in the living room, almost everything was built in. A studio couch which looked as though it could also serve as a bed had certainly seen better days. There were two battered easy chairs which did not match and a corner cupboard full of knick-knacks. Apart from a record player and a radio that was all. No pictures on the walls; only professional photographs of Debbie stuck on with sellotape. They were all signed in an affected scrawl, 'Debbie'. Seen full-faced she was broad across the forehead and between her high cheekbones but her face narrowed quickly to a small, pointed chin which gave her a puckish look, mischievous with more than a hint of malice. The photographs showed an evolutionary trend from the all-revealing to the almost total cover-up. Her most recent photographs (they were all dated) showed her in a white gown which swept the floor.

'Franks is taking his time, isn't he?'

'He was at a meeting in the hospital.'

Wycliffe looked round the flat.

In the bedroom there was a travelling case open on the floor by the wardrobe and partly packed. Other items, waiting to be packed, were laid out on the bed and these included a white evening gown in a polythene dust-cover. The bed was double and made up for two. In the wardrobe, hanging with her clothes, he found a man's dressing gown, soiled and shabby with a cigarette burn in the lapel. On the floor of the wardrobe, with a dozen pairs of her shoes, there was a pair of men's slippers, the soles worn through. They were on the small side, six-and-a-half or seven.

From the bedroom he went to the bathroom, the lavatory and he even snooped in a small closet used for storing junk. His impression was one of tattiness and neglect. What furniture there was could have been bought in the nearest sale room. Whatever else Debbie Joyce had been she was not house-proud.

He went back to the living room, lit his pipe and stood, staring out of the window. Night was closing over the city although it was still short of five o'clock.

31

There was an office block not far away which looked like a layer cake—alternate bands of light and dark. He could see into one large office where rows of girls sat at typewriters, and on another floor men were working at drawing boards clamped in special stands like easels.

At about this time a week ago Debbie Joyce had been in her bedroom packing a case for her trip to London. Somebody had rung the doorbell and she had answered it. Either she knew her visitor or he had told a good enough tale to be invited in and offered a cup of tea. (Wycliffe was quite sure that it was not a woman's crime.) Surely they must have been acquainted, well enough acquainted for the man to have a motive for murder.

She had gone into the kitchen to make tea. Perhaps they continued to talk through the open door; then, quite naturally, he had joined her . . .

Someone she trusted or someone who seemed harmless.

Wycliffe turned away from the window. 'I'll be back.'

Scales smiled. He had worked with Wycliffe for long enough to know his ways.

604 had a card on the door also. Mr and Mrs Gordon Clarke. As Wycliffe was about to ring, the door opened and he was confronted by D.C. Dixon, the youngest of his detectives. Dixon had fair hair and freckles and a seemingly incurable habit of blushing whenever he found himself in any situation in the least degree embarrassing. He blushed now.

'I'm sorry, sir.'

'What for?'

A short, plump woman, fortyish was seeing Dixon out.

'Mrs Clarke?' Wycliffe introduced himself.

'I've just told your young man all I know about it.'

'I'm sure you have but I'd like to ask you a few questions if I may.'

32

She was soft skinned and pink, inclined to wobble like a jelly and, Wycliffe suspected, as likely to laugh as cry. She was not really averse to telling her story again; she would certainly repeat it endlessly to her friends at the hairdresser's and elsewhere.

'My hubby's away a lot, he's a sales rep for Rabat Toiletries—sales manager, really—so I'm often here alone and it's nice to have someone handy who can . . .'

'You were a friend of Miss Joyce?'

'Not exactly a friend, more an acquaintance. Actually you couldn't say that she was a friendly sort of girl. In fact, at first, she was really stand-offish, quite rude, but she soon got over that.'

'Who pays for the flat?'

She chuckled, as though at a risqué joke. 'Oh, so you've tumbled to that already? Well, it's obvious somebody does, isn't it? But I don't know who ho is. These flats aren't cheap.' Her baby face became solemn. 'I shouldn't laugh, should I? But it's difficult to realise . . . You think; I've been here all week imagining about her living it up in London and all the time she's been lying there.'

'Have you seen him?'

She looked vague, momentarily. 'Her man, you mean? Oh, yes, I've seen him several times. He's about your age, distinguished-looking.'

'Could be her father.'

'Not on your life! Debbie didn't come out of the top drawer and he did, you can always tell.'

'When have you seen him here?'

'Afternoons. I often go window shopping in the afternoons and twice he's come out of the lift while I've been waiting to go down. I've also passed him two or three times in the vestibule downstairs.'

'Five or six times—in how long?'

'Spread over the eight months since we moved in.'

'Can you describe him?'

33

She screwed up her face. 'He's tall, slim but putting it on a bit round the middle. He's got a big head with tiny features all close together. Funny looking.'

'How does he dress?'

'Very quiet and expensive. Grey; either mottled or with a fine stripe. No hat. Which reminds me, he's sandy haired, going thin.'

'She never mentioned him?'

'Never. She wasn't one for telling you her business.'

'Did she have many visitors?'

'Hardly any. Of course she was working every evening; she'd come home about three in the morning and she wouldn't be up until eleven or twelve . . . you know she worked at the club?'

'The Golden Cockerel, yes, I know. Did she ever bring anybody home with her?'

Mrs Clarke seemed amused. Her manner was arch. 'Well, no, I don't think anybody came home with her.'

Wycliffe almost expected her to pat his knee and say, 'You naughty boy!'

The husband must have done pretty well out of his toiletries. The living room was expensively furnished with a large settee and easy chairs covered with real hide. There was a stereo outfit which looked like something out of science fiction and a gigantic colour television. The colour scheme was old gold from the carpet to the wallpaper, cushions and curtains. Everything was 'to tone' as Mrs Clarke would almost certainly have said. The pictures on the wall were real paintings but he was sure that she had bought them with a piece of curtain material in her hand.

'Tell me about when you last saw her.'

'Well, it was a week ago today, last Monday. She came to lunch as usual, about one . . . '

'You mean that she came in here for lunch?'

'Oh, yes, most days. That's how I came to know her as well as I do. As I said, I'm on my own most of the time and it's nice to have somebody coming in, there's no

34

satisfaction in cooking for one. When I suggested it she wasn't keen but she came round and now she seems to look forward to it—I mean she did.' She was playing with the pendant stone which hung in the plunging V-neck of her woollen dress. 'I don't think the poor girl was very domesticated; if she hadn't come here she would have been eating out of tins.'

'What about the people in the other two flats on this floor?'

She shifted her position and pulled down her dress to within speaking distance of her plump knees. 'Well, there's nobody in 601 most of the time. It belongs to Pneumax Industries and they keep it for visiting executives. In 603 there's a couple with two boys, aged seven and eleven. It's a bigger flat than this. He's the manager of a building society; they're pleasant enough people but when you try to keep your place nice you don't want two boys romping all over it. To be honest, I haven't given Mrs Woodward—that's her name—much encouragement.'

'Did Debbie tell you anything about herself or her family?'

'Practically nothing. She didn't give much away. She did say once that she'd gone to school in the city and that she'd been brought up by a maiden aunt. I can't think of anything else.'

'You must have talked about something.'

She smiled. 'Perhaps I did most of the talking. When she said anything it was usually about the club. She had a way of telling a story—laugh! Yet she hardly fetched a smile. What goes on in those places you'd never believe and Debbie had a wicked way of telling it.'

'You were going to tell me about the last time you saw her.'

'So I was. Well, as I said, she came here to lunch and by the time we'd washed up it must have been after two. She said, "I'd better be getting my skates on, I'm

35

catching the night train and I haven't done a thing about getting ready.'' Of course, I knew the club was closed and that she was going to London for a week.'

'She was going for a week?'

'That's what she said. She told me to expect her back sometime on Monday, that's today. As a matter of fact, I took in extra milk and a loaf of bread for her this morning.'

She reached for a box of cigarettes, offered them to Wycliffe and, when he refused, lit one herself. She held the cigarette awkwardly and the smoke made her cough.

'I don't smoke very often but I need something to settle my nerves.'

'When did you first hear what had happened?'

'When Stebbings, the caretaker, came ringing my doorbell looking as though he was going to pass out. He phoned the doctor from here, nothing would have persuaded him to go back in that flat.'

The light was so dim that it was becoming difficult to see across the room. Her face, as she talked, was a pale blur. He would have liked to switch on the light but he had no reasonable excuse for doing so.

'What did you think of her as a person?'

A mild exclamation of protest. 'That's a question; I don't speak ill of the living let alone the dead.'

'Unless we find out all we can about Debbie Joyce we are unlikely to discover her murderer, Mrs Clarke.'

After a time she allowed herself to be persuaded. 'Well, I must admit that Debbie had a side to her that I didn't like. You got the impression sometimes that she took a delight in hurting people. I suppose you could say that she had a mischievous streak, like people who are always playing practical jokes, but I think there was more to it than that.' She looked at Wycliffe anxiously, fearful that her candour might shock him.

'I can't forget what she told me about the pianist at the club. That really upset me. All he did was to criticise the way she sang one of her songs and she fixed it so that he lost his job, a man with a wife and two children to support.'

'What did she do?'

'Well, they were losing cigarettes from the store and Bourg, the boss, was furious about it. Anyway, Debbie took four hundred cigarettes and hid them in the pianist's locker, then tipped off the boss that they were there.' She broke off genuinely agitated. 'The worst of it was that she seemed proud of what she'd done. "Nobody treads on my neck," that was her favourite expression.'

She was silent for a while, waiting for him to speak, but then she went on, 'I don't want you to think she was always like that, she could be good company and I was glad to have her coming in but she had that other side to her.'

When Wycliffe still did not speak she said, 'Well, I suppose we've all got our faults and our funny ways, but you did ask . . .'

She could not know that Wycliffe was beginning to live a new world, a world which she was helping to create for him, the world of Debbie Joyce.

'You really have been a great help, Mrs Clarke.'

'Have I really?' She seemed pleased and surprised.

Wycliffe returned to the dead girl's flat. The case was getting under way. Inspector Scales had been joined by two more detectives and they were making a thorough search of the flat. Dr Franks, the pathologist, was examining the body prior to its removal to the mortuary and Sergeant Smith was standing by to take more photographs. In an hour or two every detail of the flat and of its contents would have been recorded on film and on paper.

As Wycliffe entered the living room Franks came out of the kitchen.

'Well?' Wycliffe greeted him.

'You can have her moved when you like.'

Franks had worked with Wycliffe so often that they were like members of the same team. They no longer needed to spell out ideas and they could sense each other's doubts and reservations but physically and temperamentally they could hardly have been less alike. The pathologist was stout, pink and shining like a precocious baby fresh from his bath. He was invincibly cheerful, he accepted things as he found them and seemed utterly lacking in any desire to change either himself or his world. By comparison, Wycliffe seemed, to himself at least, tentative, often self-conscious and given to needless worry. He was certainly aware of his own defects and frequently discouraged by the world about him.

Franks made his preliminary report.

'She died of strangulation, there can be no doubt of that, but she had a nasty bump on her head—occipital region. It must have been a fairly heavy blow. She's got a good mop of hair but it wasn't enough to cushion the impact much.'

'But it didn't kill her—the blow, I mean?'

'No, in my opinion the blow knocked her unconscious and then she was strangled.'

'How?'

'From the marks on her neck I should say by a nylon cord.'

Wycliffe nodded. 'Try this: she was making tea and while she was stooping to get a jug of milk from the refrigerator her assailant struck her across the base of the skull and she collapsed on the floor, he then strangled her with a nylon cord.'

Franks agreed. 'That would fit. Now, as to the time of death, I'll try to do better after the autopsy but at the moment I can't get closer than a few days.'

'As far as we know she was last seen alive exactly a week ago.'

'I wouldn't quarrel with that.' Franks took his coat from a chair and put it on. 'Well, I'm off. Get her over to

38

me as quickly as you can and I'll let you have my report in the morning.'

The specialist at work, clear thinking, incisive. No bumbling there. Wycliffe envied him. He turned to find D.C. Dixon standing at his elbow and spoke brusquely, 'Nothing to do, Dixon? Do you know the Golden Cockerel?'

'Night club in Judson Street, sir. Limited gaming licence. Everybody calls it the Cock.'

'Indeed.' He was always a little moved as well as irritated by Dixon's anxiety to do and say the right thing. 'Well, the proprietor is a Maltese called Bourg. I want you to get hold of him and find out what you can about the girl. I think he lives in Palmerston Crescent.'

'I know the place, sir. A great Victorian barracks with about twenty rooms. He lives there with momma and eight kids. At least it was eight at the last count. They say he's devoted to them. Apparently his wife was a real doll when he married her, now she's as broad as she's long.'

'Really.'

Even Dixon was doing it.

'Just remember one thing, Dixon, Riccy Bourg may be the ideal husband and father but he's also a crook and a clever one so don't let him put anything over.'

'You can rely on me, sir.'

'I hope so. And Dixon—ask him what happened to his pianist?'

'Sir?'

Wycliffe explained.

Dixon went out and Wycliffe watched him go with a twinge of regret. When a case was on he wanted to be everywhere and to do everything; everything but what he was expected to do, to sit in his office and issue instructions.

'Have you been in the bedroom, sir?' Scales was going through the drawers of a built-in unit in the living room.

39

'Just glanced in, why?'

'She has a man who sleeps there pretty regularly.'

'I saw the dressing gown and slippers.'

Scales nodded. 'The bed linen too. She wasn't fussy about her laundry.'

Who had shared Debbie's bed? Surely not the tall, elegant gentleman Mrs Clarke had described; yet it would be surprising if Debbie had had a lover of whom her neighbour knew nothing.

'John!'

'Sir?'

'Get on to the ground landlords and find out who holds the lease on the flat and who pays the overheads.'

'I already have. The flat is in the girl's name and she paid all the bills herself.'

'Does this place have a back entrance?'

'And a service lift, sir. I told them to bring the mortuary van round the back; they're due any minute.'

Wycliffe decided that he might really be more use in his office. He went down in the lift without seeing a soul. Outside it was still raining and people were on their way home from work, the evening rush hour was beginning. Despite the rain a small crowd had gathered on the pavement though there was nothing to see but the fluted glass of the swing doors to the foyer. A reporter from the *News* accosted Wycliffe as he was getting into his car.

'Is it true that a girl has been murdered, Mr Wycliffe?'

'Quite true.' He was never needlessly coy with the press.

'Who was she?'

'A Miss Debbie Joyce; she was a singer at the Golden Cockerel. She was strangled.'

'When did it happen?'

'Her body was discovered this afternoon but she has been dead for several days.'

'Have you—?'

'I've told you all I know at the moment and I've got work to do.'

'Your man won't let me into the building.'

'There would be no point.'

CHAPTER TWO

Wycliffe's headquarters occupied the first floor of one wing of the new area police building. For almost a fortnight it had been a lifeless place. People arrived at nine in the morning and by five-fifteen most of the offices were in darkness. His staff went about with an air of listlessness as though what they were doing might just as well have been left until the next day or not done at all. It was, presumably, the same malaise which had led him to stand by his big window, watching the traffic and to murmur:

'Futile!'

But when he returned there at a little before six the change was dramatic. Lights were on everywhere, typewriters were clacking, telephones ringing and people were bustling around with a new sense of urgency and purpose. It was odd, because as yet very few of them were involved in any way with the new case. Even undertakers must get depressed when business is slack.

He had scarcely sat at his desk when W.P.C. Saxton, his clerical assistant, came in with a tray of tea.

'I thought you might be glad of that, sir.'

'Thank you, Diane.'

She was blonde, immaculate, always band-box fresh and very efficient, like a secretary in a TV commercial.

She worried him: when she was near him he could not help wondering whether his collar was clean or if he had dandruff. He could not recall in what circumstances he had ever had the temerity to start calling her by her first name.

Reports were beginning to come in. First from D.C. Fowler who had questioned the caretaker and the occupants of the other flats. There were thirty-two flats in the building and he had spoken to someone in twenty-four of them. Only one person admitted to knowing anything about Debbie Joyce, a woman doctor on the seventh floor. Like most doctors she was prickly but Fowler was an old hand.

'Yes, I know the girl, at least I know of her.'

Fowler adopted a confidential manner and outlined what had happened in the flat below.

'Well, if, as you tell me, the girl is dead, I suppose there is no reason why I shouldn't tell you what happened. It was about three months ago, early October, between five and six in the morning, when I was awakened by someone ringing my doorbell. When I went to the door I found a young man in a dressing gown; he was distraught, barely coherent, but I gathered that there was someone ill in 602 and I went down with him.

'I found a young woman lying on the floor by the bed. She was recovering from an epileptic fit. I did what was necessary and got her back to bed. By that time she had completely recovered and she told me that she had been an epileptic since childhood but that in recent years her attacks had become less frequent and she had, rightly, given up taking the drugs which had been prescribed. I suggested, a little tartly, that if she had taken her husband into her confidence she could have avoided scaring him out of his wits. Of course, it emerged that the young man was not her husband.

'Anyway, I advised the girl to see her own doctor and

43

left them to it. As far as I was concerned that was the end of the matter.'

'Could you describe the young man or would you recognise him again if you saw him?'

'I can describe him and I have seen him again.'

'When have you seen him?'

'Two or three times, the last time was a fortnight ago. On each occasion we met in the lift, going up around midnight. To be honest I doubt whether I would have noticed him had he not been looking at me with a somewhat guilty expression which drew my attention. Then he spoke.'

The description was professionally detailed:

'Short—five feet five or six. Twentyish, slim with fair, curly hair and heavy sideburns; broad features, fresh complexion and rather cow-like brown eyes. On each occasion he wore blue jeans and a leather jacket with a checked shirt. Oh, yes, I remember, he had an old scar over his left eye. He struck me as a bit dim.'

'Do you practise from here?'

'No, I'm attached to a group practice at the Horton Health Centre.'

'Then how would he know that you are a doctor?'

'He may be dim but I imagine that he can read. My name is on the board in the hall—Dr Mary Peskett.'

Wycliffe was pleased; with that sort of description it shouldn't be difficult to pick up Debbie's sleeping partner. He was also interested to learn that she was an epileptic. Would this lead Franks to change his mind about the cause of her skull injury? In a *grand mal* attack the subject often threshes about with great violence; was it possible that she had come by her injury in this way? That the killer had then taken advantage of the fact that she was unconscious to finish her off? It sounded and was, almost certainly, absurd.

The truth was that Wycliffe had been troubled about the blow on the head. It was outside the usual pattern. Stranglers generally fall into one of two categories.

44

There are those who commit an unpremeditated crime in circumstances of unendurable frustration or anger and there are others who deliberately strangle out of perverted lust. For them the act of strangulation is associated with or is a substitute for the act of sex and they will go on killing until they are caught. In neither case is the victim likely to be knocked on the head first nor attacked while in the kitchen making tea.

D.C. Dixon was back from his interview with Bourg, the proprietor of the Golden Cockerel. He had been welcomed like an honoured guest and had been introduced to all the children from Marco aged two to Elisa who was sixteen.

'Momma, you hear this terrible thing? Little Debbie who sing at the club. Such a thing to happen.'

And Momma too was deeply distressed.

'She was a good girl,' Ricky went on. 'She work for me seven—no, eight months and everybody like her. She sing songs that are a little naughty but she look so ... what is the word? Pure? Chaste—that is it. All beautiful in a white dress like a little girl at her first communion in my village where I was born. People like that, men and women. They do not know whether to laugh a little or cry a little and that is good.'

He sighed. 'She was to do something special for when we open again on Wednesday. Tomorrow she would come for rehearsal.'

Mr Bourg absolutely refused to countenance the possibility that Debbie might have involved herself in anything discreditable. About the piano player he was contemptuous.

'He was a rogue that one. If Debbie set a little trap it was to help me; for proof of something I know already. In any case he was not good on the piano. That girl, she was as another daughter to me.'

After a pause for reflection he added: 'I tell you one thing and that is gossip only, you understand. It was said that Debbie is married and that she leave her

45

husband. Who she marry I do not know but you will find out.'

Asked who passed on this gossip he professed, grandly, never to remember such details.

Another pause and Mr Bourg reached his great conclusion. 'You find that bastard, her husband, my friend, he is the one for sure. And tell Mr Wycliffe that Riccardo Bourg give you this tip for free—no strings.'

Poor Dixon had been swamped by magnanimity and Wycliffe was highly amused even by the edited version of the interview which reached him.

The pattern was growing more complex, the colours richer. Riccy Bourg, his club, his singer, his wronged piano player and Debbie's illicit lover. Now there was the suggestion of a husband in the background.

Scales came in to say that, so far, he had been unable to trace Debbie's relatives; there had been almost nothing of a strictly personal nature in the flat. There was a cheque book but few of the counterfoils had been filled in.

'In the morning you can have a word with her bank manager.'

The wheels were beginning to turn. The description of the young man was being circulated to every policeman in the city; the occupants of the flats in Grenville House were being questioned for the second time, partly because husbands would be home, partly because they could now be questioned about the young man.

'I suppose we should get out an identikit picture of him?'

Wycliffe shrugged. 'If we don't pull him in tonight we can try it.'

He gave instructions for a man to remain in the flat through the night. 'As she was expected back today he might turn up.'

'Unless he killed her.'

*　　*　　*

46

'There you are, Mr Norman.' His secretary helped him on with his overcoat, straightened his collar at the back and handed him his briefcase and gloves.

Norman glanced briefly round his office. 'You'll see that those files go back to registry, Miss Hopkins?'

'Right away, sir.'

He lingered in the doorway. 'They shouldn't be left here overnight.' A brief pause. 'Very well, nine-thirty in the morning.'

'Nine-thirty, Mr Norman. Good-night.'

Norman set off down the long corridor to the lift. He had to pass his surgical wards. The door of the television lounge was open and he could see several patients sitting round the set. The voice of a news reader reached him:

'. . . identified as Miss Debbie Joyce, a singer in one of the city's clubs. Detective Chief Superintendent Wycliffe stated that tho police are treating her death as a case of murder.'

A domestic, pushing a trolley, steered round him and looked back with curiosity. A ward sister stopped, 'Are you all right, Mr Norman?'

He looked at her sharply. 'All right? Of course I'm all right.'

He walked on to the lift. A staff nurse, already in the lift on her way down, made herself as inconspicuous as possible. On the ground floor he stepped out of the lift and crossed the vast entrance hall. The porter dashed to open one of the doors.

'Good-night, Mr Norman, sir.'

It was raining, a fine drizzle, but his car was drawn up under the canopy. A middle-aged man in a chauffeur's cap opened the car door for him.

'A nasty night, sir.'

Norman sank into the back seat and said nothing.

The telephone rang.

'Wycliffe.'

'A Mr Matthew Norman on the line for you, sir, senior consultant surgeon at Millfield General.'

'Put him through.'

A cultured voice, dry and tight. 'I understand that a Miss Debbie Joyce has been murdered.'

'That is so.'

A moment of silence, then, 'I must talk to you, perhaps I could come to your office . . . '

'I would prefer to call on you.'

'As you wish. I live at twenty-four Conniston Gardens. What I have to tell you is important so the sooner you are able to come . . . '

'I'll be with you in half an hour.'

In the bottom flat at 14 Edgcumbe Close, Elaine Bennett was studying herself in the dressing table mirror. She was flushed, and she was feeling unwell. All day she had been conscious of a constriction in her throat, now it was painful and she had a headache.

Elaine was a nurse in private practice and her present job was nightnurse to a wealthy old lady who lived at Kemsley Rise, a bus trip across the city. For the past three weeks, each night, she had left the flat at half-past nine and walked to Godolphin Road where she boarded a 622 bus which took her to the bottom of Kemsley Rise. She had no day off for she preferred to work for short, intensive spells then take a week or two off between jobs. Her present job was something of a sinecure for she could sleep most of the night.

'I think I've got a temperature, Val.'

Valerie Hughes, her flat mate, was in the sitting room watching television but the door between was open.

'I told you.'

Elaine came through from the bedroom with a thermometer in her mouth. After a while she took it out and read it.

'A hundred and one.'

'I told you.'

48

'Can't you think of anything else to say?'

'Well, you can't go to work tonight, that's for sure.'

'But the old girl depends on me. If it gets round that I don't turn up at my cases I'm sunk.'

'She won't thank you for giving her the 'flu.'

'I suppose not. I'd better go out to the phone and ring the woman who does days. She might be willing to stop on.'

'I'll do it.'

'What? Ring?'

'No, look after the old woman. I suppose she would put up with me for one night.'

'But you're on six-till-two.'

'Tomorrow's my day off.' Valerie was a nurse at Millfield General.

'You're an angel! I do feel pretty bloody.'

'You look it.'

'Listen!' Elaine's attention had been caught by the television. An announcer was reading the regional news.

'. . . The dead girl is Debbie Joyce, a night club entertainer. A police spokesman said that she had been dead for several days when her body was found in the kitchen of her flat. The police are treating her death as murder.'

'Well, I'm damned!'

Valerie looked at her friend. 'That's the girl you went to school with, isn't it?'

'No.'

'But I remember you saying that night you went to the Cock—'

Elaine was suddenly irritable. 'You don't remember me saying I went to school with her because I didn't but I did know her when we were at school. We met playing hockey and we were friendly for a time.'

'Didn't you say Joyce wasn't her real name?'

'Whatever she's called now, her name when I knew her was Rosaline Parkin.'

49

'I wonder how she got herself murdered?'

'I would imagine that's easy enough if you carry on like she did at that club.' Elaine switched off the television. 'Now, for God's sake let's forget about it.'

Valerie shrugged. 'O.K. What are we going to eat?'

James Rendell locked the door of the shop, tried it twice, then stood on the edge of the pavement in the drizzling rain, waiting for a lull in the traffic down Prince's Street. It came and he crossed to a traffic island, waited again, then finally made it to the other side. It was not far to the city centre which was a blaze of light after the dark tunnel of Prince's Street. A man was selling newspapers in a shop doorway. A scrawled news-bill read: 'City Solicitor on Fraud Charge'. News of the discovery of Debbie Joyce's body had come too late for the evening editions.

Each working day for a week Rendell had forced himself to carry on normally, never leaving the shop between nine in the morning and half-past five in the afternoon. Each evening as he walked up Prince's Street to the city centre, he steeled himself for the moment when he would come in sight of the news-vendor and be able to read the legend on the news-bill. He would deliberately avert his eyes until he was within a couple of yards, then . . .

He could think of no circumstances in which the body could have remained undiscovered for a whole week. He told himself again and again that she was dead, there could be no doubt of that, no possible doubt. He had seen . . . but he would not think about what he had seen.

On the Wednesday evening, two days after, he had gone to the Golden Cockerel with no clear object in mind. He had certainly not intended to go in but it came as a shock when from the end of Judson Street, he saw that the club was in darkness, the sign unlit. He hurried down the street, his heart thumping wildly. There was a little notice on one of the glass doors which he had difficulty in reading because of the dim light. By bringing his eyes close to the square of cardboard he could make out the words: 'The Management regrets that the club will remain closed for ten days during which time the premises will be redecorated and modernised to give patrons a better service in the future.'

For a while he was almost prepared to believe that this was part of a plan to deceive him, to lead him to some incriminating act. Was it possible that the police, for their own reasons, would hush up the fact that a crime had been committed? The thought scared him although he would not have been able to explain why.

Later that same evening he had gone to a side street from which it was possible to see the upper floors of Grenville House and for more than an hour he had stood there watching the windows which he knew belonged to her flat. They were in total darkness. On the Friday in desperation he had almost telephoned the police to lay anonymous information.

The weekend had been purgatory. How could he go on without knowing what was happening? Now it was Monday again. A whole week.

'Goodnight, guv.' The old man with the newspapers had got to know him although he never bought a paper.

He walked on. It was not far to the *Guardian* building where he lived with his sister and brother-in-law. The couple had a flat on the top floor of the office block of which they were caretakers. He took the lift and came out into a tiny vestibule on the eighth floor.

'Is that you, Jim?'

He went into his bedroom, washed, and changed his jacket for a woolly cardigan then he went through into the living room where they would soon be sitting down to their evening meal. His sister, Alice, was in the kitchen but he could talk to her through the open hatch.

'Where's Albert?'

'They got trouble with the radiators on the third. He's down there with the maintenance man. He said not to wait. Had a good day?'

'All right.'

'You don't look very well, Jim, and that's a fact.'

'I'm all right.'

He had been a fool to come to live with his sister and her husband; it would have been better if he had stayed on in his own house, alone. Now he had to keep up this constant pretence and, worse, endure their sympathy and professed understanding when they understood nothing—nothing!

The television was on as usual. The regional news. '. . . Debbie Joyce, a night club entertainer. A police spokesman said that she had been dead several days when her body was found in the kitchen of her flat. The police are treating her death as murder.'

He had been waiting so long, yet now that it had come it was like an unexpected blow. His legs would not support him and he sat down heavily.

'What was that, Jim—about a girl being murdered?'

He did not answer, he could not trust his voice.

'Weren't you listening?'

'What?'

Alice was irritated. 'It doesn't matter, forget it.'

He was recovering and experiencing a great flood of relief. His spirits rose, he began to feel almost gay.

By the time Alice had served the meal he was so excited that he could scarcely eat his food. She noticed the change in him and, as usual, misinterpreted the signs.

'What you need is a complete change, Jim. Why don't you take a few days off—go up to London and poke around the museums and art galleries? You used to love doing that.'

'I don't need a change, I'm perfectly all right.' He spoke between his teeth, he was so irritated by her chatter. Why couldn't she shut up and leave him alone?

'Old Probert would keep the shop going—do him good, he'd miss you.'

'I said I'm all right, Alice. For God's sake stop telling me what to do!'

It was so unusual for him to raise his voice that Alice was upset.

'There's no need to rave at me, Jim. I'm only trying to help you. You want me to mind my own business, all right, I will.'

'I'm sorry.' He realised that he had gone too far. 'Really.'

But he was trembling and as soon as he could he left the table.

'Are you going out?'

'I thought I would.'

He went into his bedroom and put on his mackintosh and cap. He felt in the right-hand pocket of his mackintosh and was reassured. His nerves became steadier and his hands ceased to tremble. Before leaving he looked in the living room.

'You mustn't mind me, Alice, it's very good of you and Albert to have me here. Maybe you're right, perhaps I will have a few days but I'll wait for the better weather.'

*   *   *

Wycliffe telephoned Franks but the pathologist was unimpressed by the news that Debbie Joyce had been epileptic.

'Anything else? Otherwise I'll get on . . . '

Wycliffe was unusually diffident. 'Not about the girl, at least, not directly. I wanted to ask you, do you know Matthew Norman, the senior surgeon at Millfield?'

'As we work almost under the same roof, I'd have a job not to.'

53

'What sort of man is he?'

Even close friendship fails to compete with the Masonic solidarity of the medical profession. 'He's a good surgeon, one of the best.'

'I don't doubt it, but what sort of man is he?'

'Rather severe. He sets high standards for himself and for the people who work with him. He sometimes appears patronising but I don't think that he means to be so.'

'Married?'

Wycliffe could sense the pathologist's hesitation.

'I understand that he is separated from his wife though I know very little of his private life.'

'Any gossip about women?'

'Definitely not!' It was amusing to hear the emphatic almost shocked denial from Franks whose own affairs were notorious.

'Or the other thing?'

'Nor that.'

'All right, thanks.'

But now Franks' curiosity was aroused. 'Is he supposed to be mixed up in this affair?'

'That's what I'm going to ask him.'

'Be careful. He comes from a legal family, his father was Recorder of the city and his grandfather was a high court judge.'

'I'll remember.'

It was Franks who was now reluctant to end the conversation. 'From what I've heard, he lives for his work and his pots.'

'His pots?'

'Chinese blue-and-white porcelain. He's an authority.'

Wycliffe put down the receiver with a smile on his face.

Conniston Gardens was a crescent of large, Edwardian houses on the edge of Conniston Park. Giant elms, now bare, gave the place an air of slightly decaying elegance

54

and it would have been no surprise to hear the clip-clop of horse's hooves as the brougham drew up, bringing the master from the station.

Wycliffe was received by the housekeeper and taken to a back room where Norman waited. He was very tall, slim but slightly pot-bellied. His head was abnormally large but his features were small and close together, a ready-made caricature. No need to look further for Debbie's well-dressed visitor.

'Good of you to come, chief superintendent. Sherry?'

There were enough books to call the room a library; the bookshelves reached to within a yard of the high ceiling and blue-and-white vases and jars were disposed along the tops of the bookcases. Glass-fronted cabinets on either side of the chimney breast housed smaller pieces. A large gas fire burned cosily in a fireplace framed by a huge white-marble mantelpiece. Above the fireplace there was a portrait in oils of a man in legal gown and wig. A severe, distinguished face whose features resembled Norman's but were more fittingly proportioned and disposed.

Wycliffe watched the surgeon with bland, expressionless eyes. Norman was finding it difficult to begin, he was the sort of man who would abhor any discussion of his intimate life.

'I heard on the television news that a young woman by the name of Joyce had been found dead in her flat. It was said that she had been murdered.'

'That is so.'

'I hoped that you would be prepared to give me more information.'

Wycliffe was cool. 'If I am satisfied that you are entitled to it.'

'She was my wife.'

'I see.'

Norman had got over the first hurdle and his manner became noticeably less tense. 'We were married a year ago but we separated after three months.'

'How long since you last saw your wife, Mr Norman?'

'A little over a week.'

'You visited her regularly?'

'Fairly regularly?'

'Why?'

A flicker of annoyance. 'She was my wife, the fact that we were separated did not mean that I was indifferent to her welfare.'

'Or she to yours?'

He ignored the question.

Wycliffe's manner was brusque, almost rude. Norman moved in a world where his word was law. Doctors, nurses and patients, patients in particular, held him almost in reverence. Daily, life and death lay, literally, in his hands. In those circumstances a man is bound to develop an armour of self esteem. To get him to talk freely about himself it was essential to break through.

'You have always lived in this house?'

'I was born here, my father was Recorder of the city.' He glanced up at the portrait over the mantelpiece.

'You live alone?'

A mild show of well-bred irritation. 'My housekeeper and her husband have a flat upstairs.'

Wycliffe was trying to picture the dead girl in these surroundings, sharing them with this man. If, as her neighbour had suggested, she enjoyed hurting people she had a ready-made victim in her shy, sensitive husband.

'Why did you marry her?'

Norman's anger flared. 'I really do not see . . . '

'Your wife has been murdered and such questions will have to be answered.'

He pursed his lips and seemed to consider. 'I suppose that you are right. It would be foolish to hamper the investigations in any way.'

Thank God for the objectivity of a trained mind.

'You were a man in your late forties, a bachelor, living in the house where you were born—'

It was Norman's turn to interrupt. 'Because a man is a bachelor, it does not necessarily follow that he wishes to be so.'

'But a girl in her twenties with a totally alien background . . .'

Outside it was quite dark but the curtains had not been drawn. Norman stood up, went to the window and swept them together in a single vigorous movement.

'A man comes to terms with circumstances. Perhaps he solves his problems by pretending that they do not exist then something happens and pretence is no longer possible.'

Wycliffe looked instinctively at the shelves of books, the valuable porcelain, the desk and the well-worn swivel chair. His glance did not escape Norman who smiled, wryly.

'It wasn't enough.'

'How did you meet her?'

'By the most improbable chance. From time to time the staff at the hospital organise a dance and the consultants are expected to look in. A gesture. On this occasion Debbie was there, she had been invited by one of my juniors.' He broke off. 'Perhaps I should tell you that although she insisted on being called Debbie, it was not her real name. She was Rosaline Parkin, and she adopted the name Debbie Joyce for professional reasons. Anyway, she was there and it happened that I was standing by the buffet when she was choosing what she would have. She made it her business to draw me into conversation. At first I was a little distant but before long I found myself talking freely. Someone had told her of my interest in Chinese blue-and-white and she asked me several intelligent questions. It was clear that she knew nothing about the subject but her interest seemed genuine. To my own astonishment I found

57

myself asking her to come and see my collections.' He gestured helplessly. 'She came and we went on from there.'

The sound of a table being laid came from an adjoining room, the rattle of crockery and cutlery.

Wycliffe was asking himself whether the interview could have gone quite in this way if Norman had murdered his wife. He had to admit that he had no data to go on. The Normans of this world are not often involved with the police and so in dealing with them there are few precedents.

But the surgeon's manner had changed. He was much more relaxed. Wycliffe suspected that this introspective and essentially solitary man was finding a certain relief in unburdening himself in a strictly professional context.

'For the first time in my life I fell in love. The phrase is an apt one, it precisely describes what happened to me—I fell, as helpless to control or influence my fate as a man who steps off a cliff.' He paused. 'It was a devastating experience. Do you find that absurd, superintendent?'

'If I found human nature absurd I should not be doing this job.'

Norman looked at him appreciatively. 'No, I suppose not; nor I mine.'

He pointed to the decanter. 'Are you sure that you won't?'

'Very well, thank you.'

They were silent while he poured the sherry with that economy of movement and precision which is only found in people who daily rely on the skill of their hands.'

'Somebody said that a fool at forty must be a fool indeed. Of course, I asked her to marry me and she agreed. I did not question my fortune any more than one questions waking on a spring morning. Little things might have warned me but I was in no mood to be warned. We were married.'

A long pause during which he sipped his sherry and stared at the fire.

'It was like having a chair snatched from under you when you are about to sit down. Overnight she seemed to become a different person. You asked me why I married her, the question for me is, why did she marry me? I asked myself that question many times during each day and night that we were together and I still do not know the answer. It is true that I am comfortably off but she was not interested in my money. I have some status but she did not care about that either. She married me yet she seemed to have hated me—why?'

'Why, indeed?

'When she left me my first feeling was one of relief.' He gestured weakly with his long, white hands. 'But you cannot live with a girl like her, even as we lived, without missing her when she goes.'

'You tried to persuade her to come back?'

He nodded without speaking.

Wycliffe looked up at the Recorder's portrait and wondered what genetic cookery had produced this chancy blend of sophistication and naivety, of priggishness and sensuality, of pedantry and quirkish humour.

'Did you visit your wife last Monday?'

'Last Monday? Is that when ... '

Wycliffe said nothing.

'No, I did not see her on Monday, I was at the hospital all day, at least, until half-past six or seven in the evening.'

'Just one more thing. Can you tell me anything of her background, her relatives, where she went to school and who her friends were?'

Norman shook his head. 'I must confess that I knew very little about her and the fact worried me. One's wife ... But she was secretive. She told me once that she had lost her parents when she was a baby and that she had been brought up by a maiden aunt. That was all.'

'Did she leave any of her personal things here—letters, documents, that sort of thing?'

'She took everything with her, not that she had much. When she left her belongings went into two suitcases.' He looked at Wycliffe then at his room, stored with possessions. 'That moved me deeply.'

'Is that why you set her up in the flat and paid her bills?'

Resentment flickered again then died. He nodded. 'I made her an allowance and I bought the flat in her name. It was the least I could do.'

Another silence, so profound that they could hear the faint hissing of the gas fire.

'How did she die?'

'She was strangled after being knocked unconscious by a blow to the head.'

'Have you any idea who might have killed her?'

'None.'

'The club where she worked has an unsavoury reputation.'

'All the possibilities are being investigated.'

'Of course.' Norman came with him to the gate. 'Thank you for coming.'

'You realise that you may be the subject of further investigation?'

'Yes.'

The rain had almost stopped and a pale radiance in the sky betrayed the position of the moon above the clouds.

He drove home slowly. The move which had cost him his office in a Queen Anne crescent had enabled him to become the proud owner of the Watch House, an old coastguard house built on the slopes overlooking the narrows through which all the shipping entering and leaving the port had to pass. A half acre of ground went with the house and, altogether, it was a great consolation to him on days when he threatened himself with an early retirement.

Ever since their marriage their home had been a place where he could relax. He took it for granted, scarcely realising that it was a rare talent of his wife's which made it so. In more than twenty years, even through the twins' most difficult periods, there had been few crises and none which threatened their marriage.

'Back to normal?'

'A girl strangled in one of the new flats in the city centre.'

'Is Jimmy Gill back?'

'No, but he will be as soon as he hears about this.'

He bathed, had his meal, helped to wash up then they sat together in front of the fire, reading and listening to records.

At nine o'clock he switched on the television for the news. The finding of Debbie Joyce's body was mentioned again. 'The police are treating it as a case of murder.'

Just after ten the telephone rang. It was Gill.

'I'm at the office. I heard about the girl so I looked in to see what was going on. I'd no sooner arrived than another report came through, an attack on a girl in the Godolphin Road area. She's been taken to Millfield. I gather that she made the 999 call herself so she can't be all that bad but I thought you'd better know.'

CHAPTER THREE

Valerie came back into the sitting room dressed for the street. 'Three aspirins, a glass of hot milk and bed for you. And don't forget to use disinfectant when you wash up.'

Elaine smiled weakly. 'Thanks, Val.'

Valerie opened the street door and banged it shut behind her. The air was moist and chilly but the rain had stopped. A thin mist drifted tenuously between the houses and haloed the street lamps. She hurried up the Close to a point where a convenient footpath cut through to Godolphin Road saving a quarter of a mile of walking. It led through allotments between ragged privet hedges. As she turned into the path it started to rain again, sweeping across the open ground. She was not a nervous girl but she did not care for this walk at night. The street lamps in Godolphin Road seemed a long way off. But who would be out on a night like this unless they had to be? She focused her thoughts on the winter coat she had bought in the sales and plodded on through the darkness.

She was half way through the allotments when a sudden movement, very close, startled her. She did not cry out and when she would have done it was too late, all she could manage was a choking gurgle. Her face was pressed hard against the material of a man's raincoat and there was something round her neck which made it almost impossible to breathe. She knew that he was trying to strangle her but she could not really believe it. The cord, or whatever it was, cut into the back of her neck but in front her coat collar had caught in it. All the same ... She struggled and her waterproof hat fell off. Her head felt as though it would burst but she had not lost consciousness. Then the pressure was suddenly released and a man's voice said, 'Oh, God! Oh, God!' He moved away from her and she slipped to the ground in a sitting position, her head fell back into the privet bush and the twigs scratched her face and ears. She heard the man pounding off in the direction of the Close.

The odd thing was that she did not feel very frightened but she could not muster the strength to shout or move. After a little while she was able to drag herself to her feet. She had been sitting in mud which stuck to her clothing and she muttered to herself, 'Christ, I'm in a mess.' The thing was to get to a telephone.

She could not bring herself to go in the direction which her attacker had gone so she made for Godolphin Road. She remembered that there was a call-box where the footpath joined the main road. She felt weak and sick and giddy and her throat was painful but she made it. Godolphin Road was utterly deserted and she had difficulty in opening the door of the call-box but she got inside, lifted the receiver and dialled 999.

'Which service do you require?' The voice, cool and detached.

'Police.'

She managed to answer their questions then collapsed on the floor of the box leaving the receiver dangling on its cord. She did not lose consciousness, only the ability to move. She heard the police car arrive and she was afraid they would not see her but she could not call or get up. However there was no need; a

63

constable bent over her and a little later she heard the ambulance.

In the end they put her to bed in the accident ward of her own hospital. She sat up, not displeased with the attention she was getting and rather glad that the scratches on her face and neck and the bruises on her throat made her look worse than she felt. But she was enough of a nurse to know that it would be a different story in the morning.

A plain-clothes policeman came in and sat by her bed. A nurse drew the curtains round her bed to give some privacy. The policeman told her that he was Detective Superintendent Wycliffe but he looked an amiable and kindly man.

'What about telling your parents where you are?'

She was not a local girl, her parents lived in Bristol and she said that the ward sister had arranged for them to be told.

'Now, if it doesn't upset you too much I want you to tell me what happened in as much detail as you can remember.'

She did so and her story was coherent and told with remarkable self-possession.

'That's fine, now two or three questions and I'll leave you in peace.' He smiled encouragement. 'Did you see his face? . . . Was he much taller than you? . . . You say that you had your face pressed against his coat . . . '

She tried to explain that, in fact, she had seen nothing. The man must have been a good deal taller than she was but that meant little for she was only five feet two.

'You said just now that your hat fell off.'

'Oh, yes it did. My waterproof hat, a sort of sou'-wester.'

'I know, one of our chaps picked it up. Was it immediately after your hat fell off that he let you go?'

She considered, her forehead wrinkled under blonde hair. 'Yes, I think it was—it must have been.'

'He let you go, you slipped to the ground and you heard him say, "Oh, God!"—twice, then he ran off. Is that it?'

'Yes.'

Wycliffe wished that he might smoke. 'I would like you to think about my next question very carefully before you answer. Did you get any impression—any impression at all—as to why he released you?'

Again the puzzled frown. 'I've thought about it, of course.'

'It wasn't that you succeeded in breaking free from him?'

'Oh, no, he could have done it if he'd wanted to.' She shuddered without affectation. 'I can't say for certain but it seemed to me that he could have been shocked and frightened by what he was doing. Does that sound silly?'

'Not a bit! You mean that he could have been someone subject to fits of violence and that, fortunately, he came out of this particular fit and was horrified by what he found himself doing?'

'Yes, does it seem likely?'

Wycliffe did not say but he thought not. Certainly there are psychopathic killers who appear to be quite normal and to have little or no recollection of their crimes between attacks, but Dr Jekyll does not supplant Mr Hyde *in the act*.

'You don't think that he mistook you for someone else and that when your hat fell off he realised his mistake?'

He saw from her expression that he had hit the mark.

'It was Elaine he was after! He must have stopped when my hat fell off because he saw my fair hair—Elaine is dark.'

'Elaine?'

'The girl I share a flat with. She should have been going through the allotments at that time, not me.' She explained.

'I'll be back.' He pushed through the curtain and looked up and down the ward for the sister. He met her in the passage and she must have been impressed by his gravity of manner for when he snapped, 'Telephone!' she led him to her office without a word and left.

He was put through to headquarters and to Gill. 'This attack, Jimmy, it looks as though he went for the wrong girl, he was after her flat mate, Elaine Bennett . . . '

'They've just found her.'

'Found her?'

'I sent a crime car to Edgcumbe Close to break the news—to tell this Bennett girl that her pal was in hospital. Constable Allen couldn't get any answer although there were lights on in the flat. When he pushed the door he found that it was unlatched and there she was, lying in the hall, strangled.'

'How long since?'

'Allen's message was timed at 22.31. I got the circus on the road and I was just going to phone you when your call came through.'

'Are you going there?'

'I'm on my way.'

Wycliffe was shaken. The cold resolution behind the killing dismayed him. A mistake, rectified as soon as possible. Logic. But what logic!

He went back to the ward, his every move watched by the other patients.

'I've just thought of something else,' Valerie said. 'A funny smell . . . it was when my face was against his raincoat.'

'What sort of smell?'

It was not the first time he had faced the problem of getting a witness to describe a smell. What an opportunity for some ingenious boffin to contrive an odour identikit!

'It could have been paint or varnish, or even the polish they sometimes use on floors.'

'You mean wax polish?'

'Yes, I suppose I do.'

A moment of silence while she looked at him with worried eyes.

'Why did he want to kill Elaine?'

'I don't know.'

'Have you told her?'

'One of our cars called round some time ago.'

'She would have been in bed. You know she's got the 'flu?'

'You told me.'

Before leaving the hospital he talked with the sister. Under her professional gloss she seemed perturbed. 'No, I agree, it would be most unwise to tell her tonight; she's had enough, poor girl!' But Wycliffe had the impression that her thoughts were elsewhere. In the end it came. 'I think that I have probably been foolish . . .'

He waited.

'A few minutes ago a man telephoned to enquire after Valerie. He knew her name, he spoke of her as "Valerie Hughes, the girl who was attacked on the allotments".'

'What did he want?'

'Just to know how she was, he seemed concerned.'

It might be significant. Valerie had dragged herself to a call-box in Godolphin Road and dialled 999. A patrol car and ambulance had been sent but there had been few people about to see. Not many could know of the attack even now and who would know the identity of the girl?

'You told him she was in no danger?'

'I am afraid I did.'

'What was his reaction?'

'He seemed relieved.'

'The call came through the switchboard?'

'Of course!'

The switchboard operator remembered the call. 'He wanted to know if the girl who had been attacked on the allotments had been admitted. He sounded genuinely

67

worried and I saw no harm in putting him through to the ward sister.'

'Call-box or private subscriber?'

The operator reflected. 'Private, I'm sure of that. I mean, I didn't have to wait for the call-box routine.'

'Can you place the time of the call?'

'It was a few minutes after eleven.'

The girl's 999 call had been logged at 21.43 which meant that the attack had probably taken place at 21.30 or thereabout. If the call to the hospital had been made from the man's home—and from where else could such a call have been made?—it meant that he had gone to the house in Edgcumbe Close, committed the second crime and reached home in an hour and a half. Not much to go on, especially as there was nothing to show whether he had a car, used public transport or merely walked. But that was the kind of evidence the police were good at getting. Even on a dark, misty night it was unlikely that he could have moved about much without being seen by somebody. There was a chance.

He was inclined to believe that the call to the hospital had come from the killer and that it was made out of concern for the girl he had mistakenly attacked. But other interpretations were possible and to guard against a second attack on Valerie Hughes he arranged for a round-the-clock police guard at the hospital.

Edgcumbe Close was near the hospital, a quiet cul-de-sac of small, detached villas, several of them converted into flats to attract hospital staff. Number fourteen had been properly converted with separate access to the top flat by an outside staircase at the back. The close was crowded with police vehicles, a van which looked like a black maria, waiting for the body, a Range Rover and three patrol cars. A uniformed policeman at the gate saluted Wycliffe. The mist was turning to rain again.

'They're using the window, sir.'

To avoid the hall where the body was, Wycliffe

climbed in. The front room seemed to be full of men and he could hear Smith, the photographer, cursing the hall. 'Not enough bloody room to stand sideways . . . you need a sodding skyhook in this place!'

Franks was there and came over to Wycliffe. 'We seem to be back in business with a vengeance. Not much I can tell you. She was strangled, no doubt of that, but no blow to the head this time. Death occurred between, say half-past nine and ten. I arrived here about five minutes to eleven.'

Wycliffe nodded and turned to Scales who looked pale and weary. 'Go home, get some rest. Where's Mr Gill?'

'Mr Gill is upstairs talking to the girls in the upper flat. They are both nurses and they were on the two-till-ten shift. They arrived home about twenty minutes past ten but there's a separate entrance to their flat and they had no idea that anything was amiss.'

Smith was packing up his photographic gear. Wycliffe went out into the hall. Elaine's body was lying where it had fallen, one leg doubled under her, her back against the wall. She was wearing a green dressing gown over a baby-doll nightie. She must have been going to bed or already in bed when her murderer arrived. From where he stood the mop of black curls almost covered her face. Despite his years in the force he always found it hard to come to terms with violent death, especially of the young and this was the second body he had seen in a single day.

Gill's voice came through from the front room and Wycliffe went to join him.

'Nobody seems to have heard a thing. There was nobody upstairs when it happened and the neighbours are blind and deaf. These bloody suburbs, nobody cares a fart whether you live or die.' Gill too, was moved by the senseless killing.

Wycliffe went through into the room behind the sitting room to which there was a communicating door.

A bedroom with twin beds. Bright and chintzy but almost squalid in its untidiness. Powder spilled on the carpet, clothes all over the place. One of the beds had the clothes thrown back. There was a second door into a bathroom and loo for midgets. He had to go out into the hall again to reach the kitchen which had the things kitchens usually have and a sink-full of dirty dishes. What is it which turns bachelor girls into house-proud mums?

The front door was open, rain blew into the hall. They were moving the body.

'There's nothing for us here.'

'Nothing.'

James Rendell sat on the stairs in the front hall of the suburban house. The front door and the door leading into the sitting room were both shut and there was just room for a hall-stand and a telephone table. The hall lantern was fitted with ruby glass but the man's features were grey, scarcely warmed by the reddish glow. He wore a wet mackintosh and he held his hands tightly clasped between his knees to stop them trembling. For a long time he had been staring at the black and white tiles on the floor which seemed to change their pattern as he watched, then when it seemed, at last, that he was sufficiently composed he reached for the telephone and dialled a number. He listened while the instrument went through its repertoire of click and burrs.

'Millfield Hospital.'

He made a tremendous effort to keep his voice steady. 'I wanted to enquire about Valerie Hughes—the girl who was attacked on the allotments.'

'Hold on, please.'

An interval of silence than a woman's voice. 'Ward sister speaking. Are you a relative?'

He hesitated. 'A friend—a friend of the family.'

'Miss Hughes is suffering from shock.'

'She'll be all right?'

Oh, yes. She needs rest and quiet.'

'Thanks—thank you.'

'Who shall I say—'

He dropped the receiver. He was shivering now, his hands once more clasped between his knees, his body doubled up, contracted as though he would shrink into himself.

The minutes passed. A car stopped nearby, he heard voices, doors slamming then silence once more. He was becoming calmer but the dampness seemed to be seeping through to his bones.

He reached for the telephone again and dialled.

'474655.' A woman's voice.

He did not answer at once for, suddenly, his voice had let him down. The number was repeated on a rising note of impatience.

'Is that you, Alice?'

'Who'd you think it is, the Queen of Sheba?'

'It's Jim.'

'You don't say!'

'I think I'll stay here for the night, I don't feel like coming back just now.'

The woman sighed. 'You're being silly, Jim. What good can it do? You'll just brood over there on your own and make yourself worse. The last bus hasn't gone yet, you could still make it . . .'

'No, I think I'll stay, just for tonight.'

'All right, if you must. Make sure you have a hot drink before you go to bed. And what about breakfast? Have you got any eggs?'

'I've got everything I need thanks.'

'Well, all right. What else can I say?'

'Nothing. See you tomorrow evening after work.'

'Yes. All right. Good-night Jim.'

'Good-night, Alice.'

'And Jim . . .'

'What is it?'

'You won't do anything silly, will you?'

'Of course not.'

Wycliffe drove slowly through the wet, all but deserted streets, to his headquarters.

In the darkened building the C.I.D. floor was a brilliant band of light. Wycliffe went through the duty room and up the stairs to his office. It was rarely that he used the lift. Another protest against something indefinable, part of his resentment of this crude, new, impersonal building in which he had to work; in which, perhaps, he saw some threat to his identity.

Gill joined him in his office.

'Elaine Bennett, twenty-five, free-lance nurse, at present nursing an old woman out at Kemsley Rise. She's been on that job for the past three weeks and each night she's taken the route through the allotments to pick up a bus in Godolphin Road. I got this from the girls upstairs. They also told me that her parents ran a bakery business in the city until a couple of years ago, now they've retired and they've got a little bungalow at Paignton.'

'Have they been told?'

'I passed it to the Paignton nick, they'll see to it.' He took out a cheroot and lit it, flicking the match on the carpet.

Wycliffe filled his pipe. Two girls murdered and a third attacked, apparently in error. A week separated the two killings. Were they linked? There was nothing to suggest it except the improbability that there were two killers loose in the city and the fact that both girls had been strangled.

'The girls upstairs also told me that Elaine had a boyfriend, a chap called Nigel something, they can't remember what but they think it's Sears or Swears. They don't know where he lives or where he works but they gave me a passable description and he's got a red Mini.

72

'They're naturally a bit coy about speaking their minds now but it's obvious they didn't like her. She was a staff nurse at Millfield and chucked up her job to go into private nursing. The girls obviously feel that the hospital wasn't good enough for her.'

The telephone rang.

'Wycliffe.'

It was D.C. Dixon. Wycliffe had forgotten all about him, spending the night in Debbie Joyce's flat.

'He walked in ten minutes ago, sir, opened the door with his own key.'

'Who walked in?'

'Debbie's boyfriend, sir, the man she's been sleeping with. He's with me now and he's had quite a shock.'

'I'll send a car, you can pack up at the flat and bring him in.'

No sooner had Wycliffe passed on the news to Gill than they were interrupted again, this time by the press and Wycliffe had to go out to give them a statement.

It was one o'clock when Dixon arrived with the young man who had been Debbie's sleeping partner. Wycliffe saw Dixon in his office, alone, before tackling him.

'He took it badly, sir. I'd say he'd had the shock of his life. He's called Frisby, Donald Frisby, and he's been spending most of his nights at the flat for the past four months. He's an assistant projectionist at the Ritz cinema and he shares a flat with three other chaps; a real bachelor pad if you ask me.'

All these young people belonged to the same age group as Dixon yet his attitude towards them was that of an older man, censorious and a little patronising. It was the policeman talking. Was he the same off duty?

'He knew that she should be back today?'

'Yes, sir. He says she told him that she would be in London for a week and that she would be back in the flat tonight.'

The doctor's description had been accurate. The

73

dark brown eyes and blond, curly hair were in striking contrast. His build was slight and there was something vaguely feminine about him. He wore the same clothes as the doctor had described: blue jeans, checked shirt and leather jacket. He looked pale and confused, no more than a boy.

Wycliffe had had tea sent up and offered him a cup. He drank it down greedily.

'I can't think why anybody wanted to kill her.' His lip was trembling.

'You know that she was married?'

'Married? Debbie? I can't believe that!'

'But it's true, I was talking to her husband earlier this evening. Her husband bought the flat and paid the expenses but they lived separately.'

The rather vacant face darkened. 'Was it him?'

Wycliffe answered obliquely. 'I don't think he knew of your existence.'

Frisby looked at the chief superintendent, his eyes troubled. 'I don't know what to say. She went to London to look for a job in one of the clubs. If she got one she was going to move up there and I was going to join her later on. We were going to set up together.'

'Where did you meet?'

'At a party, one Sunday. You know how it is, there was a swop round of partners and I found myself with Debbie. I don't usually get that sort of luck.'

'When was this party?'

He looked vague. 'I can't remember exactly. September some time, I think.'

'She gave you a key to her flat?'

'After a bit. You see, she works till two in the morning and I'm not through at the cinema till half-eleven so I took up to go round to the Cock to pick her up. The trouble with that was that it cost money; Riccy, that's her boss, don't like to see people just sitting, you got to be spending money one way or another. Anyway, Debbie said if I had a key I could go straight to

74

the flat and that's what I've been doing.' He brought out a packet of cigarettes then thought better of it and put them away again.

'Smoke if you want to.'

'Thanks.'

'What time did you leave the flat each morning?'

'Between ten and eleven as a rule.'

'It's odd that Debbie's neighbour doesn't seem to know about you.'

He smiled, sheepishly. 'You mean the old dear in 604? Debbie made sure of that, she used to keep cavy for me every morning. Just out of devilment to keep the old so and so guessing, she said.'

'Do you know a girl called Elaine Bennett? She's a nurse.'

'Can't say I do. I don't know any nurses.'

'You didn't sleep at the flat while Debbie was away?'

'No, she wouldn't have liked that.'

'Why not?'

It was too much for him but he tried, 'Well, I know it sounds a bit odd, specially seeing she's ... what I'm trying to say is, she liked to run things. I mean, you had to remember ... '

'To remember what?'

He shifted uncomfortably in his chair. 'It's hard to say.'

'You had to remember that she was boss, is that it?'

'I suppose so.' He studied the end of his cigarette for a moment. 'She wasn't exactly bossy but she liked to set the pace, if you understand me.'

'How old are you. Twenty?'

'Nineteen.'

Wycliffe questioned him for the better part of an hour then let him go. He learned very little.

Poor sap. '"She liked to set the pace",' Wycliffe muttered, 'I'll bet she did. In every way.'

Donald Frisby, 19, Assistant Projectionist at the Ritz Cinema.

Matthew Norman, 48, Senior Consultant Surgeon at Millfield General.

An object lesson in the irony of sex but there was more to it than that.

A middle-aged man, inhibited and shy; a not very bright youngster of nineteen who could scarcely be regarded as a type specimen of male virility. Lady Bountiful distributes her largesse. The message was clear. No male chauvinist pigs need apply.

Wycliffe sat alone in his office with only the green-shaded desk lamp lighting the big room. It was utterly quiet, the world could have died around him.

When he heard of Elaine's death, while he was still at Valerie Hughes' bedside, his first reaction had been disbelief followed by dismay. It was the cold resolution of the killing which had dismayed him—like an execution.

The killer must have rung the doorbell more than once. Elaine had gone to bed and it would have taken her a while to get up, put on a dressing gown and answer the door. Meanwhile he had stood waiting in the rain. What had he said to her? He must have been intensely excited. Had he managed to disguise his feelings? At least sufficiently for her to admit him without creating a major scene on the doorstep. The fact that he had used Valerie's name in ringing the hospital meant that he knew the girls and probably the set-up at the flat.

'I wanted to let you know that Valerie has had an accident.'

'An accident? You'd better come in.'

And then in the little hall, she, totally unsuspecting . . .

No need of a preliminary blow to prevent a struggle or to stop her from screaming. Before she could scream it was too late.

And what about the other case? The murder of Debbie Joyce or Rosaline Norman née Parkin. Here too the killer had been admitted to the girl's flat. She was, it seemed, making him a cup of tea. Did this mean that she knew him? Not necessarily, but if not he must have told a convincing story. But here the circumstances were very different from the murderer's point of view. He was on the sixth floor of a large building with people coming and going all the time. There were probably people in the flats above and below and on the other side of the thin partitioning walls. There must be no struggle, no possibility that she would scream. At a suitable moment, when she was stooping getting milk from the refrigerator, he struck. Again, in the cold, calculating efficiency of the crime there was the suggestion of an execution.

Wycliffe smiled sourly. He had at least talked himself round to the conviction that both crimes were the work of the same hand.

He drove home through empty streets. The rain had stopped and it was turning colder. As he got clear of the city he could see the moon riding high through a rift in the clouds and when he turned off the road into his own, private lane the Watch House lay below him, white in the moon-light and the navigation lights in the estuary were pale and insignificant.

He undressed in the bathroom and posted himself between the sheets but Helen woke.

'What time is it?'

'Half-past two.'

'Sure you wouldn't like something?'

'Yes, six hours sleep.'

She kissed him lightly and turned over. Within minutes her regular breathing told him that she was asleep.

He was not so lucky. How long was it since he had stood by his window, watching the traffic and complaining of futility? Less than twelve hours. But during that time the body of a murdered girl had been discovered, another girl had been brutally attacked and a third had been murdered. During that time . . . as often when he tried to reconstruct events in a coherent and orderly fashion his mind was invaded by a series of pictures, like slides put into a projector at random, out of sequence. Phrases came back to him, often meaningless, always out of context.

Debbie Joyce lying on the tiled floor, her black hair almost hiding the unspeakable things which had happened to her face.

'Debbie liked to set the pace—'

'You got the impression sometimes that she took a delight in hurting people.'

'Why did she marry me? I asked myself that question many times during each day and night that we were together and I still do not know the answer.'

Elaine Bennett. Her body too was crumpled up on a tiled floor. She too, had dark hair.

Both girls were twenty-five years old.

One thing seemed certain, the killer was not a homicidal maniac killing at random.

Sleep came at last, it must have done, for the next thing he knew was being awakened by Helen with a cup of coffee.

'It's eight o'clock.'

CHAPTER FOUR

The information Wycliffe had given to the press was necessarily scanty and it made headline news only in the local paper. The London dailies gave it a paragraph in the stop press. But this was the lull before the storm. Once the reporters had had time to dig around, the 'City of Fear' or something like it would be on every front page. Two killings and an abortive attack were more than enough to resurrect Jack the Ripper.

Mr Bellings, the deputy chief, always sensitive to publicity of any kind, looked in on Wycliffe to say that they must be careful not to foster a mood of hysteria on the strength of two killings. Wycliffe suggested that he might like to issue a statement but Mr Bellings was too astute to be caught that way. 'I have every confidence in your discretion, Charles.'

Meanwhile routine work went ahead. An industrialist chemist was preparing a number of pieces of material very lightly impregnated with various solvents and resins for Valerie to smell. The area where the attack on her had been made, fenced off and guarded through the night, was now being thoroughly studied and searched. Through the night also the flat in Edgcumbe Close had been explored in meticulous detail. The detectives' reports were on Wycliffe's desk, so were reports from the pathologist and from forensic.

They amounted to very little, no new information. The killer had left no identifiable trademark and, what was equally important, Elaine Bennett, like Debbie Joyce, seemed to have lived only from day to day. No letters, no mementoes to shed light on her twenty-five years of life. Debbie, at least had her professional photographs. Wycliffe could only marvel at the way these young people lived their complex lives out of a suitcase when his continuing sense of individuality seemed to depend on a lorry load of books, papers, photographs, notebooks, ornaments and pictures. But Mr and Mrs Bennett had come over from Paignton during the night and he was hopeful that they might fill some of the gaps.

W.P.C. Saxton came in with another batch of reports. Her blue uniform, a faultless fit, looked as though it had just come off a Hartnell peg; her ash-blonde hair was like 'after' in the shampoo advertisements and her skin, even in this winter weather, was slightly tanned. Sometimes he almost wished her on Bellings who coped with a middle-aged dragon. He was unintentionally brusque.

'Do you live at home?'

'No, sir, I live in lodgings during the week but I go home most weekends.'

'Have you kept a lot of things from your childhood and schooldays—books, school reports, photographs —that sort of thing?'

She showed no surprise. 'No, sir, that's what mothers do, isn't it? My mother has a hoard of such stuff from my first pair of shoes onwards.' She hovered. 'If you're thinking of Elaine Bennett, sir, I doubt if you've found much in her flat but I wouldn't mind betting that her mother will have a real store of this sort of thing.' She smiled.

W.P.C. Burden had been given the job of visiting the hospital and breaking the news to Valerie Hughes. Sue Burden was the same age as the girls, pleasant, homely and, by nature, sympathetic.

'You mean that after he left me he went to the flat and ...' Valerie's brow wrinkled in an effort of comprehension. 'I can't believe it, truly, I can't.' She sat, propped up by pillows, staring at the foot of the bed.

'I mean, why Elaine?'

'That's what we've got to find out.'

'This other girl, Debbie Joyce, I mean, girls like that ask for it, don't they?'

'How well did you know Elaine?'

A shrewd look from the blue eyes. 'We've shared a flat for over a year.'

'What sort of girl was she?'

'We got on.'

'Did she have a regular boyfriend?'

A small smile which quickly faded. 'There was a boy called Nigel Sears but he was just one in a long line. It wasn't serious.'

'Doing the rounds?'

'She had a regular boy a few months back. I thought she was going to settle down but something went wrong.' A thoughtful pause. 'Elaine hated the idea of being tied to anything or anybody. I mean, that's why she gave up the hospital. And it was the same with boys.'

'Sleeping around?'

'A bit.'

'Names?'

'What do you take me for?'

'We've got to know about her if there's to be any chance of finding the chap who killed her.'

A solemn nod. 'I suppose so. In any case it makes no difference now.'

But what she knew amounted to very little, a few Christian names, the makes of one or two cars owned by Elaine's boyfriends.

'Elaine knew that Debbie had been murdered?'

'We heard it on the telly last night at six o'clock.'

'Did she say anything which suggested that she knew the girl?'

'Oh, she knew her all right, they were quite friendly when they were at school.'

'You mean that they went to school together?'

'No, I don't know the details but they didn't go to the same school, I think they met playing inter-schools hockey.'

'But in that case Elaine would have known her as Rosaline Parkin, and that name wasn't mentioned yesterday.'

'No, but she'd seen her since, at the Golden Cockerel, and recognised her.'

'Was Elaine a regular at the Golden Cockerel?'

'I don't know about a regular but I think she went there fairly often.'

'Did she seem very surprised or shocked when she heard about the murder?'

Valerie frowned, trying hard to be objective. 'No, I don't think so. She said something about it being no wonder she got murdered, considering the way she carried on at the club.'

What did she mean by that?'

'I don't know. I doubt if she meant very much, Elaine liked to appear as though she had inside information about anything that happened.'

'Did you have the impression that she herself felt threatened?'

Valerie shook her head decisively, then regretted it because of the pain it caused. 'No, I don't think the idea entered her mind; I'm quite sure it didn't.'

They were silent for a time while Valerie sipped an orange drink.

'She didn't talk about herself much and rarely mentioned the past. Her father and mother were a bit of a drag, kind and all that, thought the world of her but over-protective, if you know what I mean. Not like mine—''Get out and get on with it, girl!'' She had quite

82

a good education, she took "A"-levels and she was an S.R.N., I'm only state enrolled. She'd have been a sister by now if she'd stayed with the hospital.' She shivered. 'God, I can't take it in that she's gone.'

Sue Burden reported to Chief Inspector Gill who told her that she was to take charge of Elaine Bennett's parents. 'Go back with them to Paignton or wherever it is they come from, find out what you can.'

'The trouble is, sir, I haven't a clue what it is I'm supposed to do.'

Gill put on his baby-frightening smile. 'Simple! Find out why she got herself strangled and who did it. If her mother is like most, she'll talk, all you've got to do is pin your ears back and ask the right questions. You'll also go through the girl's belongings and all the stuff her mother keeps.'

The W.P.C. frowned. 'But I don't see where it's likely to get us, sir. Surely it's obvious the man's a nutter, he wouldn't have had a *reason* for killing her, not a real motive.'

Gill grinned. 'No thinking in the ranks. Run along now and get on with it.'

She met the Bennetts and got them into a police car. He was tall and thin and pale; she was dumpy, not to say fat; and normally, one would think, cheerful. Now her cheeks were stained with tears and she had an unhealthy flush.

'She was such a good girl. Why would anybody want to . . . ?'

They accepted the young policewoman without seeming to notice her. When they reached their bungalow in Paignton, which had a view of the sea, they let her make them a cup of tea and, later, they were persuaded to eat a little of the omelette she made from cheese and eggs. Mr Bennett hovered over her as she worked in the kitchen.

'Mother's taken it very hard.' But, if anything, he was more distraught than his wife.

Unable to stay at his desk for long, Wycliffe drove out to the allotments. He approached from Godolphin Road, a fairly wide, straight road lined with semi-detached villas built between the wars. Most of them had lapwood fencing and a few shrubs in the gardens. There was a bus stop every three hundred yards or so and a telephone kiosk on a patch of waste ground where the path across the allotments joined the road. It was not an arterial road but carried a fair amount of traffic between the city and large housing developments in its eastern suburbs.

The allotments presented a bleak prospect, a biting wind swept across the almost bare soil, rattling the corrugated iron sheeting of the ugly little sheds. Policemen stood about, waiting to be of use to the experts, stamping their feet and flailing their arms to keep warm. Sergeant Smith, the sour photographer, stalked about with his cameras and cursed steadily. Gill was sitting in a patrol car by the constable on radio watch. Wycliffe got into the back seat.

'Anything?'

Gill twisted round in his seat. 'It's obvious where he stood waiting, a gap in the privet hedge. The ground is well trodden but there are no identifiable footprints. He must take a size nine or ten in shoes which means that he's no midget. Of course, we've collected an assortment of litter but there's only one item which might be useful.' He reached into the glove tray of the car and produced a transparent polythene envelope containing a smaller manilla envelope which had a little window near the top. 'It was found where he was standing. As you see, it was crumpled and it's possible that he pulled it out of his pocket with his handkerchief. Of course, it may be nothing to do with him . . .'

'What is it—a wages packet?'

'I think so. The pay card fits in so that the man's name shows through the window. If it did come from his pocket it might help.'

'I'll take this.'

'It hasn't been checked for dabs.'

'I know.'

Gill grinned. 'In any case it's a job for a D.C.'

'I know that, too. They get the best of it, don't they?' That, to a point, was genuine. As rank had separated him more and more from the spadework—and foot-work—of detection, he had felt increasingly frustrated. It would have been absurd to pretend that he did not welcome the chance to direct investigations instead of accepting direction from others but he still envied the men who worked at the level where it all happened. Occasionally, as now, he broke out.

He drove to a firm of wholesale stationers who had their offices in the city centre and was taken to the manager.

The manager only glanced at the envelope. 'No, Mr Wycliffe, we don't supply them, I wish we did.' He reached down a catalogue and flicked through the pages. 'Here we are, they're made by Deacon and Hall, part of a wages system which they supply. As far as I know there are three firms in the city using the system. The biggest is Pneumax, they make compressors and compressed air equipment. They must be the largest employers in the city; then there is Magnelec, the radio and television people, with about a thousand or fifteen hundred on their pay-roll and, finally, Goosens who assemble Italian typewriters and business machines under licence, they employ three or four hundred. The envelopes are supplied in the flat. Wages clerks lay the computer print-out on the envelope with the correct number of notes and the machine folds and seals them.'

'What about coin?'

'They don't pay coin. They have an agreement with the unions to pay to the nearest pound and carry for-ward balances.'

He was tempted to continue playing truant and to visit the three firms but his conscience got the better of him and he returned to his office and set a detective constable to work.

There were two reports in his tray amounting to new evidence. Valerie Hughes had sniffed the chemist's array of lightly impregnated fabrics and picked out turpentine as the perfume of the month. Wycliffe had little faith in the outcome but he gave instructions for the three firms using the Deacon and Hall wages system to be questioned about the use of turpentine in any of their technical processes. The other item seemed more promising. In response to an appeal on the local radio a woman had come forward who had been in Marshfield Road shortly after the time at which Elaine Bennett must have been murdered. Marshfield Road is the alternative, longer route from Edgcumbe Close to Godolphin Road.

'I was taking the dog for a little walk, poor thing, he'd been cooped up all day. Just to the main road and back. As I was coming back down the road, not far from my house, I saw this man. He was hurrying along, half running and I thought to myself he must be wanting to catch a bus in Godolphin Road. In the evenings they're few and far between.'

'Did you get a good look at him?'

'Not a good look. For one thing he was on the other side of the road but he passed under a street lamp and I could see him plain enough.'

'What did he look like?'

'Well, it's hard to say. I mean, he was just ordinary looking.'

'Tall or short, thin or fat?'

'Oh, tall and not fat. He had this long mackintosh which looked as though it was wet through and through. It was clinging about his legs.'

'Was he wearing a hat?'

'Yes, I think he had some sort of hat. I think it was a cap but I'm not sure.'

'Old or young?'

86

'Well, I don't know but I got the impression he wasn't a youngster. It went through my mind that he must be pretty fit hurrying like that and I wouldn't have thought that if he'd been a young man, would I?'

'Glasses?'

'I don't think so. I'd have noticed if he had.'

'You saw his face?'

'Well, I must have done but I can't tell you what he looked like.'

'Were there any cars parked along Marshfield Road at this time?'

'There are always cars parked there and especially at night, people are too lazy to put their cars away and they leave them in the street.'

'Could this man you saw have been running towards a parked car and not to a bus stop in Godolphin Road?'

She hesitated. 'I suppose so, but what would have boon the point of running? He was wet enough already.'

'Did you hear a car start after he passed you?'

'I might have done, I can't really say one way or the other.'

Not much but decidedly something. The bus stop where Marshfield Road joined Godolphin Road was the one before the allotments and it might be possible to get something from a conductor or driver on the route.

Whenever Wycliffe was working at headquarters he lunched at Teague's, an old-fashioned eating house, narrow, little more than a broad passage between a supermarket and a bank. Two lines of high-backed booths separated by a matted walk, a set meal each day, well prepared. There was an atmosphere of calm, almost of reverence, and people conversed in low voices as though in church. There were groups of two, three or four people, regulars, who always sat in the same booth and though each group must have been well known to all the others they rarely exchanged more than a brief nod in passing. It had taken some time to convert Gill to Teague's, and even longer for him to moderate his voice and manner to the prevailing standards.

They did not have to give an order; the waitress brought Wycliffe a lager, Gill a draught beer then the soup of the day followed by the main course.

'I've put Sue Burden on dealing with the Bennett parents,' Gill said. 'She's been with them most of the morning and now she's gone back to Paignton with them.'

'She knows what she's looking for?'

Gill shrugged. 'A motive? Links between the two girls? Her guess is as good as mine. She won't find anything, the chap is a nutter and short of a fluke we shan't get him until he gets careless and starts to show off.'

Wycliffe sipped his lager. 'He's rational to the extent that he chooses his victims; any girl won't do. He was obviously concerned about Valerie Hughes, so concerned that he seems to have telephoned the hospital for news of her.'

Gill shook his head. 'It comes to the same thing in the end. They may start by rationalising what they do but finally it comes down to what it is, the lust to kill. In any case, on what criteria does he choose his victims? As likely as not it's the colour of their hair or the way they wriggle their backsides when they walk.' He grimaced and startled a passing waitress. 'The fact is that no girl will be safe until the bastard is locked up.'

There was sense in what Gill said, sense based on experience but Wycliffe did not agree with him.

As they were returning to the office after lunch the afternoon edition of The News was already on the streets and the placards asked a succinct question:

MADMAN ON THE LOOSE?

Wycliffe and Gill were making their way among the crowds of people returning to work; everybody was in a hurry, shoulders hunched against the biting wind. There was little opportunity for talk but Gill was like a dog with a bone.

'Night patrols and decoy girls, that's the only answer to this kind of thing.'

Wycliffe was placatory. 'We may come to that, Jimmy, but we don't want to exhaust our resources just waiting for something to happen.'

The bus station enquiry was productive. At 10.05 the previous evening a conductor on a 622 bus out of the city had noticed a man near the bus stop at the junction of Marshfield and Godolphin Roads. For what it was worth the conductor's description tallied with the woman's. Tall, middle-aged to oldish, wearing a mackintosh and cap, he was hurrying in the same direction as the bus was travelling.

'We passed him before the stop and at the stop I waited for him to catch up thinking he wanted to get on.'

'But he didn't?'

'He just went by as though the bus wasn't there. I don't think he noticed.'

'What did he look like?'

'I can't tell you more than I have. The only light came from the bus and when you're standing in the light you can't see much of anything beyond it.'

A middle-aged man, fairly tall, taking size nine in shoes and active for his age. He worked for one of the three firms who used the Deacon and Hall wages system and he had recently been in contact with turpentine.

Wycliffe smiled to himself. If only it were that simple. Such a summary assumed that witnesses were accurate, that all the facts referred to the same man and that that man was a killer. Going along with the idea however, Wycliffe would have added to the list of attributes one which he regarded as important, the man had a conscience.

Nigel Sears, Elaine Bennett's current boyfriend, had been found; he was an electrician working for a firm of contractors and Gill had him picked up.

He was stocky, bullet-headed, upset and scared.

'You've heard?'

'One of my mates showed it me in the paper.' He sat, fidgeting, not knowing what to do with his hands.

'She was your girl friend; was it serious?'

'Not exactly serious; we didn't aim to get married or anything like that.'

'Why not?'

The boy shifted uncomfortably. 'Well, it wasn't like that. For one thing, Elaine had other boyfriends. I mean, I wasn't the only one.'

'Like that, was she?'

He flushed. 'She wasn't like anything, she just hadn't settled down to one bloke yet.'

'All right, don't shout at me, lad. Did you go to bed with her?'

'Once or twice.'

'And the others—did they?'

'I don't know, do I? I wasn't the first.'

'You've got a Mini, haven't you?'

'Yes, why?'

'Clapped out?'

'She's six years old, but —'

'You'd have done better with Elaine if you'd had a Jag, is that it?'

He reddened again. 'I don't see what you're getting at.'

'She liked a good time?'

'Is there anything wrong with that?'

'Ever heard of Debbie Joyce?'

'I heard that she had been found dead in her flat.'

'But before that?'

'I knew that she was a singer at the Cock.'

'So you're one of that lot, are you?'

Sears was resentful. 'I'm not one of any lot, I've been to the Cock twice.'

'With Elaine?'

'Yes, she wanted to go there but it isn't my sort of place. Too pricey for one thing.'

'Did Elaine know Debbie—apart from seeing her at the club?'

His forehead wrinkled. 'I think she might have done.'

'Think?'

'I'm pretty sure. After her act Debbie would change then come and join the customers—you know the routine. The first night I was there I thought she was coming to our table but she changed her mind and sheered off. Elaine said, ''She knows better than come here'', but she wouldn't tell me what she meant.'

Gill glared in silence at the young man for some time, then he said, 'O.K. That'll do for now but don't go swanning off to Majorca without saying good-bye.'

Gill caught Wycliffe in a reflective mood. He was standing by the big window in his office, appparently mesmerised by the endless flow of the traffic.

'Two lads in their twenties, Debbie Joyce's sleeping partner and the latest of Elaine Bennett's boyfriends, neither of them killers, psychopathic or otherwise. These crimes are the work of a mature man.'

Gill tapped ash on to the carpet. 'I'm inclined to agree, and, on the menu so far we have Papa Bourg and Mr Matthew Norman. From what you say, Norman seems well qualified by background, temperament and experience to be a nutter and Bourg might do anything in the way of business.'

Wycliffe laughed despite himself. 'Neither of them has a weekly wage packet and Bourg certainly isn't tall and thin. All the same, I agree that they should be checked out.'

'I'll have a word with Norman this afternoon.'

'Leave it to Scales.'

Gill grinned amiably. 'You think I might create a diplomatic incident?' He knew his limitations and accepted them.

'Could be. Seriously, I can see the possibility that Norman might have killed his wife but there is no evidence of any connection between him and Elaine Bennett.'

'She used to be a nurse at Millfield.'

'So did hundreds of others.'

Reports were trickling in all the time.

Scales had established that the maiden aunt who had brought up Debbie Joyce or Rosaline Parkin, was dead. She had died of a heart atack two years before. Rosaline and her aunt had lived in a dreary little terraced house near the docks where the lorries rumbled past day and night. The neighbours were full of praise for the way in which the aunt had struggled to bring up her niece.

'And what thanks did she get, poor soul? As soon as she could keep herself young madam was off and never come near the place again in five years. Not but what that could have been a blessing in disguise for even when she was at school she was always in trouble. But she was back quick enough when the old lady died, selling up her bits and pieces.'

Another neighbour had a similar view.

'So she'd changed her name, had she. I read about a Debbie Joyce in the paper but I didn't know it was her. Well, I don't wish nobody any harm but you can't help feeling sometimes that there's a sort of justice in these things. She was always out for number one and she was that rude! I remember once when ... '

Detection commonly proceeds by laborious and exceedingly tedious processes of elimination which means that, at the end of an investigation, it is usually possible to look back through the reams of paper and to show that most of the work was wasted. Yet there is no other systematic approach. An inspired guess may sometimes save days of slogging but guesses are only inspired when they turn out to be right.

So the three firms who used the Deacon and Hall

wages system were persuaded to provide lists of the names, addresses and ages of all weekly paid male employees. When these lists were to hand detectives would go through them picking out the middle-aged and those who lived in the eastern suburbs. With these new, much shorter lists, they would attempt some further elimination, say, all those men under five feet eight in height which would mean seeing the men concerned. Almost certainly all of it would prove a waste of time. They would narrow the field to two or three perfectly harmless, middle-aged men whose wildest excess was a couple of pints at the local on a Saturday night.

CHAPTER FIVE

Four or five days of almost continuous rain while the city sprawls under leaden clouds, its roofs and streets gleaming in the steely January light. Another two months of winter ahead. Then without warning, comes a golden day, the sun shines from a blue sky, the air seems to be filled with a luminous, golden haze, the buildings and streets have been washed clean and people smile at total strangers. A taste of spring and hope is reborn.

Wednesday was such a day and Wycliffe caught himself whistling as he waited patiently at a junction to join the main stream of traffic city bound. A long-haired youth in a Mini held back to let him in and he was so surprised that he missed his gear.

Sun streamed through his office window and W.P.C. Saxton had put a little cut-glass vase of snowdrops on his desk beside the daily papers. He glanced at the headlines with detachment as one does on holiday.

'Killer Terrorises City'; 'The Dangerous Age?'—a reference to the fact that the three girls attacked were twenty-five years old. 'M.P. Demands Vigilante Patrols'.

If Wycliffe was still in doubt about the kind of man he was looking for the crime reporters were not; a madman, a compulsive killer, a psychopath. One reporter claimed to have been reliably informed that young police women, in plain clothes, were acting as a bait in police traps, risking their lives each night in unfrequented streets and alleys. 'Despite the risks Chief Superintendent Wycliffe has more volunteers for the work than he can use.'

All to give the great British public a warm feeling inside to go with their cornflakes.

Against all this (and Jimmy Gill) Wycliffe's reasons for believing that he was dealing with a rational man and not a homicidal lunatic began to look thin. His only evidence was the killer's failure to finish what he had started with Valerie Hughes and the strong possibility that he had telephoned the hospital in some anxiety to find out how she was. If Wycliffe was right, the man had killed Debbie Joyce and Elaine Bennett either because they had done him some injury or because they threatened him in some way. What kind of injury? What kind of threat? Good questions. It came back to possible links between the two girls. They had not been to the same school. Debbie had passed her eleven-plus and gone to Cholsey Grammar while the Bennett's bakery had been sufficiently prosperous to send Elaine to Bishop Fuller's, a rather plush day-school for girls. But they had known each other as schoolgirls and been friendly for a time.

There was little prospect of identifying the killer on present evidence. Neither Mrs Burton, the witness in Marshfield Road, nor the conductor of the 622 bus could remember enough of the man they saw to make an identikit picture of any value. Medium height or tall, middle-aged or old, not fat, wearing a fawn or grey mackintosh and a cap. Added to that he probably took size nine in shoes and it was possible that he worked at one of the three concerns that used the Deacon and Hall wages system. That was all they had and no amount of suggestion or persuasion could make it more. All the same, detectives were touting this meagre description round the neighbourhood of Godolphin Road and a radio appeal had gone out for anyone who had seen such a man on Monday evening.

Wycliffe, still in search of his common denominator, had decided to begin with the two schools.

Cholsey Grammar had become Cholsey Comprehensive and they had moved into new buildings since Rosaline Parkin's day. A trim heap of glass-sided packing cases standing out like a very sore thumb in a semi-rural landscape on the northern outskirts of the city.

The headmaster had been reorganised with his school, but reluctantly, and Wycliffe could see in his office signs of reactionary nostalgia. Team photographs on the walls, an M.A. hood and gown behind the door and the Wadham crest on a wooden shield above the bookcase.

'I read in the newspaper what had happened to the poor girl. I remember her very well. She was dark and sallow, rather striking. Academically she was good but her background didn't help—no tradition of academic work. Of course, nowadays, we no longer expect it.' A profound sigh.

Wycliffe asked obvious questions and got obvious answers. The central heating made the room uncomfortably warm and with the sun shining on well-tended playing fields it could have been a summer's day. A teacher's voice droned monotonously in the next room and Wycliffe could imagine rows of children drowsing over their books.

'We are looking for a possible link between Rosaline and the other girl who was killed—Elaine Bennett. Elaine did not go to this school, she was a pupil at Bishop Fuller's.'

The headmaster ran a thin hand over his balding skull. 'I don't know her, of course.'

'Were there any organised contacts between the two schools—games, excursions, that sort of thing?'

'There used to be, certainly. The girls played them at hockey and, now I come to think of it, Rosaline was a good little hockey player, a winger, very fast. And that reminds me of another thing, she had fits.'

'Fits?'

'She was epileptic and she had a fit once on the hockey field. We felt that she should give up games but the school doctor said that she must be allowed to carry on a normal life.'

It is difficult to frame questions when you have no idea of what it is you are trying to find out.

'What sort of girl was she—rebellious? Conformist?' The headmaster scratched his chin. 'It was a good many years ago, remember, but as far as I can recall she was neither one nor the other. Some children, not necessarily the most worthwhile, fit into school like a hand into a glove. Rosaline was not one of those but I don't recall her as a trouble maker either.'

He frowned in an effort of recollection then reached for his internal telephone.

'I'll ask my deputy to join us, her memory is more dependable than mine.'

Miss Finch came in and was introduced. She was aptly named, her movements were quick and darting like those of a small, slightly pugnacious bird. She was plump and fiftyish with the clear skin which is sometimes the prize of life-long celibacy.

'Rosaline Parkin? I remember her very well. I saw in this morning's paper that it was she who was killed in those new flats.'

'I was saying to the superintendent that she was an intelligent girl and not, as I remember, the sort to be in trouble.'

Miss Finch smiled. 'Not the sort to be found out certainly. In my experience she was dangerous, a very bad influence in the school and usually clever enough to escape the consequences of her actions.'

97

The headmaster looked crestfallen. 'Indeed? I am surprised.'

'Surely you remember the trouble she caused on one of those vacation trips that Miss Russell organised?'

'What sort of trouble?' Mildly, from Wycliffe.

Miss Finch frowned. 'It was before my appointment as deputy head but I was here on the staff. A Miss Russell was deputy and she organised a lot of out-of-school activities. On this occasion she took a party of girls, drawn from several schools, to a hostel in Dorset for three weeks during the summer vacation. They were to experience the advantages of communal living of which, as day-school pupils, they had been deprived.' Miss Finch's lip curled.

'What happened?'

'I did not hear all the details. Miss Russell dealt with the matter herself but I do know that the parents of a girl from another school complained that their daughter had been harassed and bullied by a group of girls of whom Rosaline Parkin was the ringleader. There was a good deal of very unpleasant gossip.' Miss Finch paused and smoothed the skirt of her Jaeger two-piece. 'I'm afraid it emerged that the whole trip had been something of a disaster and Miss Russell could not entirely escape responsibility.'

'What happened to the girl—to Rosaline?'

Miss Finch pursed her lips. 'Nothing happened to her. She was not punished in any way.'

The headmaster was embarrassed. 'Now you mention it I do remember there was a complaint from a parent which I passed to Miss Russell. I had no idea that it had turned out to be as serious as you say.'

Miss Finch shrugged. 'That *is* interesting. I had supposed that Miss Russell would keep you informed.'

'Do you remember the name of the parents who complained?'

'No, I do not, nor the school from which the child

came. Like most things in school it was a nine-day wonder.'

'Perhaps some other member of your staff?'

'I think it very unlikely, there are only two or three of us left from the old days.'

'This Miss Russell, did she leave to take up another appointment?'

The headmaster nodded. 'Oh, yes, a school somewhere near Cambridge. I could look it up if it is of any interest to you.'

Miss Finch intervened. 'No need. She went as deputy head to Lady Margaret's near Huntingdon. She was very fortunate to get such an appointment, very fortunate indeed.'

Wycliffe stood up. 'Perhaps you will have a word with other members of staff who were here when Rosaline was a pupil and telephone me if there is anything further you can tell me.'

The headmaster escorted him to the main entrance through hordes of children swarming the corridors during a change of lessons.

The atmosphere at Bishop Fuller's was different. Miss Buckley, the headmistress, had her office in the Georgian mansion which formed the nucleus of the school. A shabbily elegant room with panelled walls, glass-fronted bookcases and tall windows.

'Elaine Bennett—when you telephoned I got out her file.' She fingered a blue folder on her desk. 'Of course I heard what had happened to her and I imagine that is why you are here.'

A few minutes introductory fencing.

'She was not a particularly able girl—five Ordinary level passes but she failed her Advanced levels.'

'What about her as a person?'

A miniscule shrug. 'She was not a popular girl either with her contemporaries or with the staff. Over-indulgent parents. Elaine behaved as though she had a prescriptive right to special treatment. Needless to say, she didn't get it here.' No false sentiment with Miss Buckley.

'Did she play hockey?'

He received the what-have-I-missed-here look and Miss Buckley put on her library spectacles to refer to the file. 'Yes, she did, she was a member of our first team.'

'Would she have been likely to have played in matches against Cholsey Grammar?'

Another inquisitive glance. 'Presumably, since that was one of the schools on our fixture list at that time.'

'Can you tell me if she took part in any joint excursions or school visits with girls from Cholsey?'

Miss Buckley did not conceal her impatience. 'Really, superintendent, we are dealing with events which occurred nine or ten years ago. It is quite likely that she would have taken part in joint school activities, we did a great deal of that sort of thing.'

'But you have no records?'

'Good heavens, no! I suppose it's just possible that something of the sort might have been mentioned in her testimonial.'

Again a reference to the file.

'Yes, as it happens there is something here. Her house-mistress says that she took part in our German exchange programme, if that is of any interest.'

'Nothing else?'

'Nothing here.'

'Does the name Rosaline Parkin mean anything to you?'

She frowned. 'Wasn't that the real name of the girl who was murdered in the Grenville flats? I think I saw it in the paper this morning.'

'Apart from that?'

'She was not a pupil here.' For Miss Buckley that closed the subject.

A bell rang and he became aware of a rising tide of movement through the building and beyond.

100

'Rosaline was a pupil at Cholsey while Elaine was here.'

Miss Buckley was unimpressed. 'I think I see your drift, superintendent, but surely it is unlikely that events so far back should have any significance now.'

Wycliffe ignored that one. 'Presumably there are members of your staff who were here in Elaine's day?'

'Of course, most of them. We are a very stable institution.'

Of course. That was what middle-grade executives and prosperous trades people paid for and skimped to do it. Stability and tradition.

'Then perhaps you would ask them if they remember any occasion when, in joint activities with Cholsey, something notable occurred involving Elaine?' It sounded thin, thin as railway soup.

'Notable? In what way?'

Wycliffe sympathised with pupils of Miss Buckley's faced with her uncompromising specificity.

'I've no idea, probably something unpleasant, perhaps something which might have given rise to a deeply felt grievance.'

Miss Buckley closed Elaine's file. 'I doubt if they will be able to help but I will do as you ask.'

Wycliffe drove back to his headquarters through streets transformed by the winter sunshine. People strolled along the pavements and there were gossiping groups at the street corners. The women were dressed more colourfully and the whole population seemed to be a little high, mildly intoxicated by the warmth and the golden light.

On his desk a report summarised the conclusions of the detectives who had worked on the lists provided by the three firms using the Deacon and Hall wages system.

1. The three firms between them employ 3,600 persons.

2. 2,928 are paid weekly and of these 1,974 are men.
3. 953 of the men are over forty years of age and 521 are over 45.
4. The individuals in the second category of 3 are being further investigated.

Wycliffe turned to W.P.C. Saxton who was waiting to deal with the post. 'When I was at school it was all about filling a bath from two taps with the plug out.'

'Sir?'

'Never mind.'

Five hundred and twenty-one men. If one of them took size nine in shoes, was tall, thin and active and smelt of turpentine, then God help him.

Lies, damned lies and statistics. Wycliffe's sentiments exactly.

Despite the euphoric effect of the weather he was not optimistic about the case. Unless the killer made some further move . . .

He got a copy of an Educational Year Book and looked up Lady Margaret's School which the knowledgeable Miss Finch had said was near Huntingdon. He found it. Lady Margaret's School for Girls, Lynfield House, near Huntingdon. 650 girls. Boarding with some day pupils. Headmistress: Miss D.M. Lester-Brown, M.A., B.Lit., Oxon.

He telephoned and after some brief negotiation spoke with Miss Lester-Brown.

'Miss Russell? Miss Dorothy Russell? Yes, I remember her very well.' The headmistress was suave, courteous and guarded. Even over the telephone he could sense that Miss Lester-Brown was marshalling her defences. 'No, she is not with us now, unfortunately she stayed with us for only one year . . . She resigned . . . No, as far as I know she did not leave to take up another teaching post . . . No, I have no idea what she did . . . In her letter of resignation she

102

mentioned personal reasons . . . No, I am afraid that I do not have her present address.'

'Thank you,' Wycliffe muttered as he put down the receiver.

Perhaps after all there was light ahead.

He picked up the telephone again and asked to be put through to the Headmaster of Cholsey Comprehensive.

'Wycliffe again. I'm sorry. This Miss Russell who was once your deputy, when she was appointed you must have had a good deal of information about her—her background, where she came from, that sort of thing . . .'

The headmaster muttered something about confidentiality. Wycliffe was as bland as milk.

'I quite understand but all I want is to get in touch with her . . . No, she is not still at Huntingdon and they have no idea what has happened to her. It is, or could be, very important indeed. If you could tell me her home town it might help—where she went to school.'

Reluctant assent. 'It will take me some time to find the papers, after all it was several years ago.'

'You will ring me back?'

'As soon as I can.'

'One more thing, don't teachers have service numbers?'

'They do, indeed.'

'Then perhaps you would let me have hers.'

Bread upon the waters.

He made one more telephone call, to Huntingdon C.I.D., asking them to make discreet enquiries concerning Miss Russell's stay at Lady Margaret's.

He lunched at Teague's and returned to deal with some of the accumulated paper-work. His industry earned the approval of W.P.C. Saxton who worried about it more than he did.

The Headmaster of Cholsey Comprehensive telephoned with the information he had requested. Miss Russell had been appointed in 1960 and she had left in

103

1966. Before coming to Cholsey she had held appointments in Surrey and Bristol.

'Where was she at school, herself?'

'The Celia Ayrton Grammar School for Girls, near Lincoln. She left in 1944 to go up to Cambridge.'

'And her service number?'

The headmaster gave it.

Wycliffe telephoned the Department of Education asking for news of Miss Russell and spoke to a gloomy official who took a poor view of his enquiry and told him that it could only be considered if it came through the Home Office. Finally he put through a call to Lincoln C.I.D. for any information they could give him about Miss Russell and her family.

By the time W.P.C. Saxton left at half-past five, the mound of paper had been reduced to manageable proportions. He lit a pipe and stood by his window watching the home-going traffic. It was dark and the sky had remained clear so there was frost in the air. Everything sparkled, the car lights seemed brighter, more intense, the scene was vivid, cheerful, purposeful; these people were going home to wives, families, sweethearts, after a day's work. No longer did he murmur as he watched them, 'Futile!'

He was about to leave himself when the telephone rang.

'The editor of The News for you, sir.'

'Put him through.'

They were old acquaintances and both understood the rules of the game.

'I've a note here which purports to come from the killer, chief superintendent. I shall print it, of course but, as always, I want to co-operate. It's too late tonight but it will appear in our morning editions. I thought you might like to see it first.'

'I'll be over.'

The last edition was going out on the streets and the

building was almost deserted. In the editor's office he was offered sherry.

'When we saw what it was we didn't maul it.'

The note lay in a polythene cover on the editor's desk and the envelope, crumpled and evidently rescued from the wastepaper basket, was beside it. The note and the address on the envelope had been written in block capitals using a soft pencil and the paper of the note was thick and of coarse texture like duplicating paper. The writing was neat and the message clear and concise:

I DO NOT WANT TO TERRORISE PEOPLE. THEY SAY THAT I AM A PSYCHOPATHIC KILLER BUT THIS IS NOT TRUE. IF I HAD BEEN I WOULD HAVE KILLED THE WRONG GIRL ON MONDAY NIGHT. THE WOMEN WHO DIED ARE TWO OF THE GUILTY ONES. PEOPLE CANNOT DESTROY LIVES OF OTHERS WITHOUT BEING PUNISHED.

The editor looked at Wycliffe with the air of one who, having delivered the goods, expects to see the colour of the other chap's money.

'What's all this about the wrong girl?'

'Presumably he made a mistake in attacking Valerie Hughes and when he discovered his mistake he let her go.'

'You knew this?'

'It was a possibility.'

'And Elaine Bennett was the right girl?'

'Presumably.'

'Why?'

'I've no idea.'

The editor was chagrined or pretended to be. 'If you would rather have your chaps followed round by reporters ...'

Wycliffe said nothing.

'It looks as though this fellow is working off some sort of vendetta.'

'Perhaps. When did you get this?'

'It was delivered by hand to our street office before they closed at five-thirty this evening.'

'You mean that it was handed over the counter?'

'No, it was pushed through the letter box. One of the girls noticed it in the little wire cage when she was locking up. I've had a photostat done so you can take the original.'

Wycliffe nodded. 'This is obviously a reply to what you and others printed this morning.'

'Are you prepared to comment on what he has to say?'

'No, but thanks for the letter and the sherry.'

'They were both investments,' the editor said.

Back in his office Wycliffe treated the note very seriously. The note and the envelope were photographed then sent at once to forensic where they would be minutely examined and made to yield every scrap of information which they held. But he did not expect much. Here was a man who realised that block capitals give very little away. It is a waste of time to cut letters out of newspapers. A man with that much sense would be unlikely to give himself away through elementary carelessness.

Wycliffe sat at his desk with only the green-shaded desk lamp alight. He had not drawn the curtains over the big window behind him and the headlights of passing cars made wild patterns on the ceiling and walls. The subdued light fell on his blotter and on a photostat of the killer's declaration.

THE WOMEN WHO DIED ARE TWO OF THE GUILTY ONES.

Specific, unambiguous. You had to take this man seriously, to believe him, to believe at least that he meant what he wrote at the time of writing it.

They were not dealing with an indiscriminate killer, that much was confirmed.

THE WOMEN WHO DIED . . .

Debbie Joyce and Elaine Bennett were both twenty-five years old. How had they harmed a middle-aged man? Wycliffe was more than ever convinced that he was middle-aged or older; these were not the crimes of youth.

PEOPLE CANNOT DESTROY THE LIVES OF OTHERS WITHOUT BEING PUNISHED.

Perhaps it was not the killer himself who had been harmed but someone he loved. He saw himself as meting out justice.

He was right about a common denominator but had he been right in going back to the girls' schooldays? At least they knew each other at school. It was imperative now to follow that lead both through the schools and in the later lives of the girls.

TWO OF THE GUILTY ONES . . .

The implication was that there were others.

Finally, I AM NOT A PSYCHOPATHIC KILLER.

The need to defend himself drove him to the risky business of writing to *The News*. He could not bear to be misjudged even in anonymity.

As he stared at the note Wycliffe began to see a vague picture through the eye of his mind. Tall, lean, fastidious, gentle . . . Gentle! Yes, in spite of everything. A man to whom something had happened so devastating that he is completely thrown off balance, knocked off the rails. He has to rationalise his tragedy and, justly or unjustly, apportion the blame. It is in this process that he becomes obsessed.

For the past six months he had lodged with his sister and her husband in their little flat at the top of the *Guardian* building which Albert, his brother-in-law, called their penthouse.

He went up in the lift, took off his mackintosh and put it on a hanger in the hall cupboard.

'Is that you, Jim?'

His sister. Always the same welcome.

107

He went into his bedroom to wash and change his jacket.

Although he had lived there only half a year his room had acquired a distinctive character. There was a neat row of his books on the chest of drawers and two photographs in silver frames, one of a rather plain girl with short, straight hair and the other of a middle-aged woman with large, sad eyes. On the walls were reproductions of famous paintings, Vermeer, Canaletto, Hobbema.

He went into the living room which had a tiny dining alcove where the table was laid for the evening meal and Albert was already in his place. The television was on and the news had just started. The economic situation, a row in the U.N., a strike, the divorce of a famous actress.

Alice pushed two plates of pie through the hatch. 'You two get started, I'll be there in a minute.'

Albert was a stocky little man with black, curly hair and features which seemed to have been made of lumps of plasticene. He always looked very serious and solemn but he had a puckish sense of humour and Alice said that he ought to have been a clown.

'How's gaffer, Jim?'

'All right.' He could never accustom himself to Albert's familiarity. He was a formal person and though he did not resent his brother-in law's manner it embarrassed him because he could not reply in kind.

Alice came in with her plate. The general news had ended and the regional news began.

' . . . tension is mounting in the city. A spokesman at police headquarters said today that the possibility of further attacks could not be excluded. While there was no cause for panic it was hoped that young women in particular would behave sensibly and not go about alone or in unfrequented parts of the city after dark.'

'Terrible!' Alice said. 'Makes you afraid to put your face outside the door.'

Albert chuckled. 'You don't have to worry, old girl, he's after tender meat.'

The meal came to an end and Alice went to make coffee. Albert became serious.

'You thought any more about what I said to you?'

'Not really.'

'Of course it's your business but there's no sense leaving a house like that and nobody living in it—costing you money and nothing coming in.'

'I'll have to think about it.'

'Eighteen thousand, perhaps more, Freddie Miller reckoned you'd get, easy as falling off a log. Eighteen thousand at seven per cent free of tax would be over a thousand a year—a nice bit of extra. Or you could use your capital to expand the business.'

Jim said nothing and after a little while Albert tried again.

'If you're really determined not to sell you could let. I mean there must be some good tenants and you could pick and choose. I mean, it's not as though you was thinking of getting married again . . . '

'I've got to live somewhere.' He gestured vaguely. 'I mean, given time, when I've got used to the idea I might go back.'

'On your own in a house that size? And there's the rates—going up all the time.'

'Yes, the rates are high.'

'There you are! I mean, it doesn't make sense, does it?'

'I'll think about it.'

Alice came in with the coffee.

'I was just saying to Jim about the house—'

Alice frowned. 'Oh, leave it, Albert. It's Jim's business after all.' She picked up the newspaper. 'What's on the telly?'

Looking back Wycliffe could point to a moment in each of his major cases when he had experienced an abrupt

109

change of outlook, achieved a fresh point of view, and a new *gestalt*. It was the moment when he ceased to be a detached investigator and became involved, seeing the case from the inside. Helen, his wife, and his close colleagues never failed to observe the change in him even if they did not understand its cause. He became reserved, taciturn, brusque, he rarely went home for meals and he walked a great deal hardly ever taking his car from the park except to go home at night.

In the present case the change came while he was sitting at his desk that evening, staring at the photostat of the killer's message to the press.

He picked up the telephone and asked for his home number.

'Is that you? I ought to have rung before, I'm afraid I shan't be home for a meal.'

'Now he tells me!'

'Sorry.'

'When shall I see you?'

'Probably lateish. Don't wait up.'

He put back the receiver with a feeling of release. It was odd but it was not new.

He glanced up at the clock. Five minutes to seven. He got his overcoat, opened the case file and extracted a couple of photographs which he put in his pocket then he switched off the desk lamp and left. He went down the stairs, through the duty room and out through the swing doors. The duty officer called 'Good-night, sir', but received no answer.

It was certainly frosty, he pulled up the collar of his overcoat and walked quickly in the direction of the city centre. As he approached the centre he turned off up Middle Street which ran behind a block of departmental stores. It was a remnant of the pre-war city and on the corner at the far end there was a pub which he had visited once or twice before. The frontage was faced with ornate green and buff tiles and the windows were frosted with elaborate scroll patterns. The Market

110

Arms. During the day it was popular with people from the pannier market but at night there was a select clientele made up of shop-keepers and tradesmen who still lived in the district.

Wycliffe unbuttoned his overcoat and took his beer and sandwiches to a little tile-topped table near the stove. Close by four men were playing whist for penny points. They took it in turn to examine Wycliffe with sidelong glances. Men in their forties and fifties who made enough to live in reasonable comfort and security without being affluent.

The fat man with a red face and an enormous signet ring was dealing. He seemed to obliterate the cards with his short fat fingers and he kept the tip of his tongue between his lips while he concentrated on the deal, like a child taking his first steps in drawing or writing. His partner was lean, colourless, with thinning grey hair and a straggly moustache stained with nicotine.

'Amy tolls me your Joan is getting herself married.'

The fat man halted the deal. 'Saturday week at St Paul's. Chap who works in Finley's. He's only twenty-four but he's a buyer for their food hall. Done well for himself.'

'Might do a bit for you on the side.' The sally came from the third man, a bald, lugubrious individual who would have made a good undertaker. 'The odd box of oranges, a few trays of peaches off the back of the lorry.'

The fat man's face darkened. 'None of that, Sam, I run an honest business and always have.'

'No offence. Only a joke.'

'I hope so.'

They picked up their cards, counted them and found there had been a misdeal. They threw in, the fat man shuffled, baldy cut and the deal was restarted.

The fourth man who had not spoken so far, small dark with curly hair, said, 'There was hell up at my place before I left this evening. The wife wouldn't let

111

Tessa go out. Afraid she'd be picked up by the lunatic.'

'Quite right too,' the fat man said. 'It's a disgrace the way the police let these bloody perverts run loose. What are they paid for? As far as I can see all they bloody do is go to football on Saturday afternoons.'

'Can I get you another, superintendent?'

The landlord had come, diplomatically, to put coke on the stove. The message was not lost on the fat man who looked sheepishly at Wycliffe and received a blank stare in return.

There were three or four other tables occupied. One couple played draughts, the others sat, mostly in silence, drinking from time to time.

Why had he come here? He wanted a drink and a bit to eat, but why here? He asked himself the question and got only a vague answer. In fact he had formed a clearer picture of the man he wanted than he was prepared to admit. A solitary man, marked off from his fellows by events, but needing the reassurance of their presence. Where better than in a quiet pub like this one? He would not be among the card players but sitting alone, watching. If he was approached he would make an excuse . . . But Wycliffe was the only one sitting alone in this bar. He shrugged with self impatience. What a nonsensical way to go on!

When he had finished his sandwiches he got up, buttoned his overcoat, said good-night to the landlord and left. Conversation would break out as soon as he closed the door.

He cut through one of the narrow, communicating lanes to the city centre, crossed over and walked up Judson Street with the yellow glare fom the Golden Cockerel ahead of him. Riccy Bourg was having his grand reopening.

The club entrance was squeezed between a male boutique and a music shop which had a window full of guitars and electronic gadgetry. The doorman, a pug

112

in a monkey suit which was too small for him, met him just inside the door.

'Are you a member, sir?'

Wycliffe showed his warrant card and followed it with a photograph of Elaine Bennett. 'Have you seen this girl at the club?'

The pug held the photograph at arm's length.

'I seen her a few times.'

'When and who with?'

'She's been coming here off and on for months, a couple of times she was with a young man but most often she's with a party, several men and girls together. That sort turn up lateish, to finish the night off like.'

'There must be scores of girls who come in and out of this place in the run of a week.'

'Hundreds.'

'Then how do you remember this one?'

The pug looked knowing. 'Well sho caused trouble, didn't she, and Mr Pirelli, the floor manager, pointed her out to me.'

'What sort of trouble?'

'Well I wasn't there, was I? I mean, I'm down here, but I heard she was drunk and made a scene with Debbie Joyce.'

'Is Mr Bourg in the club?'

The man made a move to the stairs. 'I'll see if he's there, sir.'

'You stay where you are.'

Wycliffe went upstairs and through the swing doors into a foyer where the smell of fresh paint struggled with a drench of commercial perfume. A girl in red, skin-tight pants and the sketch of a bra' asked for his membership number but settled for his warrant card and his coat. As she turned to hang up the coat he saw that she had a golden cockerel embroidered across her bottom; very fetching. What price women's lib?

Another set of swing doors and he was in the main room of the club. Plush lined booths round the walls, a

113

dance floor in the middle and a band on a raised dais at the far end. Subdued lighting and a decor in red and gold. The night was young and there seemed to be more girls in red pants than customers. A young man in a red dinner jacket with a frilly shirt and a hairdo and beard like Disraeli's showed him to a booth and offered him a menu and wine list the size of a newspaper.

'Drinks are served at the tables, meals are available from ten until one. Our hostesses are delighted to partner unaccompanied gentlemen and the cabaret starts at ten. Games of chance in our salon through the curtained doorway by the dais.'

Wycliffe lit his pipe. One of the hostesses, a tall brunette with a sulky expression, came over to him.

'Care to buy me a drink?'

'Sit down.'

He showed her his warrant card. 'Police.'

'Just my luck.'

She was pretty under her make-up but her skin must have been very pale for the lighting only succeeded in making her look pink and naked.

'What's your name?'

'Della—Della Paterson.'

'How long have you worked here?'

'Just over a year.'

'So you knew Debbie Joyce pretty well.'

'I knew her all right.'

'How did you get on with her.'

'She was a bitch. The fact that she's dead won't alter that.'

'Is that your opinion or do the others share it?'

'Nobody liked her, she would do the dirt on anybody.'

'Like the pianist?'

She looked at him, surprised. 'So you've heard about that. He was in good company. I could write a book about her dirty tricks.'

'She seems to have got on with the boss.'

114

The girl nodded. 'He thought she was special. According to him she was what the customers came to see.'

'And was she?'

We shall soon find out, shan't we?'

'Did she sleep with Bourg?'

The question really surprised her. 'With Bourg? You must be joking! He never looks at anybody but his wife. As far as he's concerned we're just part of the furniture. Hey up! Here he is.'

Riccy Bourg had come through the curtains by the dais and was crossing the floor towards Wycliffe all smiles. He signed to the girl and she got up and went.

'Mr Wycliffe!'

'Your people must be slipping, I've been here ten minutes.'

'They jest tell me. I am much pleased to see you but we talk better in my office.'

'We talk better or, at least quicker, here.'

Riccy sighed and took his considerable weight off his feet.

'It's about poor Debbie. Why you come to me I don't know, I tell your young man—'

'It's about this girl, Elaine Bennett.' Wycliffe put Elaine's photograph on the table in front of him. Bourg looked at it with distaste.

'Who is this? She is not working for me.'

'Have you seen her in the club?'

He spread his hands. 'You ask me? Hundreds of girls come through that door. You expect that I remember?'

'This one, yes. Your muscle man remembers her very well.'

'Pouf! He is only bone above the neck that one but I will put on my glasses and look again.'

He produced a spectacle case and took from it a pair of spectacles with the thickest horn rims Wycliffe had ever seen.

'Now, I look'

But at that moment a party of six or eight came into the room. The glasses came off, the band seemed to be rejuvenated, Bourg signalled frantically to the young Disraeli and it was some time before his thoughts returned to the photograph.

'Yes, she has been here. Half a dozen times, maybe more.'

Things were beginning to warm up. Two men came through the swing doors, laughing, saw Wycliffe and went out again.

'There, you see? You are bad for my business sitting there, Mr Wycliffe.'

'So the sooner you tell me what I want to know . . . '

'But I do tell you.'

'Not enough. What was the connection between her and Debbie?'

'Connection? What is this?'

'Something happened between them—here.'

Bourg looked at Wycliffe then at another group which had just arrived. 'It was nothing.'

'Tell me about it.'

Bourg looked at the ceiling. 'She was drunk, the girl in the picture. Six months ago, maybe more. She is in big party, you understand, three, four tables. Much laughing and a little fooling. No harm. There is cabaret and Debbie is singing. When she is finished singing, Debbie visit the tables, talk to the customers, have a little drink with them. They like that and it is good for business. Well, this night she join the table where your girl is with her friends and after a short time there is commotion and I go over to see. Your girl is more drunk than I think so I am very smoothing and I ask her what is wrong. She is very excited and she tell me that Debbie is under false pretences. She is not Debbie but is called Rosaline something.' He smiled broadly. 'Well, this is not news to me. This I know. Debbie Joyce is professional name but I cannot make the drunk girl under-

116

stand this and so I ask her friends to take her home. There is no more trouble.

'Afterwards Debbie say she knew the girl when they was at school.'

'The girl has been back several times since.'

'Of course. Why not? No more trouble. When you are drunk you sometimes get very fixed idea that something is important then, when you are not drunk — pouf! All forgot.'

'You know that this girl has been murdered also?'

A calculating look from the brown eyes. 'I see it in the paper.' He shifted uncomfortably. 'I'm sorry but it has not to do with me.'

'This is a case of double murder, Mr Bourg, it would be very unwise to play games.'

But Wycliffe knew better than to see Bourg's attitude as necessarily sinister. His reflex response to the police was defensive and he was likely to appear most guilty when he had least to hide.

His chat with Bourg seemed to confirm that the only significant contact between the two girls had been while they were at school. But how did they become 'two of the guilty ones' nine years later?

'My men will have to question your staff about what you have told me.'

Bourg shrugged. 'But not tonight, eh? Tonight I get back some of the money I spend on making the place look so good.'

The club was filling and the cabaret started as Wycliffe was leaving. A stand-up comic with an Irish accent and a florid complexion told blue jokes one after the other.

Outside Wycliffe looked round for a bar, he wanted to get the feel and taste of the place out of his system. Tolerant of most things, he had difficulty in finding any common ground with the habitué of places like the Golden Cockerel. Vice in a cellophane wrapper with a red ribbon made him sick.

CHAPTER SIX

Thursday was another fine day but the wind had gone round to the north-east and strengthened, a bitter wind, dry and searching, probing every crack and crevice, stirring the dust in the streets and whipping up white horses in the estuary.

The News on Wycliffe's desk bleated triumphantly:

> DRAMATIC DEVELOPMENT IN CITY MURDERS
> EXCLUSIVE!
> 'I AM NOT A PSYCHOPATH!'

A photograph of the note was given a three-column spread in the middle of the front page.

More encouraging, W.P.C. Burden had returned from Paignton with a snapshot she had found amongst the mountain of stuff which Elaine's mother had treasured. Three girls of fifteen or sixteen, dressed in jeans and T-shirts, sprawled on a grassy slope in front of a disused hut that was half ruin. In the background, rocky outcrops and a moorland scene.

The girl with the mop of dark curls had been identified by her mother as Elaine, the second was Debbie Joyce, he could not think of her as Rosaline Parkin, less still as Rosaline Norman. The broad, high cheek-bones and the pointed chin were unmistakable.

The third girl, fair, plump and smiling was a stranger and somebody must have taken the snap.

Mrs Bennett was unhelpful. 'We never knew any of Elaine's friends. She never confided in us. I don't understand it really . . . we did all we could.'

Mrs Bennett did, however, remember Elaine spending a holiday after her 'O' levels at a hostel in Dorset, but she had not heard of any trouble there.

Wycliffe gave instructions for enlargements of the photograph to be made and for one to be sent to *The News*, others to the regional TV stations.

WHO IS THE THIRD GIRL?
NUMBER THREE—DO YOU KNOW THIS GIRL?
DID YOU TAKE THIS SNAP?

Ready-made headlines and almost certainly the quickest way to get answers.

He telephoned the editor of *The News*.

'Exclusive?'

'Not this time.' All the same it was from the local press that he expected results.

'You are taking over my front page.' Editors feel compelled to grumble even when good copy falls like manna from the skies.

Two girls had been murdered and in the mind of their killer they had been killed as a punishment—*two of the guilty ones*. Presumably there were others. Wycliffe had started from the assumption of a link between the two girls and it seemed logical to suppose that a similar link must exist between the dead girls and others marked down by the killer. If the nature of the link could be firmly established, if the real common denominator could be found then it should be possible to anticipate the killer, to know his intended victims and to protect them. So far it had been shown that Debbie Joyce and Elaine Bennett had known each other when they were schoolgirls and they had since met at Bourg's club. But Wycliffe was not entirely satisfied

119

with Bourg's account of the clash between the two girls. Without some deeper cause of enmity it was unlikely that Rosaline Parkin, merely by changing her name, would provoke such a demonstration from Elaine drunk or sober. He sent for Dixon.

'Della Patterson is a hostess at the Golden Cockerel. I've no idea where she lives but you can find out either from the club or from Bourg. Find her and ask her for her version of why Elaine Bennett and Debbie Joyce were at daggers drawn.'

'You think she'll know, sir?'

'I'll be surprised if she doesn't, she's been at that club for more than a year and I'll bet there isn't much she doesn't know.'

Dixon was on his way out when Wycliffe called him back.

'Are we keeping you busy, Dixon?'

Dixon studied the floor. 'I seem to have plenty to do, sir.'

'Don't you think that might mean that we find you useful?'

Dixon flushed to the roots of his blond curls. 'I hope so, sir. Thank you very much.'

Wycliffe thought of his own apprenticeship when any hint of approval from his superiors would have been interpreted by him and his contemporaries as softening of the brain. Times change.

Gill came in wearing a new suit which would soon acquire the slept-in look which distinguished all his clothes.

'I've had Lincoln C.I.D. on the phone; a chap called Evans—a Taff—says he worked with you when Noah wore rubber drawers.'

'Has he got anything for us?'

Gill sat down. 'Little enough. The Russells have lived in Saxby, near Lincoln, for generations. Dolly's father and mother kept an hotel. She was an only child. They retired some years ago and went to live on the coast but they're both dead now. There are still relatives about but they have no knowledge of or interest in our Dolly. I gather that she was unpopular —stuck up.' Gill paused to light a cheroot which he had been waving about in his hand. 'One of the relatives, a maiden aunt, says she had a letter from Dolly some time ago. It was an odd sort of letter and she ignored it.'

'How do you mean, odd?'

'I gather that it was about money but the old lady can't remember the details. She's going to try to find it but Evans says her house is like the bloody British Museum without a catalogue.'

The connections between the two murdered girls seemed slender enough but Wycliffe felt that it was the line to follow, and if he was right, the school teacher might turn out to be an important source of information. It was certainly more promising than a massive deployment of manpower to offer the public the illusion of security. Such exercises cannot be maintained and they are notoriously ineffective in catching criminals.

All the same he realised that he would have to make some move in that direction and with the co-operation of the uniformed branch and by drafting in men and cars from divisions outside the city he was able to muster a substantial force of mobiles which would patrol the city at night without exhausting his resources too rapidly. The administrative arrangements took him most of the morning and he handed over the operational planning to Gill.

Among the reports which came in was one from Scales. He had interviewed the surgeon, Matthew Norman, who appeared to have been thoroughly co-operative. Norman stated that he had been on an emergency case in the theatre at Millfield from half-past eight until gone eleven on the night Elaine Bennett was murdered. Enquiries at the hospital confirmed that Norman had successfully operated on the victim of a car crash who had suffered extensive abdominal injuries. He had been in the theatre for nearly three hours.

Exit Norman as a suspect in the Elaine Bennett case but Wycliffe had never taken the possibility of his guilt very seriously.

He was completely immersed in the case now, so much so that he was irritated by the intrusion of anything not strictly relevant. Usually he followed the national and international news with closest attention, eight in the morning on the radio, nine at night on the telly, these were sacred hours. But he had not heard a news bulletin for more than twenty-four hours. His responses to the world about him were automatic and disinterested except as they concerned or might concern his case.

Mr Bellings, the deputy chief, telephoned. 'You are an elusive fellow, Charles!'

Wycliffe, never communicative, was almost mute with Bellings.

'I think we can expect trouble from the press, Charles.'

'I don't doubt it.'

'So far they are being kind to you but it won't last . . .'

Bellings did not finish his thought. He had a stock of unfinished sentences which enabled him to make various points without actually saying anything quotable. He was saying now that another killing was almost inevitable and that it would do Wycliffe's reputation a lot of harm and not only in the press. If you listened to Bellings for long you would begin to believe that every time a dip snatched an old-aged pensioner's purse there were political repercussions. Bellings had a complex mind, he and Machiavelli would have understood each other.

'Apart from the preventive measures about which I received your memo, what other steps had you in mind?'

'I thought of writing him a letter.'

'A letter? Through the press?'

'It will have to be, I don't know his address.' He thought that he had gone too far and added, 'Call it an appeal, if you like.'

'But my dear Charles, you might as well appeal to a mad dog not to bite!'

'Perhaps, but it might be worth trying. We need time.'

Bellings took it hard. 'With three separate incidents there must be some leads.'

'There are but they haven't led anywhere. You've seen my reports?'

Why did he do it? Gratuitous provocation? Not really. His approach to his job was personal and immediate, Bellings saw everything in terms of press reaction, political and administrative repercussions, statistics and reports. There was little common ground, no hope of mutual understanding. They rubbed each other the wrong way at every contact but Bellings was able to conceal his feelings more effectively because he had the instincts of a diplomat.

'I think you should put the idea to the chief before you carry it any further.'

'I shall do, if I decide that it's worth doing.'

Was he serious about writing an open letter to the killer? Almost. The idea was growing on him. The man was sensitive to public opinion and it was just possible that such a move might put him off his stroke for a day or two, perhaps long enough to pull him in. It was worth a try. He picked up the telephone to speak to the chief constable but the chief was out of town until lunch time on Friday.

He mooned about his office most of the afternoon. He had arranged for detectives to visit the secondary schools in the city in an effort to discover the name of the girl whose parents had complained about her treatment at Miss Russell's community holiday. A trivial incident nearly ten years old. Was it likely that

123

anyone would remember? His best hope was to find the school teacher herself and he had made it known to the press that the police would be glad to interview her.

Somewhere in the city there was a man who had killed twice and intended to kill again.

Intended was probably not the right word. *Would kill again, he couldn't stop himself.*

Wycliffe knew that there must be times when the man was tortured by doubts; hours or even days when he almost closed his mind to the knowledge of what he had done and so dulled the agony of remorse. Then came resolution, he would stop now. He would never kill again. He would give himself up. If they put him in prison he would be safe. But slowly, inevitably, his resolve was undermined, his conscience spoke to him with a different voice. If he stopped now he would be running away, betraying his trust. Reluctantly he would come to see that he must go on, it was his duty, part of the burden he carried. And so the way was made smooth for his next act. The mechanics of the crime, planning the where, when and how were exciting. He became intoxicated by his capacity for clear, incisive thought and for prompt, decisive action. The tension grew from hour to hour, the rhythm quickened and the climax came.

It was a cycle.

D.C. Dixon reported directly to Wycliffe on his visit to the night club hostess, Della Patterson.

'She has a bed-sitter in a house in Bear Street, sir, down by the old harbour. I got there round one and she'd just got up—'

'Did she tell you anything?'

'In the end. At first she was a bit coy, said she'd already told you all she knew about Debbie Joyce.'

'Well?'

Dixon, obviously pleased with himself, wanted to make the best of his tale.

'It seems that the real trouble between Elaine Bennett

124

and Debbie was over the floor manager, a chap called Pirelli.'

'Mr Disraeli?'

'Sir?'

'Never mind. What about him?'

'Apparently Elaine fell for him in a big way and for several weeks there was quite a thing going between them. Even some talk of marriage.'

'But Debbie put a stop to it?'

Dixon nodded. 'True to form, according to Della Patterson. She made a dead set at Pirelli and when she'd cut out Elaine she dropped him. There was no love lost between Debbie and the other girls, apparently she'd done the same thing before.'

'It's a wicked world, Dixon.'

'Yes, sir.' He lingered. 'A good many people must have felt like killing that girl, sir.'

'Fortunately there's a big gap between feeling like killing and doing it. And who felt like killing Elaine Bennett?'

'That's a more difficult one, sir.'

The telephone rang.

'Huntingdon C.I.D. on the phone for you, sir.'

After the usual preamble he asked, 'Any joy?'

'At first it didn't look very promising. Lady Margaret's is run like a nunnery, all the staff are resident and it's virtually impossible to do any unofficial snooping, but we had a stroke of luck. It turned out that our super has a friend whose daughter was involved in the Russell affair. It was largely from what she and one or two other girls told their parents that Miss Russell was asked to resign. Of course, she did and it was all smoothed over with no nasty scandal.'

'She was a lesbian?'

'So it seems. Is that what you were after?'

'I wanted to know why she resigned.'

Wycliffe asked one or two more questions but learned nothing new.

If this girl had received unwelcome attentions from Miss Russell and told her parents . . . But it all happened nearly ten years ago. He kept coming back to that.

It was dark and once more he sat at his desk with only the green-shaded desk lamp to light the big room.

In the end he went home because he could think of nothing else to do.

He drove slowly out of the city and as he got clear of the suburbs he could feel the car being buffeted by the wind.

The living room of their new home had been made by knocking two rooms into one. There was a dining area at one end and they could sit down to a meal while they watched the ceaseless flow of traffic through the narrows at the entrance to the port. Even at night, unless the weather was bad, they often left the curtains undrawn so that they could see the pattern of light-buoys and the slow procession of ships up and down the channel, marked only by the lights they carried.

'Where are they?'

The twins, both of whom were doing post-graduate courses at university, were still on Christmas vacation.

'There's a film on at the Arts they wanted to see.'

'So long as they're together.'

'You're worried about Ruth?'

'I'd just as soon she was with her brother in the evenings until they go back or until we catch this joker.'

'Any prospect of that?'

'Not so's you'd notice.'

'I'll serve. It's fresh prawns with mushrooms and a curried sauce.'

They ate in silence. Wycliffe usually made the coffee but he did not stir and she went instead. When she came back he was sitting in his armchair staring at nothing.

'Coffee?'

He took the cup mechanically. Helen washed up without his help and when she came back he was still

126

sitting. She settled down with a book—*Coastal Gardening*.

'Got a pencil?'

Helen looked up from her book. 'There's a ball-point in the magazine rack.'

'I know, how long since you've used a pencil?'

Helen closed her book on her finger. 'I can't remember, I usually use a ball-point or nylon tip. I think I saw a few pencils in one of the drawers of the cabinet.'

'In other words you don't use pencils and neither do I.'

'Is that something for the *Guinness Book of Records* or does it lead somewhere?'

'Our chap wrote his note to the paper in pencil—very soft—probably 5B.'

'Perhaps he sketches or draws or something.'

'I'd just got round to that.' He got out his pipe and started to fill it. 'Valerie what's-her-name, the girl who was attacked on the allotments, said that he smelt of turpentine.'

'So he paints as well.'

Wycliffe shrugged. 'It's a thought.'

CHAPTER SEVEN

Sheila Barker née Jukes was getting breakfast for her husband and two children. Clive, aged one year, squatted disconsolately in his play-pen, beating the bars with a plastic toy; Denise, two and a half, lying on the floor, was scraping a crayon over a black and white picture of the Magic Roundabout.

Sheila, who had changed only predictably in nine years, was fatter, her breasts sagged more heavily and her mouth was a little harder and meaner.

Her husband called down the stairs, 'There's no socks in my drawer, Sheila.'

'They're still in the airing cupboard.'

A radio on the side board churned out pop music interspersed with inanities from the duty D.J.

She went into the kitchen and returned with an egg on a spoon which she plopped into an egg cup in her husband's place. 'Your egg's ready.'

The letter box rattled and she went out into the passage, returning with the morning paper. A picture on the front page and the headline above it caught her eye: DID YOU TAKE THIS PHOTOGRAPH? DO YOU KNOW THE THIRD GIRL?

When her husband came down she was still looking at the paper, spread out on the table.

'Look at this.'

Barker was swarthy, small and bony, already thinning on top though he was still under thirty.

He glanced at the picture and the headlines. 'They're still at it, then.'

She pointed with a fat, pink forefinger, 'That's Rosaline, that's Elaine Bennett and the fair girl is Joan Simmonds. I wonder what they're after.'

Her husband sat in his place and sliced the top off his egg.

'You'd better tell 'em.'

'Why should I get mixed up in it?'

'No, I wasn't serious. It's got nothing to do with us.'

Sheila folded the paper and put it on the sideboard. 'Funny though.'

'What is?'

'Those two being killed like that. What are they supposed to have done?'

'Done?'

'In that note he wrote to the paper he said that they were the guilty ones.'

Barker laughed shortly. 'You don't want to take any notice of that nonsense. He's kinky—mad as a hatter.' He spoke with his mouth full of bread and egg. 'Just don't go gallivanting round the streets at night.'

'Fat chance I've got doing that. When will I see you again?'

'Not tonight. There's a brief session on the new promotion this afternoon and that means I shall have to stay in Bristol overnight. With luck I should be back lunch time tomorrow.'

Miss Russell and her partner were at breakfast in their high, narrow kitchen on the first floor. Originally it had been a part of a bedroom which had now been partitioned to give a kitchen and bathroom. They ate a Swiss cereal breakfast with milk but no sugar and drank black coffee.

Miss Russell, now forty-eight, had changed little

except that her hair was grey and tiny bristles sprouted on her upper lip.

'There's the paper boy, Janet.'

Miss Carter, dumpy and cheerful, waddled downstairs to collect the paper off the mat. She came back up slowly, reading the front page.

'Look at that.'

She dropped the paper by Miss Russell's plate.

DID YOU TAKE THIS PHOTOGRAPH? DO YOU KNOW THE THIRD GIRL?

Miss Russell glanced at the headlines and at the photograph.

'What will they dig up next?'

'Do you know the other girl?'

'Yes, that's Joan Simmonds, they won't find her in a hurry, she's married and living in Malta.'

'Perhaps you should tell the police.'

Miss Russell regarded her companion with scorn. 'Why should I put myself out? It's all nonsense anyway, a newspaper gimmick I shouldn't wonder.'

'Those two girls have been murdered.'

'Probably because they asked for it. That Rosaline Parkin had all the makings of a tart and, from what I saw of her, Elaine Bennett wasn't much better.'

'You saw what the killer wrote to the paper yesterday —about punishing the guilty. He must have meant something.'

'Rubbish! It probably wasn't the killer who wrote it anyway. In any case, what's it got to do with me? I happened to have taught one of the girls, that's all.'

Miss Carter, as always, was bludgeoned into agreement by her companion. 'I suppose you're right. There must be plenty of people who will recognise the girl without you being involved.'

Miss Russell glanced at her watch. 'It's time I went down, the parents will be arriving.'

Friday was a day of frustration. Although Wycliffe was

130

beginning to feel that he was on the right track and a number of leads were being followed, results were slow to come in. He feared that the third victim would be attacked over the weekend or shortly afterwards and, so far, he was helpless to prevent it.

The photograph of the three girls appeared in the morning paper:

DID YOU TAKE THIS PHOTOGRAPH?
DO YOU KNOW THE THIRD GIRL?

How long would it be before he got answers to these questions? Surely, with two girls already dead the third and whoever took the snap would lose no time in contacting the police. But Wycliffe knew from experience that many people have a surprising capacity for convincing themselves that whatever misfortunes befall others, nothing can happen to them.

But all publicity generates some response and by mid-day several women had been to their local police stations claiming to know the third girl; three, including a matron of fifty claimed to be the girl and two remembered taking the photograph. All were regulars, ready to oblige with a confession or an identification at the drop of a hat.

The Department of Education, prompted by the Home Office, came through with the information that Dorothy Russell, when she resigned from St Margaret's, had cashed her pension contributions and ceased to be a registered teacher.

After lunch Wycliffe saw the chief constable and, despite an objection from Bellings, obtained permission to publish his own letter to the killer. He spent a good deal of the afternoon drafting the letter and, when it had been typed, he sent a copy to the editor of *The News*.

In the early evening he drove idly round the city. It was not that he wanted to check on Gill's dispositions,

131

he did not, in any case, expect that they would serve any useful purpose except to reassure the public. He drove through the streets to keep contact, because he could not work from the abstractions which other people put on paper for his benefit. He passed through the city centre and down Prince's Street. There were few people about and not a lot of traffic. The wind played tricks with the litter in the gutters.

The street lighting was poor and none of the shops was lit. That girl in the light-coloured coat, hurrying along the pavement, her body slanted to the wind, she probably felt safe in one of the main thoroughfares of the city but a resolute killer might do his work and be away before anybody realised what was happening. There would be no safety until he was taken. A police car cruised slowly down the middle traffic lane.

He reached the dock gates and turned off into a maze of streets where terraces of mean little houses alternated with the blank walls of warehouses. As he made his way northward semi-detached villas with front gardens took the place of terraced houses and there were no warehouses. Before the Second World War these had been the outskirts of the city, now the urban sprawl had engulfed former villages in all directions.

The killer was a man of the suburbs, Wycliffe felt sure of that. Once he had been at home in a neatly patterned subtopia where each tiny garden had its forsythia, its flowering cherry, floribunda roses and bedding plants in season. He did not belong to the world of fish-and-chips and betting shops. There were thousands like him but he was different because he was a killer.

The crime cars and panda were geometrically spaced, weaving complex, interlacing patterns through the streets.

The killer was vastly outnumbered but he had the choice of time and place. He could say to himself at any time when the odds seemed weighted against him, 'Not tonight.'

Or could he?

Was it not more likely that each time the resolution to kill needed time to grow, time to mature and that when it had he would be driven irresistibly to act.

Wycliffe sighed. A family man without a family. The phrase came to him out of the blue and he savoured it. It expressed two paradoxical ideas which had been in his mind for some time. The killer, a family man who knew what it was to have ties and obligations, responsibilities and compelling loyalties—'People cannot destroy lives without being punished'. And the killer, a lonely man, haunted by ghosts.

But the paradox went deeper than that. From the beginning he had insisted that the man was rational to the extent that he did not kill at random; his victims were 'the guilty ones'. This had practical importance, it offered some prospect of discovering the killer through establishing his motives which was the reason for laying such emphasis on links between the victims. On the other hand Wycliffe, without splitting psychiatric hairs, was prepared to maintain that any multiple killer is mad, in particular that a multiple strangler cannot be sane. But, in his view, there was no necessary contradiction in attributing rationality to a mad man.

If he was right the crunch might come later, when the killer had run out of victims; that is to say when he had killed 'the guilty ones'. Then his madness might become irrational or, at least, require a further process of rationalisation.

At nine o'clock he made for home. The wind brought with it occasional flurries of sleet which clogged the screen-wipers. Helen saw that he was tired and dispirited and asked no questions. He allowed himself to be fussed over, dry sherry in front of the fire followed by a light meal. Fillets of sole poached in white wine with shrimps.

'*Sole dieppoise*,' Helen explained. 'I couldn't get any mussels so I used shrimps instead.'

Helen's cooking was much influenced by their last trip abroad. One year he had endured *sauerkraut* and sausages.

On the ten o'clock news they screened the picture of the three girls with the police appeal for information.

At eleven they went to bed but lay awake until after midnight listening for the twins to come in.

Prince's Street was the only one of the city's main throughfares to have escaped both the blitz and the developers. It was still a street of small shops interspersed with pubs, and many of the proprietors still lived in the rooms over their shops. The street had remained unchanged for long enough to attract the attention of conservationists and it was becoming increasingly the vogue to speak of it as 'interesting' rather than seedy.

One shop which was both interesting and seedy had changed little in fifty years. The signboard read: Probert and Rendell. Artists' Colourmen. Picture Framers and Restorers. In the shop window there was a large, gilt-framed oil-painting. It depicted a sea scene with fishing boats in the middle distance and a crowded jetty in the foreground. Exactly one half of the picture was encrusted with dirt and varnish so that the design was scarcely discernible while the other half was so clear and bright that the colours might have been just applied. Apart from the painting there were two display racks in the window showing a range of mouldings and a card which stated: Estimates free.

Jim Rendell worked in what had once been a conservatory, built on to the back of the house. His partner and former employer, now seventy-five, looked after the shop but left most of the mounting and framing and all the restoration work to him. Anyone who judged their prosperity by the number of customers coming to the shop would have been misled for they were regularly employed by collectors, galleries and even museums throughout the south.

The glass walls of the conservatory had been replaced by brick but the sloping glass roof remained. The room had been divided by a partition and in one half Rendell did the restoration and mounting while in the other he had his picture framer's bench, his tools and stocks of mouldings. A cast-iron stove with a rusty smoke-pipe heated the whole place more or less effectively except in the coldest weather. The smells of turpentine, paint and glue were blended with the slightly sickly odour of linseed oil. An alarm clock, ticking away on top of a roll-topped desk, showed half-past five.

Rendell set about making a parcel of six small watercolours which he had mounted and framed in Hogarth moulding. He worked as he always did, systematically and without haste, completely absorbed in his task. As he was tying the string Alfred Probert came in and stood in the doorway. He was short and on the stout side. Long white hair and a moustache gave him a superficial resemblance to Lloyd George which he had cultivated, believing that there had never been a real statesman since the little Welsh wizard. He took a silver watch from his waistcoat pocket and compared it with the alarm clock.

'You off then, lad?'

'I'm off.'

'Are those Mr Walton's watercolours?'

'Yes, I'll leave them in the shop, he's calling for them in the morning.'

'What's up then, won't you be here in the morning?'

'It's Saturday.'

For fifteen years Rendell had not come to work on Saturdays but each week the old man pretended to be surprised.

'Well, I'll go upstairs to my tea. Mrs Probert doesn't like to be kept waiting. You'll shut the shop? Turn the lights out and lock up?'

'Yes. Good-night.'

'Good-night, lad.'

The same ritual every night, almost the same words but he never felt impatient, he would not have had it otherwise. He had worked with Probert for thirty-nine years, first as his apprentice, then as an employee, and for the past fifteen years as a partner.

He took off the long grey overall which he wore over his suit, hung it on a nail by the door and put on his mackintosh and cap. A quick look round the two rooms and he switched the lights out. Light came through faintly from the shop. A short passage and he was behind the counter in the shop where there was nothing displayed for sale. He switched out the light, let himself out through the shop door and locked it behind him, trying the door twice before he was satisfied.

A cutting wind blew down Prince's Street and he turned up the collar of his mackintosh. The shops were poorly lit, the street lamps were meagre and lorries thundered down the broad thoroughfare on their way to and from the docks. He waited his chance, then crossed in two spurts. It was not far to the *Guardian* building.

As usual, in the city centre, he waited until he was within a few feet of the newspaper seller before he allowed himself to read the placard.

MYSTERY OF THE THIRD GIRL

He had seen the paper that morning so he knew what they were talking about. The photograph had had a strange effect on him. He had not known of its existence, there was no reason why he should have done, but the fact that the police had found and published it made him feel insecure. It was like an attack from behind, it made him realise that things were going on of which he had no knowledge.

136

He bought a paper.

The newspaper man said, 'Joining the big spenders, guv?'

He walked slowly past one of the big stores, reading in the light from the windows.

The photograph appeared for the second time under the caption: THE MYSTERY GIRL and the text went on to say that up to the time of going to press no one had come forward to identify the third girl in the picture nor had the police heard from whoever took the photograph.

If you recognise the girl or if you know anything of the circumstances in which this photograph was taken you are urged to telephone police headquarters, Telephone 323232, or get in touch with any police station.

Long-standing Vendetta?

The importance attached to this photograph by the police suggests that they take seriously the note which the killer addressed to this newspaper and which appeared in our columns yesterday . . .

His hands trembled so much that he could not continue to read. He folded the newspaper and walked on slowly, breathing deeply to restore his calm.

'Is that you, Jim?'

He changed his jacket and came slowly into the living room. Albert was there.

'What you buy a paper for? You know we always get one.'

'Don't go running off, Jim, I'm just dishing up.'

If only they would leave him alone!

* * *

In the morning, by the time they had finished breakfast, the estuary was lit by the almost level rays of the sun, emphasising the contours of the landscape through highlights and deep shadows. A Norwegian vessel, her decks stacked with timber, crept up channel against the tide; a tug, towing a train of barges made out to sea. Wycliffe stood in the window of the living room and smoked his first pipe of the day. Soon now the killer would be opening his newspaper and he would read the famous letter. But would he telephone?

'I expect that I shall be in the office all day.'

'What about tomorrow?'

'I don't know. It depends. I could have incoming calls on the special number transferred to me.'

His son, David, had left the old banger which he shared with his sister across the garage entrance. It was going to be one of those days.

He drove into the city and parked his car in the space which had his name painted on it. MR WYCLIFFE. Next to him was MR BELLINGS and next again, MR OLDROYD, the chief constable. Two other spaces were labelled; the hoi-polloi below the rank of chief superintendent had to fend for themselves. Bellings' E-type Jag was in his space but the chief's Rover was not. The chief believed that one of the privileges of rank should be a free weekend.

Wycliffe was morose, not because anything had gone wrong, not even because the case was bogged down but because he felt ineffectual and useless. All he could do was sit at the end of a telephone and wait.

At eleven o'clock he received a call purporting to come from the strangler. 'About your letter . . . '

There followed a description of what the caller proposed to do with his remaining victims. The details were obscene as well as impracticable. Telephone engineers and police were monitoring all calls to the special number and within a very short time, after dropping the receiver, a call came through on another line.

'A call-box in East Street, sir. There were two cars

138

within easy reach so they should have him by now. What do you want done with him?'

Wycliffe considered. With these chaps, fortunately, it was all in the mind. 'Tell him if we catch him again we'll do him and let him go.'

Gill came looking as though he hadn't slept. 'We seem to be getting nowhere fast.'

They had lunch of a sort sent up from the canteen.

At a quarter to two, after three more calls from kinks who claimed to be the strangler and while they were drinking a second cup of coffee, a call came through from St Thomas's Road Police Station.

'Inspector Rigg, sir. There's a young lady here who says she's got information about the photograph published in yesterday's papers.'

'Genuine?'

The inspector was careful. 'I think so, sir. She's certainly about the right age to have been at school with the girls. She seems a sensible sort . . . '

'I'll send a car to pick her up.' He signalled to Gill who had been listening on the second earpiece. Gill gave instructions over the intercom. Within twenty minutes she was in Wycliffe's office.

'Barlow—Pamela Barlow née O'Brien.'

Red-gold hair to the shoulders, green eyes and, of course, freckles. A broad forehead and a firm chin. She wore a yellow raincoat and neat little square-toed shoes with wedge heels. Good legs. A dish—an Irish dish. She certainly earned Gill's approval.

'I live at twenty-three Water Lane, not far from St Thomas's Station.'

She had a copy of *The News* of the previous day on her lap with her handbag.

'They say you want to know about the third girl and who took the snap.'

Wycliffe nodded. 'That's right.'

'Well, I took the snap and the third girl was called Joan Simmonds.' She smiled. 'At least that was her

139

name before she was married, she's called Roberts now; her husband is in the R.A.F. and they're stationed in Malta.'

'You're sure of that?'

'Of course. I had a letter from her Thursday.'

'Where was the photograph taken?'

'On the moor. It was a Saturday and the four of us were on some sort of charity walk. I can't remember the details.' She pulled her skirt over her knees. 'I know we stopped in front of that disused army hut to have our lunch.'

'Charity walks don't sound to me like Rosaline Parkin's cup of tea.' Gill was being frighteningly amiable.

She laughed. 'Well, she didn't finish the course. When we reached the road she hitched a lift back.'

'She was a friend of yours?'

'Not really. She was Elaine's friend. I went about with Joan Simmonds and Joan was friendly with Elaine. That's how it came about. In fact we went about quite a bit together at that time.' She fiddled with her handbag. 'Actually Rosaline and to a lesser extent, Elaine, had a reputation for being a bit wild and good girls were supposed to keep away.'

'And you were a good girl?'

'Mother thought so.'

Wycliffe intervened. 'Joan, Rosaline and you were all at the same school—at Cholsey Grammar, is that right?'

'Yes. Elaine was a cut above us, she went to Bishop Fuller's. She and Rosaline and Joan Simmonds met playing hockey. I was no hockey player but all four of us used to meet some weekends.'

Gill stared at the girl. Wycliffe stared at his blotter. Winter sunshine streamed in through the window. Traffic was building up on the road outside. A fine Saturday afternoon and half the population wanted to get out of the city.

'We shan't keep you long, Mrs Barlow.'

'Don't mind me, my husband is glued to the telly on Saturday afternoons.'

'Being at Cholsey Grammar, you would remember Miss Russell?'

'Oh, yes, I remember her well enough.'

'I understand that she used to organise various vacation trips. Did you go on any of these?'

She looked surprised. 'I went on two, one was a camping holiday, the other we spent three weeks in a hostel.' She smiled again. 'An exercise in communal living, she called it. It was that all right.'

'Elaine Bennett and Rosaline Parkin went on both?'

'No, neither of them was on the camping trip.' She looked at Wyclife with a puzzled frown. 'What is all this?'

Wycliffe ignored her question. 'How many girls altogether were at the hostel?'

She thought. 'Twenty-four or five, I suppose. Most of them were from Cholsey Grammar but several other schools were represented.'

'And Miss Russell was in charge?'

'Oh, yes. She was the only teacher. She organised it.'

'Did anything happen during those three weeks— anything you might think of as disturbing or even alarming?'

She pursed her lips and frowned. 'I think I know what you're after but why, I can't imagine.'

'What are we after?'

'The fuss there was about that girl.'

'What girl?'

'I can't even remember her name, she wasn't one of ours.'

'You mean that she came from another school?'

'She must have done but I can't remember which. She wasn't in the same dormitory as Joan and me, she was in with Rosaline and Elaine.'

'Tell us what happened.'

141

For the first time she hesitated. 'I wish I knew what this is in aid of. All the same, if you want the gory details ... It wouldn't mean anything unless you know that Miss Russell was a les. At least ...'

'At least what?'

'Well, it's difficult. I mean, she liked to paw some of the girls, I don't think anything very bad happened.'

'Were you one of the girls?'

Curse of red hair and freckles, she blushed. 'Yes, I didn't like it but there wasn't much you could do. I mean, she made out she was being specially nice to you. Perhaps she was in her own way.'

'Rosaline too?'

'Rosaline especially. She got really browned off with the treatment.'

'What happened?'

She was reluctant. 'It really was quite nasty when you come to look back at it. I only heard the details when it was over. Of course, Rosaline was behind it.'

The two men waited.

'This girl that all the trouble was about was a real innocent and in the dormitory with that lot she had a good deal to put up with. One of her fads was that she didn't like taking a shower with the other girls so she used to get up early before the others were about. Of course, Rosaline got hold of this. She and Elaine and a girl called Sheila Jukes worked it all out. While this girl was in the shower they pinched her dressing gown and pyjamas so that all the poor kid had was a towel. She stuck it out in the showers for a while but in the end she had to come out. She made for the dormitory but they'd locked the door. Then, along comes Rosaline and pretends to be sorry for playing the joke on her. She said, "Your things are in Miss Russell's room, all you've got to do is go in and get them."

'By this time the kid was nearly in tears and she said she couldn't go into Miss Russell's room with no clothes on but Rosaline told her not to be a fool. How

142

did she think they'd got the stuff in there if the Russell was still in bed? She'd gone to the staff bathroom and everybody knew she took ages.

'Of course it was all lies but the kid believed her and opened the door of Miss Russell's room. As she did so Rosaline called to her, she turned to answer and Rosaline took a photo—a flash photo.'

Gill grinned with unusual ferocity. 'What a pleasant little crowd! What happened?'

'Not much at first, then, a few days later, prints of Rosaline's photo appeared on the notice boards and all over the place. There was this girl with nothing on coming out of Miss Russell's room. The door, by the way, had Miss Russell's name on it.' She stopped speaking, fished in her bag and came out with a packet of cigarettes. 'Do you mind if I smoke?'

Gill lit her cigarette.

'After that I'm not entirely sure what happened. I do know that the poor kid who was the victim of it all was sent home in disgrace. Joan Simmonds and I had to go with her in a taxi to the station to make sure she got on the train. She was in a terrible state.' She drew deeply on her cigarette and exhaled with obvious pleasure. 'Nothing happened to Rosaline and the other two as far as I know. The rumour went round that Rosaline had warned Miss Russell that if she made any fuss the headmaster would get to hear one or two things. Anyway, it all seemed to die a natural death and it wasn't long afterwards that Miss Russell left to go to another school.'

Wycliffe had made one or two cryptic notes in the convolutions of an elaborate doodle.

'This Sheila Jukes you mentioned. Was she from Cholsey Grammar?'

'Oh, yes, she was another of Rosaline's cronies.'

'You haven't kept in touch with her?'

She leaned forward to tap off the ash from her cigarette. 'No, we never had much to do with each

143

other and I haven't heard of her since she left. She left in the lower sixth and I went on to ''A'' levels.' She sat back in her chair with a half smile on her lips. 'Now, do you mind telling me why you wanted to hear all this?'

Wycliffe still offered no explanation. 'We are anxious to get in touch with Miss Russell.'

'Well, that shouldn't be difficult. I saw her last week.'

'Here—in town?'

'In the central market. I spoke to her but she pretended not to see me—she was always good at not seeing people if she didn't want to.'

'You're sure it was her?'

'Positive—and she knew me, I could tell. She turned away that bit too quickly and became absorbed in a baby-wear stall.'

Wycliffe was looking at her with expressionless eyes. 'Didn't it strike you as odd that both victims of the killer should have been girls who were involved in this rather sick joke?'

She frowned. 'No, I can't say that it did, it only struck me how horrible it was that they should be two girls I knew.' She hesitated, then went on, 'You can't really think that there is any connection, surely? I mean, it would be too ridiculous, wouldn't it? After nine years!'

Wycliffe's face was still blank and his manner unusually pedantic. 'We are on the look-out for any links between the two murdered girls and you have told us of one such link, there may be others.'

'I see.' She looked doubtful and a little worried.

'Now, about this Sheila Jukes . . .'

But Pamela Barlow had told them all she knew. As she was leaving she turned to Wycliffe, the green eyes full of concern. 'You don't think it's possible . . . I mean, if he's mad . . . after all, I did come here, didn't I?'

Wycliffe was reassuring. 'I am sure you have no cause for worry, Mrs Barlow, but I will see that your house is kept under observation especially at night.'

When she had gone, Gill slumped back in his chair and

lit a cheroot. 'I agree with her, it's bloody silly. All this for some damn fool kid's prank which happened nearly ten years ago.'

Wycliffe looked at him without speaking. Gill had never seen him so sombre. His manner was almost menacing. 'At least you know what you have to do.'

A little later he stood by while Gill briefed his men for the search. 'Dorothy Russell, aged 48, and Sheila Jukes, aged 25 . . .'

When Gill had finished he turned to Wycliffe out of courtesy. 'Anything you'd like to add, sir?'

Wycliffe looked startled, as though his thoughts had been elsewhere. He snapped, 'Just find them while they're still alive.'

For the next couple of hours he haunted the control room where radio links with all the cars were maintained. From time to time the officer on duty was prompted to speak to him, to make some casual remark but Wycliffe behaved as though he had not heard.

Scales was the first to report back. 'Sheila Jukes used to live at fourteen Stokes Road, Cholsey. It's a council housing estate. Her father was—is for all I know, a welder. I got that from the headmaster at Cholsey Comprehensive and I'm on my way there now. Sergeant Ellis is gone to Harcourt Mansions, a block of flats where Miss Russell lived when she was at school. It's our only starting point.'

Stokes Road was a long, depressing string of semi-detached council houses built between the wars. Each had its little front garden bounded by concrete posts and wire mesh. There was a light in number fourteen and Scales could hear the television. A teenaged girl answered the door and looked him up and down with interest. 'Jukes? There's nobody here called that. Mam! There's a man here asking for somebody called Jukes.' She was joined by a thin, middle-aged woman with permed and dyed hair, eye-shadow and a cigarette which seemed glued to her bottom lip so that

145

it bobbed up and down as she spoke.

'Jukes? They've been gone ages. love. Emigrated. We moved in here when they went.' She considered. 'Five year ago last August.'

'Emigrated?'

She eyed him speculatively. 'Australia, I think it was. He was a welder; good trade for emigrating, they say. You a relative?'

'Police.' He produced his warrant card. 'We wanted to get in touch with their daughter, Shelia.'

'Oh, Shelia—that's different. She didn't go.' She massaged her bare arms against the cold. 'She married some fella just before they left and she stayed behind.'

'Do you happen to remember her married name?'

'No, dear, sorry. We wasn't what you might call friends. It was just when we first come to see about curtains and things they was getting ready for this wedding.'

'Was it a church affair?'

'Oh, yes, with all the trimmings. St Andrews, over across the railway.'

Scales thanked her and raised his hat.

'She's done something?'

'Oh, no. Just a routine enquiry.'

St Andrews was the parish church of what had once been the village of Cholsey. It had retained its graveyard intact with its avenue of yews and the vicarage had kept its garden but housing development pressed in on all sides. Scales reported in on his car radio.

The short drive up to the vicarage was muddy and unlit. A lighted window to the right of the front door was the only sign of life and his ring was answered by the vicar himself, a tall, spare man with fringes of grey hair, bald on top.

'Do come in!' He was taken into the room in which he had seen the light. A large room with a dusty decorated ceiling and oak panelling half way up the walls. There elegance ended and gave place to tattiness. A thread-

146

bare carpet, deal bookshelves, a cheap plastic shade where there should have been a chandelier, an ancient gas fire standing in a grate made for logs. The vicar's desk was littered with books and papers. 'I was working. You must forgive the muddle. A detective, you say, I would have taken you for a bank manager or a solicitor.' The vicar meant to be complimentary.

'You were asking about the marriage of someone called Jukes?'

'The bride was Shelia Jukes, the marriage took place about five and a half years ago and we want to know her married name.'

The vicar dangled a pair of heavy library glasses and regarded Scales with a knowing smile, 'Barker—she is now Mrs Shelia Barker.'

'You have a good memory, sir.'

'On the contrary, I have very bad memory. It happens that you are the second person to come to me with that question.'

Scale felt his spine tingling.

'Three weeks, perhaps a month ago—certainly before Christmas, a gentleman came to me with the same enquiry. He said that he was an old friend of the family and that he had lost touch. He had been told that they had emigrated but that Shelia had married and was living in the city. Like you, he wanted to know her married name so that he could find her.' The vicar paused, reasonably, for breath. 'I searched the Registers, and, of course, there it was—Jukes/Barker.' A benign smile.

'This man, could you describe him?'

'My visitor?'

Scales nodded.

'Oh, dear, this does sound ominous! I saw little enough of him. He arrived, like you, out of the night one might say. It was bitter cold and raining; he was muffled up with an overcoat and scarf. He refused to some into the house so we went straight to the vestry

147

where our parish records are kept in a safe. A very few minutes while I searched and he was off again. To do him justice, he donated two pounds to church funds.'

'Old or young?'

'A subjective question, Mr Scales. He was grey and though he was not as thin on top as I, it seemed to me that we were much or an age—fifty to fifty-five.'

'Tall? Short? Thin? Fat?'

'About my build.'

'How did he strike you? Educated? Well off?'

'Oh, dear! These are difficult questions! I would say that he could have been a superior type of workman, a tradesman with his own business, perhaps.' Momentarily the vicar saw himself in 222B Baker Street, he was pleased with himself.

'Think, if you will, sir—was there anything about him—his manner, his dress, his speech, his appearance which struck you?'

The vicar reflected. 'No, I can't say that there was. He seemed to me to be a pleasant man in a little too much of a hurry to be quite as polite as he would otherwise have been. He might, even, have been nervous.'

They went to the vestry by a muddy path still littered with rotting beech leaves. Their way was lit by the vicar's flashlight. The vestry was damp and badly lit. It was a feat of strength to open the door of the massive old safe. The records showed that Sheila June Jukes had married William Edward Barker on the 3rd July.

Wycliffe's restless prowling brought him to the radio room just as Scales' second report was coming in. He was cheered, it was progress. With any luck it would be simple to locate Sheila Jukes and they had another witness who had almost certainly seen and talked with the strangler. It might be possible to get out some sort of identikit picture but Wycliffe had little faith in that prospect. Most people do not have the kind of visual memory which is necessary.

Wycliffe went through the Voters' List. There were

148

three William Edward Barkers and one of them was listed with Sheila June Barker at 3 Parkes Road, Maudsley. Maudsley was the nearest of the eastern suburbs, only a short distance beyond Godolphin Road. He looked them up and found them in the telephone directory.

He dialled the number. A man's voice answered.

'Mr Barker . . . ? The husband of Mrs Sheila Barker?' Agreement tinged with nervousness and suspicion. 'Detective Chief Superintendent Wycliffe. I would like to talk to you and your wife . . . This evening . . . Thank you. In fifteen mintes.'

He drove out to Maudsley, along Godolphin Road, past the allotments. Although it was a fine evening there were few people about. Maudsley is a maze of roads which happened between the wars, some of them are still unsurfaced and unadopted and peter out unexpectedly into waste ground. Parkes Road was a crescent of semi-detached villas, the road lined with cars. His ring at number three was answered at once. A young man, swarthy, dark, already balding, the sort one expects to sell something. He received Wycliffe with a blend of nervousness and aggression. The sitting room was littered with children's toys. Barker waved him to a seat.

'The wife will be down in a minute. What's it all about?'

Wycliffe refused to be drawn until she arrived. She was blonde, pink and plump, running to loose fat, her eyes protruded slightly and she had a small, rather mean mouth. She looked at Wycliffe, 'Well? What are we supposed to have done?'

Wycliffe was bland. 'Nothing! Nothing at all. I want to ask you one or two questions and from what you tell me I shall know whether you need our help or not.'

She frowned. 'Why should we need your help?' And her husband demanded, 'What's all this about? We've got a right to know.'

'Did you, Mrs Barker, once know a girl called Rosaline Parkin?'

She nodded. 'I went to school with her.'

'And Elaine Bennett?'

'I didn't go to school with her.'

'But you knew her?'

'What if I did?'

'You will know that they have both been murdered.'

She looked at her husband and back to Wycliffe. 'What's that got to do with us?'

'Have you had anything to do with either of these girls since you left school, Mrs Barker?'

'No, I haven't, and anybody who says different is a liar!'

'Nobody does. The point is that we want to find out the link between the two girls—the reason why the killer chose them; then, knowing the link we might be able to make a shrewd guess at his next victim.'

They spoke together. 'Are you saying . . .?'

'Just that we have found only one real link between the two girls and that you were involved in that link.'

Barker got out his cigarettes and offered one to Wycliffe who refused. His wife's manner had undergone a complete change. 'Are you suggesting that I . . .?'

Wycliffe would not let her finish. 'I've no idea but we can't afford to take risks.'

'But the man is mad, he kills anybody . . .'

'We think not.'

Barker blew out a thin ribbon of smoke. 'You mean that Sheila and these two girls . . . but it's bloody fantastic! You heard her say yourself she hasn't had anything to do with them since she left school.'

'It's just possible that these crimes have their origin in events which took place then.'

Barker looked incredulous but his wife was worried. 'Give us a fag, Ted.' Her husband gave her a cigarette and lit it for her.

Wycliffe went on. 'You will remember a holiday with a party of girls in a youth hostel. You, Elaine Bennett and Rosaline Parkin played a cruel prank on one of the party . . .'

'I don't know about cruel, the kid was a creep, still wet behind the ears.'

'So you remember the incident?'

She smiled a little nervously. 'Yes, I remember it all right, it was a bit of a giggle.'

'I want to know the name of the girl who was your victim.'

'Look here, if my wife is in danger we want protection.'

Wycliffe was chilling. 'Your wife will be best protected if we catch the killer. Now, Mrs Barker, about this girl . . .'

She shook her head. 'I don't know her name. I don't think I ever heard it. We used to call her Buttercup which got shortened to Butters. She wasn't one of our lot.'

'What school did she come from?'

Mrs Barker looked surprised by the question. 'How should I know? She wasn't from Cholsey, I know that.'

'What was she like?'

'I told you, a dyed-in-the-wool little creep.'

'In appearance?'

'Oh, mousey—straight hair, cut fairly short; plain with freckles. Not very tall and thin—skinny.'

'Did she have any friends?'

'I shouldn't think so.' She paused. 'Wait a minute, there was a girl, another of the same sort—Buttercup and Daisy we used to call them. I haven't a clue what she was really called either.'

'Or the school she came from?'

'No, I'm sorry. It was the first polite word she had spoken.

Try as he would he could get no further and he turned, reluctantly to the question of protection.

'Are you at home each night, Mr Barker?'

'No, I'm away two or three nights a week, I'm a rep for E.C.A. detergents.'

He arranged for a police officer to be in the house day and night and for Mrs Barker to be accompanied whenever she went out.

'No, I don't go out much. The chance would be a fine thing. With two kids under school age and no car when Ted is away . . . '

Barker came to the gate with him. 'You seem to think this is pretty serious.'

Wycliffe was cool. 'Two girls have been murdered.'

'I hope there won't be any balls-up over this. If anything happens to my wife . . . '

'If anything happens to your wife, Mr Barker, I shall be most disturbed.'

He had telephoned instructions over the Barkers' phone and he waited by his car until he saw a patrol car turn into Parkes Road, then he drove back to headquarters.

The streets were quiet, the crime cars and pandas conspicuous.

Three girls had played a sadistic prank on a fourth nine years ago. A school teacher, for reasons of her own, had seemed to connive in their cruelty. Two of the girls had been murdered, one was now under police protection, that left the teacher.

Nothing new at headquarters. He decided to go home.

CHAPTER EIGHT

On Saturday morning he took his bed linen and his underclothes to the launderette. Alice would have washed them for him, gladly, but he would not allow that degree of intimacy. He bought a paper and looked with trepidation at the headlines. He received another shock:

AN OPEN LETTER TO THE KILLER
Detective Chief Superintendent Wycliffe, Head of Area C.I.D., writes to the killer of Debbie Joyce and Elaine Bennett through the columns of *The News* ...

He could scarcely believe his eyes. He stepped into a goods entrance out of the press of Saturday morning shoppers, so that he could read without being jostled.

Detective Chief Superintendent Wycliffe, Head of Area Crime Squad, writes to the killer of Debbie Joyce and of Elaine Bennett through the column of *The News*:

'I read your letter to the newspaper and I accept your word that you are not an indiscriminate killer. I believe you when you say that you do not want to terrorise innocent people. But that is what you are

153

doing. Each night thousands of girls and women are afraid to stir out of doors because of you. Two girls have died at your hand and another has suffered injury and shock because, you say, you made a mistake. You seemed to have been upset by your mistake for you telephoned the hospital to ask about her. But how does it feel to have taken the two other lives? How will it feel if and when you murder others? You say that they are guilty, but who are you to judge? Guilt is decided by the processes of law. Are you so arrogant as to believe yourself above the law? If you are not indeed a monster you must have doubts about what you have done and even graver doubts about what you intend to do. Think again. Talk to someone. If you wish to talk to me you can do so by telephoning, day or night, 323232.

Charles Wycliffe,

Detective Chief Superintendent.'

What were they doing to him? On top of the photographs of the three girls this was too much.

'You all right, mate?'

He was standing there, staring at the newspaper, while a vanman carrying a huge cardboard box tried to get past. He slipped the newspaper into the bag with his washing and rejoined the endless stream of shoppers.

After he had washed and rough dried his clothes he went to the market and bought flowers. In the afternoon he would catch a bus to Colebrook cemetery and put his flowers on the grave. All this had become routine over the past few months, his Saturday routine. Until tea time he could pass the day well enough going about the tasks he had set himself with a sense of purpose. But this letter . . . He thrust it resolutely to the back of his mind; it would be evening before he had to face its real challenge. Most evenings Albert and Alice were busy about their offices and he had the flat to himself. He read. An avid and undiscriminating reader, he went to the library twice a week and read whatever he happened to pick up there. But on Saturday evenings Albert was free and there was no place in the flat where he could read in peace. Even if he retreated into his bedroom it was not long before Albert would open the door—'Mind if I come in? I was thinking . . . '

So, after his first Saturday night in the flat he had gone out. He had wandered aimlessly around the city streets with the feeling that he was excluded from every human activity. In his wanderings he chanced on a little bar in Chester Street, between a Chinese restaurant and a bookmaker's. It was quiet there, he could sit in a corner and watch the regulars. In particular he watched four men who were there every Saturday playing solo. By listening to their conversation and without exchanging a word he had come to know a lot about them, their work and their families. It would have been the easiest thing in the world to have become involved and the possibility frightened him though he could not have said why. Whenever one or other of the card players caught his eye he frowned and looked away.

On this particular Saturday evening, between hands, they chatted about the strangler and speculated as to whether he would try again and if he did whether he would be caught.

The manager of the shoe shop, a little pot-bellied man, was dogmatic. 'It's obvious, he's a nutter. He'll go on until they catch him. That sort won't be put off. I mean, you or I would reason out our chances . . . '

The builder who, except when he was in the act of drinking, had a pipe between his teeth, shook his head knowingly. 'They never caught Jack the Ripper, did they?' He waited to let his point sink in. 'I mean, I agree with you, he's a mad man—he must be, but that doesn't mean he's stupid. They're cunning. I've got a cousin who used to work in Broadmoor and the things he told me you wouldn't believe! Like I said—cunning.'

He was not disturbed by their conversation. He listened avidly and was strongly tempted to join in. It gave him a feeling of confidence and superiority to hear their absurd comments. But he wanted to say, 'It isn't like that! You haven't the least idea . . . '

The giant with a red face who was a wholesale grocer was dealing another hand and the conversation petered out as they picked up their cards.

'What's trumps?' The fourth man looked like a prize-fighter but he was a foreman for the council.

'Clubs.'

'I'll try a solo.'

'Abundance on hearts,' from the builder.

'Pass.'

The manager of the shoe shop studied his cards. 'I'll try a mizzy.'

They played in silence and the manager made his call.

'If I had my way I'd bring back hanging. Mad or sane, they think twice if they know they're going to get the same as they dish out.'

The grocer blew out his flushed cheek and belched. 'Hanging's too good for the likes of this one. I mean, it's obvious, they don't actually say so in the papers but you can read between the lines, he's after only one thing and he's ready to kill for it. Bastard ought to be castrated!' He laughed. 'Make the punishment fit the crime, that's what they say, isn't it?' He turned toward the solitary stranger who had sat watching their play for several Saturdays. 'I can see that you agree with me, sir. Castrate the bugger!'

He felt himself trembling. 'The girls were not raped!' he spoke the words in a voice scarcely above a whisper but he saw the attention of the four men suddenly focused on him. He got up, leaving more than half his beer in the glass, and walked out.

In the street he was still trembling and his heart was

racing. He walked quickly as though he were trying to shake off all connection with the episode, as though he could leave it behind. His thoughts raced with his heart but they made little sense. He found himself muttering over and over again, 'You're a fool! You're a fool!' It was a fine evening and there were plenty of people about, twice he collided with someone and walked on with no apology.

By the time he was once more aware of his surroundings he had reached Prince's Street. Prince's Street, dimly lit, most of the shops shuttered and dark and despite the heavy traffic the pavements were like shadowy lanes except where the pubs made an orange splash of light. Now that he could think more clearly, he was afraid, afraid of the consequences of what he had done but more of the lack of control which made it possible for him to do it. What had he said? 'The girls were not raped!' And despite what the grocer had said several papers had stated that there had been no sexual assault. It was not so much what he had said as the way he had said it. And as though to dramatise the thing, to underline it, he had walked out.

'Hullo, darling.'

He stopped, confused, too absorbed in himself to realise at once what was happening.

'Hullo, darling. Want to come home?'

She was standing in a passage by the newsagent's, her thin, pale features lit by a street lamp. Then he understood and walked on. He heard her bored, indifferent voice, 'Suit yourself!'

He was tempted to turn back. Why not? He needed something to relieve the tension which had built up until it threatened his safety. It was tension—not wholly fear—but half-pleasurable excitement which kept the nerve endings tingling and seemed to cut him off from his surroundings. It was dangerous, if he had had any doubt of that this evening's episode had dispelled it. He turned, but she was already talking to another man.

157

Just as well.

He decided that he would go back to the flat. He would have his supper and by that time he could reasonably go to bed.

Albert was watching Match of the Day with a plate of sandwiches and a glass of beer on the table beside him. Alice was ironing.

'You're back early.'

'I thought I'd have an early night.'

'Good idea. There's some sandwiches; shall I get you a can of beer from the fridge?'

'No thanks, I'll just have a sandwich.'

He went to bed but it was a very long time before he got to sleep. He had kept the morning paper and he re-read the letter. He had been hurt and angered by what the newspapers had written about him and he had tried to explain. He had written to them, the anonymous thousands who read the newspapers and believe what they read. He wanted to put the record straight and he genuinely wanted to reassure people who were unnecessarily afraid. The last thing he had expected was a reply. Now it seemed almost as though he had addressed his letter to one man. He could not explain how he felt, even to himself, but this stranger, this policeman, had taken advantage to steal into his private world and to question what was already settled.

He turned off the bedside lamp and lay, staring at the ceiling. It was never dark in this room; at whatever time of night he woke he could see across it, the handbasin, the mirror gleaming, and his green-handled toothbrush. It was never silent either. Although the street below was usually quiet after midnight the main road through to the docks was less than a quarter of a mile away and the distant rumble of traffic seemed endless.

For a long time he turned and tossed in his bed. Once he got out and remade it. At all costs he had to avoid thinking about the future. Afterwards. Through most of his life he had taken a childish pleasure in looking forward to things, small things. An outing, doing a special job about the house or garden, holidays ... Several times, especially during the past day or two, he had had to struggle to extinguish the doubts which troubled him, but he had been able to fight it down.

Now ...

He felt that he was on the verge of being cheated, perhaps of cheating himself. After all the labour he had put into his plan. It had not been easy, he had traced four people who had been involved in an event which had occurred nine years ago. Four women, three of whom had since changed their names. He had gone about the task with patience and dogged persistence and he had succeeded. Now, half his plan was accomplished.

He told himself that it was too late for doubts, he had cut himself off with no place in the world for any other person. When Rosaline Parkin died he had ended the possibility of life for himself. 'There is no going back!' He found himself saying the words aloud through clenched teeth. Strange! At the start it had all seemed so straightforward and necessary.

He heard the church clock of St George's strike three on its cracked bell. Even after that it seemed that he did not entirely lose consciousness.

On Sunday morning he woke well before it was light, as on any other morning. Rather than disturb the others by moving round he read in bed until he heard Albert stirring. Albert for sure, Alice liked her bed, especially in the mornings. He joined Albert in the kitchen and they made coffee. It was the one time of day when his brother-in-law was taciturn so he did not have to talk. The day dawned fine and cold with clear skies. From the flat he could look out over the city and glimpse the sea, remote, pure and sparkling in the morning light. At nine Alice came in wearing her dressing gown with her hair in curlers. She made breakfast.

Although she was his sister, Alice irritated and

159

repelled him. She was fourteen years younger so that they had not shared their childhood. She was blonde, plump and pink skinned; secretly he thought her gross. And she offended his sense of decency when, as now, she went round the flat wearing only her dressing gown which often failed to hide her heavy breasts. He compared her with his Rose who had been slim and dark and pale.

'What's the matter, Jim? You look peaky. Doesn't he, Albert?'

'I'm all right.'

'I don't suppose you'll be in for lunch?'

'No, I think I'll go over to the house.'

'Why not stay and have a decent meal for once?'

'No, I think I'll go over, there are several things I want to do.'

She shrugged. 'It's no use arguing with you but you don't look well.'

It had been the same with small variations on each of the Sundays he had been at the flat. Each Sunday he had reached the city centre in time to catch the 622 bus at ten o'clock. He was building a new habit pattern which would soon be as inflexible and necessary to him as the one it had replaced. But how long could it last?

The streets were almost deserted and they looked shabby and unkempt in the sunlight with the litter of Saturday still lying about in the gutters and on the pavements. He went up to the top deck of the bus.

He avoided looking out of the window while the bus was in Godolphin Road. After Godolphin Road the suburban sprawl thinned for a time then congealed again into a spider's web pattern of semi-detached houses and bungalows centred on the one-time village of Maudsley. Beyond Maudsley a dreary industrial estate, then Crowley; more urbanised countryside with the mushrooming university buildings, then Rhynton. Twenty-seven years ago when he bought his house in

Rhynton it had been cheap, now there was competition to live that far out of the city.

He got off the bus by the pub and turned up Oakshott Avenue. Most of the houses in the avenue had garages and several of the men were out washing their cars on the concrete aprons. They greeted him with what seemed excessive friendliness as though they were anxious to make up for something.

Number thirty-seven was a corner house on the junction between Holland Drive and the avenue. The wooden palings were neat and well soaked with creosote and the privet hedge above them had been geometrically clipped. The windows shone and the curtains were drawn by just the right amount proclaiming that there was nothing to hide but no desire to display. He went to the front door, inserted his key, opened the door and passed inside. 'It's only me!' The house was silent but the shining black and white tiles in the hall, the well hoovered carpet on the stairs and the gleaming white paintwork all spoke of a well-cared-for home from which the housewife had popped out to the shops or, perhaps, to church.

He picked up a couple of circulars from the mat and went through to the kitchen, opened the back door and collected a pint of milk from the step. He was experiencing an odd sense of detachment, an unreal calm. He seemed to be wholly absorbed in what he was doing, leaving no room for other thoughts, yet on the very fringe of his consciousness he was dimly aware of emotional conflict, of tension and turmoil. But it seemed at the moment to have little or nothing to do with him.

He got dusters and a vacuum cleaner from the cupboard under the stairs and went upstairs to the back bedroom. He opened the casement window and let in the cold, fresh air. Then he started to dust.

It was a single room with a divan bed. The bed was covered with a blue, linen bedspread and lying on it was a pyjama case in the shape of a dog with 'Jane' embroidered across it. There was a bedside cupboard, a built-in dressing table, a chest of drawers and bookshelves, all painted white with gilt fittings. He had made them all himself in those long summer evenings and during weekends which now seemed dream-like in recollection. Everywhere he looked he was reminded of years which had been the happiest of his life. One of the walls was almost covered with pictures of Jane, beginning with her as a baby and ending with the same photograph as he had on his chest of drawers in the flat, the girl with short, straight hair. She looked sixteen or seventeen.

'The three of us'—that had been the phrase constantly on their lips. From the beginning Jane had been a participating member of the trio, loved, protected and involved. His daily work had been no more than a necessary interruption of their lives at home. He worked hard because he wanted to secure the best for the three of them. Since his marriage to Rose no voice had ever been raised in anger in their house.

But he and Rose had seen the danger of overprotectiveness too late.

He finished his dusting and started to vacuum the carpet. It was then that he seemed to reach a decision. He switched off the machine and went downstairs to the telephone in the hall. He did not need to look up the number. He picked up the receiver and started to dial then he remembered that telephone calls can be traced or he thought they could, he wasn't sure. Almost certainly the policeman who had written that letter would have his calls monitored—that was the word. He hesitated, then decided to go to a call-box. He noticed that his heart was thumping and he was trembling a little which must mean that he was excited though he didn't feel it. He put on his jacket which he had taken off to do his housework and let himself out by the front door.

There was a kiosk at the end of Holland Drive but it was too public so he cut through by a footpath to the post office which had one in a sort of yard at the back. Being Sunday, the place was deserted. He dialled 323232. He had no idea what he would say. The ringing tone, the double burr-burr repeated itself four times then there was a click as someone lifted the receiver.

'Mr Wycliffe speaking.'

A pleasant voice, kindly, he thought. His mind was racing but he could think of nothing to say. The silence lengthened and he would have dropped the receiver but the man spoke again.

'I think you must be the man who wrote to the newspaper.'

'Yes.'

'You have something you want to say to me?'

'I think so.'

'Perhaps you would like to come and see me?'

'Yes. When shall I come?'

'When you like, now if you wish.'

'This afternoon. Where?'

'At my headquarters in Morton Road, or anywhere else you prefer.'

'Out of doors. Edgcumbe Park, by the fountain.'

'When?'

'Two clock.'

'You will come?'

'I think so.'

The policeman was beginning to say something else but he dropped the receiver.

As he walked back to the house he still felt detached. It was difficult to believe that what he had just done or what he might do could really affect him.

When he arrived back at the house the boy had delivered his Sunday newspaper. It was lying on the mat. The same paper that he had taken for twenty-five years. In the beginning it had been sober, middle-of-the-road, but over the years circulation chasing had turned it into a careful blend of sex, sensationalism and sentimentality.

LETTER TO A MURDERER!
POLICE CHIEF WRITES TO STRANGLER!

In an unprecedented and highly controversial letter, published in a local newspaper, Detective Superintendent Wycliffe, Head of C.I.D., invites the killer to come and talk things over!

The letter was reproduced in small type and followed by another explosion of king-size black print:

WHAT WE THINK.

We have grown accustomed to do-gooders, egg-heads and kinks who want us to believe that violence can be met by cosy chats on the trick-cyclist's couch but this is the first time we have come across a policeman who agrees with them!

Here we have a killer, a sadistic murderer who is guilty of two vicious killings and who plans more. What does our chief of police have to say to this man? We quote:

'I BELIEVE YOU WHEN YOU SAY THAT YOU DO NOT WANT TO TERRORISE INNOCENT PEOPLE . . .'

Laughable? But will you laugh if it is your wife or your daughter who is number three? Not so funny, is it?

WHAT WE SAY . . .

The scorn, the indignation and the moralising occupied the whole of the front page and spilled over into the nearest thing the paper had to an editorial.

He stood just inside the door, reading, then he climbed the stairs and made for the smaller of the two front bedrooms, the one over the hall. His 'glory hole' they used to call it. A table, a couple of chairs, an easel

164

and a Victorian couch. On the table a jam-jar full of brushes and a box of oil-colours. On the walls, several paintings, views of the city in flat colour. In between the paintings there were framed reproductions of drawings by Michelangelo, Dürer and Leonardo. And there were shelves jammed with books.

He sat on the couch, staring at the floor between his feet. He could no longer understand his own changes of mood and they worried him. There were periods when his feelings seemed to be anaesthetised and for long spells he could go calmly about his affairs unaware, or at least insensitive to the mental conflicts and tensions which sometimes loomed so large that they threatened to overwhelm him. There were other times, brief intervals, when he was elated, when he had no doubts and his whole being was stirred to a strange excitement. Finally there were the dark times when he was weighed down by depression and doubt, when he seemed to have lost any context for his life, when there seemed to be no standards left against which he could measure his conduct or his desires. Lately these moods had succeeded each other more rapidly and with less apparent reason. But he refused to ask himself the question which lingered obstinately in the recesses of his mind.

He was vaguely aware of someone ringing the doorbell downstairs but he did nothing about it and eventually they went away.

He took his wallet from his pocket and from it he extracted a postcard photograph of a score or more girls on a beach, an older woman in the middle. Two of the girls had been ringed. A girl in the middle of the front row carried a card with 'Weymouth—1965' on it. He looked at the photograph for a long time then he got up and crossed the room to the window. The room was cold. Outside the sun shone with a brittle, frosty brilliance. Couples with children were setting out on their Sunday walks; through the centre of Rhynton and down the avenue to the river. On any fine Sunday afternoon in winter the path by the river was like a parade, prams, children, dogs.

There were shelduck, mallard and curlews out on the mudflats and solemn, tweedy men and women watched them through binoculars. He seemed to feel again a little warm hand in his.

He must have stayed in the room for a long time but when it was getting dusk he went down to the hall and dialled a number.

'Miss Coleman? Miss Dorothy Coleman? ... I'm sorry to trouble you on a Sunday evening but I understand that you run a nursery school—a school for girls ... Yes, that is what I was told. It is for my grandchild, she is four ... My daughter is a widow and she is coming to live in the city ... She has asked me to make the arrangements ... There are certain things I would rather not discuss on the telephone ... I'm afraid that I'm working all day ... If you could see me this evening ... At seven-thirty ... Yes, I understand ... My name? Oh, yes, of course—Grant—Douglas Grant.'

His hands were trembling as he replaced the receiver.

CHAPTER NINE

Wycliffe was up early for a Sunday, before it was light. He made coffee and took it into the living room to stand by the window and watch the daybreak. The contours of the hills across the estuary slowly defined themselves, the navigation lights in the channel seemed to fade. A cold, steely grey light imperceptibly and slowly changed into a radiance which flooded the landscape with colour. He could not see the actual sunrise because his house faced south-west.

He lit his first pipe of the day.

From his early days in the force, on night duty, he had enjoyed the dawn. He liked to think of people waking from sleep, returning to the world, re-establishing their identities; remembering. But each day for some there would be a sad, perhaps a terrible awakening. You have to take up where you left off. No good fairy comes in the night to spin straw into gold or dreams into reality.

Somewhere in the city the murderer must wake this Sunday morning. Would he know a few moments of innocence before memory came flooding back?

Four schoolgirls and a wicked, perverted joke seemed to have started a train of events which had cost the lives of two of them almost ten years later. Was it possible?

167

The evidence seemed now to point that way and, intuitively, he was convinced but it was difficult to rationalise the idea. There were three questions: What was the connection between the killer and the school-girls? Why did he feel justified in murder? And why nearly ten years late?

There was no doubt in Wycliffe's mind that the killer was a middle-aged man. A husband? More likely a father. He remembered that there had been a complaint from the girl's parents. But why wait ten years? It was easy to say that the man was deranged but there had to be some powerful and continuing stimulus to keep the hatred alive for that length of time and then to kill because of it.

A man with a sixteen year old daughter, an only child, doted upon, over-protected. (Perhaps a little private school—a thought there.) Then, too late, she is encouraged to 'mix'—it happens often enough. The girl does her best to adapt, tries too hard and grows more depressed with every failure. Culminating in the traumatic experience of the wretched Parkin girl's sick joke. Could this have brought about or precipitated a mental collapse? Unlikely.

But even if it did, why wait ten years to do something about it? Perhaps a slow disintegration, the man forced to watch his child gradually losing her identity in a relentless process of decline. He might feel compelled to blame someone for such a blow of fate. Rightly or wrongly (truth seldom counts in such matters) he might trace the origin of his grief back to some single incident, clearly, explicitly defined.

As an idea it was thin, but it was possible. He decided to do two things, he would get a list of the girls of the right age who had died in the city during the past year and he would get another list prepared of girls who had been admitted to mental institutions in the same period.

Taffy Evans, now Superintendent Evans, chose to

telephone Wycliffe at his home rather than talk to headquarters. After recalling incidents which Wycliffe had forgotten and in the face of unrelenting taciturnity, he came to the point.

'I spoke to your man, Gill . . . Oh, so he told you—you're lucky, boyo, my blokes tell me nothing . . . About the Russell woman, her aunt found the letter, bless her woolly vest! She was asking her aunt to put up money for a scheme to start a prep school for girls. She had a premises in view, a country house outside Hereford. She said that she had the capital her parents left her but that she needed another seven or eight thousand. Auntie didn't want to know so she didn't bother to reply.'

Wycliffe asked if the letter was dated and from what address it had been written.

'It's ancient history, boyo, 28th December 1970 and it's on hotel notopaper—Drock's Private Hotel, Market Lane, Hereford. I don't suppose she's still there but it's the best I can do for you.'

Wycliffe detested being addressed as 'boyo' and his manner was rather more curt than the circumstances merited.

But the information was of little use.

Although a police appeal had gone out on the radio and on television there had been no response from Miss Russell. If Pamela Barlow really had seen her in the city market her silence must surely be deliberate. It was understandable that if she had re-established herself in the city she might want to avoid opening old wounds but it was just possible that the killer had reached her already. A woman living alone might not be missed for some time.

He heard the door open. His daughter, Ruth, in her dressing gown. Ruth was getting to grips with herself as a woman, leaving behind the gaucherie of adolescence.

'What's the matter? Uneasy conscience?'

She grinned. 'I smelt coffee.'

They sat on either side of the electric fire, drinking coffee in cosy silence.

Afterwards he telephoned his headquarters to get them moving on his two lists—registrations of deaths and admissions to mental homes. Not that they were likely to get far on a Sunday.

The newspapers arrived and he leafed through them. On the whole, a restrained and sympathetic press. One had chosen him as this week's burnt offering. But he was too hard bitten to be bothered by it. Bellings would be agitated.

At half-past eleven the telephone rang. He was in the living room alone. Helen and Ruth were in the kitchen getting lunch, David was still in bed.

'Mr Wycliffe speaking.'

The silence told him that this was the call he had waited for.

'I think you must be the man who wrote to the newspaper.' Mustn't try to hurry him, on the other hand don't give him too long for second thoughts.

'Yes.'

'You have something you want to say to me?'

Hesitation, painful and prolonged. 'I think so.'

'Perhaps you would like to come to see me?'

The door of the living room, opened and David came in, wearing his dressing gown, dishevelled from bed. Wycliffe held up a warning finger.

'Sorry!'

'Yes. When shall I come?' The voice had increasing assurance.

'Whenever you like—now if you wish.'

'This afternoon—where?'

'At my headquarters in Morton Road, or anywhere else you prefer.'

More hesitation. 'Out of doors. Edgcumbe Park, by the fountain. Two o'clock.'

'You will come?'

'I think so.'

'You . . . ' The receiver clicked back on to its rest and Wycliffe's phone buzzed. He replaced his receiver. A brief interval than another ring.

'Wycliffe.'

'He was calling from Rhynton, sir; a box behind the post office. A call has gone out to all mobiles in the area.'

Rhynton. Subtopia with a vengeance. The tall, thin man would now be hurrying home through the suburban roads, back to his semi-detached. A fine Sunday morning, people who knew him were bound to see him but they would never suspect. A solid citizen.

At noon headquarters called to say that they had missed him. The first mobile had arrived at the post office within three minutes of the message from the monitors but too late.

It came as no surprise to Wycliffe, he had not counted on such an easy win.

'Who is in this morning?'

'Mr Gill is in his office, sir.'

'Put me through . . . Jimmy?'

Gill was sour. 'So they've balled it up.'

'You heard what he said to me?'

'I got them to play me the tape. Do you want me to put men in the park.

Wycliffe hesitated. 'One good man who knows how to keep out of where he's not wanted.' He stopped to light his pipe with the receiver wedged against his shoulder. 'We shall have to do a house-to-house in Rhynton. Get it organised, Jimmy.'

'You think he'll come?'

'I wouldn't bet on it.'

They sat down to lunch at half-past twelve. A light meal. Helen was inflexibly opposed to the traditional Sunday lunch which lays out its victims until three. The sun was shining on the water and streaming into their living room. But for the skeletal elms on the hill opposite it could have been summer.

'I thought I might work in the garden for an hour,'

Helen said. 'Are you going out?'

He nodded. With the university term looming the twins had decided to stay in and work.

Edgcumbe Park is a typical urban green space, shut off from the encircling roads by a thin belt of trees. Swings and slides for the kids, a pond with a fountain, slatted seats, wire litter baskets and lavatories tucked away behind rustic trellis next to the potting sheds.

Wycliffe arrived shortly before half-past two and sat on a seat by the pond. Even in the sun it was chilly. There were few people about, two or three children playing listlessly on the swings and half a dozen dog-walkers. There was no sign of a policeman, which was as it should be. He neither expected the killer nor did he not expect him. The man would have seen the letter the previous morning. He had taken twenty-four hours to mull it over, to have second thoughts and second second-thoughts. Small things would influence his final decision one way or another and the fact that he had screwed himself up to the point of telephoning did not mean that he would keep the appointment. He seemed to realise that himself—'I think so' was the best he could manage and Wycliffe believed that he was being entirely honest.

A distinguished looking man in a well-cut overcoat and wearing an Enoch Powell hat advanced purposefully across the turf. A military bearing and a thick, greying moustache. Momentarily Wycliffe thought that the man was making for him but then a middle-aged lady tacked into his field of view, a lady in furs and wearing a floral toque. An assignation. They met on the gravelled path two or three yards from where Wycliffe was seated and without words but by gentle smiles and muted bird-like cooing noises showed their pleasure in the meeting.

Wycliffe waited for an hour then gave up. He found Gill's detective, told him to stay around for a little longer and to radio in if he saw anyone who might be the killer. Wycliffe walked the half mile back to his headquarters through streets which were in the firm grip of Sunday afternoon melancholy. He went to his office and was joined by Gill. Already the light was failing and he switched on his desk lamp.

'No luck, sir?' The grin on Gill's face was unmistakable.

'No, and you?'

'Not so's you'd notice. What's all this about registrations of deaths and admissions to mental hospitals?'

Wycliffe told him.

At four o'clock one of his lists arrived, sent by some clerk to the Hospital Management Committee who had given up part of his Sunday to make it. Three girls between 24 and 26 years old had been admitted to the city's mental hospital during the previous year. Only one was still there and it was expected that she would be discharged soon. Wycliffe telephoned the medical superintendent at his home and after a sticky five minutes satisfied himself that none of the girls was of interest to him.

A little later he had a call from the superintendent registrar. They had met at a civic dinner and the registrar, whose favourite reading was detective fiction, was falling over himself to be helpful. Four girls of about the right age, had died during the year. One had been killed in a car smash, one had died in childbirth. The third girl, who had died of leukaemia was a newcomer to the city. Only the fourth girl looked at all promising from Wycliffe's point of view; she had died of an inoperable brain tumour. She was unmarried. Wycliffe telephoned the police station nearest her parents' home and asked them to get particulars, discreetly.

He sat doodling on his blotter. This girl, the girl who seemed to have been the unwitting cause of all the trouble, must have had a mother but so far he had thought only of the father. Was it likely that the man who committed these crimes returned home afterwards to a wife? A family man without a family—his own words. So what had happened to the wife? He had postulated some traumatic experience which had turned the man's mind and he had assumed that it had been connected with his daughter's mental breakdown or death but the final blow might equally have been a tragedy affecting his wife.

His office oppressed him, he was deadened by it, muffled. He walked along the corridor to a room at the back of the building where Sergeant Bourne, surrounded by paper and filing cabinets, looked after reports and collation for the squad. Wycliffe picked up a file labelled 'Rhynton—House to House' and leafed through it.

'The file is incomplete, sir. They are still at it. The queries are starred in the top right corner.' Bourne was only twenty-five, up and coming. He believed in team work and the divinity of the computer so there was nothing to stop him.

The starred queries referred to houses where the men had not been able to talk to anyone or where the information given was regarded as either unsatisfactory or in some other way significant.

R6 '25 Horton Drive. Householder: George Bray. 35/40. No reply. Neighbour states that the family visit relatives on Sundays.

R21 '14 Coulston Road. Householder: John Harris. 25/30. No reply. Neighbour states that Mrs Harris is in hospital having a baby. Husband is staying with parents for the time being.

R29 '9 Stacey's Road. Householder: James Higgins. 45/50. No reply. Neighbour states that the family always go out in their car on fine Sundays ... '

A desperate lot of criminals there.

Wycliffe went back to his desk, lit a pipe and started to go through the reports, starred and unstarred alike.

174

Occasionally he put one aside and ended up with four, all of them starred:

> R58 '32 Hyde Avenue. Householder: Simon Kent 50/55. Widower. Lives with unmarried daughter who is now in London staying with friends. States that he spent whole morning in greenhouse.
>
> R79 '6 Farley Close. Householder: Arnold Pearce. 40/45. Married but lives alone. Guarded when questioned about his wife. States that he spent the morning doing his chores and did not go out.
>
> R104 '37 Oakshott Avenue. Householder: James Rendell. 50/55. No reply. Neighbour states that Rendell recently lost his wife and is living temporarily with relatives.
>
> R146 '14 Holland Drive. Householder: Frederick Polski. 50/55. Widower. Married daughter and her husband share house. Polski states that he went for a long walk between ten and lunchtime. Daughter confirms that this is his habit. Married couple spent morning about the house.'

Three widowers and one man who seems reluctant to account for his wife.

Wycliffe looked at his clock, its gilded pointers stuck out from the panelling, sweeping their silent orbits over gilded cyphers. He liked a clock which ticked, with Roman numerals and fretted hands. Seven o'clock. He telephoned his wife not to expect him.

He was depressed and uneasy.

It was a fortnight since the first murder, almost a week since the second. He felt that the next, if there was to be a next, was due—perhaps overdue. Rosaline Parkin and Elaine Bennett were dead; Sheila Barker was under the strictest surveillance which might mean that they had reached stalemate unless the school teacher was on the killer's list. If she was she must be in imminent danger. After having second thoughts about giving himself up the killer might feel a compulsive

175

need to assert himself once more, perhaps even to atone for his moment of weakness.

Wycliffe rang through to Sergeant Bourne. 'Any further reports?'

'D.C. James has just come in with another batch, sir, and two checks on previous interviews.'

'Which?'

A moment's delay. 'R79 and R104, sir, Pearce and Rendell. Pearce was cagey about his wife and the reason seems to be that she's recently left him. She was twenty years younger and she's gone off with another man. Rendell's wife died six months ago and he is now living with his married sister, a Mrs Martin. She and her husband are caretakers of the *Guardian* building in the city centre; they have a flat on the top floor.'

'Has he been contacted there?'

'No, sir, he was out when D.C. James telephoned.'

'What did his wife die of?'

Hesitation. 'The report doesn't say, sir, if it's important I'll find . . . '

'Don't bother.'

He lit his pipe and wandered over to the windows. The curtains had not been drawn and he could see the brightly-lit main road with its endless stream of traffic. The windows were misted over by fine rain which refracted the light and distorted the view. He felt helpless.

If the school teacher had been living in the city for six months she should be in the Voters' List but she was not there under her own name. He returned to his desk and picked up the exchange telephone. 'I want to speak to Mr or Mrs Martin, they are caretakers of the *Guardian* building and they live on the premises.'

An interval. 'You're through, sir.'

A woman's voice.

'Mrs Martin?' He was amiable, casual. 'Is your brother there?'

'You've just missed him; he came in and went out again.'

176

'Never mind. As you know, we are making a routine check on all the occupiers of houses in the Rhynton district of the city . . .'

She sounded helpful, unflustered.

'I understand that your brother has made his home with you temporarily—since the death of his wife . . . Yes, I'm sure it would be. How long has he been with you? . . . Since the beginning of July. Did she have a long illness?'

'She took her own life.'

'I'm sorry.'

'It was very sad.' She sounded a nice woman, genuinely upset. 'Tragic really, they lost their only child, a girl, a few years back and she never got over it. Never the same afterwards.'

'Have you any idea where your brother might be or when he's likely to be back?'

'He went out for a drink, he said he was meeting a friend.'

'Which pub does he use?'

'He doesn't have a regular pub, he's not much of a drinker.'

'It doesn't matter.'

'Shall I tell him to ring you when he gets back?'

'No, don't bother, it doesn't matter.' He thanked her and rang off.

This was it. No dramatic revelations, no blinding intuitive flash, no brilliant deductive reasoning, just the result of plodding routine enquiries. The great detective has it handed to him on a plate by a small army of foot-sloggers who go about ringing doorbells like soap salesmen. Of course, he could still be wrong but he knew that he wasn't.

He telephoned Gill and arranged for a man to be put in the flat and for the house in Oakshott Avenue to be watched. 'The sister will have to be told and we shall want a full description for circulation, photograph if possible.'

Back to the school teacher. It was disturbing that she had not been found and it seemed fairly certain that she could not be living in the city under her own name. If her professional career had ended under a cloud she might well want the past forgotten. In his experience women were singularly unimaginative in the use of an alias. A married woman usually went back to her maiden name, a single woman would often as not chose her mother's. It was worth a try. Without much enthusiasm he put through a call to Superintendent Evans at his home number and sat smoking while he waited for it to come through.

'Her mother's name? I don't have to find out, boyo, I know. Her mother was a Coleman, well known local family, farmers in a big way of business.'

And there she was in the telephone directory, or so he told himself. Miss Dorothy Coleman, The Nursery School, 6 Poulton Avenue. A woman running a nursery school would probably be obsessively concerned to avoid any breath of scandal.

He rang the duty room and told them to send a car to the school, to obtain admission if possible and to wait until he arrived. Then he collected his car from the park and drove to Poulton Avenue. It was a quarter past eight. Fine, misty rain cut down visibility and there were few people about.

Poulton Avenue consisted of large, semi-detached houses built before the first war. A neat little sign on the gate of number six showed up in the light of a street lamp: Poulton Avenue Nursery School.

A police car was parked a little way down the road, the house was in darkness and as Wycliffe drew into the curb a constable came towards him.

'Nobody home, sir. At least, I can get no answer.'

'I'll stay here, you go round the back and see if there's any sign of life there.'

Wycliffe sat in the car. The rain was so fine that it was little more than mist. The street lamps were blurred and the branches of trees overhanging from the gardens formed vague silhouettes, more like shadows.

Footsteps sounded clearly on the flagstones of the pavement and a woman, small and dumpy, stopped by the gate of number six. She looked at the car uncertainly then opened the gate. Wycliffe got out.

'Miss Coleman?'

'Is there something wrong? Who are you?'

Wycliffe introduced himself and she seemed irritated rather than surprised or concerned.

'Why are you here?'

'Perhaps we could talk inside.'

The constable returned and Wycliffe told him to wait. The woman unlocked the front door with a Yale key and switched on the hall light.

'I'm not Miss Coleman, my name is Carter—Miss Carter, I share the house and help with the school.'

The hall was bare and institutional but the stairs were carpeted and she led the way up.

'We live on the first floor.'

'Miss Coleman is not at home?'

'No, as you see, I've just come in myself but Miss Coleman usually goes out for her stroll at about this time.'

'In the rain?'

She smiled. 'It would take more than a drop of rain to put her off.'

He was taken into the front room on the first floor. It was a large room, sitting room and office combined. Old-fashioned chairs with worn upholstery, glass-fronted book-cases, a roll-topped desk with a telephone on it and gilt-framed oil paintings on the walls. Wycliffe was uneasy, partly because he was unsure of his ground. He had only flimsy reasons for supposing that Dorothy Coleman was Dorothy Russell.

'Is Miss Coleman likely to be long?'

'I shouldn't think so, she usually walks round a couple of blocks.'

She waved him to one of the easy chairs and perched herself on the edge of another, showing a lot of fat thigh above her stockings.

'How long have you known Miss Coleman?'

'Several years.'

'More than ten years?'

'Probably. Why do you ask?' Her manner was aggressive.

'Did you know her when she was Dorothy Russell?'

She dug in. 'Until you tell me why you are asking these questions I don't propose to answer any more.'

Wycliffe was bland. 'That's reasonable, I'll explain. I think that the woman who was Dorothy Russell may be in very great danger.'

She looked at him as though trying to read his mind. 'You really mean that?'

'I do.'

She seemed to relax her guard. 'I told her but she wouldn't take any notice. She's very obstinate.' She went to a side table and took a cigarette from the box. 'Smoke?'

But Wycliffe had crossed to the desk and picked up the telephone. He dialled and was answered almost at once. 'Wycliffe. I want all mobiles in Number 4 District to patrol roads within a half mile radius of Poulton Avenue. They are to look out for Miss Dorothy Coleman. Late forties . . .' He turned to Miss Carter. 'Height?'

'Five feet five.'

'Build?'

'Very thin.'

'Dressed?'

A moment of hesitation. 'Brown mackintosh with gilt buttons over a maroon trouser suit. She would be carrying an umbrella.'

He repeated the information into the telephone. 'She is to be brought here, to her home at 6 Poulton Avenue. Keep me informed at this number—347489.'

Miss Carter's aggression had disappeared, now she

looked scared. 'You really think . . . ?'

'Frankly, I've no idea but we mustn't take chances.'

Taffy Evans had said that the Russell parents had kept an hotel and the furniture here looked as though it had been rescued from the auctioneer's hammer when they sold up. A grandfather clock with a brass face, which must have come from the foyer, showed half-past eight.

'Miss Coleman knew that the police wanted to get in touch with her?'

'Oh yes, she saw it in the newspaper.'

'But she did nothing about it.'

'No, she thought it was all rather foolish.'

'The deaths of two young women?'

Miss Carter was anything but aggressive now; she flushed. 'I didn't mean that! Dot—Miss Coleman thought it was foolish to imagine that what happened to the girls had anything to do with her or with when they were schoolgirls.'

'She didn't want to get involved.'

'No, I suppose not. She can be very obstinate, as I said.' She ground out a half-smoked cigarette in the ashtray.

'What time did you go out this evening?'

'Just before six. I always go to see my mother on Sunday evenings.'

'Is everything as usual?'

She looked puzzled. 'I think so. Dot is often out when I get back.' Her expression changed suddenly. 'I've just remembered something! She had an appointment—not that it makes any difference.'

'An appointment?'

'A man phoned while we were having tea, he wanted to see the school and arrange for his granddaughter to come.' She went over to the desk and turned the pages of a desk diary. 'Here you are, Dot made a note of it—Mr Douglas Grant, seven-thirty.'

181

CHAPTER TEN

He had not eaten since breakfast and he was hungry and cold. He must force himself to behave normally or he would do something stupid as he had last night in the pub. Above all he must occupy his mind so that he would not think about what lay before him. This was a trick he had learned in childhood. When a school examination or a visit to the dentist was imminent he would lose himself in a book and when the moment of crisis came it would take him almost by surprise.

While he was upstairs he shut the windows, which he had opened to air the house, then he went downstairs, locked the back door, put on his overcoat and let himself out at the front. He walked down Oakshott Avenue with an easy stride, he looked calm and collected, he *was* calm. There were lights in most of the sitting rooms in the avenue and some had left their curtains undrawn so that he had glimpses of families gathered round television sets. He went to the bus stop in the centre of Rhynton. Another man was waiting there.

'Evening, Mr Rendell.'

'Good evening, Mr Oates.' He thought that his voice sounded quite normal. Oates had lived in Holland Drive for almost as long as he had lived in Oakshott

Avenue and the two men had been acquainted for twenty-five years.

'Been taking a look at the house?'

'Got to keep an eye on things.'

'I suppose you'll be thinking to sell.'

'I haven't thought anything yet.'

He must have sounded brusque for Oates was quick to apologise.

'None of my business, of course!'

An awkward silence before Oates added, changing the subject, 'I suppose you've had the police?'

'The police?' He felt suddenly cold inside.

'Haven't they been to you? They've been going around asking questions. Something to do with the strangler; they seem to think he might live out here.'

'Out here?' He was at a loss what to say.

The bus arrived and they got on together. Oates took a ticket to the city centre and he did the same. It carried him beyond his true destination but he could walk back.

'Shocking business, killing young women.'

'Shocking.'

'Too lax in the courts, that's more than half the trouble. They've got to take a strong line on violence. You look at some of the sentences—you'd think they wanted to encourage it.'

He peered through the window into the darkness.

'I haven't seen you to speak of since your wife . . . Very sad, terrible for you. I was saying to Marge only this morning, you've had more than your share . . . more than your share.' Oates looked away, vaguely embarrassed by his own words.

He continued to stare at the dimly reflective window. Nothing was required of him but his mind was a ferment.

'I suppose you're still with your sister?'

'For the moment—for the moment.'

They arrived at the city centre and got off together.

183

'Like a drink before you go in?'

'Thanks all the same but they will be expecting me.'

'Another time.'

'Yes.' He watched Oates as they separated and saw him turn into a bar then he walked in the opposite direction. The police. Why should they think of Rhynton? The telephone call, it must have been a trap. He was shocked, partly because he had nearly made the call from his home, partly because he felt that it was unfair. The feeling of insecurity was almost overwhelming.

His appointment was for seven-thirty but it was now scarcely six o'clock. He felt a little weak and faint, partly because he had not eaten, partly because he had been upset by what Oates had told him. It was odd, he had hardly considered the risk that he might be tracked down and caught, he had feared only that he might give himself away. He had seen the extra police patrols, the crime cars and the pandas and he knew that all this organisation was for him but he had not once felt threatened. Why should he? All his life he had been on the side of the law and he found it impossible to accept that this had fundamentally changed. But Oates' news had shaken him. He remembered the ring at the doorbell which he had ignored. What would have happened if he had gone down—totally unprepared?

He decide that he would go to the flat, get something to eat and go out again. It was a short distance away.

As he came out of the lift on the top floor he could hear a television newsreader—something about a pay claim for engineering workers. Alice was sitting on the settee, knitting.

'Hullo! You're early. Albert's gone down to set the time switch.' She turned to look at him. 'What's the matter, Jim? Still feeling seedy?'

'I'm all right.'

Her kindly, rather stupid face, expressed concern. 'You don't look it, you . . . '

The newsreader went on, 'This afternoon police made house-to-house enquiries in the Rhynton district of the city. A spokesman said that an un-named man had telephoned Detective Chief Superintendent Wycliffe from a call-box in that neighbourhood this morning.'

'They rang you here.'

'What?'

'The police rang you here, they said there was no answer at the house and a neighbour told them you were living here . . . What's the matter?'

He made a tremendous effort of control. 'You should have told me.'

'You don't give me a chance. Anyway, it's not important. They said it was just routine enquiry, just to find out where everybody was. You really do look poorly, Jim.'

His legs had all but given way and he had dropped into one of the easy chairs. 'I must admit I don't feel so good, I didn't bother with getting any lunch.'

This was a problem Alice could cope with. She bustled through into the kitchen and called to him through the hatch.

'You must have been out.'

'What?'

'When the police called at the house.'

'Yes, I went for a walk. What did they want to know when they telephoned?'

'Nothing much, just whether you were living with us and where you were.'

'What did you say?'

'That you'd gone over to the house as you did every Sunday to give it an airing and they must have missed you.'

'That was all?'

'Yes.'

He felt a little better. If anything it might tend to put them off. Looked at from their point of view it would seem normal—it *was* normal.

185

Alice brought him a plate of cold meat, some crusty bread and a glass of beer. It put new life into him.

'You're not going out again?'

'I told Jack Oates I would meet him for a drink.'

'But you're not fit, Jim!'

She was genuinely concerned, she was his sister but she meant nothing to him. All the love and affection of which he was capable had been focused on his wife and his daughter. The three of us. No need for anyone else.

He put on his overcoat once more and felt in the right-hand pocket.

The weather had undergone an abrupt change. Instead of the clear, cold frosty night which had promised it had suddenly softened. The air seemed mild and a thick mist diffused through the streets. He walked briskly away from the city centre.

There were few people about and as he got clear of the city centre he had the impression that police patrols were more numerous and obtrusive than on previous nights. He felt that he was being watched. Now and then a patrol car cruised slowly past and twice he came upon police cars parked at intersections. He was climbing a steepish hill out of the city with residential roads off on either side, semi-detached properties with tiny front gardens and narrow strips of sour soil at the back. Rather dreary Edwardian houses which had been the homes of prosperous shop-keepers and tradesmen before the first war; families able to support a couple of maids.

Dorothy Coleman lived in Poulton Avenue which was one of these roads near the top of the hill. As he turned off a police car passed him at little more than walking speed. But nothing now would put him off, he was committed. It was almost as though he had surrendered his will to external compulsion. Twice before he had known the feeling. After spells of torturing doubt his resolution seemed to form and harden of itself.

On the third or fourth gate along the road he could read by the light of a street lamp, a white painted sign:

Poulton Avenue Nursery School
Proprietors: Misses D. Coleman and J. Carter

There was a light in an upstairs room but none on the ground floor. The little front garden had been paved over. He rang the doorbell and after a moment a light flicked on behind the coloured panes of the front door which was then opened.

She was small and thin—thinner than he remembered, with close-cropped brown hair which made her face look smaller and sharper than it was.

'Miss Coleman?'

She looked up at him through thick lenses. 'Yes, and you must be Mr Grant. Please come in.' She had a rather harsh, metallic voice which must have carried without effort across many classrooms.

He refused her offer to take his coat.

'The school is here on the ground floor, I have a flat upstairs.'

The hall was bare and there was a faint smell of disinfectant but the stairs were carpeted. 'If you would like to come up to the flat we can discuss arrangements and you shall see the school afterwards if you wish.'

He followed her up to a landing and in to the front room. It was a cross between a sitting room and an office; a chesterfield and easies, an old fashioned rolltop desk. There were photographs everywhere, college groups, school groups and half a dozen large paintings in gilt frames—seascapes.

'Won't you sit down?'

He smiled vaguely but remained standing.

'About your grandchild . . .'

'Linda—yes. She is three and a half.' He was well rehearsed. 'My daughter divorced her husband . . .' He told a credible story, his voice was steady, normal. She made sympathetic noises.

'I know how difficult it is for a mother who has to work to keep herself and her child but our fees are not high. Will your daughter want Linda to come for the whole day or only part of it?'

He was still standing, showing some interest in the pictures. She seemed vaguely uneasy perhaps because of his refusal to sit down. His hand in the right-hand pocket of his raincoat felt the smooth wooden toggles which he had carved himself.

He made remarks about the pictures expecting that she would join him to point out their merits but she kept her distance. 'They were painted by my father; he made quite a reputation for himself at one time.'

He was patient. No false moves. But they were running out of conversation.

'I expect you would like to see the school?'

'If I may.'

She led the way downstairs and into a room off the hall. A large room, the original dining and drawing rooms knocked into one. Little tables and chairs, an elaborate climbing frame, a magnificent rocking-horse and open shelves all round stacked with books and toys. Lively murals on the walls.

'Our rest room is through here.' A smaller room with mattresses on low wooden frames.

'In the garden we have a toddler's adventure playground.'

He murmured approval and watched her every move. 'Very nice, very suitable. I'm sure my daughter will be delighted.' They were back in the main room and it seemed that his chance would never come but he must not take any risk. Then she darted in front of him and stooped to pick up a plastic cup from the floor which some child had dropped there. In an instant he had the cord out of his pocket. No fumbling. As she straightened, with her back to him, he twisted the nylon cord round her neck and pulled on the toggles with all his strength. She let out a scream which was cut off in a fraction of a second. He had heard a similar scream once before, the girl Bennett had screamed but the first one had made no sound.

She struggled weakly, briefly, then went limp. He held the tension until his forehead was beaded with sweat then he released her. She slipped to the floor and lay sprawled and twisted, her head resting on a rocker of the big toy horse.

His heart thumped unbearably and he could feel a powerful pulse in his neck, his head swam and he was afraid that he might collapse on the floor beside her but the faintness passed.

He stooped to recover the cord and was forced to look at her face. Her eyes were wide open and staring; she looked astonished and, perhaps because her jaw sagged, rather stupid. Her glasses had fallen off. He remembered her expression nine years ago when she had said, 'The trouble with Jane is that she has been spoiled, she is a self-indulgent child and it is high time that she grew up!'

He felt no pity.

As he recovered himself a little he looked round the room to see if he had left any trace of his visit and only then did he realise that the curtains had not been drawn. He was standing in the middle of a lighted room and all that had happened might have been seen by a passer by or even by someone in the houses opposite. At this moment they might be telephoning the police. He walked to the door and switched off the light, the hall light too; then he sat on the stairs in the darkness, he needed a little more time. At last he felt calm enough to leave. He made himself move slowly and deliberately. He let himself out by the front door and shut it behind him. He stood for a moment, listening for footsteps or the sound of a car but there was nothing and he walked to the gate; he closed and latched the gate behind him. Only once more. He would not allow himself to think about that. It was of no importance anyway. He had subordinated himself, forced himself to become an instrument, a tool, and when a tool has served its purpose . . .

Wycliffe felt cold inside.

'I think that we should search the house.'

She looked vague then frightened.

'What's on the top floor?'

'What? Oh, only two attics—lumber rooms, we never go up there.'

'We'll leave those for the moment.' By talking he hoped to get her co-operation without any panic. 'This floor first, you show me.'

The first floor was a self-contained flat, kitchen, bathroom, two bedrooms and the room they had just left. Nothing remarkable except that it was obvious neither of the women had much idea about housekeeping. All the rooms were untidy and looked as though they could do with a good clean.

'Downstairs?'

'All the rooms downstairs and the garden are given over to the school.'

Wycliffe led the way downstairs and opened a door on the left of the hall.

'That's the main schoolroom.'

The room was in darkness and he fumbled for the light switch. When he found it yellow light from a small bulb lit up a large, rather bare room with toddler's tables and chairs and toys scattered about.

It was a moment before he saw her body. She was lying on the floor, her head resting on the blue-painted rocker of a magnificent rocking-horse. Miss Carter saw her at almost the same instant; she let out a gasp but made no other sound. She made no move to enter the room but stood in the doorway, staring, her fist thrust between her teeth like a little girl.

Wycliffe bent over the body but it was obvious that nothing could be done; the strangler was thorough.

190

Wycliffe went out into the hall and closed the door of the schoolroom behind him.

'Are you all right?'

Miss Carter nodded but she did not remove her hand from her mouth. Wycliffe piloted her gently up the stairs to the sitting room and persuaded her to sit down.

'Would you like something? Tea?'

She shook her head and he went to the telephone. He was put through to Gill.

'I've found her. You'd better get the lads out here and let Franks know. 6 Poulton Avenue—the nursery school . . . No, I shall stay here for the moment. I've got another job for you. Did you get a description from the sister . . . and a photograph? Good! All your mobiles—I want every pub in the city visited beginning with the city centre. They won't have a photograph but they will have the description. Get them moving, Jimmy.'

At first, as he walked, he looked nervously about him but soon he seemed to regain confidence and his whole bearing changed, he stepped out briskly and looked neither to the right nor the left. It was raining, a thin misty drizzle and though from the hill there was a view right across the city he could see only a suffused, angry glow in the sky.

By the time he reached the city centre his mood was buoyant, he felt pleased with himself. For the third time he had not flinched from a dangerous, difficult and horrifying task. He had made a plan and he had carried it through—to the letter. He had been *competent* that was the word.

He tried never to think of the girl on the allotments, the girl he had nearly killed by mistake. He wanted to blot out that memory because of the guilt he felt, the sense of guilt which had made him so quick to defend himself in the newspaper. A psychopathic killer they had called him. The accusation had frightened him because it was not only, or even mainly his mistaken attack on an innocènt girl which made him feel guilty, it was the fact that he had wanted to go on, to finish what he had begun. When the girl's hat had fallen off and he had seen the blond hair it had taken every scrap of will power he possessed to release her. He had known the urge, almost the compulsion to kill. And he had scurried off to the flat and strangled his real victim in a frightening explosion of lust without any plan and at terrible risk.

But in his good times, as now, he could believe that what he had done had been deliberate, a rational and sensible change of plan made necessary by circumstances outside his control.

Once more and it would be over.

He was tempted to finish the thing tonight but he knew that he must resist that kind of prompting. To be competent you had to be calm, that was his secret, and he realised that he was not calm now. He was excited, pleasurably but dangerously so.

But there was no question of going back to the flat—not yet. He walked on through the city centre. A wet Sunday evening and hardly anybody about. Without consciously directing his steps he found himself in Prince's Street. He liked Prince's Street after dark, it seemed to have a teeming life of its own which went on just below the surface. A life which was no more than hinted at by the furtive figures in doorways or by the girls who accosted any unaccompanied male. Now and then between the shops there was an open door into dimly lit passage and a mysterious stairway.

He walked along the pavement with a seemingly purposive stride but in fact he was looking hopefully into every doorway. At the Joiners he went in for a drink. The bar was crowded, full of noise and tobacco smoke and he had to elbow his way to the counter. But, as usual, he seemed to be invisible to the bar-girls until someone said, 'This chap was before me.' Then he ordered a whisky though he rarely drank spirits. He retreated with his drink through the crowd to a clearer space by the windows where there were marble-topped tables. It was there that he saw her, sitting with a gin glass in front of her, showing a great deal of thigh. Her pallor was striking and the great dark eyes in her thin face semed to have a monopoly of all her vitality. She sat, staring at the blank window, apparently unaware of her surroundings. Then she looked up and caught him watching her. Automatically and with scarcely any change of expression she put out her invitation and with equal inevitability he accepted. They were separated by several yards and neither had spoken. The encounter suited his mood, he could play with fire without getting burnt.

He went over to her table. 'Can I get you another drink?'

She glanced back at the crowd round the bar and shook her head. 'It's not worth it.' She stood up, adjusted her shoulder bag and said quietly, 'Just round the corner. Number nine. Open the door and go straight up the stairs.'

He was tremulous with excitement. 'Can't I walk with you?'

She looked at him in surprise. 'No skin off my nose, love, but what if your wife gets to hear of it?'

'I haven't a wife.'

She shrugged. 'Suit yourself.'

She walked quickly with small steps, her heels tapping on the paving stones. He held her arm, thin and rigid through the material of her coat sleeve. He had difficulty in adjusting his pace. It was the first time he had walked out with a woman since . . .

He was silent because he could not trust himself to speak. He had never been with another woman, only with Rose. When he married her at 25 he was a virgin, as she was. Before he married, during the war, he had had the same temptations, the same opportunities as other men but fastidiousness and fear had combined

193

to restrain him. Now for years he had lived like a monk while he watched Rose sink deeper and deeper into depression. But suddenly he was free, unshackled, there was no longer the slightest reason for restraint. He had nothing to fear and nothing to lose.

They turned into number nine. She pushed open the front door and as they entered the little hall she saw him eyeing the door of the bottom flat which was closed.

'What's the matter?'

'Is there another girl in there?'

'She laughed. 'Why? Isn't one enough for you?'

She started up the stairs and he followed. 'Aren't you nervous, going with strange men?'

'No good to be, is it?'

She led him into a bedroom where a gas fire was burning. The room looked homely and cheerful, her dressing gown was on the bed and her make-up and toilet things were spread out on the dressing table.

She had taken off her coat and was hanging it in the wardrobe. 'Four pounds, love.'

He took the notes from his wallet and handed them to her. He stammered. 'I'll give you more if . . . '

She gave him a hard look. 'If what? You're not kinky, are you?'

'No, of course not! I meant if you are . . .' He hesitated, then added, 'if you are nice to me.'

She looked doubtful but she smiled. 'We'll see.' She had put the money in a drawer and taken off her dress. Her skin was white as paper. He watched her, fascinated by her very indifference.

'Aren't you going to undress? How many times had she said those words?

He started to do so. It had not occurred to him that his attraction to this girl sprang from her resemblance to Rose. Rose as she was twenty years ago when Jane was still a little girl. His approaches to Rose had always

194

been tentative, hesitant, her gentle smiling submissiveness disarmed lust and filled him with tenderness. This prostitute, lying naked on her bed, her legs separated waiting for him, had the same effect. She saw the change in him.

'What's the matter? Can't you do it? Come here, I'll help you.'

'No.'

He came to her nevertheless and covered her body with his. He stared down into her eyes and his gaze troubled her for it expressed none of the emotions she was accustomed to read in the faces of men. He looked puzzled as though he had suddenly found something which it was very difficult to explain or understand.

'What's the matter?'

He was caressing her pale face with his hands. His thumbs ran gently down the line of her jaw on either side. It was something he remembered from long ago. His thumbs moved down the throat to where he could feel the gentle pulsing of her blood.

'Oh, Rose!'

'What are you talking about? I aren't called Rose, my name is Brenda.' She saw a change in his expression and was frightened. 'Here! What are you doing? Lay off that!' Then she screamed.

There were heavy footsteps racing up the stairs and a policeman burst into the room.

'All right, dad, we've been looking for you.'

He made no protest but started to dress without a word.

'You all right, love?'

She was sitting on the foot of the bed staring at the man, and, suddenly she started to tremble. The constable put her dressing gown round her shoulders. 'Go into the other room, love, and make yourself a hot drink. He didn't hurt you, did he?'

She shook her head. 'No.' Then she added, 'How did you know?'

'We've been looking for him and they told me in the Joiners you'd picked him up.'

In a very few minutes they were gone and she was left alone.

CHAPTER ELEVEN

Wycliffe talked to him in an interview room at head-quarters. A little room with pale green walls, brown linoleum on the floor and furnished with a table and two chairs. Wycliffe sat on one side of the table and Rendell on the other; a constable stood by the door.

'Do you smoke?'

'No, thank you.'

'Do you want to make a statement?'

'I don't know. I would rather you asked me questions.'

'In any case I must caution you.' He repeated the formula.

'How long since you had any food?'

'I don't know but I couldn't eat anything.'

'A cup of tea?'

'No, thank you.'

Rendell was 53 but he looked 60. His hair, thin on top, was uniformly grey, his features were deeply lined and he had a whitish stubble on his chin. His skin looked grey and bloodless. His eyes stared unfocused at the table top and his hands rested palms down.

'Would I have killed her?' He asked the question apologetically.

'At any rate, you didn't, you did her no harm other than shock.'

'But would I have killed her if—?'

'Perhaps.'

He smoothed the table top with his palms. 'It's been like a nightmare, haunting me. I could never be sure.'

'Of what?'

He glanced up quickly, surprised by the question.

'It's still Sunday, isn't it?'

'A quarter to eleven on Sunday evening.'

He nodded. 'It doesn't seem possible.'

Wycliffe took out his pipe and lit it.

'The newspapers said that I was a psychopathic killer.'

'And you said, "It is not true. If I had been I would have killed the wrong girl on Monday night".'

He stopped moving his hands and focused his eyes on them as though seeing them for the first time. They were well-formed hands, broad and powerful with blunt fingers. Fine brownish-grey hairs glistened in the light.

'But I nearly did kill her.'

'You stopped when her hat fell off and you saw that she had fair hair instead of dark. You realised that she was the wrong girl.'

He nodded several times and was silent for a while. 'Yes, I did stop, didn't I?' He clenched his hands. 'But I wanted to kill her, I don't know how I found the strength to stop. I wanted to kill her even after I knew.'

Wycliffe said nothing, he sat immobile, smoking his pipe in very gentle puffs.

'I didn't understand, you see.'

'What didn't you understand?'

'That it's like sex.'

There was a clock on the wall and every half-minute it made a loud click when the large hand leapt forward a little way. It seemed to distract Rendell, almost to frighten him and he moved his chair so that the clock was no longer in his line of vision.

'It was all so clear in the beginning. I had to punish

198

the ones who killed my child and my wife. It was my duty.' He stopped, dissatisfied with what he had just said. 'No, it was more than that, I can't explain. It was something I had to do, I couldn't help myself.' He looked up at Wycliffe's face to see if he had made himself understood and met the bland impassive stare. 'I'm not trying to excuse myself, I wanted to do it, I knew it was right.'

'How did they kill your child and your wife?'

He seemed to think about the question for some time before answering. 'There never was a closer family than we were. We did everything together, the three of us. Of course, I had my work and Jane went to school but what I mean is, our lives centred on each other and on our home.'

'Where did Jane go to school?'

'It was a Catholic school but they took non-Catholics. It's closed now, The School of the Sacred Heart. We wanted her to be with girls who had had a good up-bringing.

'It all started when she went away to that hostel with a lot of girls from other schools. We thought we ought to let her mix more. I find it difficult to tell you how they treated her there.' His voice faltered.

'I know about that.'

'She was never the same. A year later she was in a mental hospital. They said she had mental illness which sometimes affects young people.'

An eavesdropper could have imagined that he was outside a confessional. The subdued, continuing murmur of one voice, the occasional interjections from the priest.

'She came out after six months but she wasn't cured. She was on drugs and she wasn't our Jane any longer. Sometimes she treated us as though we were strangers, she would talk to us but a lot of it was nonsense, she would get her words wrong and her ideas all mixed up.

'She didn't get better, she got worse and they wanted

199

to have her back in hospital, but we wouldn't agree. I can't explain what she was like, she seemed to be cut off, we couldn't reach her. It went on for four years, she was twenty-one but we couldn't let her out of our sight, somebody had to be with her almost all the time. Not that we minded . . . '

He placed his palms together, carefully matching the fingers. 'She seemed to just fade away, physically and mentally, regression I think they called it.

'And then, one afternoon while I was at work, Rose slipped out to the corner shop to buy something for tea and Jane must have followed her. She walked straight out of the house in front of a van, never looked right or left.'

'And your wife blamed herself?'

'Yes. Nothing would convince her that she was not responsible.'

He looked round the room vaguely as though not quite sure where he was.

'I can't understand it.'

'What can't you understand?'

He shook his head. 'I'm not a violent man but the girl on the allotments and the woman tonight . . . After I came away from the nursery school I was worried by the way I felt. I had to prove that they were wrong.'

'Who were wrong?'

'The newspapers.'

'What happened to your wife?' The question jolted him out of his line of thought.

'Rose killed herself. They gave her tablets to make her sleep, she was always taking tablets. Then one morning after I'd gone to work she took all she had. I found her when I came home in the evening.'

'That was last July?'

'Yes.' He passed his hand over his thinning hair as though trying to brush away some irritation. 'That evening, after they had taken her away, I saw it all clearly for the first time. Ever since Jane had become ill

200

I'd been asking myself, "Why? Why should it happen?" and there it was all the time; Jane had told me—she'd told me everything.'

'What had she told you?' The priest would have said, 'Continue, my son.'

'About the three girls and that woman, how they persecuted her. Suddenly it was clear as daylight and I knew what I had to do.'

'You set about finding these people?'

He nodded. 'It took me six months but I did it.' There was a note of pride in his voice.

In the silence which followed the clock jerked forward three more times, the clicks seemed to get louder. The constable at the door cleared his throat and Rendell turned as though surprised to see him there. The silence continued and two or three times Rendell turned to look at the policeman. Finally he said, 'Does he have to be there?'

Wycliffe made a sign and the constable went out closing the door behind him.

Rendell became increasingly restless, twice he put his hand into his inside breast-pocket and withdrew it again.

'You want to show me something?"

Rendell's hand darted with bird-like swiftness and came out with his wallet. He laid it on the table, opened it and extracted a page torn from a small notebook which he placed in front of Wycliffe. The page was dog-eared and creased from constant handling and it contained three lines of meticulous writing:

A succession of frustrations or sometimes a single, severe frustration leads to a massive withdrawal from reality and sweeping regression.

The words *single, severe frustration* had been doubly underlined.

'You see? That proves it, doesn't it? I copied that out

of an encyclopaedia. Regression, they say there, that's what the doctor said about Jane.'

Wycliffe passed the paper back and Rendell restored it to his wallet with great care as though it were a precious document, but he did not put his wallet away.

He looked Wycliffe straight in the eyes. 'That's true, isn't it?'

'If you took it from a reliable encyclopaedia I suppose it must be.'

He was excited, trembling, so that his fingers fumbled as he searched his wallet a second time. He came up with a piece of paper similar to the first which he handed over.

'I copied that from a book I got out of the library.'

This piece was not dog-eared or creased, it was obviously more recent than the other.

The schizophrenic reaction is probably not inherent in all human beings. Many authorities believe that it cannot occur in the absence of certain hereditary factors.

Rendell was watching him with extraordinary intensity as he read.

'Well?'

'There are many different kinds of mental illness.'

'Schizophrenia, that's what they said it was. I read it in the letter they gave me to give to our doctor. Hebephrenic schizophrenia.'

Wycliffe's placidity was beginning to irritate him. 'Can't you see what it means?'

Wycliffe was treading warily. 'I think I understand what it means but I'm not sure what interpretation you are putting on it.'

Rendell was rocking on his chair with impatience. 'If it's true that it's hereditary then I'm to blame.'

'For what?'

'For everything! I kill for the sake of killing, I'm a

202

madman like the papers said and I fathered a child who through no fault of her own . . . '

'Rubbish!'

The word and the manner in which it was spoken stopped him like a blow. He quietened down.

'Why did you want to kill the prostitute?'

The abrupt change caught him off balance as Wycliffe intended that it should.

'Why? I don't know.'

'You always have a reason for what you do.'

He thought about that. 'Yes, I do. You are right.' His brow furrowed in an effort of concentration. 'She was dark and thin and pale—like Rose.'

'Did you want to kill Rose?'

A spasm of anger quickly evaporated. 'No! For God's sake, why should I want to kill my wife?'

Wycliffe waited, knowing that the explanation—the rationalisation—would come.

'She lay there waiting for me—resigned. Ready to give me what I had paid for.'

'Well?'

He hesitated for some time then he said in a low voice. 'Rose submitted because she was my wife. She never uttered a word of complaint but . . .

'Each time I vowed I would never make any more demands on her. I felt like a beast. But it's something you can't always control, the situation is there and before you know where you are . . . ' After a moment he added, 'Now they will lock me up and I shan't be able to kill anybody again.' He said the words as though they contained inestimable comfort.

Wycliffe went up to his office and stood by the window in the darkness. He was trying to come to terms with himself. Why had he subjected this man to an interrogation which served no recognised professional end? Out of curiosity? If that meant that he needed to understand. Surely that was more important

203

than knowing about the electrostatic detection of foot-prints or the latest methods of recording and analysing the statistics of crime.

The telephone rang and he groped for it briefly. 'Wycliffe.'

It was Gill. 'So it's all over?'

'They will say that he's unfit to plead.'

'I told you; he's a nutter. They're all the same.'

THE END

WYCLIFFE AND THE WINSOR BLUE

To my wife:
critic and collaborator

People who know the town of Falmouth may be irritated by inaccuracies in the topography. These are deliberate in order to avoid any risk that a real person might be identified with one of the characters in this book – all of whom are imaginary.

W.J.B.

CHAPTER ONE

Edwin Garland felt uneasy, a vague shapeless unease for which he could find no immediate cause.

'You haven't taken any ham, father.'

'What?'

Beryl lifted a slice of ham on to his plate. 'Are you feeling all right, father?'

'Of course I'm feeling all right! Why shouldn't I?' In fact, he was feeling quite queer.

His son, Francis, was munching away, his protuberant eyes fixed on his father in an unwavering stare.

Beryl was beginning to look like an old woman; her hair was lank and grey, and there were fine wrinkles about her mouth . . . And that nose which seemed to sharpen with the years made her look predatory . . . How old was she? Fifty-five? About that . . . Nine years older than Francis . . . That gap . . . Why was she always so damned miserable? Of course she was drinking on the sly, her and her precious friend . . .

He was really feeling strange, curiously detached, but he struggled to hold on. His thoughts seemed to wander out of control . . . They were watching him. Concentrate on something! He looked at his wife's portrait which hung on the wall opposite where he sat. Gifford Tate had painted it a few weeks before she died. A fair painting; free in style but at the same time a good likeness. Gifford had gone overboard a bit in the blues though . . . For some reason this thought made Edwin chuckle to himself.

Francis's owl-like countenance obtruded again. Francis was too fat, his face was podgy and he had a paunch. Soft! Too much food, too little exercise. Greedy from childhood . . . Hard to credit that he had once fathered a daughter – and a beautiful girl she had turned out to be – like her granny . . . Funny thing, heredity; hit and miss. Anna was twenty now, living with her mother and some randy young rooster who knew when he was well off.

His thoughts returned to his wife's portrait. The Dresden China look. 'Refinement and fragility' Gifford had said. He was right: Judith had been . . . Judith had been exquisite – that was the word. And a bitch, but that was another story.

What was the matter with him? He was confused; and that was another word, an unpleasant one in the ears of a man of seventy-five. Mealy mouthed jargon for senile. Better eat some of this bloody ham or they would think . . . He pushed it around with his fork. Soggy! How did they make the stuff hold all that water? An offence to water milk so why not ham?

Back to Beryl and Francis. What a pair! They were Judith's children, so why were they so damned unprepossessing? And they had mean, scheming little minds. He had supported them all their lives and what had they ever done for him except wait for him to die? Watching, like vultures . . . Well, they wouldn't have long to wait, now, but they had a surprise or two to come.

He caught sight of Beryl's head in profile. Her mother's daughter, but Beryl *exquisite*! He wanted to laugh. What the hell was wrong with him? Time to pull himself together.

Safer to look out of the window, concentrate on the

view; that had never let him down. The living-room was at the back of the house, overlooking the harbour, and from where he sat at table he could see right across Carrick Roads to St Just-in-Roseland. Sunlight glittered on the water and the colours . . . the colours were not bright, but the light shattered in reflection, was brilliant. How often had he struggled to make that distinction on canvas? Painting light: that was what it was all about. The Impressionists had tried, God knows! but even they . . .

'I think I shall go down to the studio.'

Beryl said: 'But you've eaten hardly anything, father! Really —'

'I've had enough.' And he added under his breath: 'More than enough!' without being quite sure what he meant.

'Shall I bring your coffee down to you?'

'No.'

'You haven't had your tablets . . .'

'For Christ's sake!'

He went down the stairs, holding tight to the bannisters and swaying slightly. He felt giddy.

He had been born and lived all his life over the shop: E. Garland and Son, Artists' Suppliers and Printers. In the little hall at the bottom of the stairs one door opened into a side passage leading to the street; the other, to the back of the shop through which he had to pass to reach the studio. The shop was closed for the lunch hour. He shuffled past well ordered, dusted shelves and racks, and past the little office where his father had sat and schemed for most of his life. The place was peopled with ghosts and soon he would be one of them. He fumbled with a key from his pocket then opened a door into another world.

Like the living-room upstairs his studio looked out

on the harbour. It was more like a workshop than a studio – a painter's workshop. There was a sturdy bench, with an orderly arrangement of tools, where he made stretchers and frames. There was an earthenware sink, a table, a couple of easels, a painter's trolley, a chest of shallow drawers. Empty frames and canvases were stacked against the walls . . . And almost every object in the room seemed to be spattered with multi-coloured splashes of paint; while the windows were covered with grime and festooned with cob-webs. A scruffy orderliness. That was how he liked it.

When Gifford Tate was alive and used to visit him, Tate had croaked through his beard: 'Why the hell don't you get yourself a decent studio, Eddie? God knows you can afford it! At least get somebody to clean the bloody windows!' And Garland had answered: 'I like it as it is, and as for the windows, that muck is a natural filter for the light and if any interfering bastard ever cleaned 'em I'd twist his credentials off.'

Entering his studio always gave his spirit a lift; it did so now.

He fetched a tobacco pouch out of his pocket and a packet of cigarette papers. With a lifetime of practice behind him he rolled a passable cigarette in his fingers and lit it.

There was a painting on one of the easels and the trolley with his brushes, tubes of paint, and palette was beside it. He pulled up a high stool and stood, his bottom propped on the stool, which he used like a shooting stick, his painting posture for these latter days. The painting seemed complete: another harbour scene. He studied it with growing distaste. 'That water . . . as exciting as a sludge pit in a sewage works.'

He closed his eyes and tried with all the concentration of which he was capable to see with his mind

10

exactly what it was that he had wanted to paint. Slowly the scene seemed to materialise once more out of his imagination: the mist, the swathe of sunlit water; the water like shot silk in the shelter of the boats; ripples elsewhere, tiny vibrant glittering crests . . . Points of pure light . . . so brilliant that they hurt the eyes . . .

God! How they hurt the eyes! But for once he believed that he was seeing as he had striven all his life to see . . . Diamond points . . . blinding! They seemed to sear into his brain. He groped vaguely with his right hand as though reaching for a brush and as he did so he experienced an intolerable contraction in his chest, a paralysing pain, and with a cry of anguish he fell, taking the stool with him.

His niece, Cathy Carne, found him when she came back to open the shop after lunch. She was surprised to see the studio door open, he always closed the door when he was working and kept it locked when he wasn't there. Then she saw him, his heavy body lying mounded over the stool which had fallen with him. His jaw sagged and his eyes stared.

Her first reaction was incredulity. The old man had been with her in the shop that morning, the same as ever, gossiping about the business, about the vagaries of their customers, the oddities of town councillors and the perverseness of families – all with a humour that was wickedly spiced. Of course he had been warned; the family had been warned, but . . .

She felt empty inside.

She went upstairs. On the landing she could hear voices coming from the living-room and she pushed open the door. Beryl was clearing the table; Francis, with his hands in his pockets, was staring out of the window. There was an atmosphere, as always when the two of them were left alone together.

11

Beryl looked at her: 'What's wrong?'

'It's uncle; he's collapsed in the studio.' She added after a pause: 'He's dead.'

Without a word Francis turned away fom the window and pushed past her. They heard his heavy footsteps descending the stairs.

Cathy picked up the telephone which stood on a side table. 'I'd better telephone Alan.'

She dialled a number and spoke to the receptionist. 'I'm speaking for Mr Garland at the art shop. Is Dr Tate there?' A pause and when she spoke again her manner was familiar: 'Oh, Alan – Cathy here. I'm afraid it's bad news . . . Yes, Uncle . . . he collapsed on the floor in the studio . . . I'm afraid so . . . If you will . . . Yes, come to the side door.'

She replaced the receiver and turned to Beryl. 'He'll be here in a few minutes.'

Beryl was standing motionless in the middle of the room, her hand on her heart. 'I knew something was going to happen; I could *feel* it! And he brought it on himself.'

Cathy said: 'We'd better go down.'

They went downstairs; Francis was standing in the doorway of the studio. 'Well, he's dead all right.'

'I telephoned the surgery.'

'Good!'

Cathy was looking past him into the studio. 'Can't we move him?'

'Better not.'

Beryl said: 'I've told him and told him but he took no notice . . . He wouldn't even take the tablets Alan gave him. He brought it on himself.'

And then it occurred to Cathy that although the old man was lying exactly as she had seen him, something had changed. Surely, there was a different picture on

12

the easel? Odd! She was on the point of saying something but changed her mind. After all, what difference could it make? If Francis was up to something it was nothing to do with her.

Francis, hands thrust deep into his trouser pockets, said: 'I thought he seemed a bit queer at lunch but I didn't expect it to come to this . . .'

They stood, silent and waiting, until the side door opened and Alan Tate came in. He was slight of build, very dark, with a sallow complexion, and meticulously dressed in a dark grey suit with a silk tie. Son of Gifford Tate, the painter, he had been the Garlands' doctor since, at his father's death, he had returned to Falmouth and set up practice in the family house.

Subdued greetings, then he went about his business. A brief examination, his movements rapid and sure. He spoke in staccato phrases: 'His heart gave out, that's what it amounts to. Bound to happen sooner or later . . . Give me a hand, Francis – get the stool out from under him; straighten him up a little.' Although first names were being used his attitude and manner were strictly professional.

Beryl said: 'We can't leave him here, he'll have to be taken upstairs.'

Tate looked up at her, his brown eyes enlarged by the lenses of his spectacles. 'He's a big man, Beryl; too much for Francis and me. The undertakers will do it and it will be more decent that way.'

Francis said: 'You'll come upstairs, Alan?'

Tate glanced at his watch. 'I can spare a few minutes.'

Cathy Carne said: 'Shouldn't we tell Uncle Thomas and Mark?'

Blank looks from Beryl and Francis.

'After all, Thomas is his brother.'

13

Beryl said: 'They'll hear soon enough.'

Cathy gave up. 'Do you want me to shut the shop?'

'The shop?' Francis turned his bulging eyes on her: 'What would be the point of that?'

Cathy stayed in the shop while the others went upstairs. Ten minutes later Tate came down alone. Cathy was in the little office and he came to stand in the doorway. 'They are both quite composed. I doubt if there will be any problem with delayed shock.' Cynical. 'You found him, I gather?'

'Yes.'

'A shock for you. They've been in touch with the undertaker and when I left they were arguing about the funeral.'

'When shall I see you again?'

Tate hesitated. 'I'll telephone.' And added, seemingly in explanation: 'Marcella is very depressed. I'm concerned about her.'

Cathy was feeling the heat; little beads of perspiration formed between her shoulder blades and breasts. She had worn a full-length coat because it was all she had that was decently subfusc; now she wished that she had been less conformist.

She was staring at the coffin, the wooden box with fancy trimmings which held the mortal remains of Edwin Garland, her uncle and employer. She wondered what his comment would have been had he been in a position to make one.

'Man that is born of woman hath but a short time to live and is full of misery . . .'

They weren't talking about Edwin Garland; Edwin had enjoyed life in his own way.

There were more wreaths than she would have expected and the flowers were already wilting in the merciless sun. She wondered who had sent them all.

Francis, as chief mourner, stood next to the vicar; his paunchiness exaggerated by an old, dark suit that was too small for him. She wondered about the bruise on his cheek: she had noticed it the evening before when he came back from his Tuesday round. 'I walked into a door.' Somebody had hit him. Interesting!

With glazed eyes he was staring into the middle distance. Day-dreaming of life after the shop? More than likely. It wouldn't be long before he closed a deal with one or other of the chain stores who had shown an interest in the site. Then there was the printing works . . . Francis had never shown any real interest in either side of the business and, as far as the shop was concerned, this had meant that Cathy had been free to go her own way under the old man's eye.

Beryl would have to move out, but she would go to live with her friend; two old-maids together. It was what they both wanted and with her share of her father's money Beryl would be well able to provide for both of them in style.

'And that leaves me . . . At thirty-six.'

She had had a letter from Edwin's solicitor asking her to come to his office the following day. It must mean that she had been mentioned in the will. A picture, probably; she had always admired his work, perhaps a little money to go with it; that would be welcome.

' . . . deliver us not into the bitter pains of eternal death.'

Yes, well, it might not be as bad as that.

It was Wednesday afternoon. In the tradition of the street Edwin was being buried on early closing day so that the other traders could attend. But the custom had lost its meaning because there were so few private traders left, and company managers are faceless men, here today and gone tomorrow. All the same, there was a good crowd, the more surprising because Francis had not bothered to organise anything properly.

It was one of the hottest days of the year and the new part of the cemetery was without trees. Most people were out enjoying themselves and she could hear children on the beach which was not far away.

Francis's illegitimate daughter, Anna, was there with her boyfriend. They stood a little way back from the others as though unsure of their right to be there at all, and they were in bizarre contrast to the rest of the mourners. The girl's fair hair was scraped back and held with a slide; she wore a grey shirt, open half-way down the front, and bleached jeans. Her boyfriend had his hair down to his shoulders and wore a bandeau. His sweat-shirt carried the slogan: 'No! to Trident!', and his jeans seemed about to fall apart. Both of them were so beautifully and evenly brown that clothes seemed superfluous.

Cathy looked at them with a mixture of envy and doubt. At their age she had already spent four years working in her uncle's shop. But what would they be doing at thirty-six?

Also standing well back from the grave, Mike Treloar, the printing works foreman, supported himself on a stick. As a boy he had been crippled by polio.

Cathy was almost opposite Alan Tate and he was watching her, or seemed to be. It was hard to tell because of the sun glinting on his glasses. Looked at objectively there was nothing special about him: a smallish man, slight of build, dark-brown hair *en brosse*, spectacles with thick lenses and a broad, carefully trimmed moustache. Everything about him was meticulous, as though the parts had been made and assembled with scrupulous care. Cathy sometimes

16

wondered why women found him so attractive, why she herself did.

He was with Marcella, his father's second wife and widow. In her late thirties, she was two or three years younger than her step-son. Once she had been attractive, with a good figure: now she was painfully thin and her sharp features gave her a pinched look. She did nothing to improve her appearance; her flaxen hair was cut short so that it fitted her head like a helmet and accentuated the angularity of her features.

Cathy was surprised how ill she looked, there was an area of paleness about her eyes, and her nose was pinched and reddened about the nostrils; perhaps a summer cold, though Alan had said she was depressed.

'Forasmuch as it hath pleased Almighty God of his great mercy . . .'

When the service was over there was the ritual of shaking hands with the vicar. Francis spoke with his daughter and the boy. Beryl chatted with one or two of the bystanders then lingered to look at the cards on the wreaths and this annoyed Francis.

'Come *on*, Beryl! The undertaker will give you a list.'

Franics had not hired cars and Cathy joined him and Beryl in his ten-year-old saloon. As they drove away from the cemetery she spotted the clapped-out van belonging to Anna's boyfriend parked some distance from the gates, a large CND symbol painted on its side.

Beryl sat in the back of the car, her large black handbag with brass fittings balanced on her knees. She delved into the bag and came up with a packet of pastilles which she began to suck, filling the car with a sickly sweet smell.

She said: 'The Tates were there and they sent a big wreath; we ought to have invited them back with us.'

Francis did not answer.

Beryl went on: 'I saw you talking to Anna and that boy. Very friendly all of a sudden.' It was an accusation.

'Why not? She's my daughter, isn't she?'

Conversation between brother and sister was conducted at a level of mutual aggression which stopped just short of exploding into a row. An exercise in brinkmanship.

'What did she say?'

'Not a lot.'

'Did she ask where you got your bruises from?'

At first it seemed that Francis was going to leave it at that, the ball in his court, but in fact he was trying to decide which would annoy her most: being kept in the dark about his conversation with Anna or knowing the truth. He decided to speak: 'She said she'd had a letter from the lawyer.'

Beryl was roused. 'Why should Shrimpton write to her?'

'I suppose father has left her something; he had a soft spot for Anna, he said she looked like mother.'

Beryl made an angry movement. 'I only hope he's had more sense than to leave her money! She may look like mother, but mother would have turned in her grave if she could have seen that girl today!'

Cathy said: 'I had a letter from Shrimpton, myself. It simply asked me to come to his office tomorrow afternoon at half-past two.'

Beryl was dismissive. 'Yes, dear, that was to be expected. He was bound to remember you with a little legacy. This is quite different! Quite different!'

To further annoy his sister, Francis said: 'Anna is his granddaughter after all.' But the exchange had sown a tiny seed of doubt in his own mind . . .

Francis parked the car and they walked along the

18

street to the shop. When they were in the little hall at the foot of the stairs Francis said: 'Is father's studio locked, Cathy?'

'I don't think so, but the key is in the door.'

'Then lock it and bring the key up with you.'

Beryl said: 'What's this about?'

He turned his sullen gaze on her but did not answer.

Upstairs, Beryl's friend had made coffee and sandwiches for them.

Francis stood by the window. 'There's a mist coming in.'

Beryl's friend said: 'Yes, but they said on the radio that it would be fine again tomorrow.'

Francis sat at his desk making entries on index cards. He wrote in a small, neat, but cramped hand, pausing now and then to refer to one or other of the books and papers spread on his desk. On a two-deck trolley to his right a V.D.U. stood above a computer keyboard. The screen displayed columns of figures against groups of code letters and from time to time Francis referred to these, scrolling the display on or back.

The room in which he worked had been his bedroom since infancy, though now the only evidence of its primary purpose was a narrow divan bed. One wall was wholly taken up with books while the other walls were hung with home-produced charts in which numbers and symbols formed elaborate geometrical patterns. There was a bank of card-index drawers and a multi-drawer filing cabinet.

Francis seemed wholly absorbed, yet once or twice he sat back in his chair and told himself: 'My father is dead!' It was as though he could not be convinced; as though he could hardly accept the fact that his father was no longer there, the final arbiter of all that happened in the business and in their domestic lives. He was like a goldfish, suddenly tipped out of its bowl into a pond, conditioned to continue swimming in circles. Yet his father's death should not have come as a surprise. Six months ago Alan Tate had said: 'His heart is by no means strong and his blood pressure being what it is . . . If only he would discipline himself to regular medication and give up smoking . . .' Of course Francis had thought about it as something that was inevitable, and he had plans, but they had never seemed very real and he had looked on them as castles in the air. Now . . .

His desk was placed near the window, overlooking the narrow canyon of the street. At this time of night the street was quiet: the occasional car, and now and then a group of rowdy youths asserting their masculinity like stags in rut. Although it was dark outside he had not drawn the curtains. Silvery streaks of rain appeared out of the darkness and trickled down the shining panes. A wall clock ticked loudly: a few minutes to nine. Mitch, his black and white terrier, was asleep in a wicker basket on the floor. Beryl and her friend were in the living-room, across the passage.

At a quarter past nine there was a tap at the door; Beryl came in and stood waiting for his attention. She wore a long raincoat which drooped from her thin shoulders and she carried a small overnight bag. Her pale face was blotched and her lips were moist. When he turned towards her she said: 'I'm not staying in the house tonight, Francis, I'm too upset. I'm going back with Celia but I shall be here in time to get your breakfast in the morning.'

He merely stared at her with his bulging eyes and she went on: 'There are biscuits in the tin by the cooker and there is plenty of milk if you want to make yourself a hot drink.'

In a flat voice, the more insulting by its indifference, he said: 'You don't have to bother about me. Move in with Celia whenever you want.' And he turned back to his desk.

She would have liked to make some cutting rejoinder but none came to mind so she went out, closing the door behind her.

At ten o'clock he switched off his computer and put away his books. Mitch skipped out of his basket, tail wagging, and they went downstairs together. In the little hall, Francis put on a waterproof coat and cap and they went out by the back door.

The shops on the Garlands' side of the street backed on the water and only a narrow paved walk separated them from the harbour. At ten o'clock each evening, except in the very worst weather, Francis and his dog took their walk along the waterfront as far as the yacht marina and returned by the street.

It was dark for an August night. The lights at the docks twinkled mistily, and some of the larger craft at moorings carried lights, but for the most part the harbour was a broad plain of darkness. It was of no consequence; Garland knew every step of the way and Mitch trotted ahead, pursuing an erratic course as he nosed out the rich odours brought to him on the moist air.

For Francis this nightly constitutional had its place in a larger fantasy. He liked to imagine himself an academic, working after dinner in one of those elegant book-lined rooms of an Oxford college. As the clocks chimed and struck all over the city he would stroll down the Broad, along St Giles and round by the Parks . . . Nature, he thought, had intended him for scholarship yet here he was at forty-six, still a small-town trades-man.

21

Well that at any rate would change.

'My father is dead!' Well, he couldn't be expected to shed any tears.

There had been offers for the shop which his father had consistently turned down. Offers for the site, not the business. One, a very good one from a firm of chain-store chemists, was still open. In a few months he could leave those rooms over the shop and the shop itself for ever. Of course Cathy Carne was being difficult, already there had been an outburst over something he had said. The old man had spoiled her and it was high time that she faced facts.

Then there was the printing works: it had kept pace with the changing times and if it was put on the market there would be plenty of interest. Then he would be free! As far back as he could remember, those phrases 'the shop' and 'the works' had been spoken by his parents with a certain solemnity, as some speak of 'the church' or 'the monarchy'. Well, all that was over.

Their walk along the wharf was interrupted by a car-park where a scatttering of vehicles gleamed in the jaundiced light of a sodium lamp. To his surprise he recognised the battered old van which belonged to Anna's boyfriend and he wondered what it was doing there. Then he saw the glowing tip of someone's cigarette behind the windshield. He continued his walk and thought no more about the van.

'My father is dead!'

In a year the shop would be no more, lorries would carry away the rubble to which it had been reduced, leaving a gap to be filled by yet another chain store. Would he then feel a certain sadness? He thought not: at this moment the prospect afforded him a satisfaction that was almost spiteful in its intensity.

Sentiment and nostalgia are for pleasant memories.

A white yacht carrying navigation lights glided in ghostly silence through the seeming maze of moored craft, putting out to sea. He stopped to watch her until she disappeared in the darkness. The tide was lapping the harbour wall within a yard of his feet.

He would have enough money to live comfortably and he would never be bored. For many years his studies had absorbed every moment of his spare time, now they would be his full-time occupation. He would be able to visit libraries, museums and institutions all over Britain and make contact with other numerologists. Even abroad . . . He was resolved to meet every possible criticism in advance and, eventually, his conclusions would be presented to the world in a scholarly book.

And if in this new life he was to be alone . . . well, he had been alone for most of his life. In his twenties he had taken up with a girl called Freda and got her pregnant. She had given birth to a daughter but Freda had been no more anxious to marry than he had. Since then she had married someone else and been widowed, but she still lived in the district with their daughter, Anna. He saw Anna occasionally but he had not seen Freda for years though he had to admit that he might not have recognised her had he passed her in the street.

Recently he had formed another attachment, one which he valued more. But there was a price to be paid in this relationship and he wasn't sure . . . He couldn't stand scenes; violence of any sort appalled him . . .

Involuntarily he raised his hand to his face.

They were approaching a point where the wharf walk was bridged over by scaffolding erected to repair the back wall of Benson's furniture shop. Warning lights on the steel supports blinked feebly through the mist.

Mitch growled, then yelped.

'Quiet, boy!'

He had no sense of foreboding, no intimation of danger; on the contrary he felt light hearted, even light headed as vistas of freedom seemed to open ahead of him. Mitch scampered under the scaffolding and Garland followed. The lowest tier of planks cleared his head by at least a foot.

As he emerged at the other end he was aware of a frightful, blinding, stunning pain in his head, and then nothing.

CHAPTER TWO

Chief Superintendent Wycliffe's driver pulled into the car park, which had been closed to the public, and joined a line of police vehicles. A uniformed man, there to ward off sightseers, saluted.

On his way down to take part in an official inspection, Wycliffe had monitored reports on his car radio and so arrived at the scene of crime before his headquarters had got a team together. The Deputy Chief Constable, in his parade uniform, would have to manage the inspection without the assistance of his head of C.I.D.

Falmouth: a town he liked. J.B. Priestley once said that it could never quite make up its mind whether it was a port or a resort, but that very ambivalence had saved it from the worst pitfalls of both. The harbour looked mysterious: the sun had broken through but mist still lay over the docks. Massive superstructures; squat, tapering funnels; slender masts, and the jibs of cranes, merged in a ghostly silhouette. Elsewhere in the harbour the moored yachts, the power boats, launches and dinghies, regimented by the tide, matched colourful reflections in the water.

Wycliffe was reminded of a busman's holiday he had spent, not so long ago, across at St Mawes.

Appraised by bush telegraph or E.S.P. of his advent, Divisional Chief Inspector Reed hurried along the wharf to greet him.

'A nasty business, sir. Very nasty!'

A shaking of hands and a brief excursion into reminiscence. 'This way . . . He's just beyond that scaffolding . . . The surgeon has been and gone, he reckons death probably took place early in the night; the coroner has been informed, and the scenes-of-crime chaps are on the job . . .'

They walked together along the wharf; the two men, in striking contrast. Reed was built on an over-generous scale, bull-necked and bulging in his grey pinstripe; Wycliffe, slight of build, and rather pale, was more likely to be taken for an academic than a policeman; hard to believe that he had served a tough apprenticeship on the beat in a Midland city.

The scenes-of-crime van was parked as near the site as it could get, planks had been laid on the ground approaching and under the scaffolding to preserve whatever evidence there might be, and the area where the body was had been screened off. The scenes-of-crime officers had photographed the dead man and the ground for some distance around. Footprints, found in soft mud under the scaffolding, had been photographed and casts made though there was little doubt that they belonged to the victim, not the killer. There were dog prints too. The whole area was littered with fragments of mortar which had been chipped out of the wall by workmen getting it ready for re-pointing.

Behind the screen Wycliffe looked down at the dead man: middle or late forties, probably above average height, bony, but with a tendency to corpulence – sedentary: the disease of modern man. He wore a fawn waterproof, cord trousers, and good quality brown shoes. The left side of his face, in the region of the jaw articulation, looked at first sight as though it had been smashed by a blow, but Wycliffe recognised it as the

26

wound of exit of a bullet which had probably ricochetted inside the skull. Bending down, he looked for and found the wound of entry, a small round hole in the top of the head towards the back. The thin, fair hair had been singed and stained around the wound.

The undamaged part of the face had a puffy softness, an appearance of immaturity, accentuated by a fair moustache of wispy growth. There was an area of bruising below the right eye but, although it was recent, Wycliffe felt sure that it had been inflicted some time before death – probably the day before.

Reed, standing behind him, said: 'A fight?'

'Perhaps, at least several hours before he was killed.'

Murder, that much was evident but the motive was not. They had found the man's wallet in the pocket of his jacket with forty pounds in notes, a credit card, and a driving licence in the name of Francis Garland.

Wycliffe brooded. In the ensuing hours and days he would get to know Francis Garland perhaps better than he knew many of his colleagues and acquaintances. His data would come from relatives and friends, from those not so friendly; from the man's habits, likes and dislikes, his loves and his hates. In the end, if this crime turned out to be something more than an abortive mugging, he would have a portrait of the victim and through that portrait some indication of why he had become one.

Reed volunteered background: 'The Garlands have a shop in the main street, a couple of hundred yards from here: artists' materials, pictures, that sort of thing; they're printers too – they have their works farther along the waterfront, just beyond Customs Quay. You can see it from here – that concrete building. Anyway, this chap lived with his father and sister in the rooms over the shop – until Saturday.'

'What happened on Saturday?'

'His father died of a stroke. A bit of a coincidence, don't you think?'

'Has anyone broken the news to the sister?'

'I've sent Pritchard; he's good on bereavements. Ought to have been an undertaker.'

'So Garland was unmarried?'

'Yes, but according to the local sergeant, there's an illegitimate daughter around somewhere.'

The first bits of the jig-saw. From now on he would be looking for some sort of pattern. He would spend a great deal of time trying to fit in fresh pieces only to find that most of them didn't belong to his picture. Criminal investigation is a sad story of false trails and dead ends.

'Was he a queer?'

'Not as far as we know, but it's possible.'

The church clock doled out ten strokes on its tinny bell. Looking down at the dead man Wycliffe felt guilty because he was experiencing a sense of mild elation. He loathed the sterile ritual of inspections, and this poor devil in his untimely end had saved him from that. He slipped easily into the routine of a murder inquiry.

'Garland's sister must have realised that her brother didn't come home last night.'

'You would think so.'

'Who found him?'

'The builder's men coming to work on this wall. They had the sense not to plough in and now they're laying off until they hear from us.' Reed removed his fisherman's hat, uncovering a bald crown and a fringe of auburn hair. With a large pocket handkerchief he wiped the perspiration from his forehead; it was getting hot.

There was blood on the ground from the exit wound

which had not been entirely washed away by the overnight rain. The man must have been shot from above at close range as he emerged from under the scaffolding. Wycliffe looked up at the first tier of planks; the shot must have been fired from up there. If the attack went wrong the assailant stood a good chance of not being identified and if it was apparently successful it would be safe to come down and make sure.

He called to Fox, the sergeant in charge of scene of crime. Fox looked like Bertie Wooster and, for some reason, was known as Brenda to his colleagues. He was good at his job, though not as good as he thought he was, and his smugness irritated Wycliffe.

'Take a look up there where the killer must have stood or knelt.'

Fox assumed a judicial air. 'I thought it better to concentrate on the ground —'

'Just do as I ask, Fox. Now, please.'

There was no point in staying at the scene. Fox and the others would do all that was necessary and a good deal that wasn't, working by the book.

He reassured Reed about local assistance. 'I know you must have a full load so I'll try not to be greedy. I'm going to talk to somebody at the shop – the sister if possible.'

He walked back along the wharf to the car park. On an R.T. link from his car he spoke to his deputy, John Scales, at headquarters. 'Who've you got for me, John?'

The composition of a team depends on who happens to be doing what at the time. Apart from Detective Inspector Kersey, Wycliffe's usual number one, Scales had sent Sergeants Shaw and Lane. Shaw was a good organiser and internal collator, well versed in computer mystique. Lucy Lane enjoyed the distinction of having convinced Wycliffe that a woman could more than hold her own in the serious crimes squad and not only in rape cases. The three of them, with four detective constables, would set the ball rolling.

Wycliffe left his car on the park and climbed the slope to the street.

Falmouth's main shopping street runs narrowly and crookedly along the waterfront with shops on both sides but with occasional tantalising glimpses of the harbour. The street is in three parts: Market Street, because there was once a market; Church Street, because of the Church of King Charles the Martyr, built at the Restoration; and Arwenack Street, because it leads eventually to Arwenack House, all that is left of the home of the Killigrews, a mixed bag of soldiers, dramatists, pirates and entrepreneurs, who founded the town and built the church.

As is usual until mid-morning, the street was jammed with vans and lorries unloading, taking up pavement as well as road, so that shoppers had to plot a course through a maze of obstacles. Tourists navigated with resigned expressions: this was Holiday and at least you could understand the lingo.

It was sixteen years since Wycliffe's last case in the town and he was recapturing the atmosphere of the place. For centuries merchant seamen from all over the world have mingled with the local population and now, in addition, for three months every year, holiday-makers flood in like the tide. Yet the substratum of true locals remains, a distinct, identifiable breed, preserving the town's unique parochialism and delighting in the frustration of imported bureaucrats.

Byron, who had no good word to say of the town itself, spoke highly of its inhabitants: '. . . both female and male, at least the young ones, are remarkably handsome, and how the devil they came to be so is a wonder.'

'E. Garland and Son: Artists' Suppliers and Printers': gilt letters on a green ground; a discreet double frontage between a supermarket and a bank. One window displayed easels, folding stools, palettes, stretched canvases, and various shoulder-bags for transporting all the impedimenta of the would-be *plein air* painter; in the other window there were paintings of varied merit and price. There was a framed notice which read: 'Orders taken for printing of all kinds, commercial and private. Estimates on request without obligation.'

Wycliffe decided to avoid the shop for the moment; the family lived in the rooms above so there was probably a separate entrance. He found it in a stone-flagged side passage, a door bearing a small brass plate: 'Garland'. He rang the bell and it was answered by a youngish woman wearing a blue overall.

'Miss Garland?'

'No, what do you want?'

Wycliffe would have been surprised if she had said yes.

He introduced himself and she responded with engaging candour: 'Cathy Carne – I work in the shop. A policeman came earlier to break the news to Miss Garland.'

The woman was slim, dark, and well made, with an air of reserve that made one take her seriously. Dark blue eyes and black lashes: a felicitous dip from the genetic bran tub.

'It must have been a shock to Miss Garland, coming so soon after her father's death.'

'It was. I suppose you want to speak to her? She has a friend with her just now.'

31

On the spur of the moment he said: 'I would like to talk to you first.'

'If you wish.'

A door from the hall opened into the back of the shop. 'Through here.' She took him into a small office with a window overlooking the harbour. Desk, typewriter, telephone, safe, filing cabinet – all very modern and giving an impression of crisp business-like efficiency.

'Do sit down.'

She picked up a cigarette pack from the desk. 'Smoke? . . . No? Do you mind if I do?' She lit a cigarette and inhaled with sensual enjoyment.

'Do you mind telling me your position here, Miss Carne?' She was clearly more than a shop assistant.

A ghost of a smile. 'I sometimes wonder. I suppose you could say that I'm a kind of manageress. Anyway I've been here twenty years – since I left school, and Edwin Garland was my uncle by marriage.'

'Do you live above the shop?'

'I do not!' Emphatic.

'When you arrived this morning did you see Miss Garland at once?'

'She was waiting for me. She said it looked as though Francis hadn't been home all night and she was worried.'

'Had she been worried all night?'

'She wasn't here. She spent the night at a friend's house – the one who is with her now. When she returned home this morning she found Francis's dog, Mitch, whimpering outside the back door. Francis always takes him for a walk last thing before going to bed. It was while we were deciding what to do that your policeman turned up with the news.'

She was calm, self-possessed, incisive, and not obviously distressed.

32

A young girl, also wearing a blue overall, came into the office. After a brief apology she said: 'Is it all right to allow credit for this, Miss Carne?' She held out a bill form.

'Yes, that will be all right, Alice, but get Mrs Wilson to sign the bill and make sure the signature comes through on the carbon.'

Wycliffe said: 'Could anyone who knew your cousin's habits rely on him taking the same walk at approximately the same time each night?'

'Short of an earthquake or a deluge.'

'Do you know of any reason why he might have been killed?'

She shook her head. 'No. Francis wasn't the sort to make friends and influence people but I can't believe that anybody would want to murder him.'

'Somebody already has,' Wycliffe said. 'I'm told that there is a daughter?'

'It didn't take you long to find that out. Anna is twenty.'

'She lives with her mother?'

'And her boyfriend. By the way, somebody should tell her. After all he was her father.'

'Did he keep in touch with her?'

She trickled out a spiral of smoke and watched it rise. 'She kept in touch with him – at intervals.'

'Filial affection?'

She laughed outright. 'I'm in no position to say. My guess would be an upsurge of sentiment whenever the money was getting tight. But then, I'm a cynic.'

'They live near here?'

'In Flushing, just across the water. Shortly after Anna was born her mother married, and a year or so ago her husband died leaving her the house and a little money. The boyfriend moved in at the beginning of the

33

summer; he gets by doing casual work on the farms.' She was watching him through the cigarette smoke to judge the effect she was producing.

A capable woman, nobody's fool; but was she adopting a deliberate pose? And if so, for what purpose?

'Does Anna have a job?'

'She's on the check-out in one of the supermarkets but I think she's on holiday this week.'

'Any other relatives?'

She smiled. 'Yes, but not acknowledged. Edwin's younger brother Thomas and his son, Mark. Mark is about my age and also unmarried.'

'Local?'

'Oh, yes. The two of them live in a house near the docks. Thomas is a retired schoolteacher and Mark is a chiropractor – some sort of osteopath.'

'You said they weren't acknowledged; what's wrong with them from the Edwin Garlands' point of view?'

'Thirty years ago Thomas contested his father's will, he lost but his action split the family; I don't think there's been any contact since.'

'Thomas didn't go to his brother's funeral?'

'No, but I saw Mark lurking in the background as though he didn't want to be seen. He's an odd fish.'

Wycliffe changed the subject. 'You don't seem very distressed by your cousin's death.'

She considered this. 'I suppose not. Of course I'm very sorry but our relationship has never been close. I worked for his father – my uncle, not for Francis.'

'But surely Francis was involved?'

She tapped ash from her cigarette. 'With the printing and outside sales. Two days a week – Mondays and Tuesdays – he went out with the van delivering orders to customers and taking new ones for both the printing and the art sides. The rest of the week he was at the printing works. He didn't interfere here, Uncle saw to that, so I've had a free hand in the shop and although I say it myself I've made a go of it.'

She made an irritable movement. 'There's no point in mincing words. Francis has never been interested in the business and he's never pulled his weight. Although he was supposed to be in charge of the printing works it was the foreman, Mike Treloar, who ran it with Uncle keeping an eye on things and deciding policy. Francis's one idea, if he'd lived, would have been to sell out. The printing works is a good investment for anybody's money and this site is a key one in the street. Uncle had several offers but he turned them all down.'

'When we found Francis his face was marked by fairly recent bruising. Do you know how and when it happened?'

'No, I saw the bruise when he came back to the shop on Tuesday evening and I asked him what he'd done to himself. He just growled something about having walked into a door.'

Wycliffe was trying to make up his mind about Cathy Carne. A good business woman, intelligent, unmarried . . . But there was nothing of the old maid about her. Her figure, her posture, her attitude to him as a man, all suggested sexual awareness but she had a waspish tongue.

'You live near here?'

'A flat over the printing works. The foreman used to live there until he got married and needed a bigger place, then Uncle let me have it.'

'You live alone?'

A thin smile. 'Of course.'

'From your flat I suppose you can see the back of Benson's where Francis was killed.'

35

'If I look out of the right window.'

'Did you look out of the right window last night?'

'I didn't see Francis or anything happening to him if that's what you're getting at. In any case it was dark well before ten.'

'You didn't come to work by the way of the wharf walk this morning?'

'I never do.'

'Isn't it the quickest way?'

'Marginally, perhaps, but I always come by the street and pick up uncle's paper from the newsagent on my way.' She pointed to *The Times*, still neatly folded on her desk, and smiled: 'I still do it – force of habit, I suppose.' She crushed out the dog-end of her cigarette and turned towards him, perfectly composed.

'If the business had been shut down and the premises sold, what would have happened to you?'

She grimaced. 'It's not a question of what would have happened if, it's what *will* happen. I shall be out of a job and out of a home. Beryl won't keep the shop on. I suppose I shall get something in the way of redundancy pay but it won't amount to much.'

Wycliffe changed the subject. 'Your uncle died of a stroke?'

'Actually it was coronary thrombosis; he collapsed in his studio.'

'Studio?'

'My uncle used to paint, his studio is next door to this.'

'And he died there?'

'I found him when I came back from lunch. It looked as though he had collapsed while painting.' For the first time she showed emotion.

'Had he been ill?'

'He had high blood pressure and he suffered from

36

angina. It was made worse because he wouldn't do what the doctor told him. He was obstinate.'

'You were fond of him?'

She nodded.

'Presumably the doctor was satisfied that he died as a result of his illness?'

She looked at him oddly. 'Of course! The doctor issued a certificate which gave coronary thrombosis as the cause of death.'

'I'm sorry, but one has to ask these questions. Anyway, thank you for your help. Just one more thing: I would like a list of customers regularly visited by your cousin. Could you have it ready by this afternoon?'

She looked surprised but she agreed.

'Thank you. Now, perhaps, you will ask Miss Garland if she will see me.'

Miss Garland would.

The stairs and landing, lit by a murky skylight, were rarely cleaned, in sharp contrast with the office and shop. Beryl Garland was waiting for him on the landing, a lean, bony woman with uncared-for greying hair, a pallid complexion blotched with an unnatural pink, and restless suspicious eyes.

'Come into the living-room.'

The living-room had once been almost elegant: high, with a deep frieze, plaster cornice, and an elaborate ceiling rose, reminders of a time when even prosperous merchants lived over their shops. The window faced north across the harbour and the water, sparkling in the sunshine, made the room itself seem dark. The furniture was genteely shabby and not very clean. A black and white rough-haired terrier was asleep on the hearth rug.

'My friend, Miss Bond, Superintendent.'

Miss Bond, who was standing when he entered the

room, was the perfect complement to Beryl, plump instead of lean, dainty instead of gaunt, amiable instead of forbidding.

'We've known each other most of our lives and we were at school together, so we've no secrets.'

It dawned on Wycliffe that the room was smelling strongly of whisky, and that Miss Bond had probably hidden bottle and glasses while he was being received on the landing.

He was directed to a leather armchair by the empty fireplace while the two women seated themselves on dining chairs at the table. Their movements were deliberate and careful and Wycliffe had the impression of figures in slow motion, indeed of a whole existence that proceeded at a slower pace, muted, subdued, and infinitely depressing.

He expressed sympathy and it was received with complacency. 'My two closest relatives inside four days. Father died on Saturday of a coronary. Of course he's not been well for some time and he didn't take care of himself.' She lowered her voice. 'Blood pressure.' After a pause she went on: 'And angina; he was a difficult man! Wasn't he, Celia?'

Miss Bond shifted her position slightly and smiled but did not reply.

'I've given my life to looking after my father and my brother. I was thirty when mother died . . . Nobody can say I haven't done my duty.'

He led her to speak of her brother: 'I understand there is a daughter.'

'Ah! So they've told you that already. Francis was a young man when that happened and I can't see what it's got to do with this.'

'I believe the girl lives locally and that she has kept in touch with her father.'

'For what she could get! She and that boy were at the funeral yesterday. You never saw anything like it – the way they were dressed; and their hair! A disgrace! wasn't it, Celia?'

Miss Bond said: 'You know I wasn't there, dear.'

'No, well it was . . . At a funeral – it was an insult!'

For Beryl Garland the whole of reality was contained within the narrow horizons of her direct experience and her judgements were absolute.

'When was the last time you saw your brother, Miss Garland?'

'Yesterday evening at about nine o'clock. He was working in his room and I went in to tell him that I was going to spend the night with Miss Bond – I was upset, you understand. I came back at about eight this morning in time to get his breakfast and found the dog outside the back door, whining.'

'Has your brother seemed worried or nervous lately? Have you noticed any change in him?'

She shook her head with decision. 'No.'

'And last night when you spoke to him he was just as usual?'

'Just as usual, Superintendent.' She placed a bony hand firmly on the table top and fixed Wycliffe with her grey eyes. 'Francis was killed by hooligans. There's been a lot of that sort of thing in the town lately, and the police . . .' She decided not to finish that sentence.

Wycliffe said: 'But nothing was taken; his wallet, his money, his keys —'

She cut him short. 'Because the dog would have started to bark and frighten the ruffians off. That's what happened.' She turned to her friend. 'Miss Bond agrees with me, don't you Celia?'

Miss Bond nodded. 'It's true that there have been

39

several unpleasant incidents, mostly with young drunks.'

It was odd; Beryl's determination to convince him that her brother had been the victim of a random attack.

He was learning something of the dead man's background, admittedly from a biased witness, but any policeman knows that all witnesses are biased in some degree. He wanted to get the feel of the place, to find out what it was like to be Francis Garland, living with his father and sister in these rooms over the shop.

Beryl caught him looking at a painting hanging above the mantelpiece, a portrait of a middle-aged woman of exceptional beauty. 'My mother, just before she died at the age of fifty.' After a pause, she added in a church whisper: 'It was a growth – very quick.' She went on: 'Gifford Tate painted that. He was a great friend of my father's. Before Gifford had his stroke they used to go painting together all over the place. He's famous now, his pictures fetch thousands.'

Beryl having said her piece, silence took possession of the room; the two women sat, staring in front of them, scarcely moving a muscle. A trapped fly buzzed intermittently against the window panes and on the other side of the window the life of the harbour went on its unhurried way. The sounds from the street were muted.

Wycliffe, in the big black leather armchair by the empty grate, wondered if he was sitting in the old man's chair. Had Edwin spent idle hours in this room while his daughter made a great parade of doing the housework and kept up a running vituperative commentary on the last person or event to incur her displeasure? Or had he got the old man all wrong? He realised that he knew even less about the father than the son. He realised too that he needed to know about both. Father and son had died within a few days of each other . . .

Beryl broke the silence. 'I have to see father's lawyer this afteroon about the will. Of course Francis should have been there as well.' She looked down at her hands, resting on the table. 'I don't think Francis ever made a will so I suppose his share will come to me.' She shifted uneasily on her chair then, with a quick glance at Wycliffe: 'Is that right?'

'You will have to ask the solicitor about that, Miss Garland.'

'But you're a policeman; you must have some idea of the law. Celia thinks they'll say his illegitimate daughter is next-of-kin. That would be wicked! I mean, she's never done a hand's turn for her father or her grandfather —'

Miss Bond intervened. 'I really don't think the superintendent can help you, dear. You'll have to wait until you see Mr Shrimpton.'

Wycliffe said: 'Is he your father's solicitor?'

'Arthur Shrimpton, yes. The Shrimptons have looked after our affairs ever since my great grandfather started the business in 1900. In those days they lived next door but now they've only got their offices there. Over the bank.'

'Mr Shrimpton also acted for your brother?'

She looked at him in mild surprise at the question. 'Of course!'

Wycliffe said: 'I should like to see your brother's room, Miss Garland.'

'His room? What for?'

'In the circumstances the police need to know everything possible about your brother. It is one of the

41

ways in which we can hope to find out why he was killed.'

'I've told you why he was killed.'

Wycliffe's bland stare decided the issue. She got up from her chair. 'You'd better come with me.'

He followed her across the landing where she opened one of three doors. 'There you are!' Despite her pique about his refusal to discuss the will, she took a certain pride in showing him her brother's room. 'All these books . . . and a computer. Francis spent a lot of time in here studying. All about numbers.'

'Was he a mathematician?'

'Oh, no. He worked on numbers because he thought they controlled people's lives. More like astrology I think it was.'

Wycliffe walked over to the bookshelves. The books fell into two roughly equal groups: occult studies and lives of famous and infamous men and women through history. The occult section was dominated by works on numerology. He glanced over the titles: Gibson's *Science of Numerology*, Cheiro's *Book of Numbers*, Driver's *Sacred Numbers and Round Figures*, and perhaps 40 others. A good collection of scholarly nonsense.

He turned to the desk where there were several index cards in a little pile. Beryl was watching him with suspicious eyes. The cards were all concerned with Frederick the Great; the first, a sort of curriculum vitae, the others dealing with aspects of his character and the principal events in his life. Each entry was marked with a series of numbers. A nest of metal drawers contained several hundreds of such cards in which the lives of other distinguised men and women had been similarly dissected.

She asked: 'Do you understand it?'

'No.'

Beryl was smug. 'I didn't think you would.'

Wycliffe said: 'Did your brother go out much, apart from the travelling he did for the firm?'

'He took the dog for a walk every night.'

'Apart from that.'

'Apart from that he went out every Sunday after breakfast and he usually came back late. I've no idea where he went.'

'Presumably he had friends?'

'If he did he didn't tell me about them.'

'Didn't people come to see him, or telephone?'

'He sometimes had telephone calls but who from or what about I don't know. I don't listen at doors.' She added after a moment: 'I do know he wasn't liked; even as a boy he had no friends.' She said this with relish.

'Do you know if he had any contact with his relatives?'

She turned on him: 'Relatives?'

'I understand that you have an uncle and a cousin who live near the docks.'

'We don't acknowledge them!' Her contempt was regal. 'I'm sure he never went near them.'

'Just one more question: did your father or your brother own a gun of any sort?'

'A gun? Certainly not!'

'To your knowledge there has never been a gun in this house?'

'Never!'

He moved towards the door. 'I'm afraid we shall have to keep this room locked for a day or two.'

'*Locked*?'

'Until we've had a chance to go through his papers. It's quite usual; we shall try to cause as little trouble as possible.'

'It seems to me that it is we who are being treated like criminals but I don't suppose I have any choice.'

A final glance around the room, the books, the charts, the computer, the filing system . . . He had the impression of something out of key – not exactly false, but contrived. As though the setting was more important than the work.

He locked the door and slipped the key into his pocket. 'I assure you that we will add to your distress as little as possible, but we shall be here from time to time and you will also be asked to make a formal statement.' Impossible not to be pompous with this damned woman!

She looked at him with silent aggression and he left it at that. There were many questions he wanted to ask her but he needed ammunition.

She stood on the landing, watching him as he went down the stairs and out by the side door. He wondered if he would find anyone to grieve for either father or son.

As he passed the bank next door he noticed that it too had a side passage, but this one was decked out with tiles and had painted walls. A brass plate on the door, worn but shining, read: 'Shrimpton and Nicholls: Solicitors and Commissioners for Oaths.'

The street was slightly less congested, the time for unloading had passed and the lorries were gone. People ambled along, indulging in the local pastime of frustrating car drivers who had the temerity to attempt a breakthrough. Cars, of course, could and should have been excluded but that would have spoiled the fun.

Wycliffe had other preoccupations. A man of seventy-five dies of a heart condition and inside four days his son is shot dead. An actuary, assuming no casual connection, might calculate the odds against such a coincidence. Wycliffe thought they would be pretty high, so probability favoured a link. The most obvious one would be the will, but murder by advantaged legatees is a risky business. *Cui bono*? has a too obvious answer. All the same . . .

On the wharf activity was dying down. The body had been removed to the mortuary where Dr Franks would carry out the post mortem. A batch of film had gone for processing along with footprint casts and soil samples believed to be contaminated with blood or other tissue. Fox had found a bullet bedded in the ground and a cartridge case to go with it. It seemed that Francis had been shot with a self-loading pistol. a .32. They would know more when they had the report from Ballistics.

Now, one man was examining the steel tubes and struts of the scaffolding, dusting the surfaces with aluminium powder and squinting at the result through a lens; another was on his knees scrutinising the staging planks in case some fibres from the killer's clothing had become caught in the rough grain of the wood. Real Sherlock Holmes stuff! In reality, slow, monotonous, painstaking work which would almost certainly prove unrewarding.

'Check the register for licensed hand-guns of medium calibre.'

The headquarters team had arrived. Detective Inspector Kersey got out of one of the cars and came towards him. 'We're all here, sir. Lucy Lane is at the local nick taking over the paper work. Shaw is negotiating for that hen house over there.' Kersey pointed to a large portable building adjacent to the carpark. 'It seems a firm of accountants hired it as temporary accommodation while their offices were being refurbished and it's due to be removed. It would suit us better than one of our own mobile sardine cans.'

Kersey and Wycliffe had worked together for several years and their temperaments complemented each other. To Wycliffe's austere, almost puritanical approach, Kersey opposed an earthy realism and both were sufficiently tolerant to make the combination work.

'So, where do we go from here?'

'I'm going to take a look at the Garland printing works but I'll pick you up here in about half-an-hour and we'll go to lunch.'

Wycliffe had to make his way past a small crowd of would-be sightseers held well back by a uniformed policeman. A few yards off-shore several small craft provided others with vantage points but, as a spectacle, a scene of crime study ranks about level with a hole in the ground.

The printing works was a fairly modern concrete building with all the external charm of an army blockhouse, but the receptionist in the outer office was briskly efficient.

'I'll see if Mr Treloar is free.'

A brief exchange on the house telephone, a short delay, then Treloar joined them. A middle aged man in a grey overall, bald, very thin, with a conspicuous adam's apple; he walked with a limp. His manner was that of a man resigned to repeated interruptions: 'I suppose this is about Mr Francis; you'd better come into the office.'

The foreman's office was partitioned off from the shop floor and from it one could see the men at work on the machines – five or six of them – but part of the floor was screened off by large canvas sheets suspended from the roof trusses.

Treloar waved a despairing hand. 'It's chaos! We're having new photo typesetting equipment put in . . . A fine time for all this!'

46

His table was set out with batches of proof sheets clipped together, the ashtray was full of stubs, and there was a cup half full of coffee which looked as though it had gone cold hours before.

He drew up a chair for Wycliffe and sat down himself. 'I don't understand economics, Superintendent: why is it that in a country with three million on the dole some of us don't have time to breathe? Something wrong somewhere! Now, sir, how can I help you?'

Wycliffe said: 'Obviously you've heard about Francis Garland – how did you hear, by the way?'

'Cathy Carne rang me – sometime after nine.'

'The news came as a shock?'

Treloar brought out a packet of cigarettes, offered them to Wycliffe, then lit up himself. 'Not a shock exactly, a surprise, certainly.'

Obviously a man who chose his words with care.

'As far as you know did he have any enemies?'

'As far as I know he didn't have enemies or friends either, but I didn't know him very well.'

'You worked with him.'

A slow smile. 'You could say that. He spent three days a week here, more or less. I don't want to speak ill of the dead but as far as the work was concerned I have to say that he won't be missed.'

'What exactly did he do?'

'He saw commercial reps and talked to customers but he always called me in before he put in an order or gave an estimate.'

'So he knew his limitations.'

Treloar trickled smoke from between his lips. 'His father pointed them out to him often enough and he knew that things would drop on him from a great height if he put a foot wrong.'

'Edwin took an active part in the management here?'

A steady look from the grey eyes. 'He was the brains. I ran the place day to day, he decided policy. As long as you remembered that, everything was fine.'

'He came here often?'

'Every morning at half-past ten he would walk in through that door. He'd spend half-an-hour with me and another going round the machines, talking to the men. Apart from that he would be in touch by telephone.'

'You liked him?'

Hesitation. 'I admired him; he was a clever man and he was as good as his word. As to liking, I always had the feeling – I can't quite express it – the feeling that in his eyes I was all right – useful in fact, but that I didn't matter in myself. He had a way of looking at people as though they amused him, just like you might look at the antics of white mice in a cage. Sounds ridiculous, doesn't it?'

'Not to me.'

Treloar smoked for a while in silence, then he said: 'I suppose that was the man's nature but I've wondered sometimes whether it was why Francis turned out so bloody useless . . . if he was made to feel like that from childhood – insignificant, a bit of a joke.'

'What will happen now? Are you worried?'

Treloar pouted. 'Beryl will sell. As to being worried – no. I'm good at my job and anybody who wants to run this place would have to recognise the fact. Not that I welcome change; I was very satisfied as things were but it was obvious they wouldn't go on indefinitely.'

They chatted for a few minutes but Treloar had nothing more to say. One of his men was waiting to see him, there was a telephone call, a customer was asking for him, and the receptionist was getting agitated.

Wycliffe said: 'Just one more thing then I'll leave you to it. I understand Cathy Carne lives above this?'

'She has a flat up there but most of that floor is a store-room.'

'Surely she doesn't have to come through this lot to go to her flat?'

'Hardly! The flat is self-contained and there's an outside staircase on the other side of the building.'

Wycliffe thanked him and left. Outside he walked round the building. In the end facing the harbour steel doors stood open and he could see men at work inside, installing the new machines. The entrance to Cathy Carne's flat was around the corner – a wooden stairacse, well maintained, with a canopied landing at the top. He climbed the stairs but could see nothing through the hammered glass panels of the front door. The flat was at the quay end of the premises and from its windows there would be splendid views of the harbour, the waterfront, and the docks. It seemed that Cathy had a lot to lose through her uncle's death.

Brooding, Wycliffe walked back along the wharf to join Kersey in search of lunch.

Cathy Carne stood in the middle of the shop. It was a quiet time and Alice was re-stocking the shelves. Cathy stared into vacancy, seeing nothing. She was trying to grasp the radically changed situation with which she must come to terms. Edwin dead, Francis dead, and in such a short space of time. Four days ago in a similar quiet period she had been gossiping with her uncle, listening to his barbed comments on affairs, on the art world, and on his family. Now she was perplexed and afraid; perplexed because she did not understand what had happened, and afraid of what it might mean if she did.

She realised with a slight shock that she was staring straight at a man who was looking in through the shop window, staring back. It was Mark Garland of the excluded Garlands. She lifted a hand in acknowledgement, and this was all the encouragement he needed to come in.

Mark Garland was slight of build, very fair, good looking in a feminine way. He wore spectacles with thin gold rims which seemed to stress his femininity. Cathy had the impression that he was struggling to control extreme nervousness and his approach was absurdly tentative.

'I wondered whether to risk coming in or not. I didn't know what sort of reception I should get.'

Cathy was brusquely reassuring. 'There's no quarrel between us. Why should there be?'

'No, of course not! It's all very distressing. I'm very upset about Francis . . . more upset than I can say.'

Cathy waited for him to enlarge. He intrigued her, he was such a rabbit, yet Edwin had told her that he was subject to outbursts of violent temper.

'I wonder if you think I could have a word with Beryl? I would very much like to.' Another weak little smile. 'We haven't spoken since I was a child, Beryl and I. Absurd, isn't it?'

'There's no harm in trying; she won't eat you.'

'No . . . How should I go about it?'

'I'll call her if you like – or would you rather go up?'

He hesitated, looking round the shop as though it might help him to a decision. 'No, I'd rather you called her if you don't mind.'

Cathy went into the little hall and called up the stairs.

Beryl's voice answered. 'What is it?'

'Mark Garland is here and he would like a word with you.'

50

'Well, I don't want a word with him. Nothing has changed; he needn't think it has; I don't want to hear or see anything of him or his father – ever. You can tell him that!' A door slammed upstairs.

Cathy returned to the shop. 'You heard? Sorry!'

He nodded, resigned. 'It's a pity . . . I was hoping to explain . . .' He went out of the shop, head bent, shoulders drooping.

Miss Bond had gone out to buy something simple for their lunch. 'A few sandwiches from Marks and Spencer, dear – but nothing with salmon. You know I daren't touch salmon.'

Beryl was restless and apprehensive, trying hard to find firm ground, and Mark Garland turning up like that had upset her. The gall of these people! Her feeling of insecurity had started some time before her father's death with a suspicion, soon amounting to certainty, that something was going on behind her back. It was mainly due to a subtle change in Francis. She had denied anything of the kind to the police but it was real enough. She knew him and his little moods so well: he had become more aggressive, more overtly secretive – and smug. When he was young he would say: 'I know something you don't!' Not so blatant now, but it meant the same.

And there was his behaviour since their father's death: odd little things she had scarcely noticed at the time but now they began to acquire significance in her mind. She glanced at the clock: five minutes to one. Soon Cathy Carne would be shutting shop to go to lunch. Beryl went downstairs and into the shop. Cathy was in the office.

'Anything I can do, Beryl?'

'No, I just wanted the key to father's studio.'

'But I haven't got it. If you remember, yesterday afternoon, after the funeral, Francis asked me to lock the studio and bring him the key. I did, and he put it on his ring.'

'Isn't there a spare?'

'Not as far as I know. Uncle always kept the studio locked and carried the key about with him.'

To this point Beryl's manner had been almost peremptory, now she became more relaxed and confiding. 'There's something I want to ask you, Cathy. When you came upstairs to say father had collapsed, didn't you think it was very odd, the way Francis rushed down without a word?'

Cathy was cautious. 'No, it didn't strike me like that. I thought he wanted to see if he could help his father, but it was too late.'

Beryl persisted. 'And when we came down together, after you'd telephoned Alan . . . You remember?'

There was a brief pause before Cathy replied. 'Yes, I remember. What about it?'

'You looked very puzzled about something. I saw you staring at Francis; I couldn't make it out.'

Cathy was dismissive. 'I don't know how I looked but I was shocked. We all were.'

Beryl lingered, her grey eyes fixed on Cathy for some time, then she said: 'I see. Well, you'll be wanting to go to your lunch. You'll be at Shrimpton's this afternoon?'

'Yes.'

'I suppose Alice is capable of looking after the shop?'

The first time Beryl had shown the slightest concern for the business. A straw in the wind?

Anna was in the kitchen preparing vegetables, and from where she stood at the sink she could look across the water to Falmouth, a few hundred yards away: the

52

Greenbank Hotel, the Royal Yacht Club, the new flats on the Packet Quays, then the backs of High Street and the pier. The narrow strip of water between was dotted with small craft of every description, all facing upstream. The sun shone and everywhere there was stillness. Life seemed suspended and she had a disquieting sense of being quite alone. She switched on the radio to recover normality.

Her grandfather's death had affected her more than she would have thought possible. She had heard the news with regret, with sadness, but hardly with grief. After all, old men die. A month ago he had come to see her and now she understood for the first time that what he had said to her then would change her life. At the funeral (she had never been to a funeral before) it had come to her quite suddenly that something was ending in herself, that she was being challenged to take hold of her life, to make decisions, and she had quarrelled with Terry because of it.

The front door opened then slammed. Her mother had been to Falmouth shopping. She was back early. She burst into the kitchen, two shopping bags in one hand and one in the other.

'You're early.'

Freda dropped her bags and slumped on a chair. She was flushed and breathing hard. 'I got the first ferry I could after I heard . . . Shut that damn thing off, Anna!'

Anna switched off the radio.

In the silence she could hear her mother wheezing as she breathed. Freda was grossly overweight. An elaborately floral dress exposed great volumes of lobster-coloured flesh.

'What did you hear?' Anna was accustomed to her mother's histrionics.

'It's about your father.'

'What about him?'

'He's dead, Anna – murdered.'

Anna stood motionless, potato in one hand, knife in the other. There was nothing she could say, nothing she could think because she felt nothing. Only in her mind's eye she saw the image of her father, rather big, fleshy, with bulging expressionless eyes.

'The police are all over the place. I thought they might have got here before I did.'

Anna said nothing.

'He was shot last night when he was taking the dog for a walk.'

'Shot? On the wharf?'

'Yes.'

'Do they know who did it?'

'How should I know?'

Anna picked up the saucepan into which she had been putting potatoes and transferred it to the stove. Her mother watched her.

'In some ways you're just like your father, Anna. You never *feel* anything. You're cold inside!' Freda started to unpack her shopping. At one of the cupboards, with her back to the room she said: 'Terry didn't come home last night.'

Anna said nothing.

'Have you seen him this morning?'

'No.'

'What happened?'

'We had a row.'

'What about?'

'Nothing – everything. I was fed up.'

'Where would he sleep?'

'In the van, I suppose. He's done it often enough before.'

She was thinking of the periodic visits she had made to her father; they were all the same; their conversations could have been scripted:

'How is your mother?'

'All right.'

'And you?'

'I'm all right.'

'Good!' Then when the silence became uncomfortable he would reach into his pocket for his wallet. 'There, now! Buy yourself something.' He thought it was what she had come for. Perhaps he was right . . . Yet there must have been something more. Now he was dead.

Anna started to slice up runner beans. Freda said: 'You'll still go to the lawyer's this afternoon?'

'I suppose so.'

'Your grandfather thought a lot of you. He remembered you every Christmas and birthday . . . He must have left you something and you might as well know what.'

There was a knock at the front door. Freda said: 'There they are! The police.'

CHAPTER THREE

Wycliffe was watching two men in a rowing boat. One rowed while the other held a rope over the stern. They would row about fifty yards in one direction, then turn round and row back, seemingly over the same ground. What were they doing? Were they trawling for something? A lost moorings, perhaps? That was the trouble with harbour-watching, there were so many inexplicable activities carried on at a stately pace and with the deliberation of a choreographed performance.

The team had acquired the use of the large Portakabin recently occupied by a firm of accountants while their offices were being refurbished. Although all fittings and furniture had been removed it was Ritzy accommodation compared to a mobile incident van or the decayed huts and barn-like halls to which they were accustomed. There was even a screened-off cubicle which could be used as an interview room. More to the point, it was next door to the car-park and overlooked the harbour within two hundred yards of the Garlands' shop. A pantechnicon from central stores had delivered the official ration of battered furniture and a communications unit with office equipment, stationery and the basic materials for preparing police tea. A large-scale map was pinned to one wall and there was a blackboard for briefings.

By mid-afternoon they were in business.

Uniformed men and Wycliffe's detective constables

were questioning the very few people who actually lived in the street. Publicans whose premises backed on the harbour were interviewed and, over local radio, people were being asked to come forward if they had been in the neighbourhood the night before, especially those who had used the car-park. It was quite possible that the killer had come and gone by car. On the assumption that he or she might not have carried the murder weapon away Wycliffe had ordered a search of the foreshore, and a police frogman was floundering about in the shallow off-shore waters like a porpoise on the point of stranding.

'The dead man spent two days a week travelling for the firm, taking orders and delivering goods. I will let you have a list of his customers and I want them contacted, in the first instance by telephone. Find out when he last called and try to get an impression of what they thought of him. Get them to talk, and if there is a hint of anything unusual report to me.' Kersey, briefing his troops.

'We also want to know exactly how Garland spent his time from Saturday afternoon when his father died to last night when somebody shot him on the wharf. I shall draw up a timetable, hour by hour, and allowing for the fact that he must have slept, I expect to see the spaces filled in.

'The shot that killed Garland was fired at a few minutes past ten. Most of the people who were in the street at that time would have been in one or other of the pubs, but don't forget that the harbour is full of craft of all sorts and there are sure to have been people aboard some of them.'

Wycliffe dealt with the media. Interest was minimal; the fatal shooting of a small-town shopkeeper wouldn't make much of a splash, the ripples would scarcely extend to the National dailies.

Wycliffe's table was placed against the row of windows at one end of the temporary building. He had the pathologist's preliminary report which had been dictated over the telephone. 'A single wound of entry situated in the right parietal bone just anterior to the lambdoid suture and close to the saggital suture. The nature of the wound suggests a bullet of medium calibre fired at close range, under 60 centimetres. The bullet traversed the skull and was deflected in its passage to emerge on the left side, shattering bones in the area of articulation of the lower jaw.

'This would be consistent with the victim having been shot from above and slightly behind. Death must have been instantaneous.

'The facial bruising was caused 24-36 hours before death and is typical of injury brought about by a blow from a human fist.'

Already officers were returning from enquiries with completed interview-forms and Lucy Lane was going through them as they came in. Kersey was briefing himself from the paperwork so far.

Detective Sergeant Lucy Lane was still well under thirty. A good school record; university. Then what? Something constructive – working with people. But having no wish, as Virginia Woolf put it, 'to dabble her fingers self-approvingly in the stuff of other souls' and believing in the stick and carrot philosophy of human conduct, she joined the police. Oddly, her outlook was more authoritarian than her chief's. After thirty years in the force Wycliffe still held fast to a lingering hope that man may yet prove perfectable; woman too. Lucy, probably influenced by her parson father, was more inclined to a belief in original sin.

'Look at this, sir.' She passed over two reports with items marked in red.

58

The first concerned the landlord's wife at the Packet Inn. At about ten-fifteen the previous evening she had heard a 'crack' followed by a dog barking – yapping, she said. It had gone on for some time, she couldn't say how long. She was busy serving and really didn't think much about it.

The other report was from the DC who had called on Garland's daughter, Anna, and her mother. They had already heard the news and seemed to take it calmly. The officer had not seen the girl's boyfriend and was told that they did not know where he was.

'So?' Wycliffe returned the sheets.

'Just that Sergeant Shaw checked with Records. This young man, Terrence John Gill, has a conviction. Two years ago he was convicted of causing a breach of the peace at St Mawgan airfield during a CND demo.'

'What happened in court?'

'He was bound over.'

'I don't suppose that makes him a potential killer but we need to find him. Put somebody on to it.'

He thought of Beryl and the need to come to grips with the Garland set-up as it had been before the old man's death. Beryl needed firm handling but losing father and brother inside four days must mean something more than the prospect of a secure income. Lucy Lane with her stick and carrot philosophy might be the best one to deal with her.

'I want you to talk to Beryl Garland. We want background. We also want her formal statement. Take a DC with you and get started on turning over Francis's room. On second thoughts, take Shaw and see what he can make of that computer thing.'

Wycliffe had little patience with and no interest in technological gadgetry. He believed that the human capacity for moral, social, and political adaptation had been stretched to its limit in the first century of the Industrial Revolution and fatally outstripped since.

'Will we be looking for anything in particular, sir?'

'Use your imagination. Whatever Beryl believes or pretends to believe about her brother being mugged, he was in fact deliberately murdered by someone lying in wait for him on the scaffolding. There must have been an involvement in something sufficiently profitable or menacing or both to lead somebody to murder. I've got an appointment with Shrimpton, the lawyer, at four and I shall look in at the shop afterwards.'

He arrived on time for his appointment and he was not kept waiting; the receptionist introduced him at once.

Shrimpton was in the mid-forties, overweight, and slightly larger than life, a sociable type. His skin was bronzed, his thinning hair was bleached by sun and sea, and Wycliffe felt sure that he spent as little time as possible away from boats, the sea, and the club bar. Of course his office overlooked the harbour and was hung with enlarged photographs of yachts and of sailing occasions.

'Smoke? . . . I will if you don't mind.' He lit a small cigar. 'I know why you're here and I might tell you I've had one hell of an afternoon.' He blew out a cloud of smoke. 'I suppose you know our Beryl?'

'I've spoken to her briefly.'

'Then you know her. Edwin was a crafty old so-and-so and he didn't like his children very much – not that I blame him – so I thought I'd better get the beneficiaries together and explain. We had a date for this afternoon but when I heard about Francis it seemed the decent thing to postpone the arrangement. I rang Beryl with condolences and the suggestion that we should meet

60

later in the week. Not on your life! You'd think I was proposing to give away her share to a cats' home. So we went ahead as planned: Beryl, Cathy Carne – you've met Cathy? Great girl! Anna – Francis's side-kick – Alan Tate and Mike Treloar, the foreman at the printing works. Of course Francis should have been with us.'

Wycliffe said: 'Alan Tate?'

'Gifford Tate's son. Gifford and old Edwin were life-long buddies. Alan is a doctor and he lives with his stepmother in the family house – up the hill towards Wood Lane.'

'And Alan Tate is a beneficiary under the will?'

'In a small way.' He broke off, staring out of the window. 'See that?'

A heavily built boat, painted slate-blue, cutter rigged, was gliding downstream. 'That's one of the Falmouth Quay Punts. She's at least eighty years old, of course she's been restored. Before the days of radio, boats like her would race down-channel as far as the Lizard to get first contact for the ship-to-shore trade from vessels making port. Wonderful craft! I envy old Podgy Hicks that boat.

'But perhaps you're not addicted.' Reluctantly he brought his attention back to business. 'Yes, well, Edwin's testament.' He glanced at the document in front of him. 'The will was made about a year ago and this is what it amounts to: "The shop premises and stock and all assets pertaining to the business together with the contents of my studio excepting only my tube of Winsor blue to my niece and dear friend Cathy Carne".'

Shrimpton looked up. 'You can imagine how that ruffled Beryl's feathers! For a moment I thought she was going the same way as her father. Then, £10,000 to

Anna, £5,000 to Mike Treloar, and £1,000 to Alan Tate – "the son of my friend Gifford Tate together with my tube of Winsor blue" —'

'What's all this about Winsor blue? It sounds like a butterfly.'

Shrimpton grinned. 'One of the old man's little jokes. Typical! As I said, Gifford Tate and he were buddies, and it was some argument they had about colours. Winsor blue is a colour used by painters. Of course old man Tate died years ago.

'There's another legacy of £1,000, this time to his friend Martin Burger, "more than enough for that new pair of spectacles which I hope may improve his judgement and help him to see the obvious." Burger wasn't here this afternoon; he's a bit doddery on his legs and doesn't get about much.

'Anyway, the printing works and the business associated with it together with the residue of the estate after discharge of all debts and liabilities are left jointly to Beryl and Francis. That's it.'

'Is the residue going to amount to much?'

'I wouldn't mind it coming my way. Edwin owned the freehold of another property in the street, let on a fat lease, there is more property on the sea-front, and a nice carefully nurtured portfolio of equities. The Garlands have been in this game for eighty years – accumulating, not spending. Edwin liked to pretend that the art business and the printing were his livelihood, in fact they probably represent less than half his assets.'

'Isn't it a bit odd to leave property to joint heirs with no conditions laid down for its distribution?'

Shrimpton nodded. 'I tried to persuade him out of it but he wouldn't budge. A recipe for in-fighting that's what it is, and that's what the old devil intended, although he wouldn't admit it. I think he saw himself, sitting up there, watching the fun. Of course now it's going to be a damn sight funnier than even he imagined.'

'How come? With Francis out of the way —'

Shrimpton tapped ash off his cigar. 'With Francis out of the way Beryl will have to come to terms with his heir and to the best of my belief Francis never made a will. He meant to. He was in this office a fortnight ago saying that it was about time as his father was getting on and one never knew, et cetera et cetera . . . He promised to bring me a few notes from which I could prepare a draft but he never did.'

'So?'

'You know the answer to that, and so does Beryl now, though I wrapped it up a bit to save her having a fit on the spot. Young Anna is going to be well heeled but she will have to come to some arrangement with Beryl and Beryl would prefer, much, to deal with the devil himself. If the old man really is up there watching he's in for some good laughs.'

'What was Anna's reaction?'

Shrimpton grimaced. 'Hard to tell. I half thought the implications of Francis's death hadn't got through to her, but that girl doesn't give much away.'

'How did Cathy Carne receive her bit of glad news? Do you think it was a complete surprise?'

Shrimpton was emphatic. 'I'm certain! I've never seen anyone so astonished unless it was dear Beryl. I can't imagine what Francis's reaction would have been. I can't help being thankful I didn't have to cope with it. Incidentally, the old man wrote Cathy a letter which I was charged to pass over unopened. And one other thing you should know for the record: Jimmy Rowe, the old man's accountant, and I are joint executors, God help us!'

Wycliffe was grateful and said so. 'Now I'm going to ask you to be indiscreet. If Francis had made a will have you any idea how it would have gone?'

Shrimpton threw away the stub of his cigar. 'You are asking me to be clairvoyant as well as indiscreet. Francis told me nothing of his intentions so I can only guess.'

'And?'

A broad grin. 'You know nothing of any woman in his life?'

'Nothing. Was there one?'

'I'm not sure, but from things he let drop from time to time I think there probably was. Once or twice lately he's mentioned the possibility that he might "change his way of life" which could mean that he intended to get married, but with Francis it could equally mean that he was thinking of taking up golf or ludo.'

'I gather you were not fond of him.'

'I was not. I went to school with Francis and he was always odd man out. He wasn't very bright and he was more than a bit of a bore with it.'

'A couple of adjectives to describe him?'

Shrimpton laughed outright. 'You're a bloody old copper, I must say! Well, it can't do him any harm where he's gone. Two adjectives . . . devious is one, he was certainly that; and I'm afraid the other would have to be spiteful. You can add secretive for good measure though he hadn't much to be secretive about.'

'Somebody killed him.'

'Yes, and I must admit that surprises me. Francis could have been involved in something a bit shady but nothing that would have brought him within range of any violence. He was a timid soul.'

'One more question, then I won't bother you any

more. Can you tell me about the Garland relatives – Thomas's side of the family?'

'Not a lot. Thomas was a younger son and it seems he had no interest in the business; he went to university and became a teacher. At some stage he came back to Cornwall and taught. His son, Mark, trained as an osteopath or something and set up in practice here. Thomas's wife died and he and Mark continued to live in the family house down by the railway station.

'The trouble began when grandather Garland died about thirty years ago – in my father's time – and left almost everything to Edwin. Thomas felt hard done by, contested the will and lost. I don't think the two sides of the family have had anything to do with each other since.'

They parted on the best of terms. Shrimpton came with him to the top of the stairs. 'If you fancy a bit of sailing while you're here you know where to come.'

Wycliffe was anxious to talk to Cathy Carne again. Since his meeting with her that morning she had learned that she would become the owner of the business and premises. If the news was really unexpected she would be off balance and it is at such times that people are most likely to speak the truth.

As he entered the shop the young girl assistant came forward; she recognised him at once. 'Miss Carne is in the office.'

He went through and tapped on the office door.

A listless 'Come in!'

He found her sitting at the desk which was quite clear. 'Oh, it's you. I let your inspector have the list of Francis's customers you asked for.' She drummed on the desk with her fingers. 'I suppose you've heard?'

'I've just left Shrimpton. Was it totally unexpected?'

She turned on him irritably. 'Of course it was unexpected! What the hell do you think? I'd hoped for a little money, at the very most, a thousand. I can't take it in. I should be over the moon; instead . . .'

'What about Beryl?'

She reached for her cigarettes. 'Yes. What about Beryl? You may well ask. She's moving in with Celia Bond at the end of the month – or so she says. I told her she's welcome to stay up there just as long as she wants and what she said wouldn't bear repeating. I feel guilty, though God knows why I should. I've put more into this place than she and her brother together; a damn sight more!' She lit a cigarette and smoked in short, angry puffs.

Wycliffe sat down without being invited. 'My people are upstairs talking to Beryl and going through Francis's room, looking for anything which might explain why he was murdered. In my own mind I can't separate his death from his father's.'

She looked at him sharply. 'You're not suggesting —'

'That your uncle was murdered? No, merely that there is some sort of connection. He died in his studio; did he spend much time there?'

'A great deal.'

'Doing what?'

'Well, for one thing he did all our framing and there's quite a lot of that, but he painted too.'

'Did he sell his pictures?'

'Oh, yes. A number were sold through the shop though he would never have them put on display; others went to shops and commercial galleries in this part of the world. Of course he never made a name for himself, like Gifford Tate, though Tate himself reckoned uncle was the better painter. They were great friends – there were three of them: Uncle, Gifford

66

Tate, and Papa Burger – I don't know why "papa" but they always called him that. He had money and was always a bit of a dilettante. They used to go off painting together at week-ends, often in Burger's boat, and they spent quite long holidays abroad. Of course Tate died seven or eight years ago. In his will he appointed Uncle Edwin as his art executor.

'Incidentally there's an exhibition of Tate's work starting in the town next week. After that it goes on tour: Plymouth, Cardiff, London, Newcastle and Glasgow. A big affair. Uncle was really responsible for getting it organised – sponsorship and so forth. He was really looking forward to that exhibition.'

'And Burger?'

'Oh, Papa is still living up at Wood Lane. Didn't Shrimpton tell you Uncle left him £1,000 to buy a pair of spectacles? A joke, of course. He's lost the use of his legs and doesn't get about much but Uncle went to see him two or three times a week.'

'What do you know about Winsor blue?'

She laughed, the tension suddenly released, and it occurred to Wycliffe that she was very attractive when she laughed. 'It's another joke they had, like Papa Burger and the spectacles. Winsor blue is a trade mark for an artists' colour which was first marketed sometime in the thirties. Gifford Tate started to use it as soon as it came out, he reckoned it brought him luck. Uncle used to tease him about it and it became a standing joke.'

'So leaving Alan Tate a tube of Winsor blue —'

'I suppose it was a way of wishing him luck.'

'Alan Tate is a doctor?'

'That's right. He was Uncle's doctor. Mine too, for that matter.'

'Did he issue the death certificate?'

'Of course!'

Wycliffe was impressed by her seemingly transparent honesty and by her spontaneity that had something refreshingly youthful about it. He could understand Edwin entrusting her with his business.

'I believe your uncle left a letter for you.'

'Yes.' The shutters came down.

'You've read it?'

'Yes; and destroyed it as he asked me to do.'

'You were in a hurry.'

'I did what I was asked to do.'

'Are you prepared to tell me what was in it?'

She hesitated. 'It gave me some advice about dealing with problems which might arise.'

'With the family?'

'Yes, and that is all I am prepared to say.'

'Just one more thing: what exactly was Francis doing with his books, his filing system and his computer?'

'I suppose the short answer would be, conning himself. In a burst of confidence one day he told me that he was working out a new system of numerology, developed from a study of people whose lives have been well documented. His father used to say that he was so desperately anxious to amount to something that he chose a subject about which critical people knew nothing and cared less.'

'Sounds a bit harsh.'

'Uncle didn't suffer fools gladly.'

Wycliffe stood up. 'Thanks for your help. I want a word with my people upstairs.'

As he was leaving the office he stopped by another door. 'The studio?'

'Yes, I'm afraid it's locked and Francis had the key.'

'It doesn't matter. I expect we shall come across it.'

He went upstairs. After the crisp freshness of the

68

shop, the flat had a musty stale smell. Edwin must have been struck by the contrast each time he climbed the stairs.

Lucy Lane and Shaw were at work in Francis's room which overlooked the street. The shops were closing and there was that burst of activity before things settled down to the evening calm. Lucy Lane was sitting at the desk, turning the pages of a loose-leaf manuscript file. She looked like a schoolgirl doing her homework. By contrast, Shaw, communing with the computer and making a new friend, looked like one of those whiz-kids who, from their glass and concrete towers, manipulate the world's money markets. It sometimes came as a slight shock to Wycliffe to have this paragon of the modern virtues working under his direction.

He said: 'Anything for me?'

Lucy Lane answered: 'He was writing a book on numerology. To me it's all gobbledegook, but here's the title.'

She held out the first page of the manuscript file for him to read. It was written in a careful script, meticulously spaced: 'A New System of Numerology by Francis Garland.' And there followed a paragraph in smaller script: 'Derived by the inductive method from studies of the lives of famous and infamous men and women, past and present, and including a new Universal Alphabet which disposes of the conflict between the "Hebrew" and the "Modern" systems.'

Wycliffe said: 'You need a dedication to a Noble Lord to go with that.'

Lucy Lane laughed. 'Quarto, with fine portrait vignette on title. Bound in contemporary calf . . .' She closed the file and put it aside. 'He also kept a diary of sorts though most of the entries don't tell you much.' She picked up a hard-covered exercise book. 'It looks as though he had a woman friend; he refers to her as "M". She's mentioned frequently but he never gives any clue as to who she is or the nature of their relationship.'

Wycliffe said: 'The lawyer thought there was a woman but he had no idea who she might be. We must try to find out. Anything else?'

'There's an earlier entry about his father.' She turned back through the pages. 'It's dated July 15th – just over a year ago – and he writes: "Today father told me something about himself which I can scarcely believe. It's incredible to think that it's been going on all these years! And when I asked him what would happen if it got known he just smiled and said I could talk if I wanted to. But why tell me? And why now?"'

'Dramatic! What do you make of it?'

Lucy Lane sucked the top of her ball-point. Meditative. 'A man of seventy-five, a widower, well off – what secrets would a man like that be likely to have? I mean, what would make him vulnerable? Unless he was keen on little boys or little girls. . . .'

'Talk to Beryl. She probably won't tell you anything but you may be able to judge whether she knows anything, and if she does, the sort of area we are in.'

He turned to Shaw who had not ceased his manipulations of the keyboard. 'And the oracle?'

Shaw said: 'It's difficult to work out his programme but it seems that he analysed his subjects and classified their attributes, their doings, and the major events in their lives by coded numbers. He used the computer to establish correlations. That's about as far as I've got.'

'Don't spend to much time on it unless it seems to have more relevanace to the case. Any correspondence?'

Lucy Lane said: 'There's a drawer full of letters all

jumbled together; we haven't got round to them yet.'

He decided to leave them to it, and as he came out on the landing he almost collided with Beryl who must have been eavesdropping. She was flushed, her eyes were moist and her hair was wild.

She attacked at once: 'I suppose she's told you that this is no longer my home so you think you can come and go as you please. Well, I shall move out when it suits me but I want you to know that the *contents* of these rooms are mine and I shall fight for them in Court if need be.'

Wycliffe felt sorry for her; self-centred and cantankerous as she was, she had suffered some shocks. 'I merely wanted a word with my people who are working on your brother's papers.'

Beryl made a derisive sound. 'That girl of yours asked me for a statement and I gave her one – more than she bargained for, and I made her take it all down.'

'I would like to ask you one or two more questions if I may.'

She was about to refuse but thought better of it. 'You'd better come in here.'

He followed her into the living-room but she did not ask him to sit down. 'Well?'

'In your brother's papers there is mention of something your father told him about a year ago which greatly surprised and puzzled him. From the context it is clear that the secret, whatever it was, was of long standing.'

He saw the change in her expression; antagonism replaced by . . . by fear? Was that too strong? At any rate she cut him short: 'Are you saying that my father had a shameful secret of some sort?'

'No, I am not; merely that there was something he

71

had previously kept to himself which he confided to your brother. I am wondering if you have any idea of what it could be?'

Beryl was staring at him, her lips were trembling and it was clear that she was deeply disturbed. In the end she said: 'This is all nonsense! Wicked nonsense! Francis was a fool!'

'So you know of nothing which your father might have confided to Francis which would greatly disturb him?'

'Of course I know of nothing! Francis was always stirring, trying to score off people . . .' She broke off, on the verge of tears.

Impossible to judge whether she knew or did not know whatever it was that Francis had been told, and there was nothing to be gained by turning the screw too hard.

'Have you noticed any change in your brother recently – say in the last few months? Any change in his relations with his father?'

'I've noticed nothing and I certainly would have if there was anything to notice!'

Back in the street workmen were stretching a banner between the shops above the traffic: 'The Gifford Tate Exhibition of Paintings; Open 11th–22nd August. Admission Free.'

Wycliffe felt that he was getting to know the people who had been closest to the dead man. Eight hours ago he had never heard of any of them, now he was thinking of them by their first names: Francis, Edwin, Beryl, Anna, Cathy . . . And he was able to fit a face and provisionally a temperament to four of them. Francis Garland was the victim and therefore the central figure in the case. Always start with the victim

72

and try to trace around him the web of relationships in which he was involved. That was how he worked, but in this case he could not free himself of the notion that although Francis was the victim he might not be the central figure. His father seemed a more promising candidate for that role and he had died a natural death. Did that mean that the murder was . . . was peripheral?

He promised himself that he would devote at least as much attention to the father as to the son.

CHAPTER FOUR

'What do you want me for?'

'Where did you sleep last night?'

'In my van.'

'On this car-park?'

'Yes.'

'Do you usually spend your nights in the back of your van?'

'No. I live with my girlfriend and her mother in Flushing.'

'So why weren't you there last night?'

'We had a row.'

'About what?'

'God knows! What are rows usually about?'

'Money in my experience.'

Once it was known that Terry Gill was wanted for questioning, a young constable who knew him, all bright eyed and bushy tailed, pointed out that his van had been parked in the car-park all day within fifty yards of the Incident Room.

'I know him, sir. We keep an eye on him.'

So all they had needed to do was wait and, at five o'clock, the wanted man had turned up. Now he was being interrogated by Kersey in the make-shift interview room.

'Where have you been all day?'

'In Redruth to see an old mate of mine.'

'How did you get there without the van?'

'By bus. My dynamo has been dodgy and it finally packed up. I was short of a few quid to do anything about it so my mate lent me the money, we went to a scrap yard, picked up a spare and he delivered me back here in his motor, then your chaps picked me up.'

'What time did you leave this morning?'

'Early. Sevenish. I couldn't sleep so I thought I might as well get going.'

For all his long hair, bandeau and earrings which made him look like a weedy Viking, Terry Gill was a very ordinary young man, and pathetic; pathetic because he so obviously wanted to amount to something and had no idea what. Kersey would have written him off as harmless had it not been for his extreme wariness. Each question seemed to come as a relief, as though he had expected something more dangerous.

'So last night at, say, ten o'clock, where were you?'

'In my van, I expect. I'm not very good on time.'

At that point, Wycliffe joined them. Kersey looked up. 'This is Terry Gill, sir, Anna's boyfriend. He's telling us how he spent last night here, on the car-park, in his van.'

'So if you were in your van you couldn't have been two hundred yards away on the scaffolding behind Benson's furniture shop?'

This was the bull's eye. The boy looked from one to the other of them and it was a moment or two before he could find his voice, then: 'I don't know what you mean.'

'What are you so frightened of?'

'I'm not frightened.'

'You could have fooled me.' Kersey leaned forward across the table, his rubbery features close to the boy. 'Look, sonny, it sticks out a mile that you want to get something off your chest but you're scared to hell what will happen to you if you do. All I can say is the longer you mess me about the worse it will get. Now let's be serious. Take it a step at a time. When did you last see your girlfriend's father?'

'At the old man's funeral yesterday. He came and spoke to us – to Anna and me.'

'What did he say?'

'He was very friendly and nice; he wanted to know if Anna had been asked to come to the lawyer's about her grandfather's will.' Terry was recovering his voice if not his composure.

'And had she?'

'Yes.'

'So she had expectations.'

'Of something, I suppose.'

'Is that what you quarrelled about?'

'I don't think so. She was very queer after the funeral. I couldn't make her out.'

Wycliffe said: 'Anna's share in her grandfather's will was £10,000.'

The boy looked amazed. 'That's money! I don't think she was expecting anything like that.'

'But now she will get a lot more than that.'

'More?'

'From her father. It seems he didn't make a will and if that's the case Anna will get his share.'

'But her father isn't dead.' The words were spoken mechanically as though by a bad actor.

Kersey cut in. 'But he is, you know. Somebody shot him by the scaffolding behind Benson's just after ten last night.' Kersey's face split into a grin that would have intimidated a gorilla. 'So that brings us back to where we started.'

'You mean he was murdered?' Weakly.

'I mean he was murdered. As if you didn't know!'

76

'You don't think I . . . I mean, if I'd had anything to do with it do you think I'd have left my van here and come back —'

Kersey cut him short. 'Killers are usually stupid but some people might think it was a clever move to do just that. Did you know that Garland took his dog for a walk along the wharf every night?'

'No – yes.'

'We takes our choice. And you ask us to believe that out of a dozen car-parks and hundreds of side streets you could have chosen you picked this place by chance? Try telling that to your lawyer.'

'My God, I didn't kill him!'

'No? So what did you do?'

The boy paused and seemed to be gathering his wits. 'I admit I wanted to speak to him.'

'What about?'

He hesitated. 'We had that row – Anna and me. She said there was no future for us; me with no proper job and no prospects.'

'Well?'

'There's a cottage with three acres going on the Helston road. I know about market gardening and I could make a go of that. Vegetables for the health shop market, organically grown – that sort of thing.' He looked dubiously at Kersey as though he feared the very idea might provoke him to violence.

'And you thought your girl's father might put up the money?'

'As a loan – an investment.'

'Why not go and see him in the proper way instead of lurking around by night?'

He shook his head. 'I couldn't face Anna's aunt Beryl – she hates me – or Cathy Carne either, for that matter.'

77

'So what happened?'

'I saw him as he was crossing the car-park with his dog.' He was silent for a while and they could hear someone on the telephone in the main room.

Kersey prompted him: 'And?'

'I followed him some way behind.'

'How far?'

'To just past Spargo's; I couldn't raise the nerve to catch him up and speak to him. All of a sudden it seemed to be the wrong time and the wrong way to go about it, what with it being the day of the old man's funeral and everything . . . I decided after all it would be better to go and see him in the shop like you said—'

'If you got as far as Spargo's you must have seen him go under the scaffolding.'

'No, I didn't. I was some way behind, it was misty, and when I got there I couldn't see him. Then, all of a sudden, there was a sort of bang and the dog started yelping and I thought he must have fallen or something and that he might be hurt. I started running and when I reached this end of the scaffolding I saw a woman bending over something on the ground at the other end. I think she must have heard me because she ran off like the clappers towards the quay.'

'You said a woman.'

'I thought it was a woman at the time. Of course I could be wrong I suppose.'

'Wearing a skirt or trousers?'

'Oh, not a skirt – jeans I thought.'

'Thin or fat?'

'Not fat, definitely.'

'Short or tall?'

Time to ponder, then: 'Medium height, perhaps on the tall side for a woman.'

'Was he or she carrying anything?'

'Not that I could see.'

The questions were pressed but they could get nothing more definite: 'It looked like a woman.'

'Go on.'

He drew a deep breath. 'I went to look and though it was pretty dark I could see enough. It made me want to throw up. I wanted to get out. I went back to the van and the bloody thing wouldn't start so I waited there till morning when I could catch a bus and . . . and, well, just get out.'

At last he was packed off to sub-division: held for questioning.

Wycliffe said: 'Before we have to turn him loose – which we shall, get Lucy Lane over to Flushing to talk to the girl.'

Wycliffe drove the sixty miles home to another estuary while his team was given lodgings in the town.

The Wycliffes lived in The Watch House, a former coast-guard property overlooking the narrows on the Cornish side. They had a half-acre of garden, which Helen had planned and sedulously cultivated with shrubs and trees, and a plot for vegetables and fruit. Only a little-used footpath separated their garden from the shore.

He pulled into his drive as the church clock at St Juliot was striking eight; a perfect summer evening with the waters of the estuary a mirror to the sky. Helen was in the kitchen preparing a sweet savour as an offering to her lord.

'How did the inspection go?'

'It didn't. I'm on a case.'

'I know; I heard on the radio. You can pour me a sherry.'

'What are we eating?'

79

'I intended a salad but I thought you might have missed out on lunch so we've got grilled lamb chops with minted potatoes and glazed carrots.'

'Smells nice.'

They sipped their sherry while Helen prepared a fresh fruit salad.

Wycliffe said: 'What do you know about Gifford Tate?'

'The painter? I know that he's dead, that he lived somewhere in West Cornwall, that his pictures are making high prices and that I wish we could afford one. I've got a catalogue of an exhibition of his somewhere and I'll look it out if you're interested. Come to think of it, I remember reading something recently about a new exhibition of his, going on tour. How's that?'

'All right for a start. Now try Edwin Garland.'

Helen frowned and pushed back the hair from her forehead, a habit she had when thinking. 'I've heard the name. Was he a painter too?'

'Was is the operative word: he died last Saturday.'

'Not murdered?'

'No, that distinction was reserved for his son. It seems that Garland and Tate were buddies in their day.'

'I'll see what I can find after we've eaten.'

The french windows of the living-room stood open while they ate and by the time they reached the coffee stage darkness had closed over the hills across the water.

'I'll get that catalogue.'

Helen was not long gone: she had a filing system which covered the composers and the painters she enjoyed. 'Here we are: retrospective at the Hayward in 1976.'

The catalogue was a glossy production with several

illustrations in colour and black-and-white. Wycliffe turned the pages. There was the usual synoptic paragraph or two: 'Born Egham 1907; studied at the Slade Schools . . . Moved to Cornwall in 1927 and came to the notice of Stanhope Forbes . . . Painted a great deal in the environs of Falmouth but also in Brittany, the Loire valley, and the Greek islands . . . Although early in his career he was regarded as a protégé of Forbes he was largely uninfluenced by the so-called "new realism" of the Newlyn school . . . Like Alfred Sisley, whom he greatly admired, Tate was a painter of nature, and his work, though late, was in the main stream of Impressionist tradition.

'Despite a disabling stroke in 1970 he continued painting and, surprisingly, his work acquired an increased vigour; he adopted a more varied palette and made use of more vivid colours. It has been said that in recent years his allegiance shifted from Sisley to Monet!'

'Interesting! Tate died the following year – 1977.'

Helen smiled. 'I've heard it said that retrospectives are bad for the health.'

She handed him a Lyle's Price Guide, open at the right page: 'It's three years out of date but look at the prices.'

There were three Gifford Tates recorded as auctioned during the year: 'The Swanpool at Falmouth – signed and dated 1938 . . . oil on canvas . . . £17,550; The Loire at Amboise . . . 1963 . . . £12,610; Helford Village, near Falmouth . . . 1973 . . . £21,200 . . .'

Wycliffe closed the book. 'I see what you mean.'

'But what's it got to do with your case?'

'Good question. It's an odd business and it seems to be mixed up with Edwin Garland's will. He left his art shop and studio to his niece with the exception of his tube of Winsor blue and he left his tube of Winsor blue with £1,000 to the son of Gifford Tate. Another £1,000 goes to his friend, Burger, to buy himself a pair of spectacles.'

'Sounds like Lewis Carroll.'

'Yes, the old man had a wry sense of humour though on the face of it the other provisions in his will are probably more important. The residue – a substantial chunk, was left jointly to his two offspring, Beryl and Francis. Now, with Francis dead, apparently intestate, his share goes to his illegitimate daughter, a twenty-year-old. She and her mother and, possibly, her boyfriend, are the only ones who obviously benefit from Francis Garland's death. The trouble is, I don't believe it's that simple.'

Wycliffe lazed in his chair, while Helen lost herself in the zany twilight world of Iris Murdoch. His mind drifted over the people whom he had heard about for the first time that morning, groping for some sort of perspective. He was intrigued by the trio: Gifford Tate, Edwin Garland and Papa Burger, their painting holidays and their week-ends in Burger's boat. Their expeditions recalled the all-male cultural sprees which were commonplace before the first war . . . In fact the whole case seemed somehow dated. The Garlands, and their shop with the rooms over, were out of period, relics of a time when the business and management of the town had been in the hands of a few prosperous traders. Wills were of immense significance and the contingent squabbles sometimes spilled over into acts of family treachery and even violence . . .

He tried to visualise the Garland household: Edwin, widower, intelligent, shrewd, inclined to be malicious, discreetly affluent . . . Despite his chosen role as a small-town shopkeeper he seemed to have been accepted on equal terms by talented cosmopolitans . . . He had married a beautiful wife.

His son, Francis: goggle-eyed, unprepossessing, in love only with himself and his notion of some sort of scholarly distinction. A youthful affair gave him a daughter, apparently without encumbrance. On two days a week he peddled art and printing materials around the country and, for the rest, he was nominally in charge of his father's printing works. Finally, according to the lawyer, it's likely that he was having a covert affair with a woman.

And Beryl . . . Beryl, with her tunnel vision in all matters of opinion and morality, played out her role of self-sacrificing daughter and sister to the men of the house. Beryl had a friend, and both were partial to little nips of whisky . . .

Downstairs in the shop, Cathy Carne, the niece, competent and a realist. She knew that her uncle's death would radically change her position but did she, as she said, believe that the change would be for the worse?

In all that, was there any motive for murder? Of the old man perhaps, but it was the son who had been shot.

Wycliffe shifted irritably in his chair. 'Let's go to bed.'

Helen put down her book 'A night-cap. Or would you prefer cocoa?'

CHAPTER FIVE

Next morning Wycliffe spent three hours at headquarters dealing with administrative routine: departmental reports, inter-departmental memoranda, overtime schedules, and duty rosters. Diane, his personal assistant, hovered ready to guide, caution and instruct. Then he spent half-an-hour with the Chief discussing the case. His lordship was moved to reflection.

'It looks like being another of your museum pieces, Charles. When you and I joined the force the majority of homicides were like that – family affairs, or at least concerned with intimate human relationships: legacies, jealousies, frustrated passions – always with a powerful personal element. What the papers called "human dramas". Now killings are more often than not anonymous, motiveless in the sense that there is no relational link between the killer and his victim. A man is murdered because he is a policeman, a security guard, a cashier, a black man, a white man, an Arab or a Jew. At the extreme, his death may be entirely incidental to some criminal lunatic making a political point, or just blind violence like the Belgian supermarket killings. Against that sort of background the old-style domestic homicide seems almost cosy.'

Wycliffe, anxious to get away, kept comment to a minimum.

The Chief sighed. 'It's part of the pattern, Charles; society disintegrates before our eyes and we are expected to paper over the cracks.'

It was mid-day before Wycliffe made his escape. He had his week-end bag in the car and, short of an emergency, it would be several days before he was home again. He lunched at a pub on the way down and arrived at the Incident Room shortly before two. Kersey and Lucy Lane were head to head over the reports. He felt that he had been a long time away.

Kersey said: 'We've no grounds for continuing to hold Terry Gill. I've got his statement and they're letting him go.'

Wycliffe turned to Lucy Lane. 'Anything from you? How did you get on with Anna? – and, by the way, what surname did she take?'

'Her mother's maiden name – Brooks; she's Anna Brooks. I got next to nothing from her, sir. Astonishment at her legacies – genuine, I'd say, though I couldn't be sure; she's a deep one. Intelligent. I must admit I liked her; she won't squander her grandfather's money, that's for sure. It seems she saw her father five or six times a year and her grandfather less often than that, though the old man used to send her substantial cash presents at Christmas and on her birthday.'

'And her mother?'

Lucy smiled. 'Fat, lives on junk foods, strong tea and gossip; short on conventional morality, I'd guess, but not a bad sort. The kind of woman I wouldn't mind having around if I was in trouble though she might be a bit of a trial at other times. She'd spread my business all round the neighbourhood but she'd lend a hand without grudging it.' Lucy was apologetic: 'I know it doesn't get us anywhere and it's subjective, but I can only say what impression I got.'

'Any mention of the boy?'

'They didn't know we'd picked him up and I didn't

tell them. Anna was tight lipped about him but mother said: "Terry is a good lad at heart. He'll be back." '

'Fair enough. The women in this case are suspects in their own right, especially if we take notice of that boy, though from what you say I can't see Anna's mother hauling herself up on the scaffolding behind Benson's, or making a run for it when the boy turned up.'

The timetable of Francis's movements after his father's death was still full of gaps but that was to be expected. Edwin Garland had been found dead by his niece at two o'clock on the Saturday. Francis spent Saturday afternoon 'making arrangements' with the undertaker. On Saturday evening he had worked in his room. Sunday was blank. On Monday morning he registered the death and spent some time with Shrimpton – the lawyer – his father's accountant, and the bank manager. In the afternoon he visited various people who had been on friendly terms with the dead man. He had used his car for these visits. On his return he wrote several letters rather hurriedly because he was anxious to catch the post. On Tuesday he seemed to resume his normal routine of business calls and brought in two or three orders. On Wednesday morning he called on Dr Tate and he had the funeral in the afternoon.

At two o'clock Wycliffe collected the dead man's keys from the duty officer and set out along the wharf. Approach from the rear. The wharf walk had remained closed to the public in case the lab boys wanted a second bite at the cherry. The weather was changing: blue-black clouds were building in the south-east and, as Wycliffe arrived at the back of the Garlands' shop, they obscured the sun. At the same time a wind blew briefly across the harbour, rippling the water and putting the gulls to squawking flight.

It was the first time he had taken a real look at the premises from the back. The building was of a slatey stone, pointed and well maintained; two floors and a couple of attics. The ground floor windows were low enough to look in and he could see into the little office, which was empty. The other windows must belong to the studio but the lower panes were dirty on the inside so that it was difficult to see anything. All the ground floor windows were fitted with iron bars, a sufficient deterrent for the average break-and-enter boys.

He tried the door of the side passage and, to his surprise, found it unlocked. He went right through the passage to the street and entered the shop like a customer. Cathy Carne and her assistant were both serving and he had to wait. Cathy was pale and drawn and she looked tired – not, he thought, like a woman who, expecting the sack, had found herself owning the business. When she was free she took him into the office and sank into a chair as though exhausted.

Wycliffe held out Francis's keys. 'Is the studio key amongst these?'

She examined the bunch and picked out a key. 'That's it, I think.'

A five-lever Chubb. The old man had believed in security, inside as well as out.

As he was about to leave the little office he turned back. 'Do you know if Francis had a woman friend?'

'I shouldn't think so.'

'There's Anna.'

'Proving that he's capable? I'd say it was interest he lacked.'

Evidently Francis had never made advances to his cousin.

A new thought occurred to Wycliffe. 'Tuesday was the day he went off in the van and came back with a bruised face; presumably you've got a record of the people he called on that day? Of course it's possible that he made other calls not in the line of business.'

'I wouldn't know about that but I can tell you the business calls he made.' From a drawer of her desk she brought out a number of pink slips clipped together and she separated the top three. 'These were his only calls – all deliveries promised for that day.'

Wycliffe looked the slips over. 'Do you know these people?'

'Only as customers. Bestway Arts and Crafts is a small business in Hayle, dealing mainly in craft stuff; they carry a stock of art materials as a sideline. It's run by a chap called Ferris . . . The Archway Studio is just outside St Ives and belongs to a woman painter called Eileen Rich. All I know about her is that she's twice a widow . . . Ah, I'd forgotten about this one: Kevin Brand, there could be a connection there. I've got a feeling he used to live in Falmouth. He has a place out on the downs between St Ives and Penzance, a school of occult studies, would you believe? He runs day classes and in the summer he takes residential students. We print his prospectus. It's possible that Francis found a kindred spirit there.'

Wycliffe made a note of the names. 'Now I'm going to take a look over the studio and I think you should be with me.'

'If you like.'

Having looked at the studio from the outside he was prepared for squalor, but a basic orderliness surprised him. It seemed to be a combination of workshop and studio. There were two easels, and the one near the door had a picture on it, a striking painting of the Falmouth waterfront. It was painted in blocks of flat colour, cleverly apposed, with more regard for pattern than form. Wycliffe was reminded of a stained glass window.

'Is this your uncle's work?'

She was examining a few canvases stacked against the wall but she looked up at his question. 'Yes.'

'Is this where you found him?'

She came over. 'Yes, he had a habit of propping himself on that stool in front of a picture and it must have gone over with him. When I found him his body was sprawled over the stool.'

'And this picture was on the easel then?'

'Yes.'

'Had he been working on it? It seems finished.'

'He may not have been working on it; more likely he was deciding how to frame it.'

Wycliffe looked at the painter's trolley drawn up by the easel. Tubes of colour laid out tidily; there were containers for oil and turps, and two jars containing brushes.

He glanced at the tubes. 'No Winsor blue?'

'No.' But she did not smile.

'And no palette.'

'What? He wouldn't have needed one if he wasn't painting, would he?' She went back to her stacked canvases.

'May I look?'

There were twelve or fifteen finished pictures, all painted in the same manner as the one on the easel, patterns of glowing colour, but the subjects ranged from harbour and river scenes to landscapes with figures.

'So this was your uncle's style?'

'Yes. It was the style he seemed to prefer though he didn't always stick to it. He was attracted to Gauguin and the Pont Aven group.'

'In contrast with Gifford Tate.'

'Yes, Tate saw himself as an Impressionist.'

'And Burger?'

'Burger wasn't in the same class as the other two, he didn't pretend to be.'

'But he must have been keen.'

'Yes, he's very knowledgeable about painting and painters but not much of a painter himself.'

Her answers were terse, her manner preoccupied, and she was restless. She moved to another part of the studio and started to turn over a number of stretched canvases, all of them blank.

'What are you looking for?'

'I'm not looking for anything.' She realised that more was called for and went on: 'I'm curious because I've never had a chance to look round here before.'

'Not when your uncle was alive?'

'No, he kept the studio locked except when he was working, then he hated to be disturbed.'

Dark clouds now covered the sky and what could be seen of the harbour was a study in greys, slate blues and silver. It was starting to rain, fat drops slid viscously down the window panes. Cathy switched on the studio lights, further exposing its tattiness but adding to its intimacy.

Wycliffe had found Edwin's books stacked on two tiers of rough shelving. All of them were the worse (or better) for much use. No glossy volumes of coloured reproductions; most were concerned with the history and philosophy of art – Tolstoy's *What is Art?* Collingwood, Roger Fry, Greenberg, Arason, Rewald . . . not forgetting Fischer with the Gospel according to the Comrades. There were studio manuals – one with a flyleaf inscription: 'To Eddie from Gifford. Christmas 1936' – and five or six sketchbooks with pencil and watercolour sketches. If, in his paintings, Garland had sacrificed form to colour and design, it was not because he couldn't draw.

Cathy was continuing her inspection as though she would make an inventory.

Wycliffe said: 'It's all yours now.'

'Yes, I suppose so.'

'Is it possible that there was some secret in your uncle's life which he confided to Francis and which Francis tried to use to his advantage?'

He wondered why portmanteau questions always turned out so damned pompous.

Cathy Carne was derisive: 'You mean did uncle have a secret, which Francis could use to blackmail somebody else? A bit unlikely, wouldn't you say? In any case if he had a secret, Francis is the last person he would have told.'

'Yet we have evidence that your uncle did tell Francis something about himself which Francis found it hard to believe.'

She became obstinate. 'In that case I've no idea what it could be. It all sounds very improbable.'

He was moving about the studio with an apparent aimlessness looking at whatever caught his eye. He examined the rack of mouldings used for making frames and seemed interested in the machine for mitreing the angles. There was a small knee-hole desk and he went through the drawers but found nothing more than discarded pens, broken pencils, old catalogues, a quantity of scrap paper, and an assortment of pins and clips.

From time to time Cathy Carne looked across at him with obvious unease. No doubt she was wondering what it was he expected to find. He wondered himself. What was he doing, prowling about the old man's studio like a nosey neighbour? Either the place was worth searching or it wasn't. Turn it over to a couple of men to take the place apart, or leave it alone. 'You lack a professional attitude, my boy!' He'd been told that often enough in the old days. Time to behave like a policeman.

'We have a witness to the killing.'

She turned abruptly. 'A witness? You mean somebody saw Francis killed?' Unbelieving.

'From a distance, yes. The witness is under the strong impression that Francis was attacked by a woman.'

'A woman? . . .' She seemed about to add something but did not.

'Where were you on Wednesday night?'

She made an angry movement but controlled herself. 'I suppose you have to ask that. I was at home all the evening.'

'Alone?'

A momentary hesitation, then: 'Yes.'

'It would be sensible to tell me the truth.'

'I've told you. I was alone.' She turned away.

'Your flat is within two hundred yards of the spot where Francis was killed. You can see the place from at least one of your windows.'

'I've told you; I knew nothing about what had happened until I was at work next morning and one of your policemen came with the news.'

'What did your uncle say in his letter to you?'

'I've told you.'

'No. Your answer was an evasion.'

'I told you that the letter gave me advice on how to deal with the family and that is all.'

'I'll leave it at that for the moment but I may have to ask you that question again. Anyway, I've finished here for the present.'

'Do I get the key of the studio now?'

'Not yet.'

Wycliffe opened the door, waited for her to switch out the lights and pass through, then he locked the door and pocketed the keys. Cathy went into the shop and Wycliffe let himself out into the little hall from which stairs led up to the flat. He happened to glance up and saw Beryl on the landing. She beckoned to him mysteriously and he went up to her.

She spoke in a low voice: 'I heard you down there with her.' It was an accusation but delivered without punch. She seemed subdued, almost amiable. 'I want to talk to you. In here . . .'

She took him into the living-room and made him sit in the black leather armchair. He thought she might be on the point of offering him a nip of whisky but she did not go that far. She remained standing, evidently not very sure how to begin.

Outside a massive pall of cloud hung low over the harbour.

At last she began: 'I've come to see things differently since I've had time to think over what was in the will. I didn't understand at first. When they were lowering my father's coffin into his grave I thought to myself "It's all over!" I should have known better; he'd worked it all out, planned it move by move, just like when he was playing chess.'

'What had he planned?'

'How he could cause the maximum unpleasantness to those he left behind – mainly to me. Nobody, of course, will believe it: "He was such a *nice* man – a bit sarcastic at times but only in a playful sort of way." That's what people said about him. Even my friend, Celia Bond, says I'm imagining things, that I'm suffering from delayed shock or some such nonsense. We had words about it and I told her to go! Of course Celia was an only child – and spoilt; she can't believe that a father would get pleasure by humiliating his children. She's no idea!'

It was astonishing. Beryl was perfectly composed; she was no longer flushed and her hair was tidy; she even had a small smile on her lips. She had found an explanation of events which satisfied her, an explanation which in a curious way brought her contentment. She was being persecuted and it was part of a carefully laid plan. She was no longer the victim of chance, of a malign fate. Someone had hated her enough to . . . She could live with that, and fight back.

Suddenly the rain came, bursting out of the sky, beating against the window panes, and lashing the surface of the harbour into misty spray.

'Why should your father want to humiliate you?'

'He's done it all my life, it's nothing new. I was not the daughter he wanted. A girl child should be soft and pretty and loving; she should learn to titillate and flatter her father . . . Of course I failed on all counts and so I was ignored most of the time – passed over. "Beryl!" . . . I can hear him saying it now as only he could, turning my name into an insult.'

'Did Francis suffer too?'

'It wasn't the same. Francis was a boy.'

'How does your father continue to humiliate you now that he is dead?'

She looked at him. 'You ask that after hearing the details of his will? I'm turned out of the house where I was born whether I want to go or no, the house and the business are handed over to . . . to that woman, and I have to share what is left in a *joint* legacy with Francis!'

She broke off as though to allow this to sink in then went on: 'Father knew perfectly well that my brother

94

and I didn't agree, that we would part as soon as possible, so he made sure that we would be tied together in all the wrangling that would go on because of the joint legacy.' She made a vigorous gesture. 'It was his idea of a good joke!'

The lawyer had said of the will: 'A recipe for in-fighting . . . I think he saw himself sitting up there, watching the fun.'

Wycliffe said, quietly: 'There will be no wrangling with Francis now.'

She took him up at once. 'No! I shall have to deal with that girl, but now I understand . . .'

'You can't blame that on your father.'

She looked at him oddly. 'You think not? Who killed Francis and *why* was he killed? I know what I said. That was when I wanted to keep whatever scandal there was, in the family. Now things have changed. When you find out why Francis was killed you'll also find that my father had a hand in it.'

She lowered her voice: 'There are still secrets. Francis knew something – he was smug enough about it. Cathy Carne had a letter handed to her by the lawyer. They are things we know about; God knows what else there is!'

'Are you saying that you feel threatened?'

She pursed her lips. 'I can take care of myself. But I shan't let him continue to ruin my life. That's what he wanted but he won't get away with it. Now that I understand I shall come to terms. You'll see! I'm not the fool he took me for!'

'Just one question: if you had inherited the shop and premises would you have kept it going?'

'Yes, there have been Garlands running that business for nearly ninety years, but it would have been run my way.'

95

'With or without Cathy Carne?'

A wrinkling of the nose. 'That would have been up to her.'

'But I understood that you intended to live with your friend after your father died.'

'That was because I assumed that the business would go to Francis and then I would have had no say in it.'

Back in the street the rain had eased but there was more to come. On his way back to the Incident Room Wycliffe had to weave a way through milling crowds who had deserted the beaches and taken to window shopping.

He was intrigued by the three old men: Edwin Garland, Gifford Tate and Papa Burger. A friendship, begun in their twenties, had been sustained throughout their lives. Week-ends and holidays were spent together, presumably to the neglect of their families; they had their private jokes, their shared experiences, and above all their obsession with art.

It sounded harmless, even pleasant. Did he have any reason to link their activities with the murder of Garland's son? To begin with, only the coincidence of the deaths of father and son within four days of each other; beyond that his notion of a connection had been no more than a hunch, and he had been in the business too long to back his hunches far ahead of evidence. But now, here was Beryl vigorously maintaining that her father had 'worked it all out – planned it move by move'. She was even ready to see her father's hand in the murder of his son. On the face of it, an absurdity, but was there an element of sense in what she had said?

The lawyer, the printing works foreman, and Beryl had each of them offered facets of the old man's character which suggested not only a cynical vein of humour and a streak of malice but a disdainful attitude to at least some of those closest to him.

There was a strong case for finding out more about Edwin and there were two sources so far untapped: Papa Burger and Edwin's brother Thomas.

The lights were on in the Incident Room. Another rain squall blotted out the harbour and water cascaded down the window panes. Now and then lightning flickered through the gloom, the lights dimmed, and thunder rattled every loose panel and plank in the building. Lucy Lane was typing a report.

'I've just come back from the Thomas Garlands' place, sir.'

'Let's hear it.'

'A modest house with a small garden where the grass looks as though it has been cut with nail-scissors and weeded with a forceps; a dolls' house, with nothing out of place, everything polished and dusted.'

Lucy Lane always set the scene and he liked that.

'We talked in the living-room which merges into a conservatory choked with potted plants like a burgeoning rain forest. Thomas is five or six years younger than his brother, knocking seventy; he's tall, lean and a bit owlish. He's not very talkative except on the subject of his plants. He used to teach English in a comprehensive school and he probably had a rough time of it.

'I was daft enough to say his plants looked healthy and I got the Ancient Mariner treatment; a squirt-by-puff account of how he managed it. Luckily, after a while, I noticed a framed photograph of a young man on the sideboard and diverted the flow by asking if it was of his son—'

She broke off as a blue lightning flash coincided with an ear-shattering thunder clap and released a fresh torrent of rain. For a moment or two they watched the rain bouncing off the waters of the harbour.

'It was a photograph of Mark and I heard how he'd qualified as a chiropractor and set up in Falmouth where it's uphill work. Then we got round to Edwin's death and Francis's murder. He seemed genuinely distressed but quite useless. He said his lawyer had persuaded him to contest his father's will and that he'd regretted it ever since. He would have liked to have gone to his brother's funeral but he thought it would only have made matters worse. As to Francis, well, it was inconceivable that such a thing could happen. Let's hope his son can be more helpful.'

'You haven't seen him?'

'No, I spoke to him on the phone. I thought it better to tackle him outside of business hours. I told him I would call at the house this evening but he said he'd prefer to come here. He's coming when he finishes work at about six.'

Wycliffe turned up the reports of telephone enquiries made among Francis's customers to find Kevin Brand of The School of Occult Studies, Carn Fellow, near Penzance. Brand had said, 'Mr Garland came here early on Tuesday afternoon; he delivered some printing work I had ordered and we had a brief conversation. He told me that his father had died over the weekend . . . Yes, I knew him when I lived in Falmouth five or six years ago . . .'

Worth following up.

Kersey came in and Wycliffe put him in the picture.

'You want me to see this guy, sir?'

'Find out what you can about him first. The local nicks at Penzance and St Ives must have some idea what goes on in a set-up like that on their doorsteps.' He turned to Lucy Lane: 'I'm leaving Mark Garland to you. For the next hour or thereabouts I shall be at the Burgers' house in Wood Lane.'

'They called me Papa because I was the eldest, three years older than Gifford, six years older than Eddie.' Then, wryly: 'There may have been another reason; even as a young man I was a staid sort of chap and they were a bit wild at times. I suppose I was inclined to lay down the law.' The old man laughed. 'I first met Eddie Garland at Lamorna, in 1931, I think it was, when we were both in an outdoor painting group with Birch. I've never been more than a dabbler but I've always had an eye for a painter and I saw at once that he was one. It turned out that we both lived in Falmouth. I was already friendly with Tate, and Eddie knew him through the shop, so we soon made a threesome and we kept together for nearly fifty years.'

Burger was very thin and very tall; he sat back in his armchair, his bony frame draped rather than clothed by a grey light-weight suit. He had kept a sufficiency of silvery hair, his aristocratic face was deeply lined and his yellowed teeth projected slightly under a clipped moustache. His voice was high pitched and from time to time he emphasised his points by restrained movements of his hands. Near his chair was a walking frame.

'My legs have let me down.'

But despite his disability his eyes had a twinkle and Wycliffe felt that he was in the presence of a truly contented man.

Wycliffe said: 'In 1931, as I work it out, Garland would have been twenty-one and already a husband and father.'

A wary look. 'Yes, that is so.'

'I've seen Gifford Tate's portrait of Garland's wife; she must have been a very lovely girl.'

'Oh, she was. Judy was beautiful.'

Mrs Burger, a little dumpling of a woman in linen trousers and a smock, like a Chinese peasant, was listening and smiling. 'Oh, don't be so stodgy, Martin! Mr Wycliffe will hear it all from someone else if you don't tell him.'

Burger deftly arranged the creases in his trousers. 'Ah! I have my brief! Well, Judy was an assistant in the shop and the two young people, both about nineteen, were drawn together. Judy became pregnant and, against his father's wishes, Edwin married her. The child, Beryl, was born and everybody seemed content except that gossip insisted the child was not Edwin's.'

Mrs Burger interrupted: 'With good reason! The girl had been seeing a lot of another young man, an estate agent called Jose, and that association continued after the marriage – long after! Long enough to explain Francis also.'

Burger spead his hands. 'My dear Penny, you have no reason to suggest any such thing—'

'Anyone who knew Jose and looks at Francis doesn't need a reason.'

Wycliffe said: 'Doesn't this imply either remarkable tolerance or remarkable ignorance on Garland's part?'

Burger did a tactical throat clearing but his wife had no qualms. 'Of course it does! But nobody has ever been able to decide which. I doubt if anyone ever dared broach the subject to Edwin and sometimes I think he simply believed what he wanted to believe, that the two were his.'

'Because he was so deeply in love with his wife?'

Burger sighed. 'My goodness, we are getting into deep water!' He glanced up at the mantel clock, then across at Mrs Burger. 'Do you think, perhaps, a cup of tea, dear? It's about our usual time.'

Mrs Burger left them alone and Burger looked at Wycliffe with a small self-conscious smile.

It was raining hard now, beating on the window panes, and the room was in semi-darkness. A pleasantly neutral room: dove grey walls, a Persian square on the floor, grey velvet curtains and white woodwork. But on the walls Edwin Garland's pictures glowed with dramatic intensity and a curious effect of translucence.

'You obviously admire Garland's painting.'

'Oh, I do! I think Garland was a truly notable painter, and very versatile. He chose to paint in this particular style but his earlier work was quite different.'

Wycliffe teased. 'All this despite your legacy?'

A dry chuckle. 'Edwin was always a joker but the point was that he seemed to undervalue his own work and to think less of my judgement because I did not. I often told him – and so did Tate – that he did himself less than justice by being content to stand in Tate's shadow. Gifford painted excellent pictures, very pleasant pictures – he was a painter of nature, but that, in my opinion, is not of itself art; I agree with Gauguin's cautionary advice to a young novice: "Don't copy nature too much. Art is an abstraction."'

'You have none of Tate's pictures?'

'Oh, yes. I have two, but not in this room. The works of the two painters don't make good stable mates. In any case my Tates are on loan to the exhibition – you know about the exhibition, I suppose?'

'Yes, indeed.'

'A big thing; Edwin was largely responsible for getting it off the ground. He put me on the committee and now they've persuaded me to open the thing.'

'Garland seems to have been a very modest man.'

Burger put the tips of his fingers together and

101

considered what he would say. 'Modest? Modest in the sense that he never proclaimed his talents – and they were real and varied: he was, I have heard, a very good businessman, and I know him to have been a first rate chess player and a notable painter.' Burger shifted his position and looked at Wycliffe with a gentle smile. 'But people who know their true worth often do not feel the need to go about asserting it. I do not think that Edwin set any great value on other people's opinions.'

'What do you know about Winsor blue? I understand that it was the subject of another of Garland's jokes?'

The old man nodded. 'Yes, it was, but it was something between Gifford and Edwin. I was never in on the joke, whatever it was. All I can tell you is that Winsor blue is one of the trade names for an intense blue pigment, copper phthalocyanine, which came into the palette sometime in the thirties. It was favoured by many painters as a substitute for prussian blue. Gifford dated his success from the time he started to use it; he signed his pictures with Winsor blue and a dab of the pure colour occurs somewhere in them, a sort of trademark.' Burger spread his hands. 'Painters are as superstitious as fishermen. By the same token, Edwin told me that Gifford stopped using it after his stroke.'

From somewhere in the house came the rattle of teacups on a tray. Burger leaned forward quickly and, lowering his voice, said: 'Returning to our earlier subject, Garland half believed himself to be impotent – he probably was, but he was obsessed by that damned girl he married and although she was good to look at, that was all – she was an immoral woman! Ah! That looks very nice, my dear! . . . Could you place that little table, Mr Wycliffe? . . . These legs of mine!'

'Lemon or milk, Mr Wycliffe?'

They drank a highly aromatic China tea and ate little

102

biscuits made with rice flour and honey, spiced with cinnamon.

Wycliffe said: 'Gifford Tate's pictures are fetching high prices. I thought any well-known painter's work tended to slump in market value for several years after his death.'

Burger sipped his tea and patted his moustache. 'Yes, but that isn't a law of nature, Mr Wycliffe; it is sometimes the result of manipulation. It gives interested parties a chance to buy in cheaply. Then, in a few years, one or two judiciously placed magazine articles, the odd programme on TV, an opportune book, and the painter is resurrected with all his best work in the right hands.'

'But Tate's pictures seem to have avoided the doldrums; his prices have much more than kept pace with inflation.'

'Because Edwin, as Gifford's art executor, was very astute and Marcella has much to thank him for. Gifford left most of his money, and the income from his pictures, to Marcella while the house went to Alan.'

'Let me see; Alan is Tate's son – the doctor.'

'Yes, the doctor – a very good one, too. Alan has compassion and that's all too rare in his profession.'

'And Marcella?'

'Marcella is Gifford Tate's wife.'

Mrs Burger amended: 'She is Gifford's *second* wife. His first left him while Alan was still at school. Gifford was sixty-one when he married Marcella, then twenty-two. So she is about the same age as her stepson. People who don't know them take them for man and wife.'

Burger smiled: 'But there will be very few who do not know if it is left to you, dear. Anyway! Tate left a number of finished canvases which had never been shown and Edwin decided to release them at the rate of one a year through Ismay Gorton's, the London gallery which handles his work. It has become a minor occasion in the art world. Each year since Tate died the "new Tate" has been unveiled with champagne and gourmet titbits for those privileged to receive tickets for the preview. I attended the first two or three, before my legs started to trouble me.'

'And these unveilings have been going on for eight years? Are there more to come?'

Burger held up a thin hand. 'I'm not sure, but Edwin told me once that there was less than a dozen pictures altogether. Meanwhile, of course, there is this touring exhibition. Will you be going to see it, by the way?'

'I shall try to.'

Burger looked at him with an odd expression. 'I think you should come to a personal preview on Sunday afternoon when I shall be there making sure everything is ready for Monday.'

Wycliffe drove back to the Incident Room with rain lashing against his windscreen. From the fading elegance of tree-lined Wood Lane to the Wharf car park is no more than 500 yards for a purposeful crow, but for a motorist on the one-way system it is the better part of a mile.

So Edwin Garland had almost certainly been incapable of fathering a child. If that was the discovery Francis had made and mentioned in his diary it might have caused him distress but it was hard to see it as providing a motive for his murder.

From his visit to the Burgers, Wycliffe had learned something about art, more about the art trade, and a good deal about Edwin Garland, but he wondered whether it had brought him any closer to establishing a motive for the murder of Francis.

Kersey, kite flying, with a wary eye on Wycliffe, expressed the same doubt. 'This guy was shot at night, on a deserted bit of the wharf. I'm not saying it was a mugging, muggers don't use guns, not on our patch they don't – yet. The chances are we shall turn up some perfectly simple motive. I don't see why we have to drag in father and father's pals with all this art business. Of course I'm only an ignorant peasant and I don't understand these things.'

Lucy Lane rose to the bait and, if she felt out-ranked, she didn't show it.

'I don't see where that argument leads. Garland was murdered because he was Garland, or it was a motiveless killing, or it was a mistake. The fact remains that he was murdered on the night after his father's funeral and if the two are unconnected we are back in the funny coincidences department. That's why father comes into the picture, art or no art.'

Kersey grinned. 'There now, see what it is to have the logic! All I'm saying is that we don't have to go groping about in corners looking for motive, there's plenty of it lying about. His daughter Anna might well have expected to benefit from his death. Her boyfriend likewise, though indirectly. Then there's Cathy Carne. According to her she was convinced that Francis would inherit and dispose of the business, but she might have thought she could do a deal with Beryl. In fact it's not impossible they had an arrangement. Although I can't see Beryl clambering over scaffolding with a .32 tucked in her pants, she'd be quite capable of doing it by proxy. Until she knew what was in the old man's will she and Cathy seem to have been matey enough. Last, but not least, there's the shadowy woman referred to in his diary.'

Wycliffe said: 'Coming down to earth, have you found out anything about Brand?'

'Nothing about the local connection yet but I've had a word with the boys at Penzance. Seems he bought a small-holding on the moor a few years back and set up these classes. I gather there are plenty of crackpots who go in for that sort of thing. It's probably harmless, even pleasantly nutty, and Brand makes a living out of them but there's another side to his business: the school attracts more than its share of gays, especially for the residential courses in the summer.'

'You're looking into the local angle?'

'Curnow's handling that, sir.'

Less than 36 hours after the discovery of the body, facts were coming in at a fair rate, though it was still not possible to decide which were relevant and which not. DS Shaw's computer, over in the corner, blank-faced and brooding, was being well fed on a mixed diet.

CHAPTER SIX

Wycliffe was booked in at a hotel on the waterfront, up river from the wharf and facing the village of Flushing across a narrow stretch of water. For a century or more, in the age of sail, the hotel had been associated with the Packet Service, when Falmouth was the port through which overseas mail and important travellers entered and left the country. Now, with its near neighbour the yacht club, it caters for nautical types of the amateur sort who enjoy messing about in boats. Appropriately the dining room seems to rise almost directly out of the water.

Wycliffe shared a table with a merchant captain whose ship was in dock, a quiet spoken man on the verge of retirement. He had a cottage in the Cotswolds waiting for him and his wife to move in.

'What will you do – in retirement, I mean?'

The Captain laughed. 'Grow roses and keep hens – isn't that the recipe for retired seamen? No; I shall be satisfied just to stop worrying about schedules, cargoes, bunkering, crews, port dues and God knows what else. I'll get by.'

They ate chicken with tarragon, followed by fresh peaches with cream, and split a bottle of Chablis between them.

The case, reported in local newspapers and on the radio, was being talked about, and Wycliffe was aware of other diners watching him. Perhaps generations of

107

detective story writers, from Wilkie Collins down, are responsible for the romantic image of criminal investigation, so that even for a modern hard-bitten public the initials C.I.D. retain a certain mystique.

'You're a celebrity,' the Captain said.

During the meal the rain stopped and the clouds cleared magically, giving way to one of those serenely peaceful summer evenings when harbour and estuary seem embalmed in golden light and one feels that the whole world is waiting.

Wycliffe decided on a walk and his walk took him along Green Bank and down the High Street, where crumbling houses and shops were being rejuvenated or demolished, into the main street.

The Captain had set him thinking about retirement. What would he do when his turn came? Living in a cottage in the Cotswolds or anywhere else isn't an occupation. In any case he was already living where he intended to retire. 'Prepare in advance, cultivate an interest – find a hobby,' the pundits said. Well, he had plenty of interests but none sufficiently systematic to qualify as a hobby. He was not a collector; he did not watch birds, badgers or insects; photography bored him; he was not very good with his hands and the do-it-yourself world of planers, drills, jig-saws, band-saws and sanders had no appeal; he enjoyed gardens, but gardening was a chore. Perhaps he would end up like Emperor Francis of Austria – making toffee.

As though his feet were programmed he found himself at the Incident Room. DC Dixon put out his cigarette and tried to look busy.

'Just one report, sir. A Mrs Richards of Clarence Villa, almost opposite where the Tates live, says she saw Francis Garland on Wednesday morning. He drove up, got out of his car and went in—'

'We know that.'

'Yes, sir, it's in the reports, but she said he was carrying a fairly large flat package – like a picture. She didn't attach any importance to it at the time and it was only when she heard we were interested in anyone who had seen Garland between Saturday and Wednesday that she thought it worth mentioning.'

If nothing else it was a cue for a visit to the Tates.

Wycliffe said: 'You come from this part of the world, don't you?'

'I was born here, sir; my parents and married sisters still live here.'

'Do you know anything about Dr Tate? I mean, is he a popular doctor?'

'Very! It's difficult to get on his list. My mother and sisters swear by him. The funny thing is, he's not very chatty or friendly; people say he's a very shy man.'

'Any gossip?'

'Only that he's living with his stepmother who's younger than he is. People talk but there's probably nothing in it.'

Lucy Lane was at her table, typing serenely: straight back, elbows to sides, using the ten digits God had given her. The only member of the squad who could; the others hammered or pecked with two fingers, swore picturesquely, and reached for the erasing fluid. Wycliffe remembered Mark Garland.

'How did you get on?'

She swivelled on her chair to face him. 'I don't think I did, sir. He's a different proposition from his father. I got the impression that chiropractice – which turns out to be spinal manipulation – isn't a money spinner in this part of the world. Either for that reason or another he's got a monumental chip on his shoulder. He reminded me of the tight-lipped heroes in war films – the name

109

and number ploy; more you will not get even if you carve strips off me. I tried to persuade him that he wasn't threatened, wasn't accused, wasn't even suspected of anything, but he wouldn't have it. He said: "If you think I killed my cousin it is up to you to prove it. I've no alibi. I was out running on Wednesday night at ten o'clock; I am most nights at that time."'

'You say he was out running?'

'He's a keep-fit buff.'

Wycliffe sighed.

'I asked him about his attitude to his cousin and he said he didn't have an attitude but that he was very upset.' Lucy swept her hair away from her face with both hands. 'He was certainly upset about something. I know it sounds thin, sir, but I spent a long time getting no further than that and I don't think we shall do better until we have an angle – some sort of leverage.'

'Not to worry. Something will turn up. Meanwhile we shall keep an eye on him. I'm on my way to talk to Dr Tate.'

'Do you want me with you, sir?'

Wycliffe hesitated but decided not. He located Tate's house on the wall map. It was at the southern end of 'the terraces' one of the older residential areas of the town, and not far from the Burgers'.

He had the choice of half-a-dozen alleys which led off the main street and climbed to the terraces. The alleys were steep and there were steps at intervals but there was a sense of achievement in reaching the top. His choice had more than its share of steps and when he eventually arrived on a pleasant terrace overlooking the harbour, a pounding in his chest reminded him once more that he was middle-aged. But the Tates' house was only a couple of hundred yards away.

Tregarthen – the house in a garden, Wycliffe's

Cornish stretched that far – stood, aloof from the terraced houses, surrounded by a stone wall topped by shrubs. Three or four pine trees created a sombre atmosphere in the evening sun. There were green-painted double gates and a wicket for pedestrians. A brass plate on the wicket: Dr Alan Tate MB, B.Ch., FRCP. A fellowship! What was he doing, slumming it as a GP? Wycliffe passed through into a large, well kept garden – too well kept for his taste: shrubs pruned, grass like a bowling green, edges trimmed. Why not do the whole thing in plastic? The gravelled drive split into two; one branch led to the front door, the other to the back of the house and, according to a finger post, to waiting room and surgery.

A newish Volvo was parked near the house, the off-side front had been damaged and the lamp-housing smashed.

The house itself was 1914 or a bit earlier, steeply pitched slate roofs and high chimneys: bijou Lutyens for the leaner purse. Wycliffe pressed a bell push in a door with stained glass panels. A dog yapped frantically somewhere inside and was subdued. A woman's voice, strident. Footsteps, then the door opened: a man, fortyish, glasses, slim, dark, meticulously groomed: tailored slacks, a silk shirt open at the neck and patent leather house shoes.

'Yes?' Distant.

'Dr Tate?' Wycliffe introduced himself.

Attention focused: 'Ah, yes, I suppose you've come about Garland. You'd better come in.'

A tiled hall with a large oak chest and a long-case clock. Hesitation about which room would be appropriate, then a decision. 'I've been working in my surgery, perhaps we could talk there.'

Tate spoke slowly and precisely as though each word

was carefully selected, examined and polished before being released.

Wycliffe followed him down a carpeted passage to a door at the end, a small room overlooking a regimented back garden with a substantial Swiss-type chalet in the middle of the lawn. Gifford Tate's studio? The surgery was equipped with the usual furniture but out of the best catalogue: desk and swivel chair for the doctor, a couple of hygienic-looking chairs for patient and friend, drugs and instrument cabinet, couch, wash basin, and glass-fronted bookcase. Parquet flooring. No dust, no smears on the polished woodwork; a faint and rather pleasing odour of antiseptic.

'Please sit down.'

Wycliffe was half expecting to be asked: 'What exactly is the trouble?' but Tate did not speak; he waited, apparently relaxed, his thin, pale hands resting on the desk in front of him.

'You attended Edwin Garland in his last illness and you were called in at his death. According to your certificate coronary thrombosis was the immediate cause of death.' Wycliffe could not have explained why he had adopted this abrupt, almost challenging approach; the doctor made him feel uneasy.

Tate still did not speak and Wycliffe was forced to enlarge. 'I'm not questioning your judgement but I have to ask whether in view of what followed you have had any doubts?'

'None whatever. Strictly speaking, Garland died of myocardial infarction resulting from a thrombus in a coronary artery.'

'Did his general condition lead you to expect something of the sort?'

Time to consider. Tate doled out words with seeming reluctance. 'Garland was seventy-five, he suffered from

112

atherosclerosis and there was a history of anginal attacks. I warned him that unless he adhered strictly to the regimen I prescribed he would be at considerable risk.' The doctor brought his hands together and seemed to study them. 'But I fail to understand your interest in all this. Surely it is Francis's death you are investigating?'

Wycliffe was brusque. 'The deaths of father and son within a few days of each other raise questions to which I have to find satisfactory answers. You were a friend of the family, I believe?'

'My father and Edwin Garland were very close friends, so much so that I was brought up to regard Beryl and Francis as cousins.'

'And when you came back here after your father's death, to set up in practice, did you resume a family relationship with the Garlands?'

A brief hesitation. 'No. We remained on first-name terms, they became my patients, but I cannot say that there was any particular relationship between us.'

'You are a beneficiary under Edwin Garland's will, I believe?'

'A thousand pounds.'

'And a tube of Winsor blue.'

A slight gesture of impatience. 'A joke.'

'Not one with much meaning for you, I imagine?'

No response.

Wycliffe was getting nowhere, though Tate was answering his questions without protest and, apparently, without guile. In fact, that was part of the trouble, more often than not it is the protestations and evasions of a witness which tell most about him. But there was more to it than that: Wycliffe had not made contact, he had not found the tender spot which, when probed, yields a reflex rather than a reasoned response.

113

He wondered if a three-cornered exchange might be more enlightening.

'I had intended to talk with Mrs Tate also; I wonder if she would join us?'

A brief frown. 'I'm afraid that isn't possible. Mrs Tate is not at all well and she has gone to bed.'

'I'm sorry! A sudden indisposition?'

A pause while he considered his reply. 'She has been unwell for some time; she is liable to spells of nervous depression. In any case I think I can answer your questions without disturbing her.' He fiddled with the batch of NHS forms in front of him. For the first time he had been nudged slightly off balance.

A difficult man to know; perhaps shy, possibly arrogant. A meticulous man, with a compelling need for orderliness, distancing himself from anything which might threaten the harmonious life he was striving to create. When and how did he unwind? And with whom? It was hard to imagine him having a casual chat with anyone, let alone a more intimate relationship. Of course there was Marcella, but one can usually tell, from the way a man speaks of a woman, if there is an emotional involvement and, despite Mrs Burger, Wycliffe felt reasonably sure that Tate did not seek release in the arms of his stepmother.

He tried again: 'When Edwin Garland collapsed in his studio and you were called in, he was lying close to one of the two easels in the studio – is that correct?'

'The one nearest the door.'

'Was there a painting on that easel?'

'Yes. I feel sure there was.'

'Can you say which painting?'

'No, I had other things on my mind.'

'I have heard that Francis Garland brought a picture here on the morning of the funeral – is that correct?'

A faint smile – the first. 'Our neighbour has been talking, but it is quite true. Francis came to tell us about arrangements for the funeral and he brought with him one of my father's pictures which had been taken to the shop for framing. It was a tradition that Edwin should frame all my father's work but his death made that impossible in this instance so Francis returned the picture.'

Game and set.

But Wycliffe fought back: 'Will the picture be in the exhibition?'

Tate's brown eyes, enlarged by his spectacles, gazed intently at Wycliffe for a moment or two before he replied: 'No. Mrs Tate has a contract with the Ismay Gorton Gallery covering all works that were not exhibited before my father's death. I believe that it is to be shown there in February.'

Something prompted Wycliffe to ask: 'May I see the picture?'

Tate was clearly surprised and irritated by the request but after a moment or two of hesitation he said: 'Very well, if you wish. I'll fetch it.'

Wycliffe was left alone. Dusk was closing in, the garden had acquired a certain mystery in the twilight and the room itself was in near darkness. He wondered why Tate had not joined a group practice like most of his colleagues. Perhaps it was just another instance of a preference for his own company.

Tate returned with the picture. It was of moderate size – about two feet by three. He switched on the light before holding up the picture for Wycliffe's inspection. 'There you are! I am afraid the lighting is not ideal.' Sarcastic.

The village of Flushing, as seen from Falmouth in the early morning, with mist rising from the harbour. A

115

good picture, Wycliffe thought, in the Impressionist style.

'Thank you. When was that painted?'

Tate put the picture down. 'I can't tell you exactly, but sometime after he had his stroke. No doubt it is in the record. I assume that it matters to your investigation?' The doctor was becoming more aggressive.

'I have no idea what matters or does not matter at this stage.'

Tate returned to his swivel chair. 'My father left his pictures to his wife; they are really not my concern. Edwin Garland was his art executor and looked after all the business arrangements.' He looked significantly at the little battery clock on his desk.

Wycliffe said: 'I won't keep you longer than necessary, but I should appreciate your opinion of Francis – the sort of man he was.'

'I am not a psychiatrist.'

'And you consider that only a psychiatrist's opinion would be of any value?'

A faint flush on the pale cheeks. 'I did not say that!'

'Francis Garland was your patient; did he often visit you professionally?'

'Very rarely. He seemed to enjoy good health.'

'I gather that he led a lonely life with few friends.'

'I believe that is so.'

'Women?'

A look of distaste. 'I'm afraid I know nothing of his sex life.'

Wycliffe got up from his chair. 'Very well, Dr Tate. I may look for another opportunity to talk to Mrs Tate.'

Concern. 'Is that absolutely necessary?'

Wycliffe did not answer. 'Good night, doctor.'

'I'll see you out.'

***

116

Wycliffe, unsettled in his mind, made a broad detour on the way back to his hotel. He walked as far as the beaches and along the deserted sea front. Wavelets swished idly over white sand and the broad plain of the sea stretched away into darkness. To his left, St Anthony lighthouse flashed at intervals, and far away to his right the sky was lit now and then by an arc of light from The Lizard. Nearer to hand Pendennis Castle, built by Henry VIII and gallantly defended by John Arundell against Cromwell's soldiers, brooded over its promontory, floodlit for the tourists.

Wycliffe began to feel at peace with himself and the world. He walked on, crossed the isthmus, and passed the entrance to the docks. There were houses with gardens on his left. He was suddenly aware of running feet behind him. He turned and saw a lithe figure in a track suit pounding the pavement towards him. The figure passed, breathing hard, and a few yards ahead turned in at one of the gates.

Mark Garland concluding his evening run.

When Wycliffe had gone, Tate returned to his surgery and to his records. He had scarcely settled to work when his stepmother came in followed by a sad-eyed little King Charles spaniel who immediately began exploring the corners of the room.

Marcella Tate was very pale and her skin was clear, almost transparent, so that fine bluish veins showed on her forehead and at the temples. She sat in the chair Wycliffe had vacated.

'Well?'

Tate said: 'I wish you wouldn't bring the dog in here, Marcella!'

She was immediately contrite: 'Sorry!' She stooped and scooped up the little dog on to her lap. 'There now,

117

Ricky, darling! . . . What did he want?'

'He knew that Garland had brought a painting here on Sunday morning.'

'And?'

'He wanted to see it and I showed it to him.'

'Is that all?'

'More or less. He asked me what I thought of Francis; whether I knew anything about his sex life.'

'What did you say?'

'That I didn't. What did you expect me to say?'

She was bending over the dog, rubbing her cheek against its head. 'Did he ask to see me?'

'Yes; I told him you were indisposed. He said that he might call on you at some other time.'

She straightened abruptly. 'Call on me? But why?' She was suddenly flushed and she let the dog slide from her lap to the floor. 'Why does he want to see me?'

Tate was staring at her, the lenses of his spectacles glittering in the reflected light. 'It's nothing to get excited about. The police talk to everybody in the hope that by hit and miss they might pick up something. You should have been here with me tonight.'

Her voice rose. 'I couldn't face it, Alan! You know I couldn't! If you—'

He came round to her side of the desk and stood by her chair. 'Don't excite yourself. You are working yourself up again. Go up to bed and I'll bring you a hot drink with something to make you sleep . . .'

The words were gently spoken and the woman pressed her head against his body with a deep sigh. 'I depend on you, Alan. You know that.'

'I know.' But he was not looking down at her, his gaze was remote; he seemed to be looking through the window into the darkness of the garden.

118

CHAPTER SEVEN

Wycliffe awoke in his hotel bedroom with a sour taste in his mouth and a leaden feeling in his head due to drinking with the Captain the night before. In a session lasting until one in the morning they had discussed Crime in Society with that lucidity which is only achieved at somewhere above the 100 mg per cent level of blood alcohol and with the comforting knowledge that one doesn't have to drive home. He squirmed as he recalled phrases he had used: 'Speaking as a policeman' . . . 'After thirty years in the Force' . . . 'When the State usurps the functions of the family' . . . and consoled himself with the thought that he never pontificated unless he was drunk. Or did he? . . .

It was seven o'clock by his travelling clock, and broad daylight. Because he had not bothered to draw the curtains there was a trembling mosaic of light on the ceiling reflected from the water outside and, by sitting up in bed, he could see out of the window across the harbour to Flushing. The view was almost identical with Gifford Tate's picture which the doctor had shown him – the picture that was to be the next 'new' Tate. The village was lit by a swathe of sunlight which cut through the morning mist. Several of the moored craft were caught in its path, others appeared only as ghostly forms.

He seemed to be up to his eyes in paintings, painters, painting materials, and even painters' jokes . . .

Incidentally, what was so funny about leaving the doctor a tube of Winsor blue? Or Burger £1,000 to buy spectacles? And had it in any case anything to do with Francis Garland being shot through the head? It was easy to be side-tracked by the more exotic elements in a case.

He got out of bed and drank two glasses of water from the tap then he put his head out of the window and sampled the morning air, tangy with the smell of salt water and seaweed. Away to his right the pier, jutting out into the harbour, hid the back of the Garlands' premises from his view, but he could see the scaffolding behind Benson's where Francis had undergone either translation or extinction.

Across the narrow stretch of water in front of him was Flushing Quay where the ferry was moored, ready for its first crossing of the day. A row of cottages backed on the water and in one of them Francis's illegitimate daughter, Anna, lived with her mother and boyfriend. He had not paid enough attention to Anna, he had not even seen the girl, and yet she was the only one to benefit obviously and directly from her father dying when he did. In a few days or weeks Francis would almost certainly have made a will and it was unlikely that Anna would have been the principal, let alone the sole beneficiary. In any case she would have had to wait, probably for many years . . .

He took a shower, shaved, and dressed in a leisurely way. The hotel was coming to life: in the next room a woman was scolding a child; there were sounds of pots and pans being shifted about in the kitchen; eventually, from down the corridor, came a rattling of cups and saucers. Early morning tea. Across the water the ferry cast off and its squat bulk made a bee-line for the pier. The mists were gone: a glorious morning, but according

120

to the forecast it would be short-lived. Rain before evening. The chambermaid brought his tea and he drank it avidly. Saturday: the third day of his inquiry. His shopping list for the day: Anna, Francis's hypothetical mistress, Marcella Tate, and Brand. He went down to breakfast and was relieved to find that the Captain had not yet come down. Kedgeree, toast and marmalade. Good coffee. It cleared his head.

He was in the main street before nine o'clock and many of the shops were not yet open; assistants were waiting in doorways for the boss to arrive with the keys. In the Incident Room DC Curnow was duty officer and Kersey, smoking his third cigarette of the morning, brooded over a stack of reports. Greetings were perfunctory, as between members of a family.

All the windows were wide open and the room was pleasantly cool. A couple of hundred yards away pleasure boats, preparing for trippers, were berthed three abreast against the pier. Small-boat owners were off at moorings indulging themselves, checking gear or tinkering with engines. The sea was bottle green and silky inshore, out of the sun, light blue and slightly rippled further out. Wycliffe sensed that feeling of child-like excitement and anticipation which seems to infect those who find themselves almost anywhere on the fringes of the sea on a fine summer morning.

Not Kersey: he was morose. 'I've never known anything like it: over two hundred interviews with people who were in the street, mostly in the pubs, at some time between nine and eleven on the night and nobody saw or heard a damn thing. Not even the usual nutters who invent something to get themselves noticed. And yesterday Dixon and Potter spent the whole bloody day chatting up shopkeepers and others about the Garlands in general and Francis in particular.

121

Nothing to show for it! The Garlands seem to have merged into the landscape. What gossip there is, is folklore: Edwin being cuckolded by an estate agent, that's still good for a laugh—'

'By the way, is that chap still around?' In order to say something.

'No, he was killed in the war. As I was saying: they dig up that and also Francis's moment of passion when he made himself a father – which must have been more than twenty years ago! If you have to go back that far to find dirt you're wasting your time. Of course they laugh at Beryl and her friend, they think Francis was a bit weird, and the old man had the name for being tight fisted, but there's no stick to beat a dog with in all that.'

Lucy Lane arrived: in a green frock figured in black, dark hair expertly set, a shoulder bag matching her frock; she looked as though she had just stepped out of her BMW runabout for a spot of window shopping. 'Good morning!' She signed the book, put her bag in a drawer, and sat at her table.

Kersey glanced at his watch. 'Nice of you to drop in.'

'I was here until after ten last night, sir.'

Wycliffe said to Kersey: 'No mistress for Francis yet?'

Kersey crushed out the stub of his cigarette. 'No, but we've turned up Brand's track record and that could mean something. When he lived in Falmouth, Brand was an art teacher, but he gave lectures on astrology and cast horoscopes in his spare time. That was probably how he met Francis, at any rate it seems they were buddies. Then, five or six years ago, Brand came into money and set up his place on the moor.'

'Where Francis visits on business. You think Francis was gay?'

Kersey said: 'I've been checking; there's nothing in

122

his diary to say that M was a woman but you can't get M out of Kevin Brand.'

'It could be a pet name, surely?' from Lucy Lane. 'My parents call me Bunny and shorten it to B.'

Kersey looked at her. 'Really? Shameful Secrets of the Manse Revealed.'

Wycliffe said: 'You'd better go and talk to him, but find somebody who knows the area or you'll spend the rest of the day chasing your tail on that moor.'

Wycliffe turned to the reports where the only item of interest was negative: not a single .32 pistol among the licensed hand guns in the register.

He put through a call to Dr Franks, the pathologist.

Franks was on the defensive: 'You've had the gist of my report, Charles. The typing is held up because my secretary has gone sick.'

'It's not your report I'm bothered about. I want some off-the-record background on Dr Alan Tate. He's fortyish, a local GP, but according to his plate he's got a fellowship. He runs a one-man practice and his patients think he's half-way between a saint and a witch doctor.'

'You think he's a quack?'

'No, I don't. All I want is some idea of why he tucks himself away down here in general practice running a one-man show—'

'You want dirt, Charles, so why not say so? I'll see what I can do.'

Wycliffe joined the trippers on the pier and made for the Flushing ferry. He had to wait a quarter of an hour, but six or seven minutes after that he was climbing the weedy steps to the quay on the other side. Although Falmouth was less than half-a-mile away there was a curious feeling of isolation. Apart from three other ferry passengers there was no one to be seen. The quay

123

was stacked with empty fish boxes, there were platform scales, a yellow dog sleeping in the sun, a small battered truck which looked as though it had found its last resting place, and a notice about rabies. He walked past the war memorial and turned off the quay along a deserted street. The houses, whose front doors opened directly on the street, were a mixed bag, ranging from cottages to substantial dwellings of some distinction, originally built for Packet skippers. Anna and her mother lived in a little detached house which looked as though it had been sliced off from some larger building.

He knocked on the door and got no reply. He stood back and glimpsed a face at an upstair window so he knocked again and after a delay he heard someone coming down the stairs. The door was opened by a fair girl in a dressing gown, her eyes puffy with sleep. Wycliffe introduced himself.

'What time is it?'

'Half-past ten.'

'God! I overslept. You'd better come in.'

In the dark little passage she hesitated outside the door of the front room. 'That room is like a morgue, let's go in the kitchen.'

The kitchen was full of sunshine and faced across the water to Wycliffe's hotel and the Yacht Club.

'Like some coffee?'

'Yes please.'

'Only Nes – nothing fancy.'

'Where's your mother?'

She was filling the kettle at the sink. 'Gone across to Falmouth shopping, I expect.'

'And Terry?'

'Gone to work.'

'So he's back.'

'Oh yes, he's back.' She sounded resigned. She spooned coffee into the cups and added hot water, pushed over the milk jug and a packet of sugar. 'Help yourself . . . Here's a spoon . . . You want to talk to me?' She swept back her tousled hair with both hands.

'Yes. I am very sorry about your father.'

She said nothing for a moment, then: 'I didn't know him very well.'

'I hear you're going to inherit quite a lot of money.'

She stirred sugar into her coffee. 'So they tell me.'

'Did you expect anything like it?'

'No, I thought my grandfather would leave me something. He told me he was going to. Of course I didn't know about the other – coming from my father, I mean.'

'When did your grandfather tell you he intended to leave you money?'

'About a month ago. He came over one morning when mother was out and Terry had gone to work – just like now.'

'Tell me about it.'

She looked at him frowning, doubtful, then made up her mind. 'Okay. It was queer at first. He sat there, where you are, just looking at me, then, very abrupt, he said "Go and brush your hair!" I thought he must have gone a bit ga-ga but there was no harm so I went up to my room and did my hair a bit. When I came down he said: "That's better. Thank you, child!" and he just went on looking at me. In the end he said: "You are very like your grandmother, do you know that?" I said I'd seen her picture. Then he asked me to kiss him on the lips and we kissed. He held me for a minute or two, quite tight, kissing and stroking my hair, then we sat down again.

'He said that his heart was dicky and that he wouldn't

125

last much longer. He asked me a lot of questions about myself – what I wanted to do with my life, that sort of thing . . . He wanted to know if I minded being illegitimate . . .'

'And do you?'

'I never really think about it. Who cares?'

'What else did he say?'

'That I would have enough money to get started in anything I really wanted to do; that he thought I had enough guts to be a success if I put my mind to it. If I wanted to squander the money in six months or a year, I could do that too, but if I did he would haunt me.'

'Did you tell anyone what your grandfather had told you?'

'No.'

'Not your mother or Terry?'

'Nobody.'

She got up from her chair, went to a cupboard and came back with a crusty roll and a dish of butter. 'Have one?'

'No, thanks.'

Wycliffe tried to recall what his own daughter had been like at twenty, which was not so very long ago. Much less at ease with others or with herself, far less pragmatic; she had wanted to meet the world on her own terms – and still did, though her capacity for acceptance was growing. Acceptance, that was Anna's secret. For Anna the world was the world was the world, and she would come to terms with it.

'Did your grandfather say anything else?'

She bit into her buttered roll scattering crumbs, and shook her head. Only after considerable hesitation did she say: 'Not really.'

'I think he did.'

She frowned, wiping her lips. 'It was odd, a bit weird.

126

As he was going – he was in the passage – he turned round and said: "I don't suppose you know that your father and your Aunt Beryl were both illegitimate. It must run in the family, don't you think?" Then he just went. He didn't even say goodbye.' She looked at Wycliffe solemnly. 'Do you believe it?'

'Why would he lie to you?'

'No reason I can think of, but why tell me?'

Good question but not one Wycliffe was prepared to discuss. He changed the subject.

'You used to visit your father occasionally, I believe?'

'Yes.'

'Why?'

She looked at him quizzically. 'That's a funny question; because he was my father, I suppose. I mean, it's odd: I used to feel sometimes I wanted to talk to him to see what he was really like but I never did. Every time it would end up with him giving me some money. He thought that was what I came for and, in a way, I suppose he was right. I wish I had talked to him though.'

'When did you last see him?'

'At the funeral, the day before he was killed.'

'You know that Terry saw it happen?'

'From a distance.'

'He thought the killer was a woman.'

'I know.'

'I have to ask: was it you?'

She made no protest. 'No. Why should I have wanted to kill him? He never did me any harm.'

'Where were you that evening?'

'Home here, with mother.' Arms on the table, she was staring out of the window with unseeing eyes then, abruptly, she turned to face him. 'That is a lie! I was in the van with Terry.'

'He didn't say so.'

A faint smile. 'He was trying to keep me out of it.'

'Did you see your father attacked?'

'No, I'd left by then.'

'You'd better tell me about it.'

With apparent concentration she circled the rim of her coffee cup with the tip of her finger. 'After the funeral we went on the beach and in the evening to a disco. The van was on the Wharf car-park. It was one of those days, I was bloody minded . . . Anyway, in the disco we began to quarrel and just after nine we packed it in and went back to the van. Of course the damn thing wouldn't start and that was the last straw. I started nagging him about money, about not having a proper job and no guts to get one . . . You know how it is . . .' She looked up to judge whether this quiet middle-aged policeman was likely to know any such thing. She was quiet for a time and when she spoke again her manner was more confiding.

'It was the money grandfather promised me I was worried about. I'd have been a lot more worried if I'd known how much it was going to be . . . I mean, Terry isn't mean or greedy or anything like that but he would see it as a sort of bonanza, a jackpot . . . I wanted him to do something on his own.

'Anyway, he didn't say much but that didn't stop me, and in the end I got out and left him there.'

'Where did you go?'

She pushed the cup and saucer away from her. 'Tommy Webber who lives next door works in the bar at The Packet so I went along there and sat in the bar until closing time then Tommy gave me a lift home on the back of his bike.'

'Did you pass under the scaffolding on your way to The Packet?'

She shivered. 'Yes, I did.'

'Did you hear anything which, looking back, might have been suspicious?'

'Nothing, but I wasn't paying any attention.'

'This story of Terry's about going after your father to ask him for a loan to buy a small-holding – what do you make of that?'

She smiled. 'That's Terry. Of course, he didn't actually do it, did he?'

'Have you any idea of the time you left the car-park?'

'The church clock was striking ten as I came up into the street from Custom House Quay.'

Wycliffe said: 'I want you to put what you have told me into a statement. I would like you to come to the Incident Room on the Wharf later today.'

When Wycliffe returned to the quay the ferry was discharging passengers, a score or more from this trip, among them some obvious visitors, but mainly women returning from shopping in Falmouth. There was a fat woman in a floral dress, pink and perspiring, weighed down by shopping bags, who looked at Wycliffe intently. Remembering Lucy Lane's description, he felt sure that she must be Anna's mother.

But he was still haunted by the scene the girl had conjured up: the old man in that bright little kitchen with its ramshackle fittings and earthenware sink: holding her, kissing her lips and her hair; then sitting at the table, questioning her, promising to leave her some money, and finally, as a parting shot, telling her casually that her father and her aunt had both been illegitimate . . .

Marcella Tate sat on the very edge of her chair clutching her little dog to her thin breast. She looked

129

from Wycliffe to Lucy Lane and back again with apprehension that was close to panic. Although her pallor and her drawn features aged her, Wycliffe had the impression of a little girl caught out in some childish fault.

They were in the big drawing-room of the Tates' house and the afternoon sun shone directly through the tall windows which were tightly shut, making the room uncomfortably warm.

Lucy Lane, trying to make contact, got up and stooped over the dog, stroking his head. 'My uncle used to breed King Charles spaniels. What's his name?' She spoke as she might have done to a nervous child.

'He's called Ricky – after my brother who was killed in a road accident when he was three.' She implanted a quick kiss on the little dog's moist nose.

'He looks in splendid condition. Have you ever thought of showing him?'

The two women talked dogs and Wycliffe listened, looking benign.

The room was as much a library as a drawing-room, with bookshelves occupying all the available wall space to within three feet of the high ceiling. As far as Wycliffe could see, the books were a rather austere collection of poetry, classical fiction, and biography. No pictures, but a small cabinet of porcelain figures. Wycliffe thought they might be Chelsea or Chelsea Derby. Helen would have known.

Only when Marcella had relaxed sufficiently to sit back in her chair and release her tight hold on the dog did he risk intervention: 'We came to talk about the Garlands.'

'The Garlands?' Did she lay stress on the plural?

'I'm told that Edwin Garland was a close friend of your late husband.'

A flicker of relief. 'Oh yes, he was; a very dear friend, he spent a lot of time here, expecially after Gifford had his stroke . . .'

No one spoke so she felt driven to continue: 'I expect you know that I was Gifford's second wife; I married him when I was only twenty-two and he was sixty-one. People said I did it for his money but that wasn't true. I admired him a great deal . . .'

'How did you meet him?' Lucy Lane, very softly.

'I went to a series of lectures on the history of art which he gave in Exeter where I was in my final year reading English. I got my degree before we married. I don't know why he picked on me; I've never been very attractive. But it wasn't sex that really mattered to either of us; he used to say that I was his insurance and consolation in old age.' Another nervous smile.

Wycliffe thought that Gifford Tate had found himself a girl wife, one who, however unconsciously, was looking for a daddy or, perhaps, a hero rather than a husband. Marcella would never grow up, but was it possible that, along with a childish naivety, she had carried forward into adult life the single-minded ruthlessness of the young?

She went on without prompting: 'Although he was a painter he was a very literary man so we had plenty in common. He was wonderful to talk to . . . He had read widely and deeply in so many subjects!' She turned to the bookcase: 'Those were his books, but after he had his stroke he couldn't read for any length of time without tiring his eyes and I used to read to him. In that last summer before he died I read him the whole of Proust . . . It was very hot that year and he liked me to sit naked on a chair in the courtyard garden while I read to him.' She glanced down at herself in disparagement. 'I wasn't like this, then.'

'You must have missed him very much.' Lucy Lane, without apparent irony.

'I did! I mean, he'd given me experiences I could never have hoped for. At first when he died I didn't know what to do with myself, I even thought . . . Anyway, when Alan suggested that he should set up in practice here it seemed a splendid idea.' Her eyes were glistening with tears.

'Did Edwin continue to visit you?'

'Oh yes. Not as often as when Gifford was alive but quite regularly.'

'When was he here last?'

She frowned, playing absently with the dog's ear. 'It must have been a week last Wednesday. He usually came on Wednesday afternoons because Alan is almost always here then.'

'Did he come to see you both?'

'Oh yes. The three of us would chat about anything and everything for a while then Alan would take him into the surgery so that they could be private.'

'You mean for a consultation about Edwin's health?'

'I suppose so; he was Alan's patient.'

'What about Francis? Was he a regular visitor?'

'Francis never came here.'

'Beryl?'

'Not Beryl either.'

'Had there been some sort of quarrel?'

'No! It was just that we had so little in common. I mean, Francis was a very different man from his father.'

'But Francis was here last Wednesday – the morning of the funeral, wasn't he?'

Her agitation was returning. 'He came to tell us about the arrangements, it wasn't very well organised

132

I'm afraid.' She said this with an air of finality as though the subject was closed.

'And to deliver a picture.'

'Well, yes. He did bring a picture with him: one of Gifford's that Edwin was going to frame for us.'

'The "new Tate" for next year?'

'Yes, but Alan will look after that now. I don't know what I should do without him. I don't think I could go on living.'

'Weren't the pictures left to you?'

'Yes, they were, but Edwin was Gifford's art executor and he looked after all the business. Gifford left me the pictures and some money, and he left Alan the house. I was afraid I would have to move when Alan came back but he wanted someone to keep house for him so it worked out very well.'

'Are there other pictures by your husband which have not yet been exhibited?'

'I don't think so. I'm fairly sure this was the last.'

'I suppose you will be at the exhibition opening on Monday?'

She frowned. 'I don't know. If I feel well enough.'

'When Francis came on Wednesday, how long did he stay?'

'About an hour, I think.'

'You were there the whole time?'

'No, I had some work to do in the kitchen and I left them here.'

'What did you talk about while you were with them?'

'About Edwin and about the funeral. That's what Francis came about. Why are you asking me all these questions?'

She was becoming worked up again and there was an element of aggression in her manner which might soon dissolve into tears.

Wycliffe became more formal. 'Mrs Tate, I have to ask you certain questions – questions which have already been put to others who were acquainted with Francis Garland, as were you and Doctor Tate. Was there any friction during Garland's visit here on Monday afternoon?'

'No! I've told you.'

'Where were you on Wednesday evening?'

Her voice was suddenly very low. 'I was here all the evening.'

'Alone?'

'No, with Alan.'

'Neither of you was out of the house after, say, half-past eight?'

'I told you we were in all the evening.'

She looked so pale that Wycliffe was afraid she might faint. He changed the subject: 'Was the chalet in the garden your husband's studio?'

She reacted with relief. 'Oh, yes. I've kept it just as it was and it's surprising how many people come to see it. Alan says we should charge . . . He's joking, of course.'

'I would like to see it if I may.'

She looked startled. 'You? Why?'

'Curiosity; interest. I admire your husband's work.'

She looked doubtful. 'I suppose it would be all right. You'd better come with me.' She led the way along the main corridor, past the surgery door. 'The key is in the kitchen; we can go out that way.'

She took the key from a hook by the kitchen door and they followed her out into a paved courtyard that was partly glazed over; there were lounging chairs, potted plants and climbers, and a sizeable lily-pond with a fountain. 'The sun comes round in the afternoon and Gifford used to spend a lot of time here after his

134

stroke. Alan and I sometimes sit out here on fine evenings.'

They crossed the grass to the studio, a substantial timber building in the style of a Swiss chalet, well preserved. Several steps led up to the door which she unlocked. The studio was a single large room open to the rafters. Windows high up in the north wall gave a diffused light. The furnishing was simple, functional and of excellent quality: two mahogany easels, a large adjustable work table, a painter's trolley, benches with shallow drawers, racks for canvases, shelves and cupboards. Two large leather-covered armchairs were placed near a cast-iron stove, and between them there was a low table with a chessboard, the pieces set up ready for play.

'This is just as it always was except that I usually have some of his sketch books, a few of his letters, and his work-book on display, but those things are on loan to the exhibition.'

She was more relaxed, taking pride in her role of showman. 'I feel like Miss Havisham – in *Great Expectations*, you know. Except that we don't have any cobwebs.' A nervous laugh.

'Is this were Edwin Garland and your husband spent their time?'

She smiled. 'Always; both of them smoking like chimneys. I fancy sometimes that I can still smell stale tobacco-smoke in here, the place is impregnated with it. Edwin rolled his own cigarettes, my husband was a pipe man. It did neither of them any good, especially after Gifford had his stroke, but there was nothing anyone could do about it.'

'Did you ever join them here?'

The idea struck her as odd. 'Good gracious, no! Gifford hated to be disturbed when he was in here whether he was with Edwin or alone.'

Wycliffe said: 'How did the stroke affect your husband, Mrs Tate?'

She frowned. 'Well, mentally not at all; physically he suffered partial paralysis down his left side. He was left-handed and so the disability was a severe blow but he used to say: "You don't paint with your hands, you paint with your heart and mind", and he proved that, didn't he?'

A good deal of wall space was taken up with framed photographs, each one labelled with a date and the location. Most we e photographs of Gifford Tate and his two friends, the settings varied from the garden of the house to the Loire Valley, and to places in the Mediterranean. Several had been taken on a yacht at sea. Women figured in some of the pictures. Marcella pointed to a rather lean, severe-looking woman with deep-set eyes. 'That's Naomi, Gifford's first wife; they separated when Alan was seventeen; she died not long afterwards.'

She opened one of the cupboards. 'This is where I keep a lot of the material for his biography. These are his sketchbooks.' A numbered series, uniformly bound in fawn linen. 'There are fifty-eight of them, dating from 1922 . . . And on this shelf I keep his letters – letters to him that is. I'm having difficulty in getting hold of letters he wrote *to* people but they are coming in slowly. I take photo-copies . . . I've got his diaries in my room; he kept a diary from the age of thirteen.'

Wycliffe thanked her for showing them the studio. 'Some of what you have told us will have to go into a statement which you will be asked to sign. This is normal procedure and need cause you no concern. You can come back with us now or you can call in at the Incident Room on the Wharf later today if you prefer.'

'I'll come this afternoon.'

Wycliffe saw Lucy Lane look at him in astonishment as he accepted the arrangement.

They were seen off after walking round the house to the front. Marcella clutching her dog, wary but to some extent relieved.

As they reached the street Lucy Lane said: 'You were in no hurry for her statement, sir.'

'What would be the point? She would only say what she has said already.'

'And this afternoon?'

'The difference, if any, will be that she will tell a story which has been revised and edited by Tate.'

'Still further from the truth.'

'Very likely; but in our business lies are often more interesting.'

At the Congress of Vienna they cut a semi-circle from one of the grand dining tables in the Hofburg to accommodate the King of Wurtemberg's belly. Detective Constable Potter would have benefited from a similar facility in the office, but his bulk was the subject of severe official disapproval and there was a parallel concern for his health and fitness. A recent medical board had told him to stop smoking, to cut down on beer, and to eat more healthily (the current euphemism for going on a diet), or else . . . But after three weeks of this Potter claimed to have lost nothing but his good humour.

'Message from Forensic, sir.' He handed Wycliffe a buff memorandum slip. 'And will you please ring Dr Franks, sir.' Morose; no hint of the chirpy fat man who had brewed more police tea than any three others, in the force, put together.

Wycliffe was moved to sympathise. 'I know how you

feel, Potter, but stick at it. I gave up my pipe last Christmas.' Smug.

Potter smiled a wan smile. 'And, with respect, sir, for the first month we all knew about it.'

'Really? Was it as bad as that?' Chastened, Wycliffe turned to his memo: 'Bullet and cartridge case submitted August 7th: Preliminary examination suggests that these belong to the same round and that the bullet was fired from a self-loading pistol of 7.65mm calibre (.32 auto. in Britain and US), probably the Mauser H.Sc. Further details later. Best – Haines.'

Haines was a friend in the right place, ready to cut a few corners and pass on information while it was still worth having.

'Call for you, sir – Dr Franks.'

'Wycliffe here.'

'Oh, Charles! A disappointment I'm afraid. Tate's reputation is impeccable, at least professionally. Trained at Kings, first class track record and his fellowship at twenty-nine. A year or two later he took up a consultancy somewhere in the Home Counties. All systems go, then his father died and he threw in his hand to set up as a GP in Falmouth.'

'Any idea of the reason?'

'A quirk of temperament apparently. Didn't like hospital work – couldn't stand colleagues – any colleagues; he's a loner. I suppose it could be that he just wants to crow in his own back yard. I don't know.'

'Anything else?'

'What more do you want? If you mean his private life he hardly seems to have had one. Dedicated or something I expect.'

CHAPTER EIGHT

'Brand bought this small-holding: house, outbuildings and a bit of land, way out on the moor. He's done a conversion job in ye-olde-worlde style, cart wheels in the yard, bare beams and brick floors, magic symbols all over the place. He runs day classes all the year round and study holidays for resident students in the summer. There are classes in astrology, the tarot, numerology, ritual magic and God knows what else.

'The attraction of the place is that it lies spot-on a ley line – an imaginary line linking a few hunks of granite scattered around the landscape, supposed to have been put there by our ancestors for their spiritual gigs. One of the features of the course is surveying, they tramp over the moor with a theodolite, a staff, surveying poles, and packed lunch, looking for other ley lines. They also go about with a galvanometer and a Geiger counter to measure "sources of power". There's a little white-washed room on the campus with a dirty great lump of granite in the middle. When they feel drained of spiritual energy the students go there and lie on the floor, their bare feet against the granite, to re-charge their batteries.'

'Sounds harmless.'

'I suppose so but the whole set-up is as camp as a field full of tents. Brand only advertises in the gay mags and, to judge from those present, that's where he gets his clients. "Most of my students come on personal

139

recommendation." I'll bet they do.'

Three o'clock in the afternoon and the weathermen had got it wrong, the sun still shone and the sky was blue. Kersey reported on his visit to Brand.

'What sort of man is he?'

Kersey lit a cigarette. 'I know gays don't wear ID tags – "no distinguishing physical characteristics" the shrinks say, but you'd spot Brand as a card-carrying queen a mile off. Slight, fair, silk shirt, tight pants, and he walks as though he wants to wee-wee. He's friendly, but wary – very.'

'Where does Francis come in?'

'He attends classes every Sunday. Brand told me that they'd been friendly from way back and when I leaned on him a bit he admitted that they'd had a thing going but it had been broken off two or three years ago.'

'Why?'

Kersey looked like a lion with a tasty Christian in view. 'Our Frankie had found a new friend; guess who?'

Wycliffe growled, 'Get on with it!'

'His cousin, Mark. Mark turned up at these Sunday classes and despite family differences they soon realised that there was a communion of souls. Mark now spends Sundays and Tuesdays there. I don't know what the financial arrangements are but he has a double role, he attends the classes but he also does spinal manipulation and massage for those of Brand's clients who need it or say they do.'

'You didn't leave it there.' Wycliffe, being patient.

'No, Brand was persuaded to unburden himself. When Frankie arrived on Tuesday afternoon with his printing order, he got hold of Mark and they went off on their own. Frankie arrived back by himself about an hour later and drove off without a word to anybody.

140

When Mark turned up he was red-eyed and in a foul temper. "I thought they must have had a quarrel," Brand said, and I had the impression he wasn't heartbroken about it.'

'We must have a word with Mark Garland.'

'Here, at his home, or in his office?'

'I don't want to upset Thomas unnecessarily; let's see him in his office or whatever he calls it.'

'Mark Garland, Chiropractor', painted on the glass door of a small shop. Both door and window were curtained so that it was not possible to see inside. There was a bell-push with the instruction: 'Please ring and wait'. They rang and waited, and after a full minute the door was opened by a man in his thirties, fair, clean shaven, medium height, and slim. He wore a white coat, and glasses which seemed disproportionately large. Wycliffe had to revise a notion based on slender evidence that all osteopaths and chiropractors have the physique of rugby players.

'Have you an appointment?'

Wycliffe showed his warrant card.

'Oh, you'll have to wait. I have a patient with me.' His manner was nervously belligerent.

They were put into a little room, no more than a cubicle, where there were two kitchen-chairs and a table with a few magazines. The partitions were thin and they could hear Garland giving instructions to his patient to make certain movements and assume certain postures. It was soon over, the patient was shown out after making a further appointment, and they were admitted.

The consulting room was as sparsely furnished as the waiting cubicle; two chairs, a desk and a telephone, in addition to the essential couch. Wycliffe and Kersey were given the two chairs while Mark Garland perched on the edge of the couch.

A one-man show, not even a receptionist.

Garland opened with a protest. 'I told your sergeant that I know nothing of my cousin's death. I am distressed enough about it without having you people coming here, interrupting my work.'

Wycliffe was looking round the room. On the walls there was a certificate from a professional institution, an advertisement calendar, and a framed photograph of the harbour. It seemed that he had not heard Garland's little speech but his gaze came round eventually.

He said: 'Let us be clear about your position, Mr Garland. I am investigating a murder. You will be asked certain questions and your answers or failure to answer will decide whether or not you go with us to a police station for further interrogation. Now, what is it to be?'

Garland took off his spectacles and cleaned the lenses with his handkerchief. 'I'll listen to your questions before I decide.'

'No, I shall decide on the basis of your answer to one question: I want to know the circumstances in which your cousin received bruises to his face on the day before he was murdered.'

'I've told you I know nothing about Francis's death.'

Wycliffe leaned forward in his chair. 'And I've told you the options, Mr Garland. We know that you quarrelled with your cousin at Brand's place; he returned from the encounter with his face severely bruised. The following evening he was shot dead while walking his dog along the wharf here. We have reasonable grounds for detaining you on suspicion unless you can satisfy us that you had no part in the shooting.'

Garland was shaken and he was still making up his mind how to react when the doorbell rang. He looked doubtfully at Wycliffe: 'My next patient.'

Kersey said: 'Your notice tells them to ring and wait. This one has rung, now he can wait.'

'It's a woman. Shall I ask her to make another appointment.'

'That's up to you.'

Garland went to the door and they heard a brief exchange. When he came back he had decided to co-operate. 'Ask me what you want to know.' He perched on the edge of the couch once more and Wycliffe realised that he was trembling.

'Why did you attack your cousin?'

'We had a row.'

'You had a homosexual relationship?'

'That's not illegal.'

'No, it's a matter of fact.'

'All right, we had a homosexual relationship and it was understood between us that as soon as it was possible we would go away together and start afresh.' He could not keep still and his eyes reddened as though at any moment he might burst into tears.

'What would have made your plans possible?'

'It was understood that we would go when his father died and the will was settled. Then, when his father did die . . . Within three days . . .' He broke off, unable to continue.

'Take your time.'

He made an effort. 'Three days after his father died, when it seemed everything would begin to come right for us, that he would be able to leave that business and I would get out of here . . .' He looked round the bleak little room in despair. 'He chose that moment to accuse me of having someone else.' He pressed a handkerchief to his eyes, sobbed, and blew his nose.

'He was jealous?'

'Yes, it was so unreasonable! To threaten everything because of wicked gossip.'

'Gossip about you and . . . ?'

A sidelong look. 'About me and Kevin Brand. Because I gave Kevin massage – I mean, that's one of the reasons I go there.'

'So you attacked your cousin.'

'Yes, I attacked him, if that's what you like to call it! I lost my temper. If it had been a man and woman relationship you would think that was understandable but we aren't expected to have feelings; if we do they're a joke.'

Wycliffe said: 'I'm only interested in what happened at Brand's place on the Tuesday because of what followed.'

Garland shook his head. 'I didn't kill him. I couldn't!'

'So where were you on Wednesday evening?'

'I told you: I went for my usual run. I left home at half-past nine and I got back about half-past ten.'

'Where did you run?'

He made a vague gesture. 'The usual: Swanpool, across to Gyllingvase, along the seafront, around Castle Drive and home.'

'Not through the main street?'

'No.'

'Do you own a gun, Mr Garland?'

'Of course not!'

'Have you ever fired one?'

'Only a .22 sporting rifle when I was at college.'

Wycliffe said: 'I want you to come back to the Incident Room with me where you will be asked to make a full statement.'

144

'Am I under arrest?'

'No, you are helping us with our enquiries.'

More fodder for the computer if nothing else. A modern investigating officer secures his rear with computer print-out. And more enquiries to be made: anyone walking or driving along the following route between nine-thirty and ten-thirty last Wednesday evening . . . A man in a track suit, running . . .

'I thought it was a woman.' The only first-hand evidence they had and that depended on the observation of a not very bright young man, on a dark misty night, at a distance of a hundred yards.

Wycliffe reviewed possible candidates: among them the women, Cathy Carne, Marcella Tate, and Anna Brooks – any one of them would have been physically capable of committing the crime and sprinting away afterwards. And which of the men might have been mistaken for a woman? As the witness concerned, Terry Gill, had to be omitted (though he remained a suspect); that left Alan Tate and Mark Garland, both of whom were of medium height, slight of build and certainly capable of the agility required.

A reconstruction? Would seeing a re-run of the incident, as he had recounted it, help Terry Gill to a firmer conclusion? Wycliffe thought not. In his experience reconstructions were little more than public relations exercises.

Marcella Tate came to the Incident Room and made her statement which added nothing to the sum of their knowledge.

Wycliffe was late for his after-dinner walk, delayed by the Captain, but he was anxious to establish an element of routine. Without a pattern, some repetitive rhythm in his days, he felt lost.

He walked down the High Street and along the Wharf with the intention of retracing Francis's footsteps on the night of the murder. The time was about right but conditions were quite different: instead of misty rain the evening was clear, the air was balmy with that silky feel, and the waters of the harbour gleamed in the darkness. He passed the barred windows of Edwin's studio; the only light in the building came from an upstairs room, the living-room, where Beryl was almost certainly sitting and brooding alone.

He imagined Francis coming out, and the dog scampering ahead through the mist. Less than 200 yards away was the car park. When he reached it there was a sprinkling of cars but no decrepit old van with a CND symbol on its side. Had Francis seen and recognised the van? Had there, despite Terry Gill's denials, been an encounter? He passed the lighted windows of the Incident Room and continued on towards Benson's. The lights on the scaffolding shone, unwinking in the still air.

It was the first day the wharf walk had been re-opened to the public and the first night without a PC on guard at the scene of the crime. Saturday night; the pubs in the street would be doing good business but it was very quiet, only a faint hiss of escaping steam coming from the docks. He reached Benson's and passed under the scaffold. Old mortar, chipped from the wall, still crunched underfoot. At this point Francis must have had about 20 seconds to live, a few more steps and he would have reached the other end which, for him, was the threshold of death.

Wycliffe always forced himself to envisage every detail of a murder so that he would never become reconciled to the enormity of the crime. Murder appalled him because it took everything from the victim with no possibility of restitution, it blotted out memories of a past and hopes for a future. It was the supreme arrogance of the killer which dismayed him. He could not imagine the stunted, blinkered, and self-regarding mind that could contemplate the killing of another human being.

He stood for a moment or two at the spot where Francis's body had been found. The first stage of the scaffolding was little more than a foot above his head. The killer must have been kneeling there, pistol at the ready, and as Francis emerged he or she had fired at a range of a few inches.

He shuddered involuntarily and walked on towards the printing works.

He could see the rectangular outline of the building and, at the top, at the harbour end, a lighted window open to the night. He had not, so far, met Cathy Carne on her home ground and now was his chance. A moment or two later he was ringing her door bell.

There was a light behind the hammered glass and he could hear Cathy Carne's voice, speaking on the telephone. He could not distinguish her words but she sounded harassed and tense. The bell probably cut short her conversation for almost at once he heard the telephone replaced and she called out: 'Who is that?'

'Superintendent Wycliffe.'

She opened the door; she was wearing a dressing gown. She looked flushed and vaguely dishevelled. 'I'm sorry, but one has to be careful about opening the door at night.'

'Of course!' He apologised for disturbing her.

'It doesn't matter; come in. I was on the telephone.'

He followed her into the living-room. It was snug: a

147

sofa, tub chairs, television, record player, and shelves full of books on either side of the chimney breast. Over the mantelpiece an Edwin Garland landscape with figures. On a low table there was a tray with a bottle of whisky and two used glasses. She whisked the tray off the table and took it away. When she returned she felt the need to explain.

'Saturday is usually hectic in the shop and I'm ready for bed and a book by ten o'clock but tonight I felt the need of a nightcap. Do sit down!'

She sat herself on the sofa and pulled the dressing gown around her legs. She was watching him closely and she was talking too much. Something had upset her and he doubted if it was his arrival.

'I didn't ask you; would you like a drink?'

'No, thanks.'

She reached for her cigarettes and lit one. 'Now, what's all this about?' Working hard at trying to sound normal.

'How well do you know Mark Garland?'

'Mark?' She seemed surprised and perhaps relieved. 'Hardly at all. Odd you should ask, though, because he was in the shop last Thursday, wanting to talk to Beryl. It was the first time I've spoken to him in years.'

'Thursday was the day after your uncle's funeral, the day Francis's body was found.'

'Yes.' She was cautious.

'I thought there was no contact between the two sides of the family.'

'There wasn't – isn't; Beryl wouldn't see him.'

'Have you any idea why he came?'

She made a vague gesture. 'No; he seemed upset, edgy. He said he wanted to explain something to Beryl but I've no idea what. When Beryl wouldn't talk to him he went away more upset than ever.'

148

Wycliffe was taking in details of the room. Self-contained was the phrase that occurred to him; everything was there to hand. The same phrase described the woman who had made it. Not that Cathy Carne was a loner, she wanted – needed human contacts, but she would have them only on her own terms. They must arrive on the doorstep, like the milk.

'Presumably you have friends – outside of business?'

Her eyes narrowed against the smoke from her cigarette. 'Naturally.'

'Did Francis or Beryl ever visit you here?'

'Never.'

'Edwin?'

'No.'

'The Tates?'

She frowned. 'What is all this?'

'A simple question. If you would prefer not to answer it . . .'

'It's not that. As a matter of fact the Tates are friends; after all I've known them for years.'

'They come here?'

She crushed out her cigarette. 'Dr Tate comes here sometimes. To be honest he's a fairly regular visitor; he's a lonely man and we have things in common.'

'Something wrong with that? Why be coy about it?'

She wore a watch with an expanding gold bracelet and she fingered it, easing the bracelet away from her wrist and examining the pattern of indentations it left on her skin. 'It's silly really, but Alan is a doctor and vulnerable to gossip, he's also a very private man.'

'Perhaps Marcella wouldn't like it.'

'What are you suggesting?'

'Only that I have an impression that she depends a great deal on the doctor.'

'She does, but there's nothing . . . there's no attachment. That is malicious gossip.' On her metal.

'Was Dr Tate here the night Francis was killed?'

'What are you getting at?'

'Again, a simple question.'

She hesitated, then: 'Yes, he was here.'

'When did he come and when did he leave?'

'He came at about seven. I had invited him for a meal, and he left around midnight.'

Wycliffe stood up and went to the window, parted the curtains, and looked out. 'I can see the back of Benson's quite clearly. It's not far, is it? There was a shot and the dog barked, but you heard nothing?'

'Not to notice. Here, by the harbour, there are all sorts of sounds from the docks and the ships, one gets to ignore them.'

He stood, looking down at her. 'And neither of you left the flat between say eight and eleven?'

'Neither of us.'

'Good! Just one more thing. The letter your uncle left you; you say you destroyed it?'

'We come back to that!'

'And we shall continue to come back to it until you tell me what was in it.'

'I've already told you.'

'You've told me nothing which would have been worth Edwin Garland taking the trouble to put into a letter and leave it with his lawyer. It's a serious matter to mislead the police in a murder investigation. Take legal advice if you want to, but I intend to know what it was that your uncle confided to you.'

There was silence during which they could hear singing coming from the street. The clock on the mantelpiece chimed and struck eleven.

Wycliffe said: 'Have you thought that you may yourself be in danger?'

'In danger? Me?' Unconvincingly dismissive. 'I don't know what you mean?'

'Your uncle, for his own reasons, confided something to Francis and Francis is dead. Perhaps it is dangerous to have information and keep it to yourself.'

She looked incredulous. 'That is nonsense!'

'Think it over. I'll say good night and I apologise for disturbing you so late.'

She came with him to the door, uneasy, perhaps scared. She watched him go down the steps. He waited until she had closed the door then went back up, making as little noise as possible. The hall light was still on and he put his ear to the letter box; he could hear her voice on the telephone but could not distinguish her words.

Two women seemed anxious to provide Tate with an alibi, or to use him as an alibi for themselves.

He walked back along the wharf.

Wycliffe spent a restless night. Although his curtains were drawn, moonlight flooded his room and each time he awoke from an uneasy sleep he thought that it was morning. Waking or sleeping his mind fretted away at the case, images drifted in and out of his consciousness, words and phrases came to mind in a confusing jumble but once, in a doze, it seemed that Beryl was actually speaking to him in her clear, cracked voice. 'He worked it all out, planned it move by move . . .'

Beryl's words had impressed him at the time because they summed up his own vague feeling that what had happened and what was happening might be consequences of the old man's cynical, even malicious contrivings. Obviously Edwin had not murdered Francis but he had created a situation in which violence was more likely.

The main provisions of the will were devisive and

151

certain to breed strife, but they provided no motive for Francis's murder. How often had Wycliffe told himself that the only obvious beneficiary from Francis's death was his daughter? But could she have known that her father had not made a will? In any case he could not believe . . . but that was not evidential.

Aside from gain the commoner motives for murder are anger, jealousy, lust and fear. The first three, in combination, or any one of them, pointed to Mark Garland. As to fear, who would have reason to fear Francis? Surely he presented no physical threat to anyone, but it was possible that he had knowledge that was threatening. His father had confided in him and Francis himself had been surprised, not only by the nature of the confidence but also by the fact that it had been made to him. 'Something about himself . . . Incredible to think that it has been going on all these years . . . He said I could talk if I wanted to . . .'

Cathy Carne had also been told something in her damned letter.

But there were other provisions of the will, dismissed as harmless jokes, but were they? A tube of Winsor blue for Alan Tate, spectacles for Burger . . . 'which I hope may improve his judgement and help him to see the obvious.' To see the obvious – Wycliffe wished that spectacles might do that for him. What was obvious? The relative merits of Tate's and Edwin's paintings? That was Burger's explanation but the truth might not be so innocent.

A tube of Winsor blue for Alan Tate – a way of wishing him luck, Cathy Carne had said.

Wycliffe resigned himself to lying awake for the rest of the night but, in fact, he fell asleep and knew nothing more until he was awakened to broad daylight and seagulls squawking outside his window.

CHAPTER NINE

Sunday morning. Wycliffe pretended to believe that there was something special about Sunday mornings, a quality in the air which he would be able to recognise however far adrift he might be from any routine or calendar. Certainly everything moved at a slower pace: the day took longer to get going; even the hotel breakfast was later than on other days; but he was on his way to the Incident Room by nine o'clock.

A newspaper seller was setting up his stand at the entrance to the pier but otherwise the street was deserted; shop blinds were drawn and a capricious breeze chased after Saturday night's litter.

Lucy Lane was already on duty, as fresh as the morning. 'There's been a call from Mark Garland's father to the local nick. Knowing our interest they passed him on and I spoke to him. Mark didn't come home last night and he's worried. At a little after eight Mark told his father he was going out; he went, and the old man hasn't seen him since.'

'He didn't say where he was going or when he could expect him back?'

'No, but that's not unusual; the most he ever says is "Don't wait up for me", though he's rarely late home.'

'Did he take anything with him?'

'Apparently not, just the clothes he was wearing.'

'We'd better talk to Thomas.'

They walked along the wharf and at the Custom

House Quay they climbed the slope to the main street past the King's Pipe, a free-standing fireplace and a chimney where, in less sophisticated times, revenue men had burned smuggled tobacco. On their right, shops gave way to large houses and on their left, to the harbour. Unhampered by buildings the breeze decided that it was a south easterly and they could see white water off Trefusis Point, a warning to small craft not to venture outside.

A row of terraced houses as they approached the docks, then one standing alone, red brick – incongruous amid all the stone and stucco.

'This is it, sir.'

Thomas opened the front door before they could ring. 'Do come in! I'm rather worried. He's never done anything like this before. I didn't realise he wasn't in until this morning . . . He wasn't home when I went to bed but that's nothing out of the ordinary because I go to bed early. There's nothing much to stay up for.'

He led the way into the living-room. 'Mark doesn't tell me anything – he never has, so when something like this happens I don't know what to do. I telephoned the police because I wondered if there could have been an accident.'

On a tablecloth, folded over part of the dining table, there was a teapot, milk jug, and a cup and saucer. Sunlight filtered through the greenery in the conservatory making a dappled pattern on the floor. A tabby cat followed in Thomas's footsteps eyeing the visitors. On the wall among a number of framed photographs there was one of a youthful Thomas in cap and gown.

'I gather that your son went out at about eight last evening and you've no idea where?'

'No idea! he doesn't go out in the evenings, much, except for his running. He was on the telephone to

154

somebody – I don't know who – I heard him say, "I'm rather worried, I would like to come and see you", and a little later he came in here, all dressed up, to say that he was going out.'

'Dressed up?'

'He was wearing a suit that he keeps for rather special occasions.'

'Did he take his car?'

'His car is in the garage.'

Suddenly Thomas remembered his manners and found seats for them but remained standing himself.

'Does he go out a lot?'

'Apart from his work he's usually out most of the day on Sundays and Tuesdays. He doesn't have patients those days, you see.'

'Do you know where he spends his time then?'

'I know that he attends classes with a Mr Brand who runs a sort of school for what they call occult studies.' A diffident gesture. 'Not something that appeals to me, but he has always shown an interest in that sort of thing.'

Wycliffe had to probe: 'Do you know that he was a close friend of Francis Garland?'

He had not known and at first he was unbelieving, but when his protests had died away he looked at Wycliffe with fresh concern. 'Are you telling me that Mark not coming home has something to do with his cousin?'

It was Lucy Lane who answered. 'We don't know, Mr Garland, but we do know that there was an intimate relationship between Mark and Francis which reached some sort of crisis last Tuesday. This happened at Brand's place, there was a scuffle and Francis came away with his face badly bruised.'

It was painful. The thirty-odd years which Thomas

155

had spent as a schoolteacher in a comprehensive school must have been perpetual torment. Shy, vulnerable, his blue eyes looked out on a world which seemed inexplicable and hostile.

He sat down by the table; the cat leapt on his lap and he stroked it absently. 'You are saying that Mark is a homosexual. Who told you all this?' He spoke sharply but he seemed less surprised than they might have expected.

Wycliffe said: 'Your son, in a statement he made early yesterday evening.'

'You've been questioning him?'

'He was at the Incident Room helping us with our enquiries into his cousin's death.'

'You're not saying that you suspected him of . . . of killing Francis?'

'No more than others.'

'And now?'

'We must find him first.'

'You're treating him as a fugitive! You think he's run away.'

Wycliffe said: 'We simply don't know what has happened. Did he seem upset or agitated when he came home yesterday evening?'

'He was just as usual, he never says much. I asked him why he was late for his meal and he said that he'd had an extra patient.'

'I gather that he took nothing with him; no suitcase – nothing. Are you quite sure of that?'

'I'm quite sure. By chance I saw him walking down the drive to the gate and he was carrying nothing.'

He was staring at his cup, turning it round and round with his fingers. 'My brother, my nephew, and now . . .'

'We don't know that anything has happened to your

son, Mr Garland. As a matter of routine I would like one of us to take a look at his room. You can be there, of course.'

Thomas hesitated then he looked at Lucy Lane: 'I would rather go up with her.'

Wycliffe waited in the living-room but they were not long gone. When they came down again Thomas had tears in his eyes. Lucy Lane said: 'The moment we have any news we'll be in touch.'

The old man stood in the doorway, holding his cat, while they walked the short distance to the gate.

Lucy Lane said: 'He's got a friend who will be coming in later. I feel very sorry for him. Sometimes the idea of being a parent scares me stiff, it's like offering yourself for vivisection.'

'You saw his room. What was it like?'

'Very ordinary; everything neat and tidy; not much of anything and nothing remarkable except a drawer full of soft porn gay magazines, and a collection of books on occult subjects. What did you expect?'

'Thomas knew about the magazines?'

'Of course. That was why he wanted me instead of you to go up with him. Do we put Mark on the telex?'

'Yes, we've got to find him, and the sooner the better; he's not just a missing man, he's a missing suspect.'

'Anything else?'

'We get Mr Kersey to have another heart to heart with Brand.'

'The telephone call – do you think he was keeping an appointment?'

'It looks like it and we have to find out who with.'

As they walked back through the street the church bells were ringing for morning service.

***

Mark Garland's description was circulated and enquiries put in hand at the railway station, and among bus drivers, taximen and hire-car firms. In their lunch-time bulletin the local radio would ask whoever spoke on the telephone to Mark Garland on Saturday evening and anyone who saw him after eight o'clock to contact the police.

Wycliffe and Kersey brooded, watching the racing yachts with their multi-coloured sails performing a lively ballet in the fresh breeze.

'Lucy Lane talked to him on Friday evening, here; I saw him with you in his consulting room yesterday and we brought him back here to make his statement. A couple of hours later, after a phone call, he walks out of his home, taking nothing with him, and disappears.'

Kersey rubbed his chin, always bristly however often he shaved. 'Do you think he's done away with himself?'

'Putting on his best suit for the occasion?'

Kersey nodded. 'That's a point. But where does it all leave us?'

'Still searching for a missing man.'

Kersey pitched the stub of his cigarette through the open window.

'Assuming his innocence, his disappearance would be convenient for whoever did shoot our Frankie.'

'The same thought occurred to me.'

At eleven o'clock there was a telephone call for Wycliffe. 'Dr Tate speaking. I've just heard that Mark Garland is missing and I think I should tell you that he was here with me yesterday evening.'

'Was he visiting you as a patient?'

'Yes, although I have no Saturday surgery—'

Wycliffe cut him short. 'It will be best that we meet and talk. I'll be at your house in a few minutes.'

'But—'

158

'If you please, Dr Tate, in a few minutes.'

'All right.' A grudging concession to the inevitable. 'But please come round the back to my surgery. I don't want Mrs Tate disturbed.'

Wycliffe said to Kersey: 'I want you to meet this man.'

They drove to Tregarthen, walked up the drive under the pine trees, and round the back of the house to a door marked 'Waiting Room. Please Enter'. Before they could do so the door was opened by Tate in person and they were ushered through the empty waiting room into his surgery.

'Please sit down.' The doctor was wasting no time.

Wycliffe introduced Kersey, and Tate looked at him with a certain wariness. 'I find myself in a rather invidious position . . .'

Tate was meticulously turned out, perfectly shaved, his hair had been recently trimmed, his pale hands were manicured and the cuffs of his shirt just showed below the sleeves of his jacket. On the desk in front of him was a medical records envelope labelled Mark Garland.

'As you know, Mark Garland is a chiropractor and though I do not subscribe to the principles of chiropractic I recognise the value of skilled manipulation in certain cases. Garland is a natural and I have referred a number of my patients to him with good results.'

'So you had a professional relationship with the missing man. How did you hear that he is missing? It is not public knowledge.'

Tate was not pleased at this brusque approach but he explained: 'Garland left his wallet behind, it must have slipped out of his jacket when he took it off for me to examine him. At any rate I found it on the floor this morning; I telephoned to tell him and spoke to his father. Of course he told me that his son was missing

159

and that you had already started an investigation.'

'What happened yesterday evening?'

A pause, then: 'He telephoned concerning a patient I had asked him to see and he took the opportunity to tell me that he was worried about his own health. After running the previous night he was experiencing certain symptoms which, he thought, might indicate heart disease. It sounded unlikely but he was clearly in an anxious state of mind so I suggested that he should come and see me right away.' Tate paused and sat back in his chair. 'He was here within fifteen minutes.'

The sun had not yet reached the back of the house so that the garden was in shadow and the room itself in a gloomy half light. No sound came from outside and Wycliffe felt that the world had been consciously excluded, that he and Kersey certainly, and even the patients who regularly gathered behind the padded door, were intruders. They might be inevitable, even necessary, but they were not welcome.

Tate was looking at Wycliffe as though he expected a question but when none came he continued: 'I examined him and decided that whatever his symptoms they were almost certainly mental rather than physical in origin. I told him as much and he admitted that he was under considerable stress. Among other things he said that he found difficulty in sleeping. I prescribed nitrazepam, to be taken for a few nights on going to bed, and told him to see me again in a week.'

Tate spread his hands. 'And that was all. He left here reassured, at least in regard to his physical well-being. I must say that it was a considerable shock to learn that he seems to be missing.'

Wycliffe said: 'What time did he leave?'

Tate considered. 'He was here for about forty-five minutes. He must have left at nine o'clock.'

Kersey said: 'Did he tell you what was worrying him?'

So far the doctor had spoken directly to Wycliffe, but from time to time he had cast uneasy glances in Kersey's direction. Certainly Kersey's presence seemed to disturb him but, after only a brief hesitation, he answered the question: 'Not in so many words.'

'But you have some idea of what it was?'

Tate looked at him blankly and said nothing.

Wycliffe intervened: 'I'm sure you understand, Dr Tate, that the confidentiality of the consulting room has no protection in law.'

Somewhere in the house a clock chimed and struck twelve.

Tate sat back in his chair as though making up his mind about something then he said: 'I am reluctant to discuss what a patient tells me in confidence but I suppose I have no choice. Garland was worried about being interrogated by the police in connection with his cousin's murder. He told me of the incident in which Francis got a bruised face and of what led up to it. All this, of course, you already know so I am really betraying no confidences.'

Wycliffe chose his words with care. 'You say that he was worried because we questioned him; would you say that his concern went deeper than that?'

Tate made a vigorous gesture of rejection. 'I know what you have in mind but I refuse to be drawn along that line. You are no longer asking me for facts but for speculation. All I can say is that he was deeply disturbed.'

Kersey tried another approach: 'As an experienced medical man and knowing your patient well, would you be surprised if it was found that he had taken his own life?'

161

Tate pushed away the folder containing Garland's medical records as though symbolically dissociating himself from the question. 'Really, you put me in an impossible position! If I had thought that there was any such risk when he was here last evening I would have taken precautions.'

'But on reflection?'

Tate placed the tips of his fingers together and regarded them. 'On reflection, I will say that I wish I had taken his mental condition more seriously. But that doesn't mean that I think he killed himself.' He got up from his chair. 'Now, Mr Wycliffe, if you will excuse me, I have some work I want to do before lunch.'

Wycliffe remained seated. 'I have some further questions for you, Dr Tate. Do you have any idea where Garland might have gone when he left you?'

Tate frowned. 'I assumed that he would have gone home. Where else? You must understand, Mr Wycliffe, that my only connection with him is by way of an occasional professional encounter. I know nothing of his private life. Your next question?'

'Did Mrs Tate have any contact with him while he was here?'

'Mrs Tate? Certainly not! It was not a social visit.'

Wycliffe stood up and so did Kersey. 'Thank you, Dr Tate; that is all for the moment.'

Tate was distant. 'I hope that Garland turns up safe and well, but there is nothing more that I can tell you.'

They were escorted out, not through the waiting room, but through the house and out by the front door.

As they walked down the drive they saw Marcella crossing the lawn with her dog. She walked with jerky self-conscious strides and made a point of not seeing them.

Wycliffe closed the wicket gate with a sigh. 'Claustrophobic, wasn't it? What did you make of him?'

Kersey took a deep breath. 'He didn't need much persuasion to overcome his professional scruples. I had the impression that he wanted to tell at least as much as he did tell, and at one point he seemed to be hinting that Mark might well have killed his cousin.'

They were in the car before he spoke again: 'It seems to me that when we know what happened to Mark Garland we shall be in business. Either he is a killer on the run, who may have done away with himself, or he's another victim.'

Wycliffe fastened his seat belt. 'Finding out which is our biggest problem.'

Kersey was driving. Wycliffe never took the wheel if he could avoid it. As they turned away from the terraces, downhill towards the town centre, Kersey said: 'If Mark Garland wasn't the killer then we are up against motive. Somebody killed Francis and presumably they had a reason. At any rate, he's dead.'

Back in the Incident Room Wycliffe slumped into a chair. The duty officer handed him a memo slip. 'Telephone message, sir.'

The message read: 'Expecting to see you at your personal preview this afternoon at 3.00. Burger.'

Kersey said: 'I get the impression that we are being taken for a nice smooth ride but unless something breaks I don't see what we can do about it. On Tuesday afternoon Mark Garland had a set-to with Francis who had bruises to show for it. Jealousy among gays can be every bit as vicious as among heteros and on Wednesday night Francis is deliberately murdered by someone lying in wait for him on the wharf. Mark is questioned a couple of times and fails to give a satisfactory account of himself but there is nothing on which to hold him, then he disappears. If he is never found there is a nice tidy case; no more police time wasted, no trial, no burned fingers, and public money saved. Nobody to complain but the lawyers, and who loses sleep over them?'

Wycliffe shook his head. 'Nobody is going to sweep this one under the carpet.'

'So what do we do?'

'At the moment what can we do, except the obvious? – enquiries in the neighbourhood of the Tate house: anybody who saw Garland arrive, anybody who saw him leave, and anything else they can pick up.'

At three o'clock Wycliffe arrived at the Gifford Tate exhibition. He was admitted by an earnest-looking young man with large spectacles and a lisp. Burger, athletically ambulant in a wheel chair, was cordial. A severe looking matron, with a plummy voice and tinted hair, was unpacking catalogues. A young woman was checking the labels on the pictures against the numbers and descriptions in the catalogue.

'You see! My helpers do all the work while I potter.' He picked up one of the catalogues in the glossy, illustrated edition, 'Have this with the compliments of the committee. The pictures are distributed over two rooms; start in this one and follow through chronologically.'

The first room housed examples of Tate's work from his student days to 1970, the year when he suffered his first stroke. The great majority of the forty-odd pictures were landscapes: river scenes, woodland glades, farmsteads, châteaux on the Loire, peasant villages in Greece, olive groves and beached fishing boats.

Wycliffe was not very knowledgeable about paintings or painters but the Impressionists had seemed to give him a glimpse of a world before the Kaiser's war, of life

164

on the other side of the Great Divide. Tate had certainly painted in the style of the Impressionists, but after his first tour of the room Wycliffe felt disappointed, without knowing why. Perhaps it was too large a dose of the same medicine, but many of the pictures struck him as sentimental and indulgently nostalgic.

Could it be that the Impressionists painted their world as they saw it while here was an imitator? He thought that over. At least it was something moderately sensible to say to Burger.

Before he could go on to the second room Burger came bowling swiftly over the polished floor. 'Well?'

The old man listened to his diagnosis with interest and some amusement. 'Poor old Gifford! "Sentimental and self-indulgent". Well, there are critics who would agree with you, but now have a look at the other room and see if you revise your opinion.'

There were fewer pictures in the second room: less than twenty, and Wycliffe was immediately struck by their greater vigour; the colours were stronger, on the whole, and there was greater contrast. Nature was still the dominant theme but these were pictures of the contemporary world seen through the eyes and with the mind of a man who happened to employ Impressionist techniques.

Burger gave him little time to consider his judgement before joining him again, and he felt like a schoolboy being tested on his homework.

Burger said: 'These strike you as very different?'

Wycliffe ventured: 'They seem to represent a change of attitude.'

'Yes. With very little change in technique; remarkable, isn't it?' Burger's grey eyes were watching him. 'Angela Bice, the art critic who did the blurb for the catalogue, puts it down to his stroke which she regards as a "seminal event in his life". Art critics talk like that. She sees it as "the first real set-back in his career and therefore a challenge".' Burger smiled. 'It's true that Gifford enjoyed a pretty smooth run until then; his father left him well off, he had good health, his pictures sold, and women found him attractive. What more could a man want?

'Then, almost from one moment to the next, he's paralysed down one side . . . He took it badly at first, and no wonder!'

'But he rose to the challenge,' Wycliffe said, in order to say something.

'And rather magnificently, don't you think?'

Burger was up to mischief, that much was clear, but Wycliffe could not fathom what particular mischief.

He went on: 'I've spent a lot of time here while they've been setting this up.' A broad gesture, taking in the whole display. 'Although I was on intimate terms with Gifford for fifty years I've never before seen the whole range of his work gathered together in one place. It's been an interesting and instructive experience to see his pictures chronologically arranged.' He looked up at Wycliffe with another of his enigmatic little smiles. 'Death and rebirth at sixty-three! I hadn't realised until now what a dramatic metamorphosis it had been. Perhaps that was why Edwin was so anxious that I should buy new spectacles.'

Wycliffe, floundering, said: 'I gather from Cathy Carne that Edwin was very much looking forward to this exhibition.'

'I'm not surprised. I don't doubt that he expected to enjoy himself enormously, though what the outcome would have been – what the outcome will be – I don't know. Incidentally, in case it interests you, both my

Tates belong to his later period. The first was painted soon after his stroke, and he very generously presented it to me, perhaps a sort of celebration of his invigorated talent.'

Wycliffe was well aware that the old man, in his oblique fashion, had been telling him something of importance; he realised, too, that direct questions would get him nowhere. He needed time to think, time at least to work out the right approach.

Almost in self-defence, he moved on to firmer, factual ground. 'There is one question I want to ask you – not about pictures: did you, or Garland, or Tate, to your knowledge, ever own a hand gun?'

A deep frown. Burger was conscious of the change of roles, he was being interrogated. He answered after a moment's thought: 'I never did, and I'm reasonably sure that Edwin didn't either.'

'And Tate?'

Burger hesitated again. 'Well, I do know that he bought a gun during our last Mediterranean trip. Our idea was to sail round Sardinia, and with all the tales of bandits one heard he thought it as well that we should have some means of defending ourselves.'

'When was that?'

'In '69, the year before he had his stroke.'

'You went in your own boat?'

'Good heavens, no! We crossed from Genoa on the regular service and hired a boat with a Sard crew-man in Asinara. It was in Genoa that Gifford bought his pistol – an automatic of some sort, I think.'

CHAPTER TEN

It was five o'clock, the wind had dropped, the sun was hot and the street was almost empty. The holiday-makers were getting what the brochures had promised. It was Sunday afternoon and Wycliffe felt the need to walk in the sunshine, to ventilate his lungs and his mind. Through the street, he went past the Thomas Garland house and the docks and across the narrow neck of land still marked by Cromwell's earthworks, thrown up when his men besieged the castle. Wycliffe arrived at the sea-front and the beaches. His mind was occupied by seemingly casual recollections of things people had said, things he had been told. He could always more easily recall the spoken than the written word. Phrases and sentences seemed to drift to the surface of his mind and he played with them, linking, rearranging, and eventually discarding those which seemed not to fit. This was the mind game which he sometimes called musical chairs.

He walked along the sea-front and stopped to lean on the rail where he could see the beach. The Falmouth beaches are small and rather steep compared with the great stretches of flat sand on the northern coast. Swimming is good, surfing almost non-existent. There is a family picnic atmosphere quite unlike the narcissistic-maximum-exposure sun cult of the other coast. Pleasantly nostalgic.

Wycliffe had started by thinking about the fringe provisions of Edwin's will:

£1,000 to Alan Tate – 'the son of my friend Gifford Tate together with my tube of Winsor blue.'

£1,000 to Martin Burger '. . . for that new pair of spectacles which I hope may improve his judgement and help him to see the obvious.'

'Winsor blue is the trade name for an artists' colour . . . Gifford Tate started to use it as soon as it came out, he said it brought him luck. Uncle used to tease him about it . . .'

'. . . the old man wrote Cathy Carne a letter which I was charged to pass over unopened.'

'I hadn't realised until now what a dramatic meta-morphosis it had been. Perhaps that was why Edwin was so anxious that I should buy new spectacles.'

'Uncle was really looking forward to that exhibition.'

'I don't doubt that he expected to enjoy himself enormously though what the outcome would have been – what the outcome will be – I don't know.'

Wycliffe sighed and continued his walk along the sea-front. Well, it might have been obvious but Burger himself had only recently tumbled to it and the old fox hadn't come out in the open even now. Only hints, with the implied invitation to make what he could of them.

He completed the circuit, arrived back in the main street, and made for the Incident Room. DC Curnow, the blond giant, was duty officer. Curnow had two obsessions, rugby and self-education. Rumour had it that he was working his way through the Encyclopaedia Britannica and that he had reached E.

Wycliffe put through a call to the Burger house and spoke to Mrs Burger: 'I wonder if it is possible to speak to your husband?'

Burger must have been close by for almost at once his suave, cultured voice came over the line. 'Mr Wycliffe?'

Wycliffe thanked him for the preview. 'I think that I have now understood your remarks but I shall be grateful if you will enlarge on them a little. If I might come and see you at some convenient time . . . ?'

Burger was polite, dry and evasive. 'If you are seeking an opinion on a series of pictures you should call in an expert. I am by no means an authority and my opinion would carry no weight.'

'I was hoping for confirmation of what I understood you to have said.'

A pause. 'I think you have understood me quite correctly but I am afraid that you must look elsewhere for verification.'

There was nothing for it but to thank the old man and leave it there. He had scarcely expected an open acknowledgement, let alone co-operation. All the same it was a set-back. Experts would take for ever and it is their function to disagree. In the meantime . . .

Cathy Carne was certainly not an expert but he suspected her of having knowledge of more practical value. He turned to Curnow: 'I shall be back in an hour if not before.'

He walked along the wharf to the printing works. Church bells were ringing for Evensong. Although sunset was still hours away an evening calm was settling over the harbour and town. On the south coast there is a serenity and a solemnity about fine summer evenings which can be vaguely depressing. It reminded Wycliffe of Heber's hymn about Saints casting down their golden crowns around a glassy sea.

Cathy Carne had lost something of that air of smooth competence which had impressed him at their first meeting. She looked tired and careworn and she was by no means pleased to see him though she did her best to conceal it. The flat, too, was showing signs of unusual neglect: the bedroom door stood open revealing an unmade bed. In the living-room the pages of a Sunday newspaper were scattered over the floor and there were crumbs on the carpet. On a low table there was a tray with a mug of tea and two or three roughly cut sandwiches on a plate.

'I was having tea. Can I offer you something?'

Wycliffe refused.

'You won't mind if I carry on?' She did it to keep in countenance.

'I suppose you have heard that Mark Garland is missing?'

'*Missing?*'

'It was on the local news at lunchtime; in any case, I thought Dr Tate might have told you.'

'I didn't listen to local radio at lunchtime and although Dr Tate is a friend we don't live in each other's pockets.' Snappish.

'So he hasn't told you either that Mark was having a homosexual affair with Francis?'

She paused with one of the sandwiches half-way to her lips. 'Mark and Francis? I can't believe it!'

'They met regularly at Brand's place. Last Tuesday they had a jealous quarrel; that was how Francis came by his bruised face.'

She gave up any pretence of continuing with her tea; she put the sandwich back on her plate, pulled down the hem of her skirt, and seemed to brace herself.

Wycliffe could not make up his mind. Was she really hearing all this for the first time?

The dark blue eyes studied him with disturbing intensity. 'You think Mark killed him; is that it?'

'That is one possibility, but there is another: that Mark too has been murdered.'

171

Her response was instant. 'I can't believe that! Why should anyone want to kill Mark?'

'Perhaps for the same reason that Francis was murdered – because he knew something which threatened the killer. I've warned you already that you may be running that kind of risk yourself.'

She turned on him angrily. 'And I have told you that I don't know what you are talking about!'

In almost convulsive movements she crossed her legs and clasped her hands about her knees. 'You don't give up, do you? As it happens I've made up my mind to tell you what was in Uncle's letter because I realise that I shall have no peace until I do.'

'Go on.'

'I didn't want to – not because it effects me but because it concerns Beryl and Francis.'

Wycliffe wondered at this sudden consideration for her cousins.

'Uncle thought that I might have misgivings about accepting a substantial share of his property and depriving them of what they might look upon as theirs by right.'

'So?'

'He told me in his letter that neither Beryl nor Francis were his children, both were illegitimate; their true father was a man called Jose, an estate agent.' She reached for her cigarettes. 'Does that satisfy you?'

'No. It's a good try but that affair between Edwin's wife and the estate agent has entered into folklore; Edwin must have known that it was common knowledge and he also knew you too well to suppose that you would be unduly troubled about your cousins' feelings anyway.'

She lit her cigarette with a concentrated effort at composure. 'Be as unpleasant as you like but I've told

172

you what there is to tell.'

'All right, leave it for the moment. Let's talk about paintings: you won't have had a chance to see the Tate exhibition yet but—'

'I have seen it; Papa Burger invited me to a sneak preview this morning.'

'Then you must have noticed the differences between the paintings in the two rooms. I'm not knowledgeable about painting but one could hardly miss them.'

She made a gesture of impatience. 'Of course there are differences. What do you expect when a man resumes painting after a severe stroke? He's not going to take up his brush just where he left off.'

Wycliffe leaned forward in his chair. 'Let's stop playing games. You've known since last Thursday, when you read your uncle's letter, that Tate never painted a single picture after his stroke. All the subsequent work attributed to him was painted by your uncle.'

She was silent for a moment or two, watching him through the haze of her cigarette smoke, then she made up her mind. When she spoke she seemed to be mentally ticking off her points, and her manner was contemptuous. 'Gifford Tate's pictures have been studied and written about by experts, there are several of his earlier and later works in national collections, here and abroad; all his pictures are handled by a prestigious London gallery and many have been bought by notable connoisseurs. Don't you think it surprising that no one has noticed a fraud?'

Wycliffe sounded bored. 'I've nothing to say about art experts and you have no need of their opinions as far as Tate's work is concerned; you know the facts, and you have the word of the man who painted about a third of the pictures in that exhibition. I doubt whether

173

his letter to you came as a complete surprise but that doesn't matter.'

'You are saying that Tate allowed my uncle to use his name and imitate his work over a period of several years – why?'

'Well, there was a very substantial income from the pictures, but I hardly think that carried a great deal of weight. From what you and others have told me about your uncle and Gifford Tate, my guess would be that it all started as a joke – a bit of fun, possibly to cheer up Tate. The first forgery – if we are to call it that – was presented to Papa Burger as a test, and the fact that it was accepted by him as the work of a re-invigorated Tate was irresistible to the jokers. If Burger was taken in it was altogether too tempting to try it on the art world at large. It seems they lapped it up, and still do. In the words of the catalogue poor old Tate's stroke was "a seminal event" in the development of his talent. Heady stuff!'

The sun had come round to shine through the westward facing window and the golden light seemed to emphasise the dust on the furniture and the fluff on the carpet in a room that was usually immaculate.

Cathy Carne sat back in her chair as though dissociating herself from all that had been said. 'If that's what you want to believe then I can't stop you but I don't know where you are going to find the evidence or why you should want it.'

Wycliffe said: 'I don't think evidence will be difficult to come by and I shall search for it because this fraud, and his knowledge of it, was responsible for Francis's death.'

She was engaged in stubbing out her cigarette and he could not judge her reaction.

'The original hoax, dreamed up by Edwin and Tate,

was so successful that they found themselves riding a tiger – not, I suspect, that they were all that anxious to get off. The whole thing appealed to their rather malicious sense of humour and it was also very profitable.'

Cathy Carne maintained a slightly amused, contemptuous attitude. 'So why was Edwin so anxious to tell me about it when he died?'

'The answer could be that a hoax loses its point if nobody realises that it is one, but I think there was more to it than that. Edwin left it until his death to confide in you, but he had told Francis a year before.'

She could no longer sit still; she got up and walked over to the window. 'As I've already told you, Francis was the very last person he would confide in about anything.'

Wycliffe went on as though she had not spoken. 'Your uncle had a low opinion of most of the people around him and he seemed to take pleasure in the prospect of frustrating them. Think of his will in which he left the residue of his estate jointly to Beryl and Francis.'

Without turning round she said: 'I agree with you there, but—'

'The way he went about exposing the picture hoax was another example. Francis was briefed first. For a year he had the satisfaction of watching Francis, primed, ready to burst, but unable to speak without risking his expectations under the will. But if, for any reason, Francis failed to speak when Edwin was dead, you had your letter and Papa Burger and Alan Tate, their enigmatic bequests. Who would do what? Another stir of the pudding. But, of course, he wouldn't be there to see.

'As his health deteriorated one has the impression

that he became more determined to get as much entertainment as possible out of the situation, to sail nearer the wind, and so we have this exhibition which he didn't live to see. Imagine him if he had, watching the reactions as this severely chronological arrangement of pictures made its impact in moving round the country. It would be seen and reviewed by the Mandarins of the art establishment. Surely somebody would have the insight – and the guts – to blow the whistle? No wonder he was looking forward to it!'

She turned away from the window with a sigh. 'I'm not going to argue with you.'

Wycliffe got up from his chair. 'No, but just think of your position: by your refusal to talk you run a serious risk of being regarded as an accessory and, if Mark Garland was murdered, you will have contributed to his death.'

'And how would Mark Garland have come by this great secret?' She was scathing.

'Pillow talk? I believe lovers are notoriously indiscreet in their confidences. What was it that Mark was so anxious to explain to Beryl? Don't you think that when he failed he might reasonably have tried elsewhere?'

She was very pale but she said nothing. She saw him to the door and stood at the top of the steps as he went down. When she closed the door did she go straight to the telephone? Tonight he was not quite so sure. He was taking a risk, but he had to get the case moving somehow or risk worse to come.

DC Curnow handed him a polythene envelope containing a sheet of mauve writing paper. 'Pushed through the letter-box earlier this evening, sir. Just folded across, no envelope; anonymous, of course.'

Written in a round, schoolgirlish hand, the message

176

read: 'Thelma George says she heard a shot when she passed the Tates house Saturday evening. She works in Paynes coffee shop.'

Explicit, and more literate than most, but every major case draws the fire of practical jokers and nutters. All the same . . .

Curnow went on: 'I contacted DS Lane, sir, and she traced the girl George through the owner of the coffee shop. She's gone to talk to her. She shouldn't be long.'

She wasn't. In ten minutes Lucy Lane arrived back with the girl: a fair, skinny seventeen-year old, packaged in the inevitable jeans and T-shirt. She was nervous and resentful. 'You think you got friends and this is what they do to you.' She examined the anonymous note with distaste. 'That's Sharon James, I'd know her writing anywhere. I never wanted to get mixed up with the police.'

Wycliffe was gentle. 'But you *were* outside the Tates' house sometime on Saturday evening?'

The girl looked at Lucy Lane. 'I told her.'

'At about what time were you there?'

'About half-past eight; I was on my way to a friend's place.'

'And you heard a shot?'

'I never said it was a shot; I said I thought it sounded like a shot but I don't really know what a shot sounds like, do I? It was a sort of crack, not very loud. Anyway, who'd be firing off a gun in a place like that? I didn't think any more about it.'

'But you must have mentioned it to someone.'

'Well, yes. I was out with the usual crowd this afternoon and one of the girls whose mother works at the Tates said the police had been there about that man Garland who's missing and I just said what I heard – just for the sake of something to say.'

'I'm glad you did. Now I would like you to go with Miss Lane and let her write down an account of what happened on Saturday evening for you to sign.'

'Can I go then?'

'Of course! Miss Lane will take you home.'

Lucy Lane shepherded her into the little interview room.

A shot at 8.30 on Saturday evening at the Tates' place! It was almost unbelievable but the girl, a reluctant witness – often the best, had heard something, and the time was significant. At any rate he couldn't ignore it. He contacted sub-division and arranged for the Tate house to be kept under surveillance until further notice. No need for concealmeant. It would do the doctor no harm to find a police car outside his gates.

PC Dart in his Panda Car had taken up his position outside the gates of Tregarthen at 22.00 and it was now 02.15; nearly four hours of his shift to go. He was unaccustomed to the deadly monotony of surveillance. This was the third time he had been out of his car, walking up and down to stretch his legs and keep awake. A quiet, warm, moonlit night, no one about. The great pines in the garden of Tregarthen rose out of the shadows and towered against the sky. A motor cycle engine, muted by distance, roared briefly then faded. The whole town seemed asleep. He was standing by the drive gates when he heard a scream, followed by another, abruptly cut short. He could see twinkling lights from the direction of the house which had not been there before.

On his personal radio he called his station and reported, then he entered the grounds through the wicket gate and sprinted up the drive. There were lights

178

in the house, upstairs and down. He reached the front door, put his finger on the bell, and kept it there. Three years in the force had not cured him of butterflies in the stomach when faced with a possible emergency. Apart from anything else he dreaded making a fool of himself.

He could hear a man's voice, measured, reassuring. A light went on in the hall and the door was opened by Dr Tate himself; he was fully dressed. Mrs Tate, in her nightdress with a dressing gown over her shoulders, was standing behind him. She looked desperately pale, but more or less composed. Tate said: 'I know you, don't I? PC Dart, isn't it?'

'Yes, sir; I heard screams.'

'Yes, I'm afraid you must have done. Mrs Tate had a distressing nightmare and, as you can see, she is still very upset. I'm going to get her a hot drink then, back to bed . . . Good night, and thank you for coming to our rescue.'

'Good night, sir . . . Madam.'

In other parts of the town PC Dart would have had no hesitation in logging a 'domestic' – a family row.

CHAPTER ELEVEN

Wycliffe, after an early breakfast, was at the Incident Room by eight o'clock but Kersey was ahead of him.

'I hear the Tates had a disturbed night, sir. Marcella is supposed to have had a nightmare.'

Wycliffe glanced through the report which had come through from the local station.

Kersey said: 'Do you believe it?'

'I'm reaching a point where I'm prepared to believe anything. You've heard about the girl who thinks she heard a shot?'

'Yes. Seems a bit unlikely, don't you think? I can't see Tate using a gun in his own house; too risky. It's not all that isolated and he's not stupid.'

'Nobody noticed Marcella's screams last night or, if they did, they didn't do anything about it. In any case people instinctively explain away something as unlikely as the sound of a shot, especially in that sort of neighbourhood. Anyway it's given us a lever with Tate; he's got a Panda car sitting outside his gate. Let him try living with that for a bit.'

Kersey selected a bent cigarette from a crushed pack and straightened it with loving care. He said: 'You think the solution lies in that direction?'

'Things seem to point that way. Any one of several people might have killed Francis, but, if Mark Garland was murdered, what we know so far suggests that he died on Saturday evening in the Tate house.'

'Because somebody saw him go in and nobody saw him come out?'

'There is also the girl's story of a possible shot at the critical time – 8.30 – and she sounded like a credible witness. But look at the alternative, that Mark Garland was the culprit, not another victim. If he intended to do a bunk would he put on his best suit, leave his car in the garage, and pay a call on his doctor without even a weekend bag?'

'Isn't it possible that he committed suicide?'

'You think that would make the suit and the doctor more plausible?'

Kersey's face, mobile as a clown's, expressed grudging acceptance. 'I must admit, put like that, it sounds better than I'd thought, but I would have expected something more subtle from the doctor. And what about motive?'

Wycliffe retailed the picture saga and Kersey listened with close attention but at the end he was still dubious. 'You are suggesting that Tate killed twice – for what? To cover up the fact that his father and Edwin Garland had bamboozled the art world for years. Is that it, sir?'

Wycliffe shook his head. 'That's not exactly what I had in mind. Anyway, I'm going to tackle Tate this morning and I want you to lay on a search of his premises this afternoon – I'll fix it with Tate without a warrant if possible. If Mark Garland was murdered, Tate's problem was or is to get rid of the body where no one will find it.'

'Would it matter if it was found?'

'I think so. Unless Tate faked a convincing suicide, Garland would lose his value as a scapegoat and our investigation would continue; in fact, it would be reinforced.'

Kersey said: 'It's not easy to hide a body unless you

can drop it overboard in deep water with a hefty sinker.'

'That's the point; and it's unlikely that Tate managed that or anything like it on Saturday night. It would be asking for trouble to risk trying by day, and we've had his place under surveillance since yesterday evening.'

Kersey exhaled a cloud of grey smoke and coughed. 'You think the body may still be on the premises?'

'If there is a body – I think it's possible.'

'So you want a search team for this afternoon. You think Tate will consent?'

'It will be interesting to find out. If not, we get a warrant.'

Another beautiful day, still with that morning freshness but with the promise of heat: Wycliffe upheld the dignity of the Force in a light-weight grey suit, with collar and tie, and knew that he would regret it later. A trickle of people made their way to the beaches, lobster-coloured parents and trailing children. He drove up to the terraces and parked near a Panda car outside the Tates'.

'PC Gregory, sir. PC Dart was relieved at six.'

'Anything happening?'

'Nothing much, sir. At 07.30 the woman who works here arrived. At 08.00 Dr Tate came out and asked me what I was doing here. I told him I was on duty and he went in again. At 08.40 a young chap in overalls drove up in a junior Volvo. He opened the big gate and was about to drive in. I asked him what was going on and he said he was from Barton's Garage. He'd come to collect Dr Tate's car for repair and he was going to leave the other as a temporary replacement. A few minutes later he came out driving the doctor's big Volvo and I saw that the off-side bumper was sagging a bit, the headlamp was smashed and the bodywork damaged.'

'I know, I saw it earlier.'

'Since then, nothing except that the receptionist turned up for work at 08.50.'

Wycliffe walked up the drive to the front door and rang the bell. It was answered by a thin, grey-haired woman wearing an overall. He said: 'Chief Super-intendent Wycliffe.'

She looked at him with unconcealed antagonism. 'I know who you are. I must say, you choose your time. The doctor has his surgery and there's a waiting-room full of patients. It's none of my business but I should think the police had something better to do than come pestering people like the doctor.'

Obviously a disciple.

'Who are you?'

'Me? I'm Mrs Irons. I come in daily to help out – except Sundays that is.'

Wycliffe said: 'Will you ask Mrs Tate if she will see me?'

She gave him a dubious look, unsure how safe it was to trifle with a chief superintendent. 'She's not well; she shouldn't be worried.'

'Ask her.'

He waited in the black-and-white tiled hall, listening to the grandfather clock as it grudgingly doled out the seconds. A couple of minutes went by before Mrs Irons came back.

'All right. She'll see you in her room. You'd better come with me.'

Marcella's room was between the drawing-room and the dining-room and it had a french window opening to the garden at the side of the house. Marcella, wearing a shabby, green housecoat, was sitting at a knee-hole desk with an exercise book open in front of her. Her little dog was alseep in a basket at her feet. She got up to greet him.

Wycliffe said: 'I'm sorry to intrude; I gather you had a disturbed night.'

A self-conscious laugh. 'I had a nightmare. Absurd really! I dreamt that I was being suffocated and I was terrified. I haven't had anything like it since I was a young girl and I feel really silly.'

Her voice was unnaturally loud and her manner was tense – brittle.

'Do sit down.' She pointed to a chair and sat down herself.

'It must have given Dr Tate a fright.'

'Yes, it did. Luckily he hadn't gone to bed; he was working in his surgery. Paper work; you wouldn't believe! He really needs more help. At least one night a week he's up until the small hours.'

He was shocked by the change in her appearance. In her shapeless and worn housecoat which hung about her in folds, with her haggard features and untended hair, she looked like a severely harassed housewife cultivating an addiction to Valium. But she was more ready to talk than she had been during his last visit; perhaps too ready.

'Will you tell me what happened on Saturday evening?'

She frowned, obviously simulating an effort of memory. 'Saturday evening was when Mark Garland came. I was out, taking Ricky for a walk. I went out soon after eight; I prefer it when there are not too many people about, don't you?'

'Where did you go?'

'Oh, the usual – across the sea-front. It was a lovely evening and we sat, Ricky and I, in one of the shelters for a while.'

'When did you get back?'

'After nine.'

'Was Mark Garland here then?'

'Oh, no; he'd gone. Alan told me what he'd come about but I've forgotten.'

She was well briefed.

'Did you meet anyone you knew while you were out?'

'I don't think so. I talked to a lady in the shelter but she was a visitor, staying in one of the sea-front hotels I think.'

The room was sparsely furnished: the desk, bookshelves, and two or three unmatched chairs. A couple of pictures and a few photographs impressed some individuality on the room which was otherwise tasteless and institutional. But Marcella's pictures were Tates: head and shoulders portraits; one of her, younger and plumper; the other, obviously a self-portrait, of a gentleman with a spade beard and an elaborately cultivated moustache. Looking at the man it was easy to see where Alan Tate had got his large, doggy-brown eyes.

She saw his interest. 'Gifford did them especially for me; he didn't usually do portraits and I wouldn't part with them whatever happened!'

'Of course not.'

She was staring up at the portrait of her husband with a reflective air. She said: 'I know people don't believe it but I loved Gifford, really loved him, and we only had two years together before his stroke.'

'That was very sad.'

She looked quickly at him and away again, bird like. It was odd; her naivety seemed blended with a shrewd concern about the impression she made.

'And yet his stroke made no real difference. In a way

it was better for me because he needed me and I had him more to myself . . . You see, he'd done everything for me, everything!' She spoke haltingly and in a low voice that was almost reverential.

'I mean, I was brought up by my mother in a council flat on social security. I never knew my father. I was very lucky to go to university but it was only like a continuation of school – I couldn't mix much because I never had any spending money.' Another fleeting glance to see the effect of her words.

'It was only after I met Gifford that I realised what real life could be like.' She picked up the exercise book from her desk. 'I told you I was writing his biography, didn't I? This is one of his diaries. There's a bit in here about the first time we met; he took the trouble to mention it in his diary. I'll read it to you.' She found the page and read a passage which she obviously knew by heart: '"After the lecture a sweetly plain little mouse with flaxen hair came up to me and asked questions in the most earnest fashion possible. She said her name was Marcella! What pretentious names parents give their children nowadays!"' She blushed shyly and closed the book. 'He got to like my name later.

'I'm going to call the biography "Renewal" because I remember him saying once: "Who could possibly want eternal life? I should be bored to distraction! Eternal renewal – well, that's a different matter. I think I might settle for that." And in a way he experienced a renewal, didn't he?' Once more she looked Wycliffe in the eyes.

'You've no idea what it all means to me!' She was on the verge of tears. 'Almost everything in this house is as it was when he was alive; the studio and his bedroom are exactly as they were . . . Sometimes in the evenings, when I am in the house alone, I can believe

186

that *nothing* has changed. I feel that he is *here*, that I have really found a way—'

There was a knock at the door, it was opened, and Tate's receptionist came in, blonde, white coated, and peremptory: 'Excuse me. The doctor will see you now, Mr Wycliffe.'

Wycliffe said: 'I'll be along in a few minutes.'

Marcella immediately became agitated. 'No! No! You must go now. You must! You Must!' In her excitement she stood up and almost shooed him from the room.

In the corridor Wycliffe said: 'Has the doctor finished with his patients early?'

'No, he's seeing you between patients and I hope you won't keep him long; he's very busy and grossly overworked.'

Another disciple.

Tate was sitting at his desk with a selection of patients' records in front of him. He was distant but civil. He indicated a chair with a gesture.

'I suppose your visit concerns Mrs Tate's distressing experience last night though why that should interest the police I don't know.'

It was clear that he was under stress; his movements were restrained and precise, his words as carefully chosen as ever, but he looked very tired and even his spectacles failed to hide a darkening about the eyes.

Wycliffe said: 'I am here about Mark Garland's disappearance. I don't think you need me to explain your position, Doctor, but I have an obligation to do so. Mark Garland was seen arriving here, as you yourself said he did, at about eight o'clock on Saturday evening. Despite widespread enquiries we have been unable to find anyone who has seen him since. In the circumstances it is natural that we should begin our

187

enquiry into his disappearance where he was last seen.'

Tate was looking at him with attention but with no hint of concern. 'So what do you propose to do?'

An observer might have thought that they were discussing some academic problem of no great moment to either of them.

'There is another fact to be taken into account: a passer-by, at about eight-thirty on Saturday evening, says she heard a sound like a shot which seemed to come from this house.'

'A shot?' Incredulous.

'Yes, and that information taken with the fact that on present evidence Garland was last seen in this house, makes a search of your premises inevitable. If I apply to the magistrate for a warrant I have no doubt that it would be granted but I would much prefer to conduct a search with your consent.'

Tate smiled. 'I don't doubt it. If I agree, the police have nothing whatever to lose; if I do not agree and you are successful in obtaining a warrant but find nothing incriminatory, the police will look foolish and, with other things taken into account, it might appear that I am being unduly harassed.'

'The decision is yours.'

Tate studied his finger-nails for a moment or two, then he said: 'I am inclined to agree to your search. You are pestering me with your visits, you have a police vehicle apparently on permanent station outside my gate, and you are encouraging my neighbours to spy on me. If a search of my house will put a stop to these instrusions it might be an acceptable price to pay.'

'The search would have to be thorough and unhampered.'

'But I have nothing to hide.'

'You may wish to consult your lawyer.'

188

'I know my own mind, Mr Wycliffe.' Tate was gathering up certain of his patients' records into a neat pile; when he had done so, he slipped an elastic band around them. 'When will your search begin?'

'At two o'clock this afternoon. I will see that it is carried out with as little disturbance as possible. There's another matter: now that there is a suspicion of foul play in connection with Mark Garland's disappearance I have to ask you and Mrs Tate to put your accounts of what happened on Saturday evening into writing.'

'But Mrs Tate wasn't here, I've told you.'

'Then she can say so in writing. But we will leave it until this afternoon.'

Tate barely controlled his annoyance. 'I think you should tell me, Chief Superintendent, what possible reason I could have for wanting Mark Garland dead. Surely to qualify as a major suspect one has to satisfy criteria based on means, opportunity – and motive.'

It was Wycliffe's turn to consider his words. 'All I can say is that if Mark Garland was murdered it was because he knew why Francis Garland died and who had an interest in his death.'

'And that implicates me?'

Wycliffe returned his stare. 'Only you know the answer to that with certainty, Dr Tate. Just one more request: I would like to take another look around your father's studio while I am here.'

The doctor did not answer at once, his hands clenched but immediately relaxed again. 'If you wish. Miss Ward, my receptionist, will give you the key.'

Miss Ward met him in the passage. 'You will have to come through the kitchen.'

She gave him the key and let him out into the courtyard. 'Lock the door when you've finished and put the key in the kitchen.'

189

The sun had not yet come round to the back of the house and it was deliciously cool under the green glass roof. Presumably it was here that Gifford Tate had relaxed during his last summer, that blazing summer of '76, while his young wife sat naked in one of the cushioned chairs, reading from the page of Proust's *Remembrance of Things Past*. Refined titillation for the elderly and the impotent; a scene from a Grecian vase: Satyr with Maiden.

Wycliffe wanted to look at the studio again in the light of what he had learned from Burger. It was the place where Tate had spent most of his time after his stroke, much of it in company with Edwin Garland.

There were too many strands. Changing the metaphor, he felt like a juggler trying to keep too many balls in the air at once.

As he passed the window of the waiting-room all the chairs seemed to be occupied and he suspected that Tate had been concerned to cut short his conversation with Marcella.

He crossed the grass to the studio, climbed the steps and unlocked the door. The substantial timber building was cool in the heat and the north-facing windows excluded the glare of the sun so that the big room seemed dimly lit in contrast with outside. He had seen it all before, but now he was seeing it with new eyes: the pot-bellied iron stove, the coal bucket, the deep, leather armchairs drawn up on either side, and the chess-board between.

Gifford and Edwin. He could imagine them on a winter's afternoon in front of a glowing stove: Gifford, in the early stages of convalescence, and depressed; Edwin, trying to kindle a spark. They would be smoking, both of them against doctor's orders; Gifford, his pipe, Edwin, his homemade cigarettes. There were paper spills in a pot by the stove. From the time of Gifford's stroke it seemed they had seen less of Burger and so, perhaps, they were drawn closer together.

No doubt it began with idle talk. 'Wouldn't it be a laugh if . . . ?'

And later: 'Why not try it?'

A heartening chuckle from Gifford. 'Make a present of it to Papa and see what he makes of it.'

Schoolboys planning mischief.

Wycliffe brought himself back to the here and now. In the afternoon he would have the house and grounds searched, now was his chance to take a look around the studio. Not that he would find anything; Tate had been unconcerned about leaving him alone there. Mechanically, he went through the cupboards and drawers but he made only one discovery: a cupboard full of bottles and glasses: sherry, port, whisky, vodka, gin . . . The tuck box.

There was nowhere in the studio where a body might have been hidden; he even examined the floorboards and satisfied himself that they had not been lifted since the place was built.

With a certain reluctance, he locked the door and crossed the grass to return the key. The numbers in the waiting-room seemed hardly to have changed.

He had no doubt that Mark Garland was dead, that he had been shot, and that the shooting had taken place in or around this house. The pistol could easily be disposed of or hidden, and it might remain hidden despite his intended search. The body was a different matter. Tate was a clever man but he was not a magician, yet he seemed undisturbed at the prospect of a search.

Wycliffe entered the courtyard under a Moorish arch. It was certainly a very pleasant retreat, cool in the heat and sheltered from most winds. The sun was coming round. The gentle splash of the fountain was soothing and the falling water droplets glistened in the sunlight, sometimes with rainbow effects. There was a waterlily with white flowers and beneath its heart-shaped leaves orange and red fish lurked, half-hidden.

Mrs Irons, the daily woman, was in the kitchen and he handed her the key.

'Do you want to see anybody?'

'No, thank you, I'll go out around the back.'

'Suit yourself.'

As he turned back to the courtyard it occurred to him that the paving slabs immediately around the pool had been very recently cleaned; they were free of the dark lichen which 'ages' concrete or stone paving slabs and was present on all the others. Most people encourage it. His wife, Helen, offered libations of stale yoghurt to promote its growth, others preferred the pristine rawness of the builders' yard, but only the slabs near the pool had been scrubbed.

Marcella had said: 'Alan and I sometimes sit out here on warm summer evenings.'

Saturday evening had been warm and sunny. What could be more natural than that Garland should have been taken there instead of to the surgery or the drawing-room? A shooting indoors is likely to leave traces which are difficult or impossible to remove or disguise. How much simpler . . . And the paving slabs had been scrubbed. There was an independent witness to Garland's arrival but only Tate's word for what had happened afterwards and, according to him, he had been in the house alone.

Wycliffe looked about him with new interest. His eye was caught by something glistening on the very edge of the pool nearest to him. He stooped to see what it was and found a small groove in one of the slabs. Tiny quartz crystals in the concrete, freshly exposed, were catching the light . . . Was he letting his imagination run away with him? He went back under the green glass roof to fetch one of the lounging chairs and saw Marcella watching him through the kitchen window. Let her watch.

He placed the chair fairly close to the pool and stood behind it. The head and neck of anyone sitting in the chair would come above the back of the chair and, as far as he could tell, a bullet fired from about that position might graze the edge of the pool before entering the water . . . He put the chair back where he had found it. This was work for the experts.

He walked round the house to the drive and down towards the gates. The resinous scent of the pines, distilled by the heat, filled the air. From the drive there were tantalising glimpses of the harbour and of Trefusis fields beyond. The Tates lived in a very pleasant house in a large secluded garden; they were in good health, they were still short of middle age, and yet . . . He wasn't sure what it was he was trying to express, unless it was a sense of incongruity between these people, this setting, and violent crime.

Alan Tate seemed to value a calm orderliness in the pattern of his days. When his father died and left him the house he had given up a fairly prestigious consultancy to move back home and set up as a GP in a small town. He had kept his contacts to a minimum; he had accepted his father's young wife as housekeeper and left her free to fantasise over his father, the elderly Prince Charming who, she claimed, had awakened her to life.

For eight years it had seemed to work, until that Wednesday morning, the day of the funeral, when

Francis had arrived with a picture under his arm. Had the story which Francis had to tell come as such a devastating shock that murder seemed the only way out?

Wycliffe found himself outside the Tate's gate, standing by his car, conscious of the curious gaze of PC Gregory. He was preoccupied and decided to walk, so he left his car where it was.

Walking downhill, or down steps from the terraces, it is difficult to avoid reaching the main street, so he did not plot a course and, half-way down, after a flight of steps, he arrived in a quiet cul-de-sac, a row of colour-washed little houses opposite a disused burial ground and a yard at the end with a sign on the double gate: Barton's Garage. Car-body Repair Depot. Presumably where Tate's car was under repair. A steep slope and another flight of steps and he was in the main street.

'Fox, Curnow, Dixon and Lucy Lane, that makes four; five with you. Lucy will probably have to cope with Marcella as an extra.'

Wycliffe, Kersey and Lucy Lane in planning session. Kersey was not altogether happy. 'I take it the team will be searching for a .32 automatic and/or Mark Garland's body. Do you think they stand any chance of finding either?'

'They will also be looking for evidence that a shooting did take place on the premises and that could be a better bet.'

It was very hot in the Incident Room, all the windows were open but there was not enough movement of the air to stir the papers on the tables. The sky was blue and so were the waters of the harbour; there was an all-pervading stillness. If there was any sailing it must be going on out in the bay where they might just catch the whisper of a wind.

Kersey lit a cigarette and stared out of the window. 'Tate must have got rid of the body if there is one or he would have tried to stall the search.'

Wycliffe said: 'Has anyone found a decent place for a light lunch?'

Lucy Lane volunteered: 'If you're willing to trust my judgement, sir.'

'Implicitly.'

'It's called Twining's and it's just around the corner from here.'

She took them to a place not far from the car-park where they had a seat by a window overlooking the harbour. *Ratatouille au gratin* and a bottle of hock. They were disputing whether a light lunch could be stretched to include a dessert when Wycliffe was called to the telephone. It was Potter at the Incident Room.

'I heard you say where you were going for lunch, sir. You're wanted at the Tates' house urgently. Dr Tate has been found in his surgery, shot through the head, he's dead. PC Gregory reported on the telephone from the house just before one o'clock.'

CHAPTER TWELVE

Wycliffe stood looking down at the doctor's body which had slumped on its left side between the chair and the desk, the head towards the window, resting on the carpet which was stained with blood. There was a smallish hole in the right side of his head just above and in front of the ear pinna. His right arm rested limply behind his thigh as though it had slipped into that position as he collapsed. Wycliffe could see the pistol under the desk and slightly in front of the body. The swivel chair was farther from the desk than it would have been in use, probably pushed back as the body slumped sideways.

On the face of it, suicide.

The spectacles, their thick lenses apparently undamaged, were lying at a little distance from the dead man's face, the dark brown eyes were open and staring.

'A compassionate man,' Burger had said.

The little clock on the desk, flicking the seconds away, registered 29 minutes past one. Less than three hours earlier he, Wycliffe, had been sitting in the patients' chair on the other side of the desk. The bundle of medical records about which the doctor had slipped an elastic band was still there. Wycliffe shuddered in a brief spasm of revulsion against himself and his job; for an instant he was overwhelmed by guilt. He had not caused this man's death but if he had foreseen it, as he might have done . . . Then professionalism came to his rescue: no sign of a note.

Kersey had taken over the dining-room where there was a telephone, and Wycliffe joined him there. PC Gregory was making his report; a lean, dark man in his thirties with enough experience not to be flustered.

'At 12.45 I heard what I took to be a shot though, I must admit, if it hadn't been for all that went before, I might not have thought so. I reported in on my radio then I ran up the drive to the house. I tried the door but it was secured. I rang the bell but didn't wait for an answer. I went round to the back; the waiting-room door was locked so I found my way through the courtyard to the kitchen. That door wasn't locked but it was on a chain and I couldn't get in. In the end I smashed the glass of the kitchen window and climbed in over the sink.

'I couldn't hear anything at all. I called out but there was no answer. I went through the kitchen and into the passage and found Mrs Tate standing in the doorway of the surgery. She was sort of holding herself with both hands and when she saw me she said: "He shot himself! He shot himself!" and she kept on saying it. She seemed dazed. I could see the doctor behind the desk. I made sure nothing could be done for him then I got Mrs Tate in here and I telephoned. I called the Incident Room at 12.57.'

Kersey said: 'What time was it when you actually got into the house?'

The man shook his head. 'I don't know, sir, but with one thing and another I think it must have been at least five minutes after the shot before I was actually in the house.' He looked uneasily at Wycliffe who was gazing at him heavy-eyed.

Kersey said: 'That's honest anyway. Did Mrs Tate say anything more?'

197

'Not a word, sir. She seemed completely dazed and she let me guide her around as though she had no will of her own.'

'Any idea where the cleaning woman was in all this?'

'She left at twelve, sir. She lives close by and she goes home from twelve till two to give her husband his lunch.'

'All right, when your relief arrives, go back and write your report.'

The front doorbell rang and Wycliffe said: 'That'll be the police surgeon. Don't forget the coroner's office.' He went to meet the police surgeon, a young, unassuming Scot, sandy haired, with freckles.

'Dr McPherson.' The two men shook hands.

'He's in his surgery.'

McPherson followed him down the passage to the surgery, glanced about him with professional interest at his colleague's furniture and fittings, then bent over the body. A very brief examination with the minimum of disturbance. 'Well, you don't need me to tell you that he's dead or how, or when. It's a sad business; he'll be missed by his patients and by some of us. He was a first rate physician and a good GP. I don't mind admitting he's helped me out more than once. Will you be wanting me for the PM?'

'I think the coroner will nominate Franks.'

A look of surprise. 'For a suicide?'

'There may be wider implications.'

'I see. Well, I won't say I haven't heard talk about police interest but I never imagined . . .'

'Will you see Mrs Tate?'

'Ah, yes, Marcella. Where is she?'

'Upstairs, a woman officer is with her. I gather she's in shock.'

'I can believe it.'

Wycliffe was making a painful effort to come to terms with what he believed to be his own failure. 'A compassionate man, a first-rate physician and a good GP.'

Sergeant Fox, the scenes-of-crime officer, arrived and there was a telephone call from Dr Franks, the pathologist. Wycliffe took the call in the dining-room.

'I've just had your message, Charles. As it happens I'm in Plymouth and my secretary phoned through. I can be with you in about 75 minutes.'

Wycliffe, always mildly irritated by the ebullient doctor, snapped: 'The man is dead, there's no point in maiming somebody else to get here.'

Franks was notorious for fast driving.

'They'll direct you from the Incident Room on the Wharf car-park.'

He could hear a woman's voice raised in the kitchen and found Mrs Irons, the cleaning woman, confronting DC Curnow. She seized on Wycliffe, wide-eyed and trembling: 'He says the doctor is dead!'

'I'm afraid that's true.'

'But how? I mean, what's happened? He was all right when I left . . .'

'We don't know exactly what has happened.' He was sorry for her; she seemed deeply distressed.

'Where is Mrs Tate?'

'She's up in her bedroom; a doctor is with her.'

'Then I'm going up.' Challenging.

'Yes, I think that would be a good idea. Just a couple of questions first: When you went to lunch where were the doctor and Mrs Tate?'

Through her tears she said: 'He was in his surgery and she was in the kitchen preparing lunch.'

'Nothing unusual happened?'

'Nothing!'

'Just one more question: Where is Miss Ward, the receptionist?'

'She goes as soon as she's cleared up after morning surgery and she doesn't come back until four.'

In the surgery Fox was photographing the body from all accessible angles, and every aspect of the room. Fox was a very efficient scenes-of-crime officer; his Punch-like nose and receding chin gave him a comical profile and his conceit alienated goodwill, but he worked smoothly, with scarcely a pause, knowing precisely what he was going to do and the order in which he would do it. When he had all his photographs he recovered the pistol with the help of a long-handled forceps which gripped the trigger guard width-wise.

'I understand you don't want the body disturbed until Dr Franks arrives, sir.'

'That's right; get the pistol off to the lab straight away: dabs, and a full ballistics report.'

Fox placed the pistol on a prepared bed of cotton-wool in a cardboard box.

Wycliffe said: 'I want swabs taken from his and her hands for the rhodizinate test. Tell her that the test is routine.'

As he left the surgey Wycliffe met Dr McPherson coming to look for him.

'How is she?'

'She'll be all right. An emotional shock takes different people in different ways; her pulse rate is a bit erratic; she keeps feeling her throat, probably an hysterical constriction, and she's a bit vague. There isn't much to worry about, physically speaking, but it would be as well not to leave her alone. Rest and soothing companionship. I wondered about sending along a nurse? Mrs What's-her-name seems a decent soul but it might be better to have a professional. Do you know of any relatives?'

'None. I think she should have a nurse. What about questioning her?'

'Give her a couple of hours. I'll look in again this evening.'

Wycliffe rejoined Kersey in the dining-room.

Kersey had had time to ruminate. 'He couldn't face the prospect of a search, I suppose.' And then, as a new thought struck him, he looked up at Wycliffe. 'You're not blaming yourself?'

Wycliffe did not answer directly. 'I don't think the search had much to do with it. I think he was prepared for that.'

'What then?'

Wycliffe was standing by a french window which opened into the courtyard. 'Come out here.'

Kersey followed him out under the green glass roof. The afternoon sun was shining directly into the paved yard; the stone urns, filled with flowering geraniums and lobelias, looked like floral flags, and two lustrous dragonflies darted over the pool, dodging the water from the fountain.

Kersey said: 'Pretty! Am I supposed to see something?'

'The paving slabs near the pool, they've been scrubbed.'

'So they have!' The two of them had been associated for so long that they had evolved a pattern of almost reflex responses to each other's moods. When Wycliffe seemed more than commonly disturbed, Kersey's reaction was to fence.

Wycliffe pointed to the tiny groove in the edge of one of the slabs. 'What caused that?'

Kersey crouched down and carefully examined the scarred slab. 'A grazing bullet?'

'You think so?'

'I'm no expert but I'd be prepared to bet.'

'So the bullet, if it is one, is probably embedded in the opposite side of the pool. From this angle it would miss the fountain. It means that Garland must have been brought here when he arrived on Saturday evening.'

'Hardly the place for a medical examination.'

'No, but Garland didn't come here about his health, he came to talk about pictures. He struck me as not very bright, a rather weak character but conscientious, hard done by, and with a strain of obstinacy which made him aggressive. My guess is that he knew about the picture hoax, Francis had confided in him, but with Francis dead, the secret was too much for him. He wanted somebody to tell him what to do, so he tried the people directly concerned – first Beryl, then, when she wouldn't see him, the Tates. A preparatory telephone call, his best suit to boost his ego, and he presents himself.'

'You don't think he was trying his hand at blackmail?'

'I don't, but the fact that he knew, was enough to finish him.'

Kersey indulged in one of his grotesque parodies: '"Let's talk in the courtyard, it's lovely out there this evening . . . Make yourself comfortable . . . Would you care for a drink? Long and cold? Coffee if you prefer . . ." Then the poor bastard gets it in the neck – literally.'

'It could have been something like that, I suppose.' Wycliffe shivered. 'I hate this place!'

Kersey went back under the glass roof and dragged forward one of the metal chairs with its loose, striped cushions. He placed the chair with care, eyeing the scarred slab. When he sat in the chair his head came well above the cushions.

'I think this is it, sir.'

'I went through the same antics this morning.'

'And he saw you?'

'She did.'

A quick, comprehending glance from Kersey. 'Ah! . . . So where do we go from here?'

'Tell Fox to leave the surgery for the present, that can wait until after Franks has been. Start him off on this and give him what helps he needs. I shall be back in . . . Anyway, you know what to do.'

Kersey looked at him with concern. 'Something wrong, sir?' Kersey was troubled.

'Yes, an unnecessary death.'

Wycliffe left Tregarthen and retraced the route he had taken that morning, down the steps and into the secluded cul-de-sac where Barton's had their car-body repair shops. The front doors of some of the little houses stood open to the sunshine.

A first rate physician and a good GP.

He walked to the end of the street and into Barton's yard which was built up on three sides with sheds of varied structure and size. Just inside the gate there was a little building labelled 'Office' and a young girl typist told him that the foreman was in the stores on the other side of the yard.

'Are you the foreman?'

Thirty-five, dark, wearing greasy overalls and sporting a Mexican moustache. 'That's right.'

Wycliffe showed his warrant card. 'Chief Superintendent Wycliffe. I believe one of your men fetched Dr Tate's car this morning to carry out repairs.'

'Is there something wrong about it?'

'I would like to see the car.'

The foreman, puzzled, and a little worried, led the way to another shed where Tate's car had been stripped of the front over-ride, the near side lamp housing and wing panel.

Wycliffe's manner was unusually curt, almost aggressive. The truth was that he was tense and angry but his anger was directed against himself. An unnecessary death.

'When did Dr Tate have his accident?'

The foreman inspected a job sheet clipped under the screen wiper. 'The 5th, a week ago today. It was nothing much, somebody backed into him on a car-park. The insurance rep inspected the damage at the doctor's place on Friday and authorised the repair. Dr Tate arranged for us to collect the car on the 12th – that's today, and we did.'

'When was that arrangement made?'

'He telephoned on Saturday, I took the message myself.' The foreman plucked up courage. 'Don't you think you should talk to Dr Tate about this?'

Wycliffe said: 'The doctor is not able to talk to me. How long were you expecting to keep the car here?'

'We budgeted on four days, allowing for spraying.'

Four days: days when the heat would be on; after that . . . But it would require nerve . . .

He walked round the car to the rear. 'Will you open the boot, please?'

The foreman joined him. 'I can't, sir, I don't have a key.'

'But surely your man must have had the keys to drive it here.'

'The ignition key only. Of course that opens the doors but it doesn't unlock the boot. I suppose the doctor thought we didn't need it – which we don't.'

204

Wycliffe said: 'May I use your telephone?'

'In the office.'

He had to make his call with the foreman and the typist listening.

It was Kersey who answered.

'I'm speaking from Barton's car-body repair shop in Cross Street. Has Franks arrived? . . . Good! Tell him I'll be in touch before he leaves. I want you to look in the desk for car keys, possibly a spare set; also get Franks to look in Tate's pockets . . . I'll wait while you check.'

For three, four . . . possibly five minutes the little office seemed to exist in limbo. The typist sat at her machine staring out into the sunlit yard while the foreman pretended to be occupied in turning the pages of a trade catalogue. A clock on the wall, advertising a brand of tyres, showed ten minutes to four.

Wycliffe stood by the girl's desk, still as a graven image.

A cross between a saint and a witch doctor.

Kersey came back to the phone.

'Send down what you've got . . . now, at once. I'll be in touch.'

He replaced the telephone. 'I shall be outside.' He walked out into the sunshine and stood by the gates, waiting. It was very quiet, just a murmur of traffic in the main street. One of the high days of summer, with perfect weather, one of those days which would colour the memories of thousands of people in the winter ahead and persuade them to send for next year's brochure. To him it all seemed as remote as another world.

An unnecessary death.

A police car nosed along the street and pulled up by the gates. He was handed a brown envelope. 'From Mr Kersey, sir.'

'Pull into the yard and wait.'

Two sets of keys – different, and an odd one which seemed to match one of the others. With luck . . .

The foreman, without a word, followed him back to the shed where Tate's car was. Wycliffe went to the back of the car and inserted the odd key in the lock of the boot. It fitted. He lifted the lid. The boot was large; it held a heavy-duty polythene bag and through the semi-transparent plastic he could see the form of a man crouched in the posture of an embryo in the womb.

The foreman spoke in a whisper: 'Christ Almighty!'

Back to the little office. The girl looked up at the foreman. 'What's up, Jack?'

The foreman shrugged and said nothing.

Wycliffe picked up the phone. 'Perhaps you will leave me alone in the office for a few minutes?'

The two of them went out without a word and stood in the yard, talking in low tones.

Wycliffe spoke to Kersey, then to Dr Franks; he was on the phone for nearly ten minutes. When he had finished, the girl, looking dazed, went back into her office and the foreman listlessly set about picking up bits of junk around the yard and carrying them to the scrap pile. Wycliffe had another wait in the sunshine.

Fox and Curnow arrived in the scenes-of-crime van, closely followed by Dr Franks in his Porsche. The pathologist, tubby, immaculate, and jaunty as ever, greeted Wycliffe: 'Lovely day, Charles! Too good for work. Where is he?'

Wycliffe, sombre and taciturn, led the way to the shed where Tate's car was housed.

Fox and Curnow set to work placing flood lamps in the rear of the shed where the lighting was poor. Fox, with his conspicuous nose, receding chin, and stalking gait, reminded Wycliffe of some stork-like bird absorbed in the serious business of nest building. Work in the yard had come to a stop and half-a-dozen men in overalls gathered to watch but they kept their distance.

Wycliffe called over to the foreman. 'Can the car be driven?'

'No reason why not.'

When Fox had taken his photographs of the body in situ the car was driven out of its shed; the body, still in its plastic envelope, was lifted out of the boot and laid on the floor in the empty shed so that Franks could make his preliminary examination. Apart from the pathologist only Wycliffe and Fox were in the shed with the body. It was a macabre scene with the three men bending over the encapsulated corpse under the powerful lamps.

Franks said: 'Like a giant embryo in its caul.'

The heavy polythene bag, of the sort used to pack mattresses, had been carefully sealed with a broad strip of adhesive bandage. Franks cut the bag away and exposed the body so that they saw it plainly for the first time.

No doubt about indentification; it was Mark Garland. He was fully dressed: grey pinstripe suit, grey socks and shoes, pale blue shirt and matching tie. He had been shot through the base of the skull and the bullet had emerged below the bridge of the nose, shattering a relatively small area of the face. There must have been a quantity of extruded matter for some still adhered to the bag.

Franks was straightening the limbs. 'He's been dead more than 24 hours. I'd say between 36 and 48.'

'Saturday evening at 8.30?'

'I wouldn't argue with that. No more I can do here.'

The mortuary van arrived, the body was placed in a 'shell' and driven off.

207

Wycliffe turned to Fox: 'When you've finished here get back to Mr Kersey at the house.'

Fox said: 'We've made a start there, sir, lowering the water level of the pond.'

'Good!' Wycliffe was getting used to Fox and beginning to like him. 'Tell Mr Kersey I'll be back in under the hour.'

He left the yard and continued down the steep, narrow alley to the main street. It was quiet, very little traffic, very few people; even the locals must have made for the beaches or the boats. In the art shop Cathy Carne's assistant was perched on a stool by the till, reading. She came over to him at once.

'Miss Carne is upstairs in the flat with Miss Garland and Anna.'

'Something wrong?'

A faint smile. 'I think they're having a kind of meeting.'

Coming to terms? Beryl had said: 'I shan't let him continue to ruin my life. That's what he wanted . . . I shall come to terms in a business-like way.'

Wycliffe went through to the little hall and up the stairs. He could hear someone talking in the living-room – Beryl, being dogmatic: 'We must keep lawyers out of this until we've reached agreement.'

He tapped on the door and it was answered by Beryl.

'Oh, it's you. I've got people with me.'

'I want to talk to Miss Carne.'

Reluctantly she stood back from the door. Cathy Carne was seated on one side of the table and there was a young woman opposite her. There were coffee cups and a plate of biscuits on the table. A social occasion. It took Wycliffe a moment or two to recognise Anna. Anna had taken herself in hand; a stylish hair-cut, a well-fitting cornflower-blue dress, a coral necklace, smart shoes and a handbag. A youthful version of Cathy Carne.

Cathy took his intrusion in her stride. 'Ah, Mr Wycliffe; you want to speak to me? We were talking things over, business-wise.'

Wycliffe looked at her with a leaden stare. 'In your office if you don't mind.'

She stood up. 'I'll be back as soon as I can.'

They went down the stairs and into her office. Despite her effort to appear relaxed she looked at him with apprehension.

'Dr Tate is dead.'

She stiffened; her whole body became tense. 'Alan . . . *Dead*?' She seemed to withdraw into herself like a snail into its shell.

'Shortly before one o'clock he was found dead in his surgery; shot through the head.'

She reached for her cigarettes, her fingers fumbled with the cigarette pack, then with the lighter. Only when she had taken the first draw did she look directly at him.

'His body was slumped between the chair and the desk, the bullet entered his skull just above and slightly in front of the right ear.' He was deliberately, cruelly explicit, and for an instant there was hatred in her eyes.

'The gun was on the floor beside him.'

The little office had become a focus of tension and emotion, isolated from the world.

'He shot himself?' She stumbled over the words.

'There is something else: Mark Garland's body has been found in the boot of Dr Tate's car.'

She was watching him intently and for the first time he detected fear in her eyes. 'Why are you being so brutal to me?'

'Because you have your share in what has happened.

209

You have deliberately withheld information and you have lied. I feel sure that you did not destroy your uncle's letter. Unless I misjudge you, you are not the sort to destroy evidence of any sort.'

She looked at him as though she had been paid an unexpected compliment, then she opened a drawer of her desk, took out a key, unlocked the safe and handed him an envelope. 'You are quite right, I never destroy anything.'

The letter was written on the firm's paper in the old man's powerful script:

Dear Cathy,

There is something I want you to know when I am dead (if you do not know it before). Gifford Tate did not paint any pictures after his stroke; all the work attributed to him since then is mine. It started as a joke we thought up together to have fun with Papa and with the critics who are mostly imbeciles. We were more successful than we thought possible and it was too good not to keep it going. After Gifford died without letting the cat out of the bag (I thought he would have done so in his will), I set up the Ismay-Gorton annual farce in which I play the privileged role of friend and art executor of the lamented painter. You of all people will understand what a hell of a good laugh it is! (*was,* when you read this).

But I begin to want to share the joke while I'm still around to see the red faces, so I'm opening certain lines of communication (arranging leaks). Today I told Francis the whole story. I shall be interested to see how long he can keep it to himself. My guess is that greed will outweigh his yearning for self-importance and that he will hold his tongue until I am gone and he is secure in his inheritance, but we shall see!

I am also trying to get a major touring exhibition of Gifford's(!) work to give the critics a better chance.

If despite all this I still die before the world has heard the joke it will be up to you to tell them about it with the help of one or two cryptic refrences in my will.

Love from Uncle Ed who now knows all – or nothing!

PS If they want more than the evidence of their eyes, tell them that Gifford always signed his work in Winsor blue and put a blob of it somewhere in the picture. I've never used it in my life. E.

Wycliffe folded the letter and put it back in its envelope. 'Nothing about destroying it there. Quite the contrary.'

She said nothing.

'Did Tate know about this letter?'

'No, there seemed no point in telling him; by the time I received it, the day after Edwin's funeral, Francis was dead.'

'And Francis had been to see the Tates on the morning of the funeral with a picture under his arm to tell them what he knew.'

'I didn't think it was up to me to make it worse for them.'

'Perhaps you were afraid.'

She made an irritable movement. 'All right! Perhaps I was, you kept telling me I had reason to be.'

She was making a great effort at self-control and her reactions were deliberate and slow. With uncharacteristic fussiness she brushed ash from the folds of her skirt

211

as though it were an action of importance. 'You won't believe me, but Alan told me nothing of what happened. Nothing! I've only been able to guess at what's been going on. You say I've had a share in what happened but it's been a nightmare: Alan afraid to speak, and I afraid to hear.'

'And this continued when Mark Garland went missing?'

'Just the same. We exchanged purely factual information – about your visits, what you had to say, Marcella's behaviour, that sort of thing, but nothing which committed either of us to certain knowledge.'

'Yet you knew.'

She lit another cigarette; she was very pale and her hands still trembled.

Wycliffe said: 'One more question: At what time did Tate leave you on Saturday evening – the evening Mark Garland disappeared?'

'He wasn't with me—'

Wycliffe sounded weary. 'That is what he told you to say but now that he is dead, do you still need to lie?'

She shook her head. 'No! I don't need to lie; he left me shortly after nine; he said he was worried about leaving Marcella alone.'

There was a tap at the door; Cathy's assistant was standing in the entrance to the office. 'Is it all right to shut the shop, Miss Carne? It's past closing time.'

CHAPTER THIRTEEN

As Wycliffe left the shop, pleasure boats were returning from their afternoon trips and people were streaming off the pier. In the past five days three people had died; for two of them he felt no personal responsibility; he could not have anticipated their deaths. The third was a different matter. If only that morning, in the doctor's surgery, he had foreseen the possibility . . .

An unnecessary death.

He entered one of the alleys and climbed the steep slopes as though he could appease his pent-up frustration and guilt in a furious outburst of physical energy. He arrived at the gate of Tregarthen, his heart racing, breathing hard, deeply flushed.

Now there was a uniformed constable stationed outside the gate and a string of police vehicles parked in the drive. A small crowd had collected on the opposite side of the road and people were watching from the windows of the houses. If his arrival caused a ripple of interest he was totally unaware of it.

He walked up the drive and around to the back of the house. Fox and Curnow were in the courtyard, shirt-sleeves rolled up, sweating under the afternoon sun. The fountain had been turned off and they had lowered the level of the water to expose the top three courses of brickwork. Buckets, slimy with green algae, stood in a group.

Fox stooped and pointed to a scar in the lining of the

pool where the algae had been scraped away: 'There it is, sir; no doubt about that. I think we'd better lift out the whole brick to make it easier to recover the bullet.'

He came around the pool to join Wycliffe. 'As I see it, sir, Garland was sitting in one of those lounging chairs, leaning forwards – perhaps he was watching the fish; at any rate he was shot in the back of the head and he must have pitched forward on the paving. That would explain why we've found no stained cushions: all the mess was on the paving slabs.'

Wycliffe stared at the pool and said nothing and after a moment or two Fox returned to his work.

Kersey was in the dining-room juggling with sheets of paper. 'The doctor's body has gone off to the mortuary. You know what's happening down at the garage, and you've seen Fox and Curnow out there in the court-yard. Lucy Lane has gone to break the news to Thomas.'

'Marcella?'

'Oh yes, Marcella. She's still upstairs with the cleaning woman – Mrs Irons and our woman PC from the local nick. Dr McPherson's nurse arrived but Marcella sent her packing.'

Kersey lit a cigarette. 'I'm curious about the body in the boot; was it a hunch, a tip off, or what?'

'It was a hunch which seemed so unlikely that I kept quiet about it. Tate made no real protest about the search so he must have felt reasonably safe, but I couldn't see how he'd managed it. Then it occurred to me that his car had been able to leave the premises openly, also that the repair people wouldn't want access to the boot. Taken together . . .'

Wycliffe walked over to the window and stood, looking out. 'Tate foresaw the possibility of a search, and the fact that his car was due to be in the repair shop

214

for a matter of days must have seemed providential. What he did, required nerve but, if it worked, by the time he had his car back, the heat would probably be off and he would have all the time in the world.'

'Ingenious, but I can see why you kept it to yourself.'

For once exchanges between the two men were stilted and strained. They lapsed into silence and, after a moment or two, Wycliffe said: 'I'm going upstairs.'

As he reached the top of the stairs Mrs Irons, flushed and agitated, was coming down the corridor towards him. 'I'm worried about Mrs Tate; she's behaving very queer. She wouldn't take the sedative Dr McPherson left for her and she ordered his nurse out of the house.'

She looked at him with worried eyes, wondering how far she dared confide in this grim-faced policeman. 'I think she must be out of her mind, she's talking wild and saying terrible things about the doctor. I mean, I've known him since he was a schoolboy; he might seem a cold sort of man and a bit off-hand to strangers but he wouldn't hurt a fly! Nobody knows what he's done for people. And the way he's looked after her . . . I mean, it's his house; he didn't have to let her stay on, but far from turning her out, he couldn't do enough for her. It's been more like he was living in her house. And she isn't easy to live with, I can tell you! What with her nerves and going on about Mr Gifford as though he was still alive . . . Morbid, I call it!'

'Which is her room?'

'I left her in Mr Gifford's room. It's the door facing up the passage. I'm going down to make a pot of tea.'

The door was open. Gifford's bedroom was large; the furnishing, circa 1930 was massively functional. Pyjamas were laid out on the double bed and there was a padded dressing gown thrown across the foot, all in readiness for the Master. A sectional wardrobe occu-

215

pied most of one wall and all the doors stood open; there were suits, overcoats, and shirts on hangers, trays of underclothes, a rack for ties and a number of small drawers presumably containing accessories. Two sections of the wardrobe were empty.

The WPC came in, anxious and solemn; she spoke in a low voice: 'Mrs Tate is next door, in her own room, sir. I think she's intending to move in here; she's taking all her clothes out of her wardrobe.'

'Has she said anything?'

'Only to Mrs Irons, not to me.'

'Go and have a break; come back in half-an-hour.'

The girl went out and almost at once Marcella came in loaded with an armful of dresses still on their hangers. She dropped them on the bed, then started shaking them out and hanging them one by one in an empty section of the wardrobe.

Wycliffe stood with his back to the window and at first she took no notice of him, apparently absorbed in her work. Then his continuing presence seemed to make her uneasy and from time to time she glanced across at him, her eyes half fearful, half defiant.

Abruptly, in the act of shaking out the creases from one of her dresses, she said: 'I'm moving back in here with Gifford. Of course I slept here before, but when he was ill he said he disturbed my rest so he made me move next door.'

Wycliffe said nothing and after a while she went on: 'You haven't been in this room before, have you?' It seemed that she was trying to divert his attention, perhaps his thoughts. 'Just like the studio, I've kept everything exactly the same here as it was before Gifford was taken ill . . . Look at all his clothes! He has always been very particular about his clothes. Alan was like him in that way . . . Always immaculate . . .'

After another silence, during which she went on putting away her dresses, Wycliffe said: 'Why have you been telling Mrs Irons that Alan killed Francis and Mark Garland?' He put the question almost casually.

Abruptly, she sat on the edge of the bed and ran her hands through her hair. 'I really don't want to talk about it any more! I should have thought I'd suffered enough.'

'I want you to tell me what really happened on Saturday night when Mark Garland came and what happened last night when you screamed.'

She looked at him, vaguely. 'Last night?'

'You said you had a nightmare.'

She pressed her hands to her head. 'Did I? I'm so muddled! Alan always told me what to say and now I don't know where I am. I don't know what I said and what I didn't; I don't know what I'm supposed to say.' As she spoke she was watching him through half closed eyes.

'It doesn't matter about what you are supposed or not supposed to say; you know what happened on Saturday night when Mark Garland was here, and you know what happened last night to make you scream.'

She nodded slowly. 'I know about last night!' She repeated with a curious emphasis: 'I know what happened then. I saw Alan with Mark Garland's body.'

'Let's start with the night before – Saturday night, when Mark Garland came. You said that you took your dog for a walk and that it was after nine when you came back. What happened then?'

She frowned and clasped her hands tightly together. 'Well, I just came in and went to bed.'

'Did you see Dr Tate?'

'Of course! He said I looked very tired and he insisted that I go straight up to bed. I did, and he brought me a hot drink in bed.'

'Did he say anything about Mark Garland?'

'Just that he'd been; I think he said something about Mark being ill or thinking he was ill; I can't remember.' She gave him one of her quick, appraising glances.

Wycliffe was silent for a while and, hesitantly, she got off the bed and resumed putting her clothes away. Somewhere in the house a clock chimed the half-hour. Six-thirty.

'Who scrubbed the courtyard?'

She turned to face him. 'Oh, Alan did. I heard him at it early yesterday morning before I was up.'

'Now tell me about last night.'

She sat on the bed again; placed her hands together between her knees and leaned forward. She moistened her lips. 'I suppose I've got to . . . It was about two o'clock in the morning; I woke up and I could see a faint light coming from the corridor. I always leave my door open a bit for Ricky. I got out of bed and I could see that the light was coming from downstairs. I went to the top of the stairs and called. Alan answered, he said: "It's all right, Marcella; go back to bed."'

She shook her head and in a low voice she went on. 'I didn't go back to bed. I went down the stairs, but before I got to the bottom the light was switched off and I couldn't see a thing. I worked my way along the wall to the switch and when the light came on I was standing . . . I was almost touching a great plastic bag . . .' She shivered. 'And in the bag there was a body . . . I could see it. Then I screamed.'

There was a long pause; she shuddered, and said, nodding her head as though she had settled some problem: 'Yes, that was how I knew for certain what he had done.'

Some truth and some lies; her own bewildering blend

218

of fact and fiction, reality and fairy tale. That would be the pattern of her response to all interrogation. Sometimes naive and sometimes cunning, she would rely on those quick bird-like glances to pick her way through the maze.

'Why would Dr Tate want to kill Francis and Mark Garland?'

She stiffened and looked at him, her eyes wide. She raised her voice. 'Why? I don't know! He didn't tell me; he never told me anything . . .'

'And you say you were out on Saturday night when Mark Garland came?'

'I keep telling you I wasn't here! Alan told you.'

The door opened very quietly and Mrs Irons came in with tea things on a tray. She put the tray down on the chest of drawers and stood, waiting. Marcella seemed not to see her.

In a low voice Wycliffe said: 'Mark Garland was shot at half-past eight on Saturday evening.'

She looked her question.

'We have evidence that Dr Tate didn't arrive home until well after nine o'clock.'

Marcella became excited: 'That is a lie! That's what Cathy Carne told you! She's been trying to . . . She will do anything! Look at the way she wormed her way in to get all she could from Edwin! For years she's been trying to get rid of me so that she could move in here with Alan!' In her frustration she beat on the bed-clothes with her clenched fists.

Totally unexpected, Mrs Irons spoke in her rather harsh, masculine voice: 'It's you who is telling the lies. Ever since Mr Gifford died the doctor has looked after you and let you carry on in your own sweet way, as though he didn't exist except to dance attendance on your selfishness. Any ordinary man would have kicked you out in the first six months. Lucky for you the doctor was no ordinary man, but that's neither here nor there now; what I have to say is that I saw the doctor, coming up Quay Hill at a quarter-past nine on Saturday evening. And I'll swear to that in the witness box if I have to.'

Marcella looked across at Mrs Irons, she opened her mouth but no words came; for a long moment she seemed to be frozen, petrified; then she screamed and kept on screaming. She rolled over on the bed, kicking her feet and pummelling the clothes with her fists.

Mrs Irons looked down at her, totally dispassionate. 'Don't worry! That's nothing that a good slap wouldn't cure.'

Wycliffe wondered if Mrs Irons had really seen her doctor that evening but he had no intention of trying to find out.

Wycliffe looked and felt very tired. He was back in the dining-room with Kersey.

Kersey said: 'It didn't occur to me until we were out in the courtyard this afternoon that he was covering for her. Do you think he knew – really knew that she had shot Francis?'

'I doubt if he could have lived in the house without knowing, but he felt bound to protect her. I think that was genuine; I very much doubt if an exposure of the picture fraud would have weighed with him very heavily, certainly not to the extent of compounding a murder. What he didn't know was that it hadn't ended with the shooting on the wharf. If he'd even guessed at the possibility of another killing, then things would have been different. I don't think he would have knowingly set another life at risk.'

'He must have had misgivings about the gun.'

'She would have sworn to him that she'd thrown it in the harbour. She's a convincing liar when she puts her mind to it.'

'Then the poor bastard comes home one night to find a corpse literally on his doorstep and he's committed to something far more hazardous than keeping his mouth shut – and hers.'

Wycliffe was sitting by the window staring out into the courtyard and through the Moorish arch to the garden beyond. The low sun lit up a tiny window in the gable-end of Gifford's studio so that it seemed to blaze like a fire. He said: 'It makes my flesh creep to imagine what it must have been like for Tate in this house during that 40 hours from Saturday night to lunchtime today, with him certain now that she still had the gun. By day there was almost nothing he could do, he could only use the night when they had the house to themselves, to dispose of the body; to reason, to plead – and to search.'

'You think the case against her will stand up?'

'Yes, if it ever comes to court.'

'Unfit to plead?'

'That's what the shrinks will say.'

'And what do you think?'

Wycliffe said nothing for a time then: 'The thought of her going into the surgery, hiding the pistol, saying something quite ordinary and, as he looks up from his work . . . She needed a scapegoat and her need excluded every other consideration. That to me is wickedness. There is no other word.'

There was a long silence then Wycliffe said: 'This case has been about children, about arrested development; Gifford, Edwin and Papa Burger – they didn't grow up either. All three of them needed mothers rather than wives but only Burger was lucky enough to marry one.'

And after another interval he went on: 'Three deaths to preserve this woman's fantasies. I wonder if Edwin, wherever he is, will feel now that his prank got out of hand?'

THE END

WYCLIFFE AND THE
DUNES MYSTERY

To Muriel

Prologue

The holiday chalet was perched on the fringe of the foredunes, nearer the sea than most of the others. Built on stilts for the view, as well as for protection against the invasive sand, it was reached by a long flight of wooden steps.

The weekend was GG's idea. 'Let's make it a *manic* weekend, something to remember.' Manic was her current in-word, which was odd in view of what was to happen. The arrangements had been delicate; parental concern had been allayed by ingeniously vague fabrications, and without knowing it GG's mother was contributing the use of her chalet. So early in the season there were few if any other people on the site.

There was a sense of occasion. During their five terms in the sixth form the three boys and three girls had somehow gelled into a group – almost an institution, regarded by the rest of the sixth with puzzled tolerance. Now it was almost over; in a matter of weeks A-level examinations would mark the end of their schooldays and they would be caught up in the last round of the scramble for college places or jobs.

They had just arrived at the chalet and were still lumbered with the stuff they had brought. At least the weather was holding – almost a May heatwave, and according to the pundits it would see them through the weekend.

'Let's take a photo.' Barbara, plump, fair and commonsensical, had already developed a maternal instinct for ordering and recording her chicks.

7

'Dump your bags and make a group by the steps . . . No, sit down, for God's sake! You look like a bus queue.'

Barbara had her camera on a tripod and it was fitted with a delayed action trip.

'You could look a bit more affectionate, GG; I dare say Julian could stand it. And push your hair back, I can't see you.'

GG had red hair to her shoulders and half the time her view of the world was mediated by a curtain of red strands.

'Tuck your feet in, Paul! You can cuddle up to Lisa but there's no need to look as though you're going to rape her.'

Paul was a long, lean, bespectacled youth with the solemnity of an owl.

'Julian! Try not to look like cold pudding – and Alan, make room for me, I'm setting it going . . . Ready? . . . Ten seconds!'

And so the photograph was taken which, fifteen years later, would affect all their lives.

That evening, her arms resting on the veranda rail, Lisa looked out across the bay and watched the sun go down behind St Ives. The sky was cloudless and the sea shone. As the last remnant of the disc vanished, the whole coastline was transformed into a dark and strangely fashioned cut-out.

In the room behind her the radio pumped out pop with a heavy beat. Lisa turned her head to look through the open window. GG was playing the fool, her red hair swinging about, hiding her face. She contorted her body, wriggling her hips, sticking out her breasts and bottom and making supposedly lascivious gestures with her hands and arms.

Julian, squatting Buddha-like on the sofa, watched her with more tolerance than interest.

The two were alone in the room. Barbara, in the

8

kitchen, had volunteered for the short straw taking charge of the evening fry-up; Alan and Paul were in town shopping for a few cans of beer and a couple of bottles of wine.

In the afternoon they had played games on the deserted beach. Alan and Julian had wet suits and boards; Paul and the girls fooled about in the surf, but the water was cold. Afterwards there was a fair amount of boisterous sex play. Now they would drink a little and eat a lot and eventually it would be time for bed.

Which made Lisa uneasy; there were three cubicles, each with a double bed and room for little else. Lisa was not a virgin but she was troubled at the prospect of a whole night spent with that bony body in the intimacy of a double bed. Yet it would be assumed that she and Paul . . .

Lisa sighed and wondered if she was normal.

The sky over the dunes had turned from deep blue to green and in the distance there was a vague mist, a first intimation of approaching dusk. She was mildly surprised to see a lone figure, a man, trudging across the sands from the Gwithian direction. He was young, with a mass of lank black hair; he carried a rucksack and wore an all-weather outfit of jacket and trousers which seemed slightly absurd in a heatwave. He stopped short of the chalet and looked up at her; he was very pale.

'Hullo! I don't suppose there's a chance of a glass of water? I'm parched.' A pleasant voice and an easy manner but for some reason Lisa did not care for the look of him. His deep-set eyes? Or the puckered little mouth?

'You'd better come up.'

He climbed the steps. 'Kind of you . . . I'm Cochran. I'm supposed to be walking the coast path . . .'

'I'm Lisa.'

He followed her into the living room.

'Meet Gillian, known to all as GG. And this is Julian . . . Cochran has come for a glass of water.'

She left the three of them together and joined Barbara

9

who was frying onions in the kitchen. 'We've got a visitor; he wants a drink.'

'Is he expecting to stay for the meal?'

'God! I hope not.'

'How old is he?'

'Twenty, give or take. He's a rambler of some sort. Student type. I suppose he's all right but he looks a bit odd to me. Anyway, all he asked for was a glass of water.'

'Up to you. There's enough if he does stay. Hang on, I'll take him his water.'

When Barbara entered the living room, Cochran was sharing the sofa with GG while Julian lounged in the wicker chair.

Cochran was saying, 'Only a short stint today – from St Agnes, but hard going.' He took the glass of water and drank it off. 'Thanks, that was wonderful.'

Barbara said, 'You're on your own?'

'I started out with a friend but I ditched him. You know how it is.'

Barbara was thoughtful. 'I think I must have seen your friend earlier on, fair and on the plump side. He was looking for somebody who sounded like you.'

He grinned up at her. 'Really? that was a good miss, then.'

GG laughed and drew attention back to herself. 'Cochran, that's a rather unusual name.'

'You can say that again! My mother's maiden name, wished on me by my father. At school they called me "the Cock".'

Alan and Paul returned with the drinks and were introduced. Alan, a rugby type, was naturally gregarious, while Paul had little to say.

GG said, 'Well, Barbie, can you stretch it to include Cochran?'

Barbara and Lisa exchanged looks. If the newcomer protested he was not heard.

Barbara said, 'All right. If you lot fix the table it will be ready in ten minutes.'

GG had the last word. 'What about getting us a real drink, Alan, while we do the table?'

After the meal they talked, and Cochran did tricks with coins and glasses, with playing cards and with a ring on a string.

'A chap I got to know in hospital was a professional and he taught me.'

'You've been in hospital?'

A shrug. 'A sort of hospital – a place where they're supposed to iron out one's mental kinks.'

Julian was thoughtful. 'Is your name Wilder?'

The little mouth twitched into a grin. 'You've rumbled me? "Son of MP on Theft Charges." The hospital was a cosy alternative to jail.'

Lisa thought: he wanted us to know. It's all part of the act.

'Now the witch-doctors have let me out, Papa thought it would be good for me to, as he put it, "Face some physical challenge". In the old days it would have meant the colonies, now walking the coastal path is more practicable. Of course, I had a minder but I shook him off.'

At some time after ten he looked out of the window. 'God, it's dark! I must push on; I've got to find somewhere to stay in Hayle.'

GG said, 'You can't go now. At least we can make up some sort of bed on the floor – or there's the sofa.'

It was settled.

Julian produced a cigarette pack. 'Smoke?'

Cochran fished in his pocket and came out with a slim plastic box. 'I roll my own. Like to try one, anybody?'

Julian said, 'Hash?'

'Not any old rubbish, the very best resin. I get it from—'

Julian finished for him. 'A chap you knew in hospital.'

Chapter One

On almost every morning since his retirement Jerry Cox had taken his dog for a run and a forage in the sand dunes. It had become a ritual, and when onshore gales whipped the sand off the foredunes into blinding, stinging clouds and forced them to stay indoors, they felt cheated and their whole day was spoiled. They had experienced three days of it, with westerly winds gusting above fifty knots, battering the coast, raising tremendous surf in the shallow bay, driving sand and salt before it.

Now it was over; the surf still tumbled and there were white horses out to sea, but the sun shone, the sky was an intense blue and the wind was as if it had never been. It was warm, the air was balmy, it was spring.

Smudge, an English setter, showed such impatience as was consistent with dignity and they wasted no time among the landward dunes. Stabilized by vegetation, they had been spoiled by a rash of huts and chalets built for the holiday trade and unoccupied at this time of year. The gale had changed little here; just a sprinkling of newly blown sand over the fescue grass, and little heaps of the stuff piled against the sun-bleached and sand-blasted planks of fences and walls.

Man and dog made for the sea, for the marram-grass hillocks and foredunes rising from the beach. There were new slacks and blow-outs; one dune had been sliced through, exposing a face of darker sand and a veritable delta of marram-grass roots which penetrated many yards into the mound. Jerry plodded, and picked his way between the slopes rather than pursue a punishing roller-coaster course up and down the dunes. Now and then, through a fortuitous sequence of gaps, he glimpsed the white surf and the turbulent sea beyond. Smudge lolloped ahead, diverted sometimes by a fresh scent, but anxious for that romp on the fringe of the surf which would crown their morning.

Suddenly, out of sight, Smudge started to bark – and kept it up, which was unusual. Jerry called him to heel but there was no response and the barking continued. Jerry followed the sound and came upon the dog in a shallow, recently formed blow-out. At first sight Smudge seemed to be barking at the sand itself but bending down, Jerry saw the abraded face of a watch protruding slightly from the sand, and the vague form of a hand, still buried. Gingerly, and with distaste, he brushed the sand away and exposed a leather watch-strap attached to a shrivelled and mummified wrist.

Jerry said, 'No beach for us today, Smudge.'

The time was half past eight.

At nine-fifteen Sergeant Coombes concluded, 'I reckon this one belongs to CID.'

His newly fledged constable said, 'You think it's a man, Sarge?'

'It's a man's watch. I'm not too good at sexing withered wrists.'

'And you think he was murdered?'

'Well, somebody buried him and this isn't the place I'd choose as a last resting place for a dear departed.'

The dry sand was fluid and even cautious movements on the slope set it flowing in rivulets and cascades. Coombes growled, 'We'd better get the hell out of here or Scenes of Crime will be shouting about flat-footed wooden-tops.'

It was eleven before the area was cordoned off and the full coven assembled. Policemen in shirt-sleeves played at being archaeologists, cautiously removing the sand from around the body. The aim was to expose it for examination *in situ* and to discover anything in the immediate neighbourhood which could have been associated with the dead man.

A police surgeon and a Scenes-of-Crime officer attended and Detective Inspector Gross was in charge. Three or four opportunist herring gulls kept watch from neighbouring mounds in the hope that there might be something in it for them. DI Gross, new to his rank and to the division, brooded on the prospect of sand and sky and reflected that it was just his luck to be landed with a long-dead stiff in the middle of a desert.

The man had been buried on his left side and a sheet of some sort seemed to have been put under him. Presumably it was of nylon or a similar fabric for it appeared almost unaffected by burial and the lapse of time. The body had probably been naked when buried and the degree of putrefaction varied greatly. It was almost complete in the trunk, where the skeleton was largely exposed, but minimal in the extremities where mummification had occurred and the skin, though shrivelled, was almost intact. The head hair itself, straight and dark, was scarcely affected though it had parted company with the blackened skull from which all traces of skin had disappeared. The lips, too, had vanished, exposing apparently perfect but gumless teeth.

DI Gross surveyed the body with all the professional detachment he could muster. Dr Hocking, the police surgeon, an irritable little fellow with red hair and freckles, was complaining, 'I'm not taking the responsibility for shifting him. Franks should be here.' Franks was the pathologist.

Gross was deferential. 'Can't you tell me anything, Doctor?'

The little man frowned. 'He's dead, but perhaps you can see that for yourself. It's obvious that his skull is fractured but if you ask me whether the injury was inflicted before or after death, your guess is as good as mine. As to when it all happened, God only knows. This is blown sand – a tricky medium for burial; one to be avoided if you want a pathologist to tell your friends exactly what happened when they dig you up again.'

The doctor added as an afterthought, 'And I'm not even a pathologist.'

The Scenes-of-Crime officer was taking pictures when one of the policemen, still shifting sand, said, 'There's something here.'

The man had uncovered a small area of blue-grey canvas-like material. 'Looks like a rucksack, sir.'

'All right, dig around but don't shift it.'

It was a rucksack and it had been buried close to the body. The material had stood up well and the bag bulged with whatever it contained.

Gross had already noted the untarnished gold watch and was thinking that this chap could have been no loner, unmissed and unmourned. He would certainly have appeared on somebody's missing persons list, perhaps locally. Gross would check before the big boys moved in and it would help if he had some idea of how long since. He tried again. 'Can't you give me any idea, Doctor, of how long he might have been here?'

'I've told you – not my job. Certainly many many months, quite possibly years. You'll have to get Franks in. Maybe he'll treat you to a lecture on mummification as against the formation of adipocere – I'm not going to try. Anyway, he'll need to be on the table before anybody can begin to give an opinion.' The doctor looked about him at the omnipresent sand before adding, 'Even then, coming out of this stuff, it will be no more than a guess.'

Detective Chief Superintendent Wycliffe was trying to decide how long it would be before he could decently go to lunch. For almost three weeks there had been nothing to take him away from the office and he had kept office hours. For the first few days it had been a novelty, now he was bored. He sat in his executive chair, swivelled gently from side to side and tapped his teeth with a ball-point. With supreme distaste he regarded the fat

16

pink file on his desk: *Proposals for a Revision of the Command Structure with a View to a More Efficient Use of Resources.* A note clipped to the file read: 'For suggestions and detailed comment. EAP.' Which last, in translation, meant 'Early attention please'.

'Bloody hell!'

Wycliffe rarely swore but, for some reason, this seemed a special occasion.

He looked around his office, air-conditioned, double-glazed and sound-proofed, and wondered by what strange, and presumably auspicious twists of fate he had got there. Many years ago, when he was nineteen and naïve, he had joined the police: his ambition then, to become a CID sergeant. Now he was a chief super. Some climb the ladder, others take the lift, and he supposed that he must have been one of the others. The thought did not please him and, when he had nothing more pressing to think about, his plush office troubled him.

Once or twice he had tried to share such misgivings with his wife, but her reaction had been brusque. 'Don't be absurd, Charles! You worked damned hard for what you have, surely you should find the self-confidence to enjoy it.' Perhaps she was right. Women usually are.

He opened the pink file and decided that he needed a scratch pad on which to draft the predictable puerilities required of him. He looked in the top drawer of his desk and ten minutes later he was still absorbed in the complex and largely speculative history of some of the things he found there. Among the dried-up ball-points, pencils and paper clips, there was a cotton reel, a broken comb, a couple of foreign stamps torn off an envelope, several newspaper clippings and a boiled sweet still in its wrapping . . .

Even Diane, his personal assistant, pretended ignorance of the contents of 'his desk'.

She came in now, on cue. 'What's this, then? A spot of archaeology?'

'You wanted me, Diane?' Tight-lipped.

'Mr Kersey would like a word.'

'Ask him to come in.'

He swept the random assortment of objects off his desk-top, back into the open drawer, closed it, and so ensured their preservation for another season.

DI Kersey arrived, carrying a rolled-up map. Kersey was lanky, loose, and big-boned, with deeply lined features, and the look of a man who has slept in his clothes. Differences of temperament and disparity of rank had never hindered their close relationship.

Kersey unrolled his map and spread it on the desk-top. 'St Ives Bay area, sir. Gross, the new boy down there, has inherited a corpse buried in a sandhill.' He pointed to a pencilled cross. 'That's his map reference. It's in the dunes running along the east side of the bay, not far from a bunch of holiday lets. The body was found early this morning by a dog-walker, partly uncovered by the recent gales.'

Wycliffe studied the map. 'Any clue as to who he was, what he died of, or how long he's been there?'

Kersey grinned. 'I fancy old Hocking has been giving our new boy the run-around; he won't commit himself to much more than the fact of death. But it seems obvious that the body was deliberately buried, and there's a skull fracture, though no certainty that he collected it before death. They found a rucksack near the body and it looks as though he was on some sort of walking holiday . . . Gross thinks he was an upper-crust type.'

'What gives him that idea?'

'Well, he was wearing a Rolex watch and it seems that the rucksack is a quality job. Anyway, it's a job for Franks and probably for us.'

Wycliffe did not argue. 'I'll get Franks on the line and we'll go down and take a look. Send Fox on ahead with a DC.' Fox was the squad's Scenes-of-Crime officer.

Wycliffe telephoned Franks and was in luck; the

pathologist was not only in his office but anxious to be out of it. So much so that he made an effort to be helpful. 'I'll pick you up.'

'Thanks, but no!' Franks drove a Porsche and Wycliffe professed to believe that even to sit in the thing when parked was a threat to his life expectancy.

He telephoned his wife. 'I have to go down west – St Ives Bay – No, in the dunes . . . I may not be back this evening so I'll take the emergency bag . . . Yes, I'll ring . . . And you, love.'

A spell with his deputy, a word with the chief, and not long afterwards, in his own car with Kersey driving, he was crossing the Tamar. The rail bridge, Brunel's swan-song, spanned the river just a stone's throw away. The sun shone on the broad waters below, on a host of small craft, and on a couple of pensioned-off warships looking sorry for themselves.

Wycliffe's spirits were rising, though the fact made him feel like an undertaker. He consoled himself with the Cornish wreckers' prayer: 'Lord God we pray thee, not that wrecks may happen but if wrecks there must be, that thou wilt guide them to these shores for the succour and support of thy needy servants.'

They were on the Liskeard by-pass before either of them spoke, then Wycliffe said, 'I wonder if that chap could have been there for fifteen years?'

'Would it mean anything if he had?'

'It might. Remember Cochran Wilder?'

Kersey was impressed. 'I do; he disappeared, walking the coastal path or something . . . Was that fifteen years ago?'

'It was – I checked, and he was last seen near Gwithian. We must watch our step on this one; there was enough trouble about him the first time round.'

'But we weren't involved.'

'Not directly, it was handled by the divisional people because everybody except the boy's father assumed that he'd committed suicide – drowned himself.'

'Now it looks as though the father could have been right. And he's a minister now.'

'Yes, but before we start worrying about him, let's make sure it is in fact Wilder.'

The disappearance of Cochran Wilder, son of a tub-thumping backbencher, in May 1977, had been a nine-day wonder. Inshore lifeboats, RAF rescue helicopters and coastguards had scoured the sea, the beaches and the cliffs with no result. At a lean time for more highly spiced morsels, the tabloids had dramatized the thing and even dug up parallels with the disappearance of Augustus John's son, forty years earlier.

An hour later they were on the outskirts of the little town and port of Hayle. Wycliffe had a map. 'Turn off next right across a bridge, then left, through a village called Phillack with a church and a pub. We should be almost there.'

They were. The village seemed to be little more than a single street, a row of neat cottages, each with its own tiny garden, facing south across the valley to Hayle itself. They passed the church and then the pub.

Wycliffe said, 'See the sign over that pub? The Bucket of Blood.'

It was their introduction to a certain zaniness, one of the attractions of Hayle. At the far end of the village a uniformed copper stood at a point where a strip of tarmac led off into the dunes through a scattering of chalets.

Wycliffe's car was recognized. The constable advised, 'You can drive along there for a hundred yards or so, sir. You'll see the other cars parked. From then on it's walking.'

The tarmac petered out in a small, sandy arena where the Scenes-of-Crime van, with other police vehicles, was lined up beside the Porsche.

Kersey said, 'Franks has beaten us to it.'

'So much the better.'

Despite Wycliffe's years in the south-west, the dunes were still something of a novelty. As they left the chalets behind and entered the real dunes he was touched by a sense of unreality and isolation. Great mounds of sand, crowned with spiky marram grass, hemmed them in, and the muffled sound of unseen surf seemed to come from all directions.

'Here we are.'

A white tape stretched between two posts defined the exclusion zone, beyond which the police were at work. There were human spectators now, dog-walkers in place of herring gulls; several, of both sexes, occupied vantage points on neighbouring dunes, trying to look as though they were there for the view.

Gross came to meet them. Wycliffe had last seen Gross at the promotion board when he was made up to DI. One of Wycliffe's colleagues on the board had said: 'He may be a good copper but he looks like a bloody rabbit.'

It was not only the poor man's intrusive incisors but also his pinched cheeks and conspicuous ears.

'Dr Franks is here, sir, so is DS Fox. DC Curnow is taking a statement from the man who found the body; he lives in Phillack, the village you came through on the way here.'

Franks squatted on a sandbank grinning like a plump gnome. 'What kept you? I've taken the liberty of sending for the van. There's nothing I can do here, and probably not much when I get him back. They've found his clothing bundled into a plastic bag near the rucksack and I reckon they're going to be more help to you than I am.'

Wycliffe stood over the body. 'I suppose he was left-handed . . . The watch, it's on his right wrist.'

Franks stood beside him. 'So it is; I hadn't noticed. One small step. Anyway, I don't imagine identification will be a problem, what with his teeth, his clothing and the clobber in his rucksack.'

'Have you anything at all to tell me?'

'Not a lot. He's been here a long time – years rather than months, is my guess. It's obvious that he was deliberately buried, and the sheet that's still under him

21

suggests he was carried here. Add that to a severely depressed fracture affecting the vertex of the skull and you'll have to look at unlawful killing as a strong possibility.'

Franks was looking about him at the mountains of sand. 'My parents brought me here for a holiday once, when I was a kid, and I used to slide down those dunes with a bit of driftwood under my backside imagining I was doing the Cresta Run. I wouldn't mind trying it now.'

'Fascinating! Is that all?'

Franks sighed. 'You're too intense, Charles. Where does it get you? Anyway, his teeth make it certain that he was a young man. He was about five-nine in height and probably of medium build, that would give him around a hundred and fifty to a hundred and sixty pounds or seventy kilos in new money.'

'A tidy weight to lug through the dunes. Not really a job for a man on his own.'

'I shouldn't think so, but that's your problem.'

'All right, leaving that aside, would you say that the location of the injury at the vertex suggests a blow rather than a fall?'

Franks nodded. 'Yes; fall-injuries are almost always to the sides or back of the head. As I said, at the least, you've got an unlawful killing on your hands, Charles. But turning to more immediate things, did you get any lunch?'

'No.'

'Neither did I. Where's that bloody van?'

Fox, Wycliffe's Scenes-of-Crime officer, was hovering. He was tall and so lean that he looked taller than he was; a walking, talking matchstick man with a large nose and a sad expression.

'There's not much for me here, sir, until they move the body. Divisional SOCO covered the ground. Do I have to bag the rucksack as it is or can I unpack it in my van?'

'All right, go ahead but leave the clothing for the lab.' The Scenes-of-Crime van was equipped for a certain amount of on-site work. 'Let me know immediately you find any evidence of identification. And Fox, make sure the sheet he was wrapped in is dealt with separately, urgent and special attention. It may be our main link between the body and the actual scene of the crime.'

Kersey was standing on one leg emptying sand from his other shoe. 'I've been talking to one of Gross's chaps. He says there's a handy place going begging if you decide to set up an Incident Room in the town. It's a little building belonging to the council and, until recently, it was used as a meeting house by some odd-ball religious sect. It's on the main street with plenty of parking.'

'I'll get Shaw to take a look at it.' Shaw was Wycliffe's administrative officer, quartermaster and general dogsbody. 'Meanwhile, you'd better get them to bring in a van, otherwise you'll have no home or habitation. I shall go back this evening; whether or not I come down tomorrow will depend on what we find out. For the moment I'll leave you here with Curnow.'

Three men from the mortuary service arrived with a stretcher and a plastic contrivance in which to man-handle the body back to their van. Franks supervised the removal and Wycliffe arranged for an officer to attend the autopsy.

Franks promised, 'I'll be in touch some time tomorrow.'

Men were still turning over the sand and sifting through it but there was little more that could be done on the site. Wycliffe, thoughtful, walked back to the cars and to the Scenes-of-Crime van and ran into the vanguard of the media – two local reporters.

'What we have is the body of a young man which was buried in the dunes, and uncovered by the recent gale. It's clear that the body has been there a long time but we do not know who he was, or how he came to be there. There will, of course, be a post mortem and that may tell us something of the cause of death. That is all I have for you.'

'Can we take photographs at the scene?'

'There's nothing to stop you.'

In the Scenes-of-Crime van, Fox was in his element, surrounded by artefacts in tagged polythene bags of different sizes. 'Most of the stuff in his rucksack is remarkably well-preserved and it's more or less what you'd expect, sir: change of underclothes and socks, toilet gear, a pair of house shoes, a couple of sci-fi paperbacks and a guide book to the coastal path . . . I get the impression he must have been a bit of a dandy.'

Wycliffe had learned patience in dealing with Fox. 'What's this?' He pointed to a garish picture postcard which had not yet been bagged and tagged. It was badly stained but otherwise undamaged.

'You can make out the writing; it seems to be from his sister, sir, written from Cyprus.'

Wycliffe drew a deep breath. '*Whose* sister?'

Fox turned the postcard over. 'It's addressed to Cochran Wilder at a nursing home in Kent.'

The text was brief: 'I'm here with Jem. Having a wonderful time but (believe it or not) too hot!! Delighted they're opening the cage. Don't let Dad get you down. We shall be home before you are. See you soon. Your one and only sister, Podge.'

The postmark was dated 19 April 1977.

Wycliffe said, 'Ah!' because he could think of nothing else to say that would not unnecessarily upset Fox.

The identification was enough to proceed upon.

Back in his car Wycliffe telephoned the chief. Oldroyd was not appreciative. 'God, Charles, trust you to spoil a nice day! Papa Wilder always said his boy had been murdered. And, if you're right, he'll be on my neck before I can say, "Yes, Minister". What is he now, by the way?'

'Minister of State for something or other, I can't remember what.'

'Yes, well, last time when he made such a noise he was only a backbench MP. Then he yelped at me like a bad-tempered Pekinese. Silly little man! . . .' A pause. 'All the same, if his son really was murdered . . . Everybody thought the lad had drowned himself – I mean, there was a history of instability . . . Papa Wilder spends a lot of his free time with a daughter who lives in St Germans. Of course, he won't be there now with parliament in session, but the daughter will. It might be an idea for you to talk to her. The personal touch . . . Let me think . . . My wife is on some committee with her . . . Yes, her married name is Bissett – Molly Bissett, that's right! Her husband's in the navy and away a lot . . . It's on your way home, Charles, so why not look in on her, break the news and spend tonight in your own bed?'

There was no point in argument; in any case it would be a chance to meet one of the family and to get something more on the boy's disappearance than the predigested gobbledegook on file.

He found a St Germans' Bissett in the directory and telephoned. A woman with a mellow attractive voice answered, 'Molly Bissett.'

He introduced himself. 'I would like to come and see you at about six if I may . . . It's about your brother . . .'

She was silent for a moment or two, then, 'He's been found?'

'Yes, I think so.'

Another pause, then very quietly, 'The body in the sand dunes?'

He was taken by surprise. 'Yes. I'm very sorry.'

'It was on the radio just an hour ago and it set me wondering whether it could possibly be . . . But it was such a long time ago . . .'

'Your father hasn't been told.'

'No, it will be best if you leave that to me. Thank you for telephoning; I will expect you. I live at the west end

25

of the village, near the almshouses. The house is called Franklin's.'

Kersey came to the car. 'Are you off, sir?'

'Yes, but I'd like a word . . .'

Kersey got into the passenger seat and Wycliffe brought him up to date. 'I think we can assume that the body is Cochran Wilder's, so we are dealing with an incident that happened fifteen years ago. The body was naked, it was deliberately buried, and there was a skull fracture caused apparently by a blow, so there is a strong presumption of murder or manslaughter. At the moment we've only looked at the contents of his rucksack but we've got his clothes and the contents of his pockets to come. The file on his disappearance will provide background and we still have the family. But we've got to find out what we can here, on the ground.'

'It's what we're to do here on the ground that bothers me, sir. You've got to admit there's not a lot going for us. It will be like stirring yesterday's cold pudding.'

'Yes, well, all I can suggest is that you get the locals involved. We want to know what the situation was at the time Wilder arrived. Who owned the chalets in the immediate vicinity? Which, if any, were occupied, and by whom? Sow the seed, Doug, and get the gossip started.

'Of course, it's just possible that he was dead on arrival – brought here by car as a convenient place to dispose of the body, though humping it through these dunes wouldn't be my idea of convenience.

'I know it's all pretty thin, Doug, but we've got to start somewhere. You and Curnow are on your own but when you need help, say so. What do you think?'

Kersey eased his length out of the car. 'I think it would have been better for everybody if he'd stayed buried.'

Lisa stood by the window of her living room looking across the bay to Godrevy, to Gwithian, to the sand dunes and to the wooden bungalows and chalets which dotted the sands near the Hayle estuary. As so often before she told herself that at such a distance she could not pick out a particular bungalow, one with a veranda and a flight of steps leading up to it. And when her eyes belied her she experienced a sudden emptiness inside and turned away. It was a disquieting but compulsive game which she played with herself when depressed.

Behind her the radio babbled, 'Radio Cornwall News at five o'clock.'

She kept the radio on most of the time; it was company and a reminder that life went on outside the little house in Carbis Bay in which she spent her days alone. Lisa was married to Martin Bell, a schoolteacher, and under pressure from him, she had given up her job as a nurse.

Abruptly, meaning crystallized out of the cascade of words from the radio. 'The body of a man was recovered this morning from sand dunes near the Hayle estuary. Exposed by the recent gale, the body was discovered by a local man exercising his dog. The police are unable to say how the man died, or when and in what circumstances his body came to be buried in the sand. Further information is expected from the post mortem.'

Lisa switched off the radio and stood over it. She felt faint, and steadied herself against the table. She would have liked to telephone somebody – one of the others, but it was after five and Martin would be home soon. She heard the sound of a car and made a determined effort to control herself. She went back to the window. Martin was pulling into the driveway. He got out, carrying his briefcase bulging with exercise books to be corrected. She met him at the door.

'Had a rough day?'

'Is there another kind?'

Martin would notice nothing; he could be relied upon for that. He put down his briefcase, glanced at himself in the hall mirror and patted his hair. 'I don't suppose it's started?'

'It has, actually.' Brittle.

He turned to face her. 'Thank God for that! I know

you want a child, Lisa, but I don't think I could stand you being pregnant just now.'

Dr Alan Hart was writing out a prescription for his last patient of the afternoon. At thirty-three Alan had given up rugby and taken up golf. For him medicine had been a pushover; a good memory, a strictly limited imagination, and a cheerful acceptance of mortality had proved the ideal recipe for success as a GP. In order to marry Barbara he had become a Catholic, but that only bothered him in so far as she could be difficult. He was settling into a groove; on the whole a very pleasant one, and memories only troubled him when Barbara suffered one of her occasional and irrational bouts of depression, always rooted in the same cause.

His patient was a chatty, arthritic old man. 'So they've dug some poor bloke out of the sand on the towans. Bin there for years they reckon.'

Alan looked up, suddenly tense, 'What's that?'

'Uncovered by the gale. Jerry Cox over to Phillack found 'n – or 'is dog did. I 'eard it in the pub this dinnertime. The p'lice bin out there. Some do there was an' they're still at it.'

Alan hustled the old man out with his prescription and returned to sit at his desk. Should he phone Barbara? Or go home at once? She was certain to hear and in the fourth month of pregnancy with their second child, Barbara was emotional.

'God, this is all she needs!'

He was on the point of leaving when he changed his mind and picked up the telephone. 'Oh, Joyce, will you get me Stanton and Drew, the estate agents in Hayle, please.'

The ringing tone, and a girl's voice, bored, said, 'Stanton and Drew.'

'This is Dr Alan Hart. I would like to speak to Mr Paul Drew.'

Silence, then a man's voice, slow and pedantic, 'Paul

28

Drew speaking. I know why you are calling, Alan, but I would rather not discuss the matter. In fact, the less discussion of any sort the better. I mean that very seriously and I'm sure you will see the wisdom of it . . . And, Alan, if you do have to contact me again – and I hope that won't be necessary – please ring me here and I will come to see you. I don't want Alice to be distressed by any hint of . . . um . . . difficulty.'

Alan replaced his phone. 'Bloody fool!'

Paul, lean, lanky, short-sighted and solemn, had not changed, but now he was an estate agent and he had acquired a matching wife.

Gillian Grey's up-market health shop in St Ives attracted a discerning clientele and the most discerning free-spenders among them received GG's personal attention. Hairdressers had maintained the tint if not the texture and lustre of her hair, but beauticians had failed to disguise the hardening and sharpening of her features.

In her little office behind the shop she had listened to the five o'clock local news with one ear while the other was on the shop and what her two assistants were doing there.

She was not sure how to react. She supposed that it was bound to happen at some time. But was there anything at all to connect her and the others with this fifteen-year-old corpse? The answer was a decided No! But she was uneasy. She reached for the telephone and dialled a number. She waited while the ringing tone repeated itself many times.

'The bastard is probably asleep, or in bed with his tart.'

A deep, lazy voice said, 'Studio Limbo; Julian speaking.'

'It's GG.'

'Sorry, no vacancy at the moment, love.'

GG reached out and shut the door into the shop. 'I know, I've seen her. You want to watch it, Julian; importing pets without the benefit of quarantine.'

'The same old GG, always concerned for the welfare of others. You'll wear yourself out, darling.'

'Never mind that, have you heard the news?'

'I only listen to good news and they never have any.'

GG lowered her voice. 'This is serious! The gale uncovered something in the dunes across the water.'

'So what? You'd be surprised at what I've found in those dunes. Don't worry about it. Concentrate on your hypochondriacs, GG, they pay a damn sight better than my pictures.'

St Germans village is tucked into the south-east corner of Cornwall on the borders of the Eliot estate. Unspoiled, with its almshouses and its cottages of local stone, it is a picture-book village; yet it has a remote and sombre air, as though isolated in time as well as space. It was dusk when Wycliffe arrived and there was not a soul to be seen.

Franklin's was set well back from the road with a gravelled drive and laurel hedges, a four-square house with a squat hipped roof and overhanging eaves. The lady herself answered his ring. She was on the short side, inclined to plumpness, dark, with smooth clear skin, and features set in a mould of good humour. She wore a snugly fitting cherry-coloured jumper with black trousers.

'Do come in.'

The drawing room was large, shabby and comfortable, with a random assortment of furniture that had seen better days. A black and white border collie, sprawled on the hearthrug, regarded him with a lazy eye. There was an electric fire burning on the hearth, and an open book on the floor by the chair in which Molly now sat herself.

The preliminaries over, it was she who got down to business. 'You were able to identify my brother?'

He handed her the postcard she had written fifteen years ago, now in its polythene envelope.

She was clearly moved. 'How very strange! After all

those years . . .' There was an interval before she asked, 'How did he die?'

He delayed answering with another question. 'Your brother was left-handed?'

She looked puzzled. 'Yes, he was. Why?'

'He wore a Rolex watch on his right wrist.'

She smiled. 'Of course! It was a present from father on his twenty-first birthday.'

Wycliffe decided she was not the sort to appreciate protective camouflage. 'We don't know how he died. His skull was fractured but whether that was the cause of death remains to be seen.'

'You will know after the post mortem?'

'I hope so.'

She was frowning. 'He was actually buried in the sand?'

'Yes.'

After some hesitation she asked, 'Fully clothed?'

'No, the body was naked.'

'Doesn't all this make it certain that he was murdered?'

'It makes it very unlikely that he took his own life.'

She reached for a cigarette pack from the arm of her chair. 'I still have this wretched habit. My husband tries to scare me out of it, but he's in the navy and away most of the time. Will you join me?'

He refused. She lit her cigarette and inhaled deeply. 'Father will be relieved.'

'Relieved?'

'Why do you think he was so aggressive when the idea of suicide was suggested? He was afraid that it was true and that he had driven his son to take his own life.' She smiled with tolerance. 'Father is a typical politician – when you're not sure of your ground, then you attack.'

Wycliffe said nothing and she went on, 'They never hit it off. Cocky – we always called him that though father disapproved – Cocky was to be the son who would take over the business. At that time father owned Westcountry Plastics. They have a factory just outside Plymouth . . .

Anyway, Cocky didn't measure up; he was rebellious, and often silly. There was fault on both sides. Our mother had died when Cocky was only nine so that when the crunch came he had no-one to turn to.' Her eyes were glistening.

On a side table there were photographs in silver frames. Molly was there, in her wedding dress with her newly acquired naval-officer husband, but the others recorded incidents in the public life of Wilder senior. He was portrayed planting a tree, cutting a tape, or, glass in hand, chatting with the Prime Minister . . .

Molly said, 'This is father's house, it's where he and mother settled when they were married. And, of course, it was Cochran's home.'

The curtains were undrawn and the window looked out on total darkness; no sound came from within the house or from without. The dog shifted uneasily, lifted its head and looked up at Wycliffe before going back to sleep. Did this woman spend most of her time in this house alone with her dog?

She seemed to read his thoughts. 'I'm a do-gooder, Mr Wycliffe, coffee mornings, committees, jumble sales, eating for charity . . . You know the sort; always busy doing rather futile things.' She looked at him with a sly smile. 'Pathetic, isn't it?

'Anyway, getting back to Cochran, I don't know who if anybody is to blame or whether it was some genetic thing, but in his late teens he went off the rails completely. He started to steal, pointlessly, things he couldn't possibly want; and he developed a sexual kink, forcing his attention on girls in cafés, shops and cinemas, even in the street. I distrust labels, especially when they are dished out by psychiatrists, but they said that he was manic-depressive. Of course, as you must know, he ended up in the court.'

She looked at her cigarette which was only half-smoked, and crushed it out in an ashtray. 'Fortunately, the magistrates showed a bit of sense and, after a psychiatric report, he was bound over on condition that he received treatment in an approved psychiatric hospital, and he spent just over a year there.'

'And then?'

'Shortly after he came out father had the bright idea of sending him off on this walking holiday.'

'He went with someone?'

'Oh, yes; with the Creep. That's what I call him; his real name is Leslie Mace and at the time he was working in father's office as a trainee accountant – I couldn't stand him but father thought the world of him. Of course Cocky gave him the slip and I don't blame him for that.'

'What happened to Mace?'

'He went back to his work in the office but when father sold up to go into full-time politics we lost touch. I don't know whether or not he's still there.'

'Where did your brother live after coming out of hospital?'

'Here with me. It was only for a couple of weeks.'

'How did he seem?'

She hesitated. 'He was quiet, amenable – too amenable.' She shook her head. 'I don't know. I couldn't feel at ease with him. To be honest, I don't think the so-called treatment did him much good.'

'Was he on any sort of medication?'

'I remember they gave him a lithium preparation which was supposed to help stabilize him – stave off attacks – but he said it made him feel sick.'

Wycliffe explained about the contents of the rucksack and that the young man's clothing would be available shortly.

She asked, with concern, 'Will someone have to identify the body?'

'I don't think so, merely those of his possessions which have been recovered.'

'I shall telephone father. I tried earlier but I couldn't get hold of him.'

33

Wycliffe stood up. 'I'll keep in touch and I'm very grateful for your help and understanding.'

She walked with him to the gate. It was very dark; lights were on in many of the windows in the village, the only sign of life. It was also silent, not even a breath of wind to stir the leaves on the trees. She stood by the gate and watched him drive away.

He felt depressed. Even after more than thirty years in the police he still found it hard to accept that happy families are a rare breed. It was strange the extent to which his upbringing and the stories he'd read as a child still conspired to colour his outlook on life, his judgements and his expectations.

Fifteen minutes later he passed through St Juliot and was approaching the Watch House. He could see the estuary gleaming in the darkness, the twinkling navigation lights and a vague outline of the opposite bank against the sky. He turned into his own drive and stopped by the garage. As he got out of the car Helen came towards him. 'I'd almost given you up.'

When he came downstairs after a quick shower there was a plate of sandwiches and a glass of Barsac, misted over, on the little table by his armchair.

It was good to be home.

Chapter Two

Wycliffe made the mistake of looking at himself in the bathroom mirror; really looking. It was an occasion of self-examination quite different from his daily inspection to decide whether or not he had shaved properly. In consequence he went downstairs preoccupied and unsettled.

Helen asked, 'Will you be going down west again today?'

'I've no idea.'

'Perhaps you'll let me know if you're not coming back this evening.' Tight-lipped.

He realized that this was going to be one of those mornings when tension seems to condense like mist out of clear air. He poured himself some coffee. 'I'll phone you.'

'Good!'

'The discovery, yesterday, of a body in the sand dunes near Hayle, is being linked with the disappearance, fifteen years ago, of Cochran Wilder, only son of Royston Wilder, Minister of State in the Department of Social Reconstruction. The police have so far refused to comment on—'

With an irritable jab Wycliffe throttled the radio, and buttered a piece of toast.

Helen said, 'You haven't forgotten that your daughter is arriving this evening?'

When Helen talked about 'your daughter' storm cones were being hoisted; it was high time to give domestic issues an airing. Their daughter, Ruth, was personal

35

assistant to a money man, one of the younger generation of that faceless breed of currency manipulators, and for some years she had been living with him. Now a sudden, unexplained and unaccompanied visit was causing concern.

'You think they're splitting up?' Although he would never have admitted it, Wycliffe was hopeful. He did not care for his wily unconsecrated son-in-law.

'I thought she might be pregnant.'

'After all this time?'

'Why not?'

Wycliffe decided that silence was his best option. He could hardly say that he hoped Ruth had more sense.

He left soon afterwards, and fifteen minutes later he had joined the queue for the ferry. It was raining, a continuous drizzle out of a leaden sky. He switched off the engine, glared at the back of the car in front, and brooded on life and the way he was living it. Did others feel that they had lost sight of themselves in playing roles which seemed to have been thrust upon them?

Sometimes, in such a mood, he wondered what had happened to the real Charlie Wycliffe, the genuine original. Did he still exist? What had he been like . . . ? He couldn't remember . . . Perhaps it didn't matter . . . Perhaps, after all, he was no great loss.

A tooting driver reminded him of the obligations of his present persona.

Time to move on.

His space in the car park was labelled 'Det. Ch. Supt.', and the man on the desk greeted him with instant recognition and a respectful 'sir'.

In his office, Diane was sorting the mail. She said, 'Oh, Records say you'll want the file on the Wilder disappearance and they've sent it up.'

Other people seemed to know who he was – or thought they did, so perhaps that was all that mattered. He consoled himself with the thought that there would probably have been no reserved parking for that original

Charlie Wycliffe, and it was unlikely that anybody would have called him 'sir'.

'You deal with the mail, Diane, and let me know if there is anything . . .'

Diane had worked with him for more years than he cared to remember. She had come as a girl in her twenties, obviously fair, and apparently fragile, but from the start she had run the office with ruthless efficiency and with her austere indifference to males she soon became known as the Ice Maiden. Now she was a legend in her own time.

Alone, Wycliffe opened the Wilder file at random and found himself looking down at a photograph of the young man. He gave small credence to the theories of Lombroso and his successors which relate criminal tendencies to physical types, but here, he felt sure, was the face of a maladjusted youth, more likely than not to find himself at odds with society. Lank, straight black hair framed a long narrow face, a receding forehead, deeply set eyes, a rather pinched nose and a twisted little mouth.

Wycliffe skimmed through the file. On leaving school Wilder had been entered for a course in business studies at the polytechnic and from early on he had distinguished himself by throwing lavish open-house parties, buying quantities of expensive clothes which he mostly gave away, and sleeping around. At first, his father had footed the bills under strong protest, but when the screw was finally tightened Wilder turned to shop-lifting, forging cheques and forcing himself on the girls he could no longer attract; so ending up in court.

Somebody had slipped into the file a press cutting from one of the tabloids:

Royston Wilder's Son Missing

Cochran Wilder, only son of crime-bashing MP Royston Wilder, is missing on a walking holiday in Cornwall. He was last seen on Saturday evening, on the North Cornwall coastal path between Gwithian and Hayle . . . Cochran, known as 'the Cock' to his friends, was recently discharged from a psychiatric hospital where he had been detained under a court order following convictions on a number of charges including theft and indecent assault . . .

The file was bulky; psychologists and psychiatrists were thick on the ground with the occasional probation officer thrown in. There were pages of jargon sprinkled with phrases which rolled off the tongue, and there was much hedging of bets.

'The subject, despite his youth, appears to be suffering from an affective disorder strongly suggestive of a manic-depressive psychosis . . .'

A much later pundit had written, 'In the early stages the manic phase was dominant and the situation might properly have been diagnosed as unipolar, but during hospitalization depressive episodes increased in frequency and duration, so that towards the end of hospitalization a fairly classic pattern of bipolarity was established. In these circumstances the decision to discharge the subject was, perhaps, unfortunate . . .'

In other words, the gentleman was saying that young Wilder had been let loose with a recipe for suicide in his pocket. And that seemed to have set the tone for the whole police inquiry which, from the start, was heavily biased in favour of suicide.

The telephone rang. It was Franks. 'Had a good night, Charles? – I didn't. Business is looking up all of a sudden and it was early morning before I got round to your chap. Anyway it's pretty certain that he died from brain damage resulting from a depressed fracture of the skull. In fact the table in the area of the vertex is pretty thin – not exactly egg-shell, but it wouldn't have taken much of a blow to cause the injury.'

'So it was a blow.'

'I think so; obviously, as I've said, I couldn't swear to it. Incidentally, there were fragments of some sandy substance in the wound.'

'You surprise me, especially as he was buried in the stuff.'

'*Not* sea sand, Charles! These look like fragments of concrete. I can have it checked if you like.'

'Of course I like. What are you telling me? That he was hit on the head with a concrete block?'

Franks was mild. 'I suppose there are other concrete objects more amenable to use as a weapon.'

'Anything else?'

'Not a great deal. I found no other signs of injury or disease but that isn't saying much; decomposition of the soft tissues in the trunk was complete. There was a certain amount of mummification but it was confined to the extremities.'

As Wycliffe replaced the telephone there was a tap at the door and DS Lucy Lane came in.

Lucy Lane had been involved with Wycliffe and Kersey in all the major cases of the past six years and Wycliffe had come to rely upon her no-nonsense logic which nicely opposed his own tendency to woolliness and Kersey's inclination to flog dead horses.

She was carrying a 'lab box'. 'The contents of Wilder's pockets, sir, all logged and photographed; the clothing is still under examination. Apparently it's been very well-preserved by the plastic bag in which it was found.'

'Any news of the sheet or whatever it was in which he was wrapped?'

'Only that it was a nylon bed sheet; it's not clear whether they will be able to tell us any more.'

Wycliffe said, 'I can't stand nylon bed sheets.'

Lucy removed several items from her box and laid them on the desk along with a bundle of photographs. Each item was enclosed in a separate polythene bag and carried a label. 'Take a look at this, sir.' She pushed across one of the bags for Wycliffe to examine.

Through the polythene he was looking at a necklace. It consisted of a chain made up of elaborate filigreed links and a pendant in the form of a very feline cat.

Lucy Lane said, 'It's pretty, and it must have cost a bit.' She referred to a list. 'The whole thing is in hallmarked silver and the cat's eyes are seed pearls. The back of the pendant is engraved with a monogram of the letters L.M. and a date: 1 May 1977. Somebody's birthday, I suppose.'

'And this was found in his pocket?'

'In his left trouser pocket, sir. A bit odd, don't you think? I suppose it could have been his but even if he was gay it seems unlikely.'

Wycliffe pointed to the case file. 'There's no suggestion here that he was gay, rather the contrary; in any case his initials were C.W. and he was born in November.'

Lucy grinned. 'So it doesn't add up.'

Wycliffe was looking at the file. 'That date – 1 May 1977, is less than a week before Wilder disappeared.'

'Perhaps it was a present for his girlfriend which he never got round to giving her.'

'And he carried it around, loose in his trouser pocket. Sounds a bit improbable, don't you think? Anyway, what else have you got?'

Lucy picked up a bag containing a blue plastic box. 'This was in the right-hand pocket of his jacket. It contains about fifteen grams of cannabis resin, a packet of cigarette papers, a little rolling-machine and five "joints". The box has compartments as though it was made for the purpose.'

Wycliffe said, 'No trendy young man should be without one.'

Lucy Lane went on, 'There's nothing remarkable in the other bags – nothing more than one would expect to find in his pockets – a wallet with a few pounds and a credit card, some loose change, a packet of ordinary cigarettes and a lighter . . .'

Wycliffe fiddled with the bag containing the little

40

plastic box. 'I've been thinking about the young man who was supposed to look after him – Leslie Mace. According to the report they spent their last night together at a boarding house in St Agnes. The landlady testified that they were arguing shortly after they arrived, and next morning at breakfast they scarcely spoke.'

'And what was Mace's version?'

'Mace said the argument had been about the walk, how far they would go and where they would spend their nights. That day, their last together, they had a late snack-lunch at the pub in Gwithian and when they were about to leave at around two, Wilder picked up his rucksack and said, "I'm going to the loo; see you outside in five minutes." That, according to Mace, was the last he saw of him. He says he spent most of the rest of the day searching the area along the coastal path between Gwithian and Hayle before reporting by telephone to the boy's father. He says Wilder didn't seem particularly worried, confident that his son would soon come back of his own accord.

'Mace was told to stay around the area for another day, seeing what he could pick up, but he was on no account to stir up local interest or go to the police.'

Lucy Lane pouted. 'So there's no record of anybody having seen him after two o'clock?'

Wyclife flipped the pages of the report. 'Yes, there is. A chap called Bunny – John Bunny – out walking his dog, says he saw a young man answering Wilder's description and wearing a backpack trudging along in the direction of Hayle at about eight in the evening. That was on the coastpath about two miles east of the estuary.'

'I suppose that means he would have arrived in the neighbourhood where his body was found during the next half-hour or so. It also looks as though Mace was telling the truth.'

'Yes, and the boy's father thought Mace did his job to the best of his ability. It seems that Wilder senior had a high opinion of Mace, but I had a different view from the sister when I saw her last night. She called him a creep.'

'What did you say his name was – his first name?'

'Leslie – Leslie Mace; why?'

'I don't suppose there can be anything in it, but his initials are the same as those on the pendant – L.M.'

Wycliffe was thoughtful. 'We need to know more about Mace, whatever he's like.'

The telephone rang and Lucy answered. 'A woman by the name of Bissett wants to talk to you, sir.'

'Tell them to put her through. It's the boy's sister.'

'Molly Bissett, Mr Wycliffe . . .' Her manner was relaxed, as though she had known him for years. 'I expect you'll be hearing from father, if you haven't already. He's very relieved, as I told you he would be, though he may not sound like it to you. I hope he's not too unbearable. Now, I wanted to tell you that I had a call from Leslie Mace this morning asking if the body found in the dunes was Cochran's. Of course, he was his same oily self. I suppose I'm unfair, what he said was quite kind, but it's his manner, the way he talks.'

'He's still at the plastics factory?'

'Oh, yes, and he wants me to keep in touch. He telephoned from the works where he's quite a big-shot; secretary-accountant or something.'

Wycliffe thanked her, then asked her about the pendant found in her brother's pocket.

'I'm quite sure it's nothing to do with the family and I doubt if he had it when he was here with me.' She paused. 'To be honest, I remember going through his things on the quiet. I know it was underhand but there was ten years' difference in our ages and I felt responsible.'

'Perhaps you found the little plastic box?'

'I did.'

'Did you know what it was?'

'Yes, and I must admit I was relieved. If he had been experimenting with hard drugs I wouldn't have been surprised; as a matter of fact, that's what I was looking for.'

He thanked her again, with sincerity. He liked the woman; a motherly sort with plenty of not-so-common sense. Odd that she seemed to have no kids of her own.

Wycliffe had rarely felt more helpless at the start of an investigation. He pushed the file away. 'We've got to be clear about what we are trying to do, Lucy. Franks thinks he died from the blow to the head which was probably inflicted with something made of concrete; there are concrete fragments in the wound. It could have been a fall but the fact that the injury was to the vertex and that such an elaborate attempt was made to conceal the death makes it unlikely. On the other hand, it seems the boy had a thin patch in his skull, so murder is also a doubtful starter and manslaughter more of a probability. But however he died, he didn't bury himself. A possible scenario is that the argument between him and Mace was serious and he cleared out of the Gwithian pub because he felt threatened. Mace claimed he spent most of that day searching for him without success but suppose Mace was lying, suppose he found Wilder and the argument came to a fight?'

'And there was a lump of concrete handy, and Wilder happened to be naked at the time? I suppose one could construct a scenario along those lines.' Lucy was disinclined to flights of fancy. 'Anyway, I take it, sir, that I start with Mace.'

'No, I'll attend to Mace; you concentrate on the necklace. Try to persuade the two local TV stations to put it on their early evening news and if you can get it in tomorrow's paper as well, so much the better. At the same time you might get an opinion from a jeweller about its possible provenance . . . And leave me a set of the photographs.'

'And the link with the case?'

'Found among the effects of the deceased.'

*   *   *

43

Wycliffe did not have to go in search of Mace. When Diane brought in his coffee she said, 'There's a man called Mace – Leslie Mace – downstairs, asking to see you in connection with the Wilder affair.'

'Tell them to send him up.'

'Another cup?'

'No, hold him till I've had mine.'

Diane gave him five minutes then came in, removed the tray, and almost immediately afterwards ushered in Mace.

Leslie Mace was fleshy with thinning fair hair and a large smooth face with smallish features crowded together so that the rest looked strangely naked. Wycliffe had the impression that beneath the grey suit and pinstriped shirt his whole body would be pale, and smooth and hairless. He was quick to smile, though not with his wary blue eyes, and his responses were abrupt and bird-like. From the visitor's chair his darting glances took in the whole room then his attention focused on the case file which Wycliffe had in front of him. The label on the cover was conspicuous: Missing Persons. Cochran S. Wilder. 7.5.77.

'I hesitated about coming to you, Chief Superintendent, but it seemed best to go to the top . . . It's good of you to see me; you must be a very busy man.'

Wycliffe was polite but cool. 'Have you come to obtain information, Mr Mace, or to give it?'

A brief hesitation. 'I came in case I might be helpful.'

'Good! There are one or two questions I want to ask you.' He passed over the photograph of the necklace. 'Do you know anything about the original of this?'

Mace looked at the photograph in surprise. 'No, I've never seen anything like it that I can remember.'

'It was found on the body.'

The little eyes widened and he shook his head. 'I don't know where he got it.'

'You can make no suggestion?'

There was a pause. 'I suppose you know that he . . .'

A vague gesture. 'I mean, you must know that he had been in trouble with the police for taking things . . .'

'You think he might have stolen this?'

Mace became uneasy. 'How can I say? He was supposed to have been cured.'

Wycliffe changed the subject. 'In your statement you said that the argument you had with him during that last evening at St Agnes was about planning your walk – the ground you would cover in a day, where you would stay – that sort of thing. Was that really the case?'

Mace looked down at his girlish hands with their short, tapering fingers. 'No, but if I had said what it was really about, Cochran's father would have been angry at having it made public.' There was a pause before he resumed. 'You see, he wanted to go off on his own – he didn't want me with him, he said he didn't need a keeper, but his father had insisted.'

'So?'

'He offered me money to leave him to his own devices but to report to his father as if I were still with him. When I refused he seemed to accept the position, but in the morning he was sullen and I could scarcely get a word out of him. Then, as I told the police at the time, when we arrived at the Gwithian pub he gave me the slip.' Mace looked pained. 'There was nothing I could do to prevent him going if he really wanted to, but he didn't even tell me.'

'And you spent the rest of the day looking for him without success?'

'Yes; of course it was a hopeless business, I had no real idea where to look; he could have gone anywhere.'

'Was it made clear to you by Mr Wilder senior exactly what was expected of you?'

A moment or two for thought. 'Not in so many words but I knew that he wanted me to be a friend to Cochran and to try to keep him out of trouble.'

'Were you his friend?'

A pause. 'I wanted to be, but to him I was simply his father's paid spy.'

'What kinds of trouble were you supposed to look out for?'

Mace looked down at his hands. 'Women, I suppose, and pilfering.'

'Drugs?'

A quick upward glance, apprehensive. 'He wasn't on drugs as far as I know.'

'He was smoking pot; didn't you know about that?'

He spread his hands. 'I suppose I did, but I didn't take it very seriously.'

'You know the spot where the body was found?'

Mace frowned. 'Well, I know it was in the sandhills not far from the chalets just north of Hayle.'

'You must have passed somewhere near there when you were looking for him. Did you keep to the beach or were you in sight of the chalets?'

'I was in sight of some of the chalets. I spoke to a girl from one of them.'

'Which one?'

Mace took his time. 'It was one nearer the sea than most, with steps leading up to it. The girl was halfway up the steps. I asked her if she had seen anything of Cochran – I mean, I described him. She said she hadn't seen anybody except her own friends.'

'So this chalet was definitely occupied?'

'It must have been; there was pop music coming from inside.'

'Can you remember anything about the girl?'

The moon-face furrowed in concentration. 'It's so long ago. She was a bit abrupt but girls never spend much time talking to me. She was blonde and on the plump side, and I remember she was wearing a blue T-shirt and trousers.'

'How old, would you say?'

'Eighteen? About that.'

'You have a good recall, Mr Mace.'

46

A quick smile of pleasure, like the tail-wagging of a petted dog. 'People tell me that.

'The following morning I went back to the chalet in case they had seen anything since, but it was shut up.'

'You went back the following morning – at what time?'

A furrowed brow, then, 'I stayed the night in Hayle and I started looking for him again around nine – it must have been about ten when I got to the chalet.'

Wycliffe thanked him and he left. When he was gone Wycliffe telephoned Kersey and put him in the picture.

Kersey was beginning to like Hayle, which was strange; few people are attracted to the little town at first acquaintance. Sprawled along the margins of a muddy estuary with sand dunes to the north and east and the honey-pot of St Ives over the river to the west, Hayle is for most people a place on the way to a chalet or caravan park, or to the great stretch of sand on the east side of the bay. But Kersey had found attractions which were easily overlooked: the Copperhouse Arms, a pub where neither the bar nor the beer had been plasticized by a brewery; a café where the locals gathered to eat bacon and egg at all times of day; a multiplicity of little shops instead of chain stores – and friendly natives.

The incident van was parked on waste ground between Copperhouse Pool – a tidal waterway, and the long, congested street which links the elements of the town together – originally two towns, the one called Foundry, because that was where the principal foundry was, and the other, Copperhouse, because of the copper-smelting there. The van was next to the little building they hoped to use.

Kersey had Sergeant Coombes with him, the first policeman on the scene after the discovery of the body, and they were studying a sketch plan showing the disposition of the chalets in the immediate neighbourhood of the burial.

47

Coombes was smoking a pipe, Kersey a cigarette, filling the air of the little cubicle with a menacing blue-grey haze. Outside it was raining and the windows of the van were steamed over.

Coombes pointed with a thick forefinger. 'You see, sir, there are just three chalets within a hundred yards or so of where the body was buried. The rest are well inland where the dunes are more stable.'

Kersey said, 'It's those three that interest me. Does one of them have a flight of steps leading up to it?'

Coombes nodded. 'The one called Sunset Cott.'

'That's the one, then. We know that one was occupied during the weekend when Wilder went missing. What we want to know now, is who owned it and who was in it at the time.'

Coombes, watching his words, always wary of CID types, however human they appeared, referred to his notebook. 'Actually, I've made a few inquiries about those three chalets and they all belonged to the Grey family. At that time the Greys ran a small engineering firm in Camborne, but they lived in St Ives and Mrs Grey acquired the chalets as an investment, letting them out to visitors in the summer months.'

Kersey drew curlicues with his ball-point in the margin of the plan. 'These Greys, are they still around? Do they still own the chalets?'

'I doubt it. Grey retired, sold out, and moved up north four or five years back, but their daughter is still in St Ives and she runs a health shop.' Coombes removed the pipe from his mouth and contemplated the bowl. 'My wife is a bit of a health freak, she intends living to be ninety and she's a regular customer. All I can say is the extra years don't come cheap; that shop must be a gold mine.'

Kersey said, 'It might be worthwhile looking in on the Grey girl.'

'She's no girl – wrong side of thirty, anyway.'

'Married?'

'No, but from what I hear she doesn't go short of a man in her bed.'

A couple of roundabouts and three miles or so later Kersey arrived at the outskirts of St Ives. The rain had stopped, the skies had cleared and he was looking down through pine trees at a sea of Mediterranean blue. He parked behind the Sloop Inn and set off in search of the health shop. Ambling around St Ives in the sunshine out of season is a pleasant occupation in itself and Kersey was in no hurry. The tide was out and the harbour was an expanse of yellow sand where boats careened themselves if they were not propped on stilts. On the Wharf, men in peaked caps, hands in pockets, strolled up and down, or stood in groups of two or three, arms resting on the guard rail.

Kersey found the health shop in a narrow street which bordered the sea but was totally cut off from it by houses and shops. It was larger than the others, its glass and paintwork gleamed and the inscription on the fascia had been carried out in a flowing script: St Ives Bay Health and Homoeopathic Centre.

Inside, the premises had something of the appearance of a Chinese medicine shop upgraded to Bond Street. After the more or less familiar honeys, diabetic preserves, juices and cereals, Kersey was lost before shelves stocked with pickled, dried, bottled and packeted foods and supplements of which he had never heard.

One of the two white-coated assistants serving, saw her customer out and turned to Kersey. 'Can I help you, sir?'

'I want to talk to Miss Grey.'

'She's with a client.'

A door behind the counter had a notice over it: 'Homoeopathic consultations by appointment'.

'I'll wait.'

Kersey studied the shelves and wondered at what he might be missing. Was he getting his ration of calcium, potassium, magnesium and iron? Could he do with a little lecithin or a soupçon of selenium? Then there were the vitamins, more of them than he remembered as a boy doing biology at school. And his favourite, vitamin E, had moved up in the world; in his day its sole recommendation had been a facility for enhancing the fertility of rats, now it seemed to have acquired a definite though ill-defined respectability. He was growing interested, when the door behind the counter opened and a plump matron with a mauve-tinted hair-do came out. She cooed and was being cooed over by a younger, white-coated woman with startlingly red hair. 'The same time next week, then. Thank you, Mrs Hartley. Goodbye!'

The redhead interrogated one of the girls with a look, then turned her attention to Kersey. 'Can I help you, Mr . . . ?'

'Detective Inspector Kersey . . . Miss Grey? . . . I would appreciate a word in private.'

A quick look. Apprehensive? Why should she be? She didn't look the sort to be intimidated by a mere policeman. Perhaps he was mistaken.

'You'd better come into my office.'

The room on the other side of the door was flooded with light from a window overlooking the bay. Only a footpath and a rail separated the house from the rocks and the sea. The room itself had the severe functionality of a doctor's consulting room.

Kersey was amiable. 'A pleasant room.'

'I like it.' She pointed to the client's chair across the desk from her own.

'Perhaps you have an idea why I'm here?'

'No. I'm waiting for you to tell me.'

Her manner was abrupt, down to business, but she was also sizing him up as a man. Kersey recognized the type; whatever her preoccupations, sex was never far from her thoughts.

'I expect you've heard of the discovery of a body in the dunes across the bay?'

'I heard about it.'

'Please understand that this is a purely routine inquiry. Fifteen years ago, in early May 1977, when the young man disappeared, your family owned the three chalets nearest the spot where the body was found.'

'So?'

'Is it likely that any of them could have been occupied at that time?'

With a practised movement she swept back the hair which was beginning to hide her face. 'In early May? I shouldn't think so. It's not the kind of holiday people take early in the season but I can't say that it never happened.'

'At the time, Wilder's disappearance made quite a stir and that might have helped to fix things in your memory.'

A sudden smile which softened her features. 'My dear man, I was eighteen in 1977, with other, more interesting things to think about.'

'We have evidence that the chalet called Sunset Cott was occupied during the weekend that Wilder disappeared.'

'Really? I told you I didn't know; it just sounded unlikely.'

'And your parents? Is it likely they might have some recollection?'

She thought before answering. 'It's possible. Mother kept a record of her lettings, but whether she's still got it I don't know. You can ask her if you like; they're living in Shropshire now and I'll give you their phone number.'

Kersey was puzzled. His mind told him that the woman was being as helpful as he had any right to expect but he had an uneasy feeling that in some important respects he was being taken for a ride. Perhaps it was because her attitude did not square with her hard face and harder eyes.

She was looking at him with a speculative, slightly amused expression. 'I'm afraid I haven't been much help.'

'Your mother might be. In any case at this stage we're searching for a black cat in a dark room.' Kersey stood up.

She said, 'Are you married?'

'Two daughters at university.' Kersey was proud of his daughters and he let it show.

'Really? You don't look like one who's been snared and tamed.' She got up from her chair. 'I'll see you out.'

Kersey found himself out in the narrow street, wondering.

Almost opposite the health shop a lane led up steeply to join the main street and on the corner there was a shop, straight out of Dickens, with small window panes and woodwork which looked as though it had long ago been treated with paint stripper, then forgotten. The lettering on the fascia was just decipherable, The Modelmakers. In the window there was a model of a three-masted sailing ship which had obviously been there gathering dust for years, and a notice in bold script: 'No dogs, children or food inside the shop. Casual visitors not welcome'. Kersey was aware of being watched by someone whose head came just above the screen at the back of the window.

Back in the caravan there was a call from Wycliffe and the two exchanged notes. Wycliffe said, 'So we know that one of the chalets nearest to where the body was found, the one called Sunset Cott, with steps leading up to it, was occupied at the time Wilder disappeared. We know too that the chalet belonged to this Grey family which you've dug up.'

'Yes, and there's an off-chance that Mamma Grey may have kept the records of her lettings. It's a long shot but worth trying.'

'Even if it comes off there's nothing but proximity to suggest that whoever was there had any connection with Wilder, but I agree we must follow it up.'

'Anything on the necklace, sir?'

'Lucy has fixed to have it on TV this evening and in

52

some of tomorrow's papers. Anyway, how are you getting on down there?'

Kersey laughed. 'I like it; it's odd. But, for some reason I feel that whatever Hayle once had, it was all over before I got here. By the way, Shaw has fixed up for us to have the place next door. He expects to have it equipped with all systems go by Thursday morning.'

Wycliffe made a point of being home early because Ruth was due. He found them in the garden, in the evening sunshine, admiring Helen's 'Darjeeling' magnolia, flowering for the first time since its planting a dozen years before.

Helen said, 'Isn't that rich pink wonderful with the light coming through the petals? I wasn't expecting it to flower for another year or two . . . And it's got the fragrance!'

Ruth was pale and, he thought, thinner. She said little but she hugged him and placed her cheek against his. Helen looked on and lifted her shoulders, telling him, mutely, that she was none the wiser.

'I hope you can put up with me for a while, Dad.'

'It's your home, love, whenever you want it. You know that.'

'Yes; and it's a good place to be.'

They drank sherry in the kitchen where Helen had indulged herself in a small television. The Wilder case made the national news, and so did the necklace.

'Police in Cornwall are treating the death of Cochran Wilder, son of Minister of State Royston Wilder, as a case of unlawful killing.

'Cochran Wilder disappeared fifteen years ago while on a walking holiday in Cornwall and yesterday his decomposed remains were discovered in a sand dune near the little port of Hayle. The police are anxious to trace the owner of a necklace found with the body.'

The lab photograph appeared on the screen and the newsreader continued, 'The silver pendant, in the form

53

of a cat, is inscribed on the back with the initials L.M. and—'

Ruth said, 'Are you involved in this one, Dad?'

A wry grin. 'This afternoon the minister, on the telephone, explained to me how deeply I am involved.' Wycliffe sighed, 'I can sympathize with him as a father but the man is a bombastic cretin.'

Helen said, 'Your glass needs topping up, Charles.'

Lisa was laying the table for the evening meal. Martin in an easy chair, a pile of exercise books on the floor beside him, was marking on his lap and muttering to himself at intervals. The early evening news was on the television.

Place mats, knives, forks, spoons, salt and pepper pots, sweet chutney for Martin . . . Through the window she could see the sea, a flat plain, quite still, and above it a single greyish-white cloud hanging, suspended in space. A surrealist painting. In a nightmarish fashion every movement she made seemed to bring nearer that moment when the newsreader would say . . . What would he say?

That morning there had been a photograph of Cochran Wilder in the newspaper, as he was at the time of his disappearance. Over the years she had retained only a vague idea of what he looked like. In her thoughts and nightmare dreams she saw a featureless face framed in dark hair with blood soaking through it and running in rivulets over the whiteness of his skin. But in the newspaper photograph she saw again the young man who had hailed her as she stood on the veranda of the chalet, arms resting on the rail, watching the sunset. She had disliked him on sight but he had asked for a glass of water.

She shivered. 'Do you really want the television on, Martin? You're not watching.'

Martin looked up from his marking. 'I can hear it, can't I? It's the only chance I have to catch up with the news.'

Lisa did not know what it was that she feared but she felt sure there would be something to further torment her jangled nerves. Even so, when it came, she could not restrain a little cry of shocked surprise.

'The body of a young man discovered on Monday in the sand dunes on the north Cornish coast has now been identified as that of Cochran Wilder, 21-year-old son of the minister. Cochran disappeared fifteen years ago while on a walking holiday in Cornwall. In connection with his death the police are anxious to trace the owner of a necklace found with the body.'

And there on the screen was her necklace which she had not seen for fifteen years.

The newsreader's voice, suave and indifferent, continued. 'The silver pendant, in the form of a cat, is inscribed on the back with the initials L.M. and a date, the first of May 1977 . . .'

Martin said, 'What's the matter? You look as though you were going to faint or something.'

She tried to pass it off and said, foolishly, 'I'm being silly. May the first is my birthday.'

'So what?' Martin looked blank, shrugged, and returned to his marking.

It was a quarter to nine; Alan was late, detained by an emergency house call. Daniel was in bed asleep, and there was a casserole in the oven keeping warm. Barbara could have watched television while waiting for Alan but the early evening news had been more than enough. Her first impulse when she saw the necklace had been to telephone Lisa, but Martin would have been there . . . She thought that it must be worse for Lisa; at least Alan was involved and there was no need for secrecy between them.

She had made a big thing of giving Daniel his supper, reading him his story and putting him to bed; now she was forced back on herself. She went upstairs and rummaged in the bottom drawer of the big chest on the landing. From under a mass of discarded underclothes and woollies she came up with an envelope from which she removed a photograph, and took it downstairs. Now, perched on the kitchen stool, her elbows on the worktop, she gazed at it as though she had not seen it before.

Three boys and three girls, all in their late teens, sprawled on the grass and smiled, grinned, smirked or grimaced at the camera according to their natures and their moods. She did not need the photograph to recall their faces but it was the one material link with her Pandora's box of memories.

She was there, with Alan's arm around her shoulders; a school romance which blossomed. Lisa was there. At eighteen, Lisa had shoulder-length blonde hair which accentuated her rather long face. Her lips were thin and her smile for the camera was hesitant and non-committal. Of course she was wearing her necklace. Paul Drew, lanky and serious, was pressed clumsily against her, his hand on her thigh. Luckily for Lisa, that had come to nothing, though whether she had fared any better with her schoolmaster was another matter.

That left Gillian Grey, a freckled redhead, known to everyone as GG, and Julian Angove, short, stocky, and powerful, the maverick of the party.

She heard the engine of Alan's little runabout being punished on the steep hill from the town and listened as he turned into their drive, slammed the car door and let himself into the house.

'Barbara!'

'In the kitchen.'

He stood by her, put his arm around her and kissed her hair. 'Are you all right?'

'There's a casserole in the oven, keeping warm.'

'Where's Daniel?'

'In bed asleep.'

Gently he turned her face toward him and then he saw the photograph on the bench in front of her.

'I thought we agreed to destroy that years ago.'

'I know, but I couldn't bring myself to. Don't be annoyed, Alan, please!'

'But why torture yourself like this, darling?'

56

She shuddered. 'Whenever I think of it, I can hear that awful breathing.'

They were silent for a moment or two while he continued to hold her then, abruptly, her manner seemed to change and she became aggressive. She broke away from him and pointed to Lisa in the photograph. 'You see! She's wearing that bloody necklace . . . With jeans and a T-shirt! She'd have worn it in bed if it wasn't uncomfortable.'

'And she lost it. But does that matter now?' He was treading gingerly, trying to say what was soothing and conversational.

'The police think it matters. You haven't heard; they found it with the body and they had it on TV this evening, asking people to identify it . . . When somebody does . . .' She spoke calmly again, resigned.

'But who will? Certainly none of us, nobody in the photograph. She hadn't had it more than a few days and who else would remember after fifteen years?'

She looked up. 'Somebody will . . . Somebody will.' There was certainty and resignation in her voice which troubled him. Then, 'Don't try to coddle me, Alan! I'm not a child and I've known all along that one day this would catch up with us.' She turned away and said, more quietly, 'We should never have had children; we had no right . . . Whenever I look at that snapshot – and I do sometimes – I say to myself, "That was before . . . And there's no going back." '

Chapter Three

When Wycliffe arrived in the office, Diane greeted him. 'You look a bit down this morning.'

'Anything in the mail?'

Always the same question, though the answer was laid out on his desk, opened, and arranged in classified heaps.

She pointed to the little heaps of correspondence. 'Nothing on the case.'

Wycliffe's desk calendar showed Wednesday 13 May. At least it wasn't Friday. Two days since the discovery of the body, about fifteen hours since the necklace appeared on television, and fifteen years since young Wilder's body was buried in the dunes. As a rule, if an inquiry was going to be short it was usually on the third day that things began to happen, but this one had a history. All the same, he would have expected some reaction to the necklace, if only from the nutters, but so far there was nothing.

Because of Wilder's pressure tactics Wycliffe was afraid of being forced into one of those public relations exercises in which scores of officers are committed to a lucky-dip routine, asking vague questions of unlikely people, chasing shadows; taking megabytes out of the computer software, and adding to the waste-paper mountain. Occasionally such routines pay off though usually as much would have been achieved by a few officers working in full knowledge of the case. But there are no media points in that.

The local daily was neatly folded beside his mail and

he glanced at the front page. Beneath a photograph of the necklace there was a two-column spread:

The Body in the Sand Dunes

A Suspicious Death

The body of a young man discovered in the dunes near Hayle on Monday has now been officially identified as that of Cochran Wilder, only son of Government Minister Royston Wilder. The young man went missing while on a walking holiday almost exactly fifteen years ago. Post mortem evidence suggests that he was attacked and that he died as a result of injuries received.

The police are unwilling to comment on their investigations at this stage but it is understood that in addition to their efforts to trace the owner of the necklace found with the body and shown in our photograph, they are interested in a chalet near where the body was found and thought to have been occupied at the time of the tragedy . . .

Wycliffe was puzzled. As far as he knew only two contacts could have given rise to speculation about the chalet: his interview with Mace and Kersey's with the Grey woman at the health shop. Odd. It was a small thing but leaks always troubled him; they meant watching your rear.

Lucy Lane arrived.

'Anything on the necklace, Lucy?'

'Nothing to write home about, sir. The silver carries the London hallmark and the date letter for 1859. Old Minors down at Gellet's says he's never seen anything quite like it before; he thinks it's a family piece almost certainly made to order and he says it would fetch a good price at auction.'

The house telephone rang. 'The chief would like to see

you in his office when convenient, Mr Wycliffe.' It was the chief's protective dragon, known disrespectfully as 'Queenie', but Queenie had a soft spot for Wycliffe and she added, *sotto voce*, 'I think the Minister has got him ruffled.'

Wycliffe went along the corridor and through the padded door. Queenie, with more secrets tucked away beneath her silvery hair than most, revelled in her intercessionary role. She whispered, 'He's waiting for you. Go straight in.'

Chief Constable Bertram Oldroyd was a good police-man who had built up a sound administration, leading from the front, but never interfering with a subordinate who was doing his job. He had always vigorously resisted any attempt at manipulation from Whitehall or from anywhere else, and as he neared retirement his sensitivity in such matters had increased.

'Come in and shut the door, Charles. Sit down.' It was obvious to anybody who knew him that the chief was still simmering. 'I've just been talking to Wilder. I gather that he telephoned you yesterday afternoon and that he was dissatisifed with your response.'

'Yes, I think that sums it up.'

'Well, I told him that I am fully satisfied with the way in which this investigation is being conducted and that if he's got a complaint, he should make it to the Police Authority or to the Home Office. I can sympathize with the man, but he's not going to flex his political muscle in my direction.'

Oldroyd sat back in his chair, feeling better.

Wycliffe said nothing because there was nothing that needed saying and, after a pause, the chief went on, 'Incidentally, he's arranging the funeral for Saturday morning at St Germans. I take it that raises no problems with the case?'

'No, sir. The coroner has opened the inquest and adjourned for further police investigation, but he is issuing a disposal certificate.'

'Good! Now, Charles, fill me in.'

In Hayle, Kersey finally succeeded in getting GG's mother at the end of a telephone. 'Yes, I've kept the record of my lettings but how do they concern you?' A worthy mother for the redhead, knowing precisely how many pence make a pound.

Kersey explained.

'All right. It sounds round about to me but I suppose you know your own business. Leave me your number, I shall have to ring you back.'

Obviously she would telephone her daughter. Whatever she did, it took her fifteen minutes.

'No, Inspector, none of my three chalets was let during the week which included the seventh of May 1977 or for another fortnight after that.'

'We are interested mainly in Sunset Cott, the one with a flight of steps leading up to a veranda. A witness says he saw a girl entering the chalet on the day in question and that there was music coming from inside.'

Madame was unimpressed. 'I can't help what your witness says he saw. I suppose it could have been a relative of the woman who kept the chalets clean and looked after the linen. I can only tell you what I know.'

'Yes, I understand that. So there was a woman who had a key to the chalets and looked after them?'

'I didn't do it myself.'

'Is this woman still around?'

'I suppose so; I've really no idea.'

'Perhaps you will let me have her name, and her address at the time?'

'I can't imagine what she could tell you that I can't.'

'We have to double check wherever possible.'

'Very well, her name is Maggie Reynolds – as to her address, I've got it here somewhere . . . Yes, here it is – Three Russell's Ope – that's just off Foundry Square.'

'Just one more question, Mrs Grey. Did you provide nylon bed sheets in your lets?'

She was more amused than disturbed by his question. 'We all did – those of us who supplied linen at all. They're easy to wash.'

Kersey walked to Foundry Square through drizzling rain and found Russell's Ope. It was a row of white-walled cottages fronting on the blank ramparts of a deserted foundry complex left over from the days of Hayle's greatness. Once, the vast cylinders for mine pumping engines were cast here, and it was from this foundry that the Dutch commissioned the largest pumping engine in the world, to empty their Haarlem Lake. Now it had about the same relevance to modern industry as a flint-knapper's yard.

The door of number three stood open to the living room and Kersey could see inside a heavily built man with machine-clipped white hair, sitting by an open fire. He had a tabby cat on his lap and a newspaper lay crumpled on the floor at his side.

Kersey tapped on the door.

'What do you want?' Guttural and demanding.

'Mr Reynolds?'

'That's me.'

Kersey advanced into the room and the old man turned towards him, his face round, bronzed and smooth as an apple. A real son of the soil matured in the broccoli fields. Kersey prepared to cope with rural naïvety.

'Detective Inspector Kersey.'

'What can I do for you, Mister?'

'I want to talk to your wife – Mrs Maggie Reynolds, I believe.'

'You can't talk to Maggie, she ain't here. You'll have to make do with me.'

'I'm afraid it's important that I speak to your wife, Mr Reynolds. Is there somewhere I can get in touch with her?'

'You could try the cemetery.'

Son of the soil snatches metaphorical mat from under

clever detective. Kersey had worked in the country long enough to have known better. 'I'm sorry.'

'Not half as sorry as I am, Mister. Maggie was a good wife.'

Kersey grinned. 'Let's start again.'

The old man's eyes sparkled. 'You've come about "the body in the dunes", that's what they call it in the newspaper, but where does my Maggie come in?' He shifted more comfortably in his chair and brought his great hands together, disturbing the cat but preparing to enjoy himself.

'I'm told that your wife looked after three chalets on the towans for a Mrs Grey.'

'She looked after several for different people who let – kept 'em clean and did the washing.'

'Mrs Grey tells me that none of her three was occupied at the time young Wilder disappeared but—'

'I reckon she wouldn' have much idea one way or t'other.'

'She says she kept a record, and she must have had some way of checking her bookings.'

The old man looked enigmatic. 'Bookings is one thing; they as weren't booked is another.'

Kersey had learned his lesson. 'You know something I don't.'

A deep-seated chuckle. 'It was like this, Mister, in the off season that chalet with the steps leading up to it was a sort of doss for family and friends. There was a son and a daughter – the redhead – her that's now got the shop in St Ives. It was her mainly.'

'She used to bring her boyfriends there?'

'It started when she was still a schoolgirl, and soon it was most any boy or man she happened to pick up with. Proper little tart she was – still is, from what I hear.' A long drawn-out sigh. 'Sometimes I think what I missed.'

'You're a wicked old man.'

A gust of laughter. 'P'raps I never had the chance to be a wicked young one.'

63

'Did Mrs Grey know about what was going on?'

The old man shrugged. 'Hard to say. Maggie thought so. By all accounts she weren't all that different herself.'

'These unofficial visitors to the chalet, I don't suppose you have any names?'

A shake of the head. 'They was mostly just names to me when Maggie talked about 'em; 'twas a case of in one ear and out t'other. But there was one who lasted longer than most, a fella called Penrose, a lawyer over to St Ives. But he was late on – too late to be any use to you.' The old man yawned. 'That's all I can tell you, Mister.'

Kersey thanked him and got up to go. At the door he paused, 'Shall I shut this?'

'What for? I ain't afraid of burglars.'

It was lunchtime. When did the old man eat? And what? Through the drizzle Kersey made for the pub. He was not proud of his morning's work. All he'd learned was that one of the chalets had been occupied at weekends in the off season. No dates and only one name, a lawyer who had come on the scene too late to be relevant. There was certainly nothing to connect the chalet with the death of young Wilder. On the other hand, his niggling, totally unfounded suspicion of the redhead in the health shop had somehow been rekindled. She had answered his questions and seemed willing, if not anxious, to help, but his policeman's antennae had received contradictory signals. Now she had cropped up again.

There were tasty looking pasties being served at the bar but after a suicide breakfast (the full menu with sausage and fried bread), his conscience, and thoughts of his wife, persuaded him to a sandwich and a half of bitter.

He was supposed to be listening to gossip but in the pub interest in the body in the dunes seemed to have flagged and the all-absorbing topic was the state of fishing in the port, in particular the sanding-up of the bar.

'I don't fancy it above an hour either side of high water and not then if there's any sort of a blow.'

Another skipper put down his glass and wiped his lips.

'Dredging's no answer either. What we need is the sluice and until they do something about East Quay there's not much hope o' that . . .'

Kersey was out of it, so he ate his sandwich, drank his beer, and left.

Back at the van he telephoned headquarters and reported to Wycliffe who sounded weary and mildly irritable. 'All you can do is keep at it. Tackle the Grey woman again . . . Of course there may be no connection but that's the name of the game; we soldier on and keep our fingers crossed. By the way, in this morning's paper they refer to police interest in a chalet that was occupied at the time of Wilder's disappearance. Have you said anything?'

'No, and I'm quite sure Coombes wouldn't.'

'That's what I thought. I wonder who's feeding them.'

'Anything fresh at your end, sir?'

'No, it's the same story. Lucy's team hasn't come up with much. She's been through the statements taken when Wilder disappeared, picked names out of the hat, and chased up as many as possible in case something was missed. Wilder seems to have been a Walter Mitty type with an unpleasant twist; he tried to live out his fantasies. I suppose his illness was to blame. He wasn't popular in the hospital; at one stage he was involved in a punch-up but it doesn't lead anywhere. And there's the cannabis angle, another blind alley – no ring or anything of that sort, just an opportunist user in a small way.'

Wycliffe sighed. 'It's a waste of time, Doug. If Franks is right the boy died from being hit over the head with a concrete object of some sort. Even if he was, that hardly amounts to a premeditated crime, but a spur of the moment thing. And it happened fifteen years ago.'

'What about Mace?'

'He seems a harmless type. Naturally we've done some checking and the most we could find was that his name cropped up in connection with some porn videos.'

Kersey was not the only one finding it difficult to

sustain genuine enthusiasm for a fifteen-year-old corpse. Unprofessional, of course, but some policemen are only human.

It was depressing, and by six o'clock Wycliffe was home.

With two women in the house he found the atmosphere subtly different. He was fed and watered, even cosseted, but the centre of gravity had shifted, and the household no longer revolved about him. He was not grumbling, a more peripheral role could have its advantages.

And in bed that night Helen confided Ruth's secret.

'She told me this afternoon while we were working in the garden. She and David are separated; they've been living apart for the past three months. It was all quite amicable; the flat is hers and there was a settlement. In fact he's been generous in the circumstances. Of course, the settlement includes her severance pay; she could hardly continue to work as his PA.'

'What circumstances are you talking about?'

'Well, it was Ruth who wanted it; he was anxious that they should marry and have children.'

'But Ruth didn't want that?'

'No.'

Wycliffe stopped himself just in time from sounding pleased. Instead he said, 'Why ever not?'

'I think you'd better ask her that. Anyway, she's come home because she feels she needs time to take stock.'

Thursday morning, 14 May

Wycliffe was an early riser and he was surprised to find Ruth already in the kitchen with the coffee made. Over their first cup, she asked, 'Mum told you?'

'Yes.'

'I'll put on the toast.' She busied herself cutting bread (sliced bread had never crossed the Wycliffe threshold). 'What do you think?'

'It's your life, love.'

'But you're not disappointed?'

'No, I'm not.'

She ran a hand through her hair in a gesture so like her mother's when concerned, that Wycliffe was moved. 'I've always known you didn't care for him, Dad, but although he's a hard man in business, in private life nobody could be kinder or more considerate.'

'Well, then?'

'I know. You're asking me why in that case I don't do what he wants.' She was putting slices of bread into the toaster. 'It sounds silly. I want him but I don't want his children . . .' She broke off. 'No, that's not true! What I mean is that I don't want my children brought up to believe in money as the answer to almost everything, I don't want them over-indulged. If I have children I want them to grow up wanting things they can't have – until they've learned to value what they've got.'

After a longish pause she looked up. 'Would you go along with that?'

'You don't need to ask . . . But don't leave it too late, Ruthie. You need somebody.'

After a disturbed night, spells of sleeplessness alternating with uneasy dreams, Lisa toyed with her shredded wheat and watched Martin butter a piece of toast and cut it into five equal fingers. She watched him pick up one of the fingers, bite it precisely in half, and return the remainder to his plate while he chewed and swallowed the other. She watched, as she had done hundreds of times before, and marvelled that she had never until now wanted to scream. The performance over, Martin drained his coffee cup, patted his lips and moustache with a paper tissue, looked at his watch and said, 'I must be going.'

It was a ritual as immutable as the Mass.

Lisa followed him into the hall where he picked up his

bulging bag. 'I shall be late this evening. There's a full staff meeting.'

He stooped to examine his reflection in the hall mirror and seemed satisfied with what he saw. He had shaved cleanly, his hair showed no sign of thinning or of grey streaks and his broad moustache was neatly trimmed. The black hair accentuated his natural pallor and gave him, he thought, a certain distinction.

But Lisa noticed for the first time a tiny patch of baldness on the crown of his head and experienced a tremor of uncharitable satisfaction, immediately followed by guilt.

Martin had his hand on the snap lock of the front door when the flap of the letterbox rattled and a small shower of mail dropped into the wire cage.

'Better see if there is anything . . .' He sorted through the envelopes in his large bony hands. 'Electricity bill . . . A catalogue for you . . . This is for you too – looks like a letter from your aunt . . . Bank statement . . . What's this . . . ? It's addressed to you.'

He held out a plain postcard. The address was type-written, and on the other side somebody had drawn a little map of what appeared to be a stretch of coast with a heavily indented estuary. 'What is it?'

'I've no idea.' Her voice trembled but he was too preoccupied to notice.

'I'll see you tonight, then.'

The door slammed and Lisa returned to the kitchen, the mail in her hand. She selected the postcard and dropped the rest on the table. The supposed map had no labels, no contours and no scale, but Lisa was in no doubt about what it was intended to convey. She stood, looking down at the card, feeling slightly sick, and it was some time before she could think clearly about how she would react. Do nothing? That was not in her nature. But what? She slipped the card into the pocket of her dressing gown and went upstairs.

*   *   *

68

Wycliffe arrived at the office still thinking of Ruth.

Diane said, 'You're looking more cheerful this morning. Does that mean progress?'

'Progress in what?'

'The case, of course.'

'Why bring that up? Anything in the mail?'

'Only routine stuff apart from one anonymous. I haven't opened it but it's not from one of our regulars.'

The address was typewritten, evidently on an old machine, and in the envelope there was something about the size and stiffness of a postcard. The postmark was simply 'Cornwall', the Post Office having done away with local marks in case they might be useful to somebody. He used the approved technique for opening suspicious packages and drew out a plain postcard with a section cut from a snapshot stuck to one side.

It was a photograph of a blonde girl in her late teens, seated on grass with her legs tucked in. She was smiling, a hesitant smile, a pretty girl in the inevitable T-shirt and jeans.

Wycliffe put on his spectacles which he still regarded as an expedient of last resort and saw that she was wearing a necklace which looked like the one found with the body. He thought he could make out the form of the cat and the filigree whorls of which the necklace itself was made. He was sufficiently convinced to experience a tremor of satisfaction. Apart from the grass, which looked like the fine fescue found on fixed dunes, just behind the girl's head he could make out what appeared to be a flight of wooden steps. It was enough.

Lucy Lane came in and he passed her the card. 'Keep your fingers off, but what do you make of it?'

'It certainly looks like our necklace.' Lucy was thoughtful. 'She must have been about eighteen then which would put her in her early thirties now.'

'What about the photograph itself?'

Lucy took her time. 'It's obviously been cut from a snap probably of a group. There was somebody sitting very close to her on her right, and there was somebody in front of her; I can see the top of a head.'

Wycliffe said, 'Take it upstairs and see what they make of it . . . Tell them to enhance and enlarge it to the best advantage. Say, a dozen prints to start with.'

Was this the breakthrough? If the photograph was genuine, and there was no reason to doubt it, there should be no great difficulty in identifying the girl . . . But what then? There was no proof of any direct link between her and Wilder. It was quite possible that she had lost her necklace, or had it stolen. Of course there were other, more encouraging, possibilities, but Wycliffe was the sort to see a glass half-empty rather than half-full. Either way, the photograph must be followed up and it was going to be his excuse for getting back into the field.

He telephoned Kersey. 'What's the weather like down there?'

'Drizzle.'

'Well, I'm coming down; I've got a photograph for you to look at.'

It was almost an hour before the prints were ready but still only half past ten. On the house phone he spoke to his deputy, John Scales, 'I want you to keep my chair warm for me, John . . .'

As on every other morning, Paul Drew parked his car and walked the hundred yards or so to the estate agency in which he was a partner. More than six-foot tall, he carried himself like a guardsman and proceeded with measured stride, head held high, looking neither to the right nor to the left. His sombre grey suit was creaseless and his briefcase had the sheen of well-polished leather.

As it happened, the police caravan was parked on waste ground immediately opposite his office, so that whenever he entered or left he was made uncomfortable by the feeling that he was being watched. It was absurd, he could see no-one, yet at times he could persuade himself that the police had chosen that spot solely because of him.

The office, formerly a shop, had a large window almost wholly taken up by a board displaying the usual photographs and details of properties for sale. Once inside, hidden by that display board, he felt better. He and the girl assistant shared the outer office while Stanton, the senior partner, had a room to himself.

'Your mail's on your desk.'

The girl was Stanton's niece and her treatment of him was casual. It was her job to open all the business mail and to sort it between the partners according to which of them was dealing with a particular transaction.

'There's one marked personal; I've put that separate.'

He often received personal mail at the office and he wondered vaguely why she had made the point. He sat at his desk, adjusted the position of his chair, telephone, and in-tray, and turned his attention to the mail.

The personal item was a plain postcard. On the communication side there was a sketch map and the words, poorly typewritten, 'I'll be in touch again soon.'

He felt faint. The girl looked across at him. 'What's the matter? You look awful.'

'I had a bad night – something I ate.' For a couple of minutes he went through the motions of reading and sorting his mail, then, 'I've got an appointment in St Ives; I shall be back in about an hour.'

At the door she called after him, 'Aren't you taking your briefcase?'

He went back to collect it.

'Don't you want a tape?' She handed him one of the little pocket recorders which had taken the place of notebooks.

The bloody girl was doing it on purpose and by the time he was on his way again he was so flustered that he all but tripped over the step. And still he could not keep his eyes away from the police van where a plain clothes man lounged indolently in the doorway, apparently watching him.

71

He forced himself to walk at his normal pace to where he had parked his car and as he walked he told himself repeatedly, 'Mustn't panic! Mustn't panic!' He made a short-lived effort to review and analyse rationally the significance of what had happened so far: the discovery of the body, the finding of that wretched necklace, and now, the arrival of the postcard which he carried in his wallet. In his car he sat motionless at the wheel while his mind insisted on reliving that nightmare time when, holding grimly onto his corner of the sheet, he staggered through the dunes, ghostly in the darkness, sometimes sinking up to his knees in the sand . . .

He arrived at the health shop with scarcely any memory of how he had got there, expecting to see GG at once, but she was with a client. He stood awkwardly in the shop not knowing what to do with himself. As it happened there were no customers and the two assistants watched him, exchanging amused glances.

Eventually the consultation was over and GG, with honeyed words, ushered her client into the street and turned to him. One look, and she said, 'You'd better come into my office.'

When he was seated in the client's chair she went on, 'What you need is a good cup of tea.' She called to one of the girls.

Fifteen minutes later, when Drew had left, GG picked up the telephone and dialled a number.

'Penrose, Solicitors? . . . Mr Penrose, please . . . Arnold? . . . I've had Paul here in a state . . . He's cracking up . . .'

Lisa and Martin had not shared a bedroom for three or four years though he made occasional visits to hers. She had the smaller of the two front rooms and there was a view over the bay from the window. The single divan, its duvet half on the floor, clothes littered about, a colourful twin-track cassette recorder sharing a shelf with a gaggle of paperbacks – all conspired to suggest the refuge of a teenager rather than the bedroom of a woman of thirty-three.

Lisa unlocked an old-fashioned writing case and, from among the tinted envelopes which she never used, brought out a photograph of a group of young people.

She was there, at eighteen, with Paul Drew. He was sitting uncomfortably close and his hand was on her thigh. Even now she could recall the grip of his bony fingers – possessive, not a caress. Now an estate agent, Paul had acquired a wife who might easily be mistaken for his sister.

Alan Hart had his arm around Barbara Morris and they both looked absurdly pleased with themselves. Now they were a married couple, expecting their second child, and Alan was one of the town's doctors. That left Gillian Grey – GG, and Julian Angove. The two were sitting close but there was no embrace; already they were old hands. In the following years neither had married. GG had her health shop and Julian had a queer little studio on the Wharf where he painted pot-boilers for tourists in summer, and survived the winter by courtesy of Social Security.

Lisa had made up her mind to approach one of the five, but which? Although remarkably they were all still living in the same neighbourhood – those who had gone away had come back again – they did not socialize; in fact, they seemed to avoid one another. For reasons which she preferred to leave undefined she decided on Julian, the painter. At first she thought that she might telephone, but she decided against that; she would call without warning.

She dressed rather carefully for the street, tightly fitting turquoise trousers of some stretch material, a Liberty top and a tailored jacket. But it was drizzling with rain and she had to wear a mac and carry an umbrella.

She arrived on the Wharf shortly after half past ten. Julian's studio was wedged between a shop and a café

73

and its one-room width rose to three storeys, like a slice cut from a slab cake. In the tiny shop window, displayed on an easel, a colourful picture of the harbour looked like an illustration from a child's story-book. The door was locked, though stuck to the glass was a notice which read 'Open at ten'. There was a bell-push and Lisa pushed. She heard a distant ring and waited but nothing happened. Through the glass door she could see mail lying on the mat and beyond, a dim passage-like vista; the walls were lined with framed pictures and at the far end there was a barred window.

Having made up her mind Lisa was not to be put off; she put her finger on the button and kept it there until she heard movement. Shortly afterwards, she saw Julian himself coming towards her between the rows of his pictures. He wore a dressing gown, his feet were bare, he was unshaven and his mop of dark hair framed his plump features like a corona.

He fiddled with the lock and opened the door. 'God! It's you.' He stood aside to let her in and locked the door behind her. 'What time is it?'

'A quarter to eleven.'

He looked about him, his lips moist and slack. 'I was in bed. I take it you haven't come to buy a picture, so you'd better come upstairs.'

'Aren't you going to take your mail?'

He looked at her oddly, but he stooped and collected the three or four envelopes from the mat. As far as she could see there was no card. The painter grumbled, 'Bloody bills, that's all I ever get.' He looked at her again, increasingly puzzled as he recovered his faculties. 'What brought this on? . . . Anyway, come on up. Leave your mac and umbrella here.'

At the end of the shop, by the barred window, there was an easel with a half-finished painting and, in an alcove, stairs led up to the next floor.

'After you . . .'

At the top of the stairs she found herself in a narrow

74

living room, starkly furnished, with a window over-looking the quay. More stairs led to the top storey.

'Sit you down.'

He sat beside her on a long, hard bench which must have come from a railway waiting room, and looked her over. 'I see you around sometimes. You're wearing well. From the rear you look just as you did as a schoolgirl. I fancied you then – good legs and a nice little bum. You're wasted on that constipated schoolmaster but you always went for that sort. I remember you had a thing with Paul Drew and you ended up by marrying the type specimen of the breed.'

It was strange that Lisa, a trained nurse, accustomed to slapping down randy convalescents, felt no inclination to do the same with the painter. Julian sighed, and his dressing gown parted exposing his chest and a tangled mat of hair. Lisa reminded herself of what she had come for and handed him the photograph from her bag.

He studied it intently. 'What's this in aid of?' . . . Then, under his breath, 'God, we were a smug-looking bunch!'

Lisa gave him the postcard. He looked at the sketch map, turned the card over and saw the stamp. 'So it came like this; no envelope. Somebody being a bit nasty.'

'You haven't had one?'

'No.'

There was a movement on the stairs from the room above and they both looked up. A girl was standing halfway down; she was plump, very dark, in her early twenties, and she was naked.

Julian said, 'For God's sake, Elena, put something on; we've got a visitor. Then you can make some coffee and open the shop.' He added, to Lisa, 'She's a nice kid, but not very bright.' He was still holding the card. 'Have you asked any of the others?'

'No, I was wondering what to do.'

'Nothing. Forget it! Somebody's conscience is pricking and they're trying to take it out on you.'

75

The telephone rang and he answered it. It was on a little table at the top of the stairs.

'Yes, it's me . . . A card? I don't know what you're talking about. Nobody ever writes to me . . . Others? What others?' A longer interval than before. Then, 'You can come over if you like but I don't see what I can do . . .'

He dropped the telephone and returned to the seat. 'That was GG; I fancy she's wetting her see-throughs. She's had one of your cards and I gather Paul Drew's been there looking for a shoulder to cry on.' He grinned. 'I feel left out.'

Lisa said, 'It's no laughing matter, Julian.' But she was beginning to feel relaxed, the very last thing she had expected.

Chapter Four

Thursday (continued)

The day was soft with misty rain and intervals of watery sunshine. The roads were quiet and Wycliffe made, for him, good time, so that by shortly after twelve he was in Hayle where he found Kersey installed in the newly established Incident Room. It was next to where the van was parked, an odd little building and, like a great many others in Hayle, it had experienced successive incarnations, first as a bank, then as a post office, followed by a library, a social club and, lately, a meeting place for the *Heralds of the Second Coming*.

There was a large room, almost a hall, for the *hoi polloi*, and a little one to serve as an office for whoever was in charge; also a minute kitchen and rather grim toilets. Shaw had worked his usual minor miracle in persuading central stores to disgorge the necessary equipment, and the utility services to revitalize their connections; all with a minimum of red tape.

The two sat at a table in the little room beneath a lurid print of Armageddon under which some wag had scrawled with a felt pen 'Coming Shortly'.

Kersey studied one of the prints Wycliffe had brought with him. The lab had done a good job; contrast had been enhanced and the enlargement made the most of what detail there was. Kersey said at once, 'God! She's wearing the necklace; and those steps must mean that it's the Greys' chalet.' Then, after an interval, 'Somebody's playing silly buggers.'

'In what way?'

'Trying to pull strings. Whoever sent this, knows the

77

girl. Why not give us a name? Why cut away the rest of the picture and take her out of context?'

Wycliffe said, 'I thought we'd try this out on the Grey woman. Will you see her, or shall I?'

Kersey grinned. 'Time you got to know the cast, sir, don't you think?' He was still studying the photograph and finally he muttered, 'There's a smell about this.'

Wycliffe agreed though he would not confess it. 'Is there anywhere we can get some lunch?'

They lunched off pasties in Kersey's pub. Old Reynolds was there, well-established behind a pint and a pasty in what was obviously his corner. He looked across at Kersey, raised his glass, and gave him a knowing wink.

Afterwards Wycliffe drove to St Ives and parked in the yard by the police station, which reminded him of another time and another case.* He had a soft spot for St Ives; a little town which had grown out of mining, fishing and Methodism into an integrated community. Now mining was dead and the other two were on shaky legs, but tourism had come to the rescue. The community had taken a battering, but physical aspects of the old town survived, the narrow streets and tiny, stone-built houses; and the street names remained: Bethesda Place, Fish Street, Cat Street, Salubrious Place, Teetotal Street, Virgin Street . . . He was in search of Bethel Street, leading to Skidden Hill.

He found it, and the health shop; it would have been difficult not to find the health shop, the other shops in the street were modest and restrained by comparison. Indeed the one on the opposite corner – called The Modelmakers – looked derelict.

As it happened, the redheaded woman was in the shop. He introduced himself and she looked him up and down with a searching stare which would have detected a single undone button or a refractory gravy stain. 'You'd better come into my office.'

*Wycliffe and the Scapegoat

He was momentarily distracted by the backdrop of sky and sea; the sun was struggling through a mass of dove-grey cloud in an explosion of light. He recovered himself, produced his photograph and laid it on the desk in front of her.

She did not look at it immediately. Perhaps to indicate that this was not a professional interview, perhaps for other reasons, she slipped out of her white coat and hung it in a metal cupboard. Underneath she wore a green silk blouse and a severely tailored skirt. Only when she eventually sat down did she pay any attention to the photograph.

'What do you expect me to say?'

'Whether you recognize the girl, the necklace, or both.'

A pursing of lips. 'I've seen photographs of a similar necklace in the newspapers and on TV recently.'

Wycliffe sat back in his chair. 'Miss Grey, perhaps it was as a result of the publicity given to the necklace that we received this, and unless we succeed in some other way I've no doubt that by publishing this photograph we shall identify the girl.' After a pause he went on, 'Then it could be embarrassing for those who knew her and did not volunteer the information.'

GG played with an expensive looking ball-point. 'Is that a warning? Perhaps a threat?'

'Neither, it is a statement of fact. As far as we know this girl – woman as she must be now – has done nothing wrong, but we need to identify her because the necklace she is wearing in the photograph was found in association with the body of Cochran Wilder.'

She was weakening but not quite ready to give in. 'How does that concern me?'

'Because we know that you and your friends were in the habit of using one of your mother's chalets, the chalet called Sunset Cott, which is nearest to the spot where the body was found. And, in case you were there during the critical weekend, it is natural that we should come to you for any information you may be able to give before the inquiry widens.'

Gobbledegook; but delivered slowly and with significant pauses, it sounded almost menacing. She thought it over, put down the ball-point and straightened the sleeves of her blouse.

'Very well! We agreed that if it went this far we should talk. The truth is—'

Wycliffe interrupted her with intent. 'If I thought you were about to incriminate yourself it would be necessary to warn you.'

A forced laugh. 'Set your mind at rest, Superintendent, there's no risk of that. As I was saying, the truth is that we were at the chalet – a small group of us – during the weekend that Wilder disappeared. We were sixth-formers, within a week or two of our A-level examinations, having a final fling.'

She was watching him through half-closed lids. 'Our parents had been given varying versions of how their offspring intended to spend that weekend, but they wouldn't have approved of the truth – a mixed party of six in a chalet with three double beds.' She treated him to a broad smile. 'I'm not sure what the reactions of parents would be today, but this was fifteen years ago.'

The V-neck of her blouse displayed an area of freckled skin, plague of redheads.

'Did you see anything of Cochran Wilder during your stay at the chalet?'

'I did not; neither as far as I know did any of the others.'

'Presumably you did not admit to being in the chalet at the time because of your parents' attitudes, but what has stopped you coming forward since the discovery of the body?'

She spread her hands. 'We had nothing useful to say. And would you want the indiscretions of your youth put up for public discussion without good reason? We all six of us still live in this neighbourhood; Alan Hart is a doctor, married to Barbara – one of the girls. Paul Drew is an estate agent with a dragon for a wife; Lisa, another of the girls, the one with the necklace, is married to a stuffed-shirt schoolmaster . . . That kind of publicity would do none of them any good, or me. Then there's Julian Angove, the painter.'

Wycliffe noticed that she had slipped in the names, ahead of his questions. She sounded reasonable and she was obviously regaining her confidence which had been temporarily shaken.

'Do you have a copy of the photograph from which this was taken?'

She hesitated. 'No, I think it was a snap taken by Barbara. I must have had a copy but I lost it.'

'Just one other question, Miss Grey. How do you account for a necklace belonging to one of your party being found in the possession of the dead man?'

A slight shrug. 'Do I have to account for it? Surely, that's for Lisa it was her necklace. But I do know that she lost the thing and made one hell of a fuss about it. Lisa comes from what used to be called a 'good family' and the necklace was a family hand-me-down, an heirloom if you like, given to her on her eighteenth birthday only a few days earlier. She was tedious about it; you would have thought it was part of the crown jewels. And then she went and lost the damn thing in the sandhills. But you'd better talk to her.'

It could all be genuine but Wycliffe had the impression of a very good performance. 'I must ask you for a statement setting out what you have told me, Miss Grey. Of course none of it will be made public unless it proves essential to our inquiry.' Wycliffe was at his starchiest. 'I shall also need a list of the five names you mentioned, the five people who were with you during that weekend.'

'You can have them now.' She reached for a scratch pad and began to write very rapidly. She looked up. 'By the way, unless you want a couple of marital crises on your conscience I suggest that you should be diplomatic in your approach to Lisa Bell – that's her married name – and to Paul Drew.'

She handed him a sheet torn from her pad. 'There you are!'

Perhaps she expected him to get up and go, but he sat on and she began to fidget.

'A lawyer called Penrose – do you know him?'

She immediately settled in her chair. 'You've been listening to gossip, Superintendent.'

'So you do know him?'

'Arnold is my cousin, Mr Wycliffe – his mother is my mother's sister . . . Right? And we've been good friends since we were at school.'

Wycliffe glanced at the list she had given him. 'He wasn't one of the chalet party.'

'No, Arnold went to boarding school but we saw a good deal of each other in the holidays.' She made a sudden gesture of impatience. 'Let's get this out into the open! I enjoy the company of a man, and not always the same one, so I've never married. I'm made that way – promiscuous if you like. I've never tried very hard to cover up the fact. Arnold and I have had an intermittent relationship extending over many years.'

'Presumably he feels the same as you do.'

Her lips pursed. 'Arnold is married with three children.' She broke off. 'Why this interest?'

'Your names were linked in connection with the chalet.'

She smiled. 'Yes, we used to go there at one time.'

Wycliffe stood up. 'Well, thank you for your patience.' He had his hand on the knob of the office door when he paused. 'You live above here?'

'I do. I have a very nice flat. Do you want to see it?'

'Not at the moment, thank you.'

Then he was out in the street, wondering how much he had really learned from the redhead. He crossed the road and found himself staring at the window of the derelict shop. In the window was a model sailing ship, beautifully made, but dusty and neglected, like the shop.

'No dogs, children, or food inside . . .'

A movement in the shop drew his attention. An apparently disembodied head had appeared above the screen at the back of the window. It was the head of an elderly man with sparse grey hair, thin features and a goatee beard. He looked like a desiccated Chinese mandarin. A hand and an arm joined the head, signalling peremptorily that he should come in.

When he reached the door it was open and the man, a wispy little creature wearing sagging trousers and a waistcoat over his shirt, waited for him. 'Come in and let me shut the door!'

The shop was also a workshop. Just inside the door, on shelves, there were models of small sailing craft of every description. Some were complete, finished in their colours and fully rigged, others had been abandoned in various stages of construction

'Come through.'

The workshop was spacious with a window opening on to a wilderness which had once been a garden.

'Stand in the light where I can see you.'

For some reason Wycliffe obeyed the man and submitted to an inspection. To keep in countenance he said, 'You are Mr . . . ?'

'Badger – Henry Badger. Don't bother to tell me, I know who you are.'

They were standing by a workbench equipped with a great range of small tools in racks, and the centre of the room was taken up by a table on which a large, complex model was under construction. It was not a boat, but a building, of the sort that is on display in the architectural gallery of the Royal Academy and, like everything else there, it was covered in dust and had obviously not been worked on for months, perhaps years.

'That doesn't look like a boat.' Wycliffe, being ponderously jovial.

The old man grinned. 'No, I'd call it more of a toyshop. It's the new computer centre for IPF.'

'You take commissions for that sort of thing?'

'It helps to fill the rice bowl. They want to build it on the edge of the New Forest and my model is intended to con the planners into believing that a mega chicken coop can look like a stately home.' He chuckled. 'Plenty of toy trees, that's the secret of architectural models. Of course they never plant 'em when the place is built.'

He looked Wycliffe in the eye as he spoke as though challenging him to mention the accumulated dust but Wycliffe held his peace.

Against one wall there were several shelves stacked with books; books with faded and cracked spines. Wycliffe could never resist other people's bookshelves and he was running his eye over the collection. Books on sailing ships, their history and construction, took up a lot of space but there were also works on history, archaeology and anthropology, and a great many biographies.

Badger said, 'You're interested in books? You read a lot?'

'A fair amount.'

'Biography?'

'I read biography.'

'Not the kitsch stuff from media nonentities, but the lives of real people. Is that right?'

'I suppose so – yes.'

'To find out how they managed it.'

Wycliffe was becoming irritated. 'To find out how who managed what?'

'Living – how other people manage it. Isn't that why you read 'em? I only had to look at you crossing the road to realize you're like me, a man not too sure of himself, always looking over your shoulder, in need of a prop. God knows what made you a policeman! Have you read Holroyd's biography of Augustus John? There's a man for you! I reckon if I'd read something like that when I was a youngster it would have changed my life. You must

84

have the guts to go after what you want and to hell with the consequences.'

Wycliffe had had enough. 'I understood that you wanted to talk to me.'

'I *am* talking to you. Anyway, here's what I have to say: I can't help noticing that your people are taking an interest in the Grey woman. Presumably it's about the finding of young Wilder's body in the dunes. I can't help you with that, but there's something I want you to know. I want you to know that my life may be in danger.' He held up a cautionary finger. 'I don't say that it is, but in case I'm found dead in my shop or my bed one of these days I want you to know that things may not be as simple as they seem to be.' He added after a pause, 'Just that!'

Wycliffe was disturbed; the pale grey eyes were gazing up at him with great earnestness. 'But you must tell me what you are afraid of—'

'I'm not afraid of anything, certainly not of dying. After all, life itself is a terminal illness. Time and chance, Mr Wycliffe. But I don't fancy dying as a cover-up for others.'

'What causes you to feel threatened?'

'That's my business. I'm not asking you to do anything about it; in fact I shall resent any attempt you make to pry into my affairs. All I'm asking is that *if* anything happens to me I shan't be shuffled off to the crematorium with no questions asked.'

'But—'

'There are no buts, sir! You've listened to what I had to say and you'll get no more from me on that subject.'

Wycliffe tried a different tack. 'You live over your shop?'

The old man grinned. 'Some people would say I live in it.'

'You look after yourself?'

'A woman comes in mornings. She does my shopping, cleans the place a bit – not much, as you see. Mostly she fills my freezer with prepared stuff and all I have to do is heat it up.' Another grin. 'I rarely go out by day. I'm a night bird, Mr Wycliffe.'

He was like a mischievous overgrown elf.

'Do you have friends – friends who visit you?'

The old man snapped, 'What's that to do with you?' But he relented. 'There's one chap who comes here, a young fella, Angove – a painter, he calls himself, sells pot-boilers to the tourists. Can't paint, no idea, but he's a bloody fine cartoonist. Won't take it seriously. Damn fool could make a fortune. I'll show you one day if you're still around and I'm in the mood.'

Wycliffe thought that he had seen enough and heard as much as he was likely to. At the door, the old man said, 'Your Grey woman . . . she's mixed up with a lawyer called Penrose.'

'So?'

'Just that Penrose is a shady customer . . . Now you're going to warn me about making that kind of statement, but don't bother. I can look after myself. Just remember what I've said – all of it, mind!'

As he closed the rickety door behind him Wycliffe felt like Alice after her disorientating interview with the contentious caterpillar.

Kersey lit a cigarette. 'Do you believe the Grey woman?'

'No, but they've obviously agreed a story.'

'With a tame lawyer to make sure their lies are plausible.'

'It could be.'

Kersey was reflective. 'I've never known six people hold together on the truth, let alone on a lie. So it's a question of one at a time. Is that what you think, sir?'

'Probably.' Wycliffe looked over GG's list. 'There's one name here which I'm pretty certain was mentioned by Badger as a friend of his – a painter called Angove.'

Kersey reached for the phone book and fluttered the pages. 'Here we are: Angove, Julian, Studio Limbo, The Wharf, St Ives.'

'Sounds promising.'

Kersey referred to the list. 'Paul Drew, Estate Agent – there's an estate agent across the road, Stanton and Drew. I've seen them going in and out. There's a grey-haired type in his sixties, short and sprightly; a girl with a lot of leg who shows most of it; and a six-footer-plus who looks a bit like an owl worked off a battery.'

'How old?'

'Early thirties.'

'Could be our man. Better have a word. According to the Grey woman he's got a dragon for a wife so go warily until we know more than we do now.'

Kersey said, 'How about Old Father Time in the Modelmakers? Do we take him seriously?'

Wycliffe laughed. 'Badger – Henry Badger; somehow it suits him. I must admit that he left me with a very odd impression; there's something about him that makes you feel uncomfortable. Coombes, the local sergeant, seems a dependable sort and he knows his patch. Get him in for a chat and at the same time see what he can tell us about the Grey woman's lawyer friend.'

'Will you be here, sir?'

'No, I'm going to have a look around.'

'Will you be staying overnight?'

'Yes. What's your place like?'

'Comfortable. The food's OK, the beer's drinkable and they've got room; or they did have last night.'

The telephone rang and Wycliffe answered. 'Mrs Bissett on the line, sir.'

The search-button of his memory was engaged for an instant, then he had it: St Germans. 'Put her through.'

Molly Bissett sounded relaxed, and friendly as ever. 'I hope father hasn't prejudiced you too strongly against us Wilders. I want you to do me a favour.'

'If I can.'

'Cocky's funeral is on Saturday morning at eleven. It will be a very quiet affair, just the family – such as it is, and a few close friends. The point is that father will be here all the weekend and I wondered if you would drop in some time. I think you might do him a bit of good. At the moment he's not quite sure what's happening to him and in those circumstances he's always difficult.'

Wycliffe said, 'Of course I will. Would early Saturday evening suit? Say about six?'

'Six o'clock will be fine. And thanks!'

After Wycliffe had left for St Ives, Kersey crossed the road to the estate agent's office. It was raining again: Scotch mist; Cornish drizzle. The leggy girl had a desk to the left of the door and the man had his to the right. Kersey, who despite appearances was house trained, wiped his feet.

'Can I help you, sir?' From the girl, very pert.

Kersey ignored her and turned to the man who had reacted unmistakably to his arrival. 'Mr Drew? Mr Paul Drew?'

Drew pretended to be involved in sorting through some papers and he looked up, unconvincingly surprised. 'Yes?'

Kersey, with his back to the girl, showed his warrant card. 'A routine matter, Mr Drew.'

'What is it?' In a whisper. All colour had drained from the man's face.

'A few minutes chat across the road will probably straighten it out . . . More convenient than here, don't you think?'

'Yes . . . Yes, I'll come over.' And he added in a louder voice, in an attempt to sound normal, 'I shall be glad to help if I can.'

Kersey left, with a derisory smirk at the girl who was all eyes and ears. Back in the Incident Room he waited in the outside office, and just three minutes went by before he saw Drew come out, darting glances about him like a nervous rabbit, and cross the road.

Kersey said to the duty officer, 'Wheel him into the other room, I'll see him there.'

'Mr Drew, sir.'

Drew, apprehensive, took in the features of the little room as though it might prove to be a cell. 'I'm not sure what—'

'Come in and sit down, Mr Drew . . . Cigarette?'

'I don't smoke.' He took off his heavily rimmed spectacles and began to polish them. His eyes looked naked and he blinked rapidly.

Kersey looked at a paper in front of him. 'I've got a little list, Mr Drew, and your name is on it.'

'A list?'

'A list of youngsters who spent a naughty weekend in a beach chalet fifteen years ago. Six of them – three boys and three girls.' Kersey leered.

Drew replaced his spectacles. 'I know what you are talking about but I assure you—'

'That weekend included the Saturday when Cochran Wilder disappeared, and your chalet is close to the spot where his body was recently found—'

'I must insist that—'

Kersey went on, relentless. 'As I was saying, where his body was recently found. The body was naked and it had been deliberately buried in the sand. His clothes and other possessions were buried with him. He seems to have died from a cracked skull due to a blow, not a fall.'

Drew was clasping and unclasping his long bony fingers. 'I assure you, Inspector, that I saw – that *we* saw nothing of Wilder.'

Kersey nodded. 'I know that's what you and your friends have agreed to say.' He shrugged. 'It could even be true, but you must admit it doesn't seem very likely. You are saying that all this went on within a hundred yards of you and none of you saw or heard a thing? What were you doing? Don't tell me! I've got a photo to show you.'

'A photo?'

Kersey passed over the enlargement of the fragment showing the girl with her necklace. 'Recognize her?'

89

'No . . . well, yes. It's Lisa.' He added in a confiding burst, 'She's married now, to a schoolteacher called Bell.'

'Good! We're coming on. Have you got a copy of the original snap from which this was taken, Mr Drew?'

A momentary hesitation then, 'Yes.'

'We would like to see it. No hurry, just drop it in some time – like later today.' He pushed over his list of names. 'Are these the people who were in that photo?'

Drew took the paper and studied it. 'Yes.'

'Nobody else? Not Cochran Wilder, for example?'

'I've told you he wasn't there. I've told you we *didn't see him*!'

'All right, Mr Drew; no need to get worked up.'

For some time Kersey said nothing; he sat, smoking and watching the other man as though waiting for him to make the next move. Finally Drew reached into his inside pocket and brought out a wallet. From a pocket in the wallet fitted with a zip he produced a photograph about postcard size. It was slightly bent but otherwise undamaged. He passed it to Kersey. 'There you are, you can see for yourself.'

Kersey studied the photograph; it was obvious that the fragment sent to the police had been cut from an identical print. 'Good! We're really making progress, Mr Drew, but there's one thing that still puzzles me: in the photograph Lisa is wearing her necklace, the one that was found with Wilder's body; how did he get hold of it if none of you ever saw him?'

Drew sighed. 'She lost it.'

'Where?'

'How do I know? In the dunes, I suppose. And Wilder must have picked it up.'

Kersey sighed. 'Wilder's last day on earth seems to have been pretty busy.' Abruptly he held up the enlarged fragment showing the girl with her necklace. 'Do you know how we got this? It came to us out of the blue, dropped into our laps, just a bit cut from a print like yours, and we enlarged it. We've no idea who sent it.

Somebody trying to be nasty. Do you get anonymous bits and pieces sent to you like that, Mr Drew, to jog your memory? Mementoes of times past?'

'No.' The word was barely audible.

'All right. Now, we'll just make sure I can put the right names to these faces. No doubt about which is you – you haven't changed all that much in fifteen years . . . And there's Lisa, and the Grey girl, the future Dr Hart . . . Yes, I think I've got them all.' Kersey looked up, 'Well, Mr Drew, thank you for coming over . . .'

'You mean I can go?' Slightly dazed.

'Why not? You haven't done anything that need worry us, have you?'

Kersey saw him off at the outer door. 'They tell me Wilder must have weighed between eleven and twelve stone – not a heavyweight, but quite enough to go carting around the dunes at night, don't you think?'

Given a free choice of somewhere to stay, Kersey was more likely to end up in a pub than a hotel and this time was no exception, but the dining room was at the back of the house, away from the bar, and opened on to a little courtyard garden where a tortoise chewed away at lettuce leaves watched by a bored ginger cat. There were only four tables and they had the place to themselves. But Wycliffe was moody and Kersey was mildly anxious.

'Will this do you, sir? I know it's a bit basic. We get the same food as the family. Last night it was a lamb stew, tonight it's beef steak and kidney pie. The landlady is a good cook.'

The landlady herself served them with two portions of the pie on heated plates and a large dish of mixed vegetables to share. Her voice was rich and creamy, with a lilt. 'Now eat it all up! It's a lovely bit of steak and I didn't buy it to feed to the dog. Whatever you want to drink they'll bring from the bar.'

They helped themselves to vegetables and Kersey brought him up to date on the Drew interview.

Wycliffe listened and studied the photograph. In the end he said, 'As you thought, there's something wrong in all this, Doug. Whoever sent us that bit cut from the snapshot had access to a print like this, and they also had a grudge against the girl with the necklace, and probably against the others in the group as well.'

'So?'

'I wish I knew. Now you tell me you think Drew has been getting similar reminders – in other words that he's open to blackmail.'

'Yes, I do. I tried out the idea at random and the shot went home. No doubt about that. Drew is running scared; if he isn't actually being blackmailed, he thinks he's threatened. I suppose that could apply to the others as well.'

Wycliffe laid down his fork. 'But it doesn't make sense. Assume that this group of youngsters really was criminally involved in Wilder's death and that somebody has a spot of blackmail in mind – they would all be pretty vulnerable. But why bring us into it? A blackmailer would be as anxious as his victims to keep us out.'

Kersey nodded. 'There's something in that. Could it be that there's a third party in the know? . . . You're not eating . . . Try some of these carrots. They're good . . .'

But Wycliffe was not deflected. 'Now that there is some movement we need more people on the ground. We need statements from all six in the group and we need to know more about them, their backgrounds and their relationships. Some of this is tailormade for Lucy Lane but we shall need a couple of DCs as well. I'll fix that for the morning . . . By the way, have you had that chat with the local sergeant yet? – What's his name? – Coombes?'

'Not yet.'

'Then get him into the Incident Room first thing and we'll talk to him together.'

Kersey was secretly amused by the sudden invigoration of his chief. 'Anything else?'

'Yes, find out the present owner of that chalet. Now we know that it is where the six of them stayed and we have some grounds for suspecting that the crime might have taken place there, it's reasonable to give the place a going over.'

'Fox?'

Wycliffe hesitated. 'In the first instance, but if he finds anything we'd better bring in Forensic.'

'You think they'll find anything after fifteen years?'

Wycliffe was edgy. 'If not we'd better bring in the archaeologists; they seem able to tell us what Iron Age man had for breakfast. But whether they find anything or not, if this ever comes to court, how shall we look if we ignore the probable scene of the crime?'

They finished their meal almost in silence and Wycliffe crossed to the Incident Room to do some telephoning before setting out on his evening jaunt; that ritual which was part of being away from home.

There were few people about and cars were parked along the kerb. With more than an hour of daylight left he wanted to take his own look at the area where the body was found and at the chalet with the steps. A single flying visit had done little to give him the sense of place to which he attached so much importance.

He drove along Commercial Road, deciding that Hayle was a one-off, with a quirky appeal – an opinion confirmed almost at once by two shop signs: a DIY store called the Jolly Bodger and Jungle Herbert's Reptiles and Amphibians. Add those to a pub called the Bucket of Blood!

He made his way around the Pool by the Black Bridge (built from copper-smelting slag) and up Phillack Hill to the village.

The rain had gone but a mist had closed in to eddy and swirl over the valley so that one moment he saw the town on the other side, and the next he didn't. But Phillack Church, its pub, and its cottages were serene in evening sunshine. As he drove, Wycliffe carried in his thoughts and in his pocket, the print which Paul Drew had given to Kersey.

He found the clearing where he had parked on his first visit and soon he was among the chalets. On that other visit he had not singled out any particular chalet; now his only interest was in the one with a veranda and a flight of steps. When he found it, he was struck by its comparative isolation and by the fact that it was the nearest to where the body was found. Built of lapped planks, it was raised on brick piers, and a flight of twelve steps – he counted them – led up to the veranda.

He looked at his photograph. There they were, the six young people who, fifteen years ago, had somehow been in at the start of the Wilder case. And there in the background were the brick piers supporting the chalet, and the first few steps.

An ordinary group of youngsters in their late teens, they might have come from a sixth form anywhere and there was nothing to suggest that within the next few hours they would become involved in a sordid crime.

With the help of Kersey's briefing he could now put names to all the faces: the Grey girl, of course, and next to her, Julian, now a painter and friend of the Badger. The painter looked at the camera with a tolerant grin; probably the joker in the pack . . . And there was Lisa with her necklace, and next to her, the solemn-faced, bespectacled, Paul Drew . . . The plump fair girl wearing a blue T-shirt was Barbara, sitting next to Alan Hart, her future husband.

In the late afternoon or early evening of that Saturday Mace would arrive in search of Wilder. He would speak to Barbara – from his description it could only have been her.

'She was on the way up the steps . . . I spoke to her and asked her if she had seen anything of Cochran . . .'

'So this chalet was definitely occupied?'

'It must have been; there was pop music coming from inside.'

Wycliffe climbed the steps to the veranda. It ran the whole length of the little building and from it he could look into the living room and one of the bedrooms. With his arms resting on the rail he took in the view and experienced one of those moments when he regretted having given up his pipe. The mist was confined to the estuary, leaving the sea a vast silvery plain, and the sky above St Ives was barred with clouds, touched with gold by the sun which had already set.

Could he construct a scenario for the events of fifteen years ago?

Wilder, on his imposed coast walk, having shaken off his minder, arrives in the late evening and strikes up an acquaintance with the group. Not much older than they, but more experienced and worldly wise, he impresses them. He's good company. They offer him a bed on the floor for the night . . .

But then comes the gap – more a yawning gulf, for some hours later (if the indications were to be credited) these same young people are carrying Wilder's dead and naked body, wrapped in a sheet, through the dunes and away from the chalet. In the bare sand of the foredunes they will dig a grave, and in that grave they will bury the young man's body along with his clothes and his rucksack.

And, presumably, on Monday morning they were back at school, facing the run-up to their A-levels.

Was that by any stretch of the imagination credible? Group behaviour amongst young people is always less predictable and often more violent than is the case with individuals. 'The group so easily becomes the gang.' The policeman talking. But then he tried to recall his own children as adolescents; the twins, Ruth and David. They were contemporaries of the youngsters in the chalet. The thought set him wondering . . . In retrospect the twins seemed to have led a more or less placid existence, a cycle of school, homework, television, a Saturday-night disco, a weekend with friends . . . But what had he or Helen

95

really known about them? They had been as enigmatic as they were apparently amenable. Had the parents of these youngsters seen them differently?

He could not have said how long he remained there, arms resting on the veranda rail, staring at nothing, but quite suddenly he was aware of St Ives as a mound of twinkling lights against a darkening sky.

Time he got back. Something, perhaps his copper-on-the-beat training, made him try the door of the chalet before he left and, at a slight push, it opened into the seemingly impenetrable darkness of the living room.

Damn! How often had he told himself that he should carry a pocket torch?

But even in the light there was he could see the raw wood where the flimsy door had been forced. It wouldn't have taken much; a screwdriver, even a stout knife, could have done it.

He felt for a wall switch, found and flicked it, but nothing happened. Who would leave the power on in an empty chalet? But his eyes were beginning to accommodate to the darkness and he could distinguish the sofa, the table and a couple of chairs which happened to be near the window. As a pipe smoker he had once carried matches and a lighter; not now.

It was possible that this was no more than a random break-in; equally possible that the break-in was connected with his case; and here he was blundering about in the darkness. Common sense told him to return to his car and call out the troops; have the place made secure, then let Fox loose in the morning. But he could now see the door into what was presumably the kitchen, and it was open. Curiosity killed the cat.

Two or three steps, and he was standing inside the doorway; he could see the outline of the kitchen window, a sink with a gleaming tap, and there was a glass panel, presumably in the back door. That was as far as he got; he was aware of a swift movement close at hand, followed at once by a blow to the back of his head. He tottered forward, coming down heavily on his hands and knees. He did not lose consciousness but he was dazed. He heard something clatter to the floor, running footsteps, then someone almost slithering down the steps outside, followed by silence.

He picked himself up, his head was sore and throbbing and he felt queasy. He had been wearing his hat, otherwise he wouldn't now be on his feet, feeling sorry for himself. It was a minute or two before he began cursing himself for a fool.

He made for the front door and stood, supporting himself on the veranda rail. St Ives looked the same as it had done a minute or two earlier, twinkling away, remote and indifferent. He practised deep breathing and it helped; at least the nausea was passing off; but his head hurt and he felt fragile. After a while he went down the steps, clinging to the handrail.

By the time he reached his car and clumped into the driving seat the worst seemed to be over. On the car phone he spoke to the St Ives' nick. An hour or two later and the smaller stations would have shut up shop for the night, and he would have been telling his tale to a desk sergeant at Division, to be stored away and embroidered, a good in-house story for the boys.

The thought was salutary. For the moment, he would tell no-one of the attack. He would report the break-in and arrange for the place to be under observation until it was made secure. He decided that he was well enough to drive back to the pub; and he did, with such circumspection that he was unlikely to attract the attention of any marauding patrol crew hoping for a driving drunk to break the monotony.

Kersey was in the bar. 'Are you all right? You look awful. What you need is a stiff whisky.'

'What I need is bed.'

He made his usual good-night call to Helen from a little booth off the bar and contrived to sound almost normal.

'How's Ruth?'

'No different from when you saw her this morning.'
Helen seemed amused.

'David hasn't phoned?'

'No. We had a letter on Tuesday.'

'Yes, of course . . .'

He went to bed with a couple of diazepams, kept
for emergencies, and after a prolonged struggle to
find a comfortable position where his head didn't hurt,
he slept.

Barbara came into the lounge where Alan was watching
television. She looked tired – near the end of her tether.
He thought: this bloody business is getting her down. He
patted the settee beside him. 'Do come and sit down,
love.'

'I can't, Daniel has woken up. Will you go up to him?'

He was halfway up the stairs when the telephone rang.
There was one in the hall, so he took it there. 'Dr Hart
speaking.'

It was Paul Drew, very excited. 'I'm in a phone box;
I must see you, Alan. I haven't been home; I can't face
Alice . . .'

'Have you been drinking?'

'No, but I can't go through the night without talking
to somebody. I've been questioned . . . They know . . .
They're just playing with us and I've done something
terrible . . . You've got to help me.'

'Be at the surgery in ten minutes . . . All right?'

'I've been to the bloody surgery and it's all locked up.'

'Just be there! And for God's sake, calm down!'

Barbara had come into the hall. 'Trouble?'

'A patient. Sounds drunk to me but I'd better take a
look at him.'

He was gone for the better part of two hours and
Barbara was anxious.

'What happened?'

'The man is a bloody nuisance.'

'Who was it?'

'Just a patient; you wouldn't know him.'

Henry Badger was finishing his evening meal; a fish pie from the freezer which he had heated in the oven. With it he had drunk a couple of glasses of moselle, his regular tipple, and read a few pages of Fiona MacCarthy's biography of Eric Gill, sculptor and craftsman; another man who fascinated him. Such books had become his addictive tranquillizer, his literary Valium. He read and reread them as the devout read their sacred texts. But this evening the prescription had failed him; he remained uneasy, deeply troubled within himself.

Sometimes he wondered if he was going queer in the head. He would do things on the spur of the moment, silly things, for no apparent reason. Talking to that policeman was only the latest example; he had called him in off the street and said certain things . . . At such times he experienced an overwhelming need to be noticed; he would strive to be interesting, to say things that sounded dramatic, though they were rarely more than half-truths if not total fabrications. It could be dangerous.

But more worrying still, as time went on he seemed less able to distinguish between actual events and the fictions of his mind, between his dreams and his waking experience. He felt that he was getting out of step with life around him, becoming a stranger to normality. Had he reached that stage which the mealy-mouthed call confused?

He told himself that he was old and that he was alone. There was no cure for old age but finding company would have presented no problem. The truth was that generally he preferred to be alone but, as with everything else, there was a price to be paid.

The percolator had completed its vulgar repertoire; he poured himself a cup of strong black coffee and took it into his workshop and stood over the half-finished model. Not only was there dust, but a spider had spun its web between two of the skeletal struts. The web was perfect; a structure which in design, execution and sheer beauty should shame every architect and structural engineer. He reached out a hand to brush it away, then shook his head and let it be. He sipped his coffee and muttered to himself, 'They must've built the bloody thing by now.'

With no clear intention, he returned to the kitchen and climbed the stairs to the next floor. On the landing he switched on the light, a dim bulb coated with grime. Three doors stood open, one to his bedroom and an unmade double bed, another to a sitting room which had only been used during the brief period of his marriage, and the third to his bathroom and WC. There was an all-pervasive sour smell which he had lived with for so long that he was unaware of it.

Another flight of even narrower stairs led up from the landing to an attic; the door of the attic was immediately at the top of the stairs so that he had to stand on the top step to open it. The woman who looked after him was never allowed upstairs.

He entered the attic room and switched on the lights, two bulbs high in the rafters. The room, with its sloping roof, dwarf walls and dormer window, was large. Through the grimy panes of the window, Godrevy lighthouse flashed its warning out to sea, and away to his left half the town glittered under the night sky. There was a desk and chair by the window and a wooden filing cabinet stood against one wall, with a cupboard next to it. Much of the rest of the wall space was taken up by bookshelves and framed drawings.

Badger spent some time choosing a book from the hundreds on the shelves and having made his choice he carried it to the desk. Next, he unlocked the cupboard with a key from his pocket. The shelves were stacked solid with old magazines but in the bottom of the cupboard there were several bottles. Badger took one of them and cradled it in his hands for a moment or two before placing it on the desk by the book. The whole procedure had the appearance of a well-rehearsed ritual. An electric radiator placed near the desk was switched on, and he brought out a brandy goblet from one of the desk drawers.

Minutes went by before he was settled. He rolled the goblet between his hands; then came the first sip. He read a few words; another sip; a few more words, and a sense of calm began to take possession of his mind as the warmth spread through his body.

Chapter Five

In the morning Wycliffe had a dull ache at the back of his skull and a nasty bump to show for it. Over breakfast he gave Kersey an unvarnished account of his performance in the chalet. 'I was a fool. The man had broken in at the front and was in the kitchen when I blundered in. He couldn't get out that way without making a row because the back door was locked; he was trapped and I walked right into it.'

Kersey said, 'You still look pretty groggy. Surely you should see a doctor?'

'I intend to. I'm going to phone Dr Alan Hart and ask for an appointment.'

'That should be interesting. And the case aspect?'

'The local chaps will have informed the present owner of the chalet. We must get Fox out there and see what sort of tale he has to tell.'

'You saw nothing of the guy who attacked you? Got no impression at all?'

Wycliffe felt as moronic as the average witness appears to be. 'No, I did not!' With finality. 'But I'll tell you this, Doug, I don't like being hit on the head and I want to know where each of our precious six was last evening between nine and ten.'

'Could it have been a woman?'

This set Wycliffe wondering again. 'I don't think so . . . No! The footsteps were those of a man. So let's say we need to know where the three men were – at least, where they claim to have been.' And a moment later he added, 'You can leave Hart to me. But apart from all that, this fellow, whoever he was, must have walked or driven there, and the road to the towans at this time of year isn't exactly the M25. He or his car must have been seen. Get somebody on to it.'

After a meagre breakfast but with more coffee than was good for him, he telephoned the doctor.

'Dr Hart?'

'Speaking.'

Wycliffe introduced himself. 'I have acquired a nasty bump on the head and I shall be most grateful for your opinion.'

Did that sound as ambiguous as was intended? At any rate Hart took a while to digest it, then, 'I could see you at nine o'clock. My surgery is just off Island Square.' Click. Not exactly a warm reception.

Wycliffe drove into St Ives and found the surgery without difficulty, a stone-built cottage which had been gutted inside and extended at the back. He was not kept waiting. The receptionist said, 'Dr Hart will see you now.'

The surgery did not look out on to anything, and the window was fitted with hammered glass panes. Hart left his chair to stand over his patient. He was tall and fairly heavily built, but his hands were long and slender, the fingers eminently tactile. They investigated the back of Wycliffe's skull.

'Ah, yes. As you say, a nasty bump. How did you manage to hit yourself there?'

'I didn't. Somebody did it for me.'

'Really?' No obvious interest. The fingers continued to explore his skull and neck.

Wycliffe said, 'I think you must know the place where it happened, Doctor, a chalet, called Sunset Cott, on the towans.'

'No sign of an extradural haemorrhage . . . Headache?'

'Yes, but it's going off. Last evening, quite by chance, I discovered that the place had been broken into. Foolishly, I tried to investigate in the dark and I was attacked.'

'We had better take a look at your pupils. Open your eyes wide and look at the light . . . An almost normal pupillary reflex. Did you get a look at this chap who attacked you?'

'Unfortunately, no.'

'Pity! Strictly speaking I should tell you to have the day in bed but I suspect that would be a waste of my breath. It won't hurt to take an aspirin or two if the headache troubles you, but no alcohol, at least until tomorrow.'

'Where were you say, after nine o'clock yesterday evening, Doctor?'

Hart had returned to his chair and he greeted the question with an uncertain smile. 'I am becoming confused as to which of us is exercising his professional skills in this consultation, Mr Wycliffe. However, until well after ten o'clock I was here, dealing with some of the paperwork we have to cope with these days. After that I was at home. Now, I'm afraid I have calls to make before my regular surgery . . . If you will be good enough to fill in the form my receptionist will give you—'

'Thank you, Doctor.' But Wycliffe did not move. 'As you know, I am investigating the death of Cochran Wilder. We have established that at the time of his disappearance you, and five of your fellow sixth-formers, were occupying the chalet close to where his body was found.'

'So?' Hart's face was expressionless.

Wycliffe ignored the question. 'You will also know that a necklace belonging to one of the girls in the party was found with the body and that is a link which requires explanation.'

Hart would have interrupted again but Wycliffe pressed on. 'In the circumstances I shall need formal statements from the six people involved concerning the events of that weekend.'

For some reason Hart was mollified. 'I see. Well, provided there is confidentiality, I am prepared to go along with that though I'm afraid I have nothing to tell you that you do not already know.'

'At least there will be a record. I will arrange it for some time this afternoon at the local police station. One of my officers will contact you.'

The doctor shuffled the papers on his desk, his manner more diffident. 'There is just one thing. As you probably know, my wife was one of the girls in that party. At present she is pregnant and inclined to be emotional and I cannot consent to her being interviewed.'

Wycliffe nodded. 'I don't think we need insist at this stage.'

Hart was getting up from his chair. 'Now, Mr Wycliffe, I really must ask you . . .'

Wycliffe still did not move. 'I won't keep you long but there is just one other matter; I would like your opinion on a medical question which has some bearing on my case.'

Hart sat down again. 'Yes?' His manner was discouraging.

'I see from the psychiatric reports of the time that, although he was so young, Wilder was diagnosed as a manic-depressive.'

'Indeed?'

'I've read somewhere that during a manic episode when the subject may seem to be expansive and convivial, the life and soul of the party in fact, a trifling frustration may provoke a disproportionate response; aggression, and even violence. Would you say that is broadly true?'

The grey eyes were wary. 'I am not a psychiatrist, Mr Wycliffe.'

'No, but I'm sure that your experience must have brought you into touch with such cases.'

A pause, then, 'Very well. What you say is, I believe, characteristic of the disorder in certain of its forms.'

When Wycliffe had gone Hart continued sitting at his desk and for the first time since the discovery of Wilder's body he experienced real fear, an emptiness inside, and with it a feeling of helplessness, almost of resignation. Drew, idiot though he was, had been right. They knew. The policeman had been sure of his ground and at the right moment, a moment of his choosing . . . That cretin had played into their hands by breaking into the bloody chalet!

He dialled Drew's office. 'I'm sorry, Mr Drew is not in today . . . He's unwell . . . If you would like to leave a message, or speak to our senior partner, Mr Stanton . . .' Hart replaced his phone and sat for a while staring at it before trying again. This time he looked up and dialled Drew's home number. 'Mrs Drew? . . . I wonder if your husband is available? This is Dr Hart speaking.'

A slightly cracked voice, resolutely refined. 'I'm sorry, Doctor, but he is not at home. Could I take a message?'

Hart hesitated, wary of creating domestic strife, but there were more important things at stake. 'I'm anxious to get in touch with him and they told me at his office that he was unwell.'

There was silence at the other end for a while, then, 'I told them that. I didn't know what else to say.'

'*Is* he ill?'

She answered, aggression beginning to surface, 'I don't know whether he's ill or not, Doctor. I don't even know where he is. I'm ashamed to admit it, but that's the truth!' The veneer was cracking. 'He came in yesterday evening, late, looking and behaving very oddly. I've never seen him like it before . . . Never! It was intolerable! . . . I know that you are one of his friends so I suppose I can talk to you. He said that he was going straight to bed but half an hour later I heard the car moving out of the drive, and he was gone . . . He must have crept downstairs like a . . . like a *thief*! And I haven't seen him since. I can't believe—'

Hart cut her short. 'Did he take anything with him? Clothes? Money?'

She snapped, 'I don't *know* what he's taken. I haven't looked!'

'I think we should talk, Mrs Drew; I may be able to help. If I called at the house within the next hour?'

After sitting and staring at nothing for a while, Hart dialled another number. 'Is that you, Julian? . . . This is Alan Hart. I'm coming round . . .'

The painter said, 'To what do I owe this distinction?'

Hart snapped, 'Don't play the bloody fool! You know what this is about and it's serious.'

When Wycliffe arrived at the Incident Room, Kersey and Coombes were standing looking up at the print of Armageddon, and as he joined them Coombes was saying, 'The second coming. The ones who put this up were a queer lot, but I suppose it's nice to have something to look forward to.'

Kersey reported, 'Coombes has got one of his chaps out at the chalet, sir, and Fox is due with Lucy and a couple of DCs at about eleven.'

'How about the owner of the chalet?'

'No problem there. The woman who owns it has recently lost her husband and she's got other things to think about. She says we can do what we like provided we make good any damage.'

Wycliffe's head still ached but he concentrated his wits and tried to recall the questions he wanted to put to Coombes. 'This chap Badger, at the Modelmakers in St Ives – do you know him?'

Coombes grinned. 'Who doesn't? He and his shop are part of the scenery.'

'He doesn't seem anxious for custom.'

'Certainly not over the counter. I don't know how things are now but at one time he used to sell most of his ship models through an agent in London, and he also made models of buildings for architects. I've heard that he was an architect himself once.'

It was a fine morning and the sun was striking through the window. Coombes ran a finger round inside his collar. 'But whatever he does or doesn't do I don't think the bailiffs will be troubling him. It was before my time here but while he was still a youngish man he married a widow, and not too long afterwards she died leaving him a nice bit of property and money to go with it. As far as I know he's never been much of a spender.'

'A local man?'

'The Badgers were local. He had two sisters; one married Penrose, the lawyer – the present one's father. She lives with her son and his family here in town. The other sister is the one who owned the chalets – Mrs Grey, mother of the health shop woman. She moved up north when they sold up in Camborne.'

'So Badger is uncle to Arnold Penrose and to the Grey woman in the health shop?'

Kersey took his cue from Wycliffe. 'Any idea what relations are like between uncle and nephew?'

Coombes looked blank. 'All right as far as I know. I've never heard anything different. Of course the old boy must be a bit of a problem. He's come near to being in trouble with us from time to time.'

'What for?'

Coombes spread his hands. 'Being a bloody nuisance about sums it up, sir. He gets ideas into his head – takes against people and harasses them, sends them threatening letters accusing them of taking bits of his land or of tipping rubbish on it. Once or twice he's written what you might call poison-pen letters to councillors about alleged backstair deals in planning . . . So far Penrose has managed to keep his uncle out of court but it can't have been easy.'

Wycliffe said, 'Badger told me he feels his life might be in danger. Does that surprise you?'

The sergeant hesitated. 'I'm not surprised that he said it.'

'But you think it's all in his imagination. On the other

hand, if he turns up with his throat cut tomorrow morning we mustn't blame you.'

'You put that very well, sir.'

Wycliffe tried again. 'Badger made sure I knew that Penrose was, as he put it, "mixed up" with the Grey woman and he went out of his way to warn me that Penrose was a shady customer. Any comment on that?'

Coombes grinned broadly. 'You're putting me on the spot, sir. It's all more or less in keeping with what we know of the old boy. Penrose inherited a good practice from his father and he seems a good lawyer. Of course there's gossip about him and his cousin – the redhead in the health shop; and I reckon he must have his problems with his posh house, expensive wife and three kids, but I suppose mother pays her way, and probably a bit more.'

Wycliffe said, 'You evidently know your patch. Just one more thing; I want to get some contemporary background on the chalet party, the six when they were teenagers. Any idea what school they would have gone to?'

'Sure to have been John Harvey's, sir. It used to be a grammar school, now it's a comprehensive.'

'Good. That's it then. I want your chaps to keep an eye on the Modelmakers in a general way, and let me know of anything that comes up in connection with the six who seem to be concerned in all this.'

The telephone rang and Wycliffe picked it up. 'Mr Arnold Penrose would like to speak to you, sir.'

Wycliffe said, 'Talk of the devil. Put him through.'

'Mr Wycliffe? . . . Arnold Penrose, Penrose and Son, Solicitors . . . I wondered if I might call at your office for a word – some time this morning . . .'

Wycliffe said, 'I shall be in St Ives later on; it would be more convenient for me to call on you . . . Shall we say about midday?' He put down the phone. 'Penrose seems bothered. Worried about his girlfriend?'

* * *

At shortly before eleven, Lucy Lane arrived with two DCs – the over-weight Potter, and Iris Thorn, a recent transfer from Traffic. Thorn was black, tall and slender, with a calm bearing and a serene expression. A smile seemed to play constantly around her lips, but her colleagues had already discovered that she was not always amused.

On Wycliffe's instructions Lucy Lane had brought with her the necklace, still in its polythene bag, but now officially logged.

Fox, in the Scenes-of-Crime van with Collis, his apparently willing serf, had gone directly to the chalet.

In the little office Wycliffe and Kersey brought Lucy Lane up to date and Wycliffe summed up, 'It seems clear that the six young people who stayed at the chalet during the weekend Wilder disappeared were in some degree involved in his death and that it was they who buried him with his belongings in the sand.

'But that's a very different matter from framing charges and formulating a case which would stand up in court. The six are now adult, almost certainly advised by a lawyer and fully aware of their rights. So we start with their versions of the story on paper. That means formal statements from five of the six. The doctor's wife is pregnant, so leave her out for the moment.'

Wycliffe massaged the back of his skull and decided to treat himself to a couple of aspirins before seeing Penrose.

'In addition, I think we should know more about the background of those six teenagers, and their school might be the place to start.' He turned to Kersey, 'That's all work for the DCs but I want you to talk to the painter and Lucy can pay a visit to Lisa Bell – after she's been with me to see Penrose. Show her the necklace, Lucy, get her to identify it, and see what else you can get. No pressure until we are more sure of our ground.'

Wycliffe was pleased to have Lucy Lane in his immediate team again. He could not have identified the particular gap which seemed to exist when she wasn't at hand on a case but whatever it was, she filled it. It was the same with Helen when he was at home. Perhaps it was that particular brand of female logic which is more direct, with fewer reservations and conditional clauses than the male brand.

Lucy drove him to St Ives; they left the car in front of the police station and walked down to the Wharf. The sun shone out of a cloudless sky and the tide was spreading over the yellow sand of the harbour where many of the craft now grounded would be afloat within the hour.

Wycliffe pointed out Studio Limbo as they passed, wedged between a café and a gift shop.

'Julian, the painter,' Lucy said, as though responding to a catechism.

A door next to an arcade of small shops carried a worn brass plate: 'Penrose and Son, Solicitors and Commissioners for Oaths', and a small notice beside it read, 'Please ring and walk up'.

At the top of the stairs on a carpeted landing a young blonde sat behind a desk, her fingers pecking away at the keys of a word processor. 'Can I help you?' And then, 'I'll see if he's free.'

Almost at once Penrose came out of one of the offices, hand held out, his features creased in a broad smile. To Wycliffe's surprise he was plump, almost rotund and slightly balding. No Romeo.

'A pleasure to meet you, Chief Superintendent. Of course I hear a lot about you in legal circles . . .'

To which the correct reply would have been, 'Some of it good, I hope!' But Wycliffe didn't speak the language. He introduced Lucy Lane.

'Do come in . . . Do come in!'

The office overlooked the harbour, now seen through slatted blinds.

Seated, Wycliffe said, 'You wanted to talk to me.'

Penrose ran a hand through his dark, thinning curls

then straightened some files on his desk. 'This is difficult.'

'I presume that it has some connection with the discovery of Cochran Wilder's body in the sandhills.'

Penrose smiled an uneasy smile. 'Yes. What absurd names some parents wish on their children! One is inclined to wonder what effect a name like that might have had on the poor boy's future.' A throat clearing. 'Yes, well, you will understand, Mr Wycliffe, that I have no official standing in the matter. It just happens that your inquiries have involved people who are friends of mine and I thought that a little chat might be useful to them and perhaps to you.'

Wycliffe let in a cold draught. 'I assume that your friends are among the six people who, fifteen years ago, during the weekend that Wilder disappeared, were occupying the chalet nearest to where his body was recently found.'

Penrose studied the superintendent for a moment or two before saying, 'I suppose you could put it that way.'

'But you don't represent these people professionally?'

'No.'

'So, presumably you have some information which you think might be helpful?'

Things were not going the way Penrose had hoped; the atmosphere was decidedly chilly. He drummed on the desk-top with his finger tips. 'I should make it clear that I am only anxious to see your inquiry brought to a speedy conclusion so that my friends can get on with their lives without this cloud hanging over them. Although I am naturally concerned for my friends, I have good reason to believe that all six of those involved are in a similar position.'

'So what position is that?'

The telephone rang and irritably Penrose reached for the receiver. 'No calls, Delia!' He turned again to Wycliffe. 'You are not making it easy for me, Mr Wycliffe. However, I intended to be helpful and I shall be.' There was a pause while he studied his chubby hands which looked as soft and tender as a young girl's. 'As you might expect, these people, some of them well known in the district, are embarrassed by your inquiries, and their situation is being aggravated by anonymous communications.'

'What sort of communications? Abusive? Threatening?'

'Judge for yourself.' Penrose took an envelope from a drawer and passed it over. The envelope was unsealed and Wycliffe slipped its contents on to the desk-top – two plain postcards. Both were stamped and franked, and addressed on a typewriter to Miss Gillian Grey, The Health Shop, Bethel Street, St Ives. On the correspondence side of the first card was an outline map of a stretch of coastline with an arrow indicating a certain point, and on the other card was a question, again in type, 'Who killed the Cock?' followed by, 'I shall keep in touch.'

Penrose said, 'I know that four of the others have received similar cards. Julian Angove, the painter, has refused to say one way or the other.'

Wycliffe, still holding the cards, said, 'There appears to be no suggestion of blackmail.'

'How could there be without evidence of guilt? And there can be no such evidence because there is no guilt. I mean, who could believe that these six young people . . .' The plump hands were dismissive. 'It would be too absurd! . . . All the same, Mr Wycliffe, you must agree that communications of this sort, on top of your inquiries, are bound to be very disturbing to people with professional responsibilities in the district.'

Lucy Lane had watched and listened but Wycliffe had refrained from giving her any cue to intervene. Evidently she was there to observe, so observe she did and came to the obvious conclusion that Wycliffe was deliberately pushing the lawyer off balance.

Wycliffe held up the cards. 'I may keep these?' Polite.

'Of course.'

Wycliffe slid them into the envelope and put the envelope in his pocket. He took his time about it and all the while his eyes never left the lawyer's. Finally he said, 'Do you have any idea who might have sent these, Mr Penrose?'

'Certainly not!'

There was an uneasy silence during which they could hear people talking on the Wharf below. Abruptly Wycliffe changed his manner, becoming conversational as though the business of the visit was over. 'The other day I was in that extraordinary shop – opposite where your Miss Grey has her premises. It's run by an elderly man called Badger. Odd sort of chap, eccentric, but obviously very intelligent. Did I hear that he's a relative of yours?'

Penrose did not relax; if anything he seemed troubled by the change of topic. 'Henry Badger is my uncle, my mother's brother. As you say, he's an eccentric.'

'I was impressed by his miniature ship models, and by the architectural model he is building.' Wycliffe sounded chatty.

A forced laugh. 'The IPF computer centre. He hasn't touched it for years and the place is probably built by now. That was his last commission and he never finished it.'

'Obviously a very skilled man.'

'Yes, he trained as an architect, but at heart he was a craftsman and he had considerable talent. Unfortunately he gave up work quite suddenly, almost from one day to the next. I've no idea why.'

Wycliffe said, 'He seems to be something of a recluse; he told me that he rarely goes out by day and that he lives alone with just a woman coming in for an hour or two, mainly to do his shopping.'

Penrose nodded. 'That's quite true and it seems to be as he wants it. But occasionally, for two or three days together, he will lock himself in and see nobody, not even the woman who is supposed to look after him. At least I assume that he locks himself in, but I suppose it's possible that he goes away. But where would he go? Anyway, it can be very awkward. If he is there he doesn't even answer the phone.'

Wycliffe was tentative. 'I believe you've had problems with him writing letters – letters which could have led to legal complications.'

'Letters which did lead to legal complications though I was able to avoid the courts. But I see your drift, Mr Wycliffe; for a moment I was beginning to think that we were just chatting about a difficult relative. I should have known. You are hinting at the possibility that he might be responsible for these cards.'

'Is it a possibility?'

Penrose played with the cord of his telephone. 'I think it's very unlikely. I can't imagine why he should feel animosity towards the people concerned. On the other hand, if there is the slightest chance of such a thing I shall be glad of a little time to look into the matter.'

'Does he own a typewriter?'

'A typewriter? Oh, I see what you mean. I couldn't say for certain but I shouldn't think he'd give such a thing houseroom – he's always prided himself on his calligraphy.'

Wycliffe had not quite finished. 'There is, of course, another difficulty: how could your uncle have got hold of the information that these young people were occupying the chalet at the time Wilder disappeared?'

Penrose nodded, thoughtful. 'That *is* a point, certainly. On the other hand, I have to admit that it may not be an insurmountable one. You see, Julian Angove, one of the six, is a regular visitor at the Modelmakers – almost the only one. I've never understood the nature of the attraction, unless it's a common tendency to make mischief.'

Wycliffe seemed satisfied. 'Very well, Mr Penrose; I think we understand each other.'

As Wycliffe was on the point of leaving he said casually, 'Oh, perhaps I should tell you that there's been a break-in at the chalet – Sunset Cott. I was out there yesterday evening and I found that the door had been forced. I was foolish enough to investigate in the dark and I collected a blow to the back of my head.'

Penrose appeared genuinely shocked, and it was a moment or two before he said, 'I'm very sorry to hear that. Of course there has been a good deal of vandalism and some trouble with dossers out there recently. I hope it's nothing serious?'

'Oh, no. Dr Hart thinks I shall live.'

When they were once more out on the Wharf Lucy said, 'You made a contest of that, sir; but not knowing the rules of the game it was difficult to follow. Was it chess, or snakes and ladders?'

Wycliffe growled, 'I haven't made up my mind myself.'

'Do you think your Modelmaker man is harassing these people, sir?'

Your Modelmaker. For Lucy, and almost certainly for Kersey, Badger had become his private property, a fringe character who happened to have caught his imagination. He passed Lucy's question back. 'Do you?'

Lucy gave up and they ambled along the Wharf with the visitors.

They reached the painter's studio and Wycliffe hesitated.

'Are you going in?'

Another pause then, 'No, I think we'll leave him to Mr Kersey.'

They arrived at the lifeboat station and Wycliffe stopped again. 'Now you can go along to see Lisa Bell. As I said, tackle her about the necklace but don't put her under too much pressure, just get her talking.'

'But the Bells live in Carbis Bay; will you drop me off?'

'No. You take the car and I'll get a patrol car to run me back.'

When Lucy had gone, instead of turning up the hill to the town, Wycliffe followed the footpath past the public toilets along the border of the sea.

Blackened and jagged rocks and a stretch of yellow sand separated the raised walk from the sea. Gulls swooped and planed overhead, apparently for fun, and a few tourists strolled along the path with less obvious pleasure.

Wycliffe told himself, I can't get to grips with this. A young man disappears and fifteen years later his body is found buried in the dunes. During those years only the father talked about possible foul play, and that was because he couldn't accept the implications of suicide. In fifteen years there have been no accusations, yet within a day or two of the discovery of the body, people who could have been involved were being targeted with veiled threats and a photograph was sent to me, obviously with the intention of setting the police on their tails.

Surely whoever was doing all this now must have been in a position to do it at any time?

He passed the back of GG's health shop with the window of her office overlooking the sea, then turned up into Bethel Street where her shop and Badger's faced each other on diagonally opposite corners. He crossed the road and made to enter the Modelmakers but the door was locked. Then he noticed a fly-blown card which read 'Closed'.

Was Badger's involvement anything more than a fanciful idea which had come to him after a chance encounter? The lawyer, while denying its likelihood, had given the idea greater substance. Not only was the old man's niece one of the six but Angove, the painter, was a regular visitor at the model shop.

Wycliffe stood back to take stock of the property. There was a high stone wall reaching some distance up the hill behind the shop, presumably the length of Badger's wilderness garden. Wycliffe walked to the end of it and found an alley which separated the backs of the properties in Bethel Street from those in the street running parallel to it. The alley, carpeted with weeds and grass, was too narrow for a vehicle; it ran between six-foot stone walls, with plank doors into the premises on either side. Wycliffe tried Badger's door and found it secured.

He walked back down the hill with the intention of enquiring after Badger's likely whereabouts at the health shop, but changed his mind and went instead to a newsagent and tobacconist next door.

The owner looked like a retired wrestler. 'Is the old fool gone off again? All I know is that he was there yesterday. Anyway, if he runs to form, he'll be back Monday.'

'You've no idea where he goes?'

The man's face went blank. 'To be honest, Mister, for all I know he might still be in there. He's a pain, always complaining about other people, and look at the state of his place. I mean, it lets down the whole bloody street.'

'Can you remember when you last saw him?'

'Yes. It was the night before last, about eight. He was off on his usual. Every night he goes off somewhere about that time. God knows where . . .'

'You didn't see him last night?'

'No, I didn't, but that don't mean he wasn't around. It means I wasn't.'

Kersey arrived at Studio Limbo, pushed open the glass door, and found himself in the passage-like interior with paintings crowding in on either side. He waited but nobody came so he walked down the shop until he arrived at the stairs and called, 'Anybody home?'

There was a strong smell of frying. A stocky young man came to the top of the stairs and Kersey held up his warrant card. 'Police. Detective Inspector Kersey.'

'Oh, I thought we were overdue for a visit. You'd better come on up.' At the top of the stairs Kersey entered the long narrow room. At the end opposite the window a door was open into a tiny kitchen where a girl wearing an apron manipulated the contents of a wok on a stove. A table was set for a meal by the window; all very cosy and domesticated.

The painter pointed to the long bench. 'Take the weight off your feet.'

Kersey, unprepared for this casual reception, tried to play the heavy. 'I think you know why I'm here.'

Angove sat beside him on the bench. 'I suppose it's about this nonsense over the body they've dug out of the dunes.'

'We don't regard an investigation into violent death as nonsense, Mr Angove.'

The painter was unperturbed. 'Neither do I. It's the fact that some busybody who chooses to send anonymous bits of crap through the post is taken seriously.'

'This busybody of yours is in possession of information which gives substance to his crap as you call it.'

Angove had the mobile features of a clown and he looked at Kersey with amused surprise. 'What information? The fact that fifteen years ago half a dozen adolescents spent a sexy weekend in a beach chalet.'

'It is ready.' The girl, standing in the doorway of the kitchen, spoke with clipped precision. 'I must serve out or it will spoil.' She was slim and dark. South-east Asian? Filipino? As well as an apron she wore a jade green frock, sleeveless and brief.

The painter said, 'This is Elena. Can you stretch it for the inspector?'

'Of course.'

'There you are then, Inspector – diced pork with bean sprouts, onions, mushrooms and noodles.'

The smell was mouth-watering and Kersey was tempted, but declined.

'Then you'll have to watch us eat. It's too good to spoil. If you want to talk at the same time you'd better pull up a chair.'

Kersey pulled up a chair and talked to keep himself in countenance. 'You are taking your own position and that of your friends too lightly, Mr Angove. Wilder was killed in some sort of tussle by a blow on the head. The indications are that he died and was buried on the

Saturday evening of the weekend you spent at the chalet – the nearest, incidentally, to where the body was found.'

Angove and the girl went on with their meal showing as little concern as if Kersey had been talking about the weather. With his mouth full the painter said, 'I don't see what connects all this with our chalet party. The chap had a row with somebody in the dunes which turned into a fight, and presumably he got the worst of it.'

'A pretty violent row it must have been, and only a hundred yards or so from your chalet, but you heard and saw nothing. A bit surprising, don't you think? Of course Wilder was naked when he was found, so perhaps he and his opponent were indulging in some sort of ceremonial combat. His body was wrapped in a nylon bed sheet which they no doubt brought along as part of the ritual, and the concrete fragments embedded in Wilder's cracked skull must surely mean that the *coup de grâce* was administered with a ceremonial concrete block.'

The painter was grinning broadly while the girl continued eating her food with demure precision as though unaware that anything unusual was taking place. Angove said, 'Very funny!'

But Kersey became serious. 'Not so funny, really. Whatever sort of scrap Wilder was involved in took place in one of the chalets. I'm not saying that it was murder, it could have been manslaughter or even self-defence. That will be for the coroner, and perhaps a jury, to decide when we get that far. But however he died, his body was wrapped in that bed sheet and carried to a convenient place for burial in the foredunes.'

Kersey sat back in his chair allowing time for this to sink in, then went on, 'Just add the famous necklace found in Wilder's trouser pocket and it seems to me we're not all that far from identifying the chalet where it all began.'

The painter, wrestling with some reluctant noodles, remained silent and Kersey was forced to continue. 'The position of you and your friends would have been more credible if, when Wilder's body was found or when photographs of the necklace appeared on TV and in the press, you had come forward and told us that you were in the chalet during that weekend instead of waiting for our inquiries to lead us to you.'

Angove gave him a quizzical look. 'Are you married, Inspector? Do you live in a cosy little village or in a suburb where everybody knows you as the police inspector? Would you want the bloody-fool antics of your youth broadcast? It's not the sort of thing to worry me but I'm a professional drop-out.'

Kersey said, 'You should have been a lawyer, Mr Angove. But think over what I've said. For the moment, there's just one other point: I believe that you are on friendly terms with Henry Badger at the Modelmakers, and we know that Mr Badger has something of a reputation as a letter writer . . .'

The painter was amused. 'What naughty thoughts you policemen have! Ingenious, too. But a non-starter. I've got nothing against my former schoolmates and, if I had, I wouldn't involve poor old Badger.'

Kersey stood up. 'Very well, I shall leave you to it. We need a formal statement confirming what we already know plus what more you feel disposed to tell us. So let's say, at the local police station at three. I shall be sending someone along.'

The painter had finished his meal and he came down with Kersey to see him off at the shop door. 'Sure I can't interest you in original work by a local artist – a memento of your visit?'

Kersey grinned despite himself. 'Get stuffed!'

Lucy Lane drove to Carbis Bay. From a street map she discovered that Lelant Crescent was between the main road and the coast. She found it without difficulty, a row of modest semi-detached houses which, because of the steepness of the slope, had a commanding view of the bay. Like most of the others in the crescent, number fifteen had an escallonia hedge and a patch of grass with a couple of wind-blown Cordyline palms to proclaim the balmy south-west. Lucy pulled into the kerb, got out, and climbed the steep path and steps to the front door. The bell-push set off a chime which was answered almost at once.

'Mrs Lisa Bell . . . ? Detective Sergeant Lane.' Lucy showed her warrant card.

Lisa was recognizable from the snap taken fifteen years ago, the blonde hair, the rather long face and the thin, prim lips; but she was pale, her eyes were frightened and she had difficulty in finding her voice.

Lucy was taken into the lounge, a large room with the inevitable view of the bay. Otherwise it was depressingly ordinary and correct with a selection of framed prints and ornaments which could have been ordered along with the carpet and the suite.

'What a wonderful view. My name is Lucy. Do you mind if I call you Lisa?'

'If you like.' But Lisa was not interested in small talk 'Why have you come? Has something happened?'

They sat opposite each other in armchairs on either side of the unlit gas fire. 'I've come to talk to you about the necklace that was found with Cochran Wilder's body. I expect you've seen pictures of it and read the description but it's necessary that you should identify it formally.' From her shoulder bag she brought out the polythene bag containing the necklace and passed it over.

The young woman held the package in the palm of her hand, staring down at it as though it were some strange object.

'You are satisfied that it is your necklace?'

'Yes.' The word was barely audible.

'I'm afraid that it will have to remain in the custody of the police until the investigations are complete and whatever court proceedings there may be are over. Then, of course, it will be returned to you.'

Lisa continued to stare at the necklace but she said

nothing and Lucy went on, 'Although Wilder's body was naked, you probably know that his clothes were buried with him. You may not know, because it has not been mentioned by the media, that the necklace was actually found in his trouser pocket. Obviously we have to try to find out how it got there.'

Abruptly, in an uncontrolled movement, Lisa held out the bag. 'Here, take it! I don't want to see it again.' Her hands free, she thrust them together between her knees and leaned forward in her chair, every muscle tense.

Lucy said, 'How did Wilder get hold of the necklace?'

'I lost it.' She said the words as though they were a complete answer to the question.

'Where did you lose it?'

'In the dunes. I don't know where.'

'Can you tell me when and in what circumstances? I mean, when did you miss it? What had you been doing since you last had it?'

She shifted uncomfortably on the edge of her chair. 'I went for a walk. I know I was wearing it when I left the chalet and I missed it when I came back.'

'Did you walk with someone?'

'Yes, with Julian – Julian Angove, just the two of us.'

'Where did you walk?'

'Just down to the beach and back.'

'This was in the afternoon?'

She hesitated. 'In the evening.'

'Before dark?'

'Oh, yes.'

'When you got back from your walk was Barbara – Mrs Hart, as she is now – in the chalet?'

'Oh, yes. They all were.'

'Did she tell you about the man who had asked her if she had seen his friend?'

She answered quickly, 'I don't know. I mean I can't remember.'

'I suppose, Lisa, the necklace had a great deal of sentimental value for you?'

123

'Yes. It had been in the family for a long time. My parents died young and I was brought up by my grandmother so it came to me through her. She had my initials engraved on it and gave it to me on my eighteenth birthday.'

Lisa was having difficulty in holding back tears but she went on, 'I was so anxious to show it off . . . Like a fool!'

'So you must have been very upset when you lost it. Did you spend a lot of time looking for it?'

'Oh, yes, we all did.'

'In the dark?'

'Until it was dark . . . And next day.'

'Cochran Wilder must have arrived in your area at about half past eight, what were you doing at about that time?'

She hesitated briefly, then, 'We must have been searching for the necklace.'

'But you saw nothing of any stranger?'

'No.'

'How long did you stay on in the chalet on the Sunday? I mean when did you leave for home?'

The question troubled her. After an interval, she said, 'It was during the morning some time; I can't remember exactly when.'

'Was the weather still good?'

'Oh, yes.'

'But you wanted to get back?'

'Yes.'

'So you spent only the one night in the chalet – Saturday night?'

'Yes.'

'Who did you sleep with?'

She looked up, abruptly. 'Sleep with?'

'Well there were six of you and only three beds. Don't tell me that you shared your bed with a girl.'

'I slept with Paul.'

'With Paul Drew. All night?'

She flushed. 'No, we didn't stay together.' She looked at Lucy, as though in appeal. 'I couldn't stand it. He was . . . Well, it doesn't matter now.'

'So what did you do?'

'I left him and went into the living room . . . I spent the rest of the night on the sofa.'

'And you weren't disturbed? At some time during that late evening and night a man was killed and his naked body was carried through the dunes to be buried in the sand. All this within a hundred yards of the chalet, but you heard and saw nothing. Is that correct?'

Her answer was inaudible, her features creased, tears came and she covered her face with her hand. Whatever the cause she was genuinely distressed and Wycliffe had warned against applying pressure.

Lucy waited until she had recovered sufficiently to wipe her eyes and look up with a blotchy tear-stained face, then changed the subject. She asked gently, 'When did you first hear that Cochran Wilder was missing?'

'I can't remember exactly but it must have been early in the following week. His photograph was in the papers.'

'You recognized him?'

A sharp, hurt, response. 'What? No. Of course I didn't! I'd never seen him before.'

'Was the fact that Wilder went missing while you were in the chalet talked about among your sixth-form group?'

She sobbed. 'Yes, but we decided not to say anything because we shouldn't have been there.'

'Are you prepared to put all this in a statement?'

'Will it be in the papers or on the radio?' Plaintive.

'Not unless it turns out to be relevant.'

She sighed. 'All right; if I must.'

Chapter Six

It was well past one o'clock and Wycliffe was thinking about lunch. He felt better and he decided that his pride had suffered more than his skull. Still in Bethel Street, he was attracted to the Bay Wholefood Restaurant. It sounded healthy and non-alcoholic, and looking in he saw ten or a dozen marble-topped tables, most of them occupied, and plain colour-washed walls; none of the plastics and laminates which go so well with soggy chips. What more could he want?

'Just one, sir?' He was given a table for two in the fairway. 'Something to drink, sir? We do a good selection of wines including a very pleasant cottage wine made from elderflower . . .' This from a young waitress in a frilly pinafore. He must rid himself of the lingering notion that vegetarians are invariably teetotal. Many of them don't contemplate their navels either.

'Apple juice, please. And I'll have the ratatouille with garlic bread.'

While he was waiting, he took in the clientele; a mixed bag; some of them were visitors but quite a few were obvious locals – men in suits with newspapers; girls in twos and even foursomes, straight out of their shops and offices, chattering away like sparrows. At a table by the window, he spotted GG's red head and, opposite her, the sparse greying curls of her lawyer cousin. Penrose reporting? Their conversation was serious and intent.

They got up to leave when Wycliffe was halfway through his meal and they had to pass his table to reach the exit. Penrose looked vaguely embarrassed, but GG said, 'Congratulations, Superintendent! I wouldn't have put you down as a vegetarian.'

Wycliffe decided to profit from the encounter. 'I was going to phone you, Mr Penrose. I wondered if you could tell me the name of the woman who looks after your uncle?'

'Why? Is there something wrong?'

'He appears to have shut himself up again, or whatever it is he does, and I'm rather anxious to talk to him.'

Penrose looked concerned. 'I suppose he's about due for another spell, but I'm afraid the woman won't be able to help you.'

'All the same . . .'

'Very well.' Resigned. 'She's called Trewin – Elsie Trewin, I think, and she lives somewhere in Bal Lane, I've no idea of the number. It's off Norway Square.'

'I don't suppose you have access to the place, Mr Penrose?'

Penrose actually laughed. 'The very idea would give the old man a stroke!'

'What about you, Miss Grey?'

'Me?' A grim smile. 'I never go there unless I'm sent for.'

'And that happens?'

'Oh, yes, it happens; I am his niece.'

She turned to her cousin. 'We're blocking the gangway, Arnold.'

When he left the restaurant Wycliffe checked again on the Modelmakers, which was still shut up, then he strolled through the narrow main street, blocked to vehicles by a lorry unloading. There were drifting tourists, mainly pensioners, but the resident population was still in evidence, going about its business in the streets and shops, not yet submerged by the flocks of high-summer migrants.

He found Bal Lane, a double row of cottages with granite steps up to their doors. Some of them had earthenware bowls on the steps, bristling with daffodils, vivid, blatant and beautiful. Occasionally there was a cat as well; drowsily elegant. A woman, cleaning her front window, directed him to number five.

His knock was answered by Elsie herself, middle-aged, lean, dark, going grey and inclined to be waspish.

'Mr Badger? You're going to be unlucky. I couldn't get in this morning to do my work.'

'Has he gone away?'

'That's asking. What you want him for?'

'I called on him yesterday and I wanted to meet him again. Does it often happen like this – I mean that you are unable to get in?'

'Sometimes. Are you from the police? What's he done now? More letters?'

'Perhaps we could talk inside?'

'I suppose so.' Without enthusiasm she led him into the little sitting room, which after the sunlit street seemed almost dark.

Wycliffe said, 'As far as I know Mr Badger has done nothing wrong.'

'Well, that's something.' She straightened a picture over the mantelpiece and became more communicative. 'He's a bit queer. You asked me if he's gone away and the answer is I don't know for sure. I mean, it happens. Things is going on as normal for three or four weeks together then, without a word from him, for two or three days at a time, I find myself locked out. I've got used to it.'

'What happens?'

'I turn up there, usual time, and one fine morning there he is, same as ever. He always says he's been away, but it wouldn't surprise me if he just locked himself in. I mean, where would he go?' Mrs Trewin echoed the words of the lawyer. 'And there's usually some food missing out of the freezer, not much – but some; and people tell me they've seen lights on there at night when he's supposed to be away.

'I asked him once why he couldn't tell me when he

128

wasn't going to need me, and he said, "Why the hell should I? I pay you just the same." So now I don't bother. I mean, if people don't want you to take an interest . . .' She shrugged. 'Anyway, not to worry! It's Friday today, he'll be about again by Monday, that's for sure.'

Wycliffe said, 'I'm concerned about Mr Badger and I'm asking these questions in his interest. I think you know, or at least suspect, more than you've told me.'

With great care she was rearranging the window curtains to arrive at a gap which met with her approval. 'I don't want to get drawn into something, but I'll tell you this, whether he goes away or locks himself in, he looks like death afterwards. And there's always bottles in the bin-bag in the yard that he thinks I don't notice.'

'Whisky?'

She gave him a quick, appraising look. 'Brandy. But if you say I told you, I shall deny it.'

'Does he have visitors?'

'I'm only there mornings. I see the lawyer now and then, and sometimes there's the health-shop woman.'

Wycliffe returned to the sunshine and rejoined the strollers. He was in St Ives with no transport and he would have to get a lift in a patrol car. He made his way to the nick, thoughtful. So the old grey Badger went in for more or less regular but solitary binges.

So what?

All the same, the more he learned of the old man the more uneasy he became, though he had difficulty in finding any logical reason for his concern. Unless Badger was a real threat to the six, or to any one of them.

There was, as Kersey had said, a smell; something which offended that delicately sensitive organ, the copper's nose. For a fleeting moment he thought he had the glimmerings of an idea, but it faded as he tried to bring it into focus. In any case he was mixing his metaphors.

In practical terms he had to find a cast-iron link

between the dead boy and the six. It was just possible that the chalet might provide it. After all, somebody had thought it worthwhile to break in. But if nothing came out of the chalet he would have to adopt Kersey's tactic and start to turn the screw on one of the six. That, he felt sure, would be a messy business and do nothing to address what he believed to be the broader issue.

At the nick he had to wait while they called in a patrol car to take him back to Hayle and the Incident Room.

Iris Thorn, the new DC, had been given the job of getting some background on the chalet party when they were pupils in the sixth form at John Harvey's Grammar School. But police officers, like middle-aged men in plastic raincoats, tend to be suspect in the vicinity of schools. Iris was told that there was no member of staff available in a position to help. Persistent, she was given the address of a retired teacher, Geoffrey Prowse, who had been head of the sixth form in the seventies.

New to her role as a DC, she experienced a slight trepidation at the prospect of interrogating a school-teacher; it was hardly five years since she had been on the receiving end herself.

She found the Prowses in a former farmhouse off the Zennor road, overlooking the sea. Warrant card in hand, she said, 'I would like a word with Mr Prowse if that is possible.'

Mrs Prowse, plump and good-natured, looked twice, swallowed, and said, 'Oh yes, dear. Of course. The school phoned to say somebody might be coming from the police.'

She found Geoffrey Prowse in his study, seated at his desk, surrounded by books and maps which overflowed on to the floor. He seemed an amiable specimen of the breed and Mrs Prowse spoke of him as she might have done of a large pet dog. 'He spends most of his time in here when he isn't at the county records office or the museum. But he's no trouble.'

There was, of course, the standard view of the bay, a single vast sweep from Clodgy Point to beyond Godrevy.

Prowse removed his spectacles, looked from the girl to his desk then back again. 'I'm having a go at a new county history.' He said it with a mixture of bravado and diffidence. 'Quite an undertaking; there's a lot of excellent work from the past to live up to, but there are always gaps . . .'

It took a few minutes to get him orientated. 'Nineteen seventy-seven . . . That was the year before I retired . . . Give me a name . . .'

Iris had briefed herself. 'Gillian Grey, Alan Hart – there were six of them.'

A quick smile. 'I'm with you – GG and her little coterie. Odd, that was; such an unlikely grouping. Young people are so intriguing, don't you think? So unpredictable! Anyway, what do you want to know?'

It was evident that whatever rumours were circulating Prowse had not heard them. In any case he was more intrigued by his visitor. He kept looking at her and turning away quickly, as though caught out. Iris was used to it.

'This is a confidential inquiry, sir. It might be useful to know whether those six young people achieved what was expected of them in their examinations?'

Prowse, puzzled, became more wary. 'I can't imagine why you should want to know such a thing, but there can be no harm in telling you that to the best of my recollection, they did not.' He hesitated, looking at her again, this time doubtfully. 'I suppose you know about our examination system? . . . A-levels, and all that?'

'I think I have a rough idea.'

The gentle sarcasm was not lost on him. 'Of course! I'm sorry, my dear! You must excuse an old man.' After a pause he went on with a mischievous grin, 'I've accustomed myself to the invasion of this county by the Windmill Hill people, the Beaker folk, the Celts and the Saxons—'

131

'But the Afro-Caribbeans make one too many.'

They had a good laugh over this and from then on he was eating out of her hand. He got up from his chair, crossed the room to some bookshelves and came back with an exercise book. 'I suppose it's absurd, but I still keep my records of the examination results and final placings of all the sixth formers who passed through my hands while I was tutor.'

He turned the pages of neatly arranged columns. 'Here we are – A-level results for seventy-seven . . . I had forgotten how poorly . . .' He broke off. 'I suppose I ought not to enter into details, although the results of public examinations are public property. Anyway, I will tell you this much, Alan Hart got into medical school, but not the one of his choice, and only by the skin of his teeth. Julian Angove got into his art college, but there the academic requirements were not high. Of the remaining four, three who were expected to go on to university failed to secure places.'

Iris decided to push a little. 'In your opinion, was this due to last-minute nerves? Or had they thrown up the sponge earlier?'

'They certainly hadn't thrown up the sponge. I don't know about nerves but it must have been something which happened late on. I see from this that their results in the February mock examinations were fully up to expectations . . . They seemed to go to pieces in the last two or three weeks before the real thing; there was even a certain amount of absenteeism which is most unusual at such a time . . .' Prowse fiddled with the papers in front of him. 'All I can say is that I and their subject teachers were surprised and disappointed by their results.'

'And this did not apply to the other candidates?'

Prowse was emphatic. 'By no means. Seventy-seven was a good year, a very good year.' He spoke as though discussing a vintage. Then a new aspect seemed to occur to him and he became more schoolmasterish. 'But I must say, young lady, that I am at a loss to understand where all this is leading. You surely can't be investigating something in which they might have been involved all that time ago?'

Iris said something about the possibility that they had been witnesses to an incident.

Abruptly, Prowse put two and two together. 'You are talking about the body in the dunes. Oh, dear! Surely these young people could not possibly . . .' He was as much fascinated as shocked by the notion.

She said, 'To be frank, we are casting about for anybody – anybody who might help us with our investigation. At this stage there is no implication of guilt.'

But Prowse's thoughts were following their own line. He said, reflectively, 'GG – everybody called her that, even the staff – Gillian Grey; she had a good deal of charm, but I'm afraid she was not a good influence on those who became her friends.'

She thanked him and left him to his county history, with good feeling on both sides.

Kersey said, 'Fox seems to think he's struck oil and he wants to know whether to carry on or hand over to Forensic.'

'What's he found?'

Kersey grinned. 'I gather it's a hole in the floor, but you know Fox. "The preliminary indications are that there may be a link between the chalet and the crime. It is too early to speak with certainty . . ." ' Kersey mimicked Fox's precise yet elliptical style. 'I didn't bother with cross-examination on the phone; I've tried it before.'

'Shall we have a look? Take my car; you drive. But before we go, is there anything else?'

Kersey shuffled among the reports. 'There's one item that might amount to something. Potter, on house-to-house in Phillack, came across a young girl. It seems that some couples around here still go for walks instead of straight to bed—'

'Give it a rest, Doug!'

'Yes, well, this girl and her boyfriend went walking on the towans last evening and she says there was a car parked in the clearing and another tucked away in a little alley between two chalets. When they came back the car in the alley was gone, but the other was still there. She doesn't know anything about cars so Potter dug out her boyfriend. He says the remaining car was a grey Rover saloon – an up-market job.'

'Mine.'

'Looks like it, sir.' Kersey was grinning broadly. 'He wasn't sure of the other. Could have been an Escort, and probably red.'

'What time was this?'

'They were both vague about time.'

Lucy Lane had left Wycliffe's car parked by the Incident Room. He disliked motor cars but they were indispensable so he got others to drive him whenever he could.

The sun was still shining but clouds were building up from the west. The forecast, which had promised heavy showers in late afternoon, looked like being right. As he and Kersey left the car and set out for the chalet a strong gust of wind, funnelled by the dunes, rippled the surface of the sand.

When they reached the chalet they could see the sea. The scene was dramatic; blue sky and sparkling sea were being invaded from the west by masses of leaden cloud beneath which the sea was turning almost black with crests of startling whiteness. The door of the chalet was open and, just inside, Fox's photographic gear was stacked in its canvas covers. They could see through the living room into the kitchen and just beyond the spot where Wycliffe had been attacked, Collis, Fox's long-suffering assistant, was on his knees by a gap in the floorboards. He muttered something and Fox's head came round the door.

'It's all right to come in, sir. I've finished in the living room.'

The carpet in the main room had been rolled back, exposing the floorboards. On the big table, clipped to a drawing board, was a plan of the chalet, and clustered in a certain area of the plan were small, numbered crosses. Also on the table were four or five glass specimen tubes, each with a label, and each containing what looked like a quantity of soil.

Fox switched to his lecture mode. 'I've taken detailed photographs of the chalet as I found it and, as you see, sir, I am preparing the usual plan—'

'What's in the specimen tubes?'

'Ah! As you see, the carpet is rolled back. It certainly wasn't here fifteen years ago. The floorboards were treated with a wood stain and it is my belief that at that time they had mats on the bare boards—'

'And the little tubes?'

'I was coming to that. They contain material scraped from the gaps between the floorboards. As you will see, in places the boards have shrunk—'

'You had some idea in mind when you began your scraping?'

'Yes, sir, I did. I had spotted a couple of very tiny fragments of glass so I scraped every gap and collected the material.'

'You found more glass?'

'Yes, several glass fragments and others which look like bits of china. I've plotted where they were found on my plan. You will see that they are concentrated in an area where the table now stands. On the evidence I would say that there could have been some sort of struggle in which a number of glass and china utensils were smashed. Most of it was swept up but those tiny fragments remained lodged between the boards.'

Fox was very good at his job but it was hard to take

him seriously. Quite apart from his pedantic manner, he was physically a cartoon character; abnormally long and thin, his legs in particular suggested that they had been expressly designed for that discriminating stalking practised by flamingos along the margins of African lakes.

Wycliffe said, 'That's a good start. Anything else?'

'Yes, sir, there is the matter of possible bloodstains. In the same general area as I found the particles of glass, I noticed that the boards were discoloured in a way that I associate with very old bloodstains. I lifted one of the boards and found that the discoloration was more pronounced where the wood stain didn't reach.'

'The blood had seeped through?'

'If it is blood, sir. I'm by no means certain.'

'You've done very well. We must get Forensic on to the bloodstains.'

But Fox had not yet finished. 'You may have noticed that this chalet is built into the side of a small but steep dune so that although there are several steps up to the veranda, and one can even walk about under the front part of the chalet, the kitchen, which in my opinion was built on later, is on almost level ground, and its floor is nowhere much more than a foot above the sand.'

It was Kersey's turn to stem the flow. 'So you've found something under the floor in the kitchen. Is that it?'

Fox said, 'No sir, I have not found anything under the floorboards, not yet anyway.' Fox had no love for Kersey and he turned back to Wycliffe. 'The fact is, sir, a small section of the floor in the kitchen had already been lifted when I arrived. I assume that it was done by whoever was on the premises when you were here last night . . . If you will come this way . . . Watch out for the hole.'

The hole, which Collis was still investigating with a torch, had been made by removing three boards.

Fox said, 'I removed two additional boards to make it easier to see whatever might be hidden under the floor but there seems to be nothing there.'

'So?'

Fox became even more pedantic. 'I cannot, of course, speak with any certainty but in my opinion whatever was under the floor was removed by last night's intruder. In fact, I wouldn't be surprised if that was the purpose of his visit.'

Wycliffe had a disquieting vision of the intruder taking off with vital evidence under his very nose. It also occurred to him that if he had taken another step into the kitchen he would probably have had an injured leg to worry about as well as a sore head.

But Fox was still talking. 'I suspect that the object removed from under the boards was soft and compressible, perhaps a blanket or a rolled-up rug which had probably become bloodstained. The intruder, who must have known exactly where to look, had to drag it up through the narrow space, with the result that there are fibres adhering to the edges of the boards.'

It was difficult to congratulate Fox who gave the impression that such were his skills that he could effortlessly repeat these feats anywhere and at any time. Wycliffe did his best but Fox had another trick up his sleeve. From a canvas bag he produced a brace-like tool in a polythene bag. At one end it had a chisel shape and at the other a socket.

'It's a tyre lever and wheel brace, sir. From the tool kit of a car. I found it on the kitchen floor and I suspect that the intruder used it to break in and, later, to attack you. Fortunately there are good identifiable prints. It's a question of matching them against those of possible suspects.'

Kersey said, 'The red Escort.'

They had not noticed the darkening sky and suddenly the rain came, beating on the roof and blowing in through the open door. Fox rushed to close the door to protect his precious equipment. Collis had given up his hole and was hovering in the kitchen doorway.

Collis, whom Wycliffe was convinced grew physically

more like his sergeant day by day, was hesitant. 'I can see glass in the beam of the torch, Sarge, and quite large bits of china. It's some distance in and we shall have to lift other boards to get at it.'

Fox said, 'All right. I'll see to it later.'

'It could have been thrown in there when they swept up before they pushed the rug in.'

'Do you know that it was a rug, Collis? Have you become an expert on fibres?'

'Well no, Sarge, but they looked like they came from—'

'Yes, well, don't let speculation run away with you, Collis.'

Wycliffe said, 'I'll make arrangements with Forensic to examine the timbers. You'd better get your scrapings off to them right away in case they're contaminated with blood; the fibres too. They should be able to tell us what sort of material they came from.'

They scuttled back to the car through the rain. The sand was turning from almost white to pale brown. Once in the car Kersey said, 'How does Collis stick it? He tags around after Fox like a dispirited dog, and Fox treats him like one.'

'I expect he sees Fox as his pack leader.'

Kersey sighed. 'God help him!'

All the same, Fox had done a good job. The argument in favour of a struggle was strong: probable bloodstains, minute fragments of glass and china trapped between the floorboards, and larger pieces apparently hidden under the floor. Add to that a rug (or blanket) which had recently been removed and it all amounted to real evidence – for a change.

Kersey said, 'All the same it would help even more if they found a bloodstained lump of concrete under the floor.'

'True.'

When they arrived back at the Incident Room, they found DC Thorn typing a report. She stood up as they came in with the obvious intention of saying something, but Kersey cut her short.

'Did you see the school people?'

'I talked with the group's sixth-form tutor. He's retired now. He said that the six had unexpectedly poor results in their examinations.'

'I suppose it's in your report? . . . What about the statements?'

'DC Curnow and I divided the interviews between us, sir. He took Dr Hart and Lisa Bell, while I did Gillian Grey and Julian Angove—'

'What did Angove have to say? Where was he last night?'

A flicker of amusement. Iris evidently had memories of the painter. 'He said that he was in all yesterday evening – that he usually found his entertainment at home.'

'And Paul Drew?'

'We weren't able to interview Paul Drew—'

'You mean he refused?'

'No, sir. I telephoned his office and they said that he was unwell and wouldn't be in today.'

'So you went to the house?'

'No, sir. As we were told to avoid marital complications where possible we thought it best to wait for instructions, but—'

'Then we'd better find out about this illness; sounds too convenient to me. Where's DS Lane? Where's Curnow?'

'I'm trying to explain, sir.' Patient.

Wycliffe, on the sidelines, was intrigued. The girl's manner matched her presence. Unhurried and unruffled, she went on, 'Fifteen minutes ago there was a call from Mrs Drew reporting that her husband was missing. It seems that he went off in his car last night and she hasn't seen him since—'

'She took her time! So we notify all stations to look out for him. He probably hasn't gone far. Just panicked.

You've got his reg number? Where's Lucy Lane? Where's Curnow?'

'We don't have his number, sir, Mrs Drew couldn't remember it, but she did say that it was a red Escort. I gather she was very confused on the telephone and DS Lane has gone with DC Curnow to sort it all out.'

Kersey followed Wycliffe into the inner office. 'We shall have to watch that one. Too smart for her own good.' He caught Wycliffe smiling and grinned himself.

Wycliffe said, 'I only hope she hits it off with Lucy Lane.'

'Yes, well . . . Anyway, what do you make of this little lot, sir? The last couple of hours have changed things a bit, don't you think? I knew that Drew would crack one way or another and it's obvious it was he who tapped you on the head.

'Now it's a question of what's happened to him. Has he just cleared out? He can't be such a fool as to imagine he could get away with it. Suicide is more likely in my book for that type. On the other hand, it's just possible that the others saw him as an unacceptable risk.'

Wycliffe sat back in his chair and massaged the back of his skull. 'Don't be daft, Doug. Drew may be on the run, he may even have done away with himself, but as for the others having got rid of him . . . These people are not a bunch of cold-blooded killers. They're scared, perhaps too scared to think rationally, but they're hardly likely to start killing each other.'

Kersey lit a cigarette. 'I've known you a long time, sir, and I think you have a reason for holding back. We are close to being able to show that Wilder died at the chalet in violent circumstances, probably some sort of fight, and that these six were responsible for concealing his death by burying the body. We haven't got the whole story yet but there's enough to screw the rest out of them.'

Wycliffe was silent for a while, then he said, 'I'm holding back because I think that to some extent we are being led by the nose – those bits of nonsense sent through the post, appearing to threaten the six, the attempt to implicate them through a photograph sent to me . . . It's phoney, Doug – stage-managed; and I want to know who did it, and why.'

Kersey tapped ash from his cigarette into a tin lid. 'Does it matter? The pointers were in the right direction.'

Any comment from Wycliffe was rendered unnecessary by the telephone. 'The chief's on the line, sir.'

'Charles?' . . . Wycliffe signalled to Kersey to stay.

'I've been reading the reports. Anything fresh?'

Wycliffe told him.

'Then what are we waiting for, Charles? A video recording?'

Wycliffe was frosty, pushing protocol to its limit. 'I will take action, sir, when I have sufficient evidence to sustain it; in particular when I have the forensic report on material taken from the chalet. That should be early in the coming week.'

The chief capitulated. 'All right, Charles! All right! But you don't fool me; I can't help wondering just what hare you are chasing. It's as well old Wilder seems to have quietened down. With any luck I shan't have him on my back.'

Wycliffe put down the phone. 'At least we've got a stay of execution.'

'But you'll need to be careful, sir.'

'I shall be. Don't worry.'

They spent the next half-hour going through the statements and reports, which filled in gaps but told them nothing really new. It was part of the documentation process which occupies half the man-hours spent on any case, and has become a matter of obsessive concern since the Guildford Four, the Birmingham Six and the Cardiff Three.

Rain beat down on the roof of the little office which was built on to the main building. The windows were steamed over and the atmosphere was claustrophobic. Lucy Lane arrived and joined them. Wycliffe had coffee brought in and the three settled around the table.

'Well?'

Lucy made a gesture of distaste. 'That woman is impossible! I'm not surprised that Drew has cleared out; I only wonder why he waited for this. At any rate I've got the gen on his car: red Ford Escort, reg number F426 AFZ. Curnow is putting it out. As far as I can tell, Drew has taken nothing with him except the clothes he stood up in. She thinks he's got a couple of credit cards in his wallet.'

Wycliffe had rarely seen Lucy so incensed.

'She said with a sort of glee that he'd got no friends or relatives to whom he could go and she showed not the slightest interest in getting him back. She made a point of explaining that she was financially independent and that they have separate bank accounts. Her main concern was about possible publicity.'

'Did she want to know why we were involved?'

'No, she seemed to think that a missing husband was more than enough to bring us in. Incidentally, I've got a fairly recent photograph; do you want it circulated, sir?'

Wycliffe hesitated. 'Give it until morning. Has anybody talked to Drew's partner across the road?'

'Not yet, sir.'

Wycliffe glanced at his watch. 'I might catch him before he shuts up shop for the night.'

The young woman was just putting the cover on her typewriter but she was almost welcoming. 'I know who you are. You want to see Mr Stanton?' And without waiting for an answer she had picked up the telephone.

Stanton, short and stout, neat, brisk and balding, came out to greet him. 'I've been half expecting a call . . . Come through and take a pew!' He sat in his executive chair, elbows on the arms, finger tips together, judicial. 'I take it this is about my young partner. I don't mind telling you I'm worried, Superintendent – very worried. I've tried to talk to his wife but, between you and me, that woman is a fool.'

Wycliffe said, 'You may know that Mr Drew has been of some help to us in connection with the death of Cochran Wilder fifteen years ago. I am not suggesting that he was criminally involved. I understand he did not turn up for work yesterday morning and his wife told you he was unwell.'

'When I telephoned her, yes, but—'

Wycliffe cut in. 'Since then Mrs Drew has reported that she has not seen her husband since last evening when he went off in his car. Have you any idea at all where he might have gone?'

The pale blue eyes looked at him over rimless half-glasses. 'None whatever. I knew nothing of Paul's private life apart from his unfortunate marriage.'

'As a matter of routine I must ask if you suspect any irregularity, any defalcation—'

It was Stanton's turn to interrupt. 'Nothing like that, Superintendent, I've checked; though such a thing would be hardly possible with my system, anyway.' He went on, 'There is, however, one small matter that might interest you; Paul returned to the office at some time during last evening or night.'

'How do you know?'

'I think my niece might be better able to explain that, Mr Wycliffe. In the outer office. It's connected with her machine and Sandra understands it; I don't.'

Wycliffe followed him out.

'Sandra, tell Mr Wycliffe what you found when we opened this morning.'

Sandra whisked the cover off her machine like a conjuror opening his act. 'Well, that's one thing, the cover was on the floor. But he also left the machine switched on. I mean, he sometimes comes in here after hours and uses it but he'd never leave it like that unless he was in a state.'

'Is there any way of telling what he actually used it for? Isn't this a word processor? Wouldn't there be a record on disc?'

She gave him a winning smile. 'I see you know what you're talking about, Mr Wycliffe; but you can use this as an ordinary typewriter and when I came in this morning it was in the typewriting mode.' She picked up the cover to replace it. 'So, unless he used a carbon there's no way of knowing what he did.'

Wycliffe turned to Stanton. 'I suppose it's certain that it was Drew?'

'Unless someone else had his key. There are only two keys; he has one and I have the other.'

Odd. Presumably Drew had used the machine to write to someone. An explanation? A justification? A farewell note? If it had been any one of these it should turn up somewhere.

He thanked Stanton and the girl, and left.

That evening they were all three at the Copperhouse Arms. They ate in the little dining room overlooking the courtyard garden and they had it to themselves. It was still raining; no cat and no tortoise to be seen.

'Rabbit pie tonight,' the landlady said.

'*Rabbit* pie?'

'That's what I said.' She turned to Wycliffe. 'You'll remember what rabbit pie was like before the myxo – better'n any chicken, specially they battery things, an' that's what you'll have tonight. Tommy Burton from up the road do go out shooting an' he brought me in a han'som brace this lunchtime. It'll go down well with a lager or a bottle of medium to dryish white . . . Nothing too heavy – not with rabbit.'

She was right on all counts and the pie seemed to melt in the mouth.

Afterwards they settled comfortably to gossip over their coffee until Wycliffe said, later than usual, 'Time for my walk.'

But he walked only as far as his car, parked by the Incident Room, then he drove to St Ives. The roads were quiet. He left the car behind the Sloop then walked along the Wharf. A light wind blew in from the sea, sweeping curtains of misty rain before it. It was grey overhead and there were heavier clouds out to sea. Dusk was closing in and the harbour lights were on; half tide, with the water darker than the sky.

In the painter's upstairs room the curtains were undrawn, and he could distinguish two forms seated at the table by the window.

The lifeboat house, the public toilets, the footpath by the sea; a gentle surge broke in lilliputian waves against the rocks and across the sand. There was a light in a window of GG's flat and he noticed for the first time that there was a back entrance to the premises. He turned up into Bethel Street; GG's shop and the Badger's faced each other blindly across the junction. There was no-one about and apart from a solitary street lamp, no lights anywhere.

He had no particular objective in mind, but he persuaded himself that he could think more clearly about people when he shared with them the sights, sounds and smells which were the background of their lives. He felt certain Badger was at home. He was not in his shop. Was he in his workshop? In his kitchen? Or sprawled on his bed, drinking himself into a stupor?

The man both intrigued and repelled him. Badger had got under his skin, piercing the flimsy veneer of his self-confidence. It rankled. But had he truly professional reasons for his interest? It was easily possible that the old man had sent the anonymous bits of nonsense to at least five of the established citizens who had once, in their adolescence, been panicked into crime. But he suspected something more than that; something at the same time more adult and more sordid; and he saw Badger as the possible victim rather than the perpetrator.

Wondering about his true reason for being there, Wycliffe walked up the hill beside the high wall of Badger's wilderness garden and came to the alley. With no expectation that it would yield, he tried the latch of the plank door and it opened.

There was a path of sorts through the waist-high growth of weeds and he reached the back door of the house without difficulty. Again he was in luck; the door into the house was not locked. For form's sake he banged on it but there was no response so he let himself in. This time he had brought a pocket torch. He was in the kitchen. He called out, 'Anyone at home?' But his voice echoed in emptiness. He searched for a light switch and brought a forty-watt bulb to life.

Apart from a modern freezer, the kitchen could have been lifted complete out of an issue of *Ideal Home* from the early fifties. But, forty years on, neglect had brought squalor. He went through into the workshop, dimly lit by the street lamp outside, and walked past the skeletal model to the shop door. Nothing seemed to have changed. Back in the kitchen he called up the narrow stairs, again with no response. It was only when he reached the landing that he found Badger.

Badger was sprawled, head down, on the second flight of stairs. His head rested on the landing while his feet were some way up the flight. It looked as though he might have tripped at the top and fallen forwards. The stair carpet was everywhere frayed and in holes.

Wycliffe found a light switch. The old man's head was twisted sideways, his eyes were open and staring, and the hand that Wycliffe felt was cold; the fingers were flaccid. Badger had been dead for some time, long enough for rigor to become established and then to disappear.

Wycliffe looked down at the slight figure, dressed as he had first seen him in the same baggy trousers, the grubby shirt and unbuttoned waistcoat. The thin face was unshaven and his wispy grey hair stood out like a halo.

Wycliffe remembered: '. . . I don't fancy dying as a cover-up for others.' And then, 'All I'm asking is that *if* anything happens to me I shan't be shuffled off to the crematorium with no questions asked.'

There was a telephone in the workshop; he remembered seeing it on his first visit. He went back downstairs and telephoned Kersey at the pub. 'I'm at the model shop. Badger is dead. It could have been an accident, but it could equally have been arranged to look like one. We shall need the whole works.'

Chapter Seven

Friday evening

High-ranking CID officers who know their place do not discover bodies, nor do they get clobbered over the head; they have risen above such diversions. So, when he had telephoned, Wycliffe had to remind himself that this night's work might mean a court appearance with his notebook. He fished it out of his pocket and recorded incident, location and time. It was 22.09. Then he went back upstairs.

Both protocol and the Book dictated that he should now await the arrival of his experts, but if it had been his habit to heed either he would not have been there in the first place.

On the landing, looking up, he saw that the second flight of stairs ended at a door which stood open, presumably to another room. There was no landing up there so it was easy to imagine Badger, preoccupied or drunk, coming out of the room and tumbling down the stairs. In the poor light, Wycliffe could make out nothing of the interior of the room so he climbed the stairs, edging around the body, and went in. He fumbled for and found a light switch. The room was a typical attic, sloping ceiling, exposed rafters, dwarf walls and dormer window. It was large and everywhere there was chaos. Books had been swept off shelves; a filing cabinet had been emptied by the simple expedient of pulling out the drawers and upending them on to the floor; and the drawers of a desk in the dormer had been similarly treated. On the top of a wooden cupboard there was an ancient typewriter; the cupboard doors were open, and three of the shelves were empty, their former contents, a great quantity of magazines, were heaped in a mound on the floor.

On the fourth shelf, the bottom one, there were several bottles of brandy, unopened. The only other items in the room, apparently undisturbed, were a series of framed charcoal cartoons which hung above the bookshelves, presumably the work of Julian Angove which Badger had admired. One of them stood out: Badger himself, instantly recognizable; his skull-like head and skinny neck were set on a tiny body built of struts and ties like the model downstairs. The initials J.A. appeared in one corner.

The old man must have had an objective view of himself to appreciate that.

And on a grubby piece of cardboard pinned to a rafter there was a quotation, written in a good bold flowing script with a felt pen: 'All that is solid melts into air, all that is holy is profaned – Karl Marx.' No arguing with that. At least the sage got that one right.

But Wycliffe was trying to take in the message of the immediate chaos about him. It was blatant: there had been a search. Too blatant?

Anyway, one thing was clear; if he wanted to know more of what had made the strange old man at the bottom of the stairs tick, this was the place to start. He walked over to the desk. By the desk was a chair and on the desk-top a bottle of brandy, a goblet with some of the spirit remaining, and an open book – *Thomas Creevey's Papers*. It looked as though Badger had been easing himself into a literary bender.

Wycliffe returned to the typewriter: a pre-war Remington, almost a museum piece. The anonymous bits of nonsense which had been sent to five of the six, and the cut-out photograph sent to the police, had all been addressed on a vintage typewriter, the type poorly aligned and much worn. No problem for the experts to decide whether or not this was the machine.

Those messages, in particular their style, had troubled

him; there was something childish about them, reminiscent of the way one kid will sometimes hiss at another 'I know about you!'

For a little while he stood, looking out of the window. Due to the steeply rising ground and the extra storey, he was a good deal higher than any of the properties around. There was an uninterrupted view of the bay. He could see Godrevy light, and away to his left the lights of the town; while below him the narrow streets of the junction were wet and gleaming under the street lamp.

As he watched, a police car slipped into place beside the shop. No flashing lights, no siren. Sensible. Time to go down.

It was Lucy Lane with a uniformed PC. 'Mr Kersey has gone to the Incident Room; the doctor is on his way. Fox too. He and Collis finished late at the chalet so they're staying overnight with some of Fox's relatives in Hayle.'

Odd to be reminded that Fox must have relatives like other people. Wycliffe knew that he had a wife and that they were childless, but of his life away from work no-one had any inkling.

It was Lucy's first visit and she looked about her in the dark workshop with curiosity. Wycliffe was tired and his head was beginning to throb, but she looked as fresh as the girl who's had Vitabran for breakfast. He watched her as she stood looking down at the body of the old man, her expression grave and compassionate.

'So this is Badger . . . I wish I'd met him.' Then she turned to Wycliffe, 'I suppose the question now is, did he fall or was he pushed?'

Wycliffe smiled to himself. That was Lucy.

'If you look at the chaos upstairs it might help you to sort out your ideas.'

The uniformed man had been left outside to direct new arrivals and they heard somebody downstairs. Wycliffe went down. It was the irascible Dr Hocking.

'Oh, so we've got the brass here. What's happened to the old Badger to bring you in?'

'You know him?'

'I should do. He's been my patient for twenty-odd years. I suppose he's dead?' He followed Wycliffe up the first flight of stairs. A brief examination, then, 'Can I disturb him?'

'As little as possible. I want photographs.'

The little doctor shrugged. 'Well, he still stinks of drink and he was almost certainly drunk. I suppose he fell down the stairs.'

'And that killed him?'

Hocking became more cautious. 'Perhaps not, in itself. His heart was dodgy and that probably let him down finally; he's been asking for it for some time, pickling his liver in regular drinking bouts.' He looked at Wycliffe. 'I still don't understand what all the fuss is about.'

Wycliffe said, vaguely, 'It looks as though there was an intruder.'

'In other words it's not my business. All right, what do you want from me?'

'Can you give me any idea how long he's been here?'

'By divination, I suppose. Well, he's been here long enough for rigor to have come and gone, as you must know. Say twenty-four hours, which means he was killed on Thursday night. Are you going to have him shifted?'

'To the mortuary. I want Franks to do the PM.'

'So there is something fishy.'

'As far as you know, did he have any friends?'

'I believe there's a painter chap who comes here . . . Badger was a funny old bugger, a loner. Intelligent, well read . . . And a first-class craftsman . . . But there was a daft streak. Arnold Penrose, the lawyer, is his nephew and I reckon he's had his work cut out, keeping the old man out of trouble . . . Anyway, is that all? If so I'll get home to my bed.'

Wycliffe saw him to his car, and as he was returning to the house Fox arrived with his van.

From the workshop he telephoned Arnold Penrose. A female voice, incisive, non-committal, recited the number.

'Mrs Penrose? . . . This is Chief Superintendent Wycliffe. I would like to speak to your husband if he is available.'

'I'm sorry; he is not. Do you want to leave a message?'

Wycliffe did.

Penrose joined them around midnight. He looked from his uncle's body, up the stairs. 'I suppose something of the sort was bound to happen sooner or later. His heart . . .'

'I don't want to involve you in technicalities tonight, but I assume that there is no-one else we need to inform? I mean, you are looking after his affairs?'

'Yes.'

Penrose was not drunk but he had, as the Irish say so precisely, 'drink taken', and he seemed to have difficulty in focusing his ideas. 'Yes . . . Yes, I suppose so. As far as I know, there is nobody else directly concerned with his affairs.'

Fox had photographed the body, according to the Book, 'from every angle', and the mortuary van arrived shortly after Penrose.

Wycliffe said, 'There will have to be a post mortem. I shall ask the coroner to nominate Franks.'

This appeared to shake the lawyer. 'Franks? But the PM is no more than a formality, surely?'

'I would like you to take a look upstairs.'

Penrose stood in the doorway of the attic and surveyed the chaos in silence. Finally, he said, 'He must have done this himself. I mean, why would anyone . . . ?' After a pause he went on, 'Where did that typewriter come from?'

'At least you will understand that there has to be an investigation. Everything will be left as it is until the morning but there will be a constable downstairs.'

Penrose seemed dazed. 'Of course you will do as you

think necessary. I must admit this is beyond me at the moment.'

It was after one when Wycliffe and Lucy Lane returned to their cars, leaving a constable on watch. All the surrounding buildings were in darkness, the peace of the neighbourhood had not been disturbed. The rain had gone, it was a clear night and overhead there were stars.

They joined Kersey in the Incident Room where he had stayed to handle any development that might have arisen. Wycliffe gave him a brief update and all three crossed the road to the Copperhouse Arms, and bed. They had keys, so they let themselves in with as little noise as possible and for once there was no telephone call to Helen.

Wycliffe made up his mind that he would be a long time getting to sleep and he lay there staring at the dim rectangle of the window. His room was at the back of the house, away from the street lamps. Half-awake, half-dreaming, he was thinking of Badger, when the model maker's head seemed to materialize out of the darkness, the thin features, the straggling moustache and wispy beard, but as the image seemed about to come into perfect focus, it faded.

Wycliffe turned over on his side, muttering, 'Badger fell down the stairs.' And a moment later he added, 'All these steps and stairs!' And fell asleep.

Saturday morning, 16 May

Before breakfast he telephoned Helen and confessed to his knock on the head. 'In case some idiot gets it into the papers, believe me it was nothing . . . Yes, I've seen a doctor and he agrees.'

'You'll be home this evening?'

'Yes, but I have to look in at St Germans on the way. I should be home by about half-seven, but I can't say for sure at the moment.' He had to make up his mind whether to put the inquiry on hold over Sunday. Even in a murder case he had to take account of overtime as well as the need to give everybody a break.

They breakfasted in the little dining room of the pub, all three of them feeling like the morning after. Wycliffe and Lucy Lane had fruit juice, toast and coffee; Kersey ventured on a boiled egg.

Wycliffe yawned and felt his bump. 'I shall be leaving this afternoon; I have to be at St Germans by six. I want a house-to-house in the Bethel Street area. Find out if anyone saw or heard anybody or anything during the whole of Thursday evening and night. Obviously we are interested mainly in Badger's place and the health shop – remember, by the way, there's an entrance to her flat from the sea side as well as through the shop. But don't set a limit to their inquiries. Let's hear about anyone seen in the locality whom the residents can put a name to.'

'Do they tackle the lady herself?'

'Why not? Get it organized, Doug. Curnow, with the help of a uniformed man, should be able to manage that. For the rest of us, short of any dramatic developments, we shall pack it in this afternoon until Monday. We haven't had Franks's report on the Badger PM, and I doubt if we shall hear from Forensic on the chalet stuff until early next week. I'll arrange for Division to notify me if anything crops up – in particular if they pick up Drew or his car.'

He turned to Lucy Lane. 'Fox will be starting at Badger's place. For today, let Iris Thorn join the team. It will be experience for her if only in getting used to Fox's little ways.' And then, to Kersey, 'I want you to keep an eye on that set-up, Doug.'

Kersey said, 'What will they be looking for in particular?'

'Obviously, anything which links Badger with the six – anything at all. And you'd better fix for somebody to look at that typewriter and compare the type with the anonymous notes. I've no doubt they'll match, but we need to be sure. It's important that Fox should record any prints which might turn out to be identifiable.'

The rain had moved away overnight and the morning was warm and sunny. On their way to the Incident Room, Kersey, as usual, bought the *Morning News*. And on the front page, with a two-column spread near the bottom, was a report under twin headlines:

Police Chief in Mysterious Attack

Link with Wilder Tragedy?

It has just become known that on Thursday evening Detective Chief Superintendent Wycliffe was assaulted while investigating a break-in at a holiday chalet on the towans at Hayle. Mr Wycliffe, who was alone at the time, was not seriously hurt, but there has been no explanation of how a senior officer came to be involved in such an apparently trivial incident.

It is known that the police were showing considerable interest in the chalet before the attack, probably because of its proximity to the dunes in which the body of Cochran Wilder was uncovered on Monday. At present officers of the Area Crime Squad are engaged in a detailed examination of the chalet and we understand that certain objects have been removed for forensic examination . . .

Wycliffe muttered under his breath and pushed the paper aside. Kersey growled, 'And now they've got a dead Badger.'

Wycliffe was in a curious mood. Perhaps because he was tired, he felt oddly detached and yet responsible. He seemed to be watching a play in which he had no part and over which he had no control. He was trying to discover a plot which eluded him, and he felt guilty.

Badger had called him off the street to say, 'I want you to know that my life may be in danger.' Admittedly the old man had refused help and warned against interference. 'I shall resent any attempt you make to pry into my affairs.' All the same . . .

Kersey was saying to Lucy Lane, 'As I see it Badger's death at this time is the kind of coincidence that a hungry shark wouldn't swallow. Apart from anything else, are we to believe that he created all the havoc we saw last night himself?'

Lucy agreed. 'On the other hand, if somebody killed him and searched the place, what were they looking for? In the chaos they created I would have thought they were unlikely to find much.'

Kersey said, 'Panic. My money is on the estate agent, Drew. It was obvious when I talked to him that he was teetering on the edge. He decided to remove evidence from the chalet, got trapped, and landed himself in a bigger mess by clobbering the chief. Then, frantic, he turns on Badger in the belief that the old man was the other source of danger. He broke in when Badger was out for his evening walk, searched the place, and was caught in the act.'

The exchange was for Wycliffe's benefit and Kersey was coat-trailing as usual, this time with Lucy Lane aiding and abetting. But Wycliffe would not be drawn. All he said was, 'So, for one reason or another we've got to find Drew, and I don't imagine that's going to be too difficult. When we hear what Franks has to say about Badger's death and what Fox and Co find in the model shop, I hope we shall be in a better position to make up our minds.'

Restless, he decided to look in at the Modelmakers again. From the first he had been uneasy about the nature of any link Badger may have had with the dead boy or, for that matter, with the six, and he had been inclined to minimize their importance. But now Badger was dead and as Kersey said, that was a coincidence too many.

Saturday. No school, but Lisa and Martin had breakfast at the usual time. Martin had eaten his toast and was drinking his second cup of coffee. The eight o'clock news was on the radio and Lisa listened, tense in the fear that each item as it came might tell of a fresh development, a new threat. But the Wilder case was not mentioned.

She felt that she was nearing the end of her tether. In the bathroom mirror she had seen the face of an older woman, haggard; and when Martin came downstairs to breakfast he had remarked, uniquely, 'You look peaky. Don't you feel well?'

'Now the local news. A report has just come in of the death of a well-known figure in St Ives. Mr Henry Badger of the model shop on the corner of Bethel Street, who for many years has lived alone in the rooms above his shop, was found dead last night at the bottom of a flight of stairs leading to an attic. It seems likely that his death was due to falling down the stairs but the police are unable at the moment to exclude entirely the possibility of foul play. An investigation of the circumstances is under way.'

Lisa, her hands clenched beneath the table, whispered, 'Oh, God!' But she controlled herself.

Martin said, 'He was asking for it, an old man living alone like that.' He added after a pause, 'Funny old boy . . . He's been there ever since I can remember and he doesn't seem to have changed much.'

It was unusual for Martin to be so reflective.

Lisa plucked up courage. 'I don't know what you intend to do today but I saw Barbara Hart yesterday in town. She's pregnant again and I promised I would look in for a chat some time this morning. It would probably mean staying to lunch.'

Lisa was lying, and she was not very good at it, but Martin seemed not to notice. 'I thought you'd cut yourself off from your schoolfriends. You've said so often enough.'

'I know, but she was very pleasant and anxious for a bit of gossip so I didn't like to be awkward. If you could get yourself something for lunch – there's plenty of stuff in the freezer.'

'I expect I'll manage. It might even cheer you up.'

GG was in her office behind the shop. She had no client with her and she was staring out of the big window without seeing the familiar scene. People passed along the footwalk from time to time but she did not see them either. Arnold had telephoned her at two in the morning, his manner almost professional. He had offered no consolation or reassurance and he was non-committal. 'We shall have to see where this leads.'

GG told herself, 'He's washing his hands, the bastard!'

She had listened to the eight o'clock news with its hint of foul play, and their parting shot, 'An investigation of the circumstances is under way.' What circumstances? Arnold had told her no details.

Adding to her concern she had in front of her the *Morning News*, 'Police Chief in Mysterious Attack'. She looked at the telephone, she had to talk to someone. Julian was no use. Alan Hart would be in the middle of his morning surgery . . .

One of the shop girls tapped on the door and came in. 'A Mrs Bell wants to see you.'

She was about to ask who Mrs Bell was when she saw Lisa standing in the doorway. 'Lisa! I can never think of you as Mrs Bell.'

GG's welcome was unexpectedly warm; the two women had exchanged no more than a passing greeting in years.

'My dear! You look all in. Let's have some tea. I'll get one of the girls to . . .' She went through to the shop. A very different GG.

They were sitting opposite each other with their tea cups on the desk . . . Lisa was still nervous. 'I hesitated about coming. I thought you might have clients . . .'

'No clients on Saturday. Saturday is my day off.' She reached into a drawer and brought out a packet of cigarettes. 'It's the only time I can smoke in here, too. You mustn't let them smell it, and they've got noses like bloodhounds. Have one?'

'I don't, thanks.'

GG had lit up and was taking that first luxurious drag. 'It's all that keeps me sane, but most days I have to sneak upstairs.' She broke off. 'You don't have to tell me why you're here. I can guess.'

GG pushed back her mop of red hair.

Lisa said, 'I don't think I can take much more. Nothing could be worse than just sitting back and waiting for the next thing.'

GG was looking at her through a cloud of tobacco smoke. 'Keep your voice down. Those two in the shop have ears like microphones.' She pushed over the *Morning News* and pointed. 'Have you seen this?'

Lisa read the report through to the end and when she had finished she looked up. 'You think that was Paul?'

'Who else? He's crazy. He's never been normal – you, if anybody, should know that. And then he goes and marries that ghastly woman. After all, who was it who started all this?'

Lisa was shaken by the matter of fact, almost casual way in which GG referred to events of which she could not bear to think, let alone speak. And yet, the fact that it was possible to talk brought with it a feeling of release.

In a timid voice scarcely above a whisper, she asked, 'And the old man? Do you think Paul . . . ?'

GG didn't bother to answer directly. 'It's always the weak ones who turn to violence. Alan did his best to get some sense into him before it was too late but he was over the top and now he's cleared out.'

Lisa shivered. 'That night . . .'

'Don't think about it.'

'But when they catch him . . .'

'*If* they catch him.'

Lisa raised herself to the sticking point. 'You really think Badger sent us those . . . those notes?'

GG tapped ash from her cigarette. 'Arnold thinks so; although he denies it to the police. It's the kind of trick the old man's been up to lately.'

'But how did he get to know about us?'

GG frowned. 'That's a question; but we don't know what tongues have been wagging over the years. In any case, Julian has been a regular visitor across the road.'

'Julian? You can't believe that he would want to cause trouble for us.' Lisa was gathering her courage. 'And then there's the photograph – somebody cut me out of the photo Barbara took and sent it to the police. That's how they found out about the necklace.'

GG looked at her, eyes narrowed. 'I suppose Julian had a copy of the photo like the rest of us. I wonder if he's got it now.'

'But why would he want to stir up all this? It could only do him harm.'

GG stubbed out her cigarette. 'I think we should get together, all of us, and talk this out.'

Wycliffe drove to St Ives, parked his car, and walked along the Wharf. It had become almost a routine, but today the sun was shining and there was a taste of summer in the air. The little shops in Bethel Street selling paintings and books were emerging from hibernation, their windows gleamed, there were fresh pictures on show and some of the doors were open. But the Model-makers had not changed. Wycliffe went up the hill and entered by the back way. A constable in the kitchen said, 'They're upstairs, sir.'

Lucy Lane was in the sitting room on the first floor. The furniture was quality stuff from the fifties but there was a pervasive smell of damp and disuse. A bloom of mould on the arms of the leather chairs, and on the tops of little tables; peeling wallpaper, and a large damp patch on the chimney breast told their tale of neglect.

Lucy said, 'The others are up in the attic. I thought I'd take a more general look around.'

Although there was such chaos in the attic, nothing seemed to have been disturbed elsewhere. Did this mean that the searcher had found what he was looking for upstairs?

Lucy went on, 'This room sheds a different light on Badger's past.'

It did. Along with some quite acceptable landscapes on the walls there was a single framed photograph, a wedding photograph. The lean Badger, beardless, but with a good head of brown hair, middle-thirties, a figure of dignity in a well-cut suit, stood close to his bride. The bride, an attractive young woman in pale blue with a broad-brimmed hat, carried a bouquet of carnations, and the groom wore a buttonhole.

'Harry and Lydia 2 September 1951' was inscribed at the bottom.

Wycliffe protested, 'Coombes told me Badger married a widow. That girl is younger than he is.'

Lucy said, 'I suppose there are widows under thirty. But look at these.' She opened an album that was lying on an occasional table and turned the pages. 'This was in the lacquered cupboard by the window.' More photographs of the couple, mostly in climbing gear, roped together or alone on some precipitous slope, abseiling down a vertical face or clinging to invisible finger and toe holds. There were cryptic labels: 'In the Fells', 'Chamonix', 'At the Climbing School', 'Snowdonia' . . . The dates were spread over five years and the photographs covered eight or ten pages of the album; the rest was empty.

'You carry on snooping, I'll take a look upstairs.'

The attic had been tidied; Iris Thorn had piled the magazines (all architectural publications) in heaps, and was stacking them in the cupboard from which they had come. Collis was working through the books still on their shelves, examining them one at a time. Fox was still sorting the litter of folders, letters and pamphlets which had come from the filing cabinet.

He turned to Wycliffe. 'No luck, sir; nothing so far, anyway. Nothing that could connect Badger with the chalet lot.'

'The typewriter?'

'Oh, that's a different matter. I got a chap over from Redruth who knows about typewriters and he's prepared to give evidence in court if necessary. He's in no doubt that the anonymous communications were addressed on the Remington machine in the attic. He says the type itself is unusual, it's also out of alignment in distinctive ways, and at least eight of the letters have defects which identify them.'

Fox stroked his long nose. 'If you ask me, sir, whoever searched the place went off with the evidence we are looking for, evidence that would have incriminated him and his friends.'

Wycliffe was watching Collis working through his books, unhurried but never stopping: pick one up, flip through it, put it on the shelf, pick up another . . . Given the job, Collis would have worked through the Bodleian at Oxford with the same equanimity.

Wycliffe said, 'You've seen a lot of searches conducted by amateurs in your time, Fox. Did you ever see one which created the kind of senseless havoc you found here?'

'Panic, sir.'

'You think so? You don't think the whole thing was a fake? People who fabricate evidence usually over-do it.'

'I can't see the point, sir.'

'What about prints?'

'The old man's everywhere, apart from that just two strangers, a man and a woman – several specimens of the man's, only two of the woman's.'

'The keys of the typewriter?'

'Wiped clean, and that takes a bit of doing.'

'Compare those you've got with Penrose, Angove and the Grey woman.'

'Yes, sir. And still on the matter of prints, I've checked those on the wheel brace with the ones on the photograph Drew gave Mr Kersey. They match. It was Drew who clobbered you, sir. No doubt about that.'

For the first time Wycliffe took a look at the other framed charcoal drawings above the bookshelves. Badger was probably right, Julian Angove was wasting his talent on pot-boilers. Here was a series of contemporary political figures in the guise of *Alice* characters: John Major as the White Rabbit with the Maastricht Treaty under his arm, John Smith as Old Father William, balancing an eel labelled 'Middle Class' on the end of his nose . . . Lord Tebbit as the March Hare . . . Wycliffe chuckled, and earned a strange look from Fox.

Wycliffe said, 'Good! Carry on here for the rest of the day, then pack it in. Come back on Monday and work through the rest of the house.'

Wycliffe had lunch at the café in Bethel Street. Neither Penrose nor GG was there. So it was Drew who had clobbered him with the wheel brace. No surprise about that. But had he then gone on to the Modelmakers to devastate the attic and assault Badger?

After his meal Wycliffe drove back to Hayle and spent an hour with Kersey in the Incident Room. Shortly before he left, the telephone rang and he answered it. 'Put her through.'

It was Molly Bissett, sounding unusually disturbed. She spoke in a low voice. 'I wanted to make sure that you will be here this evening . . . Earlier if you can make it . . . Something has cropped up . . .' She finished hurriedly, 'I can't talk now.'

Father playing up? Trouble at the funeral? Wycliffe was puzzled. Molly Bissett was not the sort to become flustered.

He turned to Kersey. 'I'll be off then; see you on

Monday. Make the most of the weekend.' He collected his bag from the pub and set out for St Germans.

He arrived there shortly after five. The sun was shining and the street was deserted except for a car parked here and there and a dog asleep outside the pub. The white gate of Franklin's stood open. He left his car and walked up the drive between the sombre laurels. Two cars were parked in the open space before the house. Molly answered his ring almost at once. 'I'm so glad you've come.' She lowered her voice. 'He's had a very disturbing letter and it's upset him.' Then, speaking normally, she added, 'We're in the drawing room.'

This was the room he had been in before. Two men stood up as he entered. Wilder was instantly recognizable from his TV exposure, heavily built, short necked, loose jowled and florid. The other was Molly's naval-officer husband, tall, slim, greying and dignified, looking vaguely uncomfortable in civvies.

On a low table in front of the fireplace there was a decanter of whisky and glasses. Molly's introductions were perfunctory. 'You've spoken to father on the phone, now here he is in the flesh; and this is my husband, Tony; I've told you about him. He's supposed to be in Gibraltar but he flew home for the funeral.'

They were all three on edge. Wilder said, 'Drink, Wycliffe?'

'Thanks, but I still have to drive home.'

That seemed to put the damper on any thaw there might have been.

'Anyway, let's sit down.'

Molly said, 'Tony and I will leave you to it. I'll make some tea; I'm sure we can all do with a cup.'

When they had gone Wilder mumbled, 'Good of you to come, Wycliffe, in view of what's gone before . . . Anyway, I'm asking a favour.' He fished in an inside pocket and produced a folded piece of paper. 'Here, read this! It came this morning but I said nothing until after

164

the funeral. Of course you've got to see it, but I'd give a lot to keep it out of the hands of the media.'

Wycliffe unfolded the paper, obviously a piece from which a printed heading had been roughly cut away. It was typewritten and unaddressed, a statement rather than a letter. Wycliffe noted that the type itself was modern and faultless but the text was telegraphic and disjointed. The spacing was uneven and the punctuation erratic. A man at the end of his tether trying desperately to seize upon a few salient facts from the tumult of his mind and commit them to paper.

'It was an accident nobody wanted your son to die He was being turned out for what he had done to a girl he was naked and we were going to throw his clothes and his belongings after him he was standing at the top of the steps calling us names when somebody gave him a push he overbalanced and fell and hit his head on the concrete He was dead It was an accident and we were scared we were terrified. What we did after that has never been out of my mind We did not want to hurt your son it was an accident We did not . . .' And there the statement ended.

Wycliffe took time to read it and when he had finished he said, 'Very strange.'

'Is that all you can find to say?' Wilder, instantly aggressive, calmed down almost at once. 'I apologize! I'm on edge.' He looked at Wycliffe, his eyes moist and his voice barely under control. 'Do you think that's what happened? Do you think this man, whoever he is, is telling the truth?'

'I think that your son's death was accidental in the sense that it was unintentional. This is only one person's version of the circumstances, but I have no doubt that, broadly speaking, it is true.'

Wilder beat out a tattoo with his fingers on the arm of his chair. 'No, neither have I. It's got the stamp of truth. And all this happened in the chalet place they've mentioned in the papers?'

'I'm waiting for forensic confirmation but that seems to be the case.'

Wilder muttered to himself, 'A fight over a girl.'

Wycliffe said nothing. The black marble clock on the mantelpiece chimed the half-hour and abruptly Wilder leaned forward and reached for the decanter. 'Let's have a drink!' He poured whisky into two glasses. 'A small one won't push you over the limit for God's sake!'

Wycliffe would have been glad of that cup of tea but Molly was keeping away.

Wilder pointed to the typewritten sheet which now lay on the table between them. 'You know who wrote this, don't you?'

'I suspect; I don't know.'

Wilder said nothing and the silence lengthened. He sipped his drink. Once or twice he seemed to be on the point of speaking but did not. In the end it came. 'This group in the chalet on whom my son is supposed to have forced his company; how many, and how old?'

'There were six of them, all aged seventeen or eighteen; three boys and three girls. They were all at school preparing for A-levels.'

'I suppose you've talked to them. What do they say?'

'Up until now they've denied having seen your son.'

'They must be in their thirties now . . . My boy would have been thirty-six.' Wilder shifted violently in his chair. 'God, what a mess . . . This necklace all the fuss has been about – how do they account for that?'

'The girl it belonged to says she lost it in the dunes and that your son must have picked it up.'

'Do you believe that?'

It was Wycliffe's turn to remain silent.

'He was ill, Wycliffe; mentally ill. Do you think I don't blame myself for sending him off like that? . . . I thought he was cured; he was so plausible . . . The hospital . . . Bloody doctors!'

It was clear that Wilder was screwing himself up to a commitment. It came at last in the form of a question, but put so casually that it might have had no significance at all, 'Could the whole thing be dropped . . . ? If there was an open verdict from the coroner . . .'

'You know very well, sir, that it would not be up to me; it would be a matter for the Crown Prosecution Service.'

'But your private view?'

'I think that wounds should be given a chance to heal.'

Wilder looked at him. 'You're a good chap, Wycliffe.' He got up and crossed to the door which he opened, and bellowed down the corridor. 'What happened about that tea, Molly?'

Wycliffe arrived home at a little after seven. The two women were in the kitchen preparing a meal and he had a warm welcome. Even Macavity consented to purr when scratched behind the ear. Wycliffe kissed his wife and daughter and thought that Ruth looked better, less strained.

'How goes it?'

She smiled. 'Sometimes I feel as though I've never been away. Of course I miss him.'

The ritual sherry.

Helen said, 'Let me feel your head.' She did. 'Yes, well, it doesn't seem too bad but you're too old to be getting up to tricks like that. Now, by the time you've had your shower this will be ready.'

The ritual cleansing. He hoped that it might wash away a clinging sense of guilt. Badger had been put into cold storage – and that was more than a metaphor. Paul Drew was on the loose somewhere, and there were at least five other people on tenterhooks, wondering where it would all end; and that did not include Wilder. But everything stops for tea.

After their meal they walked down the garden to the water and along the tideline to St Juliot, their nearest village. Across the estuary the lights of the city flared in the night. It brought back memories of night walks along the shore when the twins were young. He felt nostalgic, sentimental, but he could not get the Wilders out of his mind.

Abruptly, he said, 'Ruth, do you remember when you were in the Sixth at school?'

'Of course I do, why?'

'I don't mean the things you did, but how you felt about certain things when you were in your late teens.'

Helen said, 'You'll have to be more specific, Charles.'

'I was afraid of that. I'll try again. Looking back, do you think that in certain circumstances, along with your friends, and out of anger or fear or even loyalty to those friends, you might, conceivably, have committed or connived in a serious criminal act?'

He thought how easy it was to make a sensible question sound like ponderous nonsense.

Ruth was silent while they crunched over the sandy gravel for another fifty yards or so, then she said, 'You sound like a policeman, Dad – or worse, like a lawyer, and I've just realized what you're getting at. It's the Wilder case, isn't it? Why not come out with it? Through listening to the news and hearing you talk I've got a pretty good idea of what's in your mind. You don't think he was deliberately killed, do you? . . . I suppose it was a fight where tempers got out of hand.'

'Not even that. As far as I can see it was no more than a quarrel which led to a scuffle in which Wilder got pushed down a flight of steps. And I've no doubt they were shocked and horrified by it. But what troubles me is their planned, cold-blooded cover-up. To take Wilder's body, wrapped in a sheet, and carry it through the dunes to a suitable spot and to bury it along with his belongings . . . To me, that seems inexplicable behaviour for a group of average sixth-formers . . . Can you understand it?'

They were passing the backs of little houses, outposts of the village, and there were lights in some of the windows. Boats were drawn up on the shingle, others were moored off, and ahead they could see the shadowy outline of the disused jetty.

Wycliffe had given up expecting a reply and when it came he was surprised by Ruth's grave, reflective manner. 'Yes. I can understand it. At that age, and in a group, I think something like it could have happened to me. With my schooldays coming to an end and my whole future suddenly under threat, I might easily have panicked and at least have followed somebody else's lead in a cover-up.'

Wycliffe would have liked to probe further but Ruth had taken his question to heart, so he said, 'I see.' And after a pause, he added, 'Interesting.'

They climbed the steps to the jetty and picked their way over its uneven surface to the road. Wycliffe was aware that by his question he had created an inexplicable tension.

Again it was Ruth who broke the silence. 'I think there's something else which could have had something to do with how your teenagers reacted. It wouldn't have been wholly out of fear for the future. Part of it might have been that they couldn't face the recriminations, especially the silent ones, from family and teachers. I don't think that parents in particular realize the burden of responsibility they put upon their children merely by being proud of them.'

She broke off with a self-conscious little laugh, then added, 'Now can we change the subject?'

They were passing the pub and Wycliffe, embarrassed by the confidences he had provoked, said, 'Why don't we go in for a drink?'

Helen, who had not spoken for some time, said, 'Yes, let's do that.'

There were three or four customers on stools by the bar and a couple playing pool, but the tables were empty and they took their drinks to a corner – two gin and tonics, and a lager.

*   *   *

Although he was tired Wycliffe lay awake. The moon had risen and despite the curtains the room was almost like day. He was thinking about the strange communication Wilder had received that morning. From Drew of course. Drew had visited the estate agent's office at some time during Thursday night in order to type it; after the fracas in the chalet, the final straw. By that time he had given up all hope, and yet he still had a compelling need to, as he saw it, put the record straight. Was that it? If so, does a man with nothing to lose always tell the truth?

'He was standing at the top of the steps . . . Somebody gave him a push . . . He overbalanced and fell . . . He hit his head on the concrete . . .'

Franks had argued that because the injury was to the vertex of the skull it was unlikely to have been caused by a fall. But a fall occasioned by a push down a flight of steps on to concrete?

There was concrete dust in the head wound. But what concrete? Wycliffe turned over heavily and Helen murmured, 'Can't you sleep?'

He wished that he had in front of him two photographs, one taken by Barbara Hart (as she now was) fifteen years ago, and one of many taken by Fox on Friday morning.

And then he thought of Drew and the declaration which he had sent to Wilder. Unsigned but unmistakably coming from him. Wycliffe's respect for the man was increasing, and his last thought before he gave up and finally drifted into sleep was, 'Poor devil!'

Sunday, another pleasant day, a late breakfast and another walk to St Juliot, this time for the papers. The church bells of St Juliot were pealing, sending their dying ripples of sound chasing each other across the estuary and the countryside. Wycliffe was aware of the Sabbath atmosphere, that sense of calm which, in the countryside at least, seems to have survived Sunday opening, Sunday sport and the Sunday supplements.

Before lunch there was a telephone call from David,

Ruth's twin, who, married with a child, was living and working in Kenya.

Jonathan piped, 'Hullo Granny!' on the telephone and, 'Thank you for your birthday present.' And afterwards Ruth talked with her brother in that cryptospeak which is only intelligible between twins.

The women spent much of the day gardening and Wycliffe was allowed to sit on the terrace, reading and dozing with Macavity for company. He spent some of the time thinking, in a drowsy sort of way – brooding was the better word. There was Helen, the girl he had met by chance more than thirty years ago. Now, like himself, she was on the wrong side of middle age, yet still he could not bear the thought of any separation. And there, working beside her mother was Ruth, their daughter, a grown woman. A little while ago he had spoken on the telephone to their son, to their son's wife, and to their grandson . . .

They were an ordinary family, and yet so very strange.

Last night it had been brought home to him how strange families are.

They had a scratch lunch, and jointly prepared their evening meal which was not entirely spoiled by too many cooks.

Chapter Eight

By previous arrangement with his deputy, John Scales, and Diane, Wycliffe was early at the office and by nine o'clock they had dealt with items which had proved too tricky for the telephone. John Scales's forte was administration, and that was lucky for Wycliffe who regarded an office chair as having all the appeal of a straight jacket.

At the door, on his way out, Wycliffe said, 'Just one more thing, John, see what you can pick up in our legal department about Penrose and Son, Solicitors. They're an old-established firm and they must be known in the fraternity.'

Wycliffe escaped, and was driving out of the car park as the chief was driving in. Just in time; another minute would have cost him at least an hour.

The morning was bright and brassy, that false start which weather watchers know only too well, and by the time Wycliffe reached the moors mist was closing in. In Hayle there was a fine drizzle, insidiously wet.

He arrived there well before eleven and outside the Incident Room he had to run the gauntlet of the press, the largest contingent so far, three men and two women.

'How did Badger die, Mr Wycliffe?'

'I don't know. He was found at the bottom of a flight of stairs with injuries consistent with a fall. I haven't yet had the report of the pathologist.'

'Is it true that his place was ransacked?'

'No. One room – an attic, was turned over.'

'Somebody looking for something?'

172

'It's possible, but if they were I don't know what.'

'Any connection with the Wilder affair?'

'I don't think that Mr Badger was in any way concerned in Cochran Wilder's death.'

'What about Paul Drew?'

'What about him? We are anxious to contact him and so far we have been unable to do so.'

'How is your head?'

'I think I shall live.'

They let him through. Kersey had driven down straight from home and was already well settled in. 'I couldn't get rid of them, they knew or guessed that you were on your way here. Anyway, Franks has been on the line and wants you to ring him back. Lucy is at the Modelmakers with Fox . . .'

'Any news of Paul Drew?'

'Yes. Curnow's house-to-house turned up two people who claim to have seen him on Thursday evening at about eleven. He was walking along Bethel Street in the direction of the Modelmakers.'

'All right! Say it. You knew that Drew was our man.'

Kersey grinned. 'No comment, sir. It's safer.'

'Any of the others seen in the neighbourhood?'

'The lawyer, Penrose. He was seen in Bethel Street around ten, apparently on his way to GG's place, and about an hour later he was seen again . . . Everybody in the neighbourhood knows the drill. He parks his car, by arrangement, in a yard close by and sometimes it's there all night. Incidentally, Curnow spoke to GG and she said she hadn't seen anybody on Thursday evening because she didn't go out.'

'It seems Penrose wasn't with her for long – under the hour according to your witnesses. Has anything come in since?'

'Nothing significant, sir. Nothing more on Drew or his car since those sightings on Thursday evening. It's odd. I could understand it if he was an old hand but the man's an innocent, he hardly knows his way in out of the wet.'

'And his wife is no help?'

'Lucy had a good go but if the woman knows or suspects anything she's keeping it to herself. But Lucy's impression was that she doesn't care a damn what's happened to him. The house is in her name and she's got money of her own. So what? Can you imagine being married to such a woman?'

'Take a look at that.' Wycliffe handed over the statement which had been sent to Wilder.

Kersey read and reread the typewritten sheet. 'Drew?'

'Who else?'

Kersey nodded. 'I could see that he couldn't hold out for much longer; he had to get it off his chest. I wonder which of the girls . . . ?'

'Didn't Lisa Bell tell Lucy that she walked out on Drew in the middle of the night? Where could she go except into the living room?'

'Where Wilder must have been dossing down on the sofa or the floor. It adds up. Are you going to tackle the girl?'

'I would like to find Drew first. In the meantime I want to get some early background on Badger: who he married, how she came to be a widow at such an early age, where her money came from and how she died. She must have been still short of forty then . . . I think I'll pay a visit to Mrs Penrose.'

'The lawyer's wife?'

'His mother. After all she's Badger's sister and it's time we talked to someone who was around when it was all happening.'

Kersey looked doubtful. 'I know you've got an idea, sir, but I can't for the life of me see where Badger's early life comes into it.'

Wycliffe ignored the implied question. 'Of course what I get from Mrs Penrose is sure to be prejudiced, but if there's anything that seems worth following up we can get Coombes to turn up an outsider who knows about the family.'

He was going through his case file. 'Before I ring Franks I want to look at a couple of photographs.' He selected the two which interested him, studied them for a moment, then passed them to Kersey. 'In the first one, the famous photograph of the six, you can see in the background the lower steps of the flight leading up to the chalet as they were fifteen years ago. In the second, taken by Fox, you can see the whole flight of steps as it is today.'

Kersey said, 'Those steps have been replaced.'

'And?'

'There used to be a concrete kerb at the bottom that isn't there now.'

'And it was on that kerb that Wilder hit his head.'

'You're not suggesting that the steps were renewed because—'

'Of course not, but it's something we should have noticed.' He reached for the telephone. 'We'll see what Franks thinks.'

Franks got in first. 'I've had a look at your Badger offering, Charles. Not much of him was there? Not in bulk anyway. So he fell head-first down the stairs; that would square well enough with his various contusions, the fracture of his right ulna and the dislocation of his right shoulder.'

'But the question is, did he fall or was he pushed?'

'I don't know, I wasn't there, but the nature of his injuries makes it clear that he went down head first and that suggests that he might have been pushed.'

'What did he die of?'

'Not as a direct result of the fall. He must have been in a pretty bad way when he reached the bottom, and with his dicky heart he wouldn't have survived for long, but somebody finished him off with a blow to the back of the neck at the base of the skull. I missed it at first but there is no doubt about it; that's what finished him off. It was not a very powerful blow but, unusually, it displaced the atlas vertebra and damaged the cord.'

'Any idea of the weapon?'

'Would you believe a blunt instrument? A stout metal rod for instance, half an inch or more in thickness, would be my guess.'

'Presumably, whoever did it needed to make sure he was dead.'

'That sounds reasonable but they needn't have bothered, the Badger wouldn't have kept them waiting long.'

Wycliffe told him about the steps at the chalet. 'Steps and stairs are a recurring theme in this case. Anyway, it seems likely that Wilder was standing at the top of those steps, being thrown out, naked, when one of the party pushed him and he went headlong down the steps, striking his head on a concrete kerb. Does that sound half-way credible to you?'

Franks hesitated. 'You can't expect a firm quotable opinion off the cuff but, between ourselves, yes, it does. The Badger affair sounds like a repeat performance but without the concrete kerb.'

'Good! That's what I wanted to hear. Thanks.'

Franks was impressed. 'What have I said to earn such effusive gratitude? I'm not used to it.'

The truth was that Wycliffe was beginning to feel on firmer ground; the pattern which he had suspected was defining itself. He turned to Kersey. 'Whether Badger was pushed or not is academic, but he was murdered by a blow to the back of the head. The weapon, according to Franks, could have been a stout metal bar of some sort. I want Fox back at the Modelmakers looking for it. There's a whole armoury of tools in the old man's workshop.'

'There is also the small matter of laying our hands on Drew, sir.'

Wycliffe was almost dismissive. 'Drew will turn up. Meanwhile, I'm going to talk to the dowager Mrs Penrose.'

Kersey said, as though it were an accusation, 'You sound positively cheerful.'

*　*　*

The Penroses lived in a pleasant house in a large garden high above St Ives; overlooking the bay, of course, but now all was shrouded in mist.

Wycliffe's ring was answered by a pretty girl with a mass of chestnut hair to her shoulders; three children in the three to six age range, trailed behind her in the hall, two girls and a boy.

'May I help you, please?' Perfect English – too perfect, the words were handled as though with chopsticks. A French *au pair*?

'Superintendent Wycliffe.' He showed his warrant card.

'Police? You wish to see Mr Penrose? I am sorry—'

'No, I would like a word with Mrs Penrose – his mother.'

'Ah, I will see . . . Be good, children!'

A very attractive girl; jeans and a T-shirt do more for some than the wiles of fashion. She flitted along a corridor and in a couple of minutes she was back. 'If you will come this way, please . . .'

He was taken to a room with a window facing towards the sea. A thin, bony, vigorous woman, waited to greet him. Her white straight hair was cut in an uncompromising 'bob' and she wore a plain grey frock, severely cut. She could have been the retired headmistress of an old-style girls' school.

'Chief Superintendent Wycliffe.'

'Clarice Penrose. I suppose it really is me that you wish to see, Mr Wycliffe?'

Wycliffe assured her.

'Well, that's something these days. Do make yourself comfortable.'

It was a comfortable room: a couple of not-too-easy chairs, a *chaise-longue*, a table and a writing desk, a workbox on casters, a television and plenty of books and magazines.

'This is my room. I come here whenever I am in people's way, or they are in mine.'

Involuntarily Wycliffe was comparing the room with Badger's attic. He expressed sympathy at the death of her brother and she thanked him. 'It is sad, even in old age, to lose someone who shared one's memories of childhood and youth. Henry was only a little older than I . . . Of course he shouldn't have been living alone, but that was his choice.'

Wycliffe avoided the mistake of speaking too soon, before he had heard all he was likely to hear, and he was rewarded.

She seemed to make up her mind to qualify what she had said by speaking plainly. 'All the same, it's no use me pretending that there was deep feeling between us. Although we both lived in the same small town we rarely saw each other.'

It made Wycliffe's task easier. 'I have to tell you that your brother's death was not an accident.'

She was disturbed. 'But he fell downstairs.'

'I don't want to distress you, Mrs Penrose, but it seems that very shortly after he fell he received a blow which was certainly not accidental, and that blow was the immediate cause of death. It raises a question as to whether the fall itself was accidental.'

'You think that he was murdered?'

'I think that is established.'

'Have you discussed this with my son?'

'No, I've come straight to you on the assumption that you and your sister in Shropshire are Mr Badger's next of kin.'

'Yes, and I've already spoken to Jennifer on the telephone.' She hesitated. 'Perhaps I ought to say that my sister and Henry were not on good terms; I doubt if she has had any contact since before they moved up north about five years ago. Of course it was only right that she should be told of his death. I told her that it was an accident because that is what I believed.'

Wycliffe said, 'You must forgive me if I probe, but I have no idea what may or may not be important. Do you know the reason for this rift between your brother and sister?'

She hesitated only briefly. 'I suppose there can be no harm in telling you; it was common gossip at the time. My brother-in-law had a small engineering works in Camborne into which Henry put some money and then, after a year or two, withdrew it for no obvious reason and almost without warning. The works had to close.'

'I see.'

The woman sat, entirely composed, with her long bony hands resting in her lap. Suddenly a fresh idea seemed to strike her. 'I hope you are not connecting my brother's death with the discovery of that young man's body . . . ? My son has told me of your suspicion that Henry might have sent certain rather childish anonymous communications, but it would be absurd to suppose that even if it were true . . .' She broke off.

'I have to look at every possibility.'

'But there must be some other explanation.'

Wycliffe was soothing. 'That is what I have to find out, and I hope that you may be able to help me. I would like to know a little more about your brother's background, his marriage, his circumstances . . .'

She was an intelligent woman and she was trying to match his words against his likely purpose, but she continued to speak with engaging frankness. 'There were no secrets in my brother's life as far as I know, Mr Wycliffe. He qualified as an architect and worked for a London firm where he seemed to do quite well. He became keen on climbing and it was at a climbing school in Scotland that he met Lydia, his wife to be. Lydia was a young widow, very well off, and within a month or two they were married.'

Wycliffe sat back in his chair looking bland and receptive. He rarely asked questions until it seemed that the other party would have no more to say.

'To everyone's surprise they decided to settle in his native St Ives. He was disillusioned with architecture, at heart he was a craftsman, and between them they started the Modelmakers. Henry used his London contacts to secure commissions for architectural models and, at the same time, they developed a profitable business in model boats – precise copies of the originals. Lydia had a flair for sales and they were soon getting orders and commissions from all over the place.'

'So the marriage was successful?'

'In business terms, certainly. I know nothing of the domestic side.' The disclaimer was tart.

There was a perfunctory tap at the door and it opened. 'Oh, I had no idea that you had someone with you . . .'

A woman in her late thirties, very fair; a good figure, well-cut skirt, silk blouse, and patterned waistcoat. A sculptured hair-do which must have presented a problem at night.

The elder Mrs Penrose was not taken in by the surprise act. Her manner was distant. 'My daughter-in-law, Mrs Catherine Penrose; Detective Chief Superintendent Wycliffe.' There was a certain emphasis on the official title. 'Mr Wycliffe has been telling me about Henry.'

Catherine Penrose looked from one to the other. 'Wouldn't it be less distressing for you, dear, to leave all this to Arnold?'

A slight gesture. 'My dear Catherine, I am not in the least distressed. We were having a most interesting conversation.'

There was an awkward pause while Catherine conceded defeat and went out, closing the door behind her.

'Where were we?'

Wycliffe said, 'I was about to ask you when, and how, did Lydia die?'

She stopped to think. 'It must have been in fifty-six. It was an accident. They were on holiday, climbing somewhere in North Wales. I don't know exactly what happened, but she fell and was dead on arrival at hospital.

There was an inquest of course, and a verdict of accidental death.'

'Your brother took it badly?'

Wycliffe was aware of her penetrating gaze. Now each question was being examined and assessed before it was answered. 'At first he seemed to carry on as before, but slowly, over many years, there was a process of what I can only call disintegration.' She made a slight gesture with her hands. 'You have seen for yourself where it led.'

Wycliffe was appreciative. 'You are being most frank and very helpful, Mrs Penrose. I have just one more question. Can you suggest any reason at all why someone might hate or fear your brother sufficiently to contrive his death?'

She pursed her lips which were lightly made up. 'No, I most certainly cannot. He rubbed a lot of people up the wrong way by writing foolish letters and by his general behaviour, but I find it very difficult to believe that anyone took him seriously.'

They parted amicably, pleased with each other. Wycliffe felt that his visit had not been wasted though there remained questions which he could only put to the lawyer.

Wycliffe had no sooner returned to his car than there was a call from the Incident Room. It was Kersey. 'I've just had word from the local nick, sir. I think we've found Drew's car. A woman who lives on the Lelant Saltings, not far from the railway halt, has reported a car parked over the weekend in the drive of an empty house next door to hers.

'She says she saw it first on Saturday morning but she didn't think much about it because it looked like the estate agent's car which, as the house is for sale, has been around several times lately. She did notice that the driver's door was wide open. Because of the trees, she can only see the drive from her attic window and she didn't happen to look again until this morning, when she saw that it was still there, looking exactly the same.

'Out of curiosity she went to take a closer look and found the driver's seat and the interior of the car on that side very wet where the rain had blown in through the open door. It was then that she rang the nick. She had the good sense to take the number. It's Drew's all right.'

'I'll join you out there.'

Wycliffe studied the map. He had to drive back through Carbis Bay to Lelant village, then turn off towards the church. Lelant Church and its churchyard, despite the ghostly mists, looked serene and peaceful enough with its weathered headstones and holm oaks, but more than once in its history it has been all but over-whelmed by sand. The road beside the Saltings is narrow, and a single-track railway separates it from the shore. On the landward side there are houses, screened by trees, and in a lay-by outside one of these Wycliffe pulled in behind a police car. There was a 'For Sale' notice secured to a tree: 'Sole Agents: Stanton and Drew, Hayle'.

The car was not visible until he had passed through the screen of trees; then, there it was, a red Escort, parked on the gravelled drive in front of a substantial Edwardian house. Kersey turned up from somewhere in the shrubbery. 'I thought I'd better wait. Once I'd made sure that we'd got it right, I sent for Fox. He's on his way.'

There was not much they could do. As the woman had said, rain had blown in through the open door soaking the upholstery. Kersey pointed out, 'He's left his keys in the ignition. I suppose as the agent he would have had a house key and he might have kipped down in there, but his car has been here since Saturday at least, perhaps earlier.'

'Let's take a look in the boot.'

With the keys from the ignition Kersey unlocked the boot. It was empty except for a rolled-up pile rug.

Kersey said, 'We know where that came from.'

Wycliffe was restless. 'You hold on here. I'll take a look around.'

A quiet and secluded neighbourhood, the brochure would say. Very. The house was attractive, steep roofs and tall chimneys; 1910 vintage. The front door was set back under a deep porch. Wycliffe tried the door but it was locked, so he went around to the back. The back door was not only unlocked, but open, and Wycliffe had a feeling of *déjà vu*. The door led into a tiled hall with the kitchen off; there was a passage through to the front of the house, and stairs to the next floor – back stairs. There would be a more impressive flight from the front hall.

Wycliffe muttered, 'They still had servants when this was built.' He called out, just in case, then he searched the ground floor: dining room, drawing room, breakfast room, and two others of indeterminate use, all as empty as the removals men could contrive. And it was the same with the first floor. He was left with a narrow flight of stairs leading to the attics.

There were four, and in these odd items of furniture remained. It was in the second of the two at the front of the house that he found Drew. The estate agent was sprawled on the floor by the window in a mess of blood, his thin, pallid features contorted in an agonized grimace, his right arm outstretched, his hand clutching a blood-stained Stanley knife. There were flies, and a smell of putrefaction.

Drew's throat was cut.

'Poor devil!' Wycliffe found himself saying it of Drew for the second time in a couple of days.

Near the body a wicker chair had been overturned. It looked as though Drew had been seated facing the window when the shock of the self-inflicted wound induced a convulsive reflex which tumbled him on to the floor.

Wycliffe looked around the bare attic. On the floor, not far from the body, there was an empty lager can lying on its side and a plastic bag about half-full of potato crisps.

'Why here?'

The situation had been chosen, everything pointed to it. Sitting in that chair Drew could look out over the trees, across the green and ochreous sandbanks and converging channels of the saltings towards Hayle, though now the town was hidden by the mist.

Suicide. It troubled Wycliffe almost more than murder. He was at a loss to understand how (except in a terminal illness) a man or woman finds the courage to choose death rather than life. But he had to be quite certain that this was suicide.

From time to time he had tried to acquaint himself with the elements of forensic pathology, mainly to keep his end up with Franks. His source was an old copy of *Taylor* and he remembered a section on incised throat wounds in which there was a gruesome table setting out the differences between the homicidal and the suicidal. For the suicide the wound or wounds tend to be at the front of the throat, not at the sides; there are often tentative preliminary cuts, and the main cut curves across the throat, deepening, and shallowing. The weapon is usually retained in the hand, firmly gripped . . .

On all counts it seemed that Drew had taken his own life.

Dr Hocking agreed with him but Wycliffe none the less went through the same ritual as he would have done in a case of suspected murder. Fox and Collis were engaged in their double act. Photographs had been taken, measurements made and prints were being sought. Franks was brought in, by which time it was mid-afternoon. Kersey, joined by the rabbit-featured DI Gross, had made the routine arrangements and Drew's car was taken for examination to the garage at Division. The rug from the boot was sent to the area lab.

Franks was puzzled. 'I don't know what you expect me to say, Charles. As you've pointed out, this has all the marks of a classic suicide.'

Wycliffe mumbled, 'All right! I needed to be sure . . .
This man's death could be convenient for someone.'
Taciturn since the discovery of the body, he had that
dogged almost sullen look, which was characteristic of
him when he had made up his mind to a course of action
that was certain to arouse opposition.

The two men were joined by Kersey on the attic
landing where they awaited the arrival of the van from
the mortuary service.

Franks said, 'I suppose you want to know how long
he's been dead?' And when there was no answer he went
on, 'All right, I'll tell you. From the general condition
of the body and the state of the extravasated blood, I'd
say he's been dead about three days. This is Monday, so
that would make it some time on Friday. Of course I
might have to think again after I've had a real look at
him.'

Wycliffe was unappreciative. 'If it really was suicide,
then all this is largely academic and we can leave it to
Gross.' He turned to Kersey, 'Tell him to make sure that
the widow is informed. I shall want you with me so that
we can get on with the real business.'

Lucy Lane and Iris Thorn, deserted by the experts, were
left at the Modelmakers to sort out the contents of the
filing cabinet which, along with everything else in the
attic, had been tumbled on to the floor in a heap. The
object was not so much to tidy the mess as to find
anything which might shed a chink of light on the
enigmatic Badger and his relationships.

'This stuff is all of it fifteen to twenty years old.' Iris
slipped another wad of papers into a file and slapped it
into the cabinet.

They were dealing with outdated correspondence with
firms and individuals, customers and suppliers; and
though the pile on the floor was getting smaller, they had
so far found nothing remotely personal.

Lucy said, 'This man is supposed to have been

well-off, with property and investments. I mean, even if his lawyer-nephew handled his affairs you would expect some correspondence and regular statements.'

In the end they found the statements, almost the last item in the heap; a neat bundle, held together by tape. They covered more than thirty tax years and they were up to date. The form of the statement had varied little and in each case the accompanying letter carried the same florid, embossed heading. The last four had been signed by Arnold Penrose, all the others, by his father.

Lucy said, 'I know nothing about accountancy but he seems to have been very well fixed. We've still found nothing really personal; surely he must have had a private bank account with a cheque book, and bank statements . . . There must have been domestic bills which he paid . . .'

Iris Thorn brushed herself off and perched on a handy stool. 'His money doesn't seem to have done him much good. Do you get many jobs like this? All this work with hardly anything to show for it?'

Lucy found a chair. 'It happens. Taking it altogether, probably more than two-thirds of our time goes in chasing rainbows and writing reports about it . . . But we have our moments.'

The two women were getting to know each other and liking what they found. Iris had a fund of anecdotes about her grandfather's early encounters in London as an immigrant bus conductor and several times Lucy had been heard to giggle, a previously all but unknown phenomenon.

Iris said, 'Feel like a coffee – or tea? There must be something down in that murky old kitchen.'

Lucy got up. 'Let's see what we can find.'

On the next landing Badger's bedroom door stood open and Iris looked in at the unmade bed with its soiled sheets and pillows. 'My dad is a jobbing plumber and he's got a little office where he does his accounts and all that, but his "papers" as he calls them, more personal things, he keeps in a tin box under the bed. It makes a bump in the mattress – very inconvenient sometimes, mum says . . . I just wondered . . .'

'It's worth a look.'

Iris got down on her knees. 'Nothing but spiders.'

But Lucy had opened the little bedside cupboard. On its single shelf there was a bulky A4 envelope, a scratch pad, a ball-point, and a few paper clips. 'Looks as though he did his office work in bed.'

The envelope carried the Penrose imprint in one corner and was labelled, 'Mitchell's Loft and 17 Bethel Street'. The envelope was sealed. Lucy hesitated, 'I suppose we should bring the lawyer in on this, but I think we'll chance it and take it with us.'

Iris Thorn said, 'Let's get that coffee.'

Chapter Nine

Monday afternoon

Instead of returning to the Incident Room as Kersey expected, Wycliffe told him to drive into St Ives. 'We are going to talk to the lawyer, so park behind the Sloop if you can.'

Kersey said, 'Did you really think Drew might have been murdered?'

'No, but I wanted there to be no possible doubt about it.'

'Surely the picture is pretty clear now: Drew does for the old man and then for himself.'

'In this panic you keep talking about.'

'Well, yes. You don't agree?'

'No.'

And that was as far as Kersey could get.

The lawyer was with a client but they had not long to wait. Immediately his client left Penrose came out. He looked a worried man. Gone was the beaming smile and the stock of small chat which had marked Wycliffe's first visit. He acknowledged Kersey, then, 'I tried to contact you over the weekend but they told me you weren't available and I had the same answer from your Incident Room this morning.'

When they were seated in the office Penrose went on, 'I'm afraid I left you with a rather bad impression on Friday night, but it was quite a shock, seeing the old man lying there. And when you seemed unwilling to agree that it was an accident, I was at a loss what to think. As well as being a relative, I look after his affairs, and it will fall to me to administer his estate. I'm naturally concerned to know the post mortem findings. Was it an accident?'

His manner was nervous and plaintive rather than aggressive.

Wycliffe said, 'It is possible that your uncle fell down the stairs accidentally but it seems more likely that he was pushed. In any case, after the fall he received a blow to the back of his head and that was the immediate cause of death according to the pathologist. In other words, he was murdered.'

Penrose shook his head. 'It's hard to believe.' He fiddled with the papers on his desk. 'Is there any news of Drew?'

'He is the reason I wasn't in touch with you earlier today.'

A quick look. 'You've got him?'

'I'm afraid Paul Drew is dead and the indications are that he committed suicide.'

'Good God! How? When?'

'This morning his car was found in the drive of an empty house on the Lelant Saltings. His body was in one of the attics of the house.'

'Bosavern.'

'I beg your pardon?'

'The name of the house – I think it's Cornish for "the house by the river". Anyway, it's where he was born and spent his childhood. The Drews were quite well off at one time. Paul's father was chairman of a small finance company that went bust in the early seventies. A few weeks after the crash the man shot himself. His widow had to get out of the house, salvaging what she could.'

Wycliffe said, 'So that is why he chose to end things there. Childhood memories.'

'It looks that way.'

Penrose ran his fingers through his sparse curls. 'God, what a mess!'

'Presumably you have your uncle's will?'

'His will? Yes, I have a will.'

'I may ask you for a copy later, but for the moment perhaps you will tell me its main provisions.'

Penrose seemed taken aback by the request as well as by the abrupt change of subject. 'Is that relevant?'

Wycliffe was emphatic. 'Mr Penrose, your uncle was murdered and it's my job to find out who was responsible.'

The lawyer looked at Wycliffe with tired eyes. 'But surely we know who was responsible.'

'Do we? Late Thursday evening your uncle was in his attic, three storeys up, with a book open in front of him and a glass of brandy at his elbow. He was not deaf, but his hearing was impaired. How much noise would a visitor have had to make in order to attract his attention and fetch him downstairs to open either the shop or the back door? There is no bell fitted to either – not even a knocker. But even assuming that the visitor was heard and admitted, without attracting the attention of the neighbourhood, which of his possible visitors would he have taken upstairs to the attic?'

Penrose was silent, staring down at his desk-top. When he spoke his voice and manner were subdued. 'I don't accept the conclusion you seem to draw from all this but I can see that you need to satisfy yourself on matters of fact. You asked for details of the will in my possession. It's not complicated. He leaves ten thousand pounds to Julian Angove; the residue to be divided equally between my mother and her sister, Mrs Jennifer Grey – Gillian's mother.'

'What will the residue amount to – very roughly?'

Penrose frowned. 'I can't give you a meaningful answer to that question until valuations have been made.'

'A substantial sum?'

'Yes.' Penrose was becoming more restive. 'You must understand, Mr Wycliffe, that my uncle was a very strange man, deliberately unpredictable – mischievous.'

'So?'

'It wouldn't surprise me if another will turned up,

more recent than the one I hold. For all I know it could be in the hands of another solicitor. He often reminded me that the will I held might not be his final word, or even his current intention . . . He delighted in mystifying people . . .'

Kersey had been listening, saying nothing because he felt out of his depth; now he seemed to touch bottom. 'Perhaps he thought he had good reason.'

Penrose bristled. 'I think you should explain that remark!'

Kersey looked across at Wycliffe for the green light and got it. 'Mr Badger confided to the police that he believed his life might be in danger. He refused categorically to enlarge on that and denied that he was asking for any sort of assistance. What he did want was an assurance that if any suspicion should attach to his death when it came, it would be thoroughly investigated.'

Penrose nodded. 'That's Badger! It doesn't really surprise me.' He turned to Wycliffe, 'Don't you see? He was always play-acting – it was all a sort of game to him.'

Wycliffe said, 'And a dangerous one apparently. Your uncle *is* dead, and he *was* murdered.'

Penrose looked at him and said, with great gravity, 'And I am confident that the man who killed him is also dead.'

Wycliffe seemed prepared to leave it at that. He stood up. 'Thank you for your time, Mr Penrose.'

Penrose followed them out to the top of the stairs, obviously taken aback by the abruptness of the leave taking. 'I hope that our conversation . . .' But Wycliffe was halfway down the stairs.

They were turning up the slope to the car park before Kersey spoke. 'We seem to be a long way from Cochran Wilder and the six youngsters in that chalet fifteen years ago.'

Wycliffe made a curious sound between a grunt and a growl. 'As far as Badger is concerned, this case was never about Wilder; that nonsense with the photograph and the cryptic messages was no more than an opportunist attempt at providing a cover. Badger's death is about money.'

'Anyway, I thought Penrose stood up to it very well.'

'He's a lawyer.'

Kersey said, 'Where to?' They were sitting in the car in the car park.

'It's gone four and we haven't had any lunch.'

Kersey said, 'I noticed.'

'Do you think a glass of beer and a sandwich?'

So they got out again and went into the Sloop. Wycliffe was subdued, almost morose. He held so many pieces. He knew why and how young Wilder had met his death; he understood why the discovery of Wilder's body had led to the anonymous communications, including the mutilated photograph which had arrived on his own desk. He thought he knew why Badger had to die. What he did not know and could not make up his mind about was who of the possible suspects had contrived his death.

He said, aloud, 'Somebody prepared to take a hell of a risk.'

They were sitting at a corner table in one of the bars; there were pictures by local painters on the walls, predecessors of Julian Angove but of greater distinction.

Kersey said, 'Penny for them.'

'You'd be robbed. I was wondering what sort of person is most likely to stake all on a real gamble. Is it always someone with nothing much to lose?'

They drove back to the Incident Room. Hayle, in the late afternoon, under a continuous drizzle, exactly suited Wycliffe's mood. In the big room, beneath the lurid print of Armageddon, Lucy Lane was concocting her report.

Laid out on a trestle table there was a collection of polythene evidence-bags of various sizes, all tagged.

'What's this?' But he knew: Paul Drew's clothes and

the contents of his pockets. There was a typed schedule and he glanced through it. 'What's this pocket tape recorder?'

Lucy Lane joined him by the table. 'Fox brought this stuff in a short time ago, sir.' She picked up a small pack containing the recorder. 'I suppose Drew carried one of these in his work. I believe a lot of estate agents do, to record details of properties instead of making notes.'

'Has anybody played this thing back?'

'Not to my knowledge, sir, but we can do it on one of ours.'

'Then we'd better do it. Take it into the little office and get somebody to bring coffee for three.'

Wycliffe sat in his chair with Lucy and Kersey opposite. When the coffee arrived he said, 'All right, Lucy; let's hear it.'

The tape began to play, there was a certain amount of mush, but the voice was clear enough.

Kersey said, 'That's Drew all right, I'd know that voice anywhere.'

The voice was subdued and the words came slowly, there were hesitations and pauses. 'I am sitting here in this attic room which was mine as a child, and it is here that I shall put an end to it all. For many years I have been conscious of people looking at me in a way that they do not look at others . . . They look at me and they say to themselves, "There goes Paul Drew, the estate agent, the man who . . ." And they smile, a horrid little inward smile. And I ask myself, "The man who what?" . . . And all the time I feel exposed as though television cameras were trained on me from every direction . . .

'Is it the way I walk? The way I look? The way I behave? Is it my marriage? Is it because they know, as my wife reminds me, that in the firm of Stanton and Drew I count for less than the girl in the office? Or is it because all those years ago my father went bankrupt and shot himself?'

There was a break, but the three who were listening

did not take their eyes off the little black box which now emitted only a faint whirring sound.

Then, abruptly, the voice resumed, more husky now, less distinct. 'I ask myself, if it is like that now, what will it be when they *know*? Not only the police, but the newspapers, Stanton, the girl, – my wife . . . I shall be, "The man who helped to bury the body . . . The man who attacked the policeman . . ." '

There was another break before the voice resumed with unexpected firmness. 'I was a fool! I tried, as they say, to put the genie back in the bottle. I went to the chalet . . . It was a futile attempt and it ended in another act of violence . . .

'From then on I behaved like a madman. I think I *was* mad . . . At one stage I drove home . . . I was going to tell everything to my wife . . . Of course I did not, and the next thing I remember is being in St Ives and telephoning Alan Hart from a box near his surgery . . . He said he would meet me there but I don't think he did . . . I know that I went into a pub and bought a can of lager and a bag of crisps . . . I think it was then that I telephoned GG . . . there was no answer but I decided to go anyway . . . I left the car and started walking . . . I walked along by the sea and when I reached the back of GG's place I could see a light in her flat . . . I rang the bell but there was no reply on her entry phone . . . I kept on ringing but it was no good. I thought she must be with Penrose . . . There was hardly anybody in the streets and I just wandered about . . . Then I saw Penrose; he was in a hurry and he passed me without seeing me . . . I thought he must have just left GG so I went back and tried again, but she still did not answer . . .'

The break this time was longer and he seemed to have finished, but after a while the voice took up the story once more.

'I walked back to the Wharf and sat in the car . . . It was then that I decided. The keys of Bosavern were in the glove compartment with two or three small tools I always keep there – *including* a Stanley knife . . . It was as though providence, or whoever looks after these things, was saying to me, "This is the way!" . . . And suddenly I was calm; I knew exactly what I must do, and I felt a tremendous sense of *relief*.

'I went to the office and typed the statement which I intended to send to Wilder's father so that he would know the truth. I put that in the post . . . and I came here.'

Lucy Lane was the first to break the silence. 'Poor man!'

It was a moment or two before anyone moved, then Lucy switched off the tape and Wycliffe, as though in a reflex response, sipped his coffee. It was cold.

Kersey said, 'That puts GG and Penrose in the frame; both or either could have been helping Badger on his way out.'

Wycliffe was staring at the recorder as though at a living witness who might be persuaded to tell more. 'Yes. The chances are that Drew was there in Bethel Street when Badger was killed . . . We must get that into type, and we shall also want certified copies of the tape. You'd better get Shaw on that.' He broke off, but it was obvious there was more to come.

'If we use this properly we can put an end to the charade we've been playing over the Wilder affair and go some way with the other.' He turned to Kersey. 'I want you to arrange for the five remaining members of the chalet party and Penrose to attend here at, say, two o'clock tomorrow afternoon. Contact them in person. They can make it under their own steam or we will fetch them, but I want them here. I don't think any of them will refuse.' He glanced at his watch. 'It's nearly six . . . We've had about enough for today . . . Nothing else, is there?'

Lucy Lane said, 'There is something which might be worth following up. When we finished in Badger's attic, Iris Thorn suggested that we should take a look around in odd places where Badger could have kept some of his more personal papers. In fact all we found was a large envelope in his bedside cupboard. Obviously he'd been looking through the papers in bed but the envelope had been resealed. It carried the lawyer's imprint, and it was labelled, Mitchell's Loft and seventeen Bethel Street.'

'So?'

'Well, I checked. Gillian Grey's health shop is seventeen Bethel Street, and Mitchell's Loft is the old name for that odd little building where Julian Angove has his studio.'

'You brought the stuff in?'

'Yes, sir. I know I should have checked with the lawyer but if it's of any importance I thought it would be safer here.'

'All right. Let's compound the offence and take a look.'

Lucy fetched the package and Wycliffe examined it. The envelope had been opened, presumably by Badger, and resealed with sticky tape. Wycliffe slit through the tape with a paper knife and tipped out the contents. There were two leases and a covering letter from Penrose. The letter was dated 8 May and headed with the addresses of the two properties and the names of the lessees. The text was simple and brief:

In accordance with our standard practice I enclose two leases which expire at Michaelmas 1992 and I shall be glad to receive your instructions concerning them so that any changes may be notified in good time to comply with the terms of the lease.

Across the bottom of the letter Badger had written two lines in his admirable script:

Mitchell's Loft. Renew. Terms as before.
17 Bethel Street. Lease to be terminated. I intend to repossess.

Wycliffe pushed the letter over to Kersey who read it and passed it to Lucy Lane.

Kersey said, 'Things are looking black for Ginger. If we can show that she had the news before dear uncle was helped over the threshold . . .'

Lucy said, 'The date is interesting – four days before the discovery of Wilder's body.'

Wycliffe was enigmatic. 'We shall have to see. Now, put that in the safe, Lucy, and let's get out of here.'

'It's spare ribs of beef tonight in my own marinade. If you don't like garlic you'd better settle for cold meat, but you'll be missing something if you do.'

They decided that they liked garlic.

'Then you're going to want a glass or two of a nice red to go with it.'

The landlady was not at all bothered by the arcane lore of the gourmet or the wine buff; she knew what she liked and her customers had better like it too. So far there were no complaints from the police contingent.

Kersey was in his element. 'That woman can cook.'

When, over coffee, they had reached the reflective stage, Wycliffe said, 'Well, Doug, do you still think Drew tried to kill the Badger?'

'No. I think he told the truth as he saw it on that tape. We are left without much choice in the way of suspects but, with what we've heard and seen in the last hour I don't suppose we need a choice. Will you tackle her in the morning?'

Wycliffe took time to think. 'No, I shall wait until we have them all together tomorrow afternoon, then let the tape do it.'

Kersey, with a wary eye on Lucy Lane, lit a cigarette. 'But the anonymous threats or whatever they were, and presumably the snapshot, did appear to come from Badger himself.'

'Only because the typing was done on his machine.'

'All right, let's assume it was GG who did it, sneaking

in when the old man was out on his evening walk. But she, after all, was one of the chalet party and by drawing attention to them she incriminates herself.'

Wycliffe agreed. 'That's a point I want to make. I realized that if we looked for Badger's killer among the chalet party it would have to be one who was prepared to have his part in the Wilder affair known, as the price of any gain from Badger's death. If Wilder had been murdered that price would be high, but if his death was accidental the only charges against the group would have to centre upon conspiracy to conceal a death.'

The landlady came over, all smiles. 'I can see you enjoyed that. Like some more coffee?'

When she had gone, Kersey, thoughtful, said, 'I suppose that after fifteen years, bearing in mind that these people were juveniles at the time with no subsequent criminal record, any court would take a lenient view.'

Wycliffe agreed. 'But there would be penalties apart from the law, the publicity and the nine-day scandal. That would bear unequally on the different individuals. The doctor and his wife would probably suffer most. They might have to move, and there could be disciplinary proceedings by his professional body. Then there is Drew, we already know how he panicked at the mere possibility of exposure.'

Lucy Lane cut in, 'And from what I saw of Lisa Bell, she isn't far from panic either.'

Kersey waved smoke away. 'Which leaves GG and Angove. I doubt if exposure would trouble either of them much. With ten grand in his pocket Angove wouldn't even notice it.'

Wycliffe said, 'But it's GG who is in the frame. All the same, a chat with the painter might not come amiss.' He turned to Lucy Lane. 'You haven't met him and neither have I. How would you feel about putting that right this evening?'

'I would like to.'

'Nothing planned?'

Lucy grinned. 'Is it likely?'

'All right, we'll meet him together.'

It was unprecedented. Wycliffe's solitary evening walks were part of an established tradition.

Kersey said, 'You'd better phone and say you're coming, otherwise he probably won't answer the door.'

The skies had cleared, as on this coast they often do in the evening of a thoroughly wet day. Lights were coming on in the streets and houses. They parked behind the Sloop and walked along the Wharf to the painter's studio. There was no breath of wind and the moored craft were dimly reflected in the still waters of the harbour. A few couples strolled along, stopping now and then to look at this or that, and Wycliffe was conscious of the fact that he and Lucy could have been just such another pair.

There was a light in the painter's upstairs room. Wycliffe rang the bell and a moment or two later the shop lit up and Angove came trundling towards them between the double row of his pictures. The door opened and he stood there, stocky and powerful as a young bull, but his manner was bantering rather than aggressive.

'I thought you lot were not supposed to disturb respectable citizens after sunset.'

'You must be thinking of search warrants, Mr Angove, and we haven't got there yet. I am Detective Chief Superintendent Wycliffe, and this is Detective Sergeant Lane.' Wycliffe showed his warrant card.

'All right. I must say I prefer the female of the species, but come on up both of you.'

They followed him through the shop and up the stairs into the long narrow room which had once been a fisherman's loft. Angove drew a heavy curtain across the top of the stairs. 'The draught comes up there like a chimney.'

A bottled-gas stove stood near the window giving out a cosy glow, and three old basket-work chairs were drawn up to it. It seemed that Angove was prepared to be hospitable.

'Elena – my girlfriend – has gone off to bed. She soon gets bored and anyway she needs her sleep.'

They sat down, and when the symphony of creaks had subsided Wycliffe said, 'A lot has happened, Mr Angove, since Inspector Kersey talked to you on Friday. I suppose you've heard that Henry Badger and Paul Drew are both dead?'

Angove contented himself with a simple 'Yes.'

'We believe that Drew took his own life but Badger's death was premeditated murder.'

'I know. Penrose told me.'

'Did he also tell you that he was in possession of Badger's will?'

'No, but I suppose he would be.'

'If no later will is found, you stand to inherit ten thousand pounds.'

It seemed that Angove was taken totally by surprise. His look of astonishment was almost comical. Then he laughed. 'The old bastard!'

Lucy Lane said, 'An odd reaction, Mr Angove.'

He turned towards her. 'I suppose it is, but I can't get over it. Three or four years back I couldn't pay my rent and Penrose was turning the screw so I took a chance and went to see the Badger. For some reason we clicked, we had the same perverted sense of humour. Anyway he told me to forget the rent and we became friends – real friends I like to think. I go to see him – went to see him – often, and he used to say, "As long as you keep me alive, boy, you can swan along doing bugger all as usual, but when I'm gone Penrose will move in with the bailiffs." '

'It seems he liked your cartoons.'

A broad grin. 'Yes, but he would also say to me, "You're the worst bloody painter in this town, and that's saying something. Why don't you sell picture postcards? At least you wouldn't be swindling the punters." '

'Did he talk much about death?' Lucy again.

The painter had been looking her over with approval ever since he had set eyes on her. 'Yes, in a cheerful, cynical sort of way. He pretended to think that there were those anxious to help him out of the world. I suppose he could have believed it, but I never took him seriously.'

'And now?'

'Well, it makes you think.'

'What does it make you think?'

Wycliffe's manner was no longer conversational and for the first time Angove became cautious. 'I'm not in the business of pointing the finger.'

Wycliffe leaned forward in his chair so that it creaked abominably. 'That finger may well point at you, Mr Angove. Think it over. Now, one or two questions: You admit to being a frequent visitor at the house, was there anyone else to your knowledge on the same footing?'

'I don't know about the same footing, whatever that was, but Penrose was there quite often. I mean, it was only natural; Badger rarely went out except for his evening walks, and Penrose, apart from being his nephew, looked after his business affairs. He was always bringing along this and that for signature.'

'Anyone else?'

'Well, GG would be called in now and then for a few minutes, just to satisfy himself that he was in control. After all she's only across the street and she was his niece.'

'You say "called in". What does that mean?'

'It means she wouldn't go there unless he asked her to. And neither would I. Unsolicited visits were not appreciated.'

'Does she have a key?'

'I've got one, so I suppose she has. If he was upstairs he didn't like having to come down to let you in.'

'It all sounds highly autocratic.'

'You could say that, but I enjoyed his company and I suppose we each had practical reasons for letting him call the tune. He must have been very profitable to Penrose, and GG and I were both in hock for our rent – for different reasons. I haven't got it and GG doesn't like spending it.'

'Did he get on with his niece?'

Angove contorted his mobile features into a grimace. 'The plain answer to that is – No! He used to bait her and she couldn't take it. He always called her "Maggie" after the Iron Lady, and that annoyed her. The two of them were like oil and water . . . Badger had a cruel streak, he liked to rile people and GG was an easy target.'

'I see. Now I have just one more question: Had you any reason to think that your lease might not be renewed in September?'

Angove looked surprised. 'No, but I hadn't given it much thought. I know GG was getting a bit edgy; she rang me up to ask if I'd heard anything. She said both our leases ran out on the same date.'

'When did she telephone?'

'A week or ten days ago, I suppose. I can't say exactly.'

Wycliffe stood up. 'Mr Angove, I want you to come to our Incident Room in Hayle at two o'clock tomorrow afternoon. In the meantime please don't discuss our conversation this evening with anyone. You understand?'

'If you say so.'

Wycliffe was making for the stairs and the painter followed, seeing them off the premises.

They were on their way back to Hayle, driving around the Causeway. Lights showed dimly from houses on the Saltings and there were odd reflections in the waters. Overhead there were stars.

Wycliffe spoke first. 'I can understand why Badger took to him.'

Lucy did not answer at once, then she said, 'A man's man.'

Wycliffe was surprised. 'You think so? He seems to have no trouble in getting female sleeping partners.'

'That's a different matter.'

Wycliffe said, 'No doubt you're right. I'm going to have a small whisky, ring home, then go to bed.'

Chapter Ten

The sun was shining, it was half past eight, and Wycliffe walked along Commercial Road on his way to the Incident Room. Kersey had stopped at a little shop to buy his newspaper and cigarettes; Lucy Lane had gone ahead of them both. It was a routine which had been repeated many times over the years in all sorts of locations over the two counties.

Wycliffe was confident now that he was dealing with two quite separate cases. Early in the Wilder investigation he had realized that he was sorting out the erratic behaviour of a bunch of teenagers, their messy emotions, unpredictable loyalties and obstinate lies. And it was strange to see them, fifteen years later, still reacting as teenagers to that traumatic episode in their lives.

But the case of Henry Badger was different; here was no hot-headed quarrel followed by a clumsy accident and cover-up, but an adult crime, premeditated, over-elaborate in its planning and carried out in cold blood. The only link between the two was a deviously contrived attempt to use the one in order to confuse the other.

There was circumstantial evidence which could point to Gillian Grey or to Penrose. Both had the opportunity, means presented no problem, and both stood to gain directly or indirectly from the old man's death. Finding the weapon and identifying it with one of them could be crucial.

Kersey said, 'I'll look in on Fox. See what's happening.'

Wycliffe was marking time and when John Scales rang

it was a relief from boredom. 'I've made a few enquiries about the Penrose firm but you know what lawyers are, even our own are cagey about discussing their kind. However, old Simmonds loosened up. It seems he started his career under Arnold's father. The word is that Arnold tends to sit on his backside and wait for business to drop into his lap, but it no longer works that way. The firm is using up accumulated fat and Arnold has acquired a taste for the good life. No crisis; but cause for concern.'

'In other words a fresh injection of capital would be more than welcome.'

'That's the message, sir.'

The morning passed. Wycliffe talked to the chief, Lucy filed reports, they drank coffee, and at half past twelve they crossed over to the pub for a snack lunch. Kersey was still at the Modelmakers.

When they got back Wycliffe asked the duty officer, 'Anything from Sergeant Fox?'

'Nothing, sir.'

Tuesday afternoon

Wycliffe waited in his little office with the door sufficiently ajar to give him a view of most of the big room. He was counting on progress but the gathering had no official status and any developments would have to be formalized through individual interviews and statements.

The first to arrive was Lisa Bell. Wycliffe had never met her but recognized her from the photograph. Lucy brought her to the table and pulled out a chair. She sat down, taut and withdrawn, handbag in lap, caught up in the dentist's waiting-room syndrome.

Julian Angove came next, looking about him in bored appraisal until he caught sight of Lisa and took the chair beside her. In no time at all they were deep in conversation that was almost animated.

At one fifty-eight by Wycliffe's watch the Harts arrived, the doctor, grave and suspicious, clearly doubting whether he should be there at all. His wife, Barbara, another whom Wycliffe had not yet met, came as a surprise; she was plump, pink and fair, inclined to be fluffy; whereas he had imagined her as a type specimen of the young matron. Her pregnancy scarcely showed.

The doctor staked out his position to Lucy. 'I hope this won't take long, it's come at a most inconvenient time.'

The Harts sat opposite the other two and there was obvious constraint. Angove's casual 'Hi, you two!' was coldly received.

Arnold Penrose and Gillian Grey came in together, both were flushed and flustered as though interrupted in mid-quarrel. Absent-mindedly they took the seats Lucy offered and fended off subdued greetings from the others.

Wycliffe gave the gathering a minute or two before taking his seat at the head of the table. When he did, he had Alan Hart on his right and GG on his left.

'Thank you for coming.' His manner was dry and distant. 'This is an unofficial gathering but it will be recorded to ensure that your rights are not infringed.'

He looked up from the notes he had in front of him. 'My investigation began with the discovery of the body of Cochran Wilder. Since then two of the people who seemed to be linked with the discovery have died. There is evidence to show that Henry Badger was murdered and that Paul Drew took his own life.'

Wycliffe had not raised his voice above a conversational level but there was no need. Whenever he stopped speaking the silence in the room was only broken by the muffled sound of passing traffic.

A brief pause and he went on, 'DS Lane will give each of you a photocopy of a statement sent by Paul Drew, shortly before his death, to the dead boy's father. You

206

will see that the statement is disjointed and reflects great distress of mind.'

The papers were distributed and read. There were audible sighs and murmurs and an appreciable time went by before anyone looked up from the few lines of type. Lisa Bell said in a whisper, 'Oh, my God!'

When eventually they had done, Wycliffe said, 'You see that Paul Drew has indicated in outline his version of what happened on that May night in 1977. Later, I shall ask for your individual recollections. I am aware that so far none of you has admitted to having seen Wilder either then or at any other time but that fiction can no longer be taken seriously.'

Lucy Lane, listening and watching, hardly recognized Wycliffe in the remote, sombre personage that now appeared. By his matter-of-fact delivery and his economy in words, he had already cut himself off totally from the emotions of his audience, so that she was beginning to feel, as they must, in a limbo of isolation.

He was speaking again. 'Staying with Paul Drew, I want you to listen to his voice on a pocket recorder which he used in his business. The tape was found on his body.'

Lucy Lane placed the little machine for the play-back in the middle of the table, switched it on, and withdrew.

If there was tension before, now it was almost tangible. It was a grey day and the lighting in the cavernous room was poor. Lucy was hearing the tape for the third time, but in these circumstances she was more than ever moved by the pathos of this man who, failing to find a human confidant, finally strips himself bare to a coil of magnetic tape.

Lucy watched the group around the table as they listened to the voice of the dead man. Each of them looked steadily at the table-top as though fearful of catching another's eye.

'. . . I shall be, "The man who helped to bury the body

. . . The man who attacked the policeman . . ." From then on I behaved like a madman . . .'

They heard about the keys of Bosavern, about the tools in the glove compartment of his car and about the Stanley knife.

'. . . And suddenly I was calm; I knew exactly what I must do, and I felt a tremendous sense of relief . . .'

When the tape had run its course there was a wave of uneasiness. Lisa Bell fumbled in her bag for a handkerchief and dabbed her eyes. GG and the lawyer looked at each other, a curious exchange. Alan Hart was the first to speak and his voice was uncertain though intended to be firm. 'I am sorry, but my wife has had enough of this and I must take her home. It was a mistake to bring her.'

Barbara flushed. 'You did not *bring* me, Alan! I insisted on coming, and I shall stay. This thing has blighted all our lives for too long and I am determined that it shall be somehow . . . somehow settled, before our child is born.'

Gillian Grey said in a harsh voice, 'I want to know what this is about.'

There was no other comment and Wycliffe resumed in the same dry, uninflected tone as before. 'The two statements from Paul Drew happen to coincide with two aspects of the investigation. The written statement sent to Wilder senior concerns what happened on that night fifteen years ago, while the recording relates to what has happened since the recovery of young Wilder's body. I want to deal with the two separately.

'You each have a copy of Paul Drew's written statement and now I want you to fill in the gaps.'

Arnold Penrose performed a metaphorical handwashing. 'I'm not sure why I am here unless it's as a lawyer. In which case I must point out that what you contribute is up to each of you. There is no legal obligation for anyone to say anything at all.'

Wycliffe sounded like the crustiest of judges

instructing a jury. 'What Mr Penrose has said about your right to remain silent is of course quite correct. In any case it has been explained to you that your attendance here is voluntary.'

He turned to speak directly to the lawyer. 'About your own status, Mr Penrose, you are not here in connection with the death of Cochran Wilder, but the murder of Henry Badger. You were closely involved with his affairs, you were a frequent visitor at his premises and you were twice seen in the locality on the night that he was murdered. I hope that you will feel able to make a statement about your movements that night.'

Penrose flushed and was about to reply but thought better of it. As Wycliffe turned back to the others he caught the ghost of a smile on GG's lips.

When it seemed that no-one would speak it was Lisa Bell who found her courage. At first she was barely audible but her voice gathered strength. 'I was on the veranda that evening when Cochran Wilder came across the dunes from Gwithian. He seemed to be worn out and he asked for a glass of water . . .'

As Lucy listened to the schoolgirlish voice, faltering at first, but growing firmer and more articulate, that May evening in the chalet on the dunes seemed to come alive. She could see the engaging stranger, worming his way into the chalet party, sharing their meal, showing off his sophistication, his conjuring tricks and his pot-smoking and ending up with a bed on the sofa . . .

Lisa said, 'I was supposed to share with Paul, but it didn't work . . . So, early in the night, I left him. I took a pillow and a blanket and tried to settle in an armchair in the living room where Wilder was. He seemed to be asleep, and eventually I dozed off.

'I woke with Wilder's hand pressed on my mouth. He was standing over me, naked, and he whispered something, but I struggled and the chair I was in turned over on us both. I think I grabbed the tablecloth; glasses and things got pulled to the floor . . .' Lisa broke off, flushed, with tears running down her cheeks.

It was not difficult to imagine the darkened room, the two figures struggling on the floor, the naked man and the girl, the girl's hand clutching at the tablecloth, the littered glasses and china, some of it broken.

Wycliffe said nothing and once more the silence waited. It was Julian Angove who finally made up his mind to speak.

He sounded quite different; subdued, with no trace of banter or cynicism. 'It woke everybody. Lisa was almost hysterical, Wilder was aggressive, and there was chaos for a bit until Alan and I bundled Wilder out of the door, naked as he was, and locked it. While Paul was collecting Wilder's clothes and belongings the two girls took Lisa into one of the bedrooms and stayed with her . . . All the time Wilder was banging on the door, and shouting . . .

'When we had his clothes and his backpack we opened the door and tried to give them to him but he struggled to get back in and one of us, perhaps both, gave him a shove . . .' Angove made an expressive gesture. 'He overbalanced . . . He overbalanced, and went head-first down the steps . . .'

The painter stopped, and Lucy realized with a sense of mild shock that the imperturbable Julian was deeply disturbed. After a moment or two he added in a cracked voice, 'It's your turn, Alan.'

The doctor passed a hand over his eyes and began to speak. 'I shall never forget that thud when his head hit the kerb at the bottom . . . We went down to him but it was impossible to see how badly he was hurt. In any case none of us had even an elementary knowledge of first aid . . . I do remember that his awful breathing scared me . . .'

They were not the words of an experienced doctor but of a frightened boy.

'We knew that we had to bring him indoors and,

somehow, we got him up the steps and into the room, where we laid him on the floor and covered him with blankets . . . He was bleeding from a wound in his head . . .

'We had to get help, and Paul was going after a telephone but as he was leaving Wilder made a sort of snorting noise and his breathing stopped . . . We knew enough to check his heart beat and pulse but there was neither . . . He was dead.'

After a longish interval Hart took the story to its conclusion. 'I can't describe our panic and I have no memory of the stages by which we reached the decision to do what we did . . . All I can say is that what we did has affected us all ever since . . . I have a recurring nightmare, endlessly trudging through the dunes in the darkness, clutching at a corner of that awful sheet . . . Then there was the digging and the running sand . . .'

It was a strange scene; the group sitting around the table seemed frozen into immobility, each still avoiding another's eyes.

Only Wycliffe appeared wholly detached, uninvolved. He looked across at GG. 'Have you anything to add, Miss Grey?'

GG swept back her hair with that practised hand. She was flushed. 'I don't know what all this is about. For fifteen years our lives have been blighted by the memory of that wretched boy and now we are assembled to listen to harrowing reminders and to the recorded meanderings of Paul Drew who broke under the strain when the body was discovered. All I can say is that if he was responsible for the death of my uncle I want that established.'

Wycliffe made no direct response. He said, 'I have arranged for your statements to be taken at the St Ives police station during the rest of today. They will be recorded and you will be asked to sign the transcripts.'

It was Barbara Hart who asked, 'And after that?'

Wycliffe shuffled together the few notes he had in front of him and stood up. 'After that, Mrs Hart, the papers concerning the Wilder affair will be passed to the Crown Prosecution Service and it will be up to them to decide what charges if any should be brought.'

It seemed almost an anti-climax, and for a while nobody moved. It was only when Lucy Lane busied herself recovering her photocopies, that the group, still almost silent, began to break up.

Wycliffe returned to his office where Kersey was waiting for him. The air was blue with cigarette smoke.

'Did it come off?'

Wycliffe shrugged. 'I think we've laid the Wilder ghost. As to the other . . . Any news from Fox?'

Kersey grimaced. 'Fox is an old woman; he's been poncing about everywhere except in the bloody workshop where we want him, but I've got him down there at last. Whether he'll find anything is another matter.' Kersey ground out a stub in the ashtray. 'Where do we go from here, sir?'

'Obviously we need to talk to Gillian Grey and Penrose again. My impression is that there's trouble between those two. They arrived together this afternoon but very flustered. They'll be making statements along with the others now so let them simmer until the morning, then we'll see.'

The telephone rang. 'Mr Penrose has come back, sir, he would like a word.'

'Show Mr Penrose in.' Wycliffe spoke to Kersey. 'He's worried.'

The lawyer looked weary, his manner of good-humoured self-satisfaction had taken a battering since their first encounter and he could hardly wait to sit down before he began to speak. 'I feel that I have put myself in an invidious position.'

Wycliffe waited, and he went on, 'In trying to protect

212

the interests of others, I have come under suspicion myself and I want to clear the air. About the night Badger was killed—'

Wycliffe interrupted, 'If you wish to clear the air, Mr Penrose, let's start further back. Let's start with the anonymous postcards which were addressed on the machine in Badger's attic. At our first meeting you told me you did not think he owned a typewriter. Later, on the night his body was discovered and you were confronted with the machine, you expressed surprise. Did you or did you not know of its existence?'

Penrose studied his hands. 'I did know that there had once been an old machine about the place but I hadn't seen it for years.' He looked up, meeting Wycliffe's gaze. 'I didn't want him accused of stirring up trouble over the Wilder business.'

'So despite your denials to me you believed that your uncle might be responsible for those cards?'

'It seemed possible, the sort of mischievous thing he could do.'

'The keys on that machine were wiped clean. What would have been the point in him doing that? In any case, where did he get his information? Whoever sent those cards knew at least the broad facts about young Wilder's death and must have had a copy of the photograph from which a cut-out was sent to me. Did you imagine that one of the six had confided in him?'

Penrose shook his head. 'Put like that it seems unlikely.'

Kersey spoke for the first time. 'Did *you* know the facts about Wilder's disappearance?'

Penrose stiffened. 'Certainly not! How could I possibly have known?'

'Pillow talk?'

Penrose flushed. 'I resent that—'

Wycliffe cut in, 'Don't bother to get excited, Mr Penrose. It was you who came here to clear the air. In my opinion Badger's killer is someone who benefits directly or indirectly from his death, someone who had access to his premises when he was out on one of his evening walks, and someone who was *either* a member of the chalet party or intimate with one of them.'

Wycliffe waited for some response but none came and he went on, 'That person saw, in the discovery of Wilder's body, the chance to kill Badger and make it appear that his death was a consequence of the anonymous cards he was supposed to have sent to five of the six members of the party. He or she underlined the connection by contriving that Badger's death looked like a repetition of Wilder's. The ransacking of the attic was, of course, an over-done attempt to suggest a frantic search for the mythical evidence in Badger's possession.'

Penrose looked up; he was clearly distressed, little beads of sweat had gathered about his eyes and he dabbed them with a handkerchief. 'I came here in good faith and at some risk to my reputation if this ever comes out in court, to tell you exactly what I did last Thursday, the night Badger died. My reception is more in the nature of an attack.'

Wycliffe was unmoved. 'No-one is attacking you, Mr Penrose. You wanted to clear the air and you know now exactly where we stand. As to what you did on that Thursday night, you were seen in Bethel Street at about ten o'clock and again at around eleven.'

Penrose nodded. 'That is correct. I arrived at Miss Grey's flat at shortly after ten and left just before eleven. I reached home shortly afterwards.'

Kersey said, 'A brief visit.'

'Yes.' He broke off, and shifted uncomfortably in his chair. 'What I came back to tell you is that she wasn't there. I didn't want it to come to this but in view of what happened here this afternoon I felt that I couldn't—'

Wycliffe was leaning forward in his chair. 'You are

saying that when you arrived at the flat around ten o'clock she didn't answer your ring?'

Penrose avoided his eyes and spoke in a lowered voice. 'I am saying that she wasn't there. I have a key and I let myself in. I waited for about an hour, then I left.'

'Had she been expecting you?'

'No, I didn't think I would be able to get away, but I do sometimes drop in like that.'

'What did you think?'

'I thought that she must have had some other engagement; we don't live in each other's pockets.'

'You've spoken about this to her since?'

'Not directly – no. She likes to maintain the idea that we have our separate lives, that we don't question each other.'

'You are willing to put this into your statement?'

'Do I have a choice?'

That evening the three of them had their last meal together in the Copperhouse Arms. Wycliffe was subdued.

Kersey said, 'What's the programme tomorrow, sir?'

'We talk to the woman.' It seemed significant that GG had become 'the woman'.

'You believe the lawyer's tale?'

Wycliffe smiled. 'You sound quite literary, Doug.'

Afterwards he went for his evening walk, along Commercial Street, across the Back Bridge and through Phillack to the dunes. On his way back he stopped at the Bucket of Blood for a drink and collected a leaflet which recorded the gruesome story of the name. He felt detached and uneasy, as though for the past few days he had been living in a book or a play, and that now he was about to return to reality.

Before going to bed he telephoned Helen. 'With any luck I shall be home by the weekend.'

215

Wycliffe was at the Incident Room by half past eight. There was a pearly mist over the estuary but the sky was bright with the promise of a fine day. On his desk were the transcripts of yesterday's statements; somebody had been working overtime. In the main they were no more than grist for the lawyers' mill. He glanced through them, spending time on only two. Penrose had stuck to his story, and GG to hers.

He said to Kersey, 'I'm going to talk to her on her own ground. There's a risk, but I don't think bringing her in for questioning is the way forward at the moment.'

'You want me?'

'No, there must be a woman. It will have to be Lucy.'

And at a little before ten, Wycliffe and Lucy Lane drove to St Ives. They parked in front of the police station and walked along the Wharf. The sun was out, the sea sparkled and gulls planed, swooped and screeched overhead. In Bethel Street a couple of cafés and boards outside advertising morning coffee and the Modelmakers looked more decrepit than ever.

'Do we call on Fox?'

'No, he'll let us know if he finds anything. He's slow but he gets there.'

There were no customers in the health shop. It was Lucy's first visit and she looked about her with interest. One of the assistants recognized Wycliffe. 'I'll tell Miss Grey.' She seemed pleased at the prospect.

GG came out, self-possessed as ever. 'You'd better come into the office.' She wore a jade-green frock under her white overall, and an antique silver necklace with a Celtic cross. In her office the curtains were drawn back and Lucy received the full impact of that framed, dazzling prospect of sea and rocks and sky.

'Please sit down.' She was assessing Lucy with a critical eye. 'I've made my statement. I don't know what more you want.'

Wycliffe said, 'On the evening your uncle died you say you were in your flat. As you heard yesterday, Drew rang your bell on two occasions but could get no reply.' She was about to interrupt but Wycliffe pressed on. 'We know that Arnold Penrose entered your flat at ten and remained there until eleven. You were not there. Where were you?'

She performed that reflex gesture, sweeping back her hair, and revealed her face, flushed and angry. 'He told you that?'

'Where were you, Miss Grey?'

A momentary hesitation, then, challenging, 'I was across the road at my uncle's.'

'Perhaps you would prefer to be questioned formally in the presence of a solicitor.'

'I can take care of myself.'

'Even so I must tell you that you do not have to answer my questions—'

'Just get on with it.'

'What were you doing at your uncle's?'

'I wanted to talk to him about my lease. I've no doubt Arnold has told you, along with everything else, that my uncle was refusing to renew it.' Her tone was bitter.

'And did you talk to him?'

'No, I did not. He was already dead.' The statement came, bald and dramatic.

Lucy could not help being impressed. It was as though a chess player had recklessly sacrificed his queen in the hope of strategic advantage.

After a pause GG continued, 'I went in by the garden door. It was unlocked and so was the back door of the house. I knew he must be in because there was a light in the attic. I called up the stairs, but there was no answer so I went up and I found him, sprawled at the bottom of the attic stairs.'

Even Wycliffe was momentarily silenced. But when a couple passed by, not far from the window, strolling along the footwalk by the sea, Wycliffe saw that she followed them with her eyes. Despite her apparent confidence, was she already beginning to feel cut off from the rest of the world?

Lucy Lane said, 'What did you do?'

'Do? My first thought was to get help, but something made me go up the stairs to the attic and I saw the chaos there. I admit I was scared. It was obvious that this was something more than an accident. I thought of Drew, and I remembered Wilder, and how he died . . .'

In the silence they could hear the vague murmur of voices from the shop, then the ringing of the telephone startled them, all three.

GG picked up the phone, muttered something, and passed it over. 'It's for you.'

The two women watched him and listened to his cryptic responses.

'Wycliffe . . . Good! . . . In the garden . . . Have you checked it over? . . . You'll get the lab to enhance . . . Yes, I agree . . .'

Once or twice during the conversation he had looked briefly, but significantly at GG. It went through Lucy's mind to wonder whether the occasion had been rehearsed although she knew that it had not.

Wycliffe replaced the telephone. 'That was the Scenes-of-Crime officer who is searching your uncle's premises. In the long grass of the garden he has found a steel bar, a case-opener, which could have been the murder weapon. It seems that there are white hairs adhering to it.' He broke off as though a fresh idea had occurred to him. 'Did you wear gloves when you visited your uncle, Miss Grey?'

'Of course not!'

'No. There are traces of prints on the weapon. It has been wiped, but not, apparently, with complete success.'

GG said nothing. Wycliffe allowed the silence to continue until it was clear that she would not speak then, at a sign from him, Lucy Lane stood up.

'Gillian Grey, you are being detained for questioning in connection with the murder of Henry Badger on or about the evening of Thursday the fourteenth of May. You do not have to say anything . . .'

For the first time GG was disorientated, but she recovered. She looked directly and steadily at Wycliffe. 'You've got a fight on your hands.'

It was Saturday before Wycliffe got home. GG had been charged, and she had made her appearance in the Magistrates' Court to be remanded in custody.

The legal processes, more ponderous than the mills of God, were trundling into action. In six or seven months' time GG would stand in the dock and barristers would display their cleverness, strutting like peacocks under the eyes of judge and jury. It would have little to do with the health shop or the Modelmakers, still less with the chalet in the dunes which had steps leading up to a veranda.

Ruth said, 'What do you think will happen about the Wilder business?'

'The CPS will decide that charges would not be in the public interest and I agree with that.'

The Wycliffes were in their living room. Outside the light was fading, the curtains were undrawn and in the garden shapes and shadows merged in the melancholy twilight. It suited Wycliffe's mood. As often before when an investigation culminated in an arrest, he was experiencing a feeling of anti-climax, even of futility. And this was especially true of the present case.

Ruth said, 'You're very quiet, Dad. Surely you feel relieved if nothing else?'

He did not answer, but spoke to Helen. 'Do you remember old Messinger?'

'He was not the sort you easily forget.'

Wycliffe turned back to Ruth. 'He was my governor at one time and he had a notice over his desk, "No situation is so bad that a policeman can't make it worse".'

Ruth said nothing, and he went on, 'Just think: if we hadn't established the link between young Wilder and the chalet crowd Paul Drew would still be alive, and it might never have occurred to GG to murder her uncle.'

Helen said, 'You're being morbid, Charles. What is it to be – St Juliot for a walk and a quiet drink, or the film on TV?'

THE END